Victoria Holt

Victoria Holt

Bride of
Pendorric

Mistress
of Mellyn

CHANCELLOR
PRESS

Bride of Pendorric first published in Great Britain
in 1963 by William Collins Sons & Co. Ltd
Mistress of Mellyn first published in Great Britain
in 1961 by William Collins Sons & Co. Ltd

This edition first published in Great Britain in 1983 by
Chancellor Press
59 Grosvenor Street
London, W.1.

ISBN: 0 907486 34 7

Printed and Bound in Great Britain by Collins, Glasgow

Victoria Holt

Contents

Bride of Pendorric

Mistress of Mellyn

Victoria Holt

Bride of Pendorric

Chapter One

I often marvelled after I went to Pendorric that one's existence could change so swiftly, so devastatingly. I had heard life compared with a kaleidoscope and this is how it appeared to me, for there was the pleasant scene full of peace and contentment when the pattern began to change, first here, then there, until the picture which confronted me was no longer calm and peaceful but filled with menace. I had married a man who seemed to me all that I wanted in a husband – solicitous, loving, passionately devoted; then suddenly it was as though I were married to a stranger.

I first saw Roc Pendorric when I came up from the beach one morning to find him sitting in the studio with my father; in his hands he held a terra-cotta statue for which I had been the original, a slim child of about seven. I remembered when my father had made it more than eleven years before; he had always said it was not for sale.

The blinds had not yet been drawn and the two men made a striking contrast sitting there in the strong sunlight: my father so fair, the stranger so dark. On the island my father was often called Angelo because of the fairness of his hair and skin and his almost guileless expression, for he was a very sweet-tempered man. It might have been because of this that I fancied there was something saturnine about his companion.

'Ah, here is my daughter Favel,' said my father as though they had been speaking of me.

They both stood up, the stranger towering above my father, who was of medium height. He took my hand and his long dark eyes studied me with something rather calculating in the intentness of his scrutiny. He was lean, which accentuated his height, and his hair was almost black; there was an expression in his alert eyes which made me feel he was seeking something which amused him, and it occurred to me that there might be a streak of malice in his amusement. He had rather pointed ears which gave him the look of a satyr. His was a face of contrasts; there was a gentleness about the full lips as well as sensuality; there was no doubt of the firmness of the jaw; there was arrogance in the long straight nose; and mingling with the undoubted humour in the quick eyes was a suggestion of mischief. I came to believe later that he fascinated me so quickly because I could not be sure of him; and it took me a very long time to discover the sort of man he was.

At that moment I wished that I had dressed before coming up from the beach.

'Mr. Pendorric has been looking round the studio,' said my father. 'He has bought the Bay of Naples water-colour.'

'I'm glad,' I answered. 'It's beautiful.'

He held out the little statue. 'And so is this.'

'I don't think that's for sale,' I told him.

'It's much too precious, I'm sure.'

He seemed to be comparing me with the figure and I guessed my father had told him – as he did everyone who admired it: 'That's my daughter when she was seven.'

'But,' he went on, 'I've been trying to persuade the artist to sell. After all, *he* still has the original.'

Father laughed in the rather hearty way he did when he was with customers who were ready to spend money, forced laughter. Father had always been happier creating his works of art than selling them. When my mother was alive she had done most of the selling; since I had left school, only a few months before this, I found myself taking it over. Father would give his work away to anyone who he thought appreciated it, and he needed a strong-minded woman to look after business transactions; that was why, after my mother had died, we became very poor. But since I had been at home, I flattered myself that we were beginning to pay our way.

'Favel, could you get us a drink?' my father asked.

I said I would if they would wait while I changed, and leaving them together went into my bedroom which led off the studio as did both our bedrooms. In a few minutes I had put on a blue linen dress, after which I went to our tiny kitchen to see about drinks; when I went back to the studio Father was showing the man a bronze Venus – one of our most expensive pieces.

If he buys that, I thought, I'll be able to settle a few bills. I would seize on the money and do it too, before Father had a chance of gambling it away at cards or roulette.

Roc Pendorric's eyes met mine over the bronze and, as I caught the flicker of amusement there, I guessed I must have shown rather clearly how anxious I was for him to buy it. He put it down and turned to me as though the statue couldn't hold his interest while I was there, and I felt annoyed with myself for interrupting them. Then I caught the gleam in his eyes and I wondered whether that was what he had expected me to feel.

He started to talk about the island then; he had arrived only yesterday, and had not even visited the villas of Tiberius and San Michele yet. But he had heard of Angelo's studio and the wonderful works of art to be picked up there; and so this had been his first excursion.

Father was flushed with pleasure; but I wasn't quite sure whether to believe him or not.

'And when I came and found that Angelo was Mr. Frederick Farington who spoke English like the native he is, I was even more delighted. My Italian is appalling, and the boasts of "English spoken here" are often . . . well, a little boastful. Please, Miss Farington, do tell me what I ought to see while I stay here.'

I started to tell him about the villas, the grottoes and the other well-known attractions. 'But,' I added, 'it always seems to me after coming back from

England that the scenery and the blue of the sea are the island's real beauties.'

'It would be nice to have a companion to share in my sight-seeing,' he said.

'Are you travelling alone?' I asked.

'Quite alone.'

'There are so many visitors to the island,' I said consolingly. 'You're sure to find someone who is eager to do the tours as you are.'

'It would be necessary, of course, to find the right companion . . . someone who really knows the island.'

'The guides do, of course.'

His eyes twinkled. 'I wasn't thinking of a guide.'

'The rest of the natives would no doubt be too busy.'

'I'll find what I want,' he assured me; and I had a feeling that he would.

He went over to the bronze Venus and began fingering it again.

'That attracts you,' I commented.

He turned to me and studied me as intently as he had the bronze. 'I'm enormously attracted,' he told me. 'I can't make up my mind. May I come back later?'

'But of course,' said Father and I simultaneously.

He did come back. He came back and back again. In my innocence I thought at first that he was hesitating about the bronze Venus; then I wondered whether it was the studio that attracted him because it probably seemed very bohemian to him, full of local colour and totally unlike the place he came from. One couldn't expect people to buy every time they came. It was a feature of our studio and others like it that people dropped in casually, stopped for a chat and a drink, browsed about the place and bought when something pleased them.

What disturbed me was that I was beginning to look forward to his visits. There were times when I was sure he came to see me, and there were others when I told myself that I was imagining this, and the thought depressed me.

Three days after his first visit I went down to one of the little beaches on the Marina Piccola to bathe, and he was there. We swam together and lay on the beach in the sun afterwards.

I asked if he was enjoying his stay.

'Beyond expectations,' he answered.

'You've been sightseeing, I expect.'

'Not much. I'd like to, but I still think it's dull alone.'

'Really? People usually complain of the awful crowds, not of being alone.'

'Mind you,' he pointed out, 'I wouldn't want *any* companion.' There was a suggestion in those long eyes which slightly tilted at the corners. I was sure, in that moment, that he was the type whom most women would find irresistible, and that he knew it. This knowledge disturbed me; I myself was becoming too conscious of that rather blatant masculinity and I wondered whether I had betrayed this to him.

I said rather coolly: 'Someone was asking about the bronze Venus this morning.'

His eyes shone with amusement. 'Oh well, if I miss it, I'll only have *myself* to blame.' His meaning was perfectly clear and I felt annoyed with him. Why did he think we kept a studio and entertained people there if not in the hope of selling things? How did he think we lived?

'We'd hate you to have it unless you were really keen about it.'

'But I never have anything that I'm not keen about,' he replied. 'Actually though, I prefer the figure of the younger Venus.'

'Oh . . . that!'

He put his hand on my arm and said: 'It's charming. Yes, I prefer her.'

'I simply must be getting back,' I told him.

He leaned on his elbow and smiled at me, and I had a feeling that he knew far too much of what was going on in my mind and was fully aware that I found his company extremely stimulating and wanted more of it – that he was something more to me than a prospective buyer.

He said lightly: 'Your father tells me that you're the commercial brains behind the enterprise. I bet he's right.'

'Artists need someone practical to look after them,' I replied. 'And now that my mother is dead . . .'

I knew that my voice changed when I spoke of her. It still happened, although she had been dead three years. Annoyed with myself as I always was when I betrayed emotion I said quickly: 'She died of T.B. They came here in the hope that it would be good for her. She was a wonderful manager.'

'And so you take after her.' His eyes were full of sympathy now and I was pleased out of all proportion that he should understand how I felt. I thought then that I had imagined that streak of mischief in him. Perhaps mischief was not the right description; but the fact was that while I was becoming more and more attracted by this man, I was often conscious of something within him that I could not understand, some quality, something which he was determined to keep hidden from me. This often made me uneasy, while it in no way decreased my growing interest in him, but rather added to it. Now I saw only his sympathy which was undoubtedly genuine.

'I hope so,' I answered. 'I think I do.'

'She must have been an excellent business woman.'

'She was.' I still could not control the pain in my voice as I remembered, and pictures of the past flashed in and out of my mind. I saw her – small and dainty, with the brilliant colour in her cheeks which was so becoming and a sign of her illness; that tremendous energy which was like a fire consuming her – until the last months. The island had seemed a different place when she was in it. In the beginning she had taught me to read and write and to be quick with figures. I remembered long lazy days when I lay on one of the little beaches or swam in the blue water or lay on my back and drifted; all the beauty of the place, all the echoes of ancient history were the background for one of the happiest existences a child could know. I had run wild, it was true. Sometimes I talked to the tourists; sometimes I joined the boatmen who took visitors to the grottoes or on tours of the island; sometimes I climbed the path to the villa of Tiberius and sat looking over the sea to Naples. Then I would come back to the studio and listen to the talk going on there; I shared my father's pride in his work, my mother's joy when she had succeeded in making a good sale.

They were so important to each other; and there were times when they seemed to me like two brilliant butterflies dancing in the sunshine, intoxicated with the joy of being alive because they knew that the sun of their happiness must go down quickly and finally.

I had been indignant when they told me I must go away to school in England. It was a necessity, my mother pointed out, for she had reached the limit of her capabilities, and although I was a tolerable linguist (we spoke English at home, Italian to our neighbours and, as there were many French and German visitors to our studio, I soon had a smattering of these languages) I had had no real education. My mother was anxious that I should go to her old school which was small and in the heart of Sussex. Her old headmistress was still in charge and I suspected that it was all very much as it had been in my mother's day. After a term or two I became reconciled, partly because I quickly made friends with Esther McBane, partly because I returned to the island for Christmas, Easter and summer holidays; and as I was a normal uncomplicated person I enjoyed both worlds.

But then my mother died and nothing was the same again. I found out that I had been educated on the jewellery which had once been hers; she had planned for me to go to a university, but the jewellery had realized less than she had hoped (for one quality she shared with my father was optimism) and the cost of my schooling was more than she had bargained for. So when she died I went back to school for two more years because that was her wish. Esther was a great comfort at that time; she was an orphan who was being brought up by an aunt, so she had a good deal of sympathy to offer. She came to stay with us during summer holidays and it helped both Father and me not to fret so much with a visitor in the studio. We said that she must come every summer, and she assured us she would. We left school at the same time and she came home with me at the end of our final term. During that holiday we would discuss what we were going to do with our lives. Esther planned to take up art seriously. As for myself, I had my father to consider, so I was going to try to take my mother's place in the studio although I feared that was something I should never be able to do entirely.

I smiled, remembering that long letter I had had from Esther, which in itself was unusual for Esther abhorred letter-writing and avoided it whenever possible. On the way back to Scotland she had met a man; he was growing tobacco in Rhodesia and was home for a few months. That letter had been full of this adventure. There had been one more letter two months later. Esther was getting married and going out to Rhodesia.

It was exciting and she was wonderfully happy; but I knew it was the end of our friendship because the only bond between us now could be through letters which Esther would have neither time nor inclination to write. I did have one to say that she had arrived, but marriage had made a different person of Esther; she had grown far from the long-legged untidy-haired girl who used to walk in the grounds of the little school with me and talk about dedicating herself to Art.

I was brought out of the past by the sight of Roc Pendorric's face close to mine, and now there was nothing but sympathy in his eyes. 'I've stirred up sad memories.'

'I was thinking about my mother and the past.'

He nodded and was silent for a few seconds. Then he said: 'You don't ever think of going back to her people . . . or your father's people?'

'People?' I murmured.

'Didn't she ever talk to you about her home in England?'

I was suddenly very surprised. 'No, she never mentioned it.'

'Perhaps the memory was unhappy.'

'I never realized it before, but neither of them ever talked about . . . before they married. As a matter of fact I think they felt that all that happened before was insignificant.'

'It must have been a completely happy marriage.'

'It was.'

We were silent again. Then he said: 'Favel! It's an unusual name.'

'No more unusual than yours. I always thought a roc was a legendary bird.'

'Fabulous, of immense size and strength, able to lift an elephant . . . if it wanted to.'

He spoke rather smugly and I retorted: 'I'm sure even you would be incapable of lifting an elephant. Is it a nick-name?'

'I've been Roc for as long as I can remember. But it's short for Petroc.'

'Still unusual.'

'Not in the part of the world I come from. I've had a lot of ancestors who had to put up with it. The original one was a sixth-century saint who founded a monastery. I think Roc is a modern version that's all my own. Do you think it suits me?'

'Yes,' I answered. 'I think it does.'

Rather to my embarrassment he leaned forward and kissed the tip of my nose. I stood up hastily. 'It really is time I was getting back to the studio,' I said.

Our friendship grew quickly and to me was wholly exciting. I did not realize then how inexperienced I was, and imagined that I was capable of dealing with any situation. I forgot then that my existence had been bounded by school in England with its regulations and restrictions, our casual unconventional studio on an island whose main preoccupation was with passing visitors, and my life with my father who still thought of me as a child. I had imagined myself to be a woman of the world, whereas no one who could lay a true claim to such a description would have fallen in love with the first man who seemed different from anyone else she had met.

But there was a magnetism about Roc Pendorric when he set himself out to charm, and he certainly was determined to charm me.

Roc came to the studio every day. He always took the statuette in his hands and caressed it lovingly.

'I'm determined to have it, you know,' he said one day.

'Father will never sell.'

'I never give up hope.' And as I looked at the strong line of his jaw, the brilliance of his dark eyes, I believed him. He was a man who would take what he wanted from life; and it occurred to me that there would be few to deny him. That was why he was so anxious to possess the statue. He hated to be frustrated.

He bought the bronze Venus then.

'Don't think,' he told me, 'that this means I've given up trying for the other. It'll be mine yet; you see.'

There was an acquisitive gleam in his eyes when he said that and a certain mischief too. I knew what he meant, of course.

We swam together. We explored the whole island and we usually chose the less well-known places to avoid the crowds. He hired two Neapolitan boatmen to take us on sea trips and there were wonderful days when we lay back in the boat letting our hands trail in the turquoise and emerald water while Guiseppe and Umberto, watching us with the indulgent looks Latins bestow on lovers, sang arias from Italian opera for our entertainment.

In spite of his dark looks there must have been something essentially English about Roc, because Guiseppe and Umberto were immediately aware of his nationality. This ability to decide a person's nationality often surprised me but it never seemed to fail. As for myself, there was little difficulty in placing me. My hair was dark blonde and there was a platinum-coloured streak in it which had been there when I was born; it had the effect of making me look even fairer than I was. My eyes were the shade of water, and borrowed their colour from what I was wearing. Sometimes they were green, at others quite blue. I had a short pert nose, a wide mouth and good teeth. I was by no means a beauty, but I had always looked more like a visitor to the island than a native.

During those weeks I was never quite sure of Roc. There were times when I was perfectly happy to enjoy each moment as it came along and not concern myself with the future; but when I was alone – at night, for instance – I wondered what I should do when he went home.

In those early days I knew the beginning of that frustration which later was to bring such fear and terror into my life. His gaiety often seemed to be a cloak for deeper feelings; even during his most tender moments I would imagine I saw speculation in his eyes. He intrigued me in a hundred ways. I knew that given any encouragement I could love him completely, but I was never sure of him, and perhaps that was one of the reasons why every moment I was with him held the maximum excitement.

One day soon after we met we climbed to the villa of Tiberius, and never had that wonderful view seemed so superb as it did on that day. It was all there for our delight as I had seen it many times before – Capri and Monte Solaro, the Gulf of Salerno from Amalfi to Paestum, the Gulf of Naples from Sorrento to Cape Misena. I knew it well, and yet because I was sharing it with Roc it had a new magic.

'Have you ever seen anything so enchanting?' I asked.

He seemed to consider. Then he said: 'I live in a place which seems to me as beautiful.'

'Where?'

'Cornwall. Our bay is beautiful – more so I think because it changes more

often. Don't you get weary of sapphire seas? Now, I've seen ours as blue
– or almost; I've seen it green under the beating rain and brown after a
storm and pink in the dawn; I've seen it mad with fury pounding the rocks
and sending the spray high, and I've seen it as silky as this sea. This is very
beautiful, I grant you, and I don't think Roman emperors ever honoured us
in Cornwall with their villas and legends of their dancing boys and girls, but
we have a history of our own which is just as enthralling.'

'I've never been to Cornwall.'

He suddenly turned to me and I was caught in an embrace which made
me gasp. He said, with his face pressed against mine: 'But you will . . .
soon.'

I was conscious of the rose-red ruins, the greenish statue of the Madonna,
the deep blue of the sea, and life seemed suddenly too wonderful to be true.

He had lifted me off my feet and held me above him, laughing at me.

I said primly: 'Someone will see us.'

'Do you care?'

'Well, I object to being literally swept off my feet.'

He released me and to my disappointment he did not say any more about
Cornwall. That incident was typical of our relationship.

I realized that my father was taking a great interest in our friendship. He
was always delighted to see Roc, and he would sometimes come to the door
of the studio to meet us after we'd been out on one of our excursions, looking
like a conspirator, I thought. He was not a subtle man and it did not take
me long to discover that some plan was forming in his mind and that it
concerned Roc and me.

Did he think that Roc would propose to me? Was Roc's feeling for me
more marked than I dared hope, and had my father noticed this? And
suppose I married Roc, what of the studio? How would my father get along
without me? – because if I married Roc I should have to go away with him.

I felt unsettled. I knew I wanted to marry Roc – but I was not sure about
his feelings for me. How could I leave my father? But I had when I was at
school, I reminded myself. Yes, and look at the result. Right from the
beginning, being in love with Roc was an experience that kept me poised
between ecstasy and anxiety.

But Roc had not talked of marriage.

Father often asked him to a meal; invitations Roc always accepted on
condition that he should provide the wine. I cooked omelettes, fish, pasta
and even roast beef with Yorkshire pudding; the meals were well cooked
because one of the things my mother had taught me was how to cook, and
there had always been a certain amount of English dishes served in the
studio.

Roc seemed to enjoy those meals thoroughly and would sit long over them
talking and drinking. He began to talk a great deal about himself and his
home in Cornwall; but he had a way of making Father talk, and he quickly
learned about how we lived, the difficulties of making enough money during
the tourist season to keep us during the lean months. I noticed that Father
never discussed the time before his marriage, and Roc only made one or two

attempts to persuade him. Then he gave it up, which was strange, because he was usually persistent – but it was characteristic of Roc simply because it was unexpected.

I remember one day coming in and finding them playing cards together. Father had that look on his face which always frightened me – that intent expression which made his eyes glow like blue fires; there was a faint pink colour in his cheeks, and as I came in he scarcely looked up.

Roc got up from his chair, but I could see that he shared my father's feeling for the game. I felt very uneasy as I thought: So he's a gambler too.

'Favel won't want to interrupt the game,' said my father.

I looked into Roc's eyes and said coldly: 'I hope you aren't playing for high stakes.'

'Don't worry your head about that, my dear,' said Father.

'He's determined to lure the lire from my pockets,' added Roc, his eyes sparkling.

'I'll go and get something to eat,' I told them, and went into the kitchen.

I shall have to make him understand Father can't afford to gamble, I told myself.

When we sat over the meal my father was jubilant, so I guessed he had won.

I spoke to Roc about it the next day at the beach.

'Please don't encourage my father to gamble. He simply can't afford it.'

'But he gets so much pleasure from it,' he replied.

'Lots of people get pleasure from things that aren't good for them.'

He laughed. 'You know, you're a bit of a martinet.'

'Please listen to me. We're not rich enough to risk losing money that has been so hard to come by. We live here very cheaply, but it's not easy. Is that impossible for you to understand?'

'Please don't worry, Favel,' he said, putting his hand over mine.

'Then you won't play for money with him any more?'

'Suppose he asks me? Shall I say, I decline the invitation because your strong-minded daughter forbids us?'

'You could do better than that.'

He looked pious. 'But it wouldn't be true.'

I shrugged my shoulders impatiently. 'Surely you can find other people to gamble with. Why do you have to choose him?'

He looked thoughtful and said: 'I suppose it's because I like the atmosphere of his studio.' We were lying on the beach and he reached out and turned me towards him. Looking into my face he went on: 'I like the treasures he has there.'

It was in moments like this when I believed his feelings matched my own. I was elated and at the same time afraid I should betray too much. So I stood up quickly and walked into the sea; he was close behind me.

'Don't you know, Favel,' he said, putting an arm round my bare shoulder, 'that I want very much to please you?'

I had to turn and smile at him then. Surely, I thought, the look he gave me was one of love.

We were happy and carefree when we swam, and later, as we lay in the sun on the beach, I felt once more that supreme happiness which is being in love.

Yet two days later I came in from the market and found them sitting at the card table. The game was finished but I could see by my father's face that he had lost and by Roc's that he had won.

I felt my cheeks aflame and my eyes were hard as I looked into Roc's face. I said nothing but went straight into the kitchen with my basket. I set it down angrily and to my dismay found my eyes full of tears. Tears of fury, I told myself, because he had made a fool of me. He was not to be trusted. This was a clear indication of it; he promised one thing and did another.

I wanted to rush out of the studio, to find some quiet spot away from everyone where I could stay until I was calm enough to face him again.

I heard a voice behind me: 'What can I do to help?'

I turned and faced him. I was grateful that the tears had not fallen. They were merely making my eyes look more brilliant, and he should not guess how wretched I was.

I said shortly: 'Nothing. I can manage, thank you.'

I turned back to the table and then I felt him standing close to me; he had gripped my shoulders and was laughing.

He put his face close to my ear and whispered: 'I kept my promise, you know. We didn't play for money.'

I shook him off and went to a drawer of the table which I opened and rummaged in without knowing for what.

'Nonsense,' I retorted. 'The game wouldn't have meant a thing to either of you if there'd been no stakes. It isn't that you enjoy playing cards. It's win or lose. And of course you both think that you're going to win every time. It seems absurdly childish to me. One of you has to lose.'

'But you must understand that I kept my promise.'

'Please don't bother to explain. I can trust my eyes you know.'

'We were gambling . . . certainly. You're right when you said it wouldn't interest us if we were not. Who do you think won this time?'

'I have a meal to prepare.'

'I won this.' He put his hand in his pocket and drew out the statuette.

Then he laughed. 'I determined to get it by fair means or foul. Fortunately it turned out to be fair. So you see I kept my promise to you, I had my gamble, and I own this delightful creature.'

'Take the knives and forks for me, will you please?' I said.

He slipped the statue into his pocket and grinned at me. 'With the greatest pleasure.'

The next day he asked me to marry him. At his suggestion we had climbed the steep path to the Grotto of Matromania. I had always thought it the least exciting of the grottoes and the Blue, Green, Yellow and Red or the Grotto of the Saints were all more worth a visit, but Roc said he had not seen it and wanted me to take him there.

'A very appropriate spot,' he commented when we reached it.

I turned to look at him and he caught my arm and held it tightly.

'Why?' I asked.

'You know,' he replied.

But I was never sure of him – not even at this moment when he regarded me with so much tenderness.

'Matromania,' he murmured.

'I'd heard that this was dedicated to Mithromania known as Mithras,' I said quickly because I was afraid of betraying my feelings.

'Nonsense,' he replied. 'This is where Tiberius held his revels for young men and maidens. I read it in the guidebook. It means matrimony because they married here.'

'There seem to be two opinions then.'

'Then we'd better give it another reason for its importance. It's the spot where Petroc Pendorric asked Favel Farington to marry him and where she said . . .'

He turned to me and in that moment I was certain he loved me as passionately as I loved him.

There was no need for me to answer.

We went back to the studio; he was elated and I was happier than I had ever been before.

Father was so delighted when we told him the news that it was almost as though he wished to get rid of me. He refused to discuss what he would do when I had gone, and I was terribly worried until Roc told me that he would insist on his accepting an allowance. Why shouldn't he from his own son-in-law? He'd commission some pictures if that would make it easier. Perhaps that would be a good idea. 'We've lots of bare wall space at Pendorric,' he added.

And for the first time I began to think seriously about the place which would be my home; but although Roc was always ready to talk of it in general, he said he wanted me to see it and judge for myself. If he talked to me too much I might imagine something entirely different and perhaps be disappointed – though I couldn't believe I could be disappointed in a home I shared with him.

We were very much in love. Roc seemed no longer a stranger. I felt I understood him. There was a streak of mischief in him and he loved to tease me. 'Because,' he told me once, 'you're too serious, too old-fashioned in many ways to be true.'

I pondered on that and supposed I was different from girls he had known, because of my upbringing – the intimate family circle, the school which was run on the same lines as it had been twenty or thirty years before. Also, of course, I had felt my responsibilities deeply when my mother had died. I must learn to be more lighthearted, gay, up-to-date, I told myself.

Our wedding was going to be very quiet; there would be a few guests from the English colony, and Roc and I were going to stay at the studio for a week afterwards; then we were to go to England.

I asked him what his family would think of his returning with a bride they had never met.

'I've written and told them we'll soon be home. They're not so surprised as you imagine. One thing they have learned to expect from me is the unexpected,' he replied cheerfully. 'They're wild with delight. You see they think it's the duty of all Pendorrics to marry, and they believe I've waited long enough.'

I wanted to hear more about them. I wanted to be prepared, but he always put me off.

'I'm not very good at describing things,' he answered. 'You'll be there soon enough.'

'But this Pendorric . . . I gather it is something of a mansion.'

'It's the family home. I suppose you could call it that.'

'And . . . who is the family?'

'My sister, her husband, their twin daughters. You don't have to worry, you know. They won't be in our wing. It's a family custom that all who can, remain at home, and bring their families to live there.'

'And it's near the sea.'

'Right on the coast. You're going to love it. All Pendorrics do, and you'll be one of them very soon.'

I think it was about a week before my wedding day that I noticed the change in my father.

I came in quietly one day and found him sitting at the table staring ahead of him, and because he had not seen me for a few moments I caught him in repose; he looked suddenly old; and more than that . . . frightened.

'Father,' I cried, 'what's the matter?'

He started up and he smiled but his heart wasn't in it.

'The matter? Why, nothing's the matter.'

'But you were sitting there . . .'

'Why shouldn't I? I've been working on that bust of Tiberius. It tired me.'

I accepted his excuse temporarily and forgot about it.

But not for long. My father had never been able to keep things to himself and I began to believe that he was hiding something from me, something which caused him the utmost anxiety.

One early morning, about two days before the wedding, I awoke to find someone moving about in the studio. The illuminated dial of my bedside clock said three o'clock.

I hastily put on a dressing-gown, quietly opened the door of my room and, peeping out, saw a dark shadow seated at the table.

'Father!' I cried.

He started up. 'My dear child, I've disturbed you. It's all right. Do go back to bed.'

I went to him and made him sit down. I drew up a chair. 'Look here,' I insisted, 'you'd better tell me what's wrong.'

He hesitated and then said: 'But it's nothing. I couldn't sleep, so I thought it would do me good to come and sit out here for a while.'

'But why couldn't you sleep? There's something on your mind, isn't there?'

'I'm perfectly all right.'

'It's no use saying that when it obviously isn't true. Are you worried about me . . . about my marrying?'

Again that slight pause. Of course that's it, I thought. Naturally he's worried. He's beginning to realize how he'll miss me.

He said: 'My dear child, you're very much in love with Roc, aren't you?'

'Yes, Father.'

'Favel . . . you're sure, aren't you?'

'Are you worried because we've known each other such a short while?'

He did not answer that but murmured: 'You'll go right away from here . . . to his place in Cornwall . . . to Pendorric.'

'But we'll come to see you! And you'll come to stay with us.'

'I think,' he went on, and it was as though he were talking to himself, 'that if something prevented your marriage it would break my heart.'

He stood up suddenly. 'I'm cold. Let's get back to bed. I'm sorry I disturbed you, Favel.'

'Father, we really ought to have a talk. I wish you would tell me everything that's on your mind.'

'You go along to bed, Favel. I'm sorry I disturbed you.'

He kissed me and we went to our rooms. How often later I was to reproach myself for allowing him to evade me like that. I ought to have insisted on knowing.

There came the day when Roc and I were married and I was so overwhelmed by new and exciting experiences that I did not give a thought to what was happening to my father. I couldn't think of anyone but myself and Roc during those days.

It was wonderful to be together every hour of the days and nights. We would laugh over trifles; it was really the laughter of happiness which comes so easily, I discovered. Guiseppe and Umberto were delighted with us; their arias were more fervent than they used to be, and after we had left them Roc and I would imitate them, gesticulating wildly, setting our faces into tragic or comic masks, whatever the songs demanded, and because we sang out of tune we laughed the more. He would come into the kitchen when I was cooking, to help me he said; and he would sit on the table getting in my way until with mock exasperation I would attempt to turn him out, which always ended up by my being in his arms.

The memories of those days were to stay with me during the difficult times ahead; they sustained me when I needed to be sustained.

Roc was, as I had known he would be, a passionate and demanding lover; he carried me along with him, but I often felt bemused by the rich experiences which were mine. Yet I was certain then that everything was going to be wonderful. I was content to live in the moment; I had even stopped wondering what my new home would be like; I assured myself that my father would have nothing to worry about. Roc would take care of his future as he would take care of mine.

Then one day I went down to the market alone and came back sooner than I had expected.

The door of the studio was open and I saw them there – my father and my husband. The expression on both their faces shocked me. Roc's was grim; my father's tortured. I had the impression that my father had been saying something to Roc which he did not like, and I could not tell whether Roc was angry or shocked. I imagined my father seemed bewildered.

Then they saw me and Roc said quickly: 'Here's Favel.'

It was as though they had both drawn masks over their faces.

'Is anything the matter?' I demanded.

'Only that we're hungry,' answered Roc, coming over to me and taking my basket from me.

He smiled and, putting his arm round me, gave me a hug. 'It seems a long time since I've seen you.'

I looked beyond him to my father; he too was smiling but I thought there was a greyish tinge in his face.

'Father,' I insisted, 'what is it?'

'You're imagining things, my dear,' he assured me.

I could not throw off my uneasiness but I let them persuade me that all was well, because I could not bear that anything should disturb my new and wonderful happiness.

The sun was brilliant. It had been a busy morning in the studio. My father always went down to swim while I got our midday meal, and on that day I told Roc to go with him.

'Why don't you come too?'

'Because I have the lunch to get. I'll do it more quickly if you two go off.'

So they went off together.

Ten minutes later Roc came back. He came into the kitchen and sat on the table. His back was to the window and I noticed the sunlight through the prominent tips of his ears.

'At times,' I said, 'you look like a satyr.'

'That's what I am,' he told me.

'Why did you come back so soon?'

'I found I didn't want to be separated from you any longer, so I left your father on the beach and came back alone.'

I laughed at him. 'You *are* silly! Couldn't you bear to be away from me for another fifteen minutes?'

'Far too long,' he said.

I was delighted to have him with me pretending to help in the kitchen, but when we were ready to eat, my father had not come back.

'I do hope he's not got involved in some long conversation,' I said.

'He couldn't. You know how people desert the beach for food and siesta at this time of day.'

Five minutes later I began to get really anxious; and with good reason.

That morning my father went into the sea and he did not come back alive.

His body was recovered later that day. They said he must have been overcome by cramp and unable to save himself.

It seemed the only explanation then. My happiness was shattered, but how thankful I was that I had Roc. I told him that I did not know how I could have lived through that time if he had not been with me. My great and only consolation was that, although I had lost my father, Roc had come into my life.

It was only later that the terrible doubts began.

Chapter Two

All the joy had naturally gone out of our honeymoon, and I could not rid myself of the fear that I had failed my father in some way.

I remember lying in Roc's arms during the night that followed and crying out: 'There was something I could have done. I know it.'

Roc tried to comfort me. 'But what, my darling? How could you know that he was going to have cramp? It could happen to anybody, and, smooth as the sea was, if nobody heard his cry for help, that would be the end.'

'He never had cramp before.'

'There had to be a first time.'

'But Roc . . . there *was* something.'

He smoothed my hair back from my face. 'Darling, you mustn't upset yourself so. There's nothing we can do now.'

He was right. What could we do?

'He would be glad,' Roc told me, 'that I am here to take care of you.'

There was a note of relief in his voice when he said that which I could not understand, and I felt the first twinges of the fear which I was to come to know very well.

Roc took charge of everything. He said that we must get away from the island as quickly as possible because then I would begin to grow away from my tragedy. He would take me home and in time I should forget.

I left everything to him because I was too unhappy to make arrangements myself. Some of my father's treasures were packed up and sent to Pendorric to await our arrival; the rest were sold. Roc saw the landlord of our studio and arranged to get rid of the lease; and two weeks later we left Capri.

'Now we must try to put that tragedy out of our minds,' said Roc as we sailed to the mainland.

I looked at his profile and for one short moment I felt that I was looking at a stranger. I did not know why – except perhaps because I had begun to suspect, since my father's death, that there was a great deal I had to learn about my husband.

We spent two days in Naples, and while we were there he told me that he was not in any hurry to get home because I was still so shocked and dazed, and he wanted me to have time to recover before he took me to Pendorric.

'We'll finish our honeymoon, darling,' he said.

But my response was listless because I kept thinking of my father sitting at the studio table in the dark, and wondering what he had had on his mind.

'I ought to have found out,' I reiterated. 'How could I have been so thoughtless? I always knew when something worried him. He found it hard to hide anything from me. And he didn't hide that.'

'What do you mean?' demanded Roc almost fiercely.

'I think he was ill. Probably that was why he got this cramp. Roc, what happened on the beach that day? Did he look ill?'

'No. He looked the same as usual.'

'Oh Roc, if only you hadn't come back. If only you'd been with him.'

'It's no use saying If Only, Favel. I wasn't with him. We're going to leave Naples. It's too close. We're going to put all this behind us.' He took my hands and drew me to him, kissing me with tenderness and passion. 'You're my wife, Favel. Remember that. I'm going to make you forget how he died and remember only that we are together now. He wouldn't have you mourn for him.'

He was right. The shock did become modified as the weeks passed. I taught myself to accept the fact that my father's death was not so very unusual. I must remember that I had a husband to consider now and as he was so anxious for me to put the tragedy behind me and be happy, I must do my best to please him.

And it was easier as we went farther from the island.

Roc was charming to me during those days; and I felt that he was determined to make me forget all the sadness.

Once he said to me: 'We can do no good by brooding, Favel. Let's put it behind us. Let's remember that by a wonderful chance we met and fell in love.'

We stayed for two weeks in the south of France, and each day, it seemed, took me a step farther away from the tragedy. We hired a car and Roc took a particular delight in the hairpin bends, laughing at me as I held my breath while he skilfully controlled the car. The scenery delighted me, but as I gazed at terraces of orange stucco villas which seemed to cling to the cliff face, Roc would snap his fingers.

'Wait,' he would say, 'just wait till you see Pendorric!'

It was a joke between us that not all the beauty of the Maritime Alps nor the twists, turns and truly majestic gorges to be discovered on the Corniche road could compare with his native Cornwall.

Often I would say it for him while we sat under a multi-coloured umbrella in opulent Cannes or sunned ourselves on the beach of humbler Menton: 'But of course this is nothing compared with Cornwall.' Then we would laugh together and people passing would smile at us, knowing us for lovers.

At first I thought my gaiety was a little forced. I was so eager to please Roc and there was no doubt that nothing delighted him more than to see me happy. Then I found that I did not have to pretend. I was becoming so deeply in love with my husband that the fact that we were together could overwhelm me and all else seemed of little importance. Roc was eager to wean me from my sorrow; and because he was the sort of man who was determined to have his way he could not fail. I was conscious of his strength, of his dominating nature, and I was glad of it because I would not have wished him to be different. He was the perfect husband and I wondered how I could ever have had doubts about him.

But I grew suddenly uneasy one night in Nice. We had driven in from Villefranche, and as we did so, noticed the dark clouds which hung over the mountains – a contrast to the sparkling scene. Roc had suggested that we visit the Casino, and I as usual readily fell in with his suggestion. He took a turn at the tables and I was reminded then of the light in his eyes when he had sat with my father in the studio. There was the same burning excitement that used to alarm me when I saw it in my father's.

He won that night and was elated; but I couldn't hide my concern, and when in our hotel bedroom I betrayed this, he laughed at me.

'Don't worry,' he said, 'I'd never make the mistake of risking what I couldn't afford to lose.'

'You're a gambler,' I accused.

He took my face in his hands. 'Well, why not? he demanded. 'Life's supposed to be a gamble, isn't it, so perhaps it's the gamblers who come off best.'

He was teasing me as he used to before my father's death, and I assured myself it was only teasing; but that incident seemed to mark a change in our relationship. I was over the first shock; there was no need to treat me with such delicate care. I knew then that Roc would always be a gambler no matter how I tried to persuade him against it, and I experienced once more those faint twinges of apprehension.

Now that the results of the shock were diminishing, I began to think of the future, and there were occasions when I was uneasy. This happened first during the night when I awoke suddenly from a hazy dream in which I knew myself to be in some unspecified danger.

I lay in the darkness, aware of Roc beside me, sleeping deeply, and I thought: What is happening to me? Two months ago I did not know this man. My home was the studio on the island with my father, and now another artist works in the studio and I have no father.

I had a husband. But what did I know of him? – except that I was in love with him. Wasn't that enough? Ours was a deeply passionate relationship and I could at times become so completely absorbed in our need of each other that this seemed all I asked. But that was only a part of marriage. I considered the marriage of my parents and remembered how they had relied on each other and felt that all was well as long as the other was close by.

And here I was waking in the night after a nightmare which hung about me seeming like a vague warning.

That night I really looked the truth in the eye, which was that I knew very little of the man I had married or of the sort of life to which he was taking me.

I made up my mind that I must have a talk with him, and when we drove into the mountains next day I decided to do so. The fears of the night had departed and somehow seemed ridiculous by day, yet I told myself it was absurd that I should know so little of his background.

We found a small hotel where we stopped to have lunch.

I was thoughtful as we ate, and when Roc asked the reason, I blurted out: 'I want to know more about Pendorric and your family.'

'I'm ready for the barrage. Start firing.'

'First the place itself. Let me try to see it and then you fill it with the people.'

He leaned his elbows on the table and narrowed his eyes as though he were looking at something far away, which he could not see very clearly.

'The house first,' he said. 'It's about four hundred years old in some parts. Some of it has been restored. In fact there was a house there in the Dark Ages I believe – so the story goes. . . . We're built on the cliff rock some five hundred yards from the sea; I believe we were much farther from it in the beginning but the sea has a habit of encroaching, you know, and in hundreds of years it advances. We're built of grey Cornish granite calculated to stand against the south-west gales; as a matter of fact over the front archway – one of the oldest parts of the house – there's a motto in Cornish cut into the stone. Translated into English it is: 'When we build we believe we build for ever.' I remember my father's lifting me up to read that and telling me that we Pendorrics were as much a part of the house as that old archway and that Pendorrics would never rest in their graves if the time came when the family left the place.'

'How wonderful to belong to such a family!'

'You do now.'

'But as a kind of outsider . . . as all the people who married into the family must be.'

'You'll soon become one of us. It's always been so with Pendorric brides. In a short time they're upholding the family more enthusiastically than those who started life with the name Pendorric.'

'Are you a sort of squire in the neighbourhood?'

'Squires went out of fashion years ago. We own most of the farms in the district, and customs die harder in Cornwall than anywhere else in England. We cling to old traditions and superstitions. I'm sure that a practical young woman like yourself is going to be very impatient with some of the stories you hear; but bear with us – we're the fey Cornish, remember, and you married into us.'

'I'm sure I shan't complain. Tell me some more.'

'Well, there's the house – a solid rectangle facing north, south, east and west. Northwards we look over the hills to the farmlands – south we face straight out to sea, and east and west give you magnificent views of a coastline that is one of the most beautiful in England and the most treacherous. When the tide goes out you'll see the rocks like sharks' teeth, and you can imagine what happens to boats that find their way on to those. Oh, and I forgot to mention there's one view we don't much like from the east window. It's known to us in the family as Polhorgan's Folly. A house which looks like a replica of our own. We loathe it. We detest it. We nightly pray that it will be blown into the sea.'

'You don't mean that, of course.'

'Don't I?' His eyes flashed, but they were laughing at me.

'Of course you don't. You'd be horrified if it were.'

'There's actually no fear of it. It has stood there for fifty years – an absolute sham – trying to pretend to those visitors who stare up at it from the beach below that it is Pendorric of glorious fame.'

'But who built it?'

He was looking at me and there was something malicious in his gaze which alarmed me faintly because for a second it seemed as though it was directed at me; but then I realized that it was dislike of the owner of Polhorgan's Folly which inspired it.

'A certain Josiah Fleet, better known as Lord Polhorgan. He came there fifty years ago from the Midlands, where he had made a fortune from some commodity – I've forgotten what. He liked our coast, he liked our climate, and decided to build himself a mansion. He did, and spent a month or so there each year, until eventually he settled in altogether and took his name from the cove below him.'

'You certainly don't like him much. Or are you exaggerating?'

Roc shrugged his shoulders. 'Perhaps. It's really the natural enmity between the *nouveaux* poor and the *nouveaux* rich.'

'Are we very poor?'

'By the standards of my Lord Polhorgan . . . yes. I suppose what annoys us is that sixty years ago we were the lords of the manor and he was trudging the streets of Birmingham, Leeds or Manchester – I can never remember which – bare-footed. Industry and natural cunning made him a millionaire. Sloth and natural indolence brought us to our genteel poverty, when we wonder from week to week whether we shall have to call in the National Trust to take over our home and allow us to live in it and show it at half-a-crown a time to the curious public who want to know how the aristocracy once lived.'

'I believe you're bitter.'

'And you're critical. You're on the side of industry and natural cunning. Oh, Favel, what a perfect union! You see, you're all that I'm not. You're going to keep me in order marvellously!'

'You're laughing at me again.'

He gripped my hand so hard that I winced. 'It's my nature, darling, to laugh at everything, and sometimes the more serious I am the more I laugh.'

'I don't think you would ever allow anyone to keep you in order.'

'Well, you chose me, darling, and if I was what you wanted when you made the choice you'd hardly want to change me, would you?'

'I hope,' I said seriously, 'that we shan't change, that we shall always be as happy as we have been up till now.'

For a moment there was the utmost tenderness in his expression, then he was laughing again.

'I told you,' he said, 'I've made a very good match.'

I was suddenly struck by the thought that perhaps his family, who I imagined loved Pendorric as much as he did, would be disappointed that he had married a girl with no money, but I was touched and very happy because he had married me who could bring him nothing. I felt my nightmare evaporating and I wondered on what it could possibly have been founded.

'Are you friendly with this Lord Polhorgan?' I asked quickly to hide my emotion.

'Nobody could be friendly with him. We're polite to each other. We don't see much of him. He's a sick man, well guarded by a nurse and a staff of servants.'

'And his family?'

'He quarrelled with them all. And now he lives alone in his glory. There are a hundred rooms at Polhorgan . . . all furnished in the most flamboyant manner. I believe, though, that dust-sheets perpetually cover the flamboyance. You see why we call it the Folly.'

'Poor old man!'

'I knew your soft heart would be touched. You may meet him. He'll probably consider that he should receive the new Bride of Pendorric.'

'Why do you always refer to me as the Bride of Pendorric – as though in capital letters?'

'Oh, it's a saying at Pendorric. There are lots of crazy things like that.'

'And your family?'

'Now things are very different at Pendorric. Some of our furniture has been standing where it does at this moment for four hundred years. We've got old Mrs. Penhalligan, who is a daughter of Jesse and Lizzie Pleydell, and the Pleydells have looked after the Pendorrics for generations. There's always a faithful member of that family to see that we're cared for. Old Mrs. Penhalligan is a fine housekeeper, and she mends the counterpanes and curtains which are constantly falling apart. She keeps the servants in order at the same time – as well as ourselves. She's sixty-five, but her daughter Maria, who never married, will follow in her footsteps.'

'And your sister?'

'My sister's married to Charles Chaston, who worked as an agent when my father travelled a good deal. He manages the home farm with me now. They live in the northern section of the house. We shall have the south. Don't be afraid that you're going to be hemmed in by relations. It isn't a bit like that at Pendorric. You need never see the rest of the family if you don't want to, except at meals. We all eat together – it's an old family custom – and anyway the servant problem makes it a necessity now. You'll be surprised at the family customs we preserve. Really, you'll think you've stepped back a hundred years. I do myself after I've been away for a while.'

'And your sister, what is her name?'

'Morwenna. Our parents believed in following the family traditions and giving us Cornish names wherever possible. Hence the Petrocs and Mor-wennas. The twins are Lowella and Hyson – Hyson was my mother's maiden name. Lowella refers to herself as Lo and her sister as Hy. I suspect she has a nickname for all of us. She's an incorrigible creature.'

'How old are the twins?'

'Twelve.'

'Are they at school?'

'No. They do go from time to time, but Lowella has an unfortunate habit of running away and dragging Hyson with her. She always says that they can't be happy anywhere but at Pendorric. We're compromised at the moment by having a governess – a trained schoolmistress. It was difficult getting the permission of the educational authorities. but Charles and Morwenna want to keep them at home for a year or so until the child becomes more stable. You'll have to beware of Lowella.'

'How?'

'It'll be all right if she likes you. But she gets up to tricks. Hyson is different. She's the quiet one. They look exactly alike, but their temperaments are completely different. Thank heaven for that. No household could tolerate two Lowellas.'

'What about your parents?'

'They're dead and I remember very little about them. My mother died when we were five, and an aunt looked after us. She still comes to stay quite often and keeps a suite of rooms at Pendorric. Our father lived abroad a great deal when Charles came in. Charles is fifteen years older than Morwenna.'

'You said your mother died when *we* were five. Who else besides you?'

'Didn't I mention that Morwenna and I were twins?'

'No. You said that Lowella and Hyson were.'

'Well, twins run in families, you know. Quite obviously they've started to run in ours.'

'Is Morwenna like you?'

'We're not identical like Lowella and Hyson; but people say they can see a resemblance.'

'Roc,' I said leaning forward, 'you know, I'm beginning to feel I can't wait to meet this family of yours.'

'That's settled it,' he replied. 'It's time we went home.'

So I was, in a measure, prepared for Pendorric.

We had left London after lunch and it was eight o'clock before we got off the train.

Roc had said that he wished we could have motored down, because he wanted to make my crossing of the Tamar something of a ceremony.

However, he had arranged that his car should be waiting at the station so that he could drive me home. Old Toms, the chauffeur-gardener and man-of-all-work at Pendorric, had driven it in that morning.

So I found myself sitting beside Roc in his rather shabby Daimler and feeling a mingling of longing and apprehension, which seemed natural enough in the circumstances.

I was very anxious to make a good impression, for in this new life to which I was going I knew no one except my husband; and I had suddenly realized what an odd position I was in.

I was in a strange country – for the island had been my home – and without friends. If Esther McBane had been in England I should not have felt quite so lonely. She would at least have been one friend. But Esther was far away in Rhodesia now, as deeply absorbed in her new life as I was becoming in mine. There had been other school friends, but none as close as Esther, and as we had never exchanged letters after we left school those friendships had lapsed.

But what foolish thoughts these were! I might not have old friends, but I had a husband.

Roc swung the car out of the station yard, and as we left the town, the quiet of the summer evening closed in about us. We were in a narrow winding lane with banks on either side which were dotted with wild roses, and there was the sweet smell of honeysuckle in the air.

'Is it far to Pendorric?' I asked.

'Eight miles or so. The sea is ahead of us, the moor's behind us. We'll do some walking on the moors . . . or riding. Can you ride?'

'I'm afraid not.'

'I'll teach you. You're going to make this place home, Favel. Some people never can, but I think you will.'

'I believe I shall.'

We were silent and I studied the landscape avidly. The houses which we passed were little more than cottages, not by any means beautiful – indeed they struck me as rather grim – all made of that grey Cornish stone. I fancied I caught a whiff of the sea as we slowly climbed a steep hill and went forward into wooded country. We were soon descending again on the other side of the hill. 'When you see the sea you'll know we're not far from home,' Roc told me, and almost immediately we began to climb again.

At the top of the hill he stopped the car, and putting his arm along the back of the seat, pointed towards the sea.

'Can you see the house there, right on the edge of the cliff? That's the Folly. You can't see Pendorric from here because there's a hill in the way; but it's a little to the right.'

The Folly looked almost like a medieval castle.

'I wonder he didn't supply a drawbridge and a moat,' murmured Roc. 'Though heaven knows it would have been difficult to have a moat up there. Still, all the more laudable that he should achieve it.'

He started up the car, and when he had gone half a mile I caught my first glimpse of Pendorric.

It was so like the other house that I was astonished.

'They look close together from here,' said Roc, 'but there's a good mile between them on the coast road – of course as the crow flies they're a little nearer – but you can understand the wrath of the Pendorrics, can't you, to find *that* set up where they just can't get it out of their sight.'

We had now reached a major road, and we sped along this until we came to a turning and began to plunge down one of the steepest hills we had come upon as yet. The banks were covered with the wild flowers which I had noticed before, and stubby fir trees with their resinous scent.

At the bottom of the hill we struck the cliff road, and then I saw the coast in all its glory. The water was quiet on that night and I could hear the gentle swish as it washed against the rocks. The cliffs were covered in grass and bracken, and dotted here and there were clumps of pink, red, and white valerian; the sweep of the bay was magnificent. The tide was out, and in the evening light I saw those malignant rocks jutting cruelly out of the shallow water.

And there half a mile ahead of us was Pendorric itself, and I caught my breath for it was awe-inspiring. It towered above the sea a massive rectangle of grey stone, with crenellated towers and an air of impregnability, noble and arrogant as though defying the sea and the weather and anyone who came against it.

'This is your home, my dear,' said Roc, and I could hear the pride in his voice.

'It's . . . superb.'

'So you're not unhappy? I'm glad you're seeing it for the first time. Otherwise I might have thought you married *it* rather than me.'

'I would never marry a house!'

'No, you're too honest – too full of common sense . . . in fact too wonderful. That's why I fell in love with you and determined to marry you.'

We were roaring uphill again, and now that we were closer the house certainly dominated the landscape. There were lights in some of the windows and I saw the arch leading to the north portico.

'The grounds,' Roc explained, 'are on the south side. We can approach the house from the south; there are four porticoes – north, south, east and west. But we'll go into the north to-night because Morwenna and Charlie will be waiting for us there. Why, look,' he went on, and following his gaze I saw a slight figure in riding breeches and scarlet blouse, black hair flying, running towards us. Roc slowed the car and she leapt on to the running-board. Her face was brown with sun and weather, her eyes were long and black and very like Roc's.

'I wanted to be the first to see the bride!' she shouted.

'And you always get your way,' answered Roc. 'Favel, this is Lowella, of whom beware.'

'Don't listen to him,' said the girl. 'I expect I'll be your friend.'

'Thank you,' I said. 'I hope you will.'

The black eyes studied me curiously. 'I said she'd be fair,' she went on. 'I was certain.'

'Well, you're impeding our progress,' Roc told her. 'Either hop in or get off.'

'I'll stay here,' she announced. 'Drive in.'

Roc obeyed and we went slowly towards the house.

'They're all waiting to meet you,' Lowella told me. 'We're very excited. We've all been trying to guess what you'll be like. In the village they're all waiting to see you too. Every time one of us goes down they say, "And when will the Bride be coming to Pendorric?"'

'I hope they'll be pleased with me.'

Lowella looked at her uncle mischievously and I thought again how remarkably like him she was. 'Oh, it was time he was married,' she said. 'We were getting worried.'

'You see I was right to warn you,' put in Roc. 'She's the *enfant terrible*.'

'And not such an infant,' insisted Lowella. 'I'm twelve now, you know.'

'You grow more terrible with the years. I tremble to think what you'll be like at twenty.'

We had now passed through the gates and I saw the great stone arch looming ahead. Behind it was a portico guarded on either side by two huge carved lions, battered by the years but still looking fierce as though warning any to be wary of entering.

And there was a woman – so like Roc that I knew she was his twin sister – and behind her a man, whom I guessed to be her husband and father of the twins.

Morwenna came towards the car. 'Roc! So you're here at last. And this is Favel. Welcome to Pendorric, Favel.'

I smiled up at her, and for those first moments I was glad that she looked so like Roc, because it made me feel that she was not quite a stranger. Her dark hair was thick with a slight natural wave and it grew to a widow's peak which in the half-light gave the impression that she was wearing a sixteenth-century cap. She wore a dress of emerald-green linen which became her dark hair and eyes, and there were gold rings in her ears.

'I'm so glad to meet you at last,' I said. 'I do hope this isn't a shock to you.'

'Nothing my brother does ever shocks us, really, because we're expecting surprises.'

'You see I've brought them up in the right way,' said Roc lightly. 'Oh and here's Charlie.'

My hand was gripped so firmly that I winced. I was hoping Charles Chaston didn't notice this as I looked up into his plump bronzed face.

'We've all been eagerly waiting to see you, ever since we heard you were coming,' he told me.

I saw that Lowella was dancing round us in a circle; with her flying hair, and as she was chanting something to herself which might have been an incantation, she reminded me of a witch.

'Oh Lowella, do stop,' cried her mother with a little laugh. 'Where's Hyson?'

Lowella lifted her arms in a gesture which implied she had no idea.

'Go and find her. She'll want to say hallo to her Aunt Favel.'

'We're not calling her aunt,' said Lowella. 'She's too young. She's just going to be Favel. You'll like that better, won't you, Favel?'

'Yes, it sounds more friendly.'

'There you see,' said Lowella, and she ran into the house.

Morwenna slipped her arm through mine, and Roc came up and took the other as he called: 'Where's Toms? Toms! Come and bring in our baggage.'

I heard a voice say: 'Ay sir. I be coming.'

But before he appeared Morwenna and Roc were leading me through the portico, and with Charles hovering behind we entered the house.

I was in an enormous hall at either end of which was a beautiful curved staircase leading to a gallery. On the panelled walls were swords and shields and at the foot of each staircase a suit of armour.

'This is our wing,' Morwenna told me. 'It's a most convenient house, really, being built round a quadrangle. It is almost like four houses in one and it was built with the intention of keeping Pendorrics together in the days of large families. I believe years ago the house was crowded. Only a few servants lived in the attics; the rest of them were in the cottages. There are six of them side by side, most picturesque and insanitary – until Roc and Charles did something about it. We still draw on them for help; and we only keep Toms and his wife and daughter Hetty, and Mrs. Penhalligan and her daughter Maria, living in. A change from the old days. I expect you're hungry.'

I told her we had had dinner on the train.

'Then we'll have a snack later. You'll want to see something of the house, but perhaps you'd like to go to your own part first.'

I said I should, and as I spoke, my eye was caught by a portrait which hung on the wall of the gallery. It was a picture of a fair-haired young woman in a clinging blue gown which showed her shapely shoulders; her hair was piled high above her head and one ringlet hung over her shoulder. She clearly belonged to the late eighteenth century, and I thought that her picture, placed as it was, dominated the gallery and hall.

'How charming!' I said.

'Ah yes, one of the Brides of Pendorric,' Morwenna told me.

There it was again – that phrase which I had heard so often.

'She looks beautiful . . . and so happy.'

'Yes, she's my great-great-great- . . . one loses count of the greats . . . grandmother,' Morwenna said. 'She was happy when that was painted, but she died young.'

I found it difficult to take my eyes from the picture because there was something so appealing about that young face.

'I thought, Roc,' went on Morwenna, 'that now you're married you'd want the big suite.'

'Thanks,' Roc replied. 'That's exactly what I did want.'

Morwenna turned to me. 'The wings of the house are all connected. You don't have to use the separate entrances unless you wish to. So if you come up to the gallery I'll take you through.'

'There must be hundreds of rooms.'

'Eighty. Twenty in each of the four parts. I think it's much larger than it was in the beginning. A lot of it has been restored, but because of that motto over the arch they've been very careful to make it seem that what was originally built has lasted.'

We went past the suit of armour and up the stairs to the gallery.

'One thing,' said Morwenna, 'when you know your own wing you know all the others; you just have to imagine the rooms facing different directions.'

She led the way, and with Roc's arm still in mine we followed. When we reached the gallery we went through a side door which led to another corridor in which were beautiful marble figures set in alcoves.

'Not the best time to see the house,' commented Morwenna. 'It's neither light nor dark.'

'She'll have to wait till the morning to explore,' added Roc.

I looked through one of the windows down on to a large quadrangle in which grew some of the most magnificent hydrangeas I had ever seen.

I remarked on them and we paused to look down.

'The colours are wonderful in sunlight,' Morwenna told me. 'They thrive here. It's because we're never short of rain and there's hardly ever a frost. Besides, they're well sheltered in the quadrangle.'

It looked a charming place, that quadrangle. There was a pond, in the centre of which was a dark statue which I later discovered was of Hermes; and there were two magnificent palm trees growing down there so that it looked rather like an oasis in a desert. In between the paving-stones clumps of flowering shrubs bloomed and there were several white seats with gilded decorations.

Then I noticed all the windows which looked down on it and it occurred to me that it was a pity because one would never be able to sit there without a feeling of being overlooked.

Roc explained to me that there were four doors all leading into it, one from each wing.

We moved along the corridor through another door and Roc said that we were now in the south wing – our own. We went up a staircase and Morwenna went ahead of us, and when she threw open a door we entered a large room with enormous windows facing the sea. The deep red velvet curtains had been drawn back, and when I saw the seascape stretched out before me I gave a cry of pleasure and at once went to the window. I stood there looking out across the bay; the cliffs looked stark and menacing in the twilight and I could just glimpse the rugged outline of the rocks. The smell and the gentle whispering of the sea seemed to fill the room.

Roc was behind me. 'It's what everyone does,' he said. 'They never glance at the room; they look at the view.'

'The views are just as lovely from the east and west side,' said Morwenna, 'and very much the same.'

She turned a switch and the light from a large chandelier hanging from the centre of the ceiling made the room dazzlingly bright. I turned from the window and saw the four-poster bed, with the long stool at its foot, the tallboy, the cabinets – all belonging to an earlier generation, a generation of exquisite grace and charm.

'But it's lovely!' I said.

'We flatter ourselves that we have the best of both worlds,' Morwenna told me. 'We made an old powder closet into a bathroom.' She opened a door which led from the bedroom and disclosed a modern bathroom. I looked at it longingly and Roc laughed.

'You have a bath,' he said. 'I'll go and see what Toms is doing about the baggage. Afterwards we'll have something to eat, and perhaps I'll take you for a walk in the moonlight – if there's any to be had.'

I said I thought it was an excellent idea, and they left me.

When I was alone I went once more to the windows to gaze out at that magnificent view. I stood for some minutes, my eyes on the horizon, as I watched the intermittent flashes of the lighthouse.

Then I went into the bathroom, where bath salts and talcum powder had all been laid out for me – my sister-in-law's thoughtfulness, I suspected. She was obviously anxious to make me welcome, and I felt it had been a very pleasant homecoming.

If only I could have thought of Father at work in his studio I could have been very happy. But I had to start a new life; I must stop fretting. I had to be gay. I owed that to Roc; and he was the type of man who would want his wife to be gay.

I went into the bathroom, ran a bath and spent about half an hour luxuriating in it. When I came out, Roc had not returned, but my bags had been put in the room. I unpacked a small one and changed from my suit to a silk dress; and I was doing my hair at the dressing-table, which had a three-sided mirror, when there was a knock at the door.

'Come in,' I called, and turning saw a young woman and a child. I thought at first that the child was Lowella and I smiled at her. She did not return the smile but regarded me gravely, while the young woman said: 'Mrs. Pendorric, I am Rachel Bective, the children's governess. Your husband asked me to show you the way down when you were ready.'

'How do you do?' I said, and I was astonished by the change in Lowella.

There was an air of efficiency about Rachel Bective, whom I guessed to be around about thirty, and I remembered what Roc had told me about a schoolmistress looking after the twins' education. Her hair was a sandy colour and her brows and lashes so fair that she looked surprised; her teeth were sharp and white. I did not warm towards her. She seemed to me to be obviously summing me up, and her manner was calculating and critical.

'This is Hyson,' she said. 'I believe you met her sister.'

'Oh I see.' I smiled at the child. 'I thought you were Lowella.'

'I knew you did.' She was almost sullen.

'You are so much like her.'

'I only *look* like her.'

'Are you ready to come down?' asked Rachel Bective. 'There's to be a light supper because I believe you had dinner on the train.'

'Yes, we did and I'm quite ready.'

For the first time since I had come into the house I felt uncomfortable, and was glad when Rachel Bective led the way along the corridor and down the staircase.

We came to a gallery and I did not realize that it was not the same one which I had seen from the north side until I noticed the picture there and I knew that I had never seen that before.

It was the picture of a woman in a riding jacket. The habit was black and she was very fair; she wore a hard black hat, and about it was a band of blue velvet which hung down forming a snood at the back. She was very beautiful, but her large blue eyes, which were the same colour as the velvet band and snood, were full of brooding sadness. Moreover the picture had been painted so that it was impossible to escape those eyes. They followed you wherever you went, and even in that first moment I thought they were trying to convey some message.

'What a magnificent picture!' I cried.

'It's Barbarina,' said Hyson, and for a moment her face was filled with vitality and she looked exactly as Lowella had when she had welcomed us.

'What an extraordinary name! And who was she?'

'She was my grandmother,' Hyson told me proudly.

'She died . . . tragically, I believe,' put in Rachel Bective.

'How dreadful! And she looks so beautiful.'

I remembered then that I had seen a picture of another beautiful woman in the north hall when I had arrived and had heard that she too had died young.

Hyson said in a voice which seemed to hold a note of hysteria: '*She* was one of the Brides of Pendorric.'

'Well, I suppose she was,' I said, 'since she married your grandfather.'

This Hyson was a strange child; she had seemed so lifeless a moment ago; now she was vital and excited.

'She died twenty-five years ago when my mother and Uncle Roc were five years old.'

'How very sad!'

'You'll have to have *your* picture painted, Mrs. Pendorric,' said Rachel Bective.

'I hadn't thought of it.'

'I'm sure Mr. Pendorric will want it done.'

'He hasn't said anything about it.'

'It's early days yet. Well, I think we should go. They'll be waiting.'

We went along the gallery and through a door and were walking round the corridor facing the quadrangle again. I noticed that Hyson kept taking covert glances at me. I thought she seemed rather a neurotic child, and there was a quality about the governess which I found distinctly disturbing.

I woke up in the night and for a few seconds wondered where I was. Then I saw the enormous windows, heard the murmuring of the sea, and it sounded like the echo of voices I had heard in my dream.

I could smell the tang of seaweed and the freshness of the ocean. The rhythm of the waves seemed to keep time with Roc's breathing.

I raised myself, and leaning on my elbow looked at him. There was enough moonlight to show me the contours of his face which looked as though it had been cut out of stone. He appeared different in repose, and, realizing how rarely I saw him thus, again I had that feeling that I was married to a stranger.

I shook off my fancies. I reminded myself that I had sustained a great shock. My thoughts were so often with my father, and I wondered again and again what he must have experienced in that dreadful moment when the cramp had overtaken him and he realized that he could not reach land and there was no one at hand to help him. He had come face to face with death, and that must have been a moment of intense horror; and what seemed so terrible was that at that moment Roc and I were laughing together in the kitchen of the studio.

If Roc had only stayed with him . . .

I wished I could stop thinking of my father, sitting in the lonely studio in the darkness, of the anxiety I had seen on his face when I had come upon him and Roc together.

I must have been dreaming about the island and my father, for what was disturbing me was the memory of relief I had fancied I saw in Roc's face at the time of the tragedy. It was almost as though he had believed it was the best possible thing that could have happened.

Surely I must have imagined that. But when had I started to imagine it? Was it that hangover from some dream?

I lay down quietly so as not to disturb him, and after a while I slept. But again I was troubled by dreams. I could hear a murmur like background music and it might have been the movement of the waves or Roc's breathing beside me; then I heard the shrill laughter of Lowella, or it might have been Hyson, as she cried out: 'Two Brides of Pendorric died young. . . . Now you are a Bride of Pendorric.'

I remembered that dream next morning, and what had seemed full of significance in my sleep now seemed the natural result of a day crammed with new experiences.

The next day the sun was shining brilliantly. I stood at a window watching the light on the water, and it was as though some giant had thrown down a handful of diamonds.

Roc came and stood behind me, putting his hands on my shoulders.

'I can see you are coming under the spell of *that* Pendorric as well as this one.'

I turned and smiled at him. He looked so concerned that I threw my arms about his neck. He waltzed round the room with me and said: 'It is good to have you here at Pendorric. This morning I'm going to take you for a drive and show you off to the locals. You're going to find them very inquisitive. This afternoon I'll have to go into things with old Charles. I've been away a long time – longer than I planned for – and there'll be a little catching up to do. You can go off and explore on your own then, or perhaps Lowella will join you.'

I said: 'The other child is quite different, isn't she?'

'Hyson? Thank heaven. We couldn't do with two like Lowella. There'd be no peace.'

'And yet they're so alike I couldn't tell which was which.'

'You get to know the slight difference after a while. Perhaps it's in the voices. I'm not sure, but we can usually tell. It's strange, but with identicals you sometimes get two entirely different temperaments. It's as though characteristics have been divided into two neat little piles – one for one, one for the other. However, Rachel takes good care of them.'

'Oh . . . the governess.'

'That makes her sound rather Victorian, and there's nothing Victorian about Rachel. Actually she's more a friend of the family. She was an old schoolfellow of Morwenna's. Ready?'

We went out of the room and I followed where Roc led, realizing that I must expect to be a little vague as yet about the geography of the house.

We were on the third floor and it seemed that there were linking doors to all wings on all floors. I looked down at the quadrangle as we passed the windows. It was true that it was quite charming in sunlight. I imagined myself sitting under one of the palm trees with a book. It would be the utmost peace. Then I looked up at the windows.

'A pity,' I murmured.

'What?' asked Roc.

'That you'd always have the feeling of not being alone down there.'

'Oh . . . you mean the windows. They're all corridor windows, not the sort for sitting at.'

'I suppose that does make a difference.'

I had not noticed that we had come round to the north wing until Roc paused at a door, knocked and went in.

The twins were sitting at a table, exercise books before them; and with them sat Rachel Bective. She smiled rather lazily when she saw me, reminding me of a tortoise-shell cat who was sleeping pleasantly and is suddenly disturbed.

'Hello, Favel!' cried Lowella leaping up. '*And* Uncle Roc!'

Lowella flung her arms about Roc's neck, lifted her feet from the ground and was swung round and round.

Rachel Bective looked faintly amused; Hyson's face was expressionless.

'Help!' cried Roc. 'Come along, Favel . . . Rachel . . . rescue me.'

'Any excuse to stop lessons,' murmured Rachel.

Lowella released her uncle. 'If I want to find excuses I always can,' she said gravely. 'That was meant to say how glad I was to see him and the Bride.'

'I want you to entertain her this afternoon,' said Roc, 'while I'll be working. Will you?'

'Of course.' Lowella smiled at me. 'I've such lots to tell you.'

'I'm looking forward to hearing.' I included Hyson in my smile but she quickly looked away.

'Now you're here,' said Roc, 'you must have a look at the old schoolroom. It's a real relic from the past. Generations of Pendorrics sat at that table. My grandfather carved his initials on it and was sternly punished by his governess.'

'How was he punished?' Lowella wanted to know.

'Probably with a big stick . . . or made to fast on bread and water and learn pages of *Paradise Lost*.'

'I'd rather the stick,' said Lowella.

'You wouldn't. You'd hate that,' put in Hyson surprisingly.

'No, I'd love it, because I'd take the stick and start beating whoever was beating me.' Lowella's eyes shone at the prospect.

'There you are, Rachel, that's a warning,' said Roc.

He had gone to the cupboard and showed me books which must have been there for years; some were exercise books filled with the unformed writing of children; there were several slates and pencil boxes.

'You'll have to have a good look when it's not lesson time, Favel. I believe Rachel's getting a little impatient with us.'

He flashed a smile at Rachel, and because I thought I saw intimacy in it I felt a pang of jealousy. Until now it had not occurred to me that the easy manner in which my friendship with Roc had progressed was due to his easygoing friendly nature. Now it occurred to me that he was very friendly with Rachel – and she with him, for if his smile for her was warm, hers was a good deal warmer. I began to wonder then how deep a friendship it was.

I was glad to leave the schoolroom, the exuberant Lowella, the silent Hyson, and Rachel who was too friendly – towards Roc. There were lots of questions I wanted to ask him about Rachel Bective but I felt that I might betray my jealousy if I did, so I decided to shelve the subject for the time being.

When I was sitting in the car with Roc I felt happy again. He was right when he had suggested that an entirely new life would help me to put the past behind me. So many new impressions were being superimposed on those old ones that they now seemed to belong to another life.

Roc put his hand over mine and I would have said he was a very contented man that morning.

'I can see you've taken to Pendorric like a duck to water.'

'It's all so intriguing, so beautiful . . . and the family is interesting.'

He grimaced. 'We're flattered. I'm going to drive you past the Folly; then you can see what a sham it is.'

We drove down the steep road and up again and then we were on a level with Polhorgan. At first glance it appeared to be as old as Pendorric.

'They've deliberately tried to make the stone look old. The gargoyles over the front porch are crumbling artistically.'

'There's no sign of life.'

'There never is from this side. The master of the house has his apartments on the south side, facing the sea. He owns the beach below and he has magnificent flower gardens laid out on the cliffs. Much grander than ours. He bought the land from my grandfather.'

'He has a wonderful view.'

'That's as well because he spends most of the time in his room. His heart won't allow him to do otherwise.'

We had passed the house and Roc went on: 'I'm taking this road which will carry us back to Pendorric because I want you to see our little village. I know you're going to love it.'

We had turned back and were going steeply down again to the coast road which led past Pendorric. I gazed at the house in a happy proprietorial way as we passed. In a short time we were roaring up the steep hill to the main road and I could see the sea on our left.

'It's the twists of our coast that make you lose your sense of direction,' Roc explained. 'This was once an area of terrific volcanic upheaval, which means that the land was flung in all directions. We've been rounding a sort of promontory and we're now coming into the village of Pendorric.'

We swooped down again and there it lay – the most enchanting little village I had ever seen. There was the church, its ancient tower, about which the ivy clung, clearly of Norman architecture, and it was set in the midst of the graveyard. On one side the stones were dark with age and on the other they were white and new-looking. There was the vicarage, a grey house set in a hollow with its lawn and gardens on an incline. Beyond the church was the row of cottages which Morwenna had mentioned; they had thatched roofs and tiny windows and were all joined together – the whole six of them. I imagine they were of the same period as the church.

Not far from the cottages was a garage with living quarters above it. 'It was once the blacksmith's forge,' Roc explained. 'The Bonds who lived there have been blacksmiths for generations. It broke old Jim Bond's heart when there were no longer enough horses in the district to make the smithy worth while, but they have compromised. The old forge is still in existence and I often pull up here to have the horses shod.'

He slowed down and called: 'Jim! Hi, Jim!'

A window above was thrown open and a handsome woman appeared there. Her black hair fell loosely about her shoulders and her scarlet blouse seemed too tight for her. She had the look of a gipsy.

'Morning, Mr. Roc,' she said.

'Why hallo, Dinah.'

'Nice to see you back, Mr. Roc.'

Roc waved a hand and at that moment a man came out to us.

'Morning, Jim,' said Roc.

He was a man in his fifties, an enormous man, just as one would have imagined a blacksmith should look; his sleeves were rolled up to display his brawny muscles. Roc went on: 'I've brought my wife along to show her the old forge and get her acquainted with the village.'

'I'm glad to see you, ma'am,' said Jim. 'Would 'ee care to come in and have a drop of our old cider?'

I said I should be delighted, and we got out of the car and went into the blacksmith's shop, where a strawberry roan was actually being shod. The smell of burning hoof filled the air, and the young man who was working at the forge said good-morning to us. He seemed to be Jim too.

I was told that he was young Jim, the son of old Jim, and that there had been Jim Bonds at the forge for as long as anyone could remember.

'And us reckons there always will be,' said old Jim. 'Though . . . times change.' He looked a little sad.

'You never know when your luck will turn,' Roc told him.

Old Jim went to a corner and came out with glasses on a tray. He filled the glasses from a great barrel with a tap at the side which stood in a corner of the shop.

'The Bonds have always been noted for their cider,' Roc explained.

'Oh yes, m'dear,' said old Jim. 'Me Granny used to keep a live toad in the barrel and 'twas said that hers was a cider as had to be tasted to be believed. Now don't 'ee look scared like. We don't use the old toad now. 'Tis just the juice of good old Cornish apples and the way we Bonds have with 'em.'

'It's as potent as ever,' said Roc.

'It's very good,' I commented.

'Sometimes a bit too much for the foreigners,' said old Jim, looking at me as though he hoped I was teetering on the verge of intoxication.

The younger man went on stolidly with his work and hardly looked at us.

Then a door opened and the woman who had looked from the window came in. Her black eyes were sparkling and she swayed her hips as she walked; she was wearing a short full skirt and her shapely legs were bare and brown; her feet, slightly grubby, were in scuffed sandals.

I noticed that all three men were intensely aware of her the moment she came in. Old Jim scowled at her and didn't seem very pleased to see her; young Jim couldn't take his eyes from her; but it was Roc's expression which was not easy to construe. I could see immediately the effect she had on the others, but not on Roc. It was my husband whom I could not understand.

She herself studied me intently, taking in each detail of my appearance. I felt she was a little scornful of my clean linen dress, as she smoothed her hands over her hips and smiled at Roc. It was a familiar and, I thought, even intimate gaze. I was a little ashamed of myself then. Was I over-jealous because I had a very attractive husband? I must stop myself wondering what his relationship had been with every young woman he had known before he met me. 'This is Dinah, young Mrs. Bond,' Roc was explaining to me.

'How do you do?' I said.

She smiled. 'I do very well,' she answered, 'and I'm terribly glad to see Mr. Roc has brought a bride to Pendorric.'

'Thank you,' said Roc. He drained his glass. 'We have a lot to do this morning,' he added.

'Can I fill up your car, sir?' asked old Mr. Bond.

'We're all right for a bit, Jim,' said Roc, and I had a feeling that he was anxious to get away.

I felt a little dizzy – it was the cider, I told myself – and I was rather glad to get out into the fresh air.

The old man and Dinah stood watching as we drove away. There was a slow smile on Dinah's face.

'Dinah rather broke up the happy party,' I said.

'The old fellow hates her, I'm afraid. Life doesn't go smoothly at the old forge since Dinah came to live there.'

'She's very attractive.'

'That seems to be the majority opinion – including Dinah's. I hope it works out, but I fancy young Jim doesn't have too good a life between the old man and the young woman. Old Jim would have liked to see him marry one of the Pascoe girls from the cottages; they'd have had a little Jim by now. But young Jim – always a docile lad till he fell in love with Dinah – married her, and that has not made for peace at the old forge. She's half gipsy and used to live in a caravan in the woods about a mile away.'

'Is she a good and faithful wife?'

Roc laughed, 'Did she give you the impression that she was?'

'Far from it.'

Roc nodded. 'Dinah wouldn't pretend to be what she isn't.'

He pulled up the car before a gate and a voice called to us: 'Why, Mr. Pendorric, how nice to see you back.'

A plump, rosy-cheeked woman who had a basket full of roses on her arm and cutters in her hand came to the gate and leaned over.

'This is Mrs. Dark,' said Roc. 'Our vicar's wife.'

'So nice of you to call so quickly. We've been so eager to meet Mrs. Pendorric.'

We got out of the car and Mrs. Dark opened the gate and took us into a garden which consisted of a lawn bounded by flower beds and enclosed by hedges of macrocarpas.

'The vicar will be very pleased to see you. He's in the study working on his sermon. I hope you'll have some coffee.'

We told her we had just had cider at the forge. 'And,' added Roc, 'I'd like to show my wife the old church. Please don't disturb your husband.'

'He'd be so sorry if he missed you.' She turned to me. 'We're so pleased to have you with us, Mrs. Pendorric, and we do hope you're going to enjoy living here and will be with us quite a lot. It's always so pleasant when the big house takes an interest in village things.'

'Favel is already enormously interested in Pendorric affairs,' said Roc. 'She's looking forward to seeing the church.'

'I'll go and tell Peter you're here.'

We walked through the garden with her, and passing through a hedge were on the lawn that sloped down to the vicarage. Opposite the house was the church, and we went towards it while Mrs. Dark hurried across the lawn to the house.

'We don't seem to be able to escape people this morning,' said Roc, taking my arm. 'They're all determined to have a look at you. I wanted to show you the church on my own, but Peter Dark will be on our trail soon.'

I was conscious of the quietness about us as we passed the yews, which had grown cumbersome with age, and crossed a part of the old graveyard and went into the church.

I immediately felt that I had stepped back in time. There was a thirteenth-century church looking little different, I imagined, from what it had in the days when it had been built. The light filtered through the stained-glass windows on to the altar with its beautiful embroidered cloth and exquisite carving. On the wall, carved in stone, were the names of the vicars from the year 1280.

'They were all local people,' Roc explained, 'until the Darks came. They come from the Midlands somewhere and they seem to know far more about the place than any of us. Dark is an expert on old Cornish customs. He's collecting them and writing a book on them.'

His voice sounded hollow, and as I looked up at him I was not thinking of the Darks, nor the church, but of the expression I had seen in Rachel Bective's eyes that morning and later in those of Dinah Bond.

He was extremely attractive; I had known that the moment I set eyes on him. I had fallen deep in physical love with him when I knew little about him. I knew little more now and I was more deeply in love than ever. I was so happy with him except when the doubts came. I was wondering now whether I had married a philanderer who was a perfect lover because he was so experienced; and it was not turning out to be such a happy morning as I had imagined it would.

'Anything wrong?' asked Roc.

'Should there be?'

He took me by the shoulders and held me against him so that I couldn't see his eyes. 'I've got you . . . here in Pendorric. How could anything be wrong with that?'

I was startled by the sound of a footstep, and breaking away I saw that a man in clerical clothes had come into the church.

'Hallo, Vicar,' said Roc easily.

'Susan told me you were here.' He advanced towards us, a pleasant-mannered man with a happy, alert expression which suggested he found his life one of absorbing interest. He took my hand. 'Welcome to Pendorric, Mrs. Pendorric. We're so pleased to have you with us. What do you think of the church? Isn't it fascinating?'

'It is indeed.'

'I'm having a wonderful time going through the records. It's always been an ambition of mine to have a living in Cornwall. It's the most intriguing of all the counties – don't you think, Mrs. Pendorric?'

'I can well believe it might be.'

'So individual. I always say to Susan that as soon as you cross the Tamar you notice the difference. It's like entering a different world – far away from prosaic England. Here in Cornwall one feels anything might happen. It's a fey country. It's due to the old superstitions and customs. There are still people here who really do leave bread and milk on their doorsteps for the Little People. And they swear it's disappeared by morning.'

'I warned you,' said Roc, 'that our vicar is enthusiastic about the customs of the place.'

'I'm afraid I am. Mrs. Pendorric, are you interested?'

'I hadn't thought much about it. But I believe I could be.'

'Good. We must have a talk some time.' We started to walk round the church and he went on: 'These are the Pendorric pews. Set apart from the rest, you see . . . at the side of the pulpit. I believe in the old days they used to be filled by the family and the retainers. Things have changed considerably.'

He pointed to one of the most beautiful of the stained-glass windows. 'That was put in in seventeen ninety-two in memory of Lowella Pendorric. I think the colouring of the glass is the most exquisite I've ever seen.'

'You've seen her picture in the north hall,' Roc reminded me.

'Oh yes . . . didn't she die young?'

'Yes,' said the vicar, 'in childbirth with her first child. She was only eighteen. They call her the First Bride. . . .'

'The first! But there must have been other brides. I understood there had been Pendorrics for centuries.'

The vicar stared blankly at the window. 'The sayings become attached and the origins are often steeped in legend. This is a memorial to another Pendorric. A great hero. A friend and supporter of Jonathan Trelawny who is himself buried at Pelynt, not so very far from here. The Trelawny, you know, who defied James II and of whom we sing:

"And shall Trelawny die?
Here's twenty thousand Cornishmen will know the reason why." '

He went on to point out other features of the church, and after renewing his wife's invitation to coffee, he left us, but not before saying that he looked forward to meeting me soon and that if I wanted any information about ancient Cornwall he would be pleased to give it to me.

I thought his kind face was a little anxious as he laid his hand on my arm and said: 'It doesn't do to take much notice of these old stories, Mrs. Pendorric. They're interesting just as curiosities, that's all.'

He left us outside the church and Roc gave a little sigh.

'He can be rather trying when he gets on to his favourite hobby. I began to think we were in for one of his longer lectures and we'd never get rid of him.' He looked at his watch. 'Now we'll have to hurry. But just a quick look round the old graveyard. Some of the inscriptions are amusing.'

We picked our way between the gravestones; some were so old that the words which had been engraved upon them were obliterated altogether; others leaned at grotesque angles.

We stopped before one which must have been more sheltered from the winds and weather than most, for although the date on it was 1779 the words were clearly visible.

Roc began to read them aloud:

> 'When you, my friends, behold
> Where now I lie,
> Remember 'tis appointed
> For all men once to die.
> For I myself in prime of life
> The Lord took me away
> And none that's on the Earth can tell
> How long they in't may stay.'

He turned to me, smiling: 'Cheerful!' he said. 'Your turn. When Morwenna and I were children we used to come here and read them to each other, taking turns.'

I paused before another stone, slightly less ancient, the date being 1842.

> 'Though some of you perhaps may think
> From dangers to be free
> Yet in a moment may be sent
> Into the grave like me.'

I stopped and said: 'The theme is similar.'

'What do you expect here among the dead? It's appropriate enough.'

'I'd rather find one that didn't harp so much on death.'

'Not so easy,' said Roc. 'But follow me.' He led the way through the long grass and eventually stopped and began to read:

> 'Though I was both deaf and dumb
> Much pleasure did I take

With my fingers and my thumb
All my wants to relate.'

We smiled. 'That's more cheerful,' I agreed. 'I'm so glad he was able to find pleasure through his misfortune.'

I turned to look at a stone nearby, and as I did so I tripped over the edge of a curb which was hidden in the long grass and I went sprawling headlong over a grave.

Roc picked me up. 'All right, darling? Not hurt?'

'I'm all right, thanks.' I looked ruefully at my stocking. 'A run-ladder. That seems to be all the damage.'

'Sure?' The anxiety in his eyes made me feel very happy and I forgot my earlier vague misgivings. I assured him that I was all right and he said? 'Now some of our neighbours would say that was an omen.'

'What sort of an omen?'

'I couldn't tell you. But falling over a grave! I'm sure they'd see something very significant in that. *And* on your first visit to the churchyard too.'

'Life must be very difficult for some people,' I mused. 'If they're continually seeing omens it doesn't give them much chance of exercising their own free will.'

'And you believe in being the master of your fate and captain of your soul, and the fault not being in your stars and so on?'

'Yes, I think I do. And you, Roc?'

He took my hand suddenly and kissed it. 'As usual you and I are in unison.' He looked about him and said: 'And that's the family vault over there.'

'I must see that.'

I made my way to it, more cautiously this time, Roc following. It was an ornate mausoleum of iron and gilt, with three steps leading down to the door.

'Locked away there are numerous dead Pendorrics,' said Roc.

I turned away. 'I've thought enough about death for one bright summer's morning,' I told him.

He put his arms round me and kissed me. Then he released me and went down the three steps to examine the door. I stood back, where he had left me, and saw that on one of the gilded spikes of the railings a wreath of laurels had been put.

I went towards it and looked at it more closely. There was a card attached to it and on it was written: 'For Barbarina.'

I did not mention the wreath to Roc when he came up to me. He did not seem to have noticed it.

I felt a strong desire to get away from this place of death; away to the sun and the sea.

Lunch was a pleasant meal served in one of the small rooms leading off the north hall. I felt that during it I became better acquainted with Morwenna and Charles, who were determined to make me feel at home. The twins and Rachel Bective ate with us. Lowella was garrulous; Hyson said scarcely a word; and Rachel behaved as though she were indeed a friend of the family. She reproved Lowella for over-exuberance, and seemed determined to be friendly with me. I wondered whether I had made a hasty judgment when I had decided I did not like her.

After lunch Roc and Charles went off together and I went to my room to get a book. I had decided that I would do what I had wanted to ever since I had seen it – sit under one of the palm trees in the quadrangle.

I took my book and found my way out. It was delightfully cool under the tree, and as I sat gloating on the beauty of the place it occurred to me there was a look of a Spanish patio about it. The hydrangeas were pink, blue, and white, and multi-coloured masses of delightful blooms; the lavender scented the air about the water over which bronze Hermes was poised; I saw the flash of gold as the fish swam to and fro.

I tried to read, but I found it difficult to concentrate because of those windows which would not allow me to feel alone. I looked up at them. Who would want to peer out at me I asked myself. And if someone did, what would it matter? I knew I was being absurd.

I went back to my book, and as I sat reading there I heard a movement close behind me, and I was startled when a pair of hands were placed over my eyes and quite unable to repress a gasp as I said rather more sharply than I intended: 'Who is it?'

As I touched the hands, which were not very large, I heard a low chuckle and a voice said: 'You have to guess.'

'Lowella.'

The child danced before me. 'I can stand on my head,' she announced. 'I bet you can't.'

She proved her words, her long thin legs in navy-blue shorts waving perilously near the pond.

'All right,' I told her, 'you've proved it.'

She turned a somersault and landed on her feet, then stood smiling at me, her face pink with the effort.

'How did you guess Lowella?' she asked.

'I couldn't think of anyone else.'

'It might have been Hyson.'

'I was certain it was Lowella.'

'Hyson doesn't do things like that, does she?'

'I think Hyson's a little shy.'

She turned another somersault.

'Are you afraid?' she asked suddenly.

'Afraid of what?'

'Being one of the Brides.'

'What brides?'

'The Brides of Pendorric, of course.'

She stood very still, her eyes narrowed, as she surveyed me. 'You don't know, do you?' she said.

'That's why I'm asking you to tell me.'

She came towards me and, putting her hands on my knees, she looked searchingly into my face; she was so close that I could see the long dark eyes which slightly resembled. Roc's, and the clear unblemished skin. I was aware of another quality which reminded me of Roc. I thought I sensed a certain mischief in her look but I was not sure.

'Will you tell me?' I asked.

For answer she looked over her shoulder and up at the windows, and I went on: 'Why did you ask me if I was afraid?'

'Because you're one of the Brides, of course. My granny was one. Her picture's in the south hall. Have you seen it?'

'Barbarina,' I said.

'Yes. Granny Barbarina. She's dead. You see, she was one of the Brides too.'

'This is all very mysterious to me. I don't know why she should die simply because she was a bride.'

'There was another Bride too. She's in the north hall. She was called Lowella and she used to haunt Pendorric until Granny Barbarina died. Then she rested in her grave.'

'Oh, I see, it's a ghost story.'

'In a way, but it's a live person's story too.'

'I'd like to hear it.'

Again she turned to look at me and I wondered whether she had been warned not to tell me.

'All right.' She spoke in a whisper. 'When Lowella in the south hall was a bride there was a great banquet to celebrate her wedding. Her father was very rich and lived in North Cornwall and he and her mother and all her sisters and brothers and cousins and aunts came to dance at a ball here at Pendorric. There were violins on the dais and they were all eating and dancing when the woman came into the hall. She had a little girl with her; it was her little girl, you see, and she said it was Petroc Pendorric's too. Not Roc's – because this was years and years ago. It was another Pendorric with that name – only they didn't call him Roc. This Petroc Pendorric was Lowella's bridegroom, you see, and the woman with the little girl thought he ought to have been hers. This woman lived wild in the woods with her mother, and the mother was a witch so that makes it a curse that works. She cursed Pendorric and the Bride and all the fun stopped then.'

'And how long ago did this happen?' I asked.

'Nearly two hundred years.'

'It's a long time.'

'But it's a story that goes on and on. It doesn't have an ending, you see. It's not only Lowella's story and Barbarina's story . . . it's yours too.'

'How could that be?'

'You haven't heard what the curse was. The Bride was to die in the prime of her life and she wouldn't rest in her grave until another Bride had gone to her death . . . in the prime of *her* life, of course.'

I smiled. I was astonished that I could feel so relieved. That ominous phrase the Brides of Pendorric was now explained. It was only this old legend which, because we were in Cornwall, where superstitions prevailed, had lived on and provided the old house with a ghost.

'You don't seem very worried. I would if I were you.'

'You haven't finished the story. What happened to that bride?'

'She died having her son exactly a year after her wedding day. She was eighteen years old, which you must admit is very young to die.'

'I expect a great many women died in childbirth. Particularly in those days.'

'Yes, but they said she used to haunt the place waiting for a bride to take her place.'

'To do the haunting, you mean?'

'You're like Uncle Roc. He always laughs at it. I don't laugh though. I know better.'

'So you believe in this haunting business.'

She nodded. 'I've got the second sight. That's why I'm telling you you won't always laugh.'

She leaped away from me and turned another somersault, her long thin legs swaying before me. I had the impression that she was rather pleased because I was going to be shocked out of my scepticism.

She came to stand before me again and with a virtuous expression said: 'I think you ought to know. You see, the Bride Lowella used to haunt Pendorric till my Granny Barbarina died. Then she rested in her grave because she'd lured another bride to take her place and do the haunting. My Granny Barbarina's been doing it for twenty-five years. I reckon she's tired. She'd want to rest in her tomb, wouldn't she? You can bet your life she's looking out for another bride to do the job.'

'I see what you mean,' I said lightly. 'I'm the bride.'

'You're laughing, aren't you?' She stepped back and turned another somersault. 'But you'll see.'

Her face seen from upside down looked jaunty as her long dark pony-tail trailed on the grass.

'I'm sure you've never seen the ghost of your grandmother – have you?'

She did not answer but regarded me stolidly for a few seconds; then she turned a rapid somersault and did a few more handsprings on the grass, going farther and farther away from me until she reached the north door. She went through this and I was alone.

I returned to my book but I found that I kept looking up at the windows. I had been right when I had thought so many windows would be disconcerting; they really were like the eyes of the house.

It's all this talk of ghosts, I thought. Well, I had been warned of the superstitions of the Cornish, and I suspected that Lowella had mischievously tried to frighten me.

The north door opened with a crash and I saw the brown face, the dark pony-tail, the light blue blouse and dark blue shorts.

'Hallo! Uncle Roc said I was to look after you in case you were lonely.'

'Well, you've been doing that after your fashion,' I told her.

'I couldn't find you. I went up to your room and you weren't there. I hunted everywhere and then I thought of the quad. So I came here. What would you like to do?'

'But you were here a little while ago.'

She looked at me blankly.

'You told me the story of the brides,' I reminded her.

She clapped her hands over her mouth. 'She *didn't*, did she?'

'You're not . . . Hyson, are you?'

'Of course not. I'm Lowella.'

'But she said . . .' Had she said she was Lowella? I was not sure.

'Did Hy pretend she was me?' The child began to laugh.

'You are Lowella, aren't you?' I persisted. 'You really are.'

She licked a finger and held it out and said:

'See my finger's wet?'

She wiped it.

'See my finger's dry?'

She drew it across her throat.

'Cut my throat if I tell a lie.'

She looked so earnest that I believed her.

'But why did she pretend she was you?'

Lowella's brows puckered, then she said: I think she doesn't like being the quiet one. So when I'm not there she thinks she'll be me. People who don't know us much can't tell the difference. Would you like to come to the stables and see our ponies?'

I said I would; I felt that I wanted to escape from the quadrangle as I had from the graveyard that morning.

Dinner that night was a comfortable meal. The twins did not join us and there were the five of us. Morwenna said that when I was ready she'd show me the house and explain how it was run.

'Roc thinks that just at first, until you've settled in, you would like things to go on as they are.' Morwenna smiled at her brother affectionately. 'But it's to be as you want. He's very insistent on that.'

'And don't think,' put in Roc, returning his sister's look, 'that Wenna will mind in the least whatever you want to do in the house. Now if you should want to root up her magnolia tree or turn the rose garden into a rockery, that would be quite another matter.'

Morwenna smiled at me. 'I've never been much of a housekeeper. Who cares? It's not really necessary. Mrs. Penhalligan's a treasure. I do love the garden, but of course if you want anything changed . . .'

'So,' cried Roc, 'the battle of the trees is about to begin.'

'Don't take any notice of him,' Morwenna said. 'He loves to tease us. But then I expect you've discovered that by now.'

I said I had and that I knew nothing of gardening and had always lived in a tiny studio which was as different from a mansion as any place could be.

I felt very happy to hear this banter between Roc and his sister because the affection which lay beneath it was very obvious. I was certain that Roc was anxious that Morwenna should not feel put out because he had brought a wife into the midst of their household, which could easily bring a lot of change. I loved him for his consideration of his sister; and when they asked me questions about Capri and were very careful not to mention my father, I guessed that Roc had warned them of my grief.

How considerate he was of us all; I loved him all the more because he never made a show of his care for us, but he hid it under that teasing manner.

Morwenna and Charles were clearly trying to make me feel at home, because they were kindly and so fond of Roc. I was less certain of Rachel. She seemed absorbed in impressing on the servants that she was an honoured member of the family; she was a little on the defensive I thought, and, when her face was in repose, I fancied I caught a bitterness in her expression.

We sat in one of the small drawing-rooms drinking coffee which was served to us by Mrs. Penhalligan while Charles and Roc talked estate business, and Morwenna and Rachel, one on either side of me, launched into a description of local affairs. I found it all very interesting, particularly after the brief glimpse I had had that morning of the little village. Morwenna said she would drive me into Plymouth when I wanted to shop because it would be better for me to have someone who knew the shops the first time I went.

I thanked her, and Rachel said that if by any chance Morwenna wasn't available I could count on her.

'That's nice of you,' I replied.

'Only too pleased to do all I can for Roc's bride,' she murmured.

Bride! Bride! I thought impatiently. Why not wife, which would have sounded so much more natural? I think it was from that moment that the eeriness of the house seemed to close in on me and I was conscious of the darkness outside.

We went to bed early, and when Roc and I were walking along the corridor on our way to our rooms on the south side I looked out of the window to the quadrangle and remembered my conversation with the twins that afternoon.

Roc stood close to me as I looked down.

'You like the quadrangle garden, don't you?'

'Apart from the eyelike windows which are watching all the time.'

He laughed. 'You mentioned that before. Don't worry. We're all too busy to peep.'

As we went along to our bedroom Roc said: 'Something's on your mind, darling.'

'Oh . . . it's nothing really.'

'There is something then.'

I tried to laugh lightly, but I was aware of the silence of that great house and I could not stop thinking of all the tragedies and comedies which must have taken place within those walls over the hundreds of years they had been standing. I could not feel indifference to the past, which in such a place seemed so much closer than it possibly could in my father's studio.

I blurted out what had happened that afternoon.

'Oh, those terrible twins!' he groaned.

'This story about the Brides of Pendorric . . .'

'Such stories abound in Cornwall. You could probably go to a dozen places and hear a similar story. These people are not cold-blooded Anglo-Saxons, you know. They're Celtic – a different race from the phlegmatic

English. I know of course that they may have haunted houses in Huntingdon, Hereford and Oxfordshire – but they're merely houses. According to the Cornish, the whole of Cornwall is haunted. If it's not the piskies it's the knackers from the mines. There are the Little People in their scarlet jackets and sugar-loaf hats. There are footlings who are born feet first, which is supposed to be a sign of their magical powers. There are pillar families – those inheriting power from fishermen ancestors who rendered some service to a mermaid; there are witches, white and black. So of course there are a few common ghosts.'

'I gather Pendorric has that kind.'

'No big house in Cornwall could possibly be without at least one. It's a status symbol. I'll bet Lord Polhorgan would give a thousand or two for a ghost. But the Cornish won't have it. He's not one of us, so he's going to be denied the privilege of being haunted.

I felt comforted, though I scorned myself for needing reassurance; but that child this afternoon had really unnerved me, chiefly because I had believed I was talking to Lowella. I thought Hyson a very strange little person indeed and I did not like the streak of mischief, the almost gloating pleasure in my uneasiness which I had noticed.

'About the story,' I said. 'After all, it concerns the Brides of Pendorric of whom I am one.'

'It was very unfortunate that Lowella Pendorric died exactly a year to the day after her wedding. That probably gave rise to the whole thing. She brought the heir into the world and departed. A common enough occurrence in those days, but you have to remember that here in Cornwall people are always looking for something on which to hang a legend.'

'And she was supposed to haunt the place after that?'

He nodded. 'Brides came and went and they must have forgotten the legend although they'd tell you now that Lowella Pendorric continued to walk by night. Then my mother died when Morwenna and I were five years old. She was only twenty-five.'

'How did she die?'

'That's just what revived the legend, I imagine. She fell from the north gallery into the hall, when the balustrade gave way. The wood was worm-eaten and it was very frail. The shock and the fall combined killed her. It was an unfortunate accident, and because the picture of Lowella hangs in the gallery the story soon got round that it was Lowella's influence that caused her to fall. Lowella was tired of haunting the house, they said, so she decided Barbarina should take her place. I am certain that the part about having to haunt the house until another bride took her place started at that time. You'll hear now that the ghost of Pendorric is my mother Barbarina. Rather a young ghost for such an old house, but you see we haunt in relays.'

'I see,' I said slowly.

He put his hands on my shoulders and laughed; I laughed with him.

Everything seemed comfortingly normal that night.

The woman in the riding jacket and blue-banded hat had begun to haunt my thoughts and I found myself drawn towards the spot where her picture hung, whenever I was alone in that part of the house. I was not anxious that anyone should guess how much the picture attracted me, because I thought it would appear that I was affected by this ridiculous legend.

It was so realistic that the eyes seemed as though they flickered as you watched them, the lips as though they were about to speak. I wondered what her feelings had been when she felt the balustrade giving way beneath her weight; I wondered if she had felt an unhealthy interest in that other bride . . . as I was beginning to feel in her.

No, I told myself. I was merely interested in the painting and I was certainly not going to allow the legend to bother me.

All the same, I couldn't resist going to look at the picture.

Roc found me there two mornings later. He put his arm through mine and said he had come to take me for a drive.

'We don't take after her, do we?' he said. 'Morwenna and I are both dark as Spaniards. You mustn't feel morbid about her. She's only a picture, you know.'

He drove me out to the moor that morning; and I was fascinated by that stretch of wild country with its tors and boulders so strangely shaped that they looked like grotesque parodies of human beings.

I thought that Roc was trying to make me understand Cornwall, because he knew that I had been upset by the legend and he wanted to make me laugh at it.

We drove for miles, through Callington and St. Cleer, little towns with grey granite façades, and out on to the moor again. He showed me the Trevethy Quoit, a Neolithic tomb made of blocks of stone; he pointed out the burial grounds of men who had lived before history was recorded; he wanted me to know that a country which could offer so much proof of its past must necessarily be one of legend.

He stopped the car high on the moor, and in the distance I could see that fantastic formation of rock known as the Cheesewring.

He put his arm round me and said: 'One day I'll take you farther west and show you the Merry Maidens. Nineteen stones in a circle which you will be asked to believe were once nineteen girls who, deciding to defy tradition and go dancing in a sacred place, were turned to stone; and indeed the stones lean this way and that as if they had been caught and petrified in the midst of a dance.' His eyes were very tender as he turned to me. 'You'll get used to us in time,' he went on. 'Everywhere you look in this place there's some legend. You don't take them seriously.'

I knew then that he was worried about me and I told him not to be because I had always prided myself on my common sense.

'I know,' he said. 'But your father's death was a greater shock than you realize. I'm going to take extra special care of you.'

'Then,' I replied, 'I shall begin to feel very precious indeed, because I fancy you have been taking rather a lot of care of me ever since that awful day.'

'Well, remember I do happen to be your husband.'

I turned to him then and said almost fiercely, 'It's something I couldn't possibly forget for a minute . . . even if I wanted to.'

He turned my face up to his and his kiss was tender.

'And you don't want to?'

I threw myself against him, and as I clung to him, his grip on me tightened. It was as though we were both trying to make each other understand the immense depth of the love between us.

It was the comfort I needed.

Roc could always emerge from an emotional scene with more ease than I could, and in a short time he was his old teasing self. He began to tell me stories of Cornish legends, some so fantastic that I accused him of inventing them.

Then we both started inventing stories about the place we passed, trying to cap each other's absurdities. It all seemed tremendous fun, although anyone listening to us would have thought we were crazy.

As we drove back in these high spirits I marvelled at the way in which Roc could always comfort and delight me.

During the next few days I spent a great deal of time in Roc's company. He would take me with him when he went on his rounds of the farms and I was welcomed everywhere, usually with a glass of some home-made wine or cider; I was even expected to eat a Cornish pasty as they came hot from the oven.

The people were warm and friendly once I had overcome a certain initial suspicion which they felt towards 'foreigners' from the other side of the Tamar. I was English; they were Cornish; therefore to them I was a foreigner.

'Once a foreigner, always a foreigner,' Roc told me. 'But of course marriage makes a difference. When you've produced a little Cornish man or woman you'll be accepted. Otherwise it would take all of fifty years.'

Morwenna and I drove into Plymouth one afternoon and stopped and had tea near the Hoe.

'Charles and I are very pleased Roc's married,' she told me. 'We wanted to see him happily settled.'

'You're very fond of him, aren't you?'

'Well, he is my brother, and my twin at that. And Roc's a rather special person. I expect you'll agree with that.'

As I agreed so wholeheartedly I felt my affection for Morwenna increasing.

'You can always rely on Roc,' went on Morwenna, and as she stirred her tea thoughtfully her eyes were vague as though she were looking back over the past.

'Were you very surprised when he wrote and said he was married?'

'Just at first, perhaps. But he's always done the unexpected. Charles and I were beginning to be afraid he'd never settle down, so when we heard, we were really delighted.'

'Even though he'd married someone who was a stranger to you.'

Morwenna laughed. 'That state of affairs didn't last long, did it? You're one of us now.'

That was a very pleasant jaunt because I was always so happy to talk about Roc and to see signs of the affection he inspired in those people who had known him all his life.

Morwenna and I called on the Darks at the vicarage and I had an interesting afternoon listening to the stories the vicar had to tell of Cornish superstitions.

'I think they're so sure that certain things are going to happen that they make them happen,' he told me.

We also talked of the people who lived on the Pendorric estate and I learned of some of the benefits which had come to them since Roc had been in control. I glowed with pride as I listened.

It was at the vicarage that I met Dr. Andrew Clement, a man in his late twenties or early thirties. He was tall, fair and friendly and we liked each other from the start.

He told me that he too was what was known as a foreigner, having come from Kent, and been in Cornwall some eighteen months.

'I come past Pendorric several times a week,' he told me, 'when I visit your neighbour, Lord Polhorgan.'

'He's seriously ill, isn't he?'

'Not so much seriously ill as in danger of becoming so. He has angina and threatening coronary thrombosis. We have to watch him very carefully. He has a nurse living there all the time. Have you met her yet?'

'No, I haven't.'

'She does occasionally come to Pendorric,' said Morwenna. 'You'll meet her sooner or later.'

That was a very pleasant afternoon, and as Morwenna and I drove back the conversation turned to the twins.

'Rachel seems to be very efficient,' I said.

'Very.'

'I suppose you're lucky to get her. A person with her qualifications must be rather difficult to come by nowadays.'

'She's here . . . temporarily. The twins will have to go to school in a year or so. They can't be at home like this for ever.'

Was it my imagination, or had Morwenna's manner changed when I mentioned Rachel?

There was a short silence between us and I reproved myself because I suspected I was becoming over-sensitive. I was beginning to look for things which didn't exist, and I wondered whether I had changed since coming to Cornwall.

I wanted to go on talking about Rachel because I was eager to know more about her. I wanted to find out what the relationship between her and Roc had been – if in fact there had been anything unusual in their relationship.

But Morwenna had dismissed the subject. She began to talk animatedly about the Darks and the changes they had made at the vicarage.

That afternoon I went to the quadrangle. I was drawn there somewhat unwillingly, for I would rather have taken a book into the garden which was on the south side and which led down to the beach. There I could have sat in one of the sheltered arbours among the hydrangeas, the buddleias and the sweet-smelling lavender, the house behind me, the sea before me. It would have been very pleasant. Yet because of that faint revulsion I had experienced in the quadrangle – mainly on account of the windows which looked down on it – I was aware of a compulsion to go there. I was not the sort of person who enjoyed feeling even vaguely afraid, and I was sure that by facing whatever disconcerted me I should more quickly overcome it.

I sat under the palm tree with my book and tried to concentrate, but once more I found myself continually glancing up at the windows.

I had not been there very long when the twins came out of the north door.

When I saw them together I had no difficulty in distinguishing between them. Lowella was so vital, Hyson so subdued. I began to wonder then whether it really had been Hyson who had warned me to beware of Barbarina, or whether it had been a mischievous trick of Lowella's to try to frighten me and then pretend that it was Hyson who had done it.

'Hallo,' called Lowella.

They came and sat on the grass and gazed at me.

'Are we disturbing you?' asked Lowella politely.

'I wasn't very deep in my book.'

'You like it here?' went on Lowella.

'It's very peaceful.'

'You're shut right in. You've got Pendorric all around you. Hy likes it here too. Don't you, Hy?'

Hyson nodded.

'Well,' went on Lowella, 'what do you think of *us*?'

'I hadn't given the matter a great deal of thought.'

'I didn't mean the two of us. I mean all of us. What do you think of Pendorric and Uncle Roc, Mummy, Daddy, and Becky Sharp?'

'Becky Sharp?'

'Old Bective, of course.'

'Why do you call her that?'

'Hy said she was like a Becky Sharp she read about in a book. Hy's always reading.'

I looked at Hyson who nodded gravely.

'She told me about Becky Sharp and I said, "That's Rachel." So I called her Becky Sharp. I give people names. I'm Lo. She's Hy. Wasn't it clever of Mummy and Daddy to give us names like that. Though I'm not sure that I like being Lo. I'd rather be Hy . . . only in my name I mean. I'd rather be myself than old Hy. She's always sitting about and thinking.'

'Not a bad occupation.' I smiled at Hyson, who continued to regard me gravely.

'I've got names for everybody – my own secret names – and Becky Sharp is one of them.'

'Have you got one for me?'

'You! Well, you're the Bride, aren't you! You couldn't be anything else.'

'Does Miss Bective like the name you've given her?' I asked.

'She doesn't know. It's a secret. But you see, she was at school with Mummy and she was always coming here and Hy said, "One day she'll come to stay because she never wants to go away." '

'Has she said so?'

'Of course not. As if she would. It's all secret. Other people never know what Becky Sharp is up to. But she wants to stay. We thought she was going to marry Uncle Roc.'

Hyson came and put her hands on my knees; she looked into my face and said: 'It was what she wanted. I don't suppose she likes it much because you did.'

'You're not supposed to say that, Hy,' Lowella warned.

'I'll say it if I want to.'

'You can't. You mustn't.'

Hyson was suddenly fierce. 'I can and I will.'

Lowella chanted: 'You can't. You can't.' And began to run round the pond. Hyson went in pursuit of her. I watched them running about the quadrangle until Lowella disappeared through the north door. Hyson made as though to follow her, hesitated, and turning stood looking at me for a few moments. Then she came back.

'Lowella's really very childish,' she told me. She knelt at my feet and looked at me, and feeling a little embarrassed by her scrutiny I said: 'You never talk very much when she's there. Why not?'

She shrugged her shoulders. 'I never talk unless I have something to say,' she murmured primly.

Now it seemed she had nothing to say for she continued to kneel at my feet in a silence which went on for several minutes, then she rose suddenly and stood looking up at the windows.

She lifted her hand and waved, and following her gaze I saw that the curtain at one of the windows was slightly pulled back and someone was standing about a foot from the window looking down. I could just make out a vague figure in a black hat with a band of blue about it.

'Who's that?' I asked sharply.

She rose to her feet and said slowly: 'That was Granny!'

Then she smiled at me and walked sedately to the north door and I was alone in the quadrangle. I looked up at the window. There was no one there and the curtain had fallen.

'Barbarina,' I murmured and I felt as though eyes were watching me, mocking me, and I did not want to stay in the courtyard any longer.

This was ridiculous, I told myself. It was a trick. Of course, Lowella had gone in and they had decided to amuse themselves at my expense.

But it had not been a child I had seen at the window. It has been a tall woman.

I hurried into the house through the south door and I paused before the picture of Barbarina. I fancied that the eyes were mocking me.

This is absurd, I said as I mounted the staircase. I was a normal, uncomplicated person who did not believe in ghosts.

Had I changed since I came to Pendorric? Was I still so self-sufficient since I had experienced emotions which had only been names to me before I met Roc Pendorric? Love, jealousy – and now fear?

Chapter Three

I went straight up to my room, and as I opened the door I gasped, for a woman was sitting in an arm-chair with her back to the light. After my experience in the courtyard I must really have been unnerved, because it seemed several seconds before I recognized Morwenna.

'I'm afraid I startled you,' she said. 'I'm so sorry. I came up to look for you . . . and sat down for a moment.'

'It was silly of me, but I didn't expect to see anyone here.'

'I came up because Deborah has arrived. I want you to meet her.'

'Who, did you say?'

'Deborah Hyson. She's my mother's sister. She spends a lot of time here. She has been away and only got back this afternoon. I think she's come back on your account. She can't bear things to be happening in the family and not take part in them.'

'Could I have seen her at one of the windows not long ago?'

'Very likely. Was it the west side?'

'Yes, I think it was.'

'Then I expect it was Deborah. She has her rooms there.'

'She was looking down on the quadrangle and Hyson waved to her, then ran off without explaining.'

'Hyson's very fond of her, and she of Hyson. I'm glad, because Lowella is usually so much more popular. Are you coming down now? We're having tea in the winter parlour, and Deborah's very anxious to meet you.'

'Let's go, then.'

We went down to the little room on the first floor of the north wing, where a tall woman rose to greet me; I was almost certain that she was the one I had seen at the window.

She was not wearing the hat now, but her abundant white hair was in a style which might have been fashionable thirty years or so ago; and I noticed too that there was an old-fashioned look about her clothes. Her eyes were very blue and her frilly *crêpe de Chine* blouse matched them perfectly. She was very tall and slender in her black tailored suit.

She took both my hands and looked earnestly into my face.

'My dear,' she said, 'how glad I am that you have come!' I was astonished by the fervour of her greeting; and I could only conjecture that, like most of the family, she was delighted to see Roc married, and therefore was prepared to accept me as a blessing. 'As soon as I heard the news I came.'

'That's very kind of you.'

She smiled almost wistfully while her eyes remained on me.

'Come and sit beside me,' she said. 'We'll have lots to talk about. Morwenna dear, is that tea coming soon?'

'Almost at once,' Morwenna replied.

We sat side by side and she went on: 'You must call me Deborah, dear. The children do. Oh, by the children I mean Petroc and Morwenna. The twins call me Granny. They always have. I don't mind in the least.'

'You don't look like a granny!'

She smiled. 'I expect I do to the twins. They think anyone of twenty somewhat aged, and after that of course quite ancient. I'm rather glad they do, though. They hadn't a granny. I supplied the need.'

Mrs. Penhalligan brought in the tea and Morwenna poured it.

'Charles and Roc won't be in for an hour or so,' she told Deborah.

'I'll see them at dinner. Oh, here *are* the twins.'

The door burst open and Lowella rushed in, followed sedately by Hyson. ''Lo, Granny,' said Lowella, and walking to Deborah's chair was embraced and kissed. Hyson followed; and I noticed that the hug she received was even more affectionate. There was no doubt that these two were very fond of each other.

Lowella went to the tea-trolly to see what there was for tea, while Hyson stood leaning against Deborah's chair.

'I must say it is pleasant to be back,' said Deborah, 'though I miss the moor.' She explained to me: 'I have a house on Dartmoor. I was brought up there and now that my parents are dead it belongs to me. You must come out and see it one day.'

'I'll come with you,' said Lowella.

'Dear Lowella!' murmured Deborah. 'She never likes to be left out of anything. And you'll come too, Hyson, won't you?'

'Yes, Granny.'

'That's a good girl. I hope you're looking after your Aunt Favel, and making her feel at home.'

'We don't call her Aunt. She's just Favel and of *course* we've been looking after her,' said Lowella. 'Uncle Roc told us we had to.'

'And Hyson?'

'Yes, Granny, I've been showing her what she ought to see and telling her what she ought to know.'

Deborah smiled and began gently pulling Hyson's pony-tail in a caressing way.

She smiled at me: 'I must show you pictures of the children. I have lots of them in my rooms.'

'On the walls,' cried Lowella, 'and in albums with writing underneath. It says "Petroc aged six." "Morwenna in the Quadrangle aged eight." And there are lots of Granny Barbarina and Granny Deborah when they were little girls – only they're in Devon.'

Deborah leaned towards me. 'There's usually a person like myself in all families: the one who did not marry but could be called in to look after the children. She keeps all the pictures and knows the dates of birthdays.'

'Granny Deborah never forgets,' Lowella told me.

'Did I see you when I was in the quadrangle?' I could not prevent myself asking, for foolish as it was, I had to satisfy myself on this point.

'Yes. I had only just arrived. I hadn't told Morwenna or Roc that I was coming to-day. I peeped out and saw you and Hyson. I didn't know you'd seen me or I should have opened the window and spoken to you.'

'Hyson waved and I looked up and saw you. I was astonished when she said you were her granny.'

'And didn't she explain? Oh Hyson, my dear child!' She went on caressing the pony-tail.

'I told her it was my granny, and it was,' Hyson defended herself.

'You're eating very little,' Morwenna scolded Deborah and me. 'Do try these splits. Maria will be hurt if we sent too many back.'

'I always say this Cornish cream isn't as good as ours in Devonshire,' said Deborah.

Morwenna laughed. 'That's sheer prejudice. It's exactly the same.'

Deborah asked me about my life in Capri and how Roc and I had met.

'How delightful!' she cried when I had answered her questions. 'A lightning romance! I think it's charming, don't you, Morwenna?'

'We're all very pleased, of course . . . particularly now that we know Favel.'

'And we were longing for the new Bride of Pendorric,' said Hyson quietly.

Everyone laughed and conversation was general while we finished tea.

When the meal was over, Hyson asked if she could help her granny unpack. Deborah was very pleased and said of course she could. She added: 'And I don't suppose Favel has seen my rooms, has she? We'll invite her to come with us, shall we, Hyson?'

I thought Hyson rather grudgingly agreed, but I accepted quickly because I was anxious to know more of this new member of the household.

The three of us went off together and soon were in the west corridor passing that very window at which Deborah had appeared and so startled me.

She opened the door of a room which had windows very like those in Roc's and my bedroom and which gave a superb view of the coastline stretching out towards the west and Land's End. My eyes went immediately to the bed – a four-poster like ours – because on the rose-coloured counterpane lay the black hat with the blue band. It was not really like the one in the picture but the colouring was similar. I felt rather foolish as well as relieved, because it was comforting to solve the mystery of the apparition so quickly, but at the same time it was disconcerting to remember how shaken I had been at the sight of it.

I saw then that a part of one of the walls was covered with photographs of all sizes and types, some being studio portraits, others snapshots.

Deborah laughed and followed my gaze. 'I have always hoarded pictures of the family. It's the same in Devonshire, isn't it, Hyson?'

'Yes, but they're all pictures of you before . . . these are after.'

'Yes, of course. Time seems rather divided like that – before Barby's marriage . . . and after.'

'Barbarina,' I murmured involuntarily.

'Yes, Barbarina. She was Barby to me, and I was Deb. No one else ever called us by those versions of our names. Barbarina was the name of an ancestress of ours. It's unusual, isn't it? Until Barbarina's marriage she and I were always together.' The blue eyes clouded momentarily and I guessed that there had been great devotion between the sisters. 'Oh well,' she went on, 'it's all so long ago. Sometimes I find it hard to believe that she is dead . . . and in her grave. . . .'

'But . . .' began Hyson.

Deborah laid her hand on the child's head and went on: 'When she . . . died, I came to live here and I brought up Petroc and Morwenna. I tried to take her place, but can anyone take the place of a mother?'

'They're very fond of you, I'm sure.'

'I think they are. Do let me show you the photographs. I think some of them are very charming. You'll want to see your husband in the various stages of his development, I expect. It's always rather fun, don't you think, to see people as they were years and years ago.'

I smiled at the mischievous-eyed boy in the open shirt and cricket flannels; and the picture of him standing side by side with Morwenna – Morwenna smiling coyly at the camera, Roc scowling at it. There was a picture of them as babies; they lay side by side and a beautiful woman was bending over them.

'Barbarina and her twins,' murmured Deborah.

'How beautiful she is!'

'Yes.' There was a note of infinite sadness in her voice. So she still mourns her sister, I thought; and there came into my mind the memory of the family vault with the laurel hanging on the spike. I guessed who had put that there.

I turned my attention to a picture of a man and a woman; I had no difficulty in recognizing Barbarina, and the man who was with her was so like Roc that I guessed he was Barbarina's husband.

There it was, the almost challenging smile, the face of a man who knew how to get the best out of life, the reckless gambler, the indefinable charm. I noticed that the ears of the man in the picture were Roc's ears, that the eyes were slightly tilted at the corners. It was a handsome face, made even more attractive by that streak of mischief . . . wickedness . . . or whatever it was that I had sensed in Roc.

'Roc's parents,' I said.

'Taken a year before the tragedy,' Deborah told me.

'It is very sad. He looks so fond of her. He must have been heartbroken.'

Deborah smiled grimly, but she did not speak.

'Aren't you going to show Favel the albums?' Hyson asked.

'Not now, dear. I've my settling in to do, and stories of the past can be a little boring, I'm afraid, to those who haven't lived them.'

'I'm certainly not bored. I'm very eager to learn all I can about the family.'

'Of course . . . now that you are one of us. And I shall enjoy showing you the albums at another time.'

It was a kind of dismissal, and I said I too had things to do and would see her later. She came towards me and, taking my hands, smiled at me affectionately.

'I can't tell you how pleased I am that you are here,' she told me earnestly; and there could be no doubting her sincerity.

'Everyone has been so charming to me at Pendorric,' I told her. 'No bride could have been more enthusiastically welcomed, and considering how sudden our marriage had been and my coming must have been rather a shock to the family, I'm very grateful to everybody.'

'Of course we welcome you, my dear.'

Hyson said earnestly: 'We've been waiting for her for years . . . haven't we, Granny?'

Deborah laughed, and gently pulled Hyson's ear. 'You take in everything, child,' she said. And to me: 'We're delighted that Roc's married. The Pendorrics usually marry young.'

The door opened and a little woman came into the room. She was dressed in black, which was not becoming to her sallow skin; her hair was what is know as iron grey and must have been almost black once; her dark bushy brows met over small worried eyes; she had a long thin nose and thin lips.

She was about to speak, but seeing me hesitated. Deborah said: 'This is my dear Carrie, who was our nurse and has never left me. Now she looks after me . . . completely, and I just don't know what I should do without her. Carrie, this is the new Mrs. Pendorric.'

The worried-looking eyes were fixed on me. 'Oh,' she murmured, 'the new Mrs. Pendorric, eh.'

Deborah smiled at me. 'You'll get to know Carrie very quickly. She'll do anything for you, I'm sure. She's a wonder with her needle. She makes most of my things as she always did.'

'I made for the two of them,' said Carrie with pride. 'And I used to say there was no one better dressed in the whole of Devonshire than Miss Barbarina and Miss Deborah.'

I noticed then the slight burr in her speech and the tenderness in her voice when she spoke of those two.

'Carrie, there's some unpacking to do.'

Carrie's expression changed and she looked almost disgruntled.

'Carrie hates leaving her beloved moor!' said Deborah with a laugh. 'It takes her quite a time to settle down on this side of the Tamar.'

'I wish we'd never crossed the Tamar,' Carrie muttered.

Deborah smiled at me and, putting her arm through mine, walked into the corridor with me.

'We have to humour Carrie,' she whispered. 'She's a privileged servant. She's getting on now and her mind wanders a little.' She withdrew her arm. 'It'll be fun showing you the pictures some time, Favel,' she went on. 'I can't tell you how pleased I am that you're here.'

I left her, feeling grateful for several reasons; not only was she affectionate and eager to be friends, but she had made me feel myself again now I was sure that it was a person of living flesh and blood who had looked down on me from the window.

The mail at Pendorric was brought up to our bedrooms with early-morning tea; and it was a few days later when Roc, looking through his, came to a letter which made him laugh aloud.

'It's come,' he called to me in the bathroom, 'I knew it would.'

'What?' I asked, coming out wrapped in a bath towel.

'Lord Polhorgan requests the pleasure of Mr. and Mrs. Pendorric's company on Wednesday at three-thirty.'

'Wednesday. That's to-morrow. Are we going?'

'Of course. I'm so eager for you to see the Folly.'

I thought very little more about Lord Polhorgan's invitation because I was far more interested in Pendorric; and I could not feel the almost malicious delight the family seemed to take in deriding the Folly and its master. As I said to Roc, if the man from Manchester, Leeds or Birmingham wanted to build a house on the cliffs, why shouldn't he? And if he wanted it to look like a medieval castle, again why shouldn't he? The Pendorrics had apparently been glad to sell him the land. It was not for them to tell him how he must use it.

As Roc and I set out that Wednesday afternoon he seemed to be enjoying some secret joke.

'I can't wait to see what you think of the set-up,' he told me.

To my unpractised eye the house looked as old as Pendorric. 'Do you know,' I said to Roc, as we approached the stone unicorns which did the same service as our battered lions, 'I shouldn't know that this wasn't a genuine antique if you hadn't told me.'

'Ah, you wait till you've had a chance to examine it.'

We pulled the bell in the great portico and heard it clanging through the hall.

A dignified manservant opened the door and, bowing his head, said solemnly: 'Good afternoon, sir. Good afternoon, madam. His lordship is waiting for you, so I'll take you up immediately.'

It took quite a long time to reach the room where our host was waiting for us; and I noticed that although the furniture was antique the carpets and curtains were expensively modern.

We were finally led to a large room with windows overlooking the beautifully laid-out cliff garden which ran down to the sea; and resting on a chaise-longue was the old man.

'My lord,' the manservant announced, 'Mr. and Mrs. Pendorric.'

'Ah! Bring them in, Dawson. Bring them in.'

He turned his head, and the intentness of those grey eyes was rather disturbing, particularly as they were directed towards me.

'Good of you to come,' he said rather brusquely, as though he didn't mean this. 'You'll have to forgive my not rising.'

'Please don't,' I said quickly, and I went to his chaise-longue and took his hand.

He had a high colour with a faint purplish tinge, and I noticed how the veins stood out on his long thin hands.

'Sit down, Mrs. Pendorric,' he said, still in the same brusque manner. 'Give your wife a chair, Pendorric. And put it near me . . . that's right, facing the light.'

I had to suppress a slight resentment that I was being put under a shrewd scrutiny, and I experienced a certain nervousness which I hadn't expected I should.

'Tell me, how do you like Cornwall, Mrs. Pendorric?'

He spoke sharply, jerkily, as though he were barking orders on a barrack square.

'I'm enchanted,' I said.

'And it compares favourably with that island place of yours?'

'Oh yes.'

'All I see of it now is this view.' He nodded towards the window.

'I can't imagine you'd find a more beautiful one anywhere.'

He looked from me to Roc; and I was aware that my husband's expression had become rather sardonic. He didn't like the old man, that much was clear; and I felt annoyed with him because I was afraid he made it obvious.

Our host was frowning towards the door. 'Late with tea,' he said. He must give his servants a difficult time, I thought, for even if he had asked for tea to be served immediately we arrived it was not very late; we had not been in the room more than three or four minutes.

Then the door opened and a tea wagon was wheeled in. It was overladen with cakes of all descriptions besides bread and butter and splits with bowls of clotted cream and jam.

'Ah,' Lord Polhorgan grunted, 'at last! Where's Nurse Grey?'

'Here I am.' A woman came into the room. She was so beautiful that for a moment I was startled. The blue in her striped dress matched her eyes, her starched apron was snowy white, and her cap, set almost jauntily on her masses of golden hair, called attention to its beauty. I had never seen a nurse's uniform worn so becomingly; then I realized that this woman would look dazzling whatever she wore, simply because she was so very beautiful.

'Good afternoon, Mr. Pendorric,' she said.

Roc had risen to his feet as she entered and I could not see his face as he looked at her. He said: 'Good afternoon, Nurse.' Then he turned. 'Favel, this is Nurse Grey, who looks after Lord Polhorgan.'

'I'm so glad to meet you.' She had a wide mouth and perfectly shaped teeth.

'What about giving Mrs. Pendorric some tea?' growled Lord Polhorgan.

'Of course,' said Nurse Grey. 'It's all here, I see. Now, Mrs. Pendorric, you'd like to sit near Lord Polhorgan. I'll put this little table here for you.'

I thanked her and she went to the tea wagon and began to pour out while Roc brought over a plate of splits and cream and jam which he set on the table.

'I don't need a nurse all the time,' Lord Polhorgan told me. 'But I may need one at any moment. That's why she's here. Quite an efficient woman.'

'I am sure she is.'

'Easy job. Gets a lot of free time. Beautiful surroundings.'

'Ideal,' I murmured, wondering how Nurse Grey liked being referred to in the third person. I glanced at her. She was smiling at Roc.

I handed Lord Polhorgan the splits, and I noticed that he moved slowly and was rather breathless as he took one.

'Shall I spread the jam and cream for you?' I asked.

'H'm!' he barked, which meant assent. 'Thanks!' he added when I had done it. 'Good of you. Now help yourself.'

Nurse Grey asked if I preferred China or Indian, and I was given delicious Mandarin Pekoe with lemon.

She then sat down near Roc. I very much wanted to hear what they were saying, but Lord Polhorgan demanded my attention by firing questions at me. He appeared to be very interested in the way we had lived on the island, and I promised to show him some of my father's work which had been sent to Pendorric.

'Good,' he said. He made me talk about my childhood and in a short time I was living it all again.

'You're not happy,' said Lord Polhorgan suddenly, and I blurted out the story of my father's death, to which he listened gravely and then said: 'You were very fond of him. Was your mother fond of him too?'

I told him something of their life together then, how they had lived for each other, how ill she had become and how they had made me aware that they wanted to live every hour to the full because they knew that the time would come when they could not be together; and as I did so I marvelled that I could talk so intimately to such a gruff old man on such short acquaintance.

He laid his veined hand on my arm. 'Is that how it is with you?' he said sharply, and he looked towards Roc, who was laughing with Nurse Grey.

I hesitated just a second too long.

'Marry in haste . . .' he added. 'Seem to have heard that said somewhere.'

I flushed. 'I'm very happy at Pendorric,' I retorted.

'You rush into things,' he said. 'Bad habit. I never rushed. Made decisions, yes . . . and sometimes quick ones, but always gave them adequate thought. You coming to see me again?'

'If you ask me.'

'Then you are asked now.'

'Thank you.'

'You won't want to, though.'

'Yes, I shall.'

He shook his head. 'You'll make excuses. Too busy. Another engagement. What would a young woman like you want with visiting a sick old man?'

'But I'd love to come.'

'You've got a kind heart. But kindness doesn't always go very deep. Don't want to hurt the old man . . . go now and then. But a bore. What a nuisance!'

'It will be nothing of the sort. You're so interested in things. And I'm attracted by this house.'

'Pretty vulgar, eh? The old man of the people who wanted to build up a bit of background. Doesn't go down well with the aristocrats, I can tell you.'

'Why shouldn't people build backgrounds if they want them?'

'Listen, young woman. There's no reason why anyone shouldn't build anything. You get your just deserts in this world. I wanted to make money and I made it. I wanted to have a family mansion . . . well, I've got it. In this world you say, I want this and I want that. And if you've got any guts you go and get it. You get what you pay for, and if it doesn't turn out as you planned, well then you have to look for where you went wrong because, you can depend on it, you've gone wrong somewhere.'

'I expect you're right.'

'I'd like you to come again even if you are bored. Perhaps you'd be less bored after a while . . . when we got to know each other.'

'I haven't started to be bored yet.'

He clenched and unclenched his hand, frowning at it. 'I'm an old man . . . incapacitated by illness . . . brought on, they tell me, by the life I've led.' He patted his chest. 'I've put a big strain on this, it seems, and now I've got to pay for it. All right, I say, life's a matter of settling bills and drawing dividends. I'm ready.'

'I can see you have a philosophy.'

'Play chess?'

'My mother taught me.'

'Your mother, eh?'

'She also taught me reading, writing and arithmetic, before I came to school in England.'

'I reckon you were the apple of her eye.'

'I was her only child.'

'Yes,' he said soberly. 'Well, if you played a game of chess with me now and then, you wouldn't be so bored with the old man's efforts at conversation. When will you come?'

I considered. 'The day after to-morrow,' I said.

'Good. Tea-time?'

'Yes, but I mustn't eat so many of these splits or I shall put on too much weight.'

He looked at me and his eyes were suddenly soft. 'You're as slight as a sylph,' he said.

Nurse Grey came over with plates of cakes, but we did not seem in the mood for eating any more.

I noticed that Nurse Grey's eyes had grown more luminous and that there was a faint pink colour in her cheeks. I wondered uneasily whether Roc had had anything to do with that, and I was reminded of Rachel Bective and Dinah Bond, the young blacksmith's wife.

The conversation became general, and after an hour we left.

Roc was clearly amused as we walked home.

'Another conquest for you,' he commented. 'The old fellow certainly took to you. I've never known him so gracious before.'

'Poor old man, I don't think people try to understand him.'

'They don't need to,' retorted Roc. 'He's as easy to read as an A.B.C. He's the typical self-made man – a character off the shelf. There are some people who mould themselves on old clichés. They decide the sort of person they're going to be and start playing the part; after a while they're so good at it that it becomes second nature. That's why there are so many stock characters in the world.' He grinned at me. 'You don't believe me, do you? Well, look at Lord P. Started selling newspapers . . . perhaps not newspapers, but some such job. It's the pattern that matters, not the detail. Never goes in for any fun, piles up the little capital to start with, and by the time he's thirty, industry and skill have turned it into a big capital and he's on the way to becoming a millionaire. That's all very well, but he can't be *himself* . . . he has to be one of the band of self-made men. He clings to his rough manners. "I came up from nothing and I'm proud of it!" Doesn't go in for the ordinary graces of conventional living. "Why should I change myself? I'm perfect as I am." Oh, I don't have to *try* to understand Lord P. If he were made of glass I shouldn't be able to see through him more clearly.'

'You don't forgive him for building his house.'

Roc shrugged his shoulders. 'Perhaps not. It's a fake and I hate fakes. Suppose all the self-made men made up their minds to build along our coast? What a sight! No, I'm against these pseudo-antiques; and to have put one on our doorstep is an imposition. Polhorgan's Folly is an outsider here on our coast with houses like Pendorric, Mount Mellyn, Mount Widden, Cotehele and the like . . . just as its master is . . . with his Midland manners calling himself Lord Polhorgan. As though Tre, Pol and Pen did not belong to Cornishmen.'

'How vehement you are!' I said, and trying to speak lightly added: 'And if *I* made a conquest, what of you?'

He was smiling as he turned to me. 'Thea, you mean?'

'You call her that?'

'That's her name, my dear. Althea Grey – Thea to her friends.'

'Of whom you are one.'

'Of course, and so will you be. As for my conquest,' he went on, 'that's one of long standing. She has been here eighteen months, you know.'

Then he put his arm about me and began to sing:

'Wherever you hear Tre, Pol and Pen
You'll know that you're with Cornishmen.'

He smiled at me and continued:

'Alas, I have to add a rider.
One can't ignore the rich outsider.'

'I think,' I said, 'that you prefer the nurse to the invalid.' I saw the teasing light in his eyes.

'With you it's exactly the reverse,' he commented. 'That's why it was such a successful visit. I took care of the nurse while you devoted yourself to your host.'

Two days later, as we had arranged, I went to play chess with Lord Polhorgan. I came back and told Roc rather defiantly that I liked the old man even more than on the first occasion; which seemed to amuse him very much. Nurse Grey was not present, and I poured out the tea. The old man was delighted when he beat me, then he looked at me shrewdly and said: 'Sure you're not humouring the old man – letting him win, eh?' I replied that I had done my best to beat him, and that satisfied him. Before I left I had promised to call again in a day or so in order to give him a return match.

I was settling into life at Pendorric. I did a little gardening with Morwenna, and it was pleasant to chat with her while we worked.

'It's a useful hobby,' she said, 'because we haven't the gardeners we once had. In my father's day there were four of them; now it's Bill Pascoe from the cottages three afternoons a week, with Toms working when he gets a chance. Both Roc and I were always fond of growing things.'

'Roc doesn't do much in the gardens now,' I put in.

'Well, there's the farm to take up his time. He and Charles work hard on that.' She sat back on her heels and smiled at the fork in her hands. 'I'm so pleased they get on well together – but then of course they're two wonderful people. I've often thought how lucky I am.'

'I know what you mean,' I answered soberly. 'We're both lucky.'

Charles was very friendly to me in a quiet and unassuming way, and I liked his chubby charm. When Roc took me round the farm for the first time I was immediately aware of the respect Charles had for Roc's judgment, and that made me like him all the more.

I even liked Rachel Bective a little better than I had in the beginning and reproached myself for a too-hasty judgment because I had fancied I detected something rather sly in her sandy looks.

On one occasion we went for a walk together and she volunteered a little information about herself, telling me how she had met Morwenna when they had been at school together and had come to spend a summer holiday at Pendorric. From then she had been there often. She had to earn her living and had decided to take up teaching, so she had agreed to come here for a year to supervise the twins' education because she knew what a trial they were to their mother.

The twins themselves had a habit of coming upon me at unexpected moments, and seemed to take a special pleasure in leaping out on me and startling me.

Lowella addressed me as Bride, which at first I thought amusing but later was not so sure; Hyson had a habit of fixing her silent gaze on me whenever she was in my company, which I also found disconcerting.

Deborah was as determined as the others to make me feel at home; she told me that she felt like a mother towards me because Roc had been like her own son. I was sitting in the quadrangle one afternoon when I suddenly had the eerie feeling that I was being watched. I shook off this feeling which was always ready to worry me when I was in the quadrangle, but it persisted, and when I looked up at the window on the west side where I had seen Deborah on the day she arrived I almost expected to see her there.

I stared for a few seconds at those curtained windows; then I turned and looked at the east side. I was certain then that I saw a movement.

I waved and continued to look, but there was no response.

Ten minutes later Deborah joined me in the quadrangle.

'How you love this spot!' she said, and she pulled up one of the white and gilded chairs to sit close to me.

'My feelings for the place are a little mixed,' I told her frankly. 'I am immensely attracted, and yet I never feel exactly comfortable here.'

'Why ever not?'

I looked over my shoulder. 'It's the windows I think.'

'I often say it's a pity that it is only corridor windows which look down on the quadrangle. It would make such a lovely view and a change from the great vistas of sea from south, west and east, and country from the north.'

'It's the windows themselves. They take away privacy.'

She laughed. 'I believe you're rather a fanciful person after all.'

'Oh no, I'm not really. Were you on the east side a little while ago?'

She shook her head.

'I'm sure someone was looking down.'

'I shouldn't think so, dear, not from the east side. Those rooms are rarely used now. The furniture's covered in dustsheets . . . except in her rooms.'

'Her rooms?'

'Barbarina's. She always liked the east side. She didn't mind Polhorgan in the least, like the others did. *They* couldn't bear to look at it. She had her music room there. She said it was ideal because she could practise there to her heart's content without disturbing anyone.'

'Perhaps it was one of the twins I saw up there.'

'That may be so. The servants don't go there very much. Carrie looks after Barbarina's room. She gets rather angry if anyone else attempts to. But you should see them. You ought to see all over the house. You are after all its new mistress.'

'I would love to see Barbarina's rooms.'

'We could go now.'

I rose eagerly and she took my arm as we walked across the quadrangle to the east door. She seemed excited at the prospect of taking me on a tour of that part of the house.

The door closed behind us and as we walked along a short corridor which led into the hall I was conscious of silence. I told myself that it had something to do with my mood, for naturally if there was no one in this wing why should the silence surprise me?

'The servants say this is now the haunted part of the house,' Deborah told me.

'And Barbarina is the ghost?' I asked.

'You know the story then? Lowella Pendorric was supposed to have haunted the house until Barbarina took her place. A typical Cornish situation, my dear. I'm glad I was born on the other side of the Tamar. I shouldn't want to be perpetually ingratiating myself with piskies and ghosties and things that go bump in the night.'

I looked about the hall, which was an exact replica of the others in its proportions. There were the steel weapons on the walls, the pewter utensils on the refectory table, the suits of armour at the foot of the staircases. The pictures in the gallery were different, of course, and I gazed casually at them as we mounted the stairs.

We reached the corridor and I glanced through the windows at the quadrangle, wondering at which one I had seen a movement.

'Barby's rooms were on the second floor,' Deborah told me. 'I used to come and stay when she married. You see we had scarcely been separated all our lives and Barby didn't see why we ever should be. This became a second home to me. I was here as much as I was in Devonshire.'

We had mounted to the second floor and Deborah opened several of the doors to show me rooms shrouded in dust-sheets. They looked ghostly, as all such rooms do in large and silent houses.

Deborah smiled at me and I guessed she was reading my thoughts and perhaps trying to prove to me that I was not as immune from Cornish superstition as I should have liked her to believe.

'Now,' she said, and threw open a door. 'This is the music room.'

There were no dust-sheets here. The huge windows gave me a view of the coast, with Polhorgan rising majestically on the cliff top; but it was not the view I looked at this time, but the room, and I think what struck me most was that it had the look of a room which was being lived in. There was a dais at one end of it and on this was a stand with a piece of music opened on it. Beside the stand, on a chair, was a violin, looking as though it had just been placed there; the case lay open on a nearby table.

Deborah was watching me gravely, and I said slowly: 'This is how it was on the day she died?'

Deborah nodded. 'A silly habit. But some people find comfort from it. At first none of us could bear to move anything. Carrie dusts and puts things down exactly where they were. Carrie feels really fierce about it and it's more for her sake than anything else that we leave it as it is. I can't tell you how devoted she was to Barbarina.'

'And to you too.'

Deborah smiled. 'To me too. But Barbarina was her favourite.'

'You were identical twins?'

'Yes. Like Lowella and Hyson. When we were young some people found difficulty in telling us apart, but as we grew older all that passed. She was gay and amusing; I was rather stolid and slow-witted. There's more to looks than features, isn't there? It's beginning to show in Hyson and Lowella. It's only when they're asleep that they seem so much alike. As I was saying, Barby was everybody's favourite, and because she was as she was ... I seemed more dull and less interesting than I should if she had not always been with me.'

'Did you resent it?'

'Resent it! I adored Barbarina with the rest. In fact she hadn't a more devoted admirer. When she was praised I was happy because in a way it seemed as though I was being praised. It's sometimes like that with twins; they can share each other's triumphs and disasters more fully than ordinary people do.'

'And did she feel the same about you?'

'Absolutely. I wish you could have known Barbarina. She was a wonderful person. She was all that I should have liked to be myself; and because she looked so like me and was my twin sister, when we were little I was quite happy that it should be so.'

'It must have been a blow to you when she married.'

'We didn't let that part us more than we could help. I had to be in Devonshire for a good part of the time because our father needed me to look after him. Our mother had died when we were fifteen and he had never really got over the shock. But whenever I could I would be at Pendorric. She was very glad to see me. In fact, I don't know what she would have done . . .' She hesitated and I had the impression that she was on the verge of confiding in me. Then she shrugged her shoulders and seemed to change her mind.

But here in Barbarina's music room I was conscious of a great desire to learn more about her. I was – although I wouldn't admit it at this stage – becoming more and more absorbed in the story of this woman who had been my immediate predecessor as a Pendorric Bride.

'Was it a happy marriage?' I asked.

Deborah turned away from me and went to the window; I was embarrassed, realizing that I had asked an awkward question, so I went to her and, laying my hand gently on her arm, said: 'I'm sorry. I'm being too inquisitive.'

She turned to me and I noticed how brilliant her eyes had become. She shook her head and smiled. 'Of course not, and naturally you're interested. After all, you're one of us now, aren't you? There's no reason why we should try to keep family secrets from you. Come and sit down and I will tell you about it.'

We sat in the window looking along the coast towards Rame Head and Plymouth. The headland jutted out darkly in the grey water and one could imagine it was a supine giantess who lay there. The tide was out and the tops of the jagged rocks were visible. I gazed at Polhorgan whose grey walls were the colour of the sea to-day.

'There's a distant family connection between the Hysons and the Pendorrics,' said Deborah. 'Cousins, many times removed. So from our childhood we knew Petroc and his family. I don't mean your Roc, of course, but his father who was Barbarina's Petroc. When he was a boy he used to stay with us. He was a year older than we were.'

'He was like Roc, wasn't he?'

'So like him that sometimes when I see Roc now I get a little shock and for the moment I think he's Petroc come back.'

'In looks, you mean?'

'Oh . . . in many ways. The voice . . . the gestures . . . his ways . . . everything. There's a very strong resemblance that runs through most of the Pendorric men. I used to hear stories of Petroc's father – another Petroc – and all that I heard could have applied to his son. Barbarina fell in love with him when she was about seven. She remained in that state until she died.'

'She must have been happy when she married him.'

'A feverish sort of ecstasy. It used to frighten me. She cared for him so much.'

'And he for her?'

Deborah smiled a little wistfully. 'Petroc liked women in general too much to care very deeply for one in particular. That's what I always felt, and so

I saw how it would be. I warned Barbarina, but she wouldn't listen of course.'

There was silence, and after a while she went on: 'We used to ride on Dartmoor. Our place is on the moor, you know. You must come and see it. The view is wonderful – if you like that kind of view. You can step from our garden right on to the moor. Once we all went riding together and they lost me. The mist came up as it does on the moor, and however well you think you know the place you can easily be hopelessly lost. You are apt to wander round and round in circles. It was really rather frightening. I found my way back but they didn't come home until next day. They'd sheltered in some hut they'd discovered, and Petroc had had the foresight to load up with chocolate. Sometimes I think he arranged the whole thing.'

'Why? I mean, if she was in love with him, couldn't he have been with her . . . more comfortably?'

Again that silence. Then she sighed and said: 'He was in love with some local girl whom he'd promised to marry. She was a farmer's daughter. But the family wanted this marriage with the Hysons because our father was well off and money was badly needed at Pendorric. Barbarina was very unhappy. She'd heard that Petroc was going to marry this girl, and she knew he must be very much in love with her because Pendorric meant a great deal to him, and it was possible that if he couldn't bring some money into the family something would have to be done about it. So she knew he must have been deeply in love with the girl to contemplate marrying someone who couldn't bring a penny into the place. He was fond of Barbarina. It wouldn't have been any hardship to marry her . . . if he hadn't been so besottedly in love with this other woman. Petroc was the sort of man who would get along with any woman . . . like . . . Well, you know the type.'

I nodded uneasily.

'Were the Pendorrics very poor then?'

'Not exactly, but the great change had set in. Things weren't what they had been for their sort of people. The house needed expensive renovations. And Petroc had gambled rather rashly in the hope of recuperating the family fortunes.'

'So he was a gambler.'

She nodded. 'As his father was.'

'And what happened after that night on the moor?'

'I think Petroc had made up his mind that he would have to marry Barbarina. Pendorric was important, so he would fall in with the wishes of his family and Barbarina's. But he couldn't tell Barbarina that . . . bluntly. So they got lost on the moors and Barbarina was seduced and . . . that made it all easy.'

'She told you this?'

'My dear Favel, Barbarina didn't have to *tell* me things. We were as close as two people can be. Don't forget that during the months of our gestation we had been as one. I knew exactly what had happened and why.'

'And after that she married him and she was happy.'

'What do you expect? Petroc couldn't be faithful. It wasn't in his nature to be, any more than it had been in his father's. He took up with the farmer's

daughter again. It was a notorious scandal. But she wasn't the only one.
Like his father he couldn't resist a woman nor a chance to gamble. Women
couldn't resist them either. I thought that when Roc and Morwenna were
born she would cease to fret for him, and for a while she did. I hoped that
she would have more children and make them her life.'

'And you were disappointed?'

'Barbarina was a good mother, don't mistake me; but she wasn't one of
those women who can ignore her husband's infidelities and become completely absorbed in her children. Petroc meant too much to her for that.'

'So she was very unhappy?'

'You can imagine it, can't you. A sensitive woman . . . in a place like this
. . . and an unfaithful husband who didn't make a secret of his infidelities;
there was nothing secret about Petroc. He never tried to pretend he was
other than he was – a reckless gambler and a philanderer. He seemed to
take up the attitude: It's a family characteristic, so there's nothing *I* can do
about it.'

'Poor Barbarina,' I murmured.

'I used to come down as often as I could, and then when my father died
I almost lived here. It was through me that she became interested in her
music again. I believe that in other circumstances she might have been a
concert violinist. She was really very good. But she had never practised
enough. However, she found great pleasure in it, particularly towards the
end. In fact she was very gifted. I remember when we were at school . . . we
must have been about fourteen then . . . she was in the school play. It was
Hamlet and she was Ophelia, a part which suited her absolutely. I was the
ghost. That was about the limit of my capabilities. I believe I was a very
poor one. But Barbarina was the hit of the show.'

'I can imagine that – from her picture, I mean. Particularly the one in the
gallery.'

'Oh, that's Barbarina as she really was. Sometimes when I look at it I
almost imagine she will step out of the frame and speak to me.'

'Yes, there's a touch of reality about it. The artist must have been a very
good one.'

'It was painted about a year before her death. She took great pleasure in
riding. In fact I sometimes felt it was a feverish sort of pleasure she was
taking in things . . . her music . . . riding, and so on. She was lovely in that
particular ensemble, and that was why she was painted in it. It was sad that
she – like Ophelia – should have died before her time. I wish you could have
heard her sing that song from the play. She had a strange voice . . . a little
off-key, which suited the song and Ophelia. I remember at the school show
how silent the audience was when she came on the stage in a flowering
gown of white and flowers in her hair and in her hands. I can't sing; but
it's that one that goes something like this:

> *"How should I your true love know*
> *From another one?*
> *By his cockle hat and staff,*
> *And his sandal shoon.*

He is dead and gone, lady,
He is dead and gone;
At his head a grass-green turf,
At his heels a stone." '

She quoted the words in a low monotone; then she flashed her smile at me. 'I wish I could make you hear it as she sang it. There was something about it that made one shiver. Afterwards it became one of her favourite songs and there was a verse which she didn't sing at the school play but she used to sing that later.

"Then up he rose, and donn'd his clothes,
And dup'ed the chamber door;
Let in the maid, that out a maid
Never departed more."

'There would be an odd little smile about her lips as she sang that, and I always felt it had something to do with that night on the moor.'

'Poor Barbarina! I'm afraid she wasn't very happy.'

Deborah clenched her fists as though in sudden anger. 'And she was meant to be happy. I never knew anyone so capable of being happy. If Petroc had been all that she hoped he would be ... if ... But what is the good? When is life ever what you hope it will be; and in any case it is all so long ago.'

'I heard about it; the balustrade was faulty and she fell to the hall.'

'It was unfortunate that it happened in the gallery where Lowella Pendorric hung. That really gave rise to all the talk.'

'It must have revived the legend.'

'Oh, it didn't take all that reviving. The people round about had always said that Pendorric was haunted by Lowella Pendorric, the Bride of long ago.'

'And now they say that Barbarina has taken her place.'

Deborah laughed; then she looked over her shoulder. 'Although I've always laughed at such talk, sometimes when I'm in this house I feel a little more inclined to accept it.'

'It's the atmosphere of old houses. The furniture is often standing in exactly the same place it was in hundreds of years ago. You can't help thinking that this house looked almost exactly the same to that Lowella whom they call the First Bride.'

'I only wish that Barbarina *would* come back!' said Deborah vehemently. 'I can't tell you what I'd give to see her again.' She stood up. 'Let's go for a walk. We're getting morbid sitting here in Barbarina's room. We'll have to get mackintoshes. Look at those clouds. The wind's in the south-west and that means rain's not far off.'

I said I should enjoy that, and we left the east wing together. She came with me to my room while I put on my outdoor things; then I went with her to hers; and when we were ready she led me round to the north wing and we paused on the gallery before the picture of Lowella Pendorric.

'This is where she fell,' explained Deborah. 'Look, you can see where the balustrade has been mended. It was woodworm, I believe. It should have been noticed long before. Actually the place is riddled with worm. It's inevitable and it'll cost a fortune to put it right.'

I looked up into Lowella Pendorric's painted face and I thought exultantly: But Roc is not really like his father and his grandfather, and the gambling, philandering Pendorrics. If he had been in his father's place he would have married the farmer's daughter, as he married me – for what had I to bring him? In ten minutes we were strolling along the cliff path, the warm sea-scented wind caressing our faces.

I had no wish to lead an idle life. On the island there had always been so much to do. I had been my father's house-keeper as well as his saleswoman. I pointed out to Roc that I wanted to do something.

'You might go down to the kitchens and have a little chat with Mrs. Penhalligan. She'd appreciate it. After all, you're the mistress of the house.'

'I will,' I agreed, 'because Morwenna won't mind in the least if I do make suggestions.'

He put his arm round me and hugged me. 'Aren't you the mistress of the house, anyway?'

'Roc,' I told him, 'I'm so happy. I wouldn't have thought it possible so soon after . . .'

Roc's kiss prevented me from going on with that.

'Didn't I tell you? And talking of having something to do . . . as Mrs. Pendorric you should take an interest in village activities, you know. It's expected, as I guess you've gathered from the Darks. I tell you, Favel, in a few weeks' time you'll not be complaining of having too little to do, but too much.'

'I think I'll begin by getting to know more of Mrs. Penhalligan and perhaps I'll call on the Darks. This afternoon, by the way, I've promised to have tea with Lord Polhorgan.'

'What, again? You really do like that old man.'

'Yes,' I said almost defiantly, 'I do.'

'Then enjoy yourself.'

'I believe I shall.'

Roc studied me, smiling as he did so. 'You certainly seem to hit it off.'

'I feel that he's really rather a lonely old man, and he seems sort of paternal.'

Roc's smile faded and he nodded slowly. 'You're still grieving,' he said.

'It's so hard to forget, Roc. Oh, I'm so happy here. I love it all; the family are so kind to me, and you . . .'

He was laughing. 'And I'm kind to you too? What did you expect? A wife-beater?'

Then he put his arms about me and held me close to him. 'Listen, Favel,' he said. 'I want you to be happy. It's what I want more than anything. I understand what you feel about the old man. He's paternal. That's what you said; and in a way he makes up for something you miss. He's lonely.

You can bet your life *he's* missed a lot. So you like each other. It's understandable.'

'I wish you liked him more, Roc.'

'Don't take any notice of what I've said. It was mostly said jokingly. When you get to know me better you'll understand what a joker I am.'

'Don't you think I know you well then?'

'Not as well as you will twenty years hence, darling. We'll go on learning about each other; that's what makes it all so exciting. It's like a voyage of discovery.'

He spoke lightly, but I went on thinking of what he had said, and I was still remembering those words when I passed under the great archway on my way out that afternoon, until I heard footsteps behind me and turning saw Rachel Bective, a twin walking sedately on either side of her.

'Hallo,' called Rachel, 'going for a walk?'

'I'm going to tea at Polhorgan.'

They caught up with me and we walked along together.

'Hope you're prepared,' warned Rachel. 'It's going to rain.'

'I've brought my mac.'

'The wind's blowing in from the south-west, and once it starts to rain here you begin to wonder whether it's ever going to stop.'

Hyson came to the other side of me so that I was in between her and Rachel; Lowella skipped on ahead.

'Do you go round by the cliff path to Polhorgan? asked Rachel. 'It's at least five minutes shorter.'

'I've always kept to this road.'

'We'll show you the short cut if you like.'

'Don't let me take you out of your way.'

'But we're only going for a walk.'

'Well, thanks – if it really won't.'

'Lowella,' Rachel called. 'We're going down Smugglers' Lane to show your Aunt Favel the short cut to Polhorgan.'

Lowella wheeled sharply round. 'Good. It'll be lovely and squelchy down Smugglers' Lane.'

'It won't. There hasn't been that much rain.'

We turned aside from the road and took a steep narrow path on either side of which the hedges had run so wild that sometimes we had to go in single file.

Lowella found a broken-off branch and went ahead of us beating the overgrown hedges and shouting: ' "Beware the awful avalanche. Beware the pine-tree's withered branch. Excelsior!" '

'Oh Lowella, do be quiet,' begged Rachel.

'Of course if you don't want me to lead you to safety, say so.'

'Hyson reads to her when they're in bed at night,' Rachel told me, 'and she goes on repeating what appeals to her.'

'You like reading, don't you?' I said to Hyson.

She merely nodded. Then she said: 'Lowella's such a child. As if this is anything like the awful avalanche!'

The path ended abruptly and we stepped on to what looked like a ledge.

Beneath us – a long way beneath us – was the sea, and beside us towering above rose the shaley face of the cliff with here and there a bush of gorse or bracken clinging to the brown earth.

'It's perfectly safe,' said Rachel Bective. 'Unless of course you have a phobia about heights.'

I told her I hadn't and added that we were several feet lower than we had been on the coast road.

'Yes, but that's a proper road. This is just a path, and a little farther on it gets even narrower. There's a notice saying use it at your own risk, but that's for visitors. Local people all use it.'

Lowella went on ahead, pretending to pick her way. 'Wouldn't it be super if we had a rope attaching us all,' she cried. 'Then if the Bride fell over the cliff, we'd haul her up.'

'That's kind of you, but I don't intend to fall.'

' "She's still the youth who bore 'mid snow and ice the banner with the strange device," ' murmured Hyson.

'Excelsior!' cried Lowella. 'Isn't it a smashing word!' She ran on, shouting it.

Rachel looked at me and shrugged her shoulders.

In a few seconds I saw what they meant about the path's narrowing; for some two yards it was little more than a shelf; we walked rather gingerly in single file; then we rounded a part of the cliff which projected over the water, and as we did so I saw that we were almost at Polhorgan.

'It's certainly a short cut,' I said. 'Thanks for showing me.'

'Shall we go back the same way?' Rachel asked the twins.

Lowella turned and was already on her way back. I heard her shouting 'Excelsior' as I went on to Polhorgan.

Lord Polhorgan was delighted to see me. I fancied the manservant treated me with rather special deference, and it occurred to me that it must be rare for his master to become so friendly in such a short space of time.

When I went into his room Nurse Grey was with him, reading to him from *The Financial Times*.

'Please don't let me interrupt,' I said. 'I must be early. I'll go and have a walk in the garden. I've always wanted to explore it.'

Lord Polhorgan looked at his watch. 'You are punctual,' he said, and waved a hand at Nurse Grey, who promptly folded the paper and rose. 'Never could abide people who have no respect for time. Unpunctuality is a vice. Glad to see you, Mrs. Pendorric. And I'd like to show you the garden, but I can't manage it these days. Too steep for me to walk; too steep for me to be wheeled.'

'I'll enjoy it from the window to-day,' I answered.

Nurse Grey must show you, one day.'

'I'd be delighted to,' said Althea Grey.

'Tell them to bring in the tea. And Nurse, there's no need for you to stay. Mrs. Pendorric will do the honours, I'm sure.'

Nurse Grey bowed her head and murmured: 'I'll hurry on the tea then.'

Lord Polhorgan nodded and the nurse went out, leaving us together.

'Tea first,' he said, 'and we'll have our chess after. Sit down and talk to me for a while. You're settling in here now. Liking it?'

'Very much.'

'All well at Pendorric?' He shot a quick glance at me from under his shaggy brows.

'Yes.' I went on impulsively: 'Did you expect it to be otherwise?'

He evaded the question. 'It's never easy settling in to a new life. Must have been very gay – that island of yours. Find it quiet here?'

'I like this quiet.'

'Better than the island?'

'When my mother was alive I was completely happy. I didn't think there was anything in the world but happiness. I was sad when I went away to school, but after a while I was used to that and being back was more fun than ever.'

He gave me a look of approval. 'You're a sensible young woman. I'm glad. Can't stand the other sort.'

'Nurse Grey seems a sensible young woman.'

'H'm. Too sensible perhaps.'

'Can one be too sensible?'

'Sometimes I wonder why she stays here. I don't think it's out of love for her patient. I'm what's known as an old curmudgeon, Mrs. Pendorric.'

I laughed. 'You can't be such a bad one, since you admit it.'

'Can't I? You forget, when a man's made money, he's invariably sur-rounded by people who are anxious to relieve him of it – or some of it.'

'And you think Nurse Grey . . .?'

He looked at me shrewdly. 'Handsome young woman . . . fond of gaiety. Not so much to be had here.'

'But she seems contented.'

'Ay, she does and all.' He nodded shrewdly. 'Often wonder why. Perhaps she thinks she won't be forgotten . . . when the great day comes.'

I must have shown my embarrassment, for he said quickly: 'A fine host I am. Why, you'll be making excuses not to come and see me if I don't watch out. Shouldn't like that . . . shouldn't like it at all.'

'I wouldn't make excuses to you. You're forthright and say what you mean, so I would try to do the same.'

'We're alike in that,' he said, and chuckled.

The tea arrived and I poured. This had become a habit which was a further indication of the rate at which our friendship had developed. He seemed to take pleasure in watching me.

While I was serving tea I saw Althea Grey walking through the gardens down to the beach. She had changed her uniform for brown jeans and a blouse the colour of delphiniums, which was a perfect foil for her fair hair, and I guessed her eyes matched the blouse. She looked back suddenly and, seeing me, waved; I waved back.

'It's Nurse Grey,' I explained to my host. 'She's off duty for a few hours I suppose.'

He nodded. 'Was she on her way down to the beach?'

'Yes.'

'Polhorgan Cove belongs to me by rights but I was soon led to understand that the natives wouldn't think very kindly of me if I made it a private beach. There's a gate and hedges shutting off the garden; but you go through the gate right on to the beach.'

'It's rather like Pendorric.'

'The same arrangement. Pendorrics own their beach and I own mine, but I don't think half the people who scramble over the rocks at low tide know that.'

'If the beaches were fenced off it would mean people couldn't walk along for very far; they'd have to keep coming up and making a detour.'

'Always believed that what was mine was mine and I had a right to say what was to be done with it. I was very unpopular when I first came, I can tell you. I've grown mellow. You learn as you get older. Sometimes if you stand out for your rights you lose what might mean more to you.'

He was momentarily sad, and I fancied that he looked a little more tired than when I had last seen him.

'Yes, I think there's a lot in that,' I said.

'There you were, with your mother and father on that island . . . perfectly happy, and I don't suppose you owned the house you lived in, let alone the ground all round and a private beach.'

'It's true. We were very poor and very happy.'

He frowned, and I wondered if I had been tactless. He went on rather brusquely: 'Nurse Grey goes down to the beach a great deal. Do you use yours much?'

'Not so far. But I shall, of course. I've hardly settled in yet.'

'I'm taking up too much of your time.'

'But I like coming and I enjoy playing chess.'

He was silent for a while, and then again he led me back to the subject of my life on the island.

I was surprised that he could be such a good listener, but while I talked he remained attentive and fired so many questions at me in his rather brusque manner that I went on talking about myself.

When the tea had been cleared away I drew up the exquisite little table on which we played; it was a dainty piece of French origin with inlaid ivory and tortoise-shell squares; I put out the ivory chessmen, which were as beautiful as the table, and the game began.

When we had been playing for about fifteen minutes, to my surprise I had him at a disadvantage. I was delightedly pursuing my strategy when, looking up, I saw that he was in considerable discomfort.

'Sorry,' he muttered. 'Please forgive me.' He was groping in his pocket.

'You've lost something?'

'A little silver box. I always keep it near me.'

I stood up and looking about me saw a small silver box on the floor at his feet. I picked it up and gave it to him. His relief was apparent as he quickly opened it and took a small white tablet from it. This he placed under his tongue. For some seconds he sat back gripping his chair.

I was alarmed because I knew that he was ill, and I got up, going to the bell to call the manservant, but seeing what I was about to do, Lord

Polhorgan shook his head. I stood uncertainly. 'Better in a minute,' he muttered.

'But you're ill. Shouldn't I . . .?'

He continued to shake his head while I stood helplessly by. In about five minutes he began to look a little better and it was as though a tension had been eased.

He drew a deep breath and murmured: 'Better now. I'm sorry.'

'Please don't be so sorry. Just tell me what I can do.'

'Just sit down . . . quietly. In a few minutes I'll be all right.'

I obeyed, watching him anxiously. The gilded French clock over the ornate fireplace ticked loudly, and apart from that there was silence in the room. From far away I could hear the gentle swishing of the waves against the rocks.

A few more minutes passed and he gave a deep sigh. Then he smiled at me. 'I'm sorry that happened while you were here. Mislaid my tablets. Don't usually stir without them. They must have dropped out of my pocket.'

'Please don't apologize. I'm the one who is sorry. I'm afraid I didn't know what to do.'

'There's nothing much anyone can do. If I'd had my box I'd have slipped a tablet into my mouth while you were busy over the game and you wouldn't have noticed anything. As it was . . . I delayed a little too long.'

'I'm glad I found them.'

'You look sad. Shouldn't, you know. I'm an old man. And one of the disadvantages of being old is that one is too old to deal with the disadvantages. But I've had my day. Besides, there's a lot of life in me yet. Don't like mislaying my tablets though. Could be dangerous.'

'What wonderful tablets they must be!'

'Not always effective. They are, ninety-nine times out of a hundred, though. T.N.T. Expand the veins and arteries.'

'And if they're not?'

'Then it's a dose of morphia.'

'I'm terribly sorry.'

He patted my hand. 'The old engine's creaking,' he said. 'I need decarbonizing. Pity I can't ask you to run me into old Jim Bond's and have it done, eh?'

'Shouldn't you rest now?'

'Don't you worry. I'll phone my doctor and ask him to come in and see me. Haven't been feeling so well this last day or so.'

'Shouldn't we phone at once?'

'Nurse Grey will do it when she comes in. Can't imagine how those tablets came to be on the floor.'

'Perhaps there's a hole in your pocket.'

He felt, and shook his head.

'You know, I think you ought to rest. Shall I go now? Or better still, telephone the doctor?'

'All right, then. His number's in the little book by the telephone. Dr. Clement.'

I went at once to the book and dialled the number. I was fortunate, for

Dr. Clement happened to be in. I told him that I was speaking from Polhorgan and that Lord Polhorgan wanted him to look in soon.

'Right,' said Dr. Clement. 'I'll be along.'

I replaced the receiver and went back to the table. 'Can I do anything for you?' I asked.

'Yes, sit down and finish the game. I'm afraid I let you get the better of me. I was thinking about my silver box. Just to show you how quickly I can recover we'll continue the game and I'll beat you yet.'

I kept taking uneasy glances at him as we played, which made him chuckle, and before we had finished the game Dr. Clement arrived.

I rose to go, but Lord Polhorgan wouldn't hear of it.

'I'm all right now,' he said. 'I only let Mrs. Pendorric call you because she was anxious about me. Tell her there's nothing to be done for me. The trouble was, Doctor, I'd mislaid my T.N.T.s and it was some minutes before Mrs. Pendorric found them.'

'You should always keep them within reach,' said Dr. Clement.

'I know. I know. Can't think what happened. Must have pulled them out of my pocket. Have some tea. Perhaps Mrs. Pendorric would ring for Dawson. That's cold by now.'

The doctor declined the tea and I said I really should go. I was certain that he would want to be alone with his patient.

'The game's unfinished,' protested Lord Polhorgan.

'We can finish it next time.'

'I've frightened you away,' said Dr. Clement almost wistfully.

I was determined to go, and I left. As I came through the portico I glanced at my watch and saw that I was half an hour earlier than I had intended to be, so instead of making my way to the road, or the path which led to the short cut Rachel and the twins had shown me that afternoon, I thought I would like to go down to the beach by way of the cliff garden and scramble over the rocks to Pendorric Cove, and through our own garden up to the house.

The tide was out, so it would be possible. I walked round to the side of the house and saw one of the Polhorgan gardeners emerging from a greenhouse. I asked him how I could get to the beach from the garden and he offered to show me the way.

He led me along a path bounded on each side by a box hedge; at the end of this path was a small gate, and passing through it I came on the cliff garden. It was a wonderful sight, for in this semi-tropical climate plants grew in profusion. There was a palm tree in a sheltered alcove which reminded me of those in the quadrangle; and the hydrangea blooms were even bigger than those at Pendorric; they flaunted their brilliant blues and pinks, whites and multi-colours. There seemed to be hundreds of fuchsias with larger flowers than I had seen before; and great white arum lilies which filled the air with their slightly funereal scent.

The path I had taken wound in zigzag fashion towards the sea to eliminate the strain of walking down such a steep slope; first I faced east, then west, then turned again as I went past borders of flowers whose names I did not know, past seats which had been set under arches and in alcoves the trellis-work of which was ablaze with Paul Scarlett, American Pillar and Golden Dawn roses.

I thought that if the sun were shining and the sea blue it would be almost too dazzling. But to-day was a grey day and the cry of the gulls seemed melancholy as they swooped and soared.

I came at length to the little gate which opened on to the beach, and as I stood in Polhorgan Cove I looked back at that wonderful garden set out on the cliff-side to the stone walls of Polhorgan's Folly looming above.

Not such a Folly, I thought. A lovely house in a lovely spot.

The tide was well out. I knew that at high tide it came up almost as far as the gates of Pendorric garden, and, I imagined, those of Polhorgan too. It was only when the tide was really out that one could walk along the beach. Even as far as I could see, the place was deserted. Ahead of me the rocks jutted out almost to the water, shutting me in the little bay which was known as Polhorgan's Cove. I guessed it would take me longer to reach Pendorric this way than by the road, so I started westwards immediately. It was not easy rounding the jagged rocks; there were so many to be climbed, and interesting little pools to be leaped over. I came to a large rock which actually did jut into the sea. It was rather difficult getting over that one, but I managed it; and then I saw our own beach, our garden, far less grand than that of Polhorgan, but perhaps as beautiful in its wild state.

I leaped on to the soft sand, and as I did so I heard the sound of laughter.

Then I saw them. She was half lying on the sand, her face propped up by her hands, and he was stretched out beside her leaning on one elbow. He looked as dark as he had when I had first seen him sitting in the studio with my father.

They were talking animatedly, and I thought uneasily: They wouldn't have expected to see me here suddenly.

I wanted them to know quickly that I was close by. Perhaps I was afraid that if I did not make my presence known I might hear or see something which I did not want to. I called out: 'Hallo.'

Roc sprang to his feet and for a few seconds stared at me; then he came running towards me, taking both my hands in his.

'Look who's here! I thought you were still at the Folly.'

'I hope I didn't startle you.'

He put his arm round me and laughed. 'In the most pleasant way,' he said.

We walked over to Althea Grey, who remained where she was on the sand. Her blue eyes, fixed on me, seemed shrewd and alert.

'Is everything all right at Polhorgan?' she asked.

I told her what had happened, and she got up.

'I'd better get back,' she said.

'Come up to Pendorric,' said Roc, 'and I'll drive you there.'

She looked up at the steep garden to the grey walls of Pendorric and shook her head. 'I don't think it would be any quicker. I'll go over the rocks.' She turned to me. 'I've done it so often, I'm becoming like a mountain goat. See you later,' she added, and started to hurry across the sand.

'You look shaken,' said Roc. 'I believe the old man often has those attacks.

He's been having them for years. Pity it happened when you were alone with him.'

We opened the gate and started the climb through the garden to the house.

'What made you come the beach way?' asked Roc.

'I don't know. Perhaps because it was a way I hadn't been before and as I was leaving a little early I thought I'd try it. Is Althea Grey a great friend of . . . the family?'

'Not of the family.'

'Only of you?'

'You know what a friendly type I am!'

He caught me to him and hugged me. Questions were on my lips but I hesitated. I didn't want him to think I was going to be foolishly jealous every time he spoke to another woman. I had to remember I had married a Pendorric and they were noted for their gallantries.

'Do you often meet on the beach?'

'This is a small place. One is always running up against neighbours.'

'I wonder why she preferred our beach to Polhorgan.'

'Ah, from Pendorric beach you can look up at real antiquity; from Polhorgan you only get the fake.'

'It's a very beautiful fake.'

'I believe you're getting very fond of his lordship.' He regarded me ironically: 'Ought *I* to be jealous?'

I laughed, but I felt almost as uneasy as I had when I had come into the cove and seen them lying there together. Was he trying to turn the tables, as guilty people often did? Was he saying: You spend your afternoon with Lord Polhorgan, so why shouldn't I spend mine with his nurse?

It was an incongruous suggestion, but he went on: 'I should be very jealous, so you mustn't provoke me.'

'I hope you will remember to do unto others as you would they should do unto you.'

'But you would never be jealous without reason. You're far too sensible.'

'Yet I suppose it would be more reasonable to be jealous of a beautiful young woman than a sick old man.'

'Often in these matters there are other factors to be considered besides personal charms.'

'Such as?'

'You don't find millionaires lurking on every rock and patch of sand.'

'What a hideous suggestion!'

'Isn't it? And I'm a beast to mention such mundane matters as money; but then, as you once said, I am a satyr, which is a form of beast, I suppose. Actually I fancied you were not very pleased to come upon Thea and me together and I wanted to tell you how ridiculous you were to be . . . not very pleased.'

'You're not hinting that you'd rather I didn't visit Lord Polhorgan?'

'Good heavens, no! I'm delighted that you do. Poor old man, he's only just beginning to realize that his millions can't buy him all he wants. He's getting more pleasure out of having a beautiful young woman to pour his tea and hover over his ivory chessmen than he's had for years. And all without paying out a penny! It's a revelation to him. It reminds me of Little Lord Fauntleroy, the terror of my youth because I was forced to read of his adventures by a well-meaning nurse. I found him particularly nauseating – perhaps because he was the opposite of myself. I could never see myself in plum-coloured velvet with my golden curls falling over my lace collar going to soften the hard heart of dear old Lord Somebody, Fauntleroy, I believe . . . old Fauntleroy. That was one thing I could never do – bring warring relations together by my childish charm.'

'Stop it Roc. Do you really object to my visits to Polhorgan?'

He picked up one of the Mrs. Sinkins pinks that grew in rather untidy clumps, filling the air with their delicious scent, and gravely put it into the buttonhole of my short linen jacket.

'I've been talking a lot of nonsense because I'm garrulous by nature. Darling, I want you to feel absolutely free. As for visiting Lord Polhorgan, don't for heaven's sake stop. I'm glad you're able to give him so much pleasure. I know he ruined our east view with his monstrosity, but he's an old man and he's sick. Go as often as he asks you.'

He leaned forward to smell the pink; then he kissed my lips. He took my hand and we climbed to the house.

As usual he had the power to make me accept what he wanted to; it was only when I was alone that I asked myself; Does he want me to visit Lord Polhorgan so that Althea Grey is free to be with him?

I went down to the kitchen one morning to find Mrs. Penhalligan at the table kneading dough, and there was the delicious smell of baking bread in the air.

The kitchens at Pendorric were enormous, and in spite of electric cookers, refrigerators and other recently installed modern equipment, looked as though they belonged to another age. There were several rooms – a bake-house, a buttery, a washhouse and another room called the dairy which had a floor of blue tiles and had once been a store-room for milk, butter, eggs and such. Across the ceiling were great oak beams supplied with hooks on which joints of meat, hams, sides of bacon and Christmas puddings had once hung.

The kitchen itself, though large, was a cosy room with its red-tiled floor and dressers, its refectory table at which generations of servants had had their meals and the wooden one scrubbed white at which, on this occasion, Mrs. Penhalligan was working. Through an open door I could see Maria preparing vegetables in the washhouse.

Mrs. Penhalligan bridled with pleasure when she saw me.

I said: 'Good morning, Mrs. Penhalligan. I thought it was about time I paid a visit to the kitchens.'

'It's good to see you, ma'am,' she answered.

'Is that bread baking? It smells delicious.'

She looked pleased. 'We've always baked our own bread at Pendorric. There's nothing like the home-baked, I always say. I bake for Father at the same time. It's always been understood.'

'How is your father?'

'Oh, fair to middling, ma'am. Don't get no younger but he be wonderful for his age. He'll be ninety next Candlemas.'

'Ninety! That's a great age.'

'And there bain't much wrong with him ... 'cept of course his great affliction.'

'Oh?'

'You didn't know, ma'am, and I reckon none as yet thought fit to tell you. Father went blind ... oh – it'll be nigh on thirty years ago. No. I bain't telling you the truth. It'll be twenty-eight years. It started ... twenty-eight years come harvest time.'

'I'm very sorry.'

'Oh, don't 'ee be. Father bain't sorry for himself. He's happy enough ... with his pipe and all he wants to eat. He likes to sit at the door on sunny days and it 'ud astonish you, ma'am, how good his hearing is. Sort of makes up for not having his sight, so it seems.'

'I expect I'll see him some time.'

'He'd be real pleased if you stopped and had a little chat with him. He's always asking about Mr. Roc's new bride.'

'I'll look for him.'

'You can't make no mistake. It's the second of the cottages down Pendorric Village. Lives all alone there. Independent since Mother went. But Maria and me, we're always in and out. And we pop over with a plate of hot something for his dinner regular as clockwork. He don't pay no rent, and he's got his bit of pension. Father's all right. He'd be wonderful ... if he had his sight.'

I was glad Mrs. Penhalligan was the loquacious type, because I had been wondering what I should say to her.

'I've been hearing about how your family have been at Pendorric for generations.'

'Oh yes ... always Pleydells at Pendorric. But then Father and Mother didn't have no son. I was their only daughter. Then I married Penhalligan, who was gardener here till he died. And we only had one too – my Maria. She'll be working here till the end ... and then that'll be the end of the Pleydells at Pendorric.'

'What a pity!'

'All things has to come to an end, ma'am. And did you want to give me some orders or something?'

'Not really. I thought I'd like to see how things were worked down here.'

'Right and proper that you should, ma'am. You be the mistress. Miss Morwenna, she was never one to take much interest. Now Miss Bective ...' Mrs. Penhalligan's face hardened ... 'she was up another street. When she first come here, it was, "Mrs. Penhalligan, we'll have this and we'll have that." But I know my place if some don't, and I take orders from the mistress of the house and none other.'

'I expect she was trying to be helpful.'

'Helpful! I don't need help in my kitchen, ma'am – no more than I've got. My Maria's been well trained and I'm not doing too bad with Hetty Toms.'

'Everything is very well organized, I'm sure.'

'And so it should be – the years I've been at it. I was in the kitchen when the other Mrs. Pendorric first come here.'

I felt excited as I always did at the mention of Barbarina. 'Was she interested in the kitchen?'

'She were like yourself, ma'am. Interested, I'd say but not one to want to change things. I remember the day she came into my kitchen, her lovely face all glowing with health; she'd come in from a ride and she was in her riding clothes . . . breeches and coat like a man's. But there was nothing of the man about her. There was a little blue flower in her buttonhole and she had one of them riding hats on with a band of yellow round it. She always wore them – like in the picture in the south hall, only she's in blue there.'

'Yes, I know the picture well.'

'A lovely lady, and it was a pleasure to serve her. It was terrible when . . . But my tongue runs away with me. Maria always says so and she's right.'

'It's pleasant to have a chat, though. That's really what I came down for.'

Mrs. Penhalligan's face shone with pleasure as her nimble fingers went on kneading the dough.

'She was like that too – always ready for a chat, particularly in the beginning. Afterwards she was . . .'

I waited, and Mrs. Penhalligan frowned down at her dough.

'She was less friendly later?' I prompted.

'Oh, not less friendly. Just sad, I think; and sometimes she wouldn't seem to see you. Reckon she was thinking of other things, poor lady.'

'Of her troubles?'

'She had those. She was very fond of him, you see. . . .' She seemed to recall to whom she was talking, and stopped. 'I suppose, ma'am, you have a preference for the wholemeal bread. I bake some white – but more wholemeal. Father, he likes white – done in the old-fashioned coburg style. Father's one to have what he wants. Though I must say now, though, that his mind wanders a bit. It's not being able to see, I think. That must make a difference.'

I said I personally preferred wholemeal, and that I thought the bread she made was the best I had ever tasted.

Nothing could have delighted her more; she was my ally from that moment. She relaxed, too; she had concluded that although I was the mistress of the house I was fond of a gossip.

'I'll certainly look out for your father when I next pass the cottages,' I told her.

'I'll tell him. He'll be that pleased. You must be prepared though for him to wander a bit. He's close on ninety and he gets a bit muddled. He's had it on his mind a bit lately. I reckon it's because there's a new bride here at Pendorric.'

'Had what on his mind?' I asked.

'Well, ma'am, you'll have heard of course how Mr. Roc's and Miss Morwenna's mother died.'

'Yes, I have heard.'

'Well, Father was there when it happened. It preyed on his mind a bit

for a time. Then he seemed to forget like . . . but things are likely to bring
it back, which is all natural. And when he heard there was a new bride at
Pendorric, you see . . .'

'Yes, I see. He was there, you say.'

'He were there. In the hall when she, poor soul, did crash from the
gallery. He weren't completely blind then neither – but almost he were. He
couldn't see clear enough, but he knew her were up there, and it was him
that gave the alarm. That's why it preyed on his mind like. That's why he
remembers now and then, though it be twenty-five years since it happened.'

'Does he believe . . . the story about the ghost?'

Mrs. Penhalligan looked surprised. 'Father knows there be such things.
I don't rightly know what he thinks about Mrs. Pendorric's fall. He don't
talk much. He just sits brooding. Can't get him to talk much about it. Might
be better if we could.'

'I shall certainly look out for him when I pass the cottages, Mrs.
Penhalligan.'

'You'll see him . . . puffing away at his old pipe. He'll be that pleased.
Maria'll just be taking the first batch out of the oven. I still use the old
cloam oven for bread. Can't be beat. Would you like to come and see it,
ma'am?'

I said I would; and as I went through the kitchens to the bakehouse and
returned the greeting of Maria and Hetty Toms, I was not thinking of them
nor the golden-brown loaves fresh from the oven; I kept seeing that beautiful
young woman crashing from the gallery, the smiling painted face of Lowella
Pendorric behind her; and in the hall, an almost sightless man, peering
towards the falling figure, trying so hard to see what was happening.

After my talk with Mrs. Penhalligan I felt that I was truly mistress of the
house. The faithful housekeeper, daughter of the Pleydells who had served
the family for generations, had accepted me. My sister-in-law had no great
desire to manage the house, and I felt delighted to have something to do.

I wanted to know every inch and corner of Pendorric. I was beginning to
love it, and to understand that a house which had stood for hundreds of
years must necessarily have a stronger appeal than one which had stood
only a few years.

I told Roc how I felt and he was delighted.

'What did I tell you?' he cried. 'The Brides of Pendorric fall fiercely in
love with the place.'

'It must be because they're so happy to have become Pendorrics.'

The remark delighted him. He put his arm about me and I felt suddenly
secure . . . safe.

'There are lots of things I want to ask you about the place,' I told him.
'Is it true that wood-worm is slowly destroying parts of it?'

'The little beasts are the enemies of the stately homes of England, darling.
They're almost as destructive as the Inland Revenue.'

'That's another thing: You did seem rather sorry because you weren't so
rich as Lord Polhorgan. Do you really think it'll be necessary to hand over
Pendorric to the National Trust?'

Roc took my face in his hands and kissed me lightly.

'Don't worry, sweetheart. We'll manage to keep the wolf from the ancestral home.'

'So we aren't living beyond our means?'

He laughed lightheartedly. 'I always knew I'd married a business woman. Listen, darling; when I've talked over this with Charles I'm going to show you how things work here. I'm going to make use of you, you see. I'm going to show you all the inner workings of an estate like ours. Then you'll see what it's all about.'

'Oh, Roc dear, I'll love that.'

'I thought you would. But first I've got to make up for my long absence from home. Then I've got to prepare old Charlie. He's a bit old-fashioned. Keep the women out of business and all that. He doesn't realize the sort of woman I've found for myself. You see, Morwenna's never been the least bit interested in anything except the gardens.'

'Do persuade him soon.'

'Trust me.' He was serious suddenly. 'I want us to be ... together in everything. Understand?'

I nodded. 'No secrets,' I added.

He held me tightly for a moment. 'Quite close ... for ever and ever until death us do part.'

'Oh, Roc, don't talk of death.'

'Only as something in the dim and distant future, my love. But you're happy now.'

'Wonderfully happy.'

'That's how I want you to stay. So no worries about the house. Don't I have you to help me? Then there's Charles. He'd die rather than see the old place go. Not that it does completely if you hand over to the National Trust. But you can't tell me your home's the same if you're going to have people wandering round from two till six-thirty every afternoon except Wednesdays.'

I felt completely happy after that talk; never had the tragedy of my father's death seemed so far behind me. My life was here at Pendorric; it was true I was a newcomer, but everyone accepted me as a member of the family and Roc had given me the comfort that only he could give.

Soon afterwards I decided I would make a tour of all the rooms and see if I could detect anything that was in need of urgent repair. I was sure it was something which should be done, for Charles was interested in the farm, Morwenna in the garden, and Roc had the entire estate to manage.

I would begin with the east wing because that was the one which was unoccupied; and after luncheon one day I came down to the quadrangle, sat by the pond for a few minutes and then entered the house by way of the east door.

As soon as that door closed behind me I began to think of Barbarina, who had loved this part of the house, and I longed to see her music room again.

I went straight to that floor, and as I mounted the stairs a sudden impulse came to me to turn back, but I quickly thrust this aside, for I was not going to feel afraid every time I came to this part of the house simply because of an old legend.

When I reached the door of the music-room, I quickly turned the handle and went in.

Everything was as it had been when I had last seen it: the violin lying across the chair, the music on the stand.

I shut the door behind me, reminding myself that I had come here for a practical purpose. Where, I wondered, would wood-worm most likely be found? In the woodwork about the windows? In the oak beams across the ceiling? In the floor perhaps, or the doors? If it did exist, the sooner it was dealt with the better.

My eyes kept straying to the music stand, and I was picturing her there, her eyes bright with inspiration, faint colour in her cheeks. I knew exactly what she looked like, and I wondered what her thoughts had been the last time she had stood there, her violin in her slim hands with their tapering fingers.

'Barbarina!' The name was spoken in a whisper.

I felt a prickly sensation in my spine. I was not alone in this room.

'Barbarina! Are you there, Barbarina?'

A movement behind me made me spin round hastily. My eyes went to the door and I saw that the handle was slowly being turned.

My hands had involuntarily placed themselves across my heart, which was beating painfully as the door was slowly opened.

'Carrie!' I cried reproachfully. 'You startled me.'

The little eyes beneath those heavy brows glinted as she looked at me.

'So it's Mr. Roc's bride,' she said. 'I thought for the moment . . .'

'You thought I was someone else?'

She nodded slowly and looked about the room as though she were seeking something.

I went on because I wanted to know what was in her mind: 'You said: "Barbarina." '

Again she nodded without speaking.

'She's dead, Carrie.'

'She don't rest,' was the low reply.

'So you believe that she haunts the house . . . haunts these rooms?'

'I know when she's getting ready to walk. There's a kind of stirring.' She came close to me and looked in my face. 'I can feel it now.'

'Well, I can't.' Then I was afraid that I had spoken rather sharply, and I remembered that she had been nurse to Barbarina and Deborah and had loved them dearly. When loved ones died, often those who had lost them made themselves believe that they could come back. I could see the devotion shining in Carrie's eyes, and I knew that when she had heard me in the music room she had really hoped it was Barbarina.

'You will,' said Carrie.

I smiled disbelievingly. 'I must get on,' I said. 'I'm rather busy.'

I walked out of the music room, but I didn't want to stay any longer in the east wing. I went back to the quadrangle and sat there; and every now and then I would find myself looking up involuntarily at those windows.

When I next called on Lord Polhorgan, Dr. Clement was there. He had tea with us and I found his company pleasant, as I was sure our host did.

I was very pleased to see that Lord Polhorgan had recovered from his recent attack and I was surprised that he could appear as well as he did.

We talked about the village and I discovered that Dr. Clement, like the Reverend Peter Dark, was very interested in the customs of the place.

He lived on the outskirts of Pendorric village in a house which he had taken over from the doctor who had retired on his arrival.

'It's called Tremethick – which is apt, because in Cornish it means the doctor's house. You must come and meet my sister sometime.'

I said I should be delighted to; and he talked of his sister Mabell, who was interested in pottery and made quite a number of the little pots and ashtrays which were for sale in some of the shops in the towns along the coast. She was something of an artist, too, and not only supplied pottery but her pictures 'on sale or return' to the shops.

'It keeps her busy – that and the house.'

She had turned the old stables into a workshop and had her oven there.

'She'll never make a fortune out of her pottery,' our host commented. 'Too much mass-production against her.'

'Not a fortune, but a lot of pleasure,' retorted the doctor. 'And it pleases her that there's a small profit in it.'

There was no chess that day, and when I got up to go, the doctor said he had his car outside and would drive me home.

I told him that there was no need, but he insisted that he went past Pendorric, so I accepted.

As we drove along he asked if I always made the journey from Pendorric to Polhorgan by the top road, and I said that there were three ways of getting there: by that road, by Smugglers' Lane and the short cut, and by way of the beach and the gardens.

'If I'm in a hurry,' I told him, 'I take the short cut.'

'Oh yes,' he said, 'you can save quite five minutes that way. Once there was a road there with houses on either side. I found an old map the other day. It gives you some idea how the sea is gradually encroaching on the land. It couldn't have been more than a hundred and fifty years old. Why not come along now and meet Mabell? She'd be delighted to see you, and I'd run you back.'

I looked at my watch, and thinking that Roc might already be home, said that I didn't really think I had time.

He dropped me at Pendorric. I thanked him and he gave me a friendly wave as his car roared away.

I turned to the house. There was no one in sight, and I stood for a while under the arch and looked up at the inscription in Cornish.

It was a grey day; there had been no sun lately; nor would there be, Roc had told me, until the wind changed. It was now blowing straight in from the south-west – soft and balmy, the sort of wind that made one's skin glow.

The gulls seemed even more mournful than usual to-day, but that may have been because of the greyness of the sea and the leaden sky.

I walked round the house to the south side and stood for a moment looking down on the garden, but even the colours of the flowers seemed subdued.

I went into the house, and as soon as I entered the hall my eyes fixed themselves on the portrait of Barbarina. I was afraid they were making a habit of doing that. The eyes in the picture followed me as I passed the suits of armour and started to go up the stairs. I went up to the gallery and stood right beneath the portrait looking up at it, and as Barbarina's eyes looked straight into mine I could almost imagine the lips curved into a smile – a warm, inviting smile.

I was really being rather silly, I told myself.

The hall was gloomy to-day because it was so grey outside. If the sun were shining through those big mullioned windows it would seem quite different.

Was Roc home, I wondered. There was a great deal to be done on the farm and about the estate, and that work was still very much in arrears, because he had been abroad so long.

I walked along the gallery to the corridor. Several of the windows were open and I could never seem to resist looking down at the quadrangle. And as I stood there I could distinctly hear the music of a violin.

I threw up the window and leaned out. Yes, there was no doubt about it; and one of the windows on the east side was opened. Was the sound coming from the east wing?

It might well be. I was sure it was. My eyes went to the second floor. If someone were playing in the music room could I hear from across the corridor and the quadrangle?

I was ashamed of feeling so frightened. I was not going to be taken in by my foolish imagination. I reminded myself of the day Carrie had come into the music room while I was there, and how scared I had been because she went creeping around calling Barbarina; as soon as I had seen that it was Carrie I had ceased to be scared; I was not the least bit taken in by her talk of 'stirring.'

I began to walk resolutely round the corridor to the east wing. As I went in I heard the violin again. I hurried up the stairs to the music room.

There was no sound of the violin now. I threw open the door. The violin lay on the chair; the music was on the stand.

There was no one in the room and I felt the stillness of the house close about me.

Then suddenly I heard the shriek of a gull outside the window.

It seemed to be laughing at me.

Because I was not anxious to stay in the house, I decided to go for a walk in the direction of the home farm, hoping to meet Roc.

As I walked I reasoned with myself: Someone in the house plays the violin, and you presumed it came from the east wing because you had seen the violin there. If you really are disturbed about it, the simplest thing is to find out who in the house plays the violin and casually mention that you heard it being played.

Out of doors everything seemed so much more rational than it did in the house. As I climbed on to the road and walked across the fields in a northerly direction I was quickly recovering my good spirits. I had not walked this way before and I was delighted to explore fresh ground. The countryside seemed restful after the rugged coast views, and I was charmed by the greenish-gold of the freshly mown fields and the scarlet of the poppies growing here and there. I particularly noticed the occasional tree, slightly bent by the south-west gales, but taller than those stunted and distorted ones which survived along the coast. I could smell the fragrance of meadow-sweet growing on the banks mingling with the harebells and scabious.

And while I was contemplating all this I heard the sound of a car, and to my delight saw it was Roc's.

He pulled up and put his head out of the window.

'This is a pleasant surprise.'

'I've never walked this way. I thought I'd come and meet you.'

'Get in,' he commanded.

When he hugged me I felt secure again and very glad I had come.

'I got back from Polhorgan to find no one around, so I decided I wouldn't stay in.'

Roc started the car. 'And how was the old man to-day?'

'He seemed to have quite recovered.'

'I believe that's how it is with his complaint. Poor old fellow, it must be a trial for him, yet he's cheerful enough . . . about his health.'

'I think he's very brave.'

Roc gave me a quick look. 'Relations still remain friendly?'

'Of course.'

'Not everyone gets along with him so well. I'm glad you do.'

'I'm still surprised that you should be when you so obviously don't like him.'

'The lady of the manor has always gone round visiting the sick. It's an old custom. You've started well.'

'Surely the custom was to visit the sickly poor and take them soup and blankets.'

Roc burst out laughing. 'Imagine your arriving at Polhorgan with a bowl of soup and a red flannel blanket, and handing them to Dawson for the deserving millionaire!'

'This is quite a different sort of visiting anyway.'

'Is it? He wants company; they wanted comforts. Same thing, but in a different form. No, really, darling, I'm delighted that you're able to bring sunshine into the old man's life. You've brought such lots into mine, I can spare him a little. What do you talk about all the time? Does he tell you about his wicked family who deserted him?'

'He hasn't mentioned his family.'

'He will. He's waiting for the opportunity.'

'By the way,' I said, 'I heard someone playing the violin this afternoon. Who would it have been?'

'The violin?' Roc screwed up his eyes as though puzzled. 'Where?'

'I wasn't sure where. I thought it was in the east wing.'

'Hardly anyone goes there except old Carrie. Can't believe she's turned virtuoso. In our youth, Morwenna and I had a few lessons. They soon discovered, in my case at least, that it was no use trying to cultivate stony ground. Morwenna wasn't bad. But she dropped all that when she married Charles. Charles is tone-deaf – wouldn't know a Beethoven concerto from "God Save the Queen"; and Morwenna is the devoted wife. Everything that Charles thinks, she thinks; you could take her as a model, darling.'

'So you're the only two who could play the violin?'

'Wait a minute. Rachel gave the twins lessons at one time, I believe. Lowella takes after me and is about as talented in that direction as a bull calf. Hyson, now . . . she's different. I think Hyson was quite good at it.'

'It could have been Hyson or Rachel I heard playing.'

'You seem very interested. Not thinking of taking it up yourself? Or are you a secret genius? There's a lot I don't know about you, Favel, even though you are my wife.'

'And there's a lot I don't know about you.'

'What a good thing we have the rest of our lives in which to discover one another.'

As we came on to the coast road we met Rachel, and Roc slowed down the car for her to get in.

'I've been looking for the twins,' she told us. 'They went shrimping this afternoon, down at Tregallic Cove.'

'I hope you took advantage of your respite,' Roc said.

'I did. I went for a long walk as far as Gorman's Bay. I had tea there and planned to pick them up on the way back. I expect they've already gone home.'

'Favel thought she heard you playing the violin this afternoon.'

I turned and looked at Rachel. Her expression seemed faintly scornful, her sandy eyes more sly than usual.

'You'd hardly have heard me on the road from Gorman's Bay.'

'It must have been Hyson, then.'

Rachel shrugged her shoulders. 'I don't think Hyson will qualify for the concert platform, and I'd be surprised if she deserted shrimps for music.'

As we were going to the house the twins arrived, with their shrimping nets and a pail in which Lowella carried their catch.

Rachel said: 'By the way, Hyson, you didn't come back and play your violin this afternoon?'

Hyson looked bewildered. 'Whatever for?' she said.

'Your Aunt Favel thought she heard you.'

'Oh,' said Hyson thoughtfully. 'She didn't hear *me* playing it.'

She turned away abruptly, and I was sure it was because she didn't want me to see that Rachel's remark had excited her.

The next day it rained without stopping and continued through the night.

'There's nothing unusual about that,' Roc told me. 'It's another old Cornish custom. You'll begin to understand why ours is the greenest grass in this green and pleasant land.'

The soft south-west wind was blowing, and everything one touched seemed damp.

The following day the rain was less constant, though the louring sky promised more to come. The sea was muddy brown about the shore, and farther out it was a dull greyish-green.

Roc was going off to the farm, and as I had decided that I would go along to Polhorgan to complete that unfinished game of chess, he drove me there on his way.

Lord Polhorgan was delighted to see me; we had tea as usual and played our game of chess, which he won.

He liked to have an inquest after it was over, and point out where I had given him the game. It put him in a good humour and I enjoyed it, because, after all, the purpose of my visits was to give him pleasure.

As I was leaving, Dr. Clement called. He was getting out of his car as I came out by the unicorns, and looked disappointed.

'Just leaving?' he said.

'Yes, I've stayed rather longer than I meant to.'

'Mabell is very much looking forward to meeting you.'

'Tell her I'm also looking forward to it.'

'I'll get her to telephone you.'

'Please do. How ill is Lord Polhorgan?'

Dr. Clement looked serious. 'One can never be sure with a patient in his condition. He can become seriously ill very quickly.'

'I'm glad Nurse Grey is always at hand.'

'It's rather essential that he should have someone in attendance. Mind you . . .'

He did not continue, and I guessed he was about to offer a criticism of Althea Grey and changed his mind.

I smiled. 'Well, I'll have to hurry. Good-bye.'

'Good-bye.'

He went into the house and I made my way towards the coast road. Then I changed my mind and decided to use the short cut.

I had not gone far when I realized I'd been rather foolish to come, for the path was a mass of reddish-brown mud and I guessed Smugglers' Lane would be even worse. I stood still wondering whether to turn back, but as I should have to plough through mud to do so I decided it couldn't be much worse if I went on. My shoes were filthy by now in any case.

I had not quite reached the narrow ledge when I heard Roc's voice.

'Favel! Stop where you are. Don't move till I get to you.'

I turned sharply and saw him coming towards me.

'What's wrong?'

He didn't answer, but coming close he put out an arm and held me tightly against him for some seconds. Then he said: 'This path is dangerous after a heavy rain. Look! Can you see the cracks in the ground? Part of the cliff has collapsed. It's unsafe even here.'

He took my arm and drew me back the way I had come, carefully picking his steps.

When we reached the beginning of the cliff path he stopped and sighed deeply. 'I was thoroughly scared,' he said. 'It suddenly occurred to me. I came hurrying over to Polhorgan and they told me you'd just left. Look back. Can you see where the cliff-side has crumbled? Look at that heap of shale and uprooted bracken half-way down the slope.'

I saw it and shuddered.

'The narrow part is absolutely unsafe,' went on Roc. 'I'm surprised you didn't see the notice. Come to think of it I didn't see it myself.'

'It always says "This path used at own risk." But I thought that was for visitors who aren't used to the cliffs.'

'After heavy rain they take that away and put up another notice: "Path unsafe." Can't understand why it wasn't done.' He was frowning, and then he gave a sudden cry. 'Good lord,' he said, 'I wonder who did this?' He stooped and picked up a board which was lying face down. There were two muddy prongs attached to it which clearly had recently been embedded in the ground. 'I don't see how it could have fallen. Thank heaven I came.'

'I was going very carefully.'

'You might have managed, but . . . oh, my God . . . the risk.'

He held me close to him and I was deeply touched because I knew he was anxious that I should not see how frightened he was. He stuck the notice-board into the ground and said gruffly:

'The car's not far off. Come on! Let's get home.'

When we drove up to the portico Morwenna was busy forking plantains from the stretch of lawn.

Roc slammed the door and shouted: 'Someone must have uprooted the danger board on the cliff path. I just stopped Favel going along it in time.'

Morwenna stood up looking startled. 'Who on earth . . .?' she began.

'Some kids, I expect. It ought to be reported. It suddenly occurred to me that she might go that way – and she did.'

'I've often been over it when the danger board's been up.'

'There was a bad landslide,' Roc said shortly. He turned to me. 'The path shouldn't be used until they've done something about it. I'm going to speak to Admiral Weston – the chairman of the local council.'

Charles had come round by the side of the house; I noticed that his boots were muddy.

'Anything wrong?'

Roc repeated the story of what he seemed to regard as my narrow escape.

'Visitors,' grumbled Charles. 'I bet it's visitors.'

'All's well that ends well,' said Morwenna, drawing off her gardening gloves. 'I've had enough for to-day. I could do with a drink. What about you, Favel? I expect Roc could do with one, and Charles never says no.'

We went into the house to a little parlour leading off the hall. Morwenna took drinks from a cabinet and while she was serving them Rachel Bective came in with Hyson. They were wearing slippers, and Morwenna's look of approval called my attention to them. I guessed they had changed at the side door where the gum-boots and house shoes were kept ready for occasions like this.

The subject of the notice-board was brought up again, and Rachel Bective did not look at me as she said: 'That could have been dangerous. It was a good thing you rememberd, Roc.' Hyson was staring at her slippers, and I fancied I saw a slight smile curve her lips.

'Where's Lowella?' asked Morwenna.

Neither Rachel nor Hyson had any idea.

It was five or ten minutes later when Lowella joined us, and she was immediately followed by Deborah. Lowella told us that she had been swimming; and Deborah had obviously just got up from her usual afternoon nap, she still looked sleepy; and no one mentioned the notice-board incident after that, but I could see that several of them hadn't forgotten it. Roc still looked worried; Rachel Bective almost rueful; and Hyson secretive, as though she knew something which she was determined not to tell.

I half wondered whether Hyson had removed the board. She knew where I had gone and that I'd probably come home by the short cut. She might even have watched me. But what reason could she possibly have for doing it? There might be more than a streak of mischief in her nature. But, I decided, Roc had made a great deal out of something not very important, simply because of his love for me.

I felt rather cosily content, until the following day, when the doubts began.

The weather had completely changed by next morning. The sky was a guileless blue, and the sea sparkled so brilliantly that it was almost too dazzling to contemplate. It was like a sheet of silk with scarcely a ripple in it. Roc took me with him to the forge, where one of his horses was being shod that morning. I was offered another glass of cider from the barrel in the corner; and while young Jim shod the horse, Dinah came into the forge to give me the benefit of her bold lustrous stare; I guessed that she was wondering about my relationship with Roc, and that made me suspect that he and she had been on intimate terms at some time and that she was trying to convey this to me.

'Maybe,' she said, 'I'll tell Mrs. Pendorric's fortune one day.'

Old Jim murmured that he doubted whether Mrs. Pendorric would be interested in such nonsense.

She ignored him. 'I'm good with the cards but it's your own hand and the crystal that's best. I could tell you a fine fortune, Mrs. Pendorric.'

She smiled, throwing back her dark head so that the gold-coloured rings in her ears danced.

'One day perhaps . . .' I murmured.

'Don't make it too long. Delay's dangerous.'

When we left the forge and passed the row of cottages I saw an old man sitting at the door of one of them.

'Morning, Jesse,' called Roc.

'Morning sir.'

'We must speak to Jesse Pleydell,' Roc whispered.

The gnarled hands were grasping the bony knees and they were trembling. I wondered why; then I saw how very old he was and thought this was the reason.

'Be that your lady as is with you, sir?' he asked gently.

'It is, Jesse; she's come to make your acquaintance.'

'How do you do,' I said. 'Your daughter was talking to me about you.'

'She be a good girl, my Bessie . . . and Maria, she be good too. Don't know what I'd do without 'em . . . now I be so old and infirm like. 'Tis a pleasure to think of her . . . up at the House.'

'We wish that you could be there too, Jesse,' said Roc, and the gentleness of his voice delighted me and made me feel as happy as I had before Dinah Bond had put misgivings into my mind.

'Ay, sir, that's where my place be. But since my eyes was took from me, it's little use I be to God or man.'

'Nonsense, we're all proud of you, Jesse. You've only got to live another twenty years and you'll make Pendorric famous.'

'Always one for a joke, Master Roc . . . like his father. Now he were one for a joke till . . .' His hands began to pluck at the cloth of his trousers nervously.

'Like father, like son,' said Roc. 'Well, we must be moving on.'

On impulse I stepped closer to the old man and laid a hand on his shoulder. He was very still, and a smile touched his lips.

'I'll come and see you again,' I said.

He nodded, and his hands began to tremble again as they sought his bony knee-caps and rested there.

''Tis like old times . . .' he murmured. ' Like old times, with a new bride up to Pendorric. I wish *you* all the best of luck, m'dear.'

When we were out of earshot I said: 'Mrs. Penhalligan told me he was in the hall at the time of your mother's accident.'

'She told you that, did she?' He was frowning. 'How they do go on about things that are past and over.' He glanced at me, and, perhaps because I looked surprised at his mild annoyance, he went on: 'I suppose so little happens in their lives that they remember every little thing that's out of the ordinary routine.'

'I should certainly hope someone's untimely death would be very much out of routine.'

He laughed and put his arm through mine. 'Remember that, when you feel tempted to go scrambling over dangerous paths,' he said.

Then we came to the Darks' house and the Reverend Peter invited us in; he was so eager to show us pictures he had taken of the Helston Furry Dancers the preceding May.

That afternoon I went to the quadrangle – not to sit, for, in spite of the warm sun of the morning, the seats had not yet dried out after the rain. Hyson followed me there and gravely walked round at my side. The hydrangeas looked fresher than ever and their colours more brilliant.

Hyson said suddenly: 'Did you feel frightened when Uncle Roc rescued you on the cliff path?'

'No. It didn't occur to me that there was any danger until he pointed it out.'

'You probably would have got through all right. It was just that there *might* have been an accident.'

'It was a good thing I was stopped from going on, then, wasn't it?'

Hyson nodded. 'It was meant,' she said, in a small hollow voice.

I looked at her sharply.

'Perhaps,' she went on, 'it was just a warning. Perhaps . . .'

She was staring at one of the windows on the east side as she had before. I looked up; there was no one there. She saw my glance and smiled faintly.

'Good-bye,' she said, and went into the house through the north door.

I felt irritated. What was the child trying to imply? I had an idea that she wanted to make an impression on me. What was she suggesting? That certain matters which were obscure to ordinary people were revealed to her? Really it was rather silly of her. But she was only a child. I must remember that; and it was rather sad if she were jealous of her sister.

Then quite suddenly I heard the voice, and for a moment I had no idea from where it was coming. It floated down to me, a strange voice singing slightly out of tune. I heard the words distinctly.

> *'He is dead and gone, lady,*
> *He is dead and gone;*
> *At his head a grass-green turf,*
> *At his feet a stone.'*

I looked up at the windows on the east side. Several of them were open.

Then I went resolutely through the east door and up the stairs to the gallery.

'Hyson,' I called. 'Are you there, Hyson?'

There was no answer; and I realized how very cool it seemed in the house after coming in from the sunshine. I was angry, telling myself that someone was trying to tease me. I was more angry than I should have been; and there, in that silent part of the house, I understood that I was so angry because I was beginning to be a little frightened.

Chapter Four

I had begun to think that someone was amusing himself – or herself – at my expense.

I had heard the playing of a violin; I had heard the singing. Why should I be the one singled out to hear these things? I was sure it was because of the legend and because I was the new Bride. Somebody in this house was trying to make me nervous.

I wondered why. Had my practical attitude, my determination not to be affected by stories of ghosts and hauntings, irritated someone? Was my scepticism a challenge? That seemed the most likely. Someone who believed in the ghost of Pendorric was determined to make me change my tune.

I wondered to whom I could talk about this subject which was beginning to take up too much of my thoughts.

If I mentioned it to Roc, he would laugh and tell me I was coming under the spell of Pendorric as all the Brides did. Morwenna was always friendly, but somehow remote; as for Charles, I saw less of him than of anyone in the household and I couldn't imagine myself chatting cosily with him. The twins? Impossible. Lowella was too much of a scatterbrain, and I could never be sure what Hyson was thinking. Indeed, if someone was trying to scare me I rather suspected it might be Hyson, for after all, there was an element of childishness in the method.

I had never liked Rachel Bective and it occurred to me that she might have sensed my dislike, returned it, and was trying to make me uncomfortable in my new home.

There seemed only one person in whom I could confide and that was Deborah. She was more affectionate than Morwenna, more inclined to share confidences; and I felt that, being a Devonshire woman, she was practical and looked on superstition much as I myself did.

There was an opportunity to talk to her when I went to her room to look at her albums, and we sat in the window-seat of her sitting-room with the books across our knees while she explained the pictures to me. They had been arranged with care, in chronological order, with a caption beneath each; and most of the early ones were of Barbarina and her husband. There were several of Barbarina and Deborah herself, and I couldn't distinguish which was which.

'That's because we're in repose,' explained Deborah. 'She was much more animated than I; she had all the charm. But you don't see that in a snapshot.'

There were many of Roc and Morwenna; and I found it absorbingly interesting to study his little face and discover there a hint of traits which were his to-day.

Then I turned a page and there were no more pictures.

'That last one was taken a week before Barbarina died,' Deborah told me. 'After that I didn't use this book. This was what I thought of as Barbarina's Book. It couldn't go on after she had gone.' She picked up another album and opened it. I looked at pictures of an older Roc and Morwenna. 'After a while,' went on Deborah, 'life started to go on in a new pattern, and I took my pictures again.'

I turned a page and stopped, for I was looking at what I thought was a group consisting of Roc, Morwenna and Barbarina.

'This one doesn't belong in this book.'

Deborah smiled. 'Oh yes it does. That isn't Barbarina. She died six months before that was taken.'

'So it's you. But you look so exactly like her.'

'Yes . . . when she was no longer there to be compared with me, people thought I was more like her than I had been before. But that was because she wasn't there, of course.' She turned the page as though she couldn't bear to look at it. 'Oh, and here's Morwenna and Charles. He's very young there.

He came to Pendorric when he was eighteen or so. Petroc's idea was to train him so that he could take over, and that was what he did. See how Morwenna gazes up at him. He was a god to her.' She laughed. 'It was rather amusing to see the effect he had on her. Every sentence she uttered began with "Charles says . . ." or "Charles does . . ." She adored him from the moment he came to Pendorric, and she's gone on doing so ever since.'

'They're very happy, aren't they?'

'Sometimes I used to think that there was too much devotion there. I remember one occasion when he went down to market and was involved in a smash-up. It was only a minor affair, and he was in hospital for less than a week, but Morwenna was . . . stricken. And I thought then: "You're not living a life of your own, my dear. You're living Charles's life. That's well enough if Charles goes on living and loving you. But what if he doesn't?" I think she'd die of a broken heart.'

'Charles seems quite devoted to her.'

'Charles would always be a faithful husband, but there are other things in his life than his marriage. He's devoted to the Church, you know. Peter Dark often says he doesn't know what he'd do without him. Charles's father was a parson, and he was very strictly brought up. He's deeply religious. In fact I wonder he didn't take holy orders. I think cultivating the land is a sort of religion with him. As a matter of fact he has moulded Morwenna to his ways. There was a time when she was as ready for mischief as her brother. I've never known her go against Charles in any way . . . except perhaps one thing.'

I waited expectantly and Deborah hesitated as though wondering whether to go on.

'I meant . . . her friendship with Rachel Bective.'

'Oh, doesn't Charles like Rachel?'

'I don't think he has any strong feelings of dislike, but at one time Morwenna used to bring her home from school for every holiday. I asked if she hadn't another friend who might come, or whether Rachel hadn't a home of her own to go to, and I remember how stubborn Morwenna was. "She *must* come here," she said. "She wants to come and she hates going to her own home." Charles didn't actually say he disapproved of her, but he never took the two of them riding or with him when he went round the farms, as he took Morwenna when she was alone. I thought that would be enough to make her stop inviting Rachel. But it wasn't.'

'And now she's living here!'

'Only until the children go away to school again. And then I expect she'll find some excuse to stay, although perhaps now you're mistress of the house . . .'

Deborah sighed, and I knew what she meant. Unprivileged Rachel had come from a poor home to Pendorric, had loved what she had seen and longed to make it her own. Had she believed that *she* might be the new Bride of Pendorric? Roc had evidently been friendly with her, and I could understand how easy it was to fall in love with him. Was Rachel in love with Roc? Or had she been at some time? Yes, I decided in that moment, Rachel Bective might have a very good reason for resenting me.

I said slowly: 'Do you remember telling me about Barbarina's playing Ophelia and singing a song from the play?'

Deborah was very still for a few seconds and I was aware that she did not look at me. She nodded.

'I thought I heard someone singing that song in the east wing. I wondered who it could be.'

The silence seemed to go on for a long time, but perhaps it was only for a few seconds. Then Deborah said: 'I suppose anyone might sing that song.'

'Yes, I suppose so.'

Deborah turned to get one of the albums which I had not yet seen; she sat beside me explaining the pictures. She evidently did not appear to think it strange that I should have heard someone singing the song.

A few days later, in response to an invitation, I called at the doctor's house. It was a charming place – early nineteenth-century – surrounded by a garden in which were beehives. Mabell Clement was a very busy person, tall and fair like her brother, and she wore her hair in a thick plait which hung half-way down her back – at least that was how it was when I first met her; on later occasions I saw it made into a knot in the nape of her neck that was always threatening to escape restriction; she wore smocks, sometimes caught in at the waist by girdles, with raffia sandals, amber beads and swinging earrings.

She was determined that everyone should recognize her as an artist, and this seemed to be her one foible, for she appeared to be good-natured, easy-going, and a good hostess. She was very proud of her brother; and he was affectionately tolerant towards her. I imagine that meals were served at odd times in that household, for Mabell admitted that when the urge to paint or pot or look after her garden came to her she simply had to obey it.

I was shown over Tremethick itself, the pottery shed, and what was called the studio, and I had an interesting afternoon.

Dr. Clement said that he would drive me back to Pendorric, but half an hour before I was due to leave, a call came through from one of his patients and he had to go off immediately.

Thus I walked back to Pendorric alone.

As I came to the village there was no sign of anyone. It was one of those still afternoons, very hot and sultry; I passed the row of cottages, and looked for Jesse Pleydell, but he was not at his door to-day. I wondered whether to call on him as I had promised to do, but decided against it. I wanted to find out from Mrs. Penhalligan or Maria what tobacco he smoked and take some along for him when I went.

The churchyard lay on my right. It looked cool and somehow inviting. I hesitated and then slipped through the lych gate. I have always been attracted by graveyards, particularly deserted ones. There seems to me to be a sense of utter peace within them, and I liked to think of all those people lying beneath the grey stones who had once lived and suffered and now were at peace.

I walked among the tombstones and read some of the inscriptions as Roc had, not very long ago; and eventually I saw ahead of me the Pendorric vault.

Irresistibly attracted I went to it. I wanted to see if the laurel wreath was still there.

It was gone, but in its place was a small wreath of roses, and as I went closer I recognized the Paul Scarlets which grew in the garden. There was no note on the flowers, but I was sure they were there in memory of Barbarina. It occurred to me then that Carrie was the one who put them there.

I heard a rustle in the grass behind me, and turning sharply saw Dinah Bond picking her way towards me. She looked even more vital here among the dead than she did in the old blacksmith's shop; she held herself erect and swung her hips as she walked, in a manner which was both graceful and provocative.

'Hallo there, Mrs. Pendorric,' she called jauntily.

'Hallo,' I answered.

'It be quiet in here . . . peaceful like.'

'I thought the village looked peaceful to-day.'

'But too hot to move about much. There's thunder in the air. Can't you feel it? All still and waiting like . . . for the storm to break.'

'I expect you're right.'

She smiled at me half insolently, and what was worse, with something which I felt might have been compassion.

'Having a look at the family vault? I often do. I bet 'ee haven't been inside, Mrs. Pendorric.'

'No.'

She laughed: 'Time enough for that, I reckon you think. It's cold as death inside . . . and all the coffins laid out on shelves. Sometimes I come and look at it . . . like this afternoon . . . just for the pleasure of knowing I'm outside and not locked in – like Morwenna once was.'

'Morwenna! Locked in! How did that happen?'

'It's years ago. I was only a kid then . . . about six, I think. When are you going to let me tell your fortune?'

'Sometime, I expect.'

'No time like the present.'

'Why are you so anxious?'

'I'm just taken that way.'

'I haven't any silver to cross your palm with.'

'That! It's just a way to get the money. I wouldn't do it for money – not for you, Mrs. Pendorric. Now I'm married to Jim Bond, I don't do it professional like. That went out when I gave up my gipsy ways.'

'Tell me about the time Morwenna was locked in the vault and who did it.'

She didn't answer, but sat down on the edge of a gravestone, and resting her chin in her hands stared broodingly at the vault.

'The key of the vault was always kept in a cupboard in Mr. Petroc's study. It was a big key. She'd come down for the holidays.'

'Who?'

'Rachel Bective.'

'How old was she then?'

'I'd say about as old as those twins are now ... perhaps a year or so younger. I was always trailing them. I think it was the colour of her hair. Mine was that black and hers was ginger colour. I wanted to keep looking at it. Not that I liked it, mind. I liked Morwenna, though. "Miss Morwenna" we were told to call her. I never did, though, and she didn't mind.

'She was like Roc – they never minded things like that. But *she* did, that ginger one. She'd say to me: "You'll call me Miss Rachel or I'll know the reason why." Miss Rachel! Who did she think she was?'

'Tell me how Morwenna came to be in the vault.'

'I was always in the churchyard. I used to come here to play among the tombstones; and one day I saw them together and I hid and listened to them talking. After that I just wanted to watch them and listen to them some more, so I was often where they were, when they didn't know it. I knew they'd be at the vault, because I'd heard about it the day before when they were in the graveyard reading the inscriptions. Morwenna told Rachel that's what she used to do with her brother, and that made Rachel want to do it, for she did always want to do everything they did. She wanted to be one of them and she couldn't ... she couldn't ever be ... no more than she can now. Oh, she be educated, I do know ... but I'd be as good as her if I'd had the schooling.'

'What has she done to you, that you hate her so much?'

''Tain't what she's done to me. Her wouldn't deign to give much thought to the likes of I, Mrs. Pendorric. It's what she'd do to others.'

'You were telling me.'

'So I were.' She held her hands in front of her, as though she were reading her own fortune. Then she went on: 'I heard 'em talking. She wanted Morwenna to get this key so that they could have a look at the vault, and Morwenna didn't want to. You see, it was in her father's study. He was away at the time – he were often away after the accident – and she said to Morwenna: "You'll be sorry if you don't." I was up in a tree and they couldn't see me, but I knew that Morwenna would get the key because she knew she would really be sorry if she didn't. Then I heard they were coming there next afternoon, so I were there too.'

'So Morwenna did get the key.'

Dinah nodded. 'I was here in the graveyard next day when they came, and they had the key. Rachel Bective opened the door of the vault and they went in, though Morwenna didn't want to much, but Rachel was saying: "You've got to. You'll be sorry if you don't," and Morwenna was saying: "I can't. Not again." Then all of a sudden Rachel laughed and ran out of the vault, slamming the door after her. Then she locked it and Morwenna was shut in.'

'It must have been a horrible experience. I hope she didn't stay there long.'

Dinah shook her head. 'No. There's a little grating in the vault and Rachel was soon at that. She kept calling out: "I won't let you out till you say you'll ask me for Christmas. I'll go back and I'll tell them I don't know where you are. Nobody'll think you're in here because I'll take the key back and put it where it belongs ... and it'll be weeks before they find you, then you'll be a skeleton like the bride in 'The Mistletoe Bough'." So Morwenna said she would do what she wanted and Rachel opened the door. I never forgot that, and I don't never pass this spot without thinking on it and how poor Morwenna had to say she would do what it was Rachel wanted, and how pleased Rachel looked in her sly way.'

'She was only a child, I suppose, and she must have longed to come to Pendorric for holidays.'

'And you reckon that excuses her ... doing a thing like that!'

'It was a childish trick ...'

'Oh, no 'tweren't. She'd have left her there if Morwenna hadn't given way.'

'I'm sure she wouldn't.'

Dinah looked at me scornfully. 'I'm beginning to read your fortune, Mrs. Pendorric, without so much as a look at your hand. You're one of them that says: "Oh no, it bain't that way" ... just when you don't want it to be. Your sort has to beware.'

'You're quite wrong. I assure you I face facts when I know they're there to be faced.'

'Ay, but it's knowing they're there that's important, don't 'ee think, Mrs. Pendorric? I'll tell 'ee this: There's people that don't change much all through their lives. You can't tell 'tis so till you've proved like ... but it don't do no harm to be on your guard. Oh, I do know a lot about Pendorrics ... living close you might say, all of me born natural life.'

'I expect there's always been a great deal of gossip about the family.'

'There was at the time, and though I was yet to be born, they were still talking of it when I were a little 'un. My mother was a sharp one. Nothing much she missed. I remember hearing her talk of Louisa Sellick, the one he were sweet on before he married Miss Barbarina.'

'Louisa Sellick?' I repeated, for I had never heard that name mentioned before.

'Oh, 'tis an old story and all happened long ago. Ain't no sense in reviving it like ... 'cept of course, you be the next Bride.'

I went over to Dinah, and looking down at her said earnestly: 'I sometimes get the impression that you're trying to warn me about something.'

She threw back her hair and laughed up at me. 'That's because I want to tell your fortune. They say "The gipsy warned me," don't 'em? 'Tis a kind of joke.'

'What do you know of Louisa Sellick?'

'Only what my mother told me. Sometimes I've been out that way ... where she do live now, and I've seen her. But that was after he were dead like ... so it weren't the same. They say he used to go out to visit her and that Barbarina Pendorric killed herself because she couldn't endure it no more ... him liking Louisa better than her. She'd thought when she first married that it was all over; that were when Louisa went out to live on the moor.'

'And is Louisa still living there?'

Dinah nodded. 'Well, least she were when I were last that way. 'Tis Bedivere House – a sizeable place. He bought it for her. 'Twas their love nest, you might say. And when he rode out on his business he'd land up at Bedivere. Perhaps there'd be mist on the moors or he was too busy to get back to Pendorric . . . see what I mean? But it was found out that she were there . . . and then things happened.'

'Do you often go out that way?'

'Not now. I got a home of me own now, remember. I married Jim Bond, didn't I? I sleep on a goose-feather bed and there's four walls all round me. But when I go out that way . . . Dozmary Pool and Jamaica Inn way . . . I see the house and I look for Louisa. She ain't so young and pretty now . . . but we none of us stay that way for ever, do us?'

I remembered suddenly that listening to Dinah's conversation I had stayed out longer than I had intended to. I looked at my watch.

'I'd no idea it was so late,' I said.

She smiled lazily. 'You'd better get back, Mrs. Pendorric. Time don't matter to me, but I know it does to the likes of you. Some folks rush about like they thought they hadn't got much time left. Perhaps they're right. Who's to say?'

She was smiling her mocking enigmatic smile.

'Good-bye,' I said, and started to pick my way through the gravestones to the lych gate.

My interest in Barbarina grew as each day passed. I went often to that room of hers and thought about her. I wondered if she had been of a passionate and jealous nature. She must have been terribly unhappy if, as Dinah had suggested, her husband had paid periodic visits to that woman on the moor.

I had heard no more violin-playing, nor singing in that strange off-key voice. Whoever had been responsible for that had evidently decided to give it a rest, and I was only faintly disconcerted because I had failed to discover who was playing the part of the ghostly musician. But I did want to know more of Barbarina.

Deborah was always willing to talk about her, and in fact obviously delighted in doing so. She was gradually building up the picture of her sister in my mind; sometimes she would even describe the dresses they had worn for certain parties, and so vividly did she talk that it was as though Barbarina materialized before my eyes.

Since my talk with Dinah the picture had become even clearer, and I knew that one day soon my curiosity would be too much for me and I should have to go out on the moor to see if I could catch a glimpse of Louisa Sellick for myself.

I had not made any excursions alone by car so far, and I couldn't very well ask Roc to take me there, nor Morwenna. I had an uneasy feeling that I'd do better to leave the past alone, and yet, because I could not suppress a feeling that I ought to know, I seemed unable to stop. Dinah's veiled warnings didn't help me to leave the subject alone, either.

There were three small cars in the garage besides Roc's Daimler and

Charles's Land-Rover; Morwenna used one of them and I had been told that the others were for general use.

I had often said that I wanted to go into Plymouth to do some shopping, and although I didn't exactly say I was going there on this occasion, I let Morwenna think so.

Roc had gone off on estate business that morning and I hadn't even told him I was going out, which, after all, did occur to me on the spur of the moment.

I had paused by the picture of Barbarina in the gallery and looked up into those sadly brooding eyes, wondering whether when she had discovered that her husband was visiting that house on the moor she had confronted him with her discovery. 'I should if I ever found that Roc was involved in such an affair,' I said to myself; and I remembered the sly looks of Rachel, the bold ones of Dinah Bond, and the beauty of Nurse Grey.

I did seem to be growing very jealous since I had arrived at Pendorric. Was I changing my nature or discovering characteristics which I had not known before that I possessed?

In any case, I assured myself, I was not the sort to suffer in silence. If I had a shred of evidence that Roc was being unfaithful to *me*, I should confront him with it and insist on the truth.

What had Barbarina done?

Was I identifying myself with Barbarina and reading things from her life into mine so that our stories were beginning to seem similar?

In any case my interest in her was becoming a little morbid.

Although this thought occurred to me it did not prevent my wanting to see the house where my father-in-law had installed her rival, but I did try to tell myself that it was really the moor that fascinated me, and it was the ideal morning for a drive.

I set out about half past ten, and branching off the road to Plymouth I was on the moor in a very short time.

It was a glorious morning. A fresh breeze ruffled the rough grass and I felt a sense of adventure as I looked ahead at the folds of moor and drove for miles without seeing any person or building.

Eventually I slowed down before a signpost, and saw that I was only a few miles from Dozmary Pool.

I drove on. I could see the hills with Brown Willy towering above them and Rough Tor in the distance. This was a very lonely spot, and looking about me I saw several mounds which earlier Roc had pointed out to me as the burial grounds of ancient Britons.

It was here that King Arthur was reputed to have fought his last battle. If it were really so, I thought, it would have looked exactly as it looked to-day.

And suddenly I saw the Pool; it was not large and I guessed that at its widest part it could not have been more than a quarter of a mile across. I stopped the car, and getting out walked to the water's edge. There was no sound but the murmur of the wind in the rough grass.

I thought of the legend as I remembered it and as I supposed thousands of visitors to this place must have done: of Bedivere standing at the edge of the water with the dying Arthur's sword in his hand, debating whether or not to throw it, as commanded, into the middle of the mere.

Finally he had done so and an arm had appeared from the centre of the Pool and grasped the sword Excalibur.

I smiled and turned away.

Bedivere, I murmured. Bedivere House. It must be fairly near; Dinah had said so.

I got back into the car and drove slowly for half a mile, and then found a narrow road which I decided to explore.

I had not gone very far when a boy came out of a narrow lane and started to walk in the direction I was going. Drawing up beside him I saw that he was about fourteen; he smiled, and right from the first moment I knew there was something familiar in that smile.

'Are you lost?' he asked.

'Not exactly. I'm just wandering round. I've come from Dozmary Pool.'

He grinned. 'Well, this is a second-class road. It doesn't lead anywhere much except to Bedivere House . . . and then back on to the main road. Only it gets a bit rougher. Your best plan, if you want to get on to the main road, is to turn back.'

'Thank you,' I said. 'But I'll go on for a bit and look at Bedivere House. What's it like?'

'Oh, you can't miss it. It's the grey house with the green shutters.'

'Sounds interesting – especially with a name like that.'

'Oh, I don't know,' he said with a grin. 'I live there, you see.'

He had his back to the light, and then I noticed that the tips of his rather prominent ears were faintly pink and pointed.

He had stepped back. 'Good-bye,' he said.

'Good-bye.'

As I started off a woman came into sight. She was tall and slim and she had a mass of white curly hair.

'Ennis,' she called. 'Oh, there you are.'

She glanced at me as I passed, and as I rounded the bend I saw the house at once. The boy had been right; there was no mistaking it. There were the green shutters. It was more than a cottage – a house of some seven or eight rooms, I imagined. There was a green gate opening on to a lawn with a flower border. Inside it were plants which looked like tomatoes; and both the doors of the glass porch and the house itself were open.

I drove a little way past, then got out of the car and, shading my eyes, looked round me at the view.

I was aware of the woman and the boy coming back; they were arm in arm; and together they went into Bevidere House.

I was certain then that I had seen Louisa Sellick; but I did wonder who the boy could be. Ennis. I believed there was a Cornish saint of that name; there was no doubt of whom he reminded me. Of some of the portraits I had seen at Pendorric – and, of course, of Roc.

I was changing for dinner when I next saw Roc, and still thinking of the boy to whom I had spoken near Dozmary. By now my imagination had made the resemblance between him and Roc more startling.

Roc must have looked exactly like that at thirteen or fourteen, I told myself. I could picture him playing in the graveyard with Rachel and Morwenna; riding his horse out to Jim Bond's when it cast a shoe; swimming, boating . . .

I was already dressed when he came into our room, and was sitting at the window watching the waves below us.

'Hallo,' he called. 'Had a good day?'

'Yes, Roc. And you?'

I stood up and found myself staring at the tips of his ears. Surely only Pendorrics had such ears.

'Very good.'

'I took the Morris on to the moors,' I told him.

'I wish I'd been with you.'

'So do I.'

He picked me up and swung me off my feet.

'It's good to have you to come home to,' he said. 'I've talked to Charlie about your looking into estate affairs with me. We'd be partners then. What do you say?'

'I'm so glad, Roc.'

'You were the brains behind that studio,' he said. 'We need brains in Pendorric.'

I had a sudden vision of my father at work in the studio, and, as whenever I thought of him I must think also of his death, I knew that a shadow passed across my face.

Roc went on quickly: 'We need brains, now that the days of the *grands seigneurs* are over. It's the farm workers who get the best end of the stick these days. They've got their unions to look after them. I've never heard of a union to protect the interest of the poor landowners. Rents must not be put up; repairs must be done. You see how we could use a business woman like you!'

'Oh Roc, I'm going to love it.'

He kissed me. 'Good. You're in business.'

'Roc, you're not worried, are you?'

'I'm not the worrying type . . . otherwise . . .'

'Otherwise you would be?'

'Oh, darling, what's the good of worrying? If we can't afford to go on in the old way, we've got to adjust ourselves to the new. Temper the wind to the shorn lamb, or is it the other way round? My God, we're shorn all right – fleeced in fact. Left, right, and centre.'

I had put my arms about his neck and my fingers almost involuntarily caught his ears – a habit they had. He was smiling and I was vividly reminded of the boy I had seen that afternoon.

'Roc,' I said, 'I saw a pair of ears exactly like yours to-day.'

He burst out laughing. Then he looked grave. 'I thought they were unique. You've always told me so.'

'They're Pendorric ears.' I touched them with my forefinger. 'And they match your eyes. They give you that satyr's look.'

'For which I have to be truly thankful, because it was that which made you fall in love with me.'

'He had the same sort of eyes . . . now I come to think of it.'

'Tell me where you found this paragon.'

'It was on the moor near Dozmary Pool. I asked him the way and he told me he lived at a place called Bedivere House and his name was Ennis.'

There was just a short pause, but during it I fancied – or did I think this afterwards? – that Roc's expression had become a little guarded.

'What a lot of information he gave! After all you only asked the way, didn't you?'

'It was all very naturally given. But the likeness was really astonishing. I wonder if he's related to you.'

'There's Pendorric blood all over the duchy,' said Roc. 'You see we were a roisterous riotous band. Not that we were the only ones. The old days were very different from these. In those days it was "God bless the Squire and his relations and make us mind our proper stations"; it was touching the forelock and thinking themselves lucky to have a place in the stables, the kitchens or the gardens. It was the *droit de seigneur*. Now of course it's "We're as good as you" and crippling taxation. Ah, the good old days have gone for ever. And talking of the rights of the squire . . . well, there's your answer. You walk round this countryside and you'll discover traces of Pendorric in half the natives. It was the order of things.'

'You sound regretful. I believe you're sighing for the old days.'

He put his hand on my shoulder and smiled at me. Did I fancy that there was a hint of relief in his face, as though he had come up to a dangerous corner and had rounded it satisfactorily?

'Since I met and married Favel Farrington,' he replied, 'I ask nothing more of life.'

And although he was smiling, I couldn't doubt that he meant what he said; and, as usual, he had the power to disperse all my doubts and fears with a look, a word and a smile.

Roc kept his promise and the next day took me with him to his study, and, as much as he could in a short time, explained certain matters about the estate. It did not take me very long to grasp the fact that although we were by no means verging on bankruptcy we were in a way fighting a losing battle against the times.

Roc smiled at me ruefully. 'It's like the tide slowly but surely creeping in. The end of the old way is not exactly imminent, but it's creeping towards us. Mind you, we've hung on longer than most. I'd be sorry if we fell to the National Trust in my time.'

'You think it's certain to happen, Roc?'

'Nothing in life is certain darling. Suppose I were to win a hundred thousand . . . I reckon that would put us on our feet for a few generations.'

'You're not thinking of gambling?' I asked in alarm.

He put his arm about me. 'Don't worry,' he said. 'I never risk what I can't afford to lose.'

'You told me that before.'

'It's only one of many things I've told you before. How much I love you, for one thing.'

'The conversation is wandering from the point,' I said with a laugh.

'That's right,' he retorted. 'I know you're going to be a good business woman. You'll keep me on the straight path, won't you? Things have been in a far worse state than they are now, I can assure you; and we've pulled through. Why, in my father's day . . .'

'What happened then?'

'We were in much greater difficulties. Fortunately my mother brought enough to put us on our feet again.'

I stared at the open book before me, and instead of the columns of figures saw that sad sweet face under the blue-banded hat. There seemed no escape from Barbarina.

Roc, who was standing behind my chair, stooped suddenly and kissed the top of my head. 'Don't let it worry you. Something will turn up, you'll see. It always does for me. Did I ever tell you I was born lucky?'

Strangely enough that was a very happy day for me, and the fact that the finances at Pendorric were not as sound as they should have been gave me a feeling of deep comfort.

I had begun to think that Roc was too much like his father and that my story was turning out to be too similar to that of Barbarina. But this was the difference: Barbarina had been married for her money when Roc's father was in love with Louisa Sellick. Roc, needing money for Pendorric, as his father had, had met me, a penniless girl, and had married her.

Oh no, my story was very different from that of Barbarina.

Mrs. Penhalligan was making Cornish pasties when I went down to the kitchen.

She looked up flushed and bright-eyed when I entered; her pink cotton sleeves were rolled up above the elbow, her short fat fingers busy.

One of the twins was sitting under the table eating a pasty.

'Good afternoon, Mrs. Pendorric,' said Mrs. Penhalligan.

'Good afternoon, Mrs. Penhalligan.'

Mrs. Penhalligan went on rolling her pastry. 'Don't do to let it hang about too long, ma'am,' she murmured apologetically. 'The secret be to make it and pop it into the oven as quick as you can. This be for Father. He's terrible particular about his pasty and he do want one regular each night. So when I bake I do four or five for him. I keep them in a tin . . . they be all nice and fresh that way, though the best is them as is eaten straight from the oven.'

'I've come to ask what tobacco your father smokes. I thought I'd go along to see him when I have the time and take him something to smoke.'

A head popped over the side of the table. 'Beware the Ides of March,' said a voice low with prophecy.

'Oh give over, Miss Lowella, do,' said Mrs. Penhalligan.

'She's been under my feet all day. Looking through the window, popping up here and there with her talk of Beware of this and that. Reckon she belongs to be in Bodmin Asylum.'

Lowella smiled and went into the bakehouse.

'I don't know,' grumbled Mrs. Penhalligan. 'That Miss Bective, she's supposed to be looking after they two. Well, where be she to, half the time, I'm wondering.'

'You were going to tell me what tobacco.'

'That I were, and right good it is of you, ma'am. 'Tis Three Nuns – the Empire, you do know. His one extravagance. But then it's only the two ounces a week he smokes and Maria and me like him to have his little treat.'

'I'll remember.'

Lowella had come back; she was holding a small pasty in her hand.

'Someone won't be wanting her supper like as not,' commented Mrs. Penhalligan.

Lowella regarded us both solemnly before crawling under the table.

'He'll be that pleased,' went on Mrs. Penhalligan. 'I reckon he'll be sitting out this afternoon. It'll make his day.'

'I'll be getting along,' I told her.

As I made for the door Lowella darted out from under the table and reached it before me.

'I say, Bride,' she said, 'I'll come with you if you like – to see old Jesse, I mean.'

'Don't bother,' I replied. 'I know the way.'

She shrugged her shoulders and went back into the kitchen, presumably to sit under the table and finish her pasty and now and then pop up to tell Mrs. Penhalligan or Maria or Hetty to beware the Ides of March.

Not far from the cottages was a house which had been turned into a general store. It was small, overcrowded, and run by a Mrs. Robinson who had come to Pendorric for a holiday twenty years before, realized that the nearest shop was two miles away, and had bought the house and made it into a shop. She sold among other things the brands of tobacco smoked by her neighbours, and kept stocks in readiness for them. So I had no difficulty in getting what I wanted.

As I came out of the shop I saw that the twins were waiting for me.

I was not pleased, for I had wanted to be alone with the old man, but there was nothing I could do but accept their company as graciously as possible.

They fell into step beside me without a word, as though we had arranged to meet.

'Where's Miss Bective?' I asked.

The twins exchanged glances as though each was waiting for the other to speak.

It was Lowella who answered. 'She's gone off in the little Morris. She said we were to pick her six different wild flowers. It's botany.'

'How many have you found so far?'

'We haven't looked yet. My dear Bride, how long do you think it's going to take *us* to find six different wild flowers? Becky won't say much if we don't find 'em anyway. She'd never say we were undisciplined, would she, because if she did they'd say we ought to go to school, and if we went to school there wouldn't be any excuse for Becky to be at Pendorric.'

'Don't you think you ought to obey her instructions? After all she is your governess.'

'You oughtn't to be worrying about *us*,' said Hyson.

Lowella leaped on ahead and ran up the bank to pick a wild rose. She stuck it in her hair and danced before us singing, 'Beware . . . beware . . . beware the Ides of March.'

Hyson said: 'Lowella is quite childish sometimes. She goes on repeating things.'

'She seems to like warning people,' I commented. 'I remember "Beware the awful avalanche!" '

'I like Ides better,' called Lowella. 'You can't have avalanches in Cornwall, but you can have Ides anywhere. Pity they're in March and this is July.'

'She doesn't *know* anything,' put in Hyson scornfully. She went on to quote:

> ' "March, July, October, May,
> The Ides fall on the fifteenth day." '

Lowella had paused. 'But what *are* Ides?'

'Just a date, stupid. Instead of saying the fifteenth, the Romans said the Ides.'

'Only a date,' wailed Lowella. 'It sounds marvellous. I thought it was something like witches . . . or ghosts. Fancy having to beware of a *date*.'

'If something was going to happen on a certain date, if it were prophesied to happen . . . that would be more frightening or as frightening as witches or ghosts.'

'Yes,' said Lowella slowly, 'I suppose it would.'

We had reached the row of cottages and old Jesse was seated at his door. I went over to him and said: 'Good afternoon. I'm Mrs. Pendorric.'

I noticed that his hands, resting on his knees, started to shake. ''Tis good of 'ee, ma'am,' he said.

'I've brought you some tobacco. I found out from Mrs. Penhalligan what brand you smoke.'

His trembling hands closed over the tin and he smiled. 'Why, 'twas thoughtful of 'ee, ma'am. I mind how kind *she* always were . . .'

Hyson had gone into the cottage and brought out a stool which she set beside the old man's chair. She nodded to me to sit down while she squatted on the other side of him. Lowella had disappeared.

'Your daughter has been baking pasties this morning,' I told him.

'A wonderful cook, my Bessie. Don't rightly know what I'd do without her. I've got a lot to be thankful for. Mr. Roc – he's been good to me. Is the little 'un here?'

'Yes, I'm here,' Hyson answered.

He nodded and turned to me. 'I hope you find this place to your liking, ma'am.'

'I'm delighted with it.'

''Tis a long time since we've had a new Bride at Pendorric.'

'There was my mother,' said Hyson, 'and before that my Granny Barbarina.'

'A sweet lady, she were. I remember the day she come.'

'Tell us, Jesse,' urged Hyson. 'The new Bride wants to hear about it.'

'Well, we'd seen her many a time. 'Twasn't like her coming from nowheres. I remember her as a little 'un, her and her sister. Used to visit us ... and master and mistress used to visit them. Hyson their name was. Such pretty names. Miss Barbarina and Miss Deborah.'

'I was named after them,' put in Hyson.

'So you were pleased when she became Mrs. Pendorric,' I said.

'I reckon I were, Mrs. Pendorric. We didn't rightly know what would happen. We knew something of how it were, and there was talk of giving up Pendorric. Pendorric as it were in the old days, that be. Us didn't know what would happen to we like. There was talk of Mr. Petroc marrying that Sellick girl and then ...'

'But he didn't,' Hyson said. 'He married my Granny Barbarina.'

'I remember the wedding. 'Twas a wonderful summer's day. It was there in the church. The Reverend Trewin were parson then. Oh, it were a grand wedding. And Miss Barbarina was a picture with Miss Deborah her maid of honour, and Mr. Petroc looking that handsome ... and it was so right and proper that it should be.'

'What about the other girl?' I asked.

'Oh, that were reckoned to be done with. She'd gone away ... and all was merry ...'

'Merry as a marriage bell,' murmured Hyson.

'A wonderful mistress she were. Kind and good ... and gentle like. She used to ride a lot and play the violin. Often I've been working on the quadrangle gardens and heard her.'

I was aware of Hyson, looking at me intently. Hyson, I thought, was it you who tried to scare me? And if so, why?

'Then she had a way of singing to herself. I remember once, coming home, I heard her singing in the graveyard. It sounded so queer and yet beautiful and like something not quite natural. I went in and saw her. She'd been putting flowers on the grave of little Ellen Pascoe from the cottages. Little Ellen had died of the meningitis, and it was her way of saying she was thinking of 'un. We thought a terrible lot of her here in the cottages.'

'You remember her very well,' I said softly.

'It seems only yesterday she were talking to me, as you be now. I was working then. Right up to the time she died I was working. But she knew I couldn't go on. I told her what was happening to me and she did comfort me. She said: "Never be feared, Jesse. I'll see that you be all right.' And every time she saw me she'd ask after me. And I was getting blind, Mrs. Pendorric. I can't even see you now. But you remind me of her in a way. You've got a kindness which was hers. Then you be happy. I can tell that.

So were she . . . at first. But it changed for her, poor gentle lady. Then she weren't happy no more. My tongue be running away with me, I fear. Bessie says I be alone so much that when people come to see me I've got so much to make up for.'

'I'm glad you want to talk,' I said. 'It's very interesting.'

'She's the new Bride, so she naturally wants to hear about the other one,' said Hyson.

'Ay,' went on the old man. 'You're happy . . . as she were when she first come. 'Twas only after, poor body . . . I wish you all happiness, Mrs. Pendorric. I wish for you to stay as you be now for evermore.'

I thanked him and asked him about his cottage; he told me that if I cared to look over it, he would be pleased. It was kept clean and tidy by his daughter and granddaughter. He rose, and taking a stick from the side of his chair led the way into the cottage. The door opened straight into the living-room; it was certainly clean and tidy. There was his armchair with his pipe-rack and ash-tray on a table beside it with a small transistor radio. There was a framed photograph on the wall, of Jesse standing, his hand resting on the shoulder of a woman sitting, whom I presumed to be his wife; they were both looking into the camera as though they were only engaged in the unpleasant duty for the sake of posterity. There were photographs of Mrs. Penhalligan at her wedding.

Leading from this sitting-room was a kitchen with a door which opened into a garden. This, like the cottage, was trim and well kept, with wallflowers and cabbage roses bordering a small lawn; a water barrel leaned against the wall to catch the rain.

There were two rooms upstairs, he told me; and he managed the stairs well enough. There was nothing wrong with him except his affliction and the fact that his memory was not what it had been.

He settled in his arm-chair and bade me be seated while he told me about his meeting and marriage to Lizzie, and how she had been under-housemaid up at Pendorric in the days when he had worked in the gardens there.

This went on for some time, and during it Hyson, presumably becoming bored, slipped away.

The old man said suddenly: 'The child has gone?'

'Yes,' I told him. 'I expect she's gone to find her sister. They're supposed to be collecting flowers for a botany lesson.'

'The little one . . . she questions and cross-questions . . .'

'She's a strange child.'

He nodded. 'She wants to know about it. It's on her mind. 'Tain't good, I reckon. Her's young. 'T'as nought to do with her.'

'I think the story has caught her imagination. It's because it's a ghost story.'

'Mrs. Pendorric.' He almost whispered my name, and I went closer to him.

'Yes, Jesse?'

'There's something I don't talk of no more. I told Mr. Petroc and he said, "Don't talk of it, Jesse. 'Tis better not." So I didn't talk. But I want to tell you, Mrs. Pendorric.'

'Why do you want to tell me, Jesse?'

'I don't know . . . but you be the next bride, see . . . and there's something tells me 'tis right and proper you should know.'

'Tell me, then.'

'My eyes was bad and getting worse. Days was when I couldn't make out shapes and such-like. I'd think I saw someone and when I come close I'd find it to be a piece of furniture. That bad they'd got to be. But the more bad they got the more I seemed to hear, and sometimes I knew summat without seeing or hearing. They say 'tis the compensation of the blind, Mrs. Pendorric.'

'Yes, Jesse, I am sure there are compensations.'

'That day I come into the hall, Mrs. Pendorric. And she were in the gallery. I knew who 'twas because I heard her speak. Low like she spoke . . . and then 'twas as though there were two shadows up there . . . I don't rightly know . . . and 'tis a long time to look back. But I believe, Mrs. Pendorric, that there were two on 'em up on that gallery a minute or two afore Mrs. Pendorric fell.'

'And you didn't make this known before?'

'Mr. Pendorric said for me not to. You see, the picture were there . . . the picture of the other bride, and they did say she'd haunted the place for more than a hundred years trying to lure a bride to take her place. There were two on 'em up there. I swear it, Mrs. Pendorric . . . but Mr. Petroc he didn't want it said. I'd always obeyed the master, as my father had and his father afore him, so I said nothing . . . but I tell *you* this, Mrs. Pendorric.'

'It's so long ago. It's best forgotten, Jesse.'

'So I thought, Mrs. Pendorric. And have thought these twenty-five years. But you being here . . . and reminding me of her . . . in a way . . . and you being so good and friendly to me like, well, I thought I should tell 'ee. 'Tis a warning like. And there's a feeling in here . . .' He tapped his chest. 'There's a feeling that I shouldn't keep 'ee in the dark.'

I couldn't see why he should feel this, but I thanked him for his concern.

I changed the subject, which wasn't difficult, for now that he had told me he seemed more relaxed as though he had done his duty. He talked of the cottage and the old days when his Lizzie had been alive; and after a time, I left.

I did not see the twins as I walked back to Pendorric.

The next day Nurse Grey telephoned me.

'Oh, Mrs. Pendorric,' she said, 'Lord Polhorgan has asked me to ring. He was wondering if you could come over this afternoon. He rather particularly wants to see you.'

I hesitated and said that I thought I could manage it, and asked how he was.

'Not quite so well. He had an attack during the night. He's resting to-day, but he says that he hoped you would be able to come, if not to-day, to-morrow.'

I set out that afternoon, wondering whether to pick some flowers from the garden to take to him; but as he had so many more than we had that seemed rather unnecessary.

When I arrived he was in his usual chair, not dressed, but wearing a Paisley silk dressing-gown and slippers. He seemed delighted to see me.

'Good of you to come so promptly,' he said. 'I was afraid you wouldn't be able to manage it.'

'I'm sorry you haven't been so well.'

'It's all ups and downs, my dear. I'll get over this little bout as I have others. They're bringing in the tea. Will you pour as usual?'

I did so and noticed that he ate very little and seemed rather more silent than usual, yet in a way expectant.

And as soon as the tea was cleared away he told me what, he said, he had been longing to ever since we had first met.

'Favel . . .' he began, and it was the first time he had used my Christian name, 'come and sit near me. I'm afraid what I have to say is going to be a great shock to you. I told you when we first met that I was an old curmudgeon, didn't I?'

I nodded.

'An impossible person. In my young days I thought of nothing but making money. It was the only thing of importance to me. Even when I married, my chief thought was to have sons . . . sons to whom I would leave my fortune . . . sons who would carry on my business and add new fortunes to the one I made. I had a successful business life, but I was not so successful in my domestic affairs. My wife left me for another man – one of my own employees. He wasn't a success. I couldn't understand why she could leave a luxurious home for him . . . but she did. I divorced her and I got the custody of our daughter, which was something she hadn't bargained for. The child was six years old at the time. Twelve years later *she* left me.'

'Doesn't it distress you to talk of the past?'

'It's a distressing subject but I want you to understand. My daughter left me because I was trying to arrange a marriage for her. I wanted her to marry Petroc Pendorric, who was then a widower. His wife had died accidentally and I thought there was a good opportunity of joining up the families. I was an outsider here, and I thought that if mine was linked with one of the oldest Cornish families I should be so no longer. Pendorric needed money. I had it. It seemed to me ideal, but *she* didn't agree.'

There was silence during which he looked at me helplessly, and for the first time since I had known him he seemed at a loss for words.

'There are often such disagreements in families,' I said.

'My wife went . . . my daughter went. You'd think I'd learned my lesson, wouldn't you? Flattered myself that in the world of commerce I'd learned all the lessons as they came along. So I had . . . But this was something I was pretty backward in. Favel, I don't know how to explain. Open that drawer. There's something in there that will tell you what I'm trying to.'

I went to the drawer, and opening it took out a photograph in a silver frame. As I stared at it I heard his voice, hoarse as I had never heard it before, with the depth of his emotion. 'Come here to me, my child.'

I came to him, and he no longer seemed the same man to me. Sitting there in that very luxurious room he had become more frail, more pitiable: and at the same time infinitely closer to me.

I acted on impulse, and going to him I took his frail body in my arms and held him against me as though he were a child and I was assuring him that he could rely on me to protect him.

'Favel . . .' he whispered.

I drew back and looked at him. His eyes were wet, so I took the silk handkerchief from the pocket of his dressing-gown and wiped them.

'Why didn't you tell me before . . . Grandfather?' I asked.

He laughed suddenly and his stern features were relaxed as I had never seen them before. 'Afraid to,' he said. 'Lost wife and daughter. Was making a bid for the granddaughter.'

It had been such a shock to me that I was still feeling all this was unreal. My thoughts were muddled. It did not occur to me in that moment to ask myself the explanation of that extraordinary coincidence which had allowed me to marry a man who came into my life by chance and turned out to be a neighbour of my grandfather. That was to come later.

'Well,' he asked, 'what do you think of your old grandfather?'

'I don't know yet what to think. I'm so bewildered.'

'I'll tell you what I think of my granddaughter, then. If I could have chosen just how I wanted her to be, she wouldn't have been different in one detail. Do you know, Favel, you're so like your mother that when you've been sitting there playing chess with me I've often found my mind slipping back . . . and I'd be thinking she'd never gone away. You've got the same fair hair, though she didn't have that white streak in it; and your eyes are the same colour . . . sometimes blue, sometimes green. And you're like her in your ways . . . the kindest heart and the impetuosity. Rushing in before you've had time to consider. I often wondered how that marriage of hers would work out. Used to tell myself it couldn't last, but it seems it did. And she chose a Cornish name for you. That shows, doesn't it, that she didn't think of the past always with regret.'

'But why was I never told? She never spoke of the past, and you . . .'

'She never told you? Nor did your father? You'd have thought they'd have mentioned it now and then. And you never asked, Favel. How was that?'

I looked back to those sunlit days of my childhood. 'I think that they felt all that had happened before their marriage was unimportant. That's how it strikes me now. Their lives were so . . . entwined. They lived for each other. Perhaps they knew she hadn't long to live. I suppose that sort of thing makes a difference. As for myself, I never thought of things being other than they were. That was why, when she died, everything changed so much for us.'

'And you were fond of your father too?' he said wistfully.

I nodded.

'He came down here to paint one summer. Rented a little place a mile or so away along the coast . . . little more than a shack. When she told me she was going to marry him I thought it was a joke at first. Soon learned it wasn't. She could be obstinate. . . . I told her she was a fool. Never stopped to think. Told her I wouldn't leave her a penny if she married this man. Told her he was after her money anyway. So they just went away one day and I never heard from her again.'

He was thinking of all the years that had been lost to him. Here he sat in the midst of his opulence – the loneliest old man I had ever met. And it need never have been.

Now he had learned that he was the one who had been foolish – not my mother and father. And pitiably he was reaching out to me to give him, for the short time left to him, the affection which more than twenty years ago he had rashly thrown away.

I turned to him impulsively and said: 'Grandfather, I'm glad I came home to you.'

'My dear child,' he murmured. 'My dearest child.' Then he went on: 'Tell me about her. Did she suffer much?'

I shook my head. 'There were several months when she knew and we knew. ... They were terrible months, particularly for my father, but it wasn't really long – though it seemed so.'

'I could have paid for the best attention for her,' he said angrily.

'Grandfather,' I replied, 'it's over. It doesn't do any good to reproach yourself – or them – or anyone. You've got to put that behind you. I'm here now. Your own granddaughter. I shall see you more often now. I shan't feel like waiting for a reasonable period before calling again. You're my very own grandfather and it's wonderful that my home is so close to yours. . . .' I stopped, picturing myself coming into the studio and seeing Roc there with my father. 'It seems so strange that Roc should have come to my father's studio . . . and that we should have married,' I said slowly. 'I mean, it seems too lucky to be true.'

My grandfather smiled. 'It wasn't just a matter of chance, my dear. Your mother never wrote to me. I had no idea where she was or what was happening to her. I had told her that if she married her artist I wanted nothing to do with her, and she took me at my word. But . . . your father wrote. It was a month or so before Roc went abroad. He told me that your mother was dead and that they had a daughter: Favel. He asked me if I would like to see you, and he gave me the address of that studio place of yours.'

'I see,' I said. 'I wonder why Father wrote.'

'I had my suspicions. I thought he was after something. People often say that men in my position are *comfortably* off. Having money isn't always comfortable, I can tell you. You're constantly watching in case you're going to lose something; you're for ever on the alert for ways of increasing what you have; and you're always suspecting that people are seeking your acquaintance because they want a little of what you've got. No. I'd say I'm *un*comfortably off. In any case I was wary of your father. I said: He wants to borrow something. Lilith wouldn't let him write when she was alive – too proud. But now she's dead he's after something. I put his letter on one side and didn't answer it. But the thought of my granddaughter kept bothering me. I wondered what she was like . . . how old she was. Your father hadn't said. And I wanted to know more about her.'

He paused and looked at me reflectively, and I said: 'So you asked Roc to . . . spy out the land?'

He nodded. 'I knew he was going to Italy, so I asked him to do me this favour. I couldn't go myself. I wanted him to find out what this studio place was like and what my granddaughter was like. My plan was that when he came back, providing I liked what he told me, I'd invite my granddaughter to Polhorgan . . . her father too, perhaps, if she wouldn't come without him.'

'So that was why Roc came to the studio.'

'That was it. But you're impetuous like your mother. You fell in love with him. So instead of his bringing back a report to me, he brought you back as his bride.'

'So Roc . . . knew . . . all the time?'

'He knew.'

'But he didn't give me a hint . . . in fact he never has.'

'Well, you see, I'd asked him not to. I didn't want you to come over to see your grandfather. I wanted us to meet as strangers. I wanted to know what you thought of me and I wanted to know what I thought of you. But the minute I saw you – you were so like your mother – I felt she'd come back to me. My dear child, I can't tell you what a difference this has made to me.'

I touched his hand, but I was thinking of Roc . . . Roc as he had come into the studio, Roc lying on the beach talking about Pendorric, about the Folly and the man who lived in it, who, he knew all the time, was my grandfather.

'So Roc was carrying out your wishes,' I said.

'He did even more than I asked. He brought you home.'

'I can understand his not telling me *that* in the beginning, but later . . .'

'I told him that I wanted to break the news to you yourself.'

I was silent. Then I said? 'You wanted my mother to marry Roc's father.'

'Ah, that was in the days when I thought I could manage people's lives better than they could themselves. I know different now.'

'So I've pleased you . . . by marrying a Pendorric.'

'Had you wanted to marry a fisherman, Granddaughter, I'd have made no objection. I learn my lessons . . . in time. All the lonely years need not have happened if I'd not tried to interfere. Fancy, if I'd raised no objections to their marrying, I'd have had them with me all those years. She might never have died. I shouldn't have had to wait till my granddaughter was a married woman before I knew her.'

'Grandfather,' I insisted, 'you wanted my mother to marry a Pendorric. Are you glad I've married Roc?'

He was silent for a few moments; then he said: 'Because you're in love with him . . . yes. I shouldn't have wanted it otherwise.'

'But you spoke of linking the families. My mother left home because you wanted her to marry Roc's father.'

'That was years ago. I suspect those Pendorrics wanted not so much my daughter as my money, and your father wanted her for herself . . . must have done, because she knew me well enough to understand that when I said there'd be nothing for her if she ran away, I meant it.'

I was silent and he lay back in his chair and closed his eyes though he had taken my hand and kept it in his. I could see how the veins stood out at his temples and that he was more flushed than usual. Such excitement was not good for him, I was sure.

My grandfather! I thought, watching him. So I had a relative after all. My eyes went round the room at the paintings on the wall. They were all of the old school. Grandfather would not buy modern paintings, which he loathed, but all the same he would have an eye for a bargain. I guessed that the pictures in this room alone were worth a fortune.

Then I thought of the studio, and my mother who had bargained so fiercely over my father's work; and it seemed to me that life was indeed ironical.

I was glad that I had a grandfather. I had liked him from the moment we met; but I wished – oh, how I wished that he were not such a rich man. I remembered what he had said about being *un*comfortably off.

Although it was less than an hour since I had discovered I was the granddaughter of a millionaire, I understood very well what he meant.

I sat with him for an hour after that; we talked of the past and the future. I told him incidents from those early days which I had not thought of telling before, because I now understood how vitally interested he was in every seemingly insignificant detail. And he told me that Polhorgan was now my home and that I must treat it thus.

I walked back to Pendorric in a state of bewilderment, and when I was midway between the two houses I looked from one to the other.

My homes, I murmured. And my pride in them was spoilt by an uneasy suspicion which was beginning to grow within me.

I was relieved, when I went up to our bedroom, to find that Roc had come in.

'Roc,' I called, and as he turned to look at me he said: 'So he's told you?'

'How did you guess?'

'My darling, you look just like a woman who has been told that she is the granddaughter of a millionaire.'

'And you knew all the time!'

He nodded, smiling.

'It seems extraordinary that you could keep such a secret.'

He was laughing as he took me by the shoulders. 'It's women who can't keep secrets, you know.'

He put his arm round me and held me against him; but I withdrew myself because I wanted to look into his face.

'I want to think about it all . . . as it happened,' I said. 'You came to the studio, looking for me. You were going to report on me to my grandfather.'

'Yes. I was going to take some pictures of you to show him. I was determined to do the job thoroughly.'

'You did it very thoroughly indeed.'

'I'm glad that you approve of my methods.'

'And my father . . .' I said. 'He knew too.'

'Of course he knew. He'd lived near Pendorric. That was how he first met your mother.'

'Father knew . . . and didn't tell me.'

'I'd explained to him my promise of secrecy.'

'I can't understand. It was so unlike him to have secrets from me.'

'This was a very important matter. I reckon he wanted you to please your grandfather. It's understandable.'

I looked at him sharply; he was smiling complacently.

'How I wish . . .' I began.

'What do you wish?'

'That you hadn't known.'

'Why? What difference does it make?'

I was silent. I felt I was going too far. I was almost on the point of asking Roc whether he had married me on account of my grandfather's money, when I didn't even know that I was his heiress. But everything was changed. When I had thought of Barbarina I had continually told myself that our positions were so different because she had been married for her money. The simple fact was that now I was beginning to wonder whether I too had been.

'What's on your mind?' persisted Roc.

'It's the shock,' I replied evasively. 'When you think you haven't any family and you suddenly find yourself confronted by a grandfather . . . it's a little bewildering. It takes time to adjust yourself.'

'You're a little aloof, you're weighing me up. I don't much like it.' He was looking at me intently, very seriously.

'Why?'

'I'm afraid of being weighed in the balance and found wanting.'

'Why should you be afraid?'

'Because you're hiding something from me – or trying to.'

'You are the one who hides things successfully.'

'Only one thing – and I had made a promise not to tell.' He laughed suddenly, and seizing me, lifted me and held me up so that I had to look down on him. 'Listen,' he said, 'and get this clear. I married you because I fell in love with you. It would have been the same if you were the granddaughter of old Bill the Beachcomber. Understand me?'

I put out my hands and touched his ears; he lowered me until my face was on a level with his. Then he kissed me; and as usual, while I was with him, I forgot my fears.

Now that the news was out, the whole of Pendorric village was agog with it. I knew that I had only to appear for the subject to be discussed. People looked at me as though they had discovered something different about me. I was the focus of attention in the neighbourhood. In the first place I had come out of the blue as the Bride of Pendorric; and now it turned out that I was the granddaughter of old Lord Polhorgan. Many of them could remember my mother's running away with the painter; and it seemed a fitting romantic sequel that I should return as a bride.

Mrs. Robinson at the general store whispered to me that my story was good enough for the television; Dinah Bond told me, when I met her one day in the village, that she knew there was something dramatic in my hand and she would have told me if only I'd let her; Morwenna and Charles appeared to be delighted; Lowella was vociferous, squealing her delight, and went about singing something about 'When Grandpappa asked Grandmamma for the second minuet,' which appeared to be quite irrelevant; Hyson regarded me with silent interest as though this new development was not entirely unexpected.

For several days everyone talked of it, but I guessed that it would turn out to be a nine days' wonder.

There were two conversations which stood out in my mind. One I had with Rachel Bective, the other I overheard.

I had gone down to Pendorric beach to swim one afternoon and as I came out of the water I saw Rachel emerge from the gardens and step on to the beach.

I looked about for the twins, but she was alone.

She came over and said: 'What's the sea like to-day?'

'Quite warm,' I answered, and lay down on the shingle.

She sat down beside me and started playing idly with the pebbles.

'What a surprise it must have been for you!' she said. 'Had you no idea?'

'None at all.'

'Well, it's not everyone who gets presented with a grandfather at your time of life. And a millionaire peer at that!'

I thought her expression a trifle unpleasant and I half rose, preparing to go up through the gardens.

'Roc knew of course,' she went on. Then she laughed. 'He must have been tickled to death.'

'You think it's an amusing situation when families are broken up?'

'I think it's amusing that Roc should go out to find you and bring you back – his bride. No wonder he has been looking so smug.'

'What do you mean?'

Her greenish eyes under the sandy brows glinted a little; her mouth was straight and grim. I thought: she is either very hurt or very angry. And suddenly I wasn't so annoyed with her as I had been a few minutes before.

She seemed to take a grip of herself. 'Roc always liked to know what other people didn't. He'd think it great fun having a secret like that, and the rest of us being in the dark. Besides . . .' I waited for her to go on, but she shrugged her shoulders. Then she gave a harsh laugh which seemed to hold a note of bitterness. 'Some people have all the luck,' she said. 'Mrs. Pendorric *and* granddaughter of Lord Polhorgan, who already dotes on her.'

'I think I'll be getting back,' I said. 'It's not so warm as I thought.'

She nodded, and as I crunched my way over the shingle she sat looking out at the sea; and I could imagine the expression on her face, for she had betrayed the fact that she was jealous of me. Jealous because I was the granddaughter of a rich man? Or jealous because I was Roc's wife?

I believed it might be for both these reasons.

The second conversation took place the following day and I heard the end of it unwittingly. I was in the quadrangle gardens and one of the windows on the ground floor of the north wing was wide open, so the voice came floating through to me and I had caught the gist of the conversation before I could get out of earshot.

It was Charles and Morwenna who were speaking, and at first I did not realize they were talking of me.

'I thought he was looking pleased with himself.' That was Charles.

'I've never known him so contented.'

'She's a pleasant creature.'

'She has everything.'

'Well, it won't be before it's needed, I can tell you. I've had some anxious moments wondering what the outcome could possibly be. Of course we're taking things rather for granted.'

'Not a bit of it. That type never leave much outside the family. After all, she's his granddaughter and he can't last much longer. . . .'

I got up and walked across to the south door, my cheeks flaming.

As I entered the house my eyes went at once to the picture of Barbarina. I stook looking up at it. I could almost fancy the expression had changed; that a pitying look was in those blue eyes, that she was saying to me: 'I understand. Who could understand better than one to whom it has all happened before?'

My grandfather wanted the whole neighbourhood to know how delighted he was to welcome his granddaughter home.

He told me that it was years since there had been any entertaining at Polhorgan and he proposed to give a ball to which he would invite all the local gentry.

'You are not nearly well enough,' I told him; but he assured me that he would come to no harm. He put his hand over mine. 'Don't try to dissuade me. It'll give me the greatest pleasure. The ball will be for you and your husband. I want you to arrange it all; I want it to be a setting for you, my dear. Please say you will.'

He looked so pleased at the prospect that I could only agree, and when I told Roc and Morwenna about it they were amused and, I could see, delighted. I had ceased to be angry with Morwenna and Charles, telling myself that loving this old house as they obviously did, it was only natural that they should be pleased because a member of the family might very possibly come into a great deal of money.

'Just fancy,' said Morwenna, 'Polhorgan is going to throw off its dust-sheets.'

The twins were delighted, and when Lowella was told that balls were not for twelve-year-olds, she boldly called on my grandfather and asked for an invitation for herself and her sister. Such conduct, which he called initiative, delighted him, and he immediately wrote to Morwenna asking her to allow the twins to attend.

Lowella was wild with excitement when she heard this; Hyson's eyes gleamed with secret pleasure. Lowella went about the house quoting in an ominous voice:

' "There was a sound of revelry by night. . . ." '

Morwenna helped arrange the list of invitations, for, as a Pendorric, she knew everyone in the neighbourhood.

'They will all want to come and see Lord Polhorgan's granddaughter,' she told me. Roc, who was present, put in: 'Nonsense. It's Mrs. Pendorric they want to see, for she's a far more important person than his lordship's granddaughter.'

'They must think it all very extraordinary,' I suggested.

'Nine days' wonder, darling,' Roc assured me. 'You know there are a lot of skeletons locked away in cupboards in these parts.'

'It's true enough,' Morwenna assured me.

Deborah was as excited as the twins at the prospect of the ball, and invited me to her room to see some material which Carrie was going to make up for her. There was a choice of two colours and she wanted me to help her decide.

Laid out on a table were two rolls of *crêpe de Chine* – one delicate mauve, the other pale pink.

I was fingering the stuff. 'One hardly ever sees it now,' I commented.

'We've had it a few years, haven't we, Carrie,' said Deborah.

I had not noticed Carrie come silently into the room; she carried a tape-measure about her neck, and a pair of scissors and a pin-cushion were attached to her belt.

'I found it in Plymouth,' she said. 'I was afraid there wouldn't be enough for the two of you.'

Deborah looked at me, smiling gently; then she laid her hand on Carrie's shoulder. 'Carrie's a wonder with her needle. I'm sure she'll make me something worthy of the ball.'

'You remember the dresses I made for the engagement party?' whispered Carrie, her eyes ecstatic. 'Empire style. You had the pink then; she had the mauve.'

'Yes, we decided we had to be different then.'

'Before that it was always the same. What one had the other had.'

'I've brought Mrs. Pendorric up to help me decide which colour,' said Deborah.

'Mauve was her colour. She wore it a lot . . . after . . .'

'Perhaps I'd better decide on the pink,' murmured Deborah.

She took me into her sitting-room, and as we sat together looking over the sea she said: 'I rather dread Carrie's making new things for me. It always brings it home to her. You see, in Devon she used to make everything in twos. She can't forget.'

When I left Deborah I ran into Rachel Bective. She gave me a grudging smile and looked almost wistful.

'Everyone's talking about the ball your grandfather's giving,' she said. 'I feel like Cinderella. Still, I suppose the governess can't expect to be invited.'

'What nonsense,' I retorted. 'Of course you're invited.'

The smile which lighted her face made her almost pretty.

'Oh,' she muttered in an embarrassed way, 'thank you I . . . I'm honoured.'

As she turned and left me I thought: Her trouble is this complex about being employed here. If only she could forget that, she'd be so much happier and I should like her so much better.

During the next few days I spent a great deal of time at Polhorgan. My grandfather was anxious that I should make a thorough tour of the house, and this I did in the company of Dawson and his wife, who were very respectful to me now that they knew I was their master's granddaughter.

Polhorgan was not built in the same mould as Pendorric. This was one large house whereas ours at Pendorric was like four smaller ones. At Polhorgan there was an immense hall which was to serve as the ballroom, and Dawson and his wife had uncovered the furniture so that I could see it in all its glory.

It was a magnificently-proportioned room, with its high vaulted ceiling and panelled walls; and there was a dais at one end which would be ideal for our orchestra. Dawson suggested that some of the exotic plants should be brought in from the greenhouses and that I might like to talk to Trehay, the head gardener, about what I should like.

Leading from this hall were several rooms which would serve as supper rooms. I could see that Mrs. Dawson was a most efficient woman and delighted at the prospect of being able to show what a skilful housekeeper she was.

She showed me the kitchens, which were models of modernity.

'All this, madam,' sighed Mrs. Dawson, 'and no one to use it for! I could have cooked for his lordship with one little stove, for all he eats. Although the nurse wants a bit of waiting on, I do assure you!'

Mrs. Dawson's lips tightened at the mention of Nurse Grey, and I began to wonder whether the nurse was generally unpopular in the household.

It was while she was showing me round that Althea Grey herself appeared. She was looking as attractive as ever in her uniform, and she gave me a pleasant smile. I was struck afresh by the perfection of her features, and I remembered uneasily the occasion when I had found her on the beach with Roc.

'So you're showing Mrs. Pendorric the house,' she said.

'Well, it looks like it, Nurse.' Mrs. Dawson's voice was tart.

'If you like I'll take over. I expect you have work to do.'

'As housekeeper I reckon it to be my duty to show Mrs. Pendorric the house, Nurse.'

Nurse Grey smiled at me and shrugged her shoulders; but as though defying Mrs. Dawson to challenge her right to be there, she remained with us.

Mrs. Dawson was put out, and behaved as though she were unaware of the nurse's presence. I wondered what Althea Grey had done to make herself so disliked.

We walked up a beautiful staircase and inspected the rooms on the first floor of the mansion with their enormous windows and those superb views to which I had become accustomed at Pendorric.

Mrs. Dawson uncovered some of the furniture and showed me beautiful pieces, mostly antique, which I guessed must be worth a great deal.

'Jewelled in every hole,' murmured Althea Grey, her lovely blue eyes mischievous.

The obvious hostility between them made me a little uncomfortable.

'I hear we're to have about sixty guests, Mrs. Pendorric,' said Althea Grey. 'It's a good thing we have a sizeable ballroom, otherwise we should be treading on each other's toes.'

'Well, Nurse,' put in Mrs. Dawson with a twitch of her nose, 'that shouldn't worry *you*, should it?'

'Oh but it will, I hate having my toes trodden on.' She laughed. 'Oh, you're thinking that as I'm merely Lord Polhorgan's nurse I shan't be there. But you're wrong, Mrs. Dawson. Of course I shall be there. I couldn't let him go without me in attendance, could I?'

She was smiling at me as though inviting me to join in her victory over Mrs. Dawson, who looked extremely put out; and I supposed this was the usual tug-of-war between two servants each of whom thought herself in a higher position than the other. That must be the reason for the animosity.

'Of course not,' I said hastily; and Mrs. Dawson's face was grim.

'I reckon, madam,' she said, 'that Nurse Grey could show you the upper rooms.'

I thanked her and assured her that I should be pleased if she stayed with us, but she muttered something about having things to see to, and left us.

Althea Grey grinned when we were alone. 'She'd make life a trial if I'd let her. Jealous old witch.'

'You think she's jealous of you?'

'They always are, you know. I've come up against this sort of thing before, nursing in private houses. They don't like it because they have to wait on us. They're anxious all the time to tell us that they're as good as we are.'

'It must be awkward for you.'

'I don't let it bother me. I can manage the Mrs. Dawson characters, I can tell you.'

In spite of her delicate beauty I was sure she could.

We had come to my grandfather's room, and when I went in with her he gave me his warm and welcoming smile, and I felt my spirits rising when I realized what a difference my coming had made to him.

Nurse Grey ordered tea and the three of us had it together. Conversation was all about the ball, and before she left us Nurse Grey warned my grandfather that he was becoming far too excited.

'You have your pills handy?' she said.

For answer he took the little silver box from his pocket and showed her. 'That's good.'

She smiled at me and left us together.

I had had a busy morning, and after lunch, because the sun was shining and it was a long time since I had been in the quadrangle, I went there and sat in my favourite spot under the palm tree.

I had not been there more than five minutes when the north door opened and a twin came out.

I was always a little ashamed of my inability to distinguish which was which when they were not together, and tried to discover without exposing my ignorance.

She came and stood before me. 'Hallo. How you like this place! But you haven't been here lately, have you?'

'I've been too busy.'

She regarded me solemnly. 'I know. It is a busy business, suddenly finding you're Lord Polhorgan's granddaughter.' She stood on one foot and hopped a few paces nearer. 'Just fancy! You might have been here always . . . if your mother and father hadn't gone away. Then we should always have known you.'

'That could easily have happened,' I admitted.

'But it was more exciting the other way. There wouldn't have been this ball perhaps . . . if you'd always been here. There wouldn't be any sense in giving a fatted-calf sort of ball if you'd never been away, would there?'

'Would you say this was like the prodigal's return?'

She nodded vigorously. 'You're rich now, aren't you; and you must have been poor, though perhaps you didn't eat the husks that the swine did eat.'

I was sure it was Lowella now. She had started to hop all round my seat, and when she was immediately behind me she stood close, breathing down my neck. 'Everybody wasn't pleased when *he* came home, were they? There was the brother who'd stayed at home. He didn't see why the fatted calf should be killed for the brother who'd run away when he wanted to.'

'Don't worry. I haven't got a brother who'll be jealous of my having a welcome.'

'There doesn't have to be a *brother*. A parable's different, isn't it? It doesn't always mean exactly what it says. You have to work it out – Becky says so. Carrie's waiting for me to try on my dress for the ball.'

'She's making it for you, is she?'

'Yes, it's gold colour. She's making two – exactly alike. It'll be fun. They won't know which is Hy and which is Lo.'

'You'd better go if Carrie wants to fit on your dress, hadn't you?'

'You come with me and see it. It's very pretty.'

She started to hop towards the west door and I rose and followed her into the house, unsure again whether I had been speaking to Hyson or Lowella.

She started to hum as we went up the stairs, and the song she hummed was the tune that I had heard in that strange, off-key voice which had startled me so. This humming was quite different, though, rather monotonous and tuneless.

'What's that you're singing?' I asked.

She stopped, turned slowly and looked down on me, for she was standing several stairs above me. I knew then that she was Hyson.

'It's Ophelia's song in *Hamlet*.'

'Did you learn it at school?'

She shook her head.

'Did Miss Bective teach it to you?' I was becoming too anxious, I realized; and she guessed it and found it amusing.

Again she shook her head. She was waiting mischievously for the next question.

I merely continued: 'It's a haunting tune,' and started up the stairs.

She ran on ahead of me until she came to the door of Carrie's sewing room.

Carrie was seated at an old-fashioned sewing machine and I saw that she was working on a gold-coloured dress.

There were two dressmaker's dummies in the room, one a child's and the other an adult's. On the smaller one was another gold-coloured dress, on the larger a mauve evening dress.

'Ah, there you are, Miss Hyson,' said Carrie. 'I've been waiting for you. Come here, do. That neck don't please me.'

'Here's Mrs. Pendorric, too' said Hyson. 'She wanted to see the dresses so I brought her up.'

I went over to the dummy on which the other gold-coloured dress had been arranged.

'It's lovely,' I said. 'This is Lowella's, of course.'

'I fitted it on Miss Hyson,' mumbled Carrie. 'Miss Lowella can't stand still for more than a second or two.'

'It's true,' said Hyson primly. 'Her mind flitters and flutters like a butterfly. She can't concentrate on anything for any length of time. Becky says it's deplorable.'

'Come here, then,' said Carrie, snipping a cotton and withdrawing the dress from the machine.

Hyson stood meekly while Carrie slipped off her dress and put on the gold-coloured silk.

'It's delightful,' I said.

'The neck's wrong.' Carrie was breathing heavily as she purred and clicked over the neck of the dress. I went over to the mauve dress and examined it. It was beautifully made, but like all Deborah's clothes it had that slightly old-world look. The rows of flounces in the long skirt would have been fashionable many years ago, so would the lace fichu at the neck. It was like a charming period piece.

'I thought you were going to make up the pink,' I said.

'Ur,' grunted Carrie, her mouth full of pins.

'I suppose Deborah changed her mind, but when I was here I thought she said she would have the pink.'

Hyson nodded at me vigorously and inclined her head towards a dress hanging behind the door. I looked and saw an exact replica of the dress, this time in pink.

I stared in astonishment.

'Carrie made two, didn't you, Carrie?' said Hyson. 'She made two gold dresses . . . one for me, one for Lowella, and she made two like that – one pink and one mauve – because ever since they left Devon they never had the same colour. It was different after they left Devon, wasn't it, Carrie?'

Hyson was regarding me almost triumphantly and I felt impatient with her.

'What on earth are you talking about?' I demanded.

Hyson became engrossed in the tips of her shoes and would not answer me.

'Carrie,' I insisted, 'I suppose Miss Deborah has had the two dresses made up. Perhaps it's as well if you've had the material for a long time – which I believe you said you had.'

'The pink's for Miss Deborah,' said Carrie. 'I like her in pink.'

'And the mauve . . .?'

Hyson darted away from Carrie and ran to me; she laid a hand on my arm and smiled up at me.

'The pink was made for Granny Deborah,' she whispered, 'and the mauve for Granny Barbarina.'

Carrie was smiling at the mauve dress as though she saw more than a dress; she said quietly: 'Mauve were your colour, my dear; and I always say there weren't two prettier maidens in Devonshire than my Miss Deborah and Miss Barbarina.'

I was suddenly impatient with the stuffy sewing room. I said. 'I've things to do,' and went out.

But when I had shut the door I asked myself what motive lay behind Hyson's strange behaviour. I could understand that Carrie's mind wandered a little; she was old; and she had clearly been devoted to Barbarina. Deborah had said that she had never recovered from the shock of her death. But where did Hyson come into this? She was just a mischievous child, I suspected; could it be that for some reason she resented my coming to Pendorric? That talk about the fatted calf – what had been the meaning behind that?

I looked over my shoulder and restrained the impulse to go back into the room. Instead I went along the corridor until I came to the door of Deborah's sitting-room.

I hesitated for a moment, then I knocked.

'Come in,' said Deborah.

She was seated at a table reading.

'My dear, what a pleasant surprise. Why, is anything wrong?'

'Oh no . . . nothing. I'm just a little puzzled, that's all.'

'Come and sit down and tell me what's puzzling you.'

'Hyson's a queer child, isn't she? I'm afraid I don't understand her.'

She shrugged her shoulders. 'It's not always easy to understand what goes on in the mind of a child.'

'But Hyson is so very strange. Lowella is quite different.'

'It's the case of the extrovert and the introvert. They are twins of entirely different character. Tell me what Hyson's been doing to upset you.'

I told her about the dress I had seen on the stand in Carrie's sewing room.

Deborah sighed. 'I know,' she said. 'She'd done it before I could stop her. I'd decided on the pink and the pattern; then I found that she was making up not only the pink but the mauve.'

'Does she really think that Barbarina is still alive?'

'Not all the time. There are occasions when she's as lucid as you or I. And at others she thinks she is back in the past. It doesn't matter. The dresses are exactly alike, so that I can wear either of them. I never scold her.'

'But, what about Hyson?' I said. 'Does Carrie talk to her?'

'Hyson understands perfectly the state of affairs. I've explained to her. But I've told her that she must never hurt Carrie's feelings. Hyson's a good child. She does her best. You look disapproving, my dear.'

'I think it's a little . . . unhealthy,' I said.

'Oh, it does no harm, and it makes Carrie happy. While she can believe that Barbarina is still with us she's contented. It's when she faces up to what really happened that she is depressed and sad. It's easier in Devonshire. There, of course, she is often under the impression that Barbarina is in Cornwall, and that we shall shortly be visiting her. Here it's not so easy, because she thinks Barbarina should be here.'

I was silent and she laid her hand over mine.

'My dear,' she went on softly, 'you're young and bursting with sound common sense. It's difficult for you to understand the vagaries of people whose minds are not quite as normal as your own. Don't let Carrie upset you. She's been like this for so long. I couldn't bear to make her unhappy . . . that's why I humour her. So I let her say: Miss Deborah shall go to the ball in the pink dress and Miss Barbarina in the mauve. It's of little consequence. And talking of dresses – tell me, what are you going to wear?'

I told her that it was a green and gold dress which I had bought in Paris during my honeymoon. I had so far had no chance to wear it and the ball seemed the ideal occasion.

'I'm sure you'll look wonderful, my dear, quite wonderful; and your grandfather and your husband will be so proud of you. Oh Favel, what a fortunate woman you are to find a husband and a grandfather all in a few months!'

'Yes,' I said slowly, 'it's certainly very strange.'

She laughed merrily. 'You see, strange things are beginning to happen to *you* since you came to Pendorric.'

It was arranged that Roc and I should go to Polhorgan half an hour before the guests were due to arrive, so that we should be there, with Lord Polhorgan, to receive them.

I bathed and dressed in good time, and was rather pleased with my appearance when I put on my dress. It was a sheath of green silk chiffon billowing out from the knees into a frothy skirt; there was a narrow gold belt at the waist and a gold tracing showed through the chiffon from the satin underskirt.

I had piled my hair high on my head, and I was delighted with the Parisian effect.

Roc came in while I was standing before the mirror, and taking my hands held me at arms' length to examine me.

'I haven't a doubt who'll be the belle of the ball,' he said. 'And what could be more apt?' He drew me to him and kissed me as lightly as though I were a porcelain figure which he feared might break under rough handling.

'You'd better dress,' I warned. 'Remember we have to be early.'

'First I want to give you this,' he said, and took a case from his pocket.

I opened it and saw a glittering necklace of emeralds and diamonds.

'Known – rather grandiosely – as the Pendorric Emeralds,' he told me. 'Worn at her wedding by her whom they call the First Bride.'

'They're exquisite, Roc.'

'I had them in mind when I suggested you should buy that dress. I don't pretend to know anything about clothes, but being green it did seem they'd match.'

'So I'm to wear them to-night?'

'Of course.' He took them from the case and fastened them about my neck. I had looked *soigné* before, but now I was regal. The emeralds did that for me.

'Why didn't you tell me that you were giving me these?'

'But in all the best scenes the jewels are clasped about the lady's neck at the precise psychological moment!'

'You have an eye for drama. Oh Roc, they're quite lovely. I shall be afraid of losing them.'

'Why should you? There's a safety chain. Pendorric brides have been wearing them for nearly two hundred years and not lost them. Why should this bride?'

'Thank you, Roc.'

He lifted his shoulders and surveyed me sardonically. 'Don't thank me, darling. Thank that other Petroc who married Lowella. He bought them for her. They're your heritage anyway. It'll be nice to show that opulent grandfather of yours that you've a husband who can give you something worth having.'

'You've given me so much that's worth having. I don't want to disparage the necklace, but . . .'

'I know, darling. Kind hearts are more than emeralds. A sentiment with which I am in complete agreement. But it's getting late, so we'll develop that line of thought later.'

'Yes, you'd better hurry.'

He went into the bathroom and I looked at my watch. We should be leaving in fifteen minutes. Knowing his tendency to talk while dressing, and feeling this would delay him, I went out of the room into the corridor and stood at the window looking down at the quadrangle. I was thinking about my grandfather and all that had happened to me in the last weeks, and it seemed to me that my life, which until then had run along expected lines, had suddenly become dramatic. I did not think I should be very surprised whatever happened to me next.

Still, I was happy. I was more deeply in love with my husband every day; I was growing fonder of my grandfather, and I found great pleasure in being the one who could bring such happiness into his life. I knew that he had changed a great deal since I had come; and, since he had revealed his relationship to me, even more. He often reminded me of a boy in his enthusiasm for simple things, and I understood that this was because he had never had time to be really young.

Some impulse made me lift my eyes from the pond and the palms. That feeling which came to me often when I was in the quadrangle was strong at that moment. I had never analysed it, but it was a feeling of eerie discomfort, a notion that I was being watched intently and not casually or in a friendly way.

My eyes went at once to the east windows . . . to that floor on which Barbarina had had her music room.

There was a movement there. Someone was standing at the corridor window – not close, but a little way back. Now the figure came nearer. I could not see the face, but I knew it was a woman because she was wearing a mauve dress.

It was the one I had seen on the dressmaker's dummy; the dress which Carrie had made for Barbarina.

'Barbarina . . .' I whispered.

For a few seconds I saw the dress clearly, for a pale hand had drawn back the curtains. I could not see the face, though . . . then the curtain fell back into place.

I stood staring at the window.

Of course, I said to myself, it was Deborah. She has decided to wear the mauve dress after all. That's the answer. But why did she not wave to me or let me see her?

It had been all over in a few seconds, hadn't it? She couldn't have seen me.

Roc came out of the room, shouting that he was ready.

I was about to tell him what I had seen, but somehow it had become unimportant. When I saw Deborah at the ball in the mauve dress I should be satisfied.

The ballroom at Polhorgan was magnificent. Trehay, eager to show off his more exotic blooms, had made a wonderful show, but it was the hydrangeas, indigenous to Cornwall, that in my opinion were the most dazzling.

My grandfather was already in the ballroom in his wheelchair with Althea Grey beside him, looking startlingly beautiful in her eggshell-blue off-the-shoulder dress, with a white camellia adorning it. Her hand was resting on my grandfather's chair in a proprietorial way.

'You look more like your mother than ever,' said my grandfather brusquely; and I knew he was moved as I stooped and kissed him.

'It's going to be wonderful,' I replied. 'I'm so looking forward to meeting all your friends.'

My grandfather laughed. 'Not *my* friends. Few of them have ever been here before. They've come to meet Mrs. Pendorric – and that's a fact. What do you think of the ballroom?'

'Quite magnificent.'

'Have you got anything like this at Pendorric, Roc?'

'I'm afraid we don't run to such glory. Our halls are tiny in comparison.'

'Like that panelling? I had that specially brought here from the Midlands. Some old mansion that was broken up. Used to say to myself, "One day that'll be mine." Well, so it was in a way.'

'There's a lesson in it,' said Roc. 'Take what you want and pay for it.'

'I paid for it all right.'

'Lord Polhorgan,' said Althea, 'you mustn't get over-excited. If you do I shall have to insist on your going back to your room.'

'You see how I'm treated?' said my grandfather. 'I might be a schoolboy. In fact I'm sure at times Nurse Grey thinks I am.'

'I'm here to look after you,' she reminded him. 'Have you your T.N.T.?'

He put his hand in his pocket and held up the silver box.

'Good. Keep them handy.'

'I shall be keeping my eye on him too,' I said.

'How fortunate you are, sir,' Roc murmured. 'The two most beautiful women at the ball to watch over you!'

My grandfather put his hand over mine and smiled at me. 'Aye,' he agreed, 'I'm lucky.'

'That sounds like the first of the guests,' said Althea.

It was. Dawson, spectacular in black livery with gold frogs and buttons, was announcing the first arrivals.

I felt very proud standing there between my grandfather and my husband as I greeted the guests. My grandfather was cold and formal; Roc quite the opposite. I was, naturally, the centre of a great deal of interest; I guessed that many of these people wanted to see what sort of woman Roc Pendorric had married. The fact that I was Lord Polhorgan's granddaughter meant that they were aware of our romantic meeting, for they all knew my mother had run away from home and had not communicated with her father again. It made a good story, and naturally there had been a certain amount of gossip about it.

Roc was told that he was lucky, and now and then I sensed the underlying significance of that remark. Polhorgan was an imposing structure, but a great many of these people possessed houses as grand. The difference was that they had been in their families for hundreds of years, while my grandfather had earned the money to build his. Moreover, it was unlikely that any of these people could match the opulence of the furnishings they now saw. It was well known that my grandfather was either a millionaire or something near it.

So when they told Roc he was lucky, I presumed my grandfather's wealth had something to do with it.

However, I was beginning to enjoy myself. The music had started and the guests were still arriving. They were not all young; indeed there were some very old people present, for the invitations had been issued to whole families. It was going to be a very mixed ball.

The party from Pendorric had arrived, and the twins came ahead, arm in arm, looking exactly alike in their gold-coloured dresses; behind them Charles and Morwenna, and then . . . Deborah.

Deborah was wearing the pink dress which Carrie had made for her, and looking as though she had stepped out of a twenty-five-year-old magazine.

But pink! Then who had been wearing the mauve?

I forced myself to smile at them; but I could not stop thinking of the vision I had seen at the window. Who could it have been?

Deborah had taken my hands. 'You look lovely, dear. Is everything all right?'

'Why yes . . . I think so.'

'I thought you looked a little startled when you saw me.'

'Oh no . . . not really.'

'It *was* something. You must tell me later. I'd better pass on now.'

More guests were approaching, and Roc was introducing me. I took the outstretched hands, still thinking of the vision I had seen in the mauve dress.

I danced with Roc and with many others that night. I was aware of my grandfather's eyes, which never seemed to leave me.

I think I was a successful hostess.

I was grateful to Deborah, who was determined to put me at my ease since I had shown her that I was disturbed.

She took the first opportunity of talking to me.

Roc was dancing with Althea Grey and I was standing by my grandfather's chair when she came up.

'While you have a moment, Favel,' she said, 'I'd like to chat. Tell me, why were you startled when you saw me?'

I hesitated, then I replied: 'I thought I'd seen you earlier in the evening at the east window – before we left Pendorric . . . in the mauve dress.'

There was silence for a few seconds and I went on: 'I was dressed and waiting for Roc when I looked out of the window and saw someone in the mauve dress.'

'And you didn't recognize who it was?'

'I couldn't see a face. I only saw the dress and that someone was wearing it.'

'What ever did you think?'

'I thought you'd decided to wear it.'

'And when I came in the pink surely you didn't think you'd seen . . . Barbarina?'

'Oh no, I didn't think that really. But I wondered who . . .'

She touched my hand. 'Of course you wouldn't think it. You're too sensible.' She paused and said: 'There's a simple explanation. I had a choice of two dresses. Why shouldn't I try on the mauve and finally decide on the pink?'

'So it *was* you.'

She did not answer; she was staring dreamily at the dancers. I realized that I didn't believe what she was hinting. She had not said that she had tried on the mauve dress, she had put it differently. 'Why shouldn't I try on the mauve . . .?' It was as though she did not want to tell a lie but at the same time was trying to set my mind at rest.

That was just a fleeting thought which came into my head as I looked at her kind, gentle face.

Almost immediately I said to myself: Of course, Deborah tried on the mauve first. It was natural. And moreover it was the only explanation.

But why should she go to the east wing to do it? Because Carrie would have put the dress there, was the obvious answer.

I dismissed the matter from my mind. Deborah saw this and seemed contented.

Grandfather said that I must not remain at his side, as he liked to see me among the dancers. I told him I was rather anxious about him, as he looked more flushed than usual.

'I'm enjoying it,' he said. 'I should have liked to have done more of this in the past. Perhaps we will now, eh, now you've come home? Where's your husband?'

He was dancing with Nurse Grey and I pointed him out. They were the most striking couple in the room, I thought; she with her fair looks, he so dark.

'He ought to be dancing with you,' said my grandfather.

'He did suggest it, but I told him I wanted to talk to you.'

'Now that won't do. Ah, here's the doctor. Nice to see you unprofessionally, Dr. Clement.'

Andrew Clement smiled at me. 'It was good of you and Mrs. Pendorric to ask me.'

'Why don't you ask my granddaughter to dance? Don't want her to be glued to the old man's chair all the evening.'

Andrew Clement smiled at me and we went on to the floor together.

'Do you think this is too much excitement for my grandfather?' I asked.

'I wouldn't say he was too excited. No, I think it's doing him good. I'll tell you something, Mrs. Pendorric; he's been much better since you've been here.'

'Has he?'

'Oh yes, you've given him a real interest in life. There were times when I was afraid he'd die of melancholia . . . sitting in that room day after day, staring out at the sea. Now he's no longer lonely. I think he's changed a great deal; he's got something to live for, and you know he's a man of immense energy. He's always gone all out for what he wants, and managed to get it. Well, now he wants to live.'

'That's excellent news.'

'Oh yes, he's told me how delighted he is with you. He wanted me to witness his signature on some important documents the other day, and I said to Nurse Grey afterwards that I hadn't found him so well for a very long time. She said it was all thanks to that granddaughter of his on whom he doted.'

'I can't tell you how happy I am if I can be of help to him. Is your sister here to-night?'

'Oh yes, though ballroom dancing isn't much in her line. Now if it were folk-dancing . . .'

He laughed, and at that moment he was tapped on the shoulder by a dark, handsome young man. Andrew Clement pretended to scowl, and said: 'Oh, is it that sort of dance?'

'Afraid so,' said the young man. 'I'm claiming Mrs. Pendorric.'

As I danced with this young man he told me he was John Poldree and that he lived a few miles inland.

'I'm home for a bit,' he went on. 'Actually I'm studying law in London.'

'I'm so glad you were home for the ball,' I told him.

'Yes, it's good fun. All very exciting too – your turning out to be Lord Polhorgan's granddaughter.'

'Most people seem to think so.'

'Your grandfather has a striking-looking nurse, Mrs. Pendorric.'

'Yes, she's certainly very beautiful.'

'Who is she? I've seen her somewhere before.'

'Her name is Althea Grey.'

He shook his head. 'Can't recall the name. The face is familiar, though. Seem to connect her with some law case or other . . . I thought I had a good memory for such things, but it seems I'm not so good as I thought.'

'I should think if you'd met her you'd remember her.'

'Yes. That's why I was so sure. Well, it'll come back I expect.'

'Why don't you ask her?'

'As a matter of fact I did. She absolutely froze me. She was certain she had never met *me* before.'

There was a tap on his shoulder, and there was Roc waiting to claim me.

I was very happy dancing with my husband. His eyes were amused and I could see that he was enjoying himself.

'It's fun,' he said, 'but I don't see half enough of the hostess. I expect she has her duties, though.'

'The same thing applies to you.'

'Well, haven't you seen me performing? I've had my eyes on every wallflower.'

'I've seen you on several occasions dancing with Althea Grey. Was she wilting for lack of attention?'

'At things of this sort, people like Althea and Rachel could be at a disadvantage. The nurse and the governess! There's a certain amount of snobbery still in existence, you know.'

'So that's why you've been looking after Althea. What about poor Rachel?'

'I'd better keep an eye on her too.'

'Then,' I said lightly, 'as you're going to be so busily engaged elsewhere I'd better make the most of the time that belongs to me.'

He squeezed my hand. 'Have you forgotten,' he asked, his lips touching my ear, 'that the rest of our lives belong together?'

Supper was very gay. We had arranged that it should be served in three of the larger rooms which adjoined the hall; they all faced south and the great french windows opened on to terraces which looked over the gardens to the sea. There was plenty of moonlight, and the view was enchanting.

Trehay's flower scheme was as beautiful in the supper rooms as it was in the ballroom; and no effort had been spared to achieve the utmost luxury. On the overladen table were fish, pies, meats and delicacies of all description. Dawson and his under-servants in their smart livery took charge of the bar while Mrs. Dawson looked after the food.

I shared a table with my grandfather, John Poldree and his brother, Deborah and the twins.

Lowella was as silent as Hyson on this occasion; she seemed to be quite overawed, and when I whispered to her that she was unusually subdued, Hyson answered that they had made a vow not to call attention to themselves, in case someone should remember that they weren't really old enough to go to balls and tell Rachel to take them home.

They had escaped Rachel, they told me, and their parents; and so would I please not call attention to them in case Granny Deborah noticed?

I promised.

While we were talking together, some of the guests strolled out on to the terraces and I saw Roc and Althea Grey walk by the window.

They stood for a while looking out over the sea and seemed to be talking earnestly, and the sight of them threw a small shadow over my enjoyment.

It was midnight when several of the guests started to leave, and finally only the Pendorric party remained.

Althea Grey hovered while we said good-bye and congratulated each other on the success of the evening. Then she wheeled my grandfather's chair to the lift which he had had installed some years before when he had first been aware of his illness, and he went up to his bedroom while we went to our cars.

It was half-past one by the time we reached Pendorric, and as we drove under the old archway to the north portico, Mrs. Penhalligan opened the front door.

'Oh, Mrs. Penhalligan,' I said, 'you shouldn't have stayed up.'

'Well, madam,' she said, 'I thought you'd like a little refreshment before settling down for the night. I've got some soup for you.'

'Soup! On a hot summer's night!' cried Roc.

'Soup! Soup! Glorious Soup!' sang Lowella.

'One of the old customs,' Morwenna whispered to me. 'We can't escape them if we want to.'

We went into the north hall and Mrs. Penhalligan led the way into the small winter parlour where soup plates had been set out; and at the sight of them Lowella danced round the room chanting: ' "There was a sound of revelry by night".'

'Oh Lowella, please,' sighed Morwenna. 'Aren't you tired? It's after one.'

'I'm not in the least tired,' insisted Lowella indignantly. 'Oh, isn't this a wonderful ball!'

'The ball's over,' Roc reminded her.

'It's not— not till we're all in our beds. There's soup to be had before that's over.'

'You'd better let them sleep late to-morrow, Rachel,' said their mother.

Mrs Penhalligan came in with a tureen of soup and began ladling it out into the plates.

'It was always like this in the old days,' said Roc. 'We used to hide in the gallery and watch them come in; do you remember, Morwenna?'

Morwenna nodded.

'Who?' asked Hyson.

'Our parents, of course. We couldn't have been more than . . .'

'Five,' said Hyson, 'You'd have to be, wouldn't you, Uncle Roc? You couldn't have been more, could you?'

'What memories these children have!' murmured Roc lightly. 'Have you been coaching them, Aunt Deborah?'

'What soup's this?' asked Lowella.

'Taste it and see,' Roc told her.

She obeyed and rolled her eyes ecstatically.

We all agreed that it was not such a bad custom after all, and that although we should not have thought of hot soup on a summer's night there was something reviving about it and it was pleasant to sit back and talk about the evening.

When we had finished the soup no one seemed in a hurry to go to bed, so we talked about Polhorgan and the people we had met there, while the twins sat back in their seats, desperately trying to keep awake, looking like daffodils which had been left too long out of water.

'It's time they were in bed,' said Charles.

'Oh Daddy,' wailed Lowella, 'don't be so old-fashioned!'

'If you're not tired,' Roc pointed out, 'others might be. Aunt Deborah looks half asleep and so do you, Morwenna.'

'I know,' said Morwenna, 'but it's so comfortable sitting here and it's been such a pleasant evening I don't want it to end. So go on talking, all of you.'

'Yes do, quick,' cried Lowella; and everyone laughed and seemed suddenly wide awake. 'Go on, Uncle Roc.'

'This reminds me of Christmas,' said Roc obligingly, and Lowella smiled at him with loving gratitude and affection.

'When,' went on Roc, 'we sit around the fire, longing for our beds and too lazy to go to them.'

'Telling ghost stories,' said Charles.

'Tell some now,' pleaded Lowella. Do, please. Daddy. Uncle Roc.'

Hyson sat forward, suddenly alert.

'Most unseasonable,' commented Roc. 'You'll have to wait a few months yet, Lo.'

'I can't. I can't. I want a ghost story – *now*!'

'It certainly is time you were in bed,' commented Morwenna.

Lowella regarded me with solemn eyes. 'It'll be the Bride's first Christmas with us,' she announced. 'She'll love Christmas at Pendorric, won't she? I remember last Christmas we sang songs as well as telling ghost stories. Real Christmas songs. I'll tell you the one I like best.'

' "The Mistletoe Bough",' said Hyson.

'You'd like that, Bride, because it's all about another bride.'

'I expect your Aunt Favel knows it,' said Morwenna. 'Everyone does.'

'No,' I told them, 'I've never heard it. You see, Christmas on the island wasn't quite like an English Christmas.'

'Fancy! She's never heard of "The Mistletoe Bough".' Lowella looked shocked.

'Think what she's missed,' mocked Roc.

'I'm going to be the one to tell her,' declared Lowella. 'Listen, Bride! This other bride played hide and seek in a place . . .'

'Minster Lovel,' supplied Hyson.

'Well, the place doesn't matter two hoots, silly.'

'Lowella,' Morwenna admonished; but Lowella was rushing on.

'They were playing hide and seek and this bride got into the old chest, and the lock clicked and fastened her down for ever.'

'And they didn't open the chest until twenty years later,' put in Hyson. 'Then they found her – nothing but a skeleton.'

'Her wedding dress and orange blossom were all right, though,' added Lowella cheerfully.

'I'm sure,' said Roc ironically, 'that must have been a comfort.'

'You shouldn't laugh, Uncle Roc. It's sad, really.'

' "A spring lock lay in ambush there",' she sang.

' "And fastened her down for ever".'

'And the moral of that,' Roc put in, grinning at me, 'is, don't go hiding in oak chests if you're a bride.'

'Ugh!' shivered Morwenna. 'I'm not keen on that story. It's morbid.'

'That's why it appeals to your daughters, Wenna,' Roc told her.

Charles said: 'Look. I'm going up. The twins ought to have been in bed hours ago.'

Deborah yawned. 'I must say I find it hard to keep awake.'

'I've an idea,' cried Lowella. 'Let's all sing Christmas songs for a bit. Everyone has to sing a different one.'

'I've a better idea,' said her father. 'Bed.'

Rachel stood up. 'Come along,' she said to the twins. 'It must be nearly two.'

Lowella looked disgusted with us because we all rose; but no one took any notice of her, and we said good night and went upstairs.

The next day I went over to Polhorgan to see how my grandfather was after all the excitement.

Mrs. Dawson met me in the hall and I congratulated her on all that she and her husband had done to make the ball a success.

'Well, madam,' she said, bridling, 'it's a pleasure to be appreciated, I must say. Not that Dawson and I want *thanks*. It was our duty and we did it.'

'You did it admirably,' I told her.

Dawson came into the hall at that moment, and when Mrs. Dawson told him what I had said, he was as pleased as his wife.

I asked how my grandfather was that morning.

'Very contented, madam, but sleeping. A little tired after all the excitement, I think.'

'I won't disturb him for a while,' I said. 'I'll go into the garden.'

'I'm sending up his coffee in half an hour, madam,' Mrs. Dawson told me.

'Very well then, I'll wait till then.'

Dawson followed me into the garden; there was something conspiratorial about his manner, I thought; and when I paused by one of the greenhouses he was still beside me.

'Everyone in the house is glad, madam, that you've come home,' he told me. 'With one exception, that is.'

I turned to look at him in astonishment, and he did not meet my eyes. I had the impression that he was determined to be the good and faithful servant, dealing with a delicate situation because this was something I ought to know.

'Thank you, Dawson,' I said. 'Who is the exception?'

'The nurse.'

'Oh?'

He stuck out his lower lip and shook his head. 'She had other notions.'

'Dawson, you don't like Nurse Grey, do you?'

'There's nobody in this house that likes her, madam . . . except the young men. She being that sort. There's some that don't look beyond a pretty face.'

I thought it was the usual story of a nurse in the house who was determined to establish the fact that she was superior to the servants. Probably Nurse Grey gave orders in the kitchen, which they did not like. It was not an unusual situation. And now that they knew I was Lord Polhorgan's granddaughter, they regarded me as the mistress of the house. This was the Dawsons' way of telling me I was accepted as such.

'Mrs. Dawson and I have always felt ourselves to be in a privileged position, madam. We have been with his lordship for a very long time.'

'But of course, you *are*,' I assured him.

'We were here, begging your pardon, when Miss Lilith was at home.'

'So you knew my mother?'

'A lovely young lady, and, if you'll forgive the liberty, madam, you're very like her.'

'Thank you.'

'That's why . . . Mrs. Dawson and I . . . made up our minds that we could talk to you, madam.'

'Please say everything that's in your mind, Dawson.'

'Well, we're uneasy, madam. There was a time when we thought she would try to marry him. There was no doubt that was what she was after. Mrs. Dawson and I had made up our minds that the minute that was decided on we should be looking for another position.'

'Miss Grey . . . marry my grandfather?'

'Such things have happened, madam. Rich old gentlemen do marry young nurses now and then. They get a feeling they can't do without them and the nurses have their eyes on the money, you see.'

'I'm sure my grandfather would never be married for his money. He's far too shrewd.'

'That was what we said. She could never achieve that, and she didn't. But Mrs. Dawson and I reckon it wasn't for want of trying.' He came closer to me and whispered: 'The truth is, madam, we reckon she's what you might call . . . an adventuress.'

'I see.'

'There's something more. Our married daughter came to see us not so long ago. . . . It was just before you came home, madam. Well, she happened to see Nurse Grey and she said she was sure she'd seen her picture in the paper somewhere. Only she didn't think the name was Grey.'

'Why was her picture in the paper?'

'It was some case or other. Maureen couldn't remember what. But she thought it was something bad.'

'People get mixed up about these things. Perhaps she'd won a beauty competition or something like that.'

'Oh no, it wasn't that or Maureen would have remembered. It was something to do with the courts. And it was Nurse something. But Maureen didn't think it was Grey. It was just the face. She has got the sort of face, madam, that once seen is never forgotten.'

'Did you ask her?'

'Oh no, madam, it wasn't the sort of thing we could ask. She would be offended, and unless we'd got proof, she could deny it, couldn't she? No, there's nothing we can put a finger on. And now you've come home it doesn't seem the same. His lordship's not so likely to get caught – that's how Mrs. Dawson and I see it, madam. But we're keeping our eyes open.'

'Oh . . . it's Mrs. Pendorric.'

I turned sharply to see Althea Grey smiling at me, and I flushed rather guiltily, feeling at a disadvantage to have been discovered discussing her with the butler. I wondered if she had overheard anything. Voices carried in the open air.

'*You* don't look as if you've been up half the night,' she went on. 'And I'm sure you must have been. What an evening! Lord Polhorgan was absolutely delighted with the way everything went off.'

Dawson slipped away and I was left alone with her. Her hair, piled high beneath the snowy cap, was beautiful; but I wondered what it was that made her face so distinctive. Was it the thick brows, several shades darker than her hair; the eyes of that lovely deep blue shade that is almost violet and doesn't need to take its colour from anything because it is always a more vivid blue than anything else could possibly be? The straight nose was almost Egyptian, and seemed odd with such Anglo-Saxon fairness. The wide mouth was slightly mocking now. I felt sure that even if she had not overheard our conversation, she knew that Dawson had been speaking of her derogatively.

It was a face of mystery, I decided, a face that concealed secrets; the face of a woman of the world, a woman who had lived perhaps recklessly and had no desire for the past to prejudice the present, or future.

I remembered that the young man with whom I had danced had mentioned something from the past too. So Dawson's suspicions were very likely not without some foundation.

I felt wary of this woman as I walked with her towards the house.

'Lord Polhorgan was hoping you'd come this morning. I told him you most certainly would.'

'I was wondering how he felt after last night.'

'It did him a world of good. He enjoyed fêting his beautiful granddaughter.'

I felt that she was secretly laughing at me, and I was glad when I was with my grandfather and she had left us alone together.

It was a week later that there was a call in the night.

The telephone beside our bed rang and I was answering it before Roc had opened his eyes.

'This is Nurse Grey. Could you come over at one? Lord Polhorgan is very ill, and asking for you.'

I leaped out of bed.

'What on earth's happened?' asked Roc.

When I told him he made me slip on some clothes, and, doing the same himself, said: 'We'll drive over right away.'

'What's the time?' I asked Roc, as we drove the short distance between Pendorric and Polhorgan.

'Just after one.'

'He must be bad for her to ring us,' I said.

Roc put his hand over mine, as though to reassure me that whatever was waiting for me, he would be there to share it.

As we drove up to the portico the door opened and Dawson let us in.

'He's very bad, I'm afraid, madam.'

'I'll go straight up.'

I ran up the stairs, Roc at my heels. Roc waited outside the bedroom while I went in.

Althea Grey came towards me. 'Thank God you've come,' she said. 'He's been asking for you. I phoned as soon as I knew.'

I went to the bed where my grandfather lay back on his pillows; he was quite exhausted and I could see that he was finding it difficult to get his breath.

'Grandfather,' I said.

His lips formed the name Favel; but he did not say it.

I knelt by the bed and took his hand in mine; I kissed it, feeling desolate. I had found him such a short time ago. Was I to lose him so soon?

'I'm here, Grandfather. I came as soon as I heard you wanted me.'

I knew by the slight movement of his head that he understood.

Althea Grey was at my side. She whispered: 'He's not in pain. I've given him morphia. He'll be feeling the effect of it now. Dr. Clement will be here at any moment.'

I turned to look at her and I saw from her expression that his condition was very grave. Then I saw Roc standing some little way from the bed. Althea Grey moved back to where he was and I turned my attention to my grandfather.

'Favel.' It was a whisper. His fingers moved in mine, and I knew that he was trying to say something to me so I brought my face nearer to his.

'Are you there . . . Favel?'

'Yes, Grandfather,' I whispered.

'It's . . . good-bye, Favel.'

'*No.*'

He smiled. 'Such a short time. . . . But it was a happy time . . . the happiest time . . . Favel, you must be . . .'

His face puckered and I bent nearer to him.

'Don't talk, Grandfather. It's too much of an effort.'

His brows puckered into a frown. 'Favel . . . must be . . . careful. . . . It'll be yours now. Make sure . . .'

I guessed what he was trying to tell me. Even when he was fighting for his breath he was preoccupied with his money.

'It's different . . .' he went on, 'when you have it. . . . Can't be sure . . . can never be sure. . . . Favel . . . take care. . . .'

'Grandfather, please don't worry about me. Don't think about anything but getting better. You will get better. You *must*. . . .'

He shook his head. 'Couldn't find . . .' he began; but his battle for breath was too much for him; his eyes were closing. 'Tired,' he murmured. 'So tired. Favel . . . stay . . . be careful. . . . It's different with money. Perhaps I was wrong . . . but I wanted . . . be careful. . . . I wish I could stay a while to . . . look after you, Favel.'

His lips were moving now but no sound came. He lay back on his pillows, his face looking shrunken and grey.

He was very near the end by the time Dr. Clement arrived.

We sat in the room where I had played so many games of chess with him – Dr. Clement, Roc, Nurse Grey and myself.

Dr. Clement was saying: 'It's not entirely unexpected. It could have happened at any time. Did he ring the bell?'

'No. Or I should have heard him. My room is next to his. The bell is always by his bed for him to ring if he wanted anything in the night. It was Dawson who went in. He said he was locking up when he saw Lord Polhorgan's light on. He found him gasping and in great pain. He called me and I saw that it was necessary to give him morphia, which I did.'

Dr. Clement rose and went to the door.

'Dawson,' he called. 'Are you there, Dawson?'

Dawson came into the room.

'I've heard that you came in and found Lord Polhorgan in distress.'

'Yes, sir. He'd snapped on the light and seeing it I looked in to make sure he was all right. I saw he was trying to ask for something, but I didn't know what, for a while. Then I found out it was his pills. I couldn't find them then so I called Nurse and came back with her. That was when she gave him the morphia.'

'So it seems as though this attack developed into a major one because he had no chance of holding it off.'

'I'd always impressed on him the need to have his pills at hand,' said Althea Grey.

Dawson was looking at her scornfully. 'I found them after, sir. After his lordship had had the morphia, that was. The box was lying on the floor. It had come open and the pills was scattered, sir. The bell was on the floor also.'

'He must have knocked them over when he reached for the pills,' said Althea Grey.

I looked at Roc, who was staring straight ahead of him.

'A sad business,' murmured Dr. Clement. 'I think I ought to give you a sedative, Mrs. Pendorric. You're looking all in.'

'I'll take her home,' said Roc. 'There's no point in waiting here now. We can do nothing till the morning.'

Dr. Clement smiled at me sadly. 'There was nothing we could do to prevent it,' he told me.

'If he had had his pills,' I said, 'that might have prevented it.'

'It might have.'

'What an unfortunate accident . . .' I began; and my eyes met Dawson's and I saw that his were gleaming with speculation.

'It couldn't be helped,' Roc was saying. 'It's easy to see how it happened . . . reaching out . . . in a hurry . . . knocking over the box and the bell.'

I shivered, and Roc put his arm through mine.

I wanted to get out of that room; there was something in Dawson's expression which frightened me; there was something too in the calm, beautiful features of Althea Grey.

I felt as though I were outside looking in on all that had happened since Roc and I came into this house. I saw myself leaning over my dying grandfather; I heard his voice warning me of some danger which he sensed ahead of me. Roc and Althea were standing together in that room of death. What words did they exchange while my grandfather told me to take care? What had been the expressions in their eyes as they looked at each other?

Dawson had done this with his hatred of the nurse, with his groundless suspicions. But did I really know that they were groundless?

I felt the cool night air on my face and Roc's tender voice beside me.

'Come on, darling, you're quite worn out. Clement's right. It has been a terrible shock to you.'

Those were sad weeks which followed, for only when I had lost him did I realize how fond I had become of my grandfather. I missed him deeply; not only his company, I began to understand; not only the complacent joy I had felt because I had brought so much pleasure into his lonely life; but he had given me a sense of security, and that I had lost. I had subconsciously felt that he was there – a powerful man of the world to whom I could go if I were in trouble. My own flesh and blood. I could have trusted him to do anything in his power to help me . . . should I have needed his help.

It seemed strange that I should have felt this need. I had a husband who could surely give me any protection I wanted; but it was the loss of my grandfather which brought home to me the true relationship between myself and my husband. To have lost him would have been complete desolation; he could amuse and delight me too, but the truth remained that I was not sure of him; I did not know him. Yet, in spite of this uncertainty I loved him infinitely, and my entire happiness depended on him. I was wretched because I must be suspicious of his relationship with Althea Grey, Rachel Bective and even Dinah Bond. And I had begun to feel – since I had discovered that

I had a grandfather – that he was someone who had for me a deep and uncomplicated affection. Now I had lost him.

I was his heir and there were many visits from his solicitors. When I heard the extent of the fortune he had left I felt dizzy at the prospect of my riches. There were several bequests. The Dawsons had been left a comfortable pension; there was a thousand pounds for the nurse who was employed by him at the time of his death; all the servants had been remembered and rewarded according to their length of service; he had left a sizeable sum to be used for the benefit of orphans – he himself had been an orphan – and I was very touched that he had remembered this charity. Death duties, I was informed, would swallow up a large proportion, but I should still have a considerable fortune.

Polhorgan itself was mine with all its contents; and this in itself was worth a great deal.

My grandfather's death seemed to have changed my whole life. I was so much poorer in affection, so much richer in worldly goods; and I was beginning to be afraid that this last fact coloured people's attitude towards me.

I fancied people like the Darks and Dr. Clement were not quite so friendly; that the people in the village whispered about me when I had passed. I had become not merely Mrs. Pendorric, but the rich Mrs. Pendorric. But it was in Pendorric itself that I felt the change most, and this was indeed disturbing. I felt that Morwenna and Charles were secretly delighted, and that the twins watched me a little furtively as though they had overheard gossip which had made them see me in a different light.

Deborah was more outspoken than the others. She said: 'Barbarina was an heiress, but nothing of course to be compared with yourself.'

I hated this kind of talk. I wished that my grandfather had not been such a rich man. I wished that he had left his money elsewhere, for I was realizing now that one of the facts which had made me so happy at Pendorric was that, although the old house and estate needed money, Roc had married me, a girl without a penny. I could no longer say to myself: 'He could only have married me for love.'

It was with my grandfather's money that the canker had touched our relationship.

It was some weeks after my grandfather's death that I had an interview with his solicitor and he brought home to me the advisability of making a will.

So I did so, and, with the exception of one or two legacies, I left the residue of my fortune to Roc.

September had come. The evenings were short and the mornings misty; but the afternoons were as warm as they had been in July.

It was two months since my grandfather's death and I was still mourning him. I had done nothing about Polhorgan, and the Dawsons and all the servants remained there; Althea Grey had decided to have a long holiday before looking for a new post and had taken a little cottage about a mile

from Pendorric, which during the months of June, July and August was let
to holiday-makers.

I knew I should have to do something about Polhorgan, and an idea had
come to me. It was to turn the house into a home for orphans – such as my
grandfather must have been – the deprived and unwanted ones.

When I mentioned this to Roc, he was startled.

'What an undertaking!' he said.

'Somehow I think it would have appealed to my grandfather because he
was an orphan himself.'

Roc walked away from me – we were in our bedroom – and going to the
window stared out at the sea.

'Well, Roc, you don't like the idea?'

'Darling, it's not the sort of project you can rush into.'

'No, of course not. I'm just thinking about it.'

'Things aren't what they used to be, remember. There'd be all sorts of
bureaucratic regulations to be got over . . . and have you thought of the cost
of running a place like that?'

'I haven't thought about anything very much. It was just a faint idea. I'm
brooding on it, though.'

'We'll have to do a lot of brooding,' he said.

I had a notion that he was not impressed with the idea, and I shelved it
for the time being, but I was determined not to give it up easily.

I often called on Jesse Pleydell, who always seemed delighted to see me
apart from the tobacco I took him. Mrs. Penhalligan said I kept him supplied
and he was grateful, though my visits meant as much to him as the tobacco.

I shall never forget that September day, because it brought the beginning
of the real terror which came into my life, and it was at this time that I
began to understand how the pleasant picture had changed piece by piece
until I was confronted with the cruellest of suspicions and horror.

The day began normally enough. In the morning I went down to Mrs.
Robinson's and bought the tobacco. Knowing that I was going, Deborah
asked me to buy some hairpins for her, and Morwenna asked me to bring
some bass she needed for tying up plants. I met Rachel and the twins as I
was setting out; they were going on a nature ramble, so they all three walked
with me as far as the shop. When I came back I met Roc and Charles going
off to the home farm together.

But I didn't leave for the cottages until after tea, and when I arrived Jesse
was sitting at his door catching the last of the sun.

I sat beside him talking for a while, and because I thought it was getting
a little chilly I went inside with him and he made me a cup of tea. It was
something he enjoyed doing, and I knew better than to offer to help. While
we sat drinking the thick brew, Jesse talked of the old days and how the
Pendorric gardens had looked in his time.

'Ah, madam, you should have been here forty years ago . . . that was the
time. I had four men working under me all the time, and the flowers in the
cliff garden were a picture . . . a real picture.'

He would go on and on in this strain, and because he enjoyed it I
encouraged him to do so. I learned a good deal about life at Pendorric forty

or fifty years ago when Jesse was in his prime. It was a more leisurely life, but even so the beginning of change had set in.

'Now when I were a boy things were different.'

That would have been about eighty years ago. Very different indeed, I thought.

'There was no talk then of not being able to keep up like,' mused Jesse. 'There was no thought that things 'ud ever be different from what they always had been. Polhorgan House wasn't here then – nor thought of – and all Polhorgan meant to us was the little old cove down there.'

I listened dreamily, staying rather longer than I had intended, and it was six o'clock when I rose to go.

It was always gloomy in the cottage on account of the small latticed windows, so I hadn't noticed how dark it had grown. The sea mist had been lurking in the air all day, but now it had thickened. It was warm and sea-scented and not by any means unpleasant; it hung in patches and in some spots was really thick. It was especially so near the church; and as I paused at the lych gate to look at the gravestones with the mist swirling about them, thinking how strangely picturesque everything was, I heard it; it seemed to be coming from inside the graveyard – singing in that strange, high voice, which was slightly out of tune.

> *'How should I your true love know*
> *From another one?*
> *By his cockle hat and staff*
> *And his sandal shoon.'*

My heart began to beat fast; my hand on the lych gate trembled. I looked about me, but I seemed to be alone with the mist.

Someone was in there singing, and I had to find out who, so I opened the lych gate and went into the graveyard. I was determined to know who it was who sang in that strange voice, and because I was sure that it was someone from the house, instinctively I made my way to the Pendorric vault. I was almost certain now that it must be Carrie. She brought wreaths for her beloved Barbarina and she would have heard her sing that song; what more natural than that hearing it often she had learned it by heart?

It must be Carrie.

As I reached the Pendorric vault, I drew up short in astonishment because the door was open. I had never seen it open before, and was under the impression that it would never be opened except when it was prepared to receive those who had died.

I went closer and as I did so I heard the voice again.

> *'He is dead and gone, lady,*
> *He is dead and gone;*
> *At his head a grass-green turf,*
> *At his heels a stone.'*

And it appeared to be coming from *inside* the vault.

I went down the stone steps. 'Who's there?' I called. 'Carrie. Are you in there?'

My voice sounded strange at the entrance of that dark vault.

'Carrie,' I called. 'Carrie.' I put my head inside and saw that four or five stone steps led down. I descended, calling: 'Carrie! Carrie! Are you there?'

There was silence. Because of the light from the open door I could see the ledges with the coffins on them; I could smell the dampness of the earth. Then suddenly I was in darkness, and for a few seconds I was so shocked and bewildered that I could not move. I could not even cry out in protest. It took me several seconds to understand that the door had closed on me and I was shut in the vault.

I gave a gasp of horror.

'Who's there?' I cried. 'Who shut the door?'

Then I tried to find the steps, but my eyes were not yet adjusted to the darkness, and groping I stumbled and found myself sprawling up the cold stone stairs.

Frantically I picked myself up. I could make out the shape of the steps now, and I mounted them. I pushed the door but it was firmly shut and I could not move it.

For some moments, I'm afraid, I was hysterical. I hammered on the door with my fists. 'Let me out of here,' I screamed. 'Let me out of here.'

My voice sounded hollow and I knew that it would not be heard outside.

I lay against the door, trying to think. Someone had lured me into this dreadful place, someone who wanted to be rid of me. How long could I live here? But I should be missed. Roc would miss me. He would come to look for me.

'Roc!' I called. 'Oh . . . Roc . . . come quickly.'

I covered my face with my hands. I did not want to look about me. I was suddenly afraid of what I might see, shut in this vault with the Pendorric dead. How long before I became one of them?

Then I thought I heard a movement near me. I listened. Was that the sound of breathing?

The horror was deepening. I did not believe in ghosts, I tried to tell myself. But it is easy to say that when you are above ground in some sunny spot, some well-lighted room. Very different, buried alive . . . among the dead!

I had never known real fear until that moment. I was clammy with sweat, my hair was probably standing on end. I did not know, because there was no room in my mind for anything but fear, the knowledge that I was locked in with the dead.

But I was not alone. I knew it. Some breathing, living thing was in this tomb with me.

I had covered my face with my hands because I did not want to see it. I dared not see.

Then a cold hand touched mine. I screamed, and I heard myself cry: 'Barbarina!' because in that moment I *believed* the legend of Pendorric. I believed that Barbarina had lured me to my tomb so that I could haunt Pendorric and she might rest in peace.

'Favel!' It was a sharp whisper and the one who said it was as frightened as I was.

'Hyson!'

'Yes, Favel. It's Hyson.'

Floods of relief! I was not alone. There was someone to share this horrible place with me. I felt ashamed of myself, but I couldn't help it. I had never been so glad to hear a human voice in the whole of my life.

'Hyson . . . what are you doing here?'

She had come up the stairs and snuggled close beside me.

'It's . . . frightening . . . with the door shut,' she said.

'Did you do this, Hyson?'

'Do it . . . do what?'

'Lock me in.'

'But I'm locked in with you.'

'How did you come to be in here?'

'I knew something was going to happen.'

'What? How?'

'I knew. I came to meet you . . . to see if you were all right.'

'What do you mean? How could you know?'

'I do know things. Then I heard the singing . . . and the door was open . . . so I came in.'

'Before I did?'

'Only a minute before. I was hiding down at the bottom of the steps when you came in.'

'I don't understand what it means.'

'It means Barbarina's lured you in. She didn't know I was here too.'

'Barbarina's *dead.*'

'She can't rest, till you take her place.'

I was recovering my calm. It was amazing what the presence of one small human being could do.

'That's nonsense, Hyson,' I said. 'Barbarina is dead and this story of her haunting the place is just an old legend.'

'She's waiting for a new bride to die.'

'I don't intend to die.'

'We'll both die,' said Hyson, almost unconcernedly; and I thought: She knows nothing of death; she has never seen death. She had looked at the television and seen people drop to the ground. Bang! You're dead. In a child's mind death is quick and neat, without suffering. One forgot that she was only a child posing as a seer.

'That's absurd,' I said. 'We shan't. There must be a certain amount of air coming into this place. They'll miss us and there'll be search parties to find us.'

'Why should they think of looking in the vault?'

'They'll look everywhere.'

'They'll never look in the vault.'

I was silent for a while. I was trying to think who could have done this, who had been waiting for me to leave Jesse Pleydell's cottage and lure me to the vault with singing, like some cruel siren of the sea.

Someone who wanted me out of the way had done this. Someone who had waited for me to enter the vault and descend the stone steps, and then glided out from some hiding place and locked the door on me.

I was recovering rapidly from my fear and realizing that I was not afraid of human scheming; I felt myself equal to deal with that. As soon as I could rid myself of the notion that I was being lured to death by someone who was dead, I felt my natural resilience returning. I was ready to match my wits with those of another human being. I could fight the living.

I said: 'Someone locked the door. Who could it be?'

'It was Barbarina,' whispered Hyson.

'That's not reasonable. Barbarina's dead.'

'She's in here, Favel . . . in her coffin. It's on the ledge with my grandfather's beside it. She couldn't rest, and she wants to. . . . That's why she's locked you in here.'

'Who opened the door?'

'Barbarina.'

'Who locked the door?'

'Barbarina.'

'Hyson, you're getting hysterical.'

'Am I?'

'You mustn't. We've got to think of how we can get out of here.'

'We never shall. Why did she lock me in too? It's like Meddlesome Matty. Granny was always warning me. I shouldn't have come.'

'You mean that then I should have been the only victim.' My voice was grim. I was ashamed of myself. It was a terrible experience for the child; and yet it was doing me such a lot of good not to be alone.

'We shall stay here,' said Hyson, 'for ever. It'll be like "The Mistletoe Bough." When they next open the vault there'll only be our bones, for we shall be skeletons.'

'What nonsense!'

'Do you remember the night of the ball? We all talked about it.'

I was silent with a new horror, because the idea flashed into my mind that on that night when we had sat drinking soup after the ball, one member of our party may have thought of the vault as a good substitute for the old oak chest.

I shivered. Could there be any other explanation than that someone wanted *me* out of the way?

I gripped Hyson's shoulder. 'Listen,' I said. 'We've got to find a way out of this place. Perhaps the door isn't really locked. Who could have locked it anyway?'

'Bar . . .'

'Oh, nonsense.' I stood up cautiously. 'Hyson,' I said, 'we must see what we can do.'

'She won't let us.'

'Give me your hand and we'll see what it's like here.'

'We know. It's all dead people in coffins.'

'I wish I had a torch. Let's try the door again. It may have got jammed.'

We stood on the top step and beat against it. It did not budge.

'I wonder how long we've been in here,' I said.

'An hour.'

'I don't think five minutes. Time goes slowly on occasions like this. But they'll miss us at dinner. They'll start searching for us in the house and then they'll be out, searching for us. I want to look round. There might be a grating somewhere. We might shout through that.'

'There'll be nobody in the churchyard to hear us.'

'There might be. And if they come looking . . .'

I dragged her to her feet and she cowered close to me. Then together, keeping close, we cautiously descended the steps.

Hyson was shivering. 'It's so cold,' she said.

I put my arm round her and we stepped gingerly forward into the darkness. I could see vague shapes about me and I knew these to be the coffins of dead Pendorrics.

Then suddenly I saw a faint light, and feeling my way towards it discovered that there was a grating at the side of the vault. I peered through it and fancied I saw the side of a narrow trench. I knew then that a certain amount of air was coming into the vault and I felt my spirits rising. I put my face close to the grating and shouted: 'Help! We're in the vault. Help!'

My voice sounded muffled as though it were thrown back at me, and I realized that however loudly I shouted I should not be heard unless someone were standing very close to the vault.

Nevertheless I went on shouting until I was hoarse, while Hyson stood shivering beside me.

'Let's try the door again,' I said. And we made our way slowly back to the steps. Once again we forced our weights against it and still it remained fast shut. Hyson was sobbing and bitterly cold, so I took off my coat and wrapped it round us both. We sat side by side on that top step, our arms about each other. I tried to comfort her and tell her that we should soon be rescued, that this was quite different from the old oak chest. We had seen the grating, hadn't we? That meant that air was coming in. Perhaps we should hear their voices. Then we would shout together.

Eventually she stopped trembling, and I think she slept.

I could not sleep although I felt exhausted, bitterly cold, stiff and cramped; and I sat there holding the body of the child against me, peering into the darkness, asking myself over and over again: Who has done this?

There was no means of knowing the time, for I could not see my watch. Hyson stirred and whimpered; I held her closer and whispered assurances to her, while I tried to think of a plan to escape from this place.

I pictured the family coming down to dinner. How upset they would be! Where was Favel? Roc would want to know. He would be a little anxious at first and then frantic with worry. They would already have been searching for us for hours.

Hyson had awakened suddenly: 'Favel . . . where are we?'

'It's all right. I'm here. We're together. . . .'

'We're in that place. Are we still alive, Favel?'

'That's one thing I'm sure of.'

'We're not . . . just ghosts, then?'

I pressed her hand. 'There are no such things,' I told her.

'Favel, you *dare* say that . . . down here . . . among them.'

'If they existed they would surely make us aware of them, just to prove me wrong, wouldn't they?'

I could feel the child holding her breath as she peered into the darkness. After a while she said: 'Have we been here all night?'

'I don't know, Hyson.'

'Will it be dark like this all the time?'

'There might be a little light through the grating when the day comes. Shall we go and look?'

We were so stiff and cramped that we could not move our limbs for some seconds.

'Listen!' said Hyson fearfully. 'I heard something!'

I listened with her, but I could hear nothing.

I felt my way cautiously down the steps, holding Hyson's hand as we went.

'There!' she whispered. 'I heard it again!'

She clung to me and I put my arm about her.

'If only we had a lighter or a match,' I murmured as we picked our way to where I thought the grating had been, but there was no light coming from the wall, so I guessed it was still dark outside. Then I saw a sudden flash of light; I heard a voice call: 'Favel! Hyson!'

The light had shown me the grating and I ran stumbling towards it shouting: 'We're here . . . in the vault. Favel and Hyson are here in the vault!'

The light came again and stayed. I recognized Deborah's voice. 'Favel! Is that you, Favel?'

'Here,' I cried. 'Here!'

'Oh, Favel! . . . thank God! Hyson . . .?'

'Hyson's here with me. We're locked in the vault.'

'Locked in . . .'

'Please get us out . . . quickly.'

'I'll be back . . . soon as I can.'

The light disappeared and Hyson and I stood still hugging each other.

It seemed hours before the door was opened and Roc came striding down the steps. We ran to him – Hyson and I – and he held us both against him.

'What the . . .' he began. 'You gave us a nice fright. . . .'

Morwenna was there with Charles, who picked Hyson up in his arms and held her as though she were a baby.

Their torches showed us the damp walls of the vault, the ledges with the coffins; but Hyson and I turned shuddering away and looked towards the door.

'Your hands are like ice,' said Roc, chafing them. 'We've got the cars by the lych gate. We'll be home in a few minutes.'

I lay against him in the car, too numb, too exhausted for speech.

I did manage to ask the time.

'Two o'clock,' Roc told me. 'We've been searching since soon after eight.'

I went straight to bed and Mrs. Penhalligan brought me hot soup. I said I shouldn't be able to sleep; in fact I should be afraid to, for fear I should dream I was back in that dreadful place.

But I did sleep – almost immediately; and I was untroubled by dreams.

It was nine o'clock that morning before the sun shining through the windows woke me. Roc was sitting in a chair near the bed watching me, and I felt very happy because I was alive.

'What happened?' asked Roc.

'I heard someone singing and the door of the vault was open.'

'You thought the Pendorrics had left their coffins and were having a little sing-song?'

'I didn't know who it was. I went down the steps and then . . . the door was locked on me.'

'What did you do?'

'Hammered on the door – called out. Hyson and I both used all our strength against it. Oh Roc . . . it was horrible.'

'Not the most pleasant spot to spend a night, I must say.'

'Roc, who could have done it? Who could have locked us in?'

'No one.'

'But someone *did*. Why, if Deborah hadn't come there looking for us we'd still be there. Heaven knows how long we should have been there.'

'We decided to search every inch of the land for miles around. Deborah and Morwenna did Pendorric village, and the Darks joined up with them.'

'It was wonderful when we heard Deborah's voice calling us. But it seemed ages before she came back.'

'She thought she needed the key, and there's only one I know of – to the vault. It's kept in the cupboard in my study, and the cupboard is locked; so she had to find me first.'

'That's why it took so long.'

'We didn't waste any time, I can tell you. I couldn't imagine who could have got at the key and unlocked the vault. The sexton borrowed it some weeks ago. He must have thought he locked it.'

'But someone locked us in.'

Roc said: 'No, darling. The door wasn't locked. I discovered that when I tried to unlock it.'

'Not locked! But . . .'

'Who would have locked you in?'

'That's what I'm wondering.'

'No one has a key except me. There has only been one for years. The key was locked in my cupboard. It was hanging on the nail there when I went to get it.'

'But Roc, I don't understand how . . .'

'I think it's simple enough. It was a misty evening, wasn't it? You passed the lych gate and went into the churchyard. The door of the vault was open because old Pengally hadn't locked it when he was there a few weeks ago and the door had blown open.'

'It was a very still evening. There was no wind.'

'There was a gale the night before. It had probably been open all day and no one had noticed it. Few people go to the old part of the graveyard. Well, you saw it open, and went inside. The door shut on you.'

'But if it wasn't locked why didn't it open when we pushed with all our strength?'

'I expect it jammed. Besides, you probably panicked to find yourself shut in. Perhaps if you'd not believed the door was locked you would have discovered it was only jammed.'

'I don't believe it.'

He looked at me in astonishment. 'What on earth's in your mind?'

'I don't quite know . . . but someone locked us in.'

'Who?'

'Someone did it.'

He smoothed the hair back from my forehead.

'There's only one person who could,' he said. 'Myself.'

'Oh Roc . . . *no!*'

He threw himself down beside me and took me into his arms.

'Let me tell you something darling,' he said. 'I'd far rather have you here with me than in that vault with Hyson.'

He was laughing; he did not understand the chill of fear which had taken possession of me.

Chapter Five

I could now no longer delude myself. I had to face up to all the fears which I had refused to look in the face during the last weeks.

Someone had deliberately lured me into the vault and locked me in, for I refused to believe Roc's theory that the door had jammed. In the first moments it was true that I may have panicked; but when I had discovered Hyson and sought to comfort her, I had regained my composure. We had both tried to open that door with all our strength and had failed. And the reason was that it had been locked.

This could mean only one thing. Someone wanted to harm me.

Suppose Deborah had not come by? Suppose she had not heard our call, how long could we have lived in the vault? There was a little air coming in, it was true; but we should have starved to death eventually, because it was a fact that few people came that way, and if they did we should not have heard them unless they had come close to the grating and called us.

It might have been one week . . . two weeks. We should have been dead by then.

I believed that that was what someone was trying to do: kill me, but in a way which, when my death was discovered, would appear accidental.

Who?

It would be the person who would benefit most from my death. Roc?

I couldn't believe that. I was perhaps illogical, as women in love are supposed to be; but I was not going to believe for one moment that Roc would kill me. He wouldn't kill anyone – least of all me. He was a gambler, I knew; he might even be unfaithful to me; but he could never in any circumstances commit murder.

If I died, he would be very rich. He had married me knowing that I was the granddaughter of a millionaire; he had brought me back to my grandfather, and it must have occurred to him that I would become his heir. He needed money for Pendorric, and Roc and I were partners so that my fortune would make certain that Pendorric remained entirely ours. This was all true; and whether I died or not, Pendorric was safe.

I refused to look beyond that; but I did believe that someone had locked me into the vault in the hope that I should not be discovered until I was dead.

That brought me back to the all-important question: Who?

I thought back over everything that had happened and my mind kept returning to the day when Roc had first come to the studio. My father must have known who he was as soon as he heard his name – there could not be many Pendorrics in the world – yet he had not told me. Why? Because my grandfather had not wanted me to know. Roc was to report on me first, take pictures of me. I smiled ruefully. That was typical of my grandfather's arrogance. As for Father, he had probably done everything he did for what he would believe to be my good.

And the day he died? Roc had seemed strange that day. Or had he? He had come back to the studio and left my father to bathe alone. And when he knew what had happened, had he seemed . . . relieved, or had I imagined it?

I must stop thinking of Roc in this way, because if I was going to find out who was seeking to harm me I must look elsewhere.

There had been an occasion when I had taken the dangerous cliff path after the rain, and the warning had been removed. I remembered how uneasy I had felt then. But it was Roc who had remembered the path and dashed after me. It was reassuring to remember that. But why should it be reassuring? Because it showed that Roc loved me and wanted to protect me; that he could not possibly have had a hand in this.

But of course I knew he hadn't.

Who, then?

My mind went at once to those women in whom, I believed, he had once been interested . . . perhaps still was. One could never be quite sure with Roc. Rachel? Althea? And what of Dinah Bond?

I remembered that she had once told me that Morwenna had been locked in the vault. What of the conversation I had heard between Morwenna and Charles? Oh, but it was natural that they should talk of my inheritance, that they should be pleased because Roc had married an heiress instead of a penniless girl. Why should Morwenna want to be rid of me? What difference could it make to her?

But if I were out of the way my fortune would go to Roc and he would be free to marry . . . Rachel . . . Althea?

Rachel had been there when we had talked about the bride in the oak chest; and if I could believe Dinah Bond, she had, long ago, locked Morwenna in the vault. She had known where to get the key; but there was only one key and Roc had that; it was an enormous key that hung in his cupboard, and the cupboard was kept locked. When they had unlocked the vault they had had to find Roc first because he had the only key.

Rachel had known this and she had managed somehow, all those years ago, to get the key from Roc's father's cupboard.

Rachel, I thought. I had never liked her from the moment I had first seen her.

I was going to watch Rachel.

Morwenna said that such an experience was bound to have shocked me, and I ought to take things easily for the next few days. She was going to see that Hyson did.

'I'd rather it had been Lowella who was locked in with you,' she told me one day when I came out of the house and saw her working on the flower-beds on one of the front lawns. 'Hyson's too sensitive as it is.'

'It was a horrible experience.'

Morwenna straightened up and looked at me. 'For both of you. You poor dear! I should have been terrified.'

A shadow passed across her face and I guessed she was remembering that occasion, so long ago, when Rachel had locked her in and refused to let her out until she made a promise.

Deborah came out of the house.

'It's a lovely day,' she said. 'I'm beginning to wonder what my own garden is looking like.'

'Getting homesick?' asked Morwenna. She smiled at me. 'Deborah's like that. When she's on Dartmoor she thinks of Pendorric, and when she's here she gets homesick for the moor.'

'Yes, I love both places so much. They both seem like home to me. I was thinking, Favel, this horrible affair . . . it's been such a shock, and you're not looking so well. Is she, Morwenna?'

'An experience like that is bound to upset anyone. I expect she'll have fully recovered in a day or so.'

'I thought of going to the moor for a week or so. Why not come with me, Favel? I'd love to show you the place.'

'Oh . . . how kind of you!'

Leave Roc? I was thinking. Leave him to Althea? To Rachel? And how could I rest until I had solved this matter? I must find out who had a grudge against me, who wanted me out of the way. No doubt it would be very restful to spend a week with Deborah, but all the time I should be longing to be back in Pendorric.

'As a matter of fact,' I went on, 'I've got such lots to do here . . . and there's Roc. . . .'

'Don't forget,' Morwenna reminded Deborah, 'they haven't been married so very long.'

Deborah's face fell. 'Well, perhaps some other time – but I thought that you needed a little rest and . . .'

'I do appreciate your thinking of it and I shall look forward to coming later on.'

'I wish you'd take Hyson,' said Morwenna. 'This business has upset her more than you think.'

'Well, I must take dear Hyson,' replied Deborah. 'But I did so want to show Favel our old home.'

I laid my hand on her arm. 'You are kind, and I do hope you'll ask me again soon.'

'Of course I shall. I shall positively pester you until you accept. Were you going for a walk?'

'I was just going over to Polhorgan. There are one or two things I have to see Mrs. Dawson about.'

'May I walk with you?'

'It would be a great pleasure.'

We left Morwenna to her flowers and took the road to Polhorgan. I felt rather guilty about refusing Deborah's invitation and was anxious that she should not think me churlish.

I tried to explain to her.

'Of course I understand, my dear. You don't want to leave your husband. As a matter of fact I'm sure Roc would protest if you suggested it. But one day perhaps later on you'll come for a week-end when he has to go away. He does sometimes, on business, you know. We'll choose our opportunity. It was just that I thought, after that . . .'

She shivered.

'If it hadn't been for you we might be there still.'

'I've never ceased to be thankful that I happened to go into the graveyard. It was just that I was determined to search every square inch. And when I think how chancey it was I shudder. I might have walked right round the vault and you might not have heard me, nor I you.'

'I don't like thinking of it . . . even in broad daylight. It's so extraordinary, too, that Roc says the door wasn't locked . . . only jammed. I must say I feel a little foolish about that.'

'Well, of course a door *could* get jammed.'

'But we were so desperate. We hammered with all our might. It seems incredible. And yet there's only the one key and that was locked in Roc's cupboard.'

'So,' she went on, 'the only one who could have locked you in would have been Roc.' She laughed at the ludicrous idea; and I laughed with her.

'There used to be two keys, I remember,' she went on. 'Roc's father kept one in the cupboard there where Roc keeps it now.'

'And who had the other?'

She paused for a few seconds, then she said: 'Barbarina.'

We were silent after that and scarcely spoke until we said good-bye at Polhorgan.

I had never enjoyed going to Polhorgan since my grandfather's death. The place seemed so empty and useless without him; it had an air of being unlived-in, which I always think is so depressing – like a woman whose life has never been fulfilled. Roc often laughed at me for my feeling about houses; as though, he said, they had a personality of their own. Well, at the moment Polhorgan's personality was a negative one. Of course, I thought, if I filled it with orphans who had never seen the sea, had never had any care and attention, what a different house it would be!

Idealistic dreams! I could hear Roc's voice. 'Wait until you see how the bureaucrats are going to punish you. This is the Robin Hood State, in which the rich are robbed to help the poor.'

I didn't care what difficulties I should encounter. I was going to have my orphans – if fewer than I had first dreamed of.

Mrs. Dawson came out to greet me.

'Good morning, madam. Dawson and I were wondering if you'd come; and as you have, would you be pleased to take a cup of coffee in our sitting-room? There's something on our minds. . . .'

I said I should be delighted to, and Mrs. Dawson told me she would make the coffee at once and send for Dawson.

Ten minutes later I was in the Dawsons' comfortable sitting-room, drinking a cup of Mrs. Dawson's coffee.

Dawson had some difficulty in getting to the point, which I quickly perceived was an elaboration of the suspicions which had occurred to him the night my grandfather died.

'You see, madam, it's not easy to put into words. A man's afraid of saying too much . . . then again he's afraid of not saying enough.'

Dawson was the typical butler. Dignified, and self-assured, he was the type of manservant my grandfather would have insisted on having, because he was what Roc would have called a *cliché* butler in the same way that my grandfather was the *cliché* self-made man.

'You can be perfectly frank with me, Dawson,' I told him. 'I'll not repeat anything you say unless you wish me to.'

Dawson looked relieved. 'I would not wish, madam, to be taken to the courts by the woman in question. Although if it should be true that she had been there before, that could well be counted in my favour.'

'You mean Nurse Grey?'

Dawson said that he meant no other. 'I am not satisfied, madam, about the nature of his lordship's death; and having talked together, Mrs. Dawson and I have come to the conclusion that it was brought about by a deliberate act.'

'You mean because the pills were discovered under the bed?'

'Yes, madam, his lordship had had one or two minor attacks during the day, and Mrs. Dawson and I had noticed that often attacks would follow closely on one another, so it seemed almost certain that he would have another attack some time during the night.'

'Wouldn't he call the nurse when he had these attacks during the night?'

'Only if the attack got so bad he needed morphia. Then he'd ring the bell on his side table. But first he'd take his pill. The bell was on the floor too, madam, with the pills.'

'Yes, and it looked as though he knocked them over when reaching for the pills.'

'That may have been how it was intended to look, madam.'

'You are suggesting that Nurse Grey deliberately put the pills and the bell out of his reach?'

'Only within these four walls, madam.'

'But why should she wish him dead? She has lost a good job.'

'She had a good legacy,' put in Mrs. Dawson. 'And what's to prevent her finding another job where she'll get another legacy?'

'But you're not suggesting that she kills off her patients for the sake of the leagacies they leave her?'

'It might be so, madam, and I feel impelled to explain my suspicions regarding this young woman, and they are that she is an adventuress who needs to be watched.'

'Dawson,' I said, 'my grandfather is dead and buried. Dr. Clement was satisfied that he died from natural causes.'

'Mrs. Dawson and I don't doubt Dr. Clement's word, madam; but what we think is that his lordship was hastened to his death.'

'This is a terrible accusation, Dawson.'

'I know, madam; and that is why I would not want it to go beyond these four walls; but I thought you should be warned of our suspicions, the young woman still being in the neighbourhood.'

Mrs. Dawson stared thoughtfully into her coffee cup. 'I was talking to Mrs. Greenock,' she said, 'who owns Cormorant Cottage.'

'That's where Nurse Grey is living now, isn't it?'

'Yes, having a little rest between posts, so she says. Well, Mrs. Greenock wasn't very keen on letting to her. She was really after a long let that would go on all through the winter, and Nurse Grey wanted it for what she called an indefinite period. But it seems Mr. Pendorric persuaded Mrs. Greenock to let Nurse Grey have it.'

I was beginning to understand why the Dawsons had wanted to talk to me. They were not only underlining their suspicions as to why my grandfather had died when he did, but were telling me that we had an adventuress in our midst, who was none too scrupulous, and was more friendly with my husband than they considered wise.

If they had wanted to make me feel uneasy they had certainly succeeded.

I changed the subject as inconspicuously as I could; we talked about the problems of Polhorgan, and I told them that I wanted them to go on as they were until I made up my mind what to do about the house. I assured them that I had no intention of selling and that I wanted them to remain there and hoped they always would.

They were delighted with me as their new employer. Mrs. Dawson told me so with tears in her eyes and Dawson implied, without sacrificing one part of his dignity, that it was a pleasure to serve me.

But I was very unhappy because I knew that they had spoken as they did out of a genuine concern for my welfare.

That afternoon I went to see the Clements because I wanted to talk to the doctor unprofessionally about my grandfather.

Mabell Clement was emerging triumphant from what she called the pot house when I arrived, her hair half up, half down, and she was dressed in a cotton blouse and bunchy yellow skirt.

'Nice surprise,' she declared breezily. 'Andrew will be pleased. Come in and I'll make you a cup of tea. It's been one of the most successful days I've had for a long time.'

Andrew came to the door of the house to meet me and told me that I'd come at a fortunate time because it was his afternoon off, and his partner, Dr. Lee, was on duty.

Mabell made the tea, and, because she couldn't find the cosy, put a woollen balaclava over the pot. There were toasted scones – a little burned – and a cake which had sagged in the middle.

'It tastes rather like a Christmas pudding,' Mabell warned.

'I like Christmas pudding,' I assured her.

I liked Mabell too; she was one of the few people who were unimpressed by my sudden wealth.

While we were having tea I told Dr. Clement that I was disturbed about my grandfather's death.

'Could he have lived much longer if he hadn't had that attack?' I asked.

'He could have, yes. But we had to expect such attacks, and their consequences could be fatal. I was not in the least surprised when I got the call.'

'No, but he might have been alive now if he had been able to reach his pills in time.'

'Has Dawson been talking to you again?'

'Dawson spoke to you about this, didn't he?' I countered.

'Yes, at the time your grandfather died. He found the pills and the bell on the floor.'

'If he had been able to reach his pills . . . or his bell . . .'

'It seemed perfectly clear that he had tried and had knocked them over. In the circumstances a major attack developed, and . . . that was the end.'

Mabell brought over the cake which was like a Christmas pudding and I took a piece.

'It's over now,' she said gently. 'It's only disturbing to go over something that's finished.'

'Yet I would like to know.'

'Actually I think the Dawsons didn't get on with the nurse,' Mabell went on. 'Nurses are notoriously bossy; butlers notoriously dignified; housekeepers tend to regard the house as their domain and resent anyone but their employers. I think it was just not very unusual domestic strife; and now the Dawsons see a chance of settling an old score.'

'You see,' said Andrew, 'Dawson could suggest she deliberately put the pills and bell out of reach; she would emphatically deny it. There could be no proof either way.'

'She looks like a piece of Dresden china but I reckon she's as sturdy as earthenware,' mused Mabell. 'It must have been a pleasant job she had with Lord Polhorgan. In any case she seemed to like it. How long had she been with him?'

'More than eighteen months,' said Andrew.

'Was she a good nurse?' I asked.

'Quite efficient.'

'She seemed . . . hard,' I suggested.

'She was a nurse, and as such had had some experience of suffering. Nurses . . . doctors . . . you know they can't feel the same as someone like yourself. We see too much of it.'

'I know I can trust you two,' I said, 'so I'll say this: Do you think that she discovered she would get a thousand pounds when my grandfather died and that made her hasten his death?'

There was silence. Mabell took a long amber cigarette holder, opened a silver box and offered me a cigarette.

'Because,' I said slowly, 'if she would do a thing like that, it's rather a sobering thought that she's going into other sickrooms, and the lives of other patients will be put into her hands.'

Dr. Clement watched me intently. Then he said: 'At the moment she's resting. She's taking a holiday before going to a new post, and I think it would be very unwise to talk of this matter beyond this room.'

Mabell changed the subject in her blunt way. 'I suppose you've quite recovered from that midnight adventure of yours.'

'Oh . . . yes.'

'An unpleasant experience,' commented Andrew.

'I shiver even now when I think of it.'

'The door was jammed, wasn't it?'

'I was certain that we were locked in.'

'All the rain we've been having might make the door jam,' said Andrew. 'Yet . . .'

Mabell thoughtfully knocked the ash from her cigarette. 'Who on earth would have locked you in?'

'That's what I've been wondering ever since.'

Andrew leaned forward. 'So you don't believe the door jammed?'

I hesitated. What impression was I giving them? First I was repeating Dawson's suggestions against Nurse Grey, and now I was hinting that someone had locked me in the vault. They were two intelligent, uninhibited people. They would think I had a persecution mania if I was not careful.

'The general opinion seemed to be that the door had jammed. There was only one key anyway, and that was locked in a cupboard in my husband's study. He brought it down to the vault and it was he who found the door wasn't locked at all.'

'Well, thank heaven they did discover you.'

'If Deborah hadn't happened to come that way – and it was really purest chance that she did – goodness knows how long we should have been there. Perhaps we should be there now.'

'Oh no!' protested Mabell.

'Why not? Such things have been known to happen.'

Andrew lifted his shoulders. 'It didn't happen.'

'In future,' Mabell put in, 'you must be very careful.'

Andrew leaned forward and there was a puzzled expression in his eyes.

'Yes,' he repeated, 'in future you must be very careful.'

Mabell laughed rather nervously and began to talk about a pot she had made which she thought was unusual. When it was fired she wanted my opinion.

I felt that when I was not there they would talk of my affairs. They would say it was surprising that the door of the vault had been jammed and not locked and, perhaps, that Roc had the only key. They would undoubtedly have heard that Roc had persuaded Mrs. Greenock to let Althea Grey have Cormorant Cottage; and they would ask themselves: What is happening at Pendorric?

My uneasiness was deepening.

I didn't want to talk any more about the disturbed thoughts which were turning over in my mind; I feared that I had already said too much to the Clements. I wished that I could have talked to Roc of my fears, but I imagined he would laugh at them – besides, he himself was so much involved.

I tried therefore to go on as normally as possible. So exactly a week after my unfortunate adventure I called on Jesse Pleydell again. He greeted me with more than his usual warmth and made it very clear that he was glad I had come. So he too had heard the story.

We no longer sat outside his cottage – the afternoon was too chilly. I was in his own arm-chair, which he insisted on giving up to me while he made me a cup of tea.

He did allow me to pour it out, and when we were sitting opposite each other he said: 'I was worried like when I heard 'em talking.'

'You mean about . . .'

''Twere the last time you did come and see me.'

'It was very unfortunate.'

He shook his head. 'I don't like it much.'

'I didn't either.'

'You see, it's like as though . . .'

'We decided the sexton left the door open when he was last there, and that it must have been open for some time. Nobody noticed because . . . nobody went near it.'

'Oh, I don't know,' murmured Jesse.

We were silent for some time, then he said: 'Well, me dear, I reckon you should take extra care like. I reckon you should.'

'Jesse, what are you thinking?'

'If only these old eyes hadn't been so blind I should have seen who was up there in the gallery with her.'

'Jesse, have you any idea who it was?'

Jesse screwed up his face and beat on his knee. 'I'm feared I do,' he whispered.

'You think it was Lowella Pendorric, who died all those years ago.'

'I couldn't see like. But I be feared, for she were the bride, and 'twas said after, that she was marked for death as soon as she was the Bride of Pendorric.'

'And you think that I . . .'

'I think you have to take care, Mrs. Pendorric. I think you haven't got to go where harm can come to 'ee.'

'Perhaps you're right, Jesse,' I said, and after a pause: 'Your Michaelmas daisies are looking a picture.'

'Aye, reckon so. The bees be that busy on 'em. I was always one for Michaelmas daisies, though 'tis sad to see them since it means the end of summer.'

I left him, and as I came past the cottages and saw the church ahead of me I stopped at the lych gate and looked into the graveyard.

'Hello, Mrs. Pendorric.'

There was Dinah Bond coming towards me. 'I heard about 'ee,' she said. 'Poor Mrs. Pendorric. I reckon you was scared in that place.' She was almost laughing at me. 'You should have let me read your hand,' she went on. 'I might have warned you.'

'You weren't anywhere around when it happened, I suppose?' I asked.

'Oh no. My Jim had taken me into market with him. We didn't get back till late. Heard about it next morning though. I was sorry because I can guess what it feels like to be in that dark place.' She came up to the lych gate and leaned on it. 'I've been thinking,' she went on, 'there's something strange about this. Has it struck you that things seem to be happening twice?'

'What do you mean?'

'Well, Morwenna was shut in the vault, wasn't her? And then you were, with Hyson. Looks as though someone remembered that and thought to try it again.'

'Do you think someone locked me in, then? The general belief is that the door jammed.'

'Who's to say?' She shrugged her shoulders. 'Then there was Barbarina being an heiress and marrying a Pendorric, and there was Louisa Sellick, who had to go and live near Dozmary because of it. Now there's you – awful rich, they tell me you be, Mrs. Pendorric – and you're the New Bride while . . .'

'Please go on.'

She laughed. 'You wouldn't let me read your hand, would you? You didn't believe I was any good. All right, you wouldn't believe what I could tell 'ee. But 'tis all of a piece and so seems as though it was meant, if you get what I mean.'

'I'm afraid I don't.'

She came through the lych gate and walked past me, smiling as she went.

'You be awful rich, Mrs. Pendorric,' she murmured, 'but you bain't very bright, I'd say.'

She looked over her shoulder at me; then she began to walk towards the

forge, swinging her hips in the provocative way which was second nature
to her.

All this did not comfort me. I was longing to have a talk with Roc and
tell him what was in my mind, but something warned me not to. It was of
course the fact that I was not at all sure where Roc fitted into this.

The house seemed quiet. Deborah had taken Hyson and Carrie with her
to Devonshire; and Lowella had refused to do any lessons since her sister
was having a holiday. 'It wouldn't be fair to Hyson,' she explained piously.
'I should go so far ahead of her that she'd never catch up.'

Morwenna, declaring that this was hardly likely, at the same time gave
way, and Lowella, who had become suddenly attached to her father – her
affections changed as frequently as the winds – insisted on spending a lot
of time at the home farm with him.

I found myself constantly listening for the sound of singing or the playing
of a violin, and I became aware that that adventure in the vault had upset
me more than I cared to admit. I wanted to get away from the house to
think, so I took the car one afternoon and went on to the moor.

In the first place I had no intention of going the way I had before. I
merely wanted to be alone to think; and I wanted to do my thinking right
away from the house, because I was beginning to suspect that the house had
an effect on me, making me more fanciful than I should otherwise have
been.

I drew up on a lonely stretch of moor, shut off the engine and, lighting
a cigarette, sat back to brood. I went over every detail of what had happened
from the first day I had seen Roc; and whichever way I looked, one thought
kept hammering in my mind: He knew that I was an heiress when he
married me.

Dinah Bond had marvelled how events repeated themselves. Barbarina
had been married for her money when her husband would have preferred
Louisa Sellick. Had I been married for mine when my husband would have
preferred . . .?

It was something I refused to accept. He could never have been such a
good actor as to deceive me so utterly. I thought of the passion between us;
I thought of the ways in which he had made love to me. Surely that could
not have been all lies. I could hear his voice coming back to me: 'I'm a
gambler, darling, but I never risk losing what I can't do without.'

He had never pretended to be a saint. He had never told me that I was
the first woman he had ever loved. He had not denied that he was a gambler.

What had happened that day when he went down to swim with my
father? What was I thinking now! My father's death had nothing to do with
all this. That had been an unfortunate accident.

I threw away my cigarette, started up the car and drove on for some miles
without noticing the direction in which I was going; then suddenly I was
aware that I was lost.

The moor looked so much the same whatever road one took. I could only
drive on until I came to a signpost.

This I did, and when I saw Dozmary on it I discovered I was very eager to have another glimpse of the boy who looked so like Roc. After all, I told myself, Louisa Sellick had played a part in the story of Barbarina, and it seemed as though her story was very closely linked with my own.

When I reached the Pool I left the car and went down to the water's edge; it looked cold and grey and the place was deserted. Leaving the car I started to walk, until I found the road which led to the house.

I started up this, then it occurred to me that if I met the boy again he might recognize me and wonder why I had come back; and as there was another path branching from this one – nothing more than a cart track – I took this and found I was mounting a slight incline.

Now I had a good view of the front of the house, although there were several large clumps of bracken between me and the road in which it stood. I sat down beside one of these clumps and looked at the house, which I could now study at my leisure. I saw a stable, and I guessed that the boy had his own horse; there was also a garage, and the garden at the front and sides of the house was well kept. I caught a glimpse of green-houses. It was a comfortable house set in rather unusual surroundings, for it didn't appear to have any neighbours. It must be rather lonely for Louisa Sellick when the boy went away to school, which I supposed he must do. Who was the boy? Her son? But he would be too young. He couldn't be more than thirteen or fourteen; surely Petroc Pendorric had been dead longer than that.

Then who was the boy? That was another of those questions which I didn't want to think too much about. There was beginning to be quite a number of them.

Suddenly the door of the glass-roofed porch opened and someone came out. It was the boy again. I could see the resemblance to Roc even from where I was. He seemed to be talking to someone in the house; then she came out. I think I must have cowered into the bracken, for I was suddenly afraid of being recognized, because the woman who had come out of Bedivere House was Rachel Bective.

She and the boy walked towards a car, and I recognized it as the little grey Morris from the Pendorric garages.

She got into it, and the boy stood waving while she drove away.

In a moment of panic it occurred to me that she might pass my car and recognize it. I ran down the cart track, and as I came to the main road I was relieved because she had gone in a direction away from where my car was parked.

I walked slowly back and drove thoughtfully home.

Why, I asked myself, was Rachel Bective visiting the boy who was so obviously a Pendorric?

Deborah and Hyson and Carrie returned to Pendorric after a few days. I thought the child looked pale and that the holiday had not done her much good.

'She misses Lowella,' Morwenna told me. 'They're never completely happy apart although they quarrel almost all the time when they're together.'

Deborah smiled sadly. 'When you're a twin you understand these things,' she said. '*We* do, don't we, Morwenna?'

'Yes, I suppose so,' replied Morwenna. 'Roc and I were very close always, though we rarely quarrelled.'

'Roc would never take the trouble to quarrel with anyone,' murmured Deborah. She turned to me: 'My dear, you're not looking as well as I should like to see you. You should have come with us. My moorland air would have done you the world of good.'

'Oh come, it's not as good as our sea air surely,' laughed Morwenna.

'It's change that's good for everyone.'

'I'm so glad you've come back,' I told Deborah. 'I've missed you.'

She was very pleased. 'Come up with me. I've brought you a little present from home.'

'For me! How charming of you!'

'It's something I treasure.'

'Then I shouldn't take it.'

'You must, my dear. What point would there be in giving you something I want to get rid of?'

She slipped her arm through mine and I thought: Perhaps I can ask Deborah. Not outright, of course, but perhaps indirectly. After all, she would know what was happening better than most people.

We went up to her bedroom, where Carrie was unpacking.

'Carrie,' cried Deborah, 'where's the little gift I brought for Mrs. Pendorric?'

'Here,' said Carrie without looking at me.

'Carrie hates leaving her beloved moor,' Deborah whispered to me.

She was holding out a small object wrapped in tissue paper. I opened it, and although it was one of the most exquisite things I had ever seen, I was dismayed. For in a frame set with jade and topaz was a delicate miniature of a young girl, her hair falling about her shoulders, her eyes serene.

'Barbarina,' I whispered.

Deborah was smiling down at the lovely face. 'I know how interested you have always been in her and I thought you'd like to have it.'

'It's a beautiful thing. It must be very valuable.'

'I'm so glad you like it.'

'Is there one of *you*? I would rather have that.'

My words evidently pleased her, for she looked very beautiful suddenly. 'People always wanted to paint Barbarina,' she said. 'Father invited lots of artists to the house – he was interested in the arts – and they used to say: "We must paint the twins, and we'll begin with Barbarina." They sometimes did; and when it was my turn, they forgot. I told you, didn't I, that she had something that I lacked. It drew everyone to her – and because I was so like her, I seemed like a pale shadow . . . a carbon copy, you might say, a little blurred, much less attractive.'

'Do you know, Deborah,' I said, 'you underrate yourself. I'm sure you were every bit as attractive.'

'Oh Favel, what a dear child you are! I feel so grateful to Roc for finding you and bringing you to us.'

'It's I who should be grateful. Everyone's been so kind to me . . . particularly you.'

'I? Boring you with my old photographs and chatter about the past!'

'I've found it immensely interesting. I want to ask you lots of things.'

'What's stopping you? Come and sit in the window. Oh, it *is* good to be back. I love the moor, but the sea is more exciting, perhaps. It's so unpredictable.'

'You must have missed the moor when Roc and Morwenna were young and you were looking after them.'

'Sometimes, but when they went away to school I'd go to Devonshire.'

'Did they go to Devon for school holidays?'

'Almost always they were at Pendorric. Then of course Morwenna started bringing Rachel for holidays, and it seemed to be a natural thing that she should come to us every time. Morwenna was extraordinarily fond of her for some reason. And she wasn't really a pleasant child. She locked Morwenna in the vault, once. Just for fun! *You* can understand how terrified poor Morwenna was. She had a nightmare soon after it happened and told me about it when I went in to comfort her. But it didn't make any difference to the friendship, and when Roc and Morwenna went to France, Rachel went with them.'

'When was that?'

'It was when they were older. They would have been about eighteen then. I always hoped that Morwenna would drop her, but she never did. And at that time the three of them became very friendly.'

'When they were about eighteen . . .'

'Yes. Morwenna was anxious to go to France. She wanted to improve her accent; and she said she'd like to go for two months. She had finished at her English boarding school and I was thinking that she might go abroad to school; but she said it would be much better for her to stay in some *pension* where she would learn the language, by mixing with people, more easily than she ever would at school.'

'And Morwenna went to France for two months.'

'Rachel went with her. So did Roc for a while. I was a bit alarmed at that time. Roc was with them so much and I was beginning to be afraid that he and Rachel . . .'

'You wouldn't have welcomed . . . that?'

'My dear, I expect I'm being rather mean, but somehow I should not have liked to see Rachel mistress of Pendorric. She hasn't the . . . charm. Oh, she's an educated girl, but there's something I don't like about her . . . something I don't altogether trust. This is strictly between ourselves, of course! I wouldn't say it to anyone else.'

'I think I know what you mean.'

'She's too sharp. One gets the idea that she's watching for the main chance all the time. I expect it's my stupid imagination, but I can tell you I had some very deep qualms at that time, because Roc was so anxious to see the girls settled in their *pension* comfortably. And he actually stayed there for a while and went back and forth while they were there. Every time he returned I was terrified that he would announce his intentions. Fortunately it all fell through.'

'It was a long time ago,' I said.

Deborah nodded.

I was thinking. They were eighteen, and the boy could be about fourteen now. Roc is thirty-two.

I had often felt that Rachel had some hold on the Pendorrics. She gave that impression. She was like a person with a chip on her shoulder and yet at the same time there was a certain truculence about her. It was as though she was continually implying: Treat me as a member of the family or else. . .!

And she visited the boy who was living with Louisa Sellick!

I said: 'I suppose at that time their father was dead . . . I mean Roc's and Morwenna's.'

'They were about eleven when he died. It was six years after Barbarina. . .'

So the boy was not his, I thought. Oh Roc, why do you keep these secrets from me? There's no need.

My impulse was to talk to Roc at the earliest opportunity, to tell him what I had conjectured.

When I went to my room I put the miniature on the mantelshelf and stood for some minutes looking into the serene eyes depicted there.

Then I decided to wait a while, to try to find out more about the nature of this web in which I was becoming entangled.

In the midst of this uncertainty Mabell Clement gave a party. When Roc and I drove over, we were both a little subdued; I felt weighed down with thoughts of the boy who lived on the moors, and conjectures as to what part Roc had played in bringing him into the world. I longed to talk to Roc and yet I was afraid to do so. Actually I was afraid to face up to the fact that Roc might not tell me the truth. I was pathetically eager that he should not lie to me, and at the same time I was desperately trying to keep intact that wonderful happiness which I had known.

As for Roc, he was telling himself that my adventure in the vault had naturally upset me a good deal and that I should need time to recover.

He treated me gently, and reminded me of those days immediately following my father's death.

Mabell, ear-rings swinging, was a wonderful hostess and there was an informal atmosphere about the party. Several of the local artists were present, for our scenery had made the district an artists' colony; and I was gratified when one of them mentioned my father and spoke with reverence of his work.

From the other side of the room I heard Roc's laughter and saw that he was the centre of a group, mainly women. He seemed to be amusing them, and I wished that I was with them. And how I wished that there were no more doubts and that I could escape from my misgivings into that complete and unadulterated happiness which no one on earth but Roc could give to me.

'Here's someone who wants to meet you.' Mabell was at my elbow and with her was a young man. I looked at him for some seconds before I recognized him.

'John Poldree, you remember?' he said.

'Why yes. The ball . . .'

Mabell gave him a little push towards me and then was gone.

'It was a wonderful ball,' he went on.

'I'm so glad you enjoyed it.'

'And very sad of course that . . .'

I nodded.

'There was something I wanted to tell you, Mrs. Pendorric. Though I don't suppose it matters much now.'

'Yes?'

'It's about the nurse.'

'Nurse Grey?'

'M'm. Where I'd seen her before.'

'And you remember?'

'Yes. It was something in one of the papers. It came back to me. Then I remembered that I was in Genoa at the time and it wasn't all that easy to get English papers. Having fixed the date I went and looked up old copies. She's the one all right. Nurse Althea Stoner Grey, Nurse Stoner Grey, she was called. If I'd heard the double-barrelled name I'd have remembered. But I couldn't mistake the face. It's rarely that you find a face as perfect as that one.'

'What did you find out?'

'I'm afraid I misjudged her. I'd got it into my head that she'd committed some crime. Hope I didn't give you the wrong impression. All the same it wasn't very pleasant. She was lucky to have a name like Stoner Grey. She could drop the first part and seem like a different person. After all, Grey's a fairly common name. Coupled with Stoner, far from it. She lost the case.'

'What was the case, then?'

'She'd been nursing an old man and he'd left her money; his estranged wife contested the will. It was only a few paragraphs and you know how disjointed these newspaper reports can be.'

'When did all this happen?'

'About six years ago.'

'I expect she's had a case or two in between that and coming to my grandfather.'

'No doubt of it.'

'Well, she must have brought good references to my grandfather, I imagine. He was the sort who would make sure of that.'

'That wouldn't be difficult with a woman like that. She's got a way of getting round people. You can see that. She's pretty hard-boiled, I should think.'

'I should think so too.'

He laughed. 'I wanted to tell you ever since I solved the mystery. I expect she's far away by now.'

'No. She's still living fairly near us. She's taking a little holiday and renting a cottage for a time. My grandfather left her a small legacy, so she probably feels she can afford a rest.'

'Must be a lucrative job – private nursing – providing you have the foresight to choose rich patients.'

'Of course, you couldn't be sure that they would conveniently die and leave the legacy.'

He lifted his shoulders. 'Smart woman, that one. I think she'd be the sort who'd choose with care.' He had picked up one of the pieces of pottery which were lying about the studio. 'Good, this,' he said.

And for him the subject was closed; but not for me. I could not get Nurse Grey out of mind, and when I thought of her I thought of Roc.

I was very quiet during the drive back to Pendorric.

I had noticed a change in Morwenna; there were days when she gave me the impression that she was walking in her sleep; and her dreams seemed to be happy ones, for at times her expression was almost rapturous. She was absent-minded, too, and I had on one or two occasions spoken to her and received no answer.

She came up to our room one evening when we were changing for dinner. 'There's something I want to tell you two.'

'We're all ears,' Roc told her.

She sat down and did not speak for a few seconds. Roc looked at me, his eyebrows raised.

'I didn't want to say anything to any of you until I was absolutely sure.'

'The suspense is becoming unbearable,' commented Roc lightly.

'I've told Charles, of course, and I wanted to tell you two before it became generally known.'

'Are we soon to hear the patter of little feet in the Pendorric nurseries?' asked Roc.

She stood up. 'Oh . . . Roc!' she cried, and threw herself into his arms. He hugged her and then began waltzing round the room with her. He stopped abruptly with exaggerated concern. 'Ah, we have to take great care of you now.' He released her and putting his hand on her shoulder kissed her cheek solemnly. 'Wenna,' he said, reverting to his childhood's name for her, 'I'm delighted. It's wonderful. Bless you.'

There was real emotion in his voice, and I was touched to see the affection between them.

'I knew you'd be pleased.'

I felt as though I were shut out of their rejoicing; and it occurred to me how very close they were, because Morwenna seemed to have forgotten my existence and I knew that when she had said she wanted to tell us first she had meant she had wanted to tell Roc. Of course, they were twins, and how true it was that the bond between twins was strong!

They suddenly seemed to remember me, and Morwenna immediately brought me into the picture.

'You'll think we're crazy, Favel.'

'No, of course not. I think it's wonderful news. Congratulations!'

She clasped her hands together and murmured: 'If only you knew!'

'We'll pray for a boy,' said Roc.

'It must be a boy this time – it must.'

'And what does old Charles say?'

'What do you think! He's rapturous. He's already thinking up names.'

'Make sure it's a good old Cornish name, but we don't want any more Petrocs about the place for a while.'

Morwenna said to me: 'After all these years. It does seem marvellous. You see, we've always wanted a boy. . . .'

We all went down to dinner together, and after the meal Roc proposed the health of the mother-to-be, and we all became quite hilarious.

Next day I had a talk with Morwenna, who had become more friendly, I thought; I liked her new serenity.

She told me that she was three months pregnant and had started to plan the child's layette; and she was so certain that it was going to be a boy that I was a little afraid for her, because I realized how disappointed she would be if it should be a girl.

'You probably think that I'm behaving like a young girl about to have her first baby,' she said with a laugh. 'Well, that's how I feel. Charles wanted a boy so much . . . and so do I, and I always felt I was letting him down in some way by not producing one.'

'I'm sure he didn't feel that.'

'Charles is such a *good* man. He would never show resentment. But I know he longed for a son. I'll have to be careful nothing goes wrong. It did about five years ago. I had a miscarriage and was very ill, and Dr. Elgin, who was here before Andrew Clement, said I shouldn't make any more attempts . . . not for some time in any case. So you see how we feel.'

'Well, you must take the greatest care.'

'Of course one can take too much care. Some people think you should carry on as normally as possible for as long as possible.'

'I'm sure you'll be all right; but suppose it should be a girl?'

Her face fell.

'You'd love it just the same,' I assured her. 'People always do.'

'I should love her, but it wouldn't be the same. I long for a boy, Favel. I can't tell you how I long for a boy.'

'What name have you decided to give him?' I asked. 'Or haven't you thought of that?'

'Charles is insisting that if it's a boy we call him Ennis. It's a name that's been given to lots of Pendorrics. If you and Roc have a son you'll call him Petroc. That's the custom: the eldest son of the eldest son. But Ennis is as Cornish as Petroc. It's rather charming, don't you think?'

'Ennis,' I repeated.

She was smiling, and the intensity of her expression disturbed me.

'He's certain to be Ennis,' she went on.

I turned to the book of baby patterns which was lying on her lap and expressed more interest in it than I really felt.

So even Morwenna's news added to my uneasiness. Ennis was a family name; and the boy on the moor had the looks as well as the name; Morwenna had taken Rachel away and Roc had been at hand to help make arrangements;

he had visited them during their sojourn abroad, and Deborah had been afraid that Roc was going to marry Rachel.

I thought I was controlling my suspicions, but I couldn't hide them from Roc.

One day he announced that he was going to take me out for the day. I mustn't imagine I knew Cornwall just because I had seen our little corner; he was going to take me farther afield.

There was an autumnal mist in the air when we left Pendorric in the Daimler, but Roc assured me that it was only the pride of the morning; the sun would break through before long; and he was right.

We drove on to the moor, and then turned northward and stopped at a country hotel for lunch.

It was over this meal that I realized Roc had brought me out to talk seriously to me.

'Now,' he said, filling my glass with Chablis, 'let's have it.'

'Have what?'

'What's on your mind?'

'On my mind?'

'Darling, innocence, in this case, is unbecoming. You know perfectly well what I mean. You've been looking at me for the last week or so as though you're wondering whether I'm Bluebeard and you're my ninth wife.'

'Well, Roc,' I replied, 'although you're my husband and we've been married quite a few months, I don't always feel I know you very well.'

'Am I one of those people who don't improve on acquaintance?'

As usual he caught me up in his mood; and I was already beginning to feel gay and that my suspicions were rather foolish.

'You remain . . . mysterious,' I told him.

'And it's time you began to clear up the mysteries, you're thinking?'

'As you're my husband I don't think there should be secrets between us.'

He gave me that disarming smile which always touched me deeply. 'Nor do I. I know what's disturbing you. You discovered that I haven't lived the life of a monk before my marriage. You're right in that. But you don't want details of every little peccadillo, do you?'

'No,' I told him, 'not every one. Only the important ones.'

'But when I met you I realized that nothing that had happened to me before was of the slightest significance.'

'And you haven't taken up the old way of life since you married me?'

'I can assure you that I have been faithful to you in thought and deed. There! Satisfied?'

'Yes, but . . .'

'So you're not?'

'There are people who seem to regard you in a certain way and I wondered whether they realize that any relationship which existed between you is now . . . merely friendship.'

'I know. You're thinking of Althea.'

'Well?'

'When she first came here to look after your grandfather I thought her the most beautiful woman I had ever seen. We became friends. The family was always urging me to marry. Morwenna had been married for years and they all implied that it was my duty to marry, but I had never felt that I wanted to settle down with any woman.'

'Until you met Althea Grey?'

'I hadn't actually come to that conclusion. But shall we say the idea occurred to me as a possibility.'

'And then my grandfather asked you to come and have a look at me, and you thought I was the better proposition?'

'That sounds a little like your grandfather. There was no question of "propositions." I had already decided that I did not want to marry Althea Grey, *before* your grandfather suggested I should come and look at you. And when I did see you, it happened. Just like that. You were the only one from then on.'

'Althea couldn't have been very pleased.'

He lifted his shoulders. 'It takes two to make a marriage.'

'I begin to understand. You must have come very near to being engaged to Althea Grey before you changed your mind. And what about Dinah Bond?'

'What about Dinah? She assisted in the education of most young men in the district.'

'I see. Not serious?'

'Absolutely not.'

'And Rachel Bective?'

'Never!' he said almost fiercely. He filled my glass. 'Catechism over?' he asked. 'Favel, I'm beginning to wonder whether you aren't somewhat jealous.'

'I don't think I should be jealous . . . without reason.'

'Well, now you know there is no reason.'

'Roc . . .' I hesitated and he urged me to go on. 'That boy I saw at Bedivere House . . .'

'Well?'

'He's so like the Pendorrics.'

'I know; you told me before. You're not imagining that he's the living evidence of *my* sinful past, Favel!'

'Well, I did wonder who he was.'

'Do you know, darling, you haven't enough to do. At the week-end I want to go out to one of the properties on the north coast. Come with me. We'll be away a couple of nights.'

'That will be lovely.'

'Something else on your mind?' he asked.

'So many things are not clear. In fact when I go back to the first time I saw you . . . it seems to me that that was when everything began to change.'

'Well obviously things couldn't be the same for either of us after we'd met. We were swept off our feet.'

'No, Roc. I didn't mean that. Even my father seemed to change.'

He looked grave suddenly; and then he seemed to come to a decision.

'There are certain things you didn't know about your father, Favel.'

'Things *I* didn't know.'

'Things he kept from you.'

'But he didn't. He always confided in me. We were so close . . . my mother, he and I.'

Roc shook his head. 'For one thing, my dear, he didn't tell you that he had written to your grandfather.'

I had to agree that this was so.

'Why do you think he wrote to your grandfather?'

'Because he thought it was time we met, I suppose.'

'Why should he think that was the time when for nineteen years he hadn't considered it necessary? I didn't want to tell you, Favel. In fact, I'd made up my mind not to . . . for years. I was going to wait until you were fifty. A nice cosy grandmother with the little ones playing at your knee. Then it would have seemed too far away to be painful. But I've come to the conclusion – in the last half-hour that there shouldn't be secrets between us.'

'I'm certain there shouldn't be. Please tell me what you know about my father.'

'He wrote to your grandfather because he was ill.'

'Ill? In what way?'

'He had caught your mother's disease through being with her constantly. She wouldn't go away from him, or he from her; they wanted to pretend that there was nothing wrong. So they stayed together and he was her only nurse until she was so very ill. He told me that if she had gone away she might have lived a little longer. But she didn't want to live like that.'

'And he too. . . . But I was never told.'

'He didn't want you to know. He was very anxious about you. So he wrote to your grandfather telling him of your existence. He hoped that your grandfather would ask you to Cornwall. He himself would have stayed in Capri; and when he became really ill you wouldn't have been there.'

'But he could have had attention. He could have gone to a sanatorium.'

'That's what I told him. That's what I believed he would do.'

'He told you all this . . . and not his own daughter!'

'My darling, the circumstances were unusual. He knew of me, and as soon as I turned up at the studio he knew why I had come. It would have been too much of a coincidence for a Pendorric to arrive only a month or so after he had sent off his letter to Polhorgan. Besides, he knew your grandfather's methods. So he guessed at once I had been sent to look round.'

'You told him, I suppose.'

'I had been asked by Lord Polhorgan not to, but it was impossible to hide it from your father. However, we agreed that we would say nothing to you, and that I should write and tell him what I had seen; then he would presumably write to his granddaughter and invite her to England. That was what your father hoped. But, as you know, we met . . . and that was enough for us.'

'And all the time he was so ill . . .'

'He knew that he was on the point of becoming *very* ill. So he was delighted when we said we were going to get married.'

'You don't think that he was made a little uneasy by it?'

'Why should he be?'

'You knew that I was the granddaughter of a millionaire.'

Roc laughed. 'Don't forget he'd had some experience of your grandfather. The fact that you were his granddaughter didn't mean that you would inherit his fortune. He might have taken an acute dislike to you, and me as his son-in-law, in which case you would have been "cut off with a shilling." No, your father was delighted. He knew I'd take care of you; and I fancy he was happier to think of you in my care than in your grandfather's.'

'I thought he was worried about something . . . just before he died. I thought he was uneasy . . . about *us*. What really happened on the day when you went down to bathe?'

'Favel, I think I know why your father died.'

'Why . . . he died?'

'He died because he no longer wished to live.'

'You mean . . .?'

'I believe he wanted a quick way out, and found it. We went down to the beach together. It was getting late, you remember. There were few people about; they were all having lunch behind the sun blinds; soon they would be deep in the siesta. When we reached the beach he said to me: "You know you'd rather be with Favel." I couldn't deny it. "Go back," he said, "leave me. I would rather go in alone." Then he looked at me very solemnly and said: "I'm glad you married her. Take care of her." '

'You're suggesting that he deliberately swam out to sea and had no intention of coming back?'

Roc nodded. 'Looking back, I can see now that he had the look of a man who has written "The End" to his life. Everything was in order.'

I was too filled with emotion to trust myself to speak. I could see it all so clearly; that day when Roc had come back to the kitchen and sat on the table watching me, his legs swinging, the light making the tips of his ears pink. He didn't know then what had happened, because it was only afterwards that one realized the significance of certain words . . . certain actions.

'Favel,' said Roc, 'let's get out of here. We'll drive out to the moor and we'll stop then and talk and talk. He trusted me to care for you, to comfort you. You must trust me too, Favel.'

When I was with Roc I believed everything he said; it was only when I was alone that the doubts set in.

If only my father had confided in me, I would never have let him do what he did. I would have cared for him, brought him to England; he could have had the best possible attention. There was no need for him to die so soon.

But had it been like that?

When I was alone I faced the fact that the talk with Roc had not really eased my fears; it had only added to them.

I couldn't help feeling that some clue to the solution of my problem might lie in that house near Dozmary Pool, and I found myself thinking of it continually – and the boy and the woman who lived there.

Suppose I called on Louisa Sellick. Why shouldn't I? I could tell her who I was; and that I had heard of her connection with Pendorric. Or could I, considering the nature of that connection?

I had caught a glimpse of her and she had appeared to be a kindly and tolerant woman. Could I go to her and say that I was constantly being compared with Barbarina Pendorric and that I was interested in everyone who had known her?

Scarcely.

And yet the idea that I should go kept worrying me.

Suppose I pretended I had lost my way. No, I didn't want to pretend.

I would go and find a reason when I got there.

I took out the little blue Morris which I had made a habit of driving and which was now looked upon as mine, and I went out to the moor.

I knew the way now and was soon passing the Pool and taking the second-class road which led to the house.

When I pulled up I was still undecided as to what I should say. What I really wanted to ask was: 'Who is the boy who is so like the Pendorrics?' And how could I do that?

While I was looking at the house the door of the glass-roofed porch opened and a woman came out. She was elderly and very plump; she had evidently seen me from a window and had come out to inquire what I wanted.

I got out of the car and said 'Good morning' as she approached.

I began: 'My name is Pendorric. Mrs. Pendorric.'

She caught her breath and her rosy face was immediately a deeper shade of red.

'Oh,' she said. 'Mrs. Sellick bain't here to-day.'

'I see. You're .. ?'

'I'm Polly that does for her.'

'You've got a wonderful view here,' I said conversationally.

'Us don't notice it much. Been here too long, I reckon.'

'So . . . Mrs. Sellick is not at home to-day.'

'She's taking the boy back to school. She'll be away to-night, back to-morrow.'

I noticed that the woman was trembling slightly.

'Is anything wrong?' I asked.

She came closer to me and whispered: 'You ain't come for to take the boy away, have 'ee?'

I stared at her in astonishment.

'You'd better come in,' she said. 'We can't talk here.'

I followed her over the lawn to the porch, and into a hall; she threw open the door of a cosy sitting-room.

'Sit down, Mrs. Pendorric. Mrs. Sellick would want me to give you something, like. Would you have coffee or some of my elderberry wine?'

'Mrs. Sellick didn't know I was coming. Perhaps I shouldn't stay.'

'I'd like to be the one to talk to you, Mrs. Pendorric. Mrs. Sellick, she'd be too proud like. She'd say, 'Yes . . . you must do what you wish . . .' and then when you'd gone she'd break her heart. No, I've often thought I'd like the chance to do the talking if this day ever come, and it seems like Providence that it has come when her's off with the boy.'

'I think there's some misunderstanding. . . .'

'There's no misunderstanding, Mrs. Pendorric. You're from Pendorric and 'tis what she's always feared. She's often said: "I made no conditions then, Polly, and I'll make none now." She talks to me about everything. I knew her from the first . . . you see. I came with her when she first came to Bedivere. That was when he married. So we've been through a lot together.'

'Yes, I see.'

'Well, let me get you some coffee.'

'I'd rather not. Mrs. Sellick might not be very pleased if she knew I'd come in like this.'

'Her's the sweetest, mildest creature I ever saw, and I don't mind telling you I've often thought her too mild. The likes of her gets put upon. But I couldn't bear it to happen, see. Not twice in one lifetime . . . first losing *him* and then the boy. It 'ud be too much. Well, she's had him since he were three weeks old. She were a changed woman when Mr. Roc brought him here.'

'Mr. Roc . . .!'

She nodded. 'I remember the day well. It was getting dusk. I reckon they'd waited till then. They'd come straight from abroad. . . . Mr. Roc was driving the car and the young woman was with him . . . nothing more than a girl, though I didn't see much of her. Wore a hat pulled down over her face . . . didn't want to be seen. She carried the baby in and put him straight into Mrs. Sellick's arms; then she went back to the car and left Mr. Roc to do the talking.'

Rachel! I thought.

'You see, she felt guilty like. She'd loved Mr. Roc's father and had thought he was going to marry her. So he would have done, it was said, but the Pendorrics wanted money in the family so he married that Miss Hyson instead. He never gave up Louisa, although there were others too, but she were the one he really cared for, and when his wife died he begged her to marry him. But she wouldn't – for some reason. She used to think that because his wife had died as she did it wouldn't be right. Then he was away a lot but he came back to see Louisa. No one could be to him what she were. You're a Pendorric yourself now and you've heard tell of all this, so there's no need for me to repeat it. When he died she were heartbroken, and she always longed for a child of his . . . even though 'twould have been born out of wedlock. She took an interest in those twins of his and they were a mischievous pair. They'd heard about their father and this house and they came out once to have a look at Louisa. That was after he was dead; and she brought them in and gave them cakes and tea. And after that they came now and then. She told them that if they were ever in trouble – and they were the kind who might be . . . of course, they've sobered down now, but 'twas different when they were young – she'd help them if it were in her power. Well then she got this letter from Mr. Roc. Here was trouble all right. A baby on the way and could she help?'

'I see.'

'Of course she could help. She wanted to help. So she took little Ennis and she's been as a mother to him ever since. It was a turning point like. She began to be happy again when that little boy came into this house. But she never stopped being afeared. You see, he grew up such a beautiful child and he weren't hers. She'd take no money for what she did; she'd make no conditions. So you see, she was always afraid that one day Mr. Roc would come and claim that boy. When she heard he was married she was certain he'd want the boy. . . . She was terrible frit, I can tell 'ee. And I'm telling 'ee all this because I've got to make 'ee *see*.'

'Did he come to see the boy?'

'Yes. He comes every now and then. Terrible fond of him he be, and the boy of him.'

'I'm glad that he didn't desert him entirely.'

'No question of that. But it's puzzling. The Pendorrics were never ones to care much about scandal. There was his father coming to see Louisa. Didn't keep it as dark as some thought he should. But I reckon it was because Mr. Roc was so young. Not much more than seventeen and Louisa advised him not to let it be known . . . for the boy's sake. He's known as Ennis Sellick and thinks Louisa's his aunt.' She stopped and looked at me beseechingly. 'Please, Mrs. Pendorric, you look kind . . . please understand that he have been here nigh on fourteen years. You can't take him now.'

'You mustn't worry about that,' I told her. 'We have no intention of taking him.'

She relaxed and smiled happily. 'Why, when you said as who you were . . .'

'I'm sorry I frightened you. As a matter of fact it was very wrong of me to call. My visit was one of curiosity. I'd heard of Mrs. Sellick and wanted to meet her. That was all.'

'And you won't take the boy?'

'No, certainly not. It would be too cruel.'

'Too cruel,' she repeated. 'Oh thank 'ee, Mrs. Pendorric. It'll be a weight off our minds. Now won't you let me give you a cup of coffee? Mrs. Sellick wouldn't like you to leave without.'

I accepted the invitation. I felt I needed it. While Polly was in the kitchen I was thinking: How can I trust him again? If he could deceive me about the boy, he could about other things. Why hadn't he told me? It would have been so much easier.

Polly returned with the coffee; she was quite happy now; at least my visit had done much to restore her contentment. She told me how she and Louisa had grown to love the moor, and how difficult it was to cultivate the garden, which was so stony.

'Moorland country bain't the most fertile ground, Mrs. Pendorric, I do assure you,' she was saying, when we heard the sound of a car drawing up outside the house.

'Why, it can't be Mrs. Sellick back already,' said Polly, rising and going to the window.

Her next words sent the blood drumming in my ears. 'Why 'tis Mr. Pendorric,' she said. 'Oh dear, I reckon he thought they wasn't going till to-morrow.'

I stood up, and my knees were trembling so much that I thought they would give way as I heard Roc's voice. 'Polly, I saw the car outside. Who's here?'

'Oh, you've come to-day, Mr. Pendorric,' answered Polly blithely. 'Well, Mrs. Sellick thought it 'ud be better to take two days over the driving, seeing it's so far. They'm staying in London and then they'll go on to the school to-morrow. Reckon you thought they wouldn't be leaving till to-day.'

He was coming through the glass-roofed porch; striding into the sitting-room in the manner of someone who well knows the way.

He threw open the door and stared at me. 'You!' he said; then his expression darkened. I had never seen him so angry.

We stood staring at each other and I think he felt the same about me as I did about him; that we were both looking at a stranger.

Polly came into the room. 'Mrs. Pendorric's been telling me as you won't want to take the boy away. . . .'

'*Has* she?' he said; and his eyes took in the used coffee cups.

'I was that relieved. Not that I thought you'd do it, Mr. Roc. It was that pleasant meeting your bride.'

'I'm sure it was,' Roc answered. 'You should have waited, darling, until I drove you over.'

His voice sounded quite cold, as it had never been before when he spoke to me.

'And you came to-day unbeknownst to each other, and there's two cars outside. Well it *is* a day!'

'Yes,' echoed Roc almost viciously, 'it *is* a day.'

'I'll heat up this coffee, Mr. Roc.'

'Oh, no thanks, Polly. I came to see the boy before he went to school, but I'm too late. Never mind. I've met my wife instead.'

Polly laughed. 'I'm sorry Mrs. Sellick didn't warn you, but she doesn't care about telephoning the house, as you know.'

'I know,' said Roc. He turned to me. 'Are you ready to go?'

'Yes,' I said. 'Good-bye, Polly, and thank you for the coffee.'

'It's been a pleasure,' said Polly.

She stood at the door smiling as we went out to the cars. Roc got into his, I into mine. I drove off and he followed me.

Near that bridge where it was said Arthur fought his last fight against Sir Mordred, Roc drove ahead of me and pulled up. I heard the door of his car slam and he came to stand by mine.

'So you lied to me,' I said.

'And you saw fit to pry into matters which are no concern of yours.'

'Perhaps they are some concern of mine.'

'You are quite wrong if you think so.'

'Shouldn't I be interested in my husband's son?'

'I would never have believed you'd do anything so petty. I had no idea I'd married a . . . spy.'

'And I can't understand why you should have lied. I should have understood.'

'How good of you! You are of course extremely tolerant and forgiving, I'm sure.'

'Roc!'

He looked at me so coldly that I shrank from him. 'There's really nothing more to be said, is there?'

'I think there is. There are things I want to know.'

'You'll find out. Your spy system seems excellent.'

He went to his car, and drove on towards Pendorric; and I followed him home.

Back at Pendorric, Roc only spoke to me when necessary. I knew that he was planning his trip to the north coast, but there was now no question of my going with him.

It was impossible to hide from the household that we had quarrelled, because neither of us was good enough at hiding our feelings; and I was sure they were all rather curious.

The next few days seemed unbearably long and I had not felt so wretched since the death of my father. Two days after that disastrous visit to Bedivere I went into the quadrangle and sat under the palm tree thinking ruefully that the summer was nearly over, and with it the happiness I had believed was mine.

The sun was shining but I could see the spiders' webs on the bushes, and beautiful as the Michaelmas daisies and chrysanthemums were they did underline the fact that winter was on the way. But because this was Cornwall, the roses were still blooming; and although the hydrangeas did not flower in such profusion, there were still some to brighten the quadrangle.

One of the twins must have seen me for she came out and began to walk unconcernedly towards the pond, humming as she came.

'Hallo,' she said. 'Mummy says we're not to sit on the seats because they're damp. We'll catch our deaths if we do. So what about you?'

'I don't think it's really damp.'

'Everything's damp. You might get pneumonia and die.'

I knew this was Hyson, and it occurred to me that since our adventure in the vault her attitude towards me had changed; and perhaps not towards me only; it seemed that she herself had changed.

'It would be one way. . . .' she said thoughtfully.

'One way of dying, you mean?'

Her face puckered suddenly. 'Don't talk of dying,' she said. 'I don't like it . . . much.'

'You're becoming awfully sensitive, Hyson,' I commented.

She looked thoughtfully up at the east windows as though watching for something.

'Are you expecting someone?' I asked.

She did not answer.

After a while she said: 'You must have been very glad that I was in the vault with you, Favel.'

'It was rather selfish of me, but I was.'

She came nearer to me and putting her hands on my knees, looking into my face. 'I was glad I was there too,' she said.

'Why? It wasn't very pleasant and you were horribly scared.'

She smiled her odd little smile. 'Yes, but there were two of us. That made a difference.'

She stepped back and put her lips in the position to suggest whistling.

'Can you whistle, Favel?'

'Not very well.'

'Nor can I. Lowella can.'

She stopped, looking up at the east windows.

'There it is,' she said.

It was the sound of the violin.

I stood up and caught Hyson's wrist. 'Who is it?' I asked.

'You know, don't you?'

'No, I don't. But I'm going to find out.'

'It's Barbarina.'

'You know Barbarina's dead.'

'Oh Favel, don't go in there. You know what it means. . . .'

'Hyson! What do you know? Who is playing the violin? Who locked us in the vault? Do you know that?'

For the moment I thought I saw a madness in the child's eyes, and it was not a pleasant sight. 'It's Barbarina,' she whispered. 'Listen to her playing. She's telling us she's getting tired. She means she won't wait much longer.'

I shook her a little because I could see that she was near hysteria. 'I'm going to find out who's playing that violin. You come with me. We'll find this person together.'

She was unwilling but I dragged her to the east door. As I opened it I could distinctly hear the sound of a violin.

'Come on,' I said, and we started up the stairs. The violin had stopped playing, but we went on to Barbarina's room; I threw open the door. The violin was lying on the chair; the music was still on the stand. The room was just as it had been when I had last seen it.

I looked at Hyson, but she had lowered her eyes and was staring at the floor.

I was more frightened than I had ever been, because never before had I felt so utterly alone. First I had had my parents to care for me; then – as I thought – a husband; finally a grandfather.

I had lost them all, for now I could no longer rely on Roc to protect me from the danger which I felt was close.

Chapter Six

Roc left for his week-end trip.

Before he went he said to me, when we were in the bedroom together: 'I don't like this at all, Favel. We've got to get it sorted out. I wish you hadn't gone snooping. It's all at such an unfortunate time.'

He was almost his old self and I immediately swung round to meet him half-way. Eagerly I waited for what he would say next.

'There's a simple explanation to all this,' he said. 'But I can't tell you yet. Will you wait a while and trust me?'

'But Roc . . .'

'All right,' he said. 'You can't. But this isn't going on. I'll think about it while I'm away; but promise me this: You won't think too badly of me, will you? I'm really not quite such a scoundrel as you believe I am.'

'Oh Roc,' I said, 'it's all so unnecessary. There was no need to tell me lies. I just wish you hadn't.'

'And you can't trust someone who has once lied, can you?'

He looked at me wistfully and I had the impression that he was trying to charm me as he had so many times before.

'Roc, tell me about it,' I pleaded. 'Tell me now. Then we can start being happy again.'

He hesitated. 'Not now, Favel.'

'But why not now?'

'It isn't only my affair. I've got to discuss it with someone else.'

'Oh, I see.'

'But you don't see. Listen, Favel. I love you. And you've got to love me too. You've got to trust me. Damn it, can't you have a little faith in me?'

I couldn't make myself say yes.

'All right.' He put his hands on my shoulders and gave me a swift kiss on the lips with nothing warm or passionate about it. 'See you on Monday or Tuesday.'

Then he was gone, leaving me as baffled and unhappy as before – or almost.

But the fact that he was away did give me an opportunity to think; and several little incidents from the past kept recurring to me. I had been in danger of losing my life on two occasions since coming to Pendorric; which was strange because it was within a very short time, and it was something which had never happened to me before in the whole of my life. I was thinking of that time when someone had removed the danger signal on the cliffs. But then it had been Roc who had *saved* me. At that time I had not known I was Lord Polhorgan's granddaughter. But Roc had, and if I had died then, Roc would have inherited nothing.

A horrible thought came to me. Was it meant to shift suspicion? Was the idea that, when later I had a fatal accident, people would remember how Roc had saved me then?

No, that was a hideous thought. I was suggesting that Roc had deliberately locked me in the vault and planned to leave me there!

It was as though my personality had split into two; there was part of me which was determined to defend Roc and prove him innocent, and another equally as determined to prove him guilty.

Who else could have locked the door of the vault? Who else could have come along and unlocked it and then pretended that it was jammed? Who else had a motive for wanting to be rid of me? On my death Roc would inherit my grandfather's fortune and be free to marry whomsoever he wished. Who would that be? Althea Grey?

Then I thought of what Polly had said that morning in Bedivere House: when Barbarina was dead, Roc's father had wanted to marry Louisa.

While I was brooding on these things there came a knock on the door and Morwenna came in. For a moment I felt envious of her radiant happiness.

'Oh hallo, Favel. I hoped I'd find you here.' She looked at me anxiously. 'Roc seems to have gone off in a bit of a huff. Why don't you make it up?'

I was silent and she shrugged her shoulders. 'It's unlike him,' she went on. 'Usually with him it's a big flare-up and then everything's as it was before. Yet this thing of yours seems to have been going on for days.'

'You mustn't let it bother you,' I said.

'Oh, I don't. It'll work itself out, I expect. But an annoying thing has happened. I've had to leave my car at the garage and I was wondering if you were using the Morris this morning.'

'Please have it,' I said. 'I can go to Polhorgan – I've got to go some time, and I don't need a car to go there.'

'Are you sure? I want to go into Plymouth. Dr. Clement says I've got to rest every day. He's going to be a bit fussy about me, so I thought I'd do a bit of knitting. It'll be something to do while I put my feet up. I want to get wools and patterns and there's so little to choose from here.'

'Do take the Morris and don't worry about me.'

She came over to me and, unexpectedly, kissed me. 'Things will soon be all right between you and Roc, I know,' she said.

When she had gone I left at once for Polhorgan. There was no sense in sitting about and brooding; I went by way of the coast road and tried to stop thinking of Roc's duplicity by planning the orphans' home I might one day have at Polhorgan.

When I arrived, Mr. and Mrs. Dawson came out to greet me, and I could tell by their portentous manner that they had been eagerly looking forward to telling me something.

I was taken to the sitting-room and given coffee, and then it came out.

'We wouldn't mention this, madam, but for the fact that Mrs. Penhalligan has been having a word with Mrs. Dawson, and that has somewhat coloured our views in the matter. It is a delicate subject, madam, and Mrs. Dawson and I trust that you will understand that it is only in our endeavour to serve you . . .'

I was anxious to cut short the circumlocution so I said: 'Oh yes, of course, I understand, Dawson.'

'Then, madam, I will tell you. I did not care to mention this before because I feared it might reflect on . . . one whom it was not my place to mention. But since Mrs. Penhalligan has spoken to Mrs. Dawson . . .'

'Please tell me all about it, Dawson.'

'Well, madam, Dr. Clement was so certain that his lordship died from natural causes and discouraged us from bringing forward what actually happened. There was no inquest, the cause of death being considered natural. But there is a way of hastening death, madam, and Mrs. Dawson and I have long been of the opinion that his lordship was hurried to the grave.'

'Yes, I know the bell and the box were on the floor, but he might very well have knocked them over when he was reaching for them.'

'So he might, madam; and who is to say he didn't? One cannot make suppositions in a court of law. But Mrs. Dawson overheard a conversation between his lordship and the nurse on the morning of the night he died.'

'Oh! What conversation?'

'His lordship threatened to dismiss her if she continued to see Mr. er . . .' Dawson coughed apologetically. 'Mr. Pendorric.'

I wanted to protest, but my throat seemed to have closed up and would not let my voice come through. I had had enough. I could not bear any more revelations.

'And it seems, madam, rather coincidental that not many hours later his lordship should be unable to reach his pills. Mrs. Dawson and I do not forget, madam, that a legacy was mentioned in that will for the nurse who was in his lordship's employ at the time of his death. . . .'

I was scarcely listening to them. I was thinking: How many lies has he told me? He did admit that he was almost engaged to Althea Grey. Then he had heard of my existence. He had married me as his father had married Barbarina. How much was he influenced by the past? It was as though we were actors in some obscure drama, playing the same parts which had been played before.

Barbarina had been married to bring money into Pendorric when her husband had been in love with Louisa Sellick. Had I been married for the same reason when *my* husband was in love with Althea Grey? Who was the vague shadow sensed by Jesse Pleydell on that day when Barbarina fell to her death? Was it her husband, Petroc Pendorric?

I'm becoming hysterical, I thought. I'm letting my imagination run away with me.

I should never have believed this of Roc before that scene in Bedivere House.

Now my thoughts would not be controlled. Had Althea Grey deliberately removed the pills, hoping to hasten his death? For he had to die, before I could inherit his money; and now . . . I had to die before it was theirs.

I wondered what gossip was going on all around me. Mrs. Penhalligan had talked to Mrs. Dawson. Did they all know, then, of the trouble between Roc and me? Did they know the reason?

The Dawsons were looking at me with concern and compassion. Were they warning me that Roc and Althea Grey were lovers? Were they suggesting that, since the nurse had had no compunction in hastening my grandfather to his death, she and her accomplice might have none in hastening me to mine?

I said: 'It was very unfortunate that my grandfather should have imagined these things. I think perhaps being such an invalid he was apt to worry over non-existent troubles. I have heard that it is a symptom of the illness he had.'

The Dawsons looked at me sorrowfully. Mrs. Dawson would have continued to speak, but Dawson was too much of a diplomatist to allow it. He lifted a hand and she was silent.

On his face was the expression of a man who can be satisfied that he has done his duty.

When I left Polhorgan I was afraid I should not be able to keep up my façade of serenity. I was too restless. There were so many things I wanted to find out and I had to go into action; one thing I could not endure was inactivity.

I wanted to talk to someone and I believed if Morwenna had not gone to Plymouth I should have sought her out and confided everything in her. There was Deborah. I could talk to her.

I hurried back to the house and went to Deborah's room. She was not in. Uncertainly I came down to the hall again, telling myself that it would be easier to think out of doors, when the hall telephone began to ring.

When I answered it there was a low chuckle at the other end of the line.

'Ah, I was hoping I'd catch you. This is Althea Grey.'

I was startled because she was so much in my thoughts and I was growing more and more certain that she was playing a big part in the tangle.

'I was wondering if you'd come and see me before I go.'

'Before you go?'

'Yes, I'm leaving very soon. To-morrow.'

'You mean leaving altogether?'

'Come along and I'll tell you all about it. I've been wanting to have a talk with you for some time. When can you?'

'Why . . . now.'

'Suits me.' Again there was that low laugh and she rang off.

I hurried out of the house, out along the coast road; and in due course came to Cormorant Cottage.

It was aptly named; even now the gulls were swooping and soaring about the little cove which lay below, and I saw some cormorants. The cottage itself was perched on a rock which jutted out over the sea; it was small and painted blue and white, and there was a steep path which led up to it. It was the ideal summer cottage.

'Hallo!' One of the windows was thrown up. 'I've been watching for you. I'll come down.'

I started up the path which was almost overgrown with St. John's Wort, and by the time I reached the door Althea was standing there.

'I'm just packing.'

'You're leaving?'

'M'm. Do come in and sit down.'

I stepped straight into a room with casement windows which looked on to the sea. It had clearly been furnished for renting with only the essentials, and everything in drab colours which wouldn't show the dirt.

'Rather a change from Polhorgan,' she commented, and held out a cigarette case while she looked at me with what seemed like amusement.

'Nice of you to come and see *me*.'

'I might say it was nice of you to ask me.'

'I was lucky to catch you in.'

'I'd only just come in. Roc's away for a few days.'

'Yes, I know.'

I raised my eyebrows, and again that flicker of amusement crossed her face. 'Grape-vine,' she said. 'You can scarcely move in this place without everyone knowing all about it. Did anyone see you come in here?'

'No. Why ... I don't think so.'

'Because if someone did there'd be speculation, you bet.'

'I had no idea you were leaving Cornwall so soon.'

She shrugged her shoulders. 'The season's over. It's lonely. You walk for miles along the cliffs without meeting anyone. You see, you didn't meet anyone coming here from Pendorric. Not my cup of tea. By the way, would you like one?'

'No, thanks.'

'Coffee?'

'No, thank you. I can't stay long.'

'A pity. We've never had a real cosy chat, have we? And it's so peaceful here. I've often thought you were rather suspicious of me. I'd like to put that right.'

'Suspicious? What do you mean?'

'Now you're playing innocent.'

'I should like to know why you asked me here. I thought you had something to tell me.'

'I have. And this is the time to tell. You see, I've got another job and I like to tidy everything up before I go.' She stretched out her long slim legs and regarded them with satisfaction. 'Rich old gentleman going on a world tour needs a nurse in constant attendance. Rich old gentlemen seem to be my speciality.'

'Don't rich young ones ever come your way?'

'The trouble with the young is that they don't need nurses.' She burst into laughter. 'Mrs. Pendorric, you *are* uneasy.'

'Uneasy?'

'Well, this is a lonely spot and I don't believe you have a very high opinion of my character. You're beginning to regret coming and are wondering how you can quietly slip away. Yet you came of your own free will, remember. In fact, you jumped at it when I asked you. It wasn't really very wise, was it? You're here and nobody knows you've come. You're rather rash, Mrs. Pendorric. You act on the spur of the moment. Do come and look at my view.'

She took my hand and pulled me to my feet. She was strong and I remembered in that moment that Mabell Clement had said she only *looked* as though she were made of Dresden china.

She drew me to the window, holding my arm in a firm grip, while with her free hand she threw open the casement window. I looked down at the sheer drop to the sea. A long way below, the waves were breaking on the jagged rocks.

'Imagine,' she said, her voice close to my ear, 'someone falling from this window! Not a chance. It wouldn't do to let this cottage to anyone with sleep-walking tendencies or to someone who was planning a little homicide.'

For a few seconds I really believed that she had lured me here to kill me. I thought: She has planned this . . . so that the way will be free to Roc and my grandfather's fortune.

That she read my thoughts was obvious; but what I saw in her face was amusement as she released my arm.

'I think,' she said slowly, 'that you would be more comfortable sitting down.'

'What was your object in asking me here?' I demanded.

'That's what I'm going to tell you.' She almost pushed me on to the dingy settee and sat in the arm-chair opposite me.

'Mrs. Pendorric,' she said, 'you can stop being scared. I only intend to talk. You really shouldn't worry about me, you know. In a few days I shall have gone right away from this place.'

'Are you sorry to be going?'

'It's a mistake to be sorry. Once a thing's over it's done with. You were always a little jealous of me, weren't you? There's no need to be. After all, you married him, didn't you? It's true he did think of marrying me once.'

'What about you?'

'Certainly. It would have been a good marriage. I don't know whether it would have suited me; though I like adventure. But it's true I'm just past thirty now, so perhaps it is time I began to think about settling down.'

'You seem to find life . . . amusing.'

'Don't you? You should. It's the only way to live it. I've made a decision, Mrs. Pendorric; I'm going to tell you all you came to hear.'

She was laughing at me, and strangely enough I was ready to believe whatever she told me: for although she seemed tough and extremely worldly, experienced and capable of almost anything, she did seem truthful – largely because she would find it more amusing to tell the truth than lies.

'What were you doing before you came to Polhorgan?' I asked.

'Nursing, of course.'

'As Nurse Stoner Grey?'

She shook her head. 'In my last case I was Grey. Stoner Grey before that.'

'Why did you drop Stoner?'

'Unpleasant publicity. Not that I minded, but it might not have been easy to get the kind of job I wanted. People have long memories. So you knew about the Stoner Grey incident. Those Dawsons told you, I bet.'

'They were a bit vague about it. It was . . . someone else.'

She nodded. 'If all had gone well I might never have had to take up nursing again. There was nothing wrong with it. The old gentleman made a will in my favour; but they found he was *non compos mentis* . . . and his wife won the case.'

'I suppose you persuaded him to make that will.'

'Well, what do you think?' She leaned forward. 'You're a nice woman, Mrs. Pendorric, and I'm . . . not so nice. You see I didn't have your advantages. No nice millionaire for a grandfather. I wasn't really the sort of girl to marry into Pendorric. I'm an adventuress because I like adventure. It adds a spice to life. I lived the early part of my life in a back street and I didn't like that much. I was determined to break away. . . . I was like your grandfather in my way. I hadn't got the business flair, though. I didn't know how to set about earning millions. But it wasn't long before I found out that I was beautiful, and that's one of the best assets a girl can have. I took up nursing, and I intended to go into private nursing, which was a way of getting what I wanted. And I saw that I got the right jobs, too. That's why I came to look after your grandfather.'

'You hoped that *he* would leave you his money?'

'One can always hope. Then there was Roc. Adventuresses always weigh up all the possibilities, you know.'

'Roc must have seemed the more hopeful of the two, surely . . . when you got to know my grandfather.'

She laughed again. 'He did. But then he's too shrewd. He saw through me. He liked me, yes. And I liked him. I'd have liked him if he'd been one of the fishermen here. But he always held back; he seemed to be aware of something in me which . . . well, how shall we say? . . . wasn't quite what a gentleman looks for in his wife – not Roc's kind anyway. So we were good friends and then he went away and when he came back he'd married you. He's got a kind heart. He wanted to be friends still, and didn't want me to feel snubbed. That was why he was extra nice to me. But I saw you were getting a little jealous.' She laughed. 'All clear now?'

'Not quite,' I said. 'How did my grandfather die?'

She looked at me very intently and seemed more serious than she had during the whole of our interview.

'I have admitted to you that I look out for chances to improve my lot,' she said firmly, 'but I'm not a murderess. I've always believed that other people's lives mean as much to them as mine does to me. If I can get the better of people . . . all well and good. But I do draw the line at murder.' Once again the smile was in her eyes. 'So that's why you were so alarmed when you came in! Then I'm doubly glad you came. I want to clear up *that* little point before I go away. Your grandfather often mislaid his little box. He did so once when you were with him. Don't you remember?'

I did remember. I had left Polhorgan early and found her with Roc on Pendorric beach.

'He dropped the pills; it agitated him that he could not find them when he needed them; and in that agitation he knocked over the bell. That was how he died, Mrs. Pendorric. I'd be ready to swear it. He was, it's true, in rather an agitated state. He was worried about you. He knew that at one time your husband and I had been friendly and he spoke to me about it. It upset him, although I assured him that there was nothing beyond friendship in our relationship. But to worry over imaginary details is a feature of his complaint. But I do assure you that I did nothing intentionally to hasten his death.'

'I believe you,' I said, because I did.

'I'm glad. I shouldn't have liked you to think me capable of *that*. Most other things . . . yes. But not murder.' She yawned and stretched her arms. 'Just think, in a month's time I'll be heading for the sun . . . when the mists swirl round Pendorric and the south-west gales batter the walls of Polhorgan. I've got loads of packing to do.'

I rose. 'Then I'd better go.'

She came to the door of the cottage with me, and when I had walked down the path we said good-bye. She stood at the door watching me.

My encounter with Althea Grey had been rather bewildering, for she had been embarrassingly frank. I had believed her while I was sitting with her, but now I wondered whether she had been amusing herself with my gullibility.

Was she really going away? At least she was not with Roc, and there was some measure of comfort in that.

The day seemed to stretch out endlessly before me. I did not want to go back to Pendorric, but there seemed nothing else to do. I thought I would go now and find Deborah and talk to her, not that I was really anxious to confide, even in her.

As I came towards the house Mrs. Penhalligan, who must have seen me approaching, came running out. She was very agitated and could scarcely speak coherently.

'Oh, Mrs. Pendorric, there's been an accident. . . .'

My heart missed a beat and then began to gallop to make up for it. Roc! I thought. I ought to have been with him. . . .

'It's Miss Morwenna, ma'am. She's had an accident in her car. It was the hospital that phoned.'

'Morwenna . . .' I breathed.

'Yes, it happened on Ganter Hill. They've taken her to Treganter Hospital.'

'She's . . .?'

'They say it's very serious. Mr. Chaston's already gone.'

'I see.'

I felt bewildered. I could not think what I should do for the best.

'The twins . . .?' I began.

'Miss Bective is with them. She's told them.'

Deborah drove up at that moment. She got out of her car and called to us: 'Isn't it warm this morning? Hallo . . . is anything wrong?'

I said: 'There's been an accident. It's Morwenna. She was driving in to Plymouth.'

'Is it bad? Is she hurt?'

I nodded. 'Charles has gone to Treganter Hospital. It's rather serious, I think.'

'Oh my God,' murmured Deborah. 'And Hyson . . . and Lowella?'

'They're with Rachel. She'll look after them.'

Deborah put her hands over her eyes. 'This is terrible.' There was a sob in her throat. 'At such a time. I wonder how badly hurt she is. It'll be tragic if this has harmed the child.'

'Do you think we ought to go to the hospital?'

'Yes,' said Deborah. 'Let's go at once. Poor Charles! Get in, Favel. It isn't very far.'

Mrs. Penhalligan stood watching us as we drove away.

Deborah looked grim and I thought: She loves Morwenna like a mother; and indeed it was natural that she should, for she had brought up Roc and his sister after their mother had died.

'I expect she was thinking of the child,' murmured Deborah. 'We ought not to have let her drive. She's been so absent-minded lately.'

'I could have driven her into Plymouth,' I said.

'Or I. Why did she want to go, anyway?'

'For knitting-wool and patterns.'

'It's so ironical. She's longed for another child, and because of it . . .'

I had suddenly remembered, and the memory struck me like a blow.

'Deborah,' I said slowly, 'Morwenna wasn't driving her own car. She was using the little blue Morris which I usually drive!'

Deborah nodded. 'But she'd driven it before. Beside, she has always been such a good driver.'

I was silent. The coincidence did not seem to impress Deborah as it did me. I was almost afraid to examine my thoughts.

I shook them off. I was becoming unnerved. At least first of all I must wait to hear what had caused the accident.

And if by any chance something in the car had gone wrong, should I be foolish to imagine that it was due to tampering, that someone, believing I should use the car, had done something which made an accident inevitable? I was not such an experienced driver as Morwenna. What would have happened if I had been in that car this morning?

Deborah had laid a hand on mine.

'Favel, we mustn't anticipate trouble dear. Let us hope and pray that she'll come through.'

That was a strange day of brooding horror. Morwenna's life was in danger; I believed mine was too, for I was certain that what had happened to her that day had been part of a plan and no accident, and that someone not very far from me was angry because the wrong person had walked into the trap.

There had been a witness of the accident. It had happened on Ganter Hill – not a very steep hill as Cornish hills go, but rather a long one which sloped gradually into Treganter. One of the local people had seen the car; there was no other involved. Suddenly it had begun to roll about the road, the steering clearly out of control; a glimpse had been caught of the frightened woman at the wheel as the car wobbled downhill and crashed into a tree.

In the late afternoon the hospital rang up, and as a result Charles took the twins to see Morwenna. Deborah and I went with them, at Charles's request. Quite clearly he feared what he would find when we arrived there.

Deborah and I did not go in to see Morwenna, because she was very weak and only her immediate family were allowed to see her.

I shall never forget Hyson's face as she came out. It was so pale, and seemed shrivelled so that she looked like an old woman. Lowella was crying; but Hyson shed no tears.

Charles told us that Morwenna's condition was still very serious, that he was going to stay at the hospital and wanted us to take the twins home; so I drove, while Deborah sat at the back, a twin on either side of her, her arms about them holding the sobbing Lowella and the silent Hyson.

When we reached Pendorric, Rachel and Mrs. Penhalligan were waiting to hear the news.

We were all very silent and upset, and Mrs. Penhalligan said we should try to eat something. We went into the winter parlour, and when we were there Hyson suddenly cried out: 'Her head was all bandaged. She didn't know me. Mummy didn't know me! She's going to die . . . and death's horrible!'

Deborah put her arms about the child. 'There, my darling, hush. You're frightening Lowella.'

Hyson broke free. Her eyes were wild and I could see that she was on the verge of hysteria. 'She should be frightened. We all should. Because Mummy's going to die and I . . . I hate it.'

'Mummy will get better,' Deborah comforted.

Hyson gazed straight before her for a few seconds and then suddenly her eyes were on me. She continued to stare at me, and Deborah, noticing this, took the child's head and held it against her breast.

'I'm going to take Hyson up to my room,' she said. 'She'll stay with me to-night. This has been terrible . . . terrible.'

She went out of the room, her arms about Hyson; but Hyson had turned once more to stare at me.

'I hate it . . . I hate it . . .' she cried.

Deborah gently led her away.

Roc came home at once, his business uncompleted, and when I saw him I realized again the depth of his affection for his sister. He was stunned by what had happened, and seemed to have forgetten all about our strained relationship.

The next days were spent in going to the hospital, although only Charles and Roc were allowed to see Morwenna. Deborah was wonderful with the twins, and I felt that Hyson needed a good deal of care during those days. I had not guessed how deep was her feeling for her mother.

It was three days after the accident when we heard that Morwenna would probably recover; but she had lost her baby; and she had not yet been told this.

I remember driving Charles home from the hospital after he had been given that information; he was very upset and talked to me more intimately than he ever had before.

'You see, Favel,' he said, 'it meant so much to her. I wanted a son, naturally; but she seemed to have a sort of obsession about it. And now there won't be any more children . . . ever. That much they can tell me.'

'As long as she recovers . . .' I whispered.

'Yes, as long as she recovers there mustn't be any more regrets.'

When we knew that Morwenna was out of danger Roc went away again. There was nothing he could do at home, he said; either he or Charles had to attend to business, and in the circumstances it was for Charles to remain at Pendorric, close to Treganter.

During the last days I had been so immersed in the tragedy of Morwenna's accident that I had not thought very much about my own position, but as soon as Roc had gone my fears began to return, especially as it seemed firmly established that it was some unusual fault in the steering that had been responsible for the accident; and I knew very well that there had been nothing wrong with the car when I had used it the day before.

I spent a sleepless night after Roc had gone, and the next morning Mabell Clement telephoned me and asked if I would come over and have morning coffee with her. She had sounded rather agitated, and when I arrived at Tremethick, Mabell took both my hands in a firm grip and said: 'Thank heaven you've come.'

'What's wrong?' I wanted to know.

'I've scarcely slept all night thinking of you. Andrew's very worried. We were talking about you nearly all last night. We don't like it, Favel.'

'I don't understand. What don't you like?'

'You know, or perhaps you don't . . . but I assure you he is, I mean Andrew. He's the most level-headed person I've ever known. And he's not satisfied. He thinks this is too much of a coincidence to be ignored.'

'You mean . . .'

'Sit down. I've got the coffee made. Andrew will be in at any moment. At least he's going to try to be. But young Mrs. Pengally's baby's due, so it's possible he'll be detained. If he is, *I've* got to make you see.'

'I've never seen you so agitated, Mabell.'

'I don't think I've ever *felt* so agitated. I've never before known anyone who's in danger of being murdered.'

I stared at her in horror, because I knew what she meant; and the fact that the thought was in her mind as well as mine gave it substance.

'We've got to be logical, Favel. We've got to look this thing right in the face. It's no use saying 'This sort of thing couldn't happen here . . . or to me.' That's what everybody says. But we know such things do occur. And you happen to be very rich. People envy money more than anything. They're ready to kill for it.'

'Yes, I think you're right, Mabell.'

'Now listen, Favel. Someone locked you in that vault and intended to keep you there, where your cries wouldn't be heard, and you would have died of fright or starvation or something. That was the plan.'

I nodded.

'If Miss Hyson hadn't happened to come that way and hear you call, you might still have been there . . . at least your body might . . . with that of the little girl.'

'I think you're right.'

'Well, suppose there was an explanation of that. Suppose the door did jam as they said it did . . .'

She paused, and I thought: As Roc said it did. Oh Roc . . . not you. That would be more than I could bear.

'. . . well, I suppose that's possible,' she continued. 'But what is so strange is that, not so long after, the car which you were expected to be driving should be involved in this accident. When Andrew and I heard what had happened we were quite stunned. You see the same idea occurred to us both.'

I tried to speak steadily. 'You think that the . . . person who locked me in the vault, tampered with the car?'

'I think two accidents like that can't be merely chance.'

'There was another.' I told her about the notice on the cliffs. 'Roc happened to remember, and came after me.'

I knew what was in her thoughts, because her mouth hardened and she said: 'It wasn't all that dangerous. It wasn't like the vault . . . and the car.'

'Still, someone did move the board. It might have been someone who knew I was at Polhorgan. And then of course there's this violin-playing and singing, and the story of the Brides.'

'As I said, we don't like it. We're very fond of you, Favel – myself and . . . Andrew. I think that someone is trying to harm you and it's someone at Pendorric.'

'It's a ghastly thought, and now that Roc's away . . .'

'Oh, so he's away?'

'Yes, he went last week-end on business and he came back when he heard about the accident. He's had to go back now.'

Mabell stood up. That hard expression was in her face again, and I knew whom she suspected.

'That nurse has left Cormorant Cottage,' she said.

'I knew she was going.'

'I wonder where she is now?'

We were silent for a few minutes, then Mabell burst out: 'I just don't like the thought of your being at Pendorric.'

'But it's my home.'

'I think you ought to get away for a bit . . . to sort things out. Why don't you come and stay here for a night or two? We could talk, and you'd feel safe here.'

I looked round the room with the pictures (which Mabell has been unable to sell) on the walls and examples of her handiwork in evidence over the brick fireplace.

It certainly seemed like a haven. I should feel perfectly at peace here. I should have time to think about what had happened, to talk about it with Mabell and Andrew; but there was no real reason why I should stay with them.

'It would seem so odd,' I began.

'Suppose I was going to paint your portrait. Would that give us an excuse?'

'Hardly. People would say I could easily come over for sittings.'

'But we hate the thought of your being there. We're afraid of what's going to happen next.'

I thought of Roc, going away on business; this time he had not suggested that I should go with him. So why shouldn't I stay with friends?

'Look,' said Mabell, 'I'll drive you back and you can pack a bag. Just your night things.'

She was so determined and I felt so uncertain that I allowed her to get out the car and drive me back to Pendorric.

When we reached the house I said: 'I'll have to explain to Mrs. Penhalligan that I shan't be home for a night or so. I'll tell her about the picture . . . only I must say it seems rather strange in the midst of all this trouble.'

'Stranger things have been happening,' said Mabell firmly.

I went up to my room and put a few things into a bag. The house seemed very quiet. I felt dazed, as I had since I had talked to Mabell. I was certain now that someone was determined to kill me; and that it could happen while I was in Pendorric. The playing of the violin, the singing – they had been the warning signs; someone had tried to unnerve me, to make me believe this story of the woman who was trying to lure me into the tomb to take her place.

But ghosts did not have keys to vaults; they did not tamper with cars.

My bag was packed. I would go down to the kitchen and tell Mrs. Penhalligan. If Morwenna had been here I should have explained to her that I was staying with the Clements for a while. I didn't want to disturb Charles. Of course I could tell Deborah.

I went along to her rooms. She was there reading when I entered, and as she looked at me the serenity faded from her face. She sprang to her feet. 'Favel, you're upset.'

'Well everything's been so upsetting.'

'My dear child.' She took my hand and led me to the window-seat. 'Sit down and tell me all about it.'

'I've just come to tell you that I'm spending a night or two with the Clements.'

She looked surprised. 'You mean the doctor and his sister?'

'Yes. Mabell's going to paint my portrait.' Even as I said the words I thought how puerile they sounded. She would know that I was making an excuse to leave Pendorric. She had always been so kind to me and I was sure she would understand if I explained to her. It was insulting to her intelligence not to tell her the truth, I felt. So I blurted out: 'As a matter of fact, Deborah, I want to get away. If it's only for a day or so I want to get away.'

She nodded. 'I understand. Things haven't been going quite smoothly between you and Roc and you're upset. And coming on top of all this . . .'

I was silent and relieved when she went on: 'It's perfectly understandable. It'll do you good, dear, to get away for a while. I feel the same myself. This anxiety about Morwenna has been . . . terrible. And now we know that she'll be all right we realize how tensed-up we've been, and we begin to feel the effects of the shock. So you're going to the Clements.'

'Yes. Mabell suggested it. I've just packed a bag.'

Deborah frowned. 'My dear, I suppose it's wise.'

'Wise?'

'Well, it's not as though Mabell's there alone, is it? You see, this is a small place and there's a lot of gossip. Quite absurd, of course, but there it is . . . and I've noticed . . . and I expect other people have too . . . that the doctor is rather interested in you.'

I felt myself flushing hotly. 'Dr. Clement!'

'He's quite young and people are so ready to talk. You might say there's always gossip about Pendorrics, and so there is. The men I mean. It's different with the women. Unfair of course, but that's the way of the world. The women have to be beyond reproach. Because of the children, my dear. This is ridiculous. It's really quite absurd, but so is the gossip and the scandal that goes on in this place. You must please yourself, Favel, but I don't really think that . . . in the circumstances . . . it would be wise for you to go to Tremethick.'

I was amazed; then I remembered the eager friendship of the Clements. Andrew Clement had always shown pleasure in my company; Mabell knew this. Was that why she had been so friendly with me?

'I'm sure Mabell Clement would understand if it were put to her,' said Deborah. 'Let's go to her and bring her in and explain.'

We did. Mabell looked surprised when we asked her in, but Deborah put the case very tactfully and, although Mabell quite clearly didn't agree, she made no attempt to persuade me.

'It's this place.' said Deborah, waving a hand. 'All small places are the same, I suppose. So little happens that people look for drama.'

'I shouldn't have said so *little* happens at Pendorric,' put in Mabell. 'Favel was shut in the vault and Morwenna has a crash that is almost fatal.'

'Such happenings give people a taste for more drama,' said Deborah. 'No, I'm certain it would be wrong. You see, my dears, suppose Favel is going to have her portrait painted, why shouldn't she come over every day?' She turned to me. 'Now if you do want to get away, dear, I'll take you to Devon for a week-end. Why not? You've always wanted to see my house. We could leave to-morrow if you liked. How would that be?'

'I'd like that,' I said.

Mabell seemed satisfied although disappointed that I was not going back with her.

'What more natural than that we should get away for a night or two,' said Deborah smiling. 'Then you'll be back by the time your husband returns.'

'It would be a . . . respite,' I said.

And Mabell agreed.

When Mabell had gone, Deborah told Charles what we planned. He thought it was an excellent idea. Rachel Bective was there to look after the twins; and he thought that by the time we returned we should know when Morwenna was leaving the hospital.

'My dear,' said Deborah, 'I don't see why we shouldn't leave to-day. Why wait till to-morrow? If you're ready to go, I am.'

I was very eager to get away from Pendorric because it was firmly in my mind that the menace which I felt close to me was somewhere in that house.

I collected together the things which I should need and Deborah went off to ask Carrie to do the same for her. Then Deborah brought her car round to the west porch, and Carrie came down with the bags.

As we drove round the side of the houe the twins came out of the north door.

They ran up to the car.

'Hallo, Granny Deb,' said Lowella. 'Hallo, Bride. We're going to see Mummy this afternoon. Daddy's taking us to the hospital.'

'That's wonderful, darling,' said Deborah, stopping to smile at them. 'Mummy will soon be home.'

'Where are you going?' demanded Lowella.

'I'm taking Favel to show her my house.'

Hyson had gripped the side of the car. 'Let me come with you.'

'Not this time, darling. You stay with Miss Bective. We'll be back soon.'

'I want to come. I want to be there. I don't want to stay here . . . alone,' said Hyson on a shrill note.

'Not this time, dear,' said Deborah. 'Take your hands away.' She touched them gently. Hyson dropped them and Deborah drove on. I turned and saw Rachel Bective come out of the house; then Hyson started to run after the car.

But Deborah had accelerated. We turned out of the drive.

We crossed the Tamar at Gunislake, and it seemed to me that as the distance between us and Pendorric grew greater, the higher Deborah's spirits rose. There was no doubt that recent events had depressed her considerably.

She talked a great deal about Morwenna, and what a relief it was to know that she was going to get well.

'When she recovers,' she said, 'I shall bring her over to the moor. I'm certain it would do her the world of good.'

I was beginning to see that she thought her moorland air the cure for all sickness, whether of the body or mind.

After passing through Tavistock we were soon on the moor. It reminded me very much of our own Cornish moors, but there was a subtle difference, Deborah told me; and you discovered it when you got to know them well. There was no moor like Dartmoor, she assured me, and insisted that Carrie corroborate this statement – which she readily did.

Carrie was excited too, and I caught their excitement and felt more at ease than I had since my quarrel with Roc.

Laranton Manor House stood alone about a mile from the village of

Laranton. It was an impressive building – Queen Anne in style – with massive iron gates at the entrance.

In the grounds was a cottage, and in this, Deborah told me, lived Mr. and Mrs. Hanson and their unmarried son, all of whom worked for her and kept the house in readiness for her return at any time.

She took out a key and opened the front door of the house about which clematis climbed. It must have been a lovely sight in season.

'Ah, it's good to be home,' she cried. 'Come along, my dear. Come in and see the old house which will always be home to me.'

I met Mrs. Hanson, who expressed no surprise to see her mistress home, and Deborah gave orders in her gentle but competent way.

'Mrs. Hanson, this is my nephew's bride. She's going to stay for a night or two. I want Carrie to get the blue room ready for her.'

'The blue room?' repeated Mrs. Hanson.

'Yes, please. I said the blue room. Carrie, put two hot-water bottles in the bed. You know how the first night in a strange bed always seems. And we should like something to eat, Mrs. Hanson. It's a fair journey from Pendorric.'

She made me sit down, for I was tired, she was sure.

'I'm going to cosset you,' she told me. 'Oh, it is fun to have you here. I've always wanted to bring you.'

I sat down in a chair near the big window which gave me a view of a neat lawn and flower-beds. 'Hanson's a good gardener, but it's not so easy to grow things on the moor as it is at Pendorric. The ground here is stony and it can be very cold in winter. Snow's a bit of a rarity at Pendorric; you should see it here in winter. There were times when Barbarina and I were kept in for a whole week – absolutely snowed up.'

I looked round the large room with its ingle-nook and pleasant furniture, and the large bowl of chrysanthemums on a gilt and marble console table.

'I've told Mrs. Hanson always to keep flowers in the house,' she told me, following my gaze. 'Barbarina used to look after the flowers, until she married. Then I took over. I didn't arrange them as artistically as she did.' She lifted her shoulders and smiled. 'I'm longing to show you your room. They should have it ready very soon. But first I'm hungry. Aren't you? It's our moorland air. Oh, it's good to be home.'

'I wonder you spend so much time at Pendorric,' I said, 'when you so clearly prefer it here.'

'Oh, it's because of the family . . . Morwenna, Roc, Hyson and Lowella! Pendorric's their home and if I want to be with them I have to be at Pendorric. I've brought Hyson here quite a lot. Lowella prefers the sea, but Hyson certainly has a taste for the moor.'

'She was very eager to come with us this time.'

'I know, dear child. But I did feel you needed a thorough rest. And with her mother in the hospital she should be there. When I'm here I feel young again. There's so much to remind me. I can almost imagine that Father is still alive and that at any moment Barbarina will come in through that door.'

'Did Barbarina come here often after her marriage?'

'Yes. She felt the same as I do about this place. After all it was home to her. She had spent the greater part of her life here. How I do harp on the past. It's a failing of the aged. Do forgive me, Favel. I want you to be happy here.'

'You're very kind.'

'My dear, I'm so fond of you.'

We were silent for a few moments and I thought that if I were with Deborah in some small country hotel I could have felt at ease. It was a pity that to escape from Pendorric I had to come to the house where Barbarina had spent the greater part of her life.

Mrs. Hanson came in to tell us that the meal was ready.

'An omelette, madam,' she said. 'If I'd had more time . . .'

'It'll be delicious, I'm sure,' smiled Deborah. 'Mrs. Hanson is one of the best cooks in Devon.'

The omelette was certainly delicious, and there was apple pie with clotted cream to follow.

'The real Devonshire cream,' Deborah told me gleefully. 'Now don't you agree it's better than the Cornish?'

I really couldn't tell the difference, so I said it was very good indeed.

'They copied it from us,' said Deborah; 'but they say we copied it from them!'

We were both growing more light-hearted, and I was sure it was a good thing that Deborah had brought me here! I could see quite clearly now that it would have been most unwise for me to have gone to the Clements'.

When the meal was over we went back to the drawing-room for coffee, and when we had finished, Deborah took me up and showed me my room.

It was right at the top of the house, very large and an odd shape. There were two windows, and the ceiling sloped slightly in a way which was charming and told me that we were immediately under the roof. The single bed at the opposite end of the room was partly in an alcove; and there was a desk, wardrobe, bedside table and dressing-table; on the bed was a blue coverlet, and the carpet was blue.

'This is delightful,' I said.

'And right at the top of the house. It's so light and airy, isn't it. Come and look out.'

We went to one of the windows, and because there was a half-moon I could see the moor stretched out beyond the gardens.

'You should see it in daylight,' Deborah told me. 'Miles and miles of moor. The gorse can be a picture, and the heather too. You can pick out the little streams. They look like flashes of silver in the sunlight.'

'I shall enjoy a good walk to-morrow.'

She didn't answer. She gazed, enraptured, at the moor.

She turned to me. 'Shall I help you unpack?'

'There's no need. I've brought very little.'

'There's plenty of room for your things.' She opened the door of the wardrobe.

I took out my night things and the two dresses I had brought with me, and she hung them on hangers.

'I'll show you the rest of the house,' she said.

I enjoyed my tour of the house. I saw the nursery where she told me she and Barbarina had played, the music room where Barbarina had learned the violin, the big drawing-room with its grand piano, and I had peered through the window at the walled garden outside.

'We used to grow lovely peaches on that wall. Our gardener saved all the best for Barbarina.'

'Weren't you a little jealous of her?' I asked.

'Jealous of Barbarina – never! Why, she and I were . . . close, as only twins can be. I could never really be jealous.'

'I think Barbarina was lucky to have you for a sister.'

'Yes, she was the lucky one . . . until the end, of course.'

'What really happened?' I felt compelled to ask. 'It was an accident, wasn't it?'

Her face crumpled suddenly and she turned away.

'It's so long ago,' she said almost piteously.

'And you still feel . . .?'

She seemed to pull herself together. 'There was a suggestion that someone was with her in the gallery at the time.'

'Did you believe it?'

'Yes.'

'Then who . . .?''

'It was never said, but lots of people had the idea that it was . . .'

'Her husband?'

'There was scandal about that woman. He was still seeing her. He never gave her up when he married Barbarina. He'd married Barbarina because of the money. He needed money. Houses like Pendorric are great monsters . . . they need continual feeding.'

'You think he killed her because he wanted to have Barbarina's fortune and marry Louisa Sellick?'

'It entered the minds of some people.'

'Yet he didn't marry her.'

'Perhaps he dared not.' She smiled at me bravely. 'I don't think we ought to be talking like this. It isn't fair to . . . Petroc.'

'I'm sorry. It's being here in her old home that reminded me.'

'Let's change the subject, shall we? Tell me what you would like to do while you're here.'

'See as much of the country as possible. I intend to be up early to-morrow. After all, I shall be here such a short time. I want to make the most of it.'

'Then I hope you get a good night's sleep. It's not always easy in a new bed, is it? I'll send Mrs. Hanson up with a nightcap. What do you like? Horlicks? Milo? Cocoa? Or just plain milk?'

I said I should prefer plain milk.

We sat talking a little while and then she said she would order the milk and take me up.

We mounted the lovely staircase right to the top of the house.

'One thing,' she told me, 'you'll be very quiet up here.'

'I'm sure I shall.'

'Barbarina always used to say that this was the room she liked best in the whole of the house. It was her room until she went to Pendorric.'

'Barbarina's room?' I said.

'The most charming of the bedrooms. That's why I gave it to you.'

'It was kind of you.'

'You . . . like it, don't you? If you don't I'll give you another.'

'I like it. . . .'

She laughed suddenly. 'It's Pendorric she's supposed to haunt. Not the old Manor.'

She drew the curtains across the windows and the room looked even more charming. Then she switched on the lamp which stood on the hexagonal bedside table.

'There! That should be comfortable. I hope you'll be warm enough. They should have put two bottles in the bed.' She prodded it. 'Yes, they have.'

She stood smiling at me. 'Good night, dear. Sleep well.'

Then she took my face in her hands and kissed it.

'The milk will be coming up. When would you like it – in five or ten minutes?'

'Five, please,' I said.

'All right. Good night, dear.'

She went out and left me. I undressed and, drawing back the curtains, stood for some seconds looking out over the moor. Peace, I thought. Here I shall be able to think about all the strange things which have been happening to me. I shall be able to make up my mind what I have to do.

There was a knock on my door and I was surprised to see Deborah, who came in carrying a glass of milk on a small tray.

She put this down on the hexagonal table.

'There you are, my dear. I thought I'd bring it myself.'

'Thank you.'

'You won't let it get cold, will you? Sleep well.'

She kissed me and went out.

I sat on the edge of the bed and, picking up the glass, sipped the milk, which was very hot.

I got into bed, but I was not in the least sleepy. I wished that I had brought something to read, but I had left Pendorric in such a hurry that I had forgotten to do so.

I looked around the room to see if I could find a book; then I noticed the drawer of the hexagonal table. Absently I opened it, and lying inside was a book with a leather cover. I took it out and saw written in a round childish hand on the fly-leaf: '*The dairy of Deborah and Barbarina Hyson*. This must be the only diary that ever has been written by two people, but of course we are not really two people in the same way that other people are. That is because we are twins. Signed: *Deborah Hyson. Barbarina Hyson*.'

I looked at those two signatures; they might have been written by the same hand.

So Deborah and Barbarina had kept a diary between them.

I was excited by my discovery; then I remembered that I was prying into something private. I shut the book firmly and drank some more milk. But I could not put the diary back into the drawer.

Barbarina had written in it. If I read what she had written I might learn something about her and she had roused my curiosity from the moment I had heard of her; now of course that curiosity was great because I had always felt that Barbarina was in some way connected with the things which were happening to me, and as I sat there in that strange bed it occurred to me that my position was not less dangerous because I had left Pendorric for a temporary respite. When I returned, more attempts might be made on my life.

I remembered that strange singing I had heard in the graveyard before I had been locked in the vault. If it was indeed true that someone was planning to murder me, then that someone was going to make it appear that my death was connected with the legend of Barbarina. And there was no doubting the fact that, if the superstitious people who lived round Pendorric were determined that the death of the Brides of Pendorric was due to some metaphysical law, they would be less likely to report any strange incident they might witness.

And as I held that book in my hand I became convinced that I should be foolish to put aside something which might help me in my need. There might be something in this book, some hint as to how Barbarina had met her death. Had she been in a position similar to mine before that fatal fall? Had she felt, as I was feeling now, that danger was creeping closer and closer, until it eventually caught up with her? If she had felt that, might she not have put it into her diary?

But this was her childhood diary; the one she shared with Deborah. There would scarcely be anything in it about her life at Pendorric.

But I was determined to see, and I opened the book.

It had probably not been intended for a diary in the first place, for there were no printed dates on the pages; but dates had been written in.

The first was September 6th. No year was given, and the entry read: 'Petroc came to-day. We think he is the best boy we have ever met. He boasts a bit, but then all boys do. We think he likes us because we are asked to his birthday party at Pendorric.'

The next entry was September 12th. 'Carrie is making our new dresses. She didn't know which of us was which. She is going to put name tabs on our clothes: Barbarina. Deborah. As if we cared. We always wear each other's things, we told her. Barbarina's are Deborah's and Deborah's Barbarina's; but she said we should have our own.'

It seemed just a childish account of their lives here in this house on the moor, of the parties they went to. I had no idea who was writing because the first person singular was never used; it was all in the first person plural. I went on reading until I came to a blank page and thought for a moment that was the end; but a few pages on there was more writing, yet it was not the same. It had matured and I presumed that the diary had been forgotten for some time and taken up again. There was more than a change in the handwriting, for I read:

'*August 13th*. I was lost on the moor. It was wonderful.' I was excited because now I could say: That was actually written by Barbarina.

Barbarina seemed to have taken on the diary from that point.

'*August 16th*. Petroc has asked Father and of course Father is delighted. He pretended to be surprised. As if it isn't what they've all wanted for so long! I'm so happy. I'm longing to be at Pendorric. Then I shall escape from Deborah. Fancy wanting to escape from Deborah who up till now has always seemed a part of me. She is in a way a part of me. That was why she had to feel as I do about Petroc. There were always two of us to go places, to get ourselves out of trouble – silly little troubles, of course, which you think are so important when you're children. But that's all changed now. I want to get away – away from Deborah. I can't stand the way she looks at me when I've been with Petroc – as though she's trying to read my mind and can't, like she used to – as though she hates me. Am I beginning to hate her?

'*September 1st*. Yesterday Father, Deborah and I arrived at Pendorric for a visit. We're going ahead fast with arrangements for the wedding and I'm so excited. I saw Louisa Sellick to-day while I was out riding with Petroc. I suppose she's what people would call beautiful. She looks sad. That's because she knows now she has lost Petroc for ever. I asked Petroc about her. Perhaps I should have said nothing. But I was never one to stay calm. Deborah was the calm one. Petroc said it was all over. Is it? If it isn't I feel I could kill her. I won't share Petroc. Sometimes I wish I'd fallen in love with some of the others. George Fanshawe would have been a good husband and he was very much in love with me. So was Tom Kellerway. But it had to be Petroc. If Tom or George would fall in love with Deborah – Why is it they don't? We look so much alike that people can't tell us apart and yet they don't fall in love with Deborah. It's the same as it was when we were young. When we were at parties she'd keep in the background. I never did. She always said: "People don't want me. I get in on your ticket." And because she believed it and acted that way, it came to be true. Now Deborah doesn't know I'm going on with our diary I can write exactly what I feel. It's such a relief.

'*September 3rd*. Pendorric! What a wonderful old house. I love it. And Petroc! What is it about him that's different from everyone else in the world! Some magic! He's so gay, but sometimes I'm frightened. He doesn't seem to be entirely with me.'

I had come to several blank pages in the book, but after that the writing went on.

'*July 3rd*. I found this old diary to-day. It's ages since I wrote in it. The last time was just before I married. I see I've only put the months and days and left out the years. How like me! Still, it doesn't matter. I don't know why I want to write in it again. For comfort, I suppose. Since the twins were born I haven't thought of it. It's only now. I woke up last night and he wasn't there. I thought of that woman, Louisa Sellick. I hate her. There are rumours about her. I suppose he's still seeing her – and others. Could anyone be all that attractive and not take advantage of it? If I'd wanted a faithful husband I ought not to have married such an attractive man as

Petroc. I notice things. I've seen people at parties talking. They brightly change the subject when I come up. I know they're talking about Petroc and me - and some woman. Louisa Sellick probably. The servants look at me - pityingly. Mrs. Penhalligan for one - even old Jesse. What are they saying? Sometimes I feel I'll go mad if I let things drift like this. When I try to talk to Petroc he'll never be serious. He says, "Well, of course I love you." And I snap back: "And how many others too?" "Mine's a loving nature," he answers. He can never be serious. Life's so amusing to him. I want to shout at him that it's not so amusing to me. When I think of the old days in Father's house I remember how I used to love parties. Everyone made a fuss of me. And Deborah was there - she used to be as pleased as I was with my popularity. Once she said: "I enjoy it just as though it were mine." And I answered "It *is* yours, Deb. Don't you remember we always used to say that we weren't two people - but one." In those days that satisfied her.'

I had been so excited by what I read that I hadn't noticed what was happening to myself. I had actually yawned several times during the reading, and my lids now seemed so heavy that I couldn't keep my eyes open.

If I had been less enthralled I should not have been surprised, but the contents of this diary should surely have kept me wide awake.

I was determined to go on reading.

'*August 8th.* Deborah has been here for the last fortnight. She seems to come more often now. There is a change in Deb. She's become more *alive*. She laughs more easily. Something has changed her. Other people may not notice - but then they don't know her like I do. She borrowed my riding hat the other day - the black one with the band of blue round it. She stood before the looking-glass and said: "I don't believe anyone would know I wasn't you - not *anyone.*" And actually she has grown more like me since she became more lovely. I know on several occasions the servants called her by my name. It amused her very much. I had an idea that she longed to be in my place. If only she knew. But that's something I wouldn't tell even her. It's too humiliating. No, I couldn't even tell Deborah about all the times when I wake up and find Petroc not with me, how I get up and walk about the room imagining what he's doing. If she knew what I had to suffer she wouldn't want to be in my place. She sees Petroc as so many others see him - just about the most fascinating man anyone could meet anywhere. It's different being his wife. Sometimes I hate him.

'*August 20th.* There was another scene yesterday. Petroc says I've got to be calm. He says he doesn't know what'll happen if I don't control myself more. Control myself! When he treats me like this! He says I'm too possessive. He says, "Don't pry into my life and I won't pry into yours." What sort of a marriage is this?

'*August 27th.* He has not been near me for more than a week. Sometimes I think everything is over between us. He can't stand scenes, he says. Of course he can't, because he's in the wrong. He just wants to go on living his own way - which is more or less the same as before he was married; but everything must seem all right on the surface. There mustn't be scandal. Petroc hates scandal. The fact is he's lazy. That's why he married me.

Pendorric needed money. I had it. It was simple. Marry money and there's no need to worry. Why does he have to be so amusing, so charming on the surface – so feckless and cruel underneath? If only I could be as light-hearted as he is! If only I could say "Oh – that's just Petroc. I must take him as I find him." But I can't. I love him too much. I don't want to share him. Sometimes I think I'll go mad. Petroc thinks so too. That's why he stays away. He hates it when I lose control. Father used to hate it too. But Father was kind and gentle with me. He used to say, "Barbarina my dear, you must be quiet. Look at Deborah. How calm she is. Be more like your sister, Barbarina." And that used to help. I'd remember that Deborah and I were like one. She had all the calmness in our nature. I was the volatile one. Father might deplore my wildness; but it was what made me attractive and Deborah a little dull. Deborah ought to comfort me now but even she has changed.

'*August 29th*. From my window I saw Deborah come back from a ride to-day. She was wearing a hat with a blue band. Not mine this time. She's got one exactly like it. As she came round from the stables the children were just going out with their nurse. They called to her. "Hallo, Mummy," they said. Deborah stooped and kissed first Morwenna, then Roc. The nurse said: "Morwenna's knee is healing up nicely, Mrs. Pendorric." Mrs. Pendorric! So the nurse and the children had mistaken her for me. I felt angry. I hated Deborah in that moment and it was like hating myself. I did hate myself. It was some minutes later when I said to myself, "But why didn't Deborah explain?" But she didn't. She just let them think she was the children's mother – the mistress of the house.

'*September 2nd*. If this goes on I think I shall kill myself. I've been thinking about it more and more. A quiet sleep for ever and ever. No more Petroc. No more jealousy. Sometimes I long for that. I often remember the Bride story. Some of the servants are sure Lowella Pendorric haunts the place. They won't go in the gallery where she hangs, after dark. This Lowella died after a year of marriage, having a son; she was cursed by her husband's mistress. The Pendorric men haven't changed much. When I think of my life at Pendorric, I'm ready to believe there might be a curse on the women of the house.

'*September 3rd*. Petroc says I'm getting more and more hysterical. How can I help that? All I ask is that he should be with me more, should love me as I love him. Surely that's not asking too much. All *he* cares about is that he should miss none of his pleasures, which means women – women all the time. Though I believe he's kept on with this Louisa Sellick. So he's faithful to her – after his fashion. There's one other thing that he cares about: Pendorric. What a fuss the other day when they discovered woodworm in the gallery. The wood's particularly bad in the balustrade – near Lowella Pendorric's picture – the one who was supposed to have died because of the curse, and haunt the place. That's what's made me think of her so much.

'*September 12th*. Deborah is still with us. She doesn't seem to want to go back to the moor. She certainly has changed. Sometimes I think she's growing more like I used to be, and I'm becoming more like she was. She's inclined to use my things as though they were hers. We did this in the old days but it was different then. She comes into my bedroom and talks. It's odd but I fancy she's trying to get me to talk about Petroc, and when I do she seems to shy away. The other day when we were talking she picked up a jacket of mine – a casual sort of thing in mustard colour. "You hardly wear it," she said. "I always like it." She slipped it on and as I looked at her I had a strange feeling that I *am* Deborah and that she's so longing to be in my place that she is Barbarina. I felt it was myself I was looking at. Is Petroc right? Is all that I'm suffering driving me crazy? Deborah took off the jacket but when she went out she slung it over her arm and I haven't seen it since.

'*September 14th*. I cry a lot. I'm so wretched. No wonder Petroc hardly ever comes near me. For some weeks he's been sleeping in the dressing-room. I try to tell myself it's better that way. Then I don't know whether he's there or not, so I don't have to wonder whom he's with. But of course I do.

'*September 20th*. I can't believe it. I must write it down. I think I'll go mad if I don't. I could bear the others; but not this. I know about Louisa Sellick and I can understand it – and up to a point forgive it. After all he wanted to marry her. It was because of Pendorric that he married me. But this. It's all so unnatural. I hate Deborah now. There isn't room for the two of us in this world. Perhaps there never was. We should have been one person. No wonder she's going about deceiving people – not correcting them when they call her Mrs. Pendorric. Petroc and Deborah! It's incredible. But of course it's not. It's inevitable in a way. After all, so much of me is Deborah and so much of her me. We are one – so why shouldn't we share Petroc as we have shared so many other things? Gradually she's been taking what's mine – not only my husband but my personality. The way she laughs now – the way she sings. That's not Deborah; it's Barbarina. I go about the house outwardly calm letting the servants think that I don't care. I stand there smiling when they talk to me and pretend to be interested as I did to-day when old Jesse talked about bringing something into the hall – some plant or other. It's getting too cold out of doors or something and he doesn't think the hothouse is quite right for it. Yes, yes, yes, I said, not listening. Poor old Jesse! He's almost blind now. I told him not to worry; we'd see he was all right. And Petroc will, of course. That's one thing about him – he's good to the servants. I'm writing trivialities to prevent myself thinking. Deborah and Petroc – I've seen them together. I know. It's her room he goes to. It leads from the gallery not far from that spot where the picture of Lowella Pendorric hangs. I lay listening last night and heard the door close. Deborah who is getting like I used to be – and Petroc. How I hate them – both! There shouldn't be two of us. I've tolerated others but I won't tolerate this. But how can I stop it?

'*September 21st*. I've decided to kill myself. I can't go on. I keep wondering how. Perhaps I'll walk into the sea. They say that after the first moment of struggle, it's an easy death. You don't feel it much. My body would be washed in and Petroc would see it. He'd never forget. I'd haunt him for the rest of his life. It would be his punishment and he deserves to be punished. It would be the legend coming true. The Bride of Pendorric would haunt the place, and I, Barbarina, would be that bride. It seems somehow right – inevitable. I think it is the only way.'

The rest of that page was blank and I thought I had come to the end of the diary. I yawned, I was very tired.

But as I turned the page I came to more writing, and what I read startled me so much that I was almost wide awake.

'*October 19th*. They think I am dead. Yet I am still here and they don't know it. Petroc doesn't know. It's a good thing that he can't bear to be near me, because he might discover the truth. He's away most of the time. He goes to Louisa Sellick for comfort. Let him. I don't care now. Everything is different. It's – exciting. There's no other word for it. I shouldn't write in this book. It's all so dangerous, but I like to go over it again and again. It's funny – really funny because it makes me laugh sometimes – but only when I'm alone. When I'm with anyone I'm calm – terribly calm. I have to be. I feel more alive now than I have for a long time – now that they think I'm dead. I must write it down. I'm afraid I'll forget if I don't. I had made up my mind how I would die. I was going to walk into the sea. Perhaps I'd leave a note for Petroc, telling him that he'd driven me to it. Then I'd be sure that I'd haunt him for the rest of his life. It all happened so suddenly. I hadn't planned it that way at all. Then suddenly I saw how it could be done. How a new bride could take the place of Lowella Pendorric, for it was time she rested in her grave, poor thing. Deborah came into my room. She was wearing my mustard-coloured jacket, and her eyes were bright; she looked sleek and contented, and I knew, as well as if she'd told me, that he'd been with her the previous night. "You're looking tired, Barby," she said. Tired! So would she, had she lain awake as I had. She'd be punished too. She would never forgive herself. I doubted whether she and Petroc would be lovers after I had gone. "Petroc's really concerned about the gallery," she said, "It'll probably mean replacing the whole thing." How dared she tell me how Petroc felt! How dared she talk in that proprietorial way about Petroc and Pendorric! She used to be so sensitive to my moods; but now her mind was full of Petroc. She picked up a scarf of mine – Petroc himself had bought it for me when we were in Italy – a lovely thing of emerald-coloured silk. She put it absently about her neck. The mustard-coloured jacket set it off perfectly. Something happened when she took that scarf. It seemed tremendously important. My husband – my scarf. I felt I hadn't a life of my own any more. I wonder now why I didn't snatch it away from her, but I didn't. "Come and look at the gallery," she said. "It's really quite dangerous. The workmen will be coming in to-morrow." I allowed myself to follow her out to the gallery; we stood beneath the picture of Lowella. "Here," she said, "Look, Barby." Then it happened. It suddenly seemed clear to me. I was going to die because there was no longer any reason to go on living. I had thought of walking into the sea. Deborah was standing close to the worm-eaten rail. It was a long drop down to the hall. I felt Lowella Pendorric was watching us from her canvas, saying: "A Bride must die that I may rest in peace." It was the old legend and there's a lot of truth in these old legends. That's why they persist. Deborah was, in a sense, a Bride of Pendorric. Petroc treated her as such – and she was part of me. There were times when

I was not sure which of us I was. I'm glad I wrote this down, although it's dangerous. This book must never be seen by anyone. It's safe enough. Only Carrie has ever seen it and she knows what happened as well as I do. When I read it, I can remember it clearly. It's the only way I can come back to what really happened on that day. I can live again that moment when she was standing there, perilously close, and I leaned forward and pushed her with all my might. I can hear her catch her breath in amazement – and horror. I can hear her voice, or did I imagine that? But I hear it all the same. "No, Barbarina!" Then I know of course that I am Barbarina and that it is Deborah who lies in the Pendorric vault. Then I can laugh and say: How clever I am. They think me dead and I am alive all these years. But it's only when I read this book that I am absolutely sure who I am.'

I felt limp with horror.

But there was more to be read and I went on reading.

'*October 20th.* I shouldn't write in the book any more. But I can't resist it. I want to write it down while I remember, because it's fading fast and I am not sure. There was someone in the hall. I was frightened. But it was only old Jesse and he couldn't see. I stood in the gallery, looking at the splintered wood. I wouldn't look down on to the hall. I didn't stay long. Old Jesse had run for help. He might not see me but he knew something was wrong. I ran into the nearest room because I had to get out of the gallery before I was seen. It was Deborah's. I threw myself on to her bed and I lay there, my heart thundering. I don't know how long I lay there but it seemed like hours. It was a few minutes actually. Voices, cries of horror. What was happening in the hall? I longed to see but I knew I must stay where I was. After a while there was a knock on the door. I was still lying on the bed when Mrs. Penhalligan came in. She said: "Miss Hyson, there's been a terrible accident." I raised myself and stared at her. "It's the gallery rail. 'Twas worse than we thought. Mrs. Pendorric—' I just went on staring at her. She went out and I heard her voice outside the door. "Miss Hyson, she be terrible shocked, poor dear. 'Tis not to be wondered at – they being so close – so near like. I for one couldn't tell one from the other."

'I went down to the sea and looked at it. It was grey and cold. I couldn't do it. It's easy to talk of dying; but when you face it – you're frightened. You're terribly frightened. I'd been so stunned by the news that they'd made me stay in bed until it was all over. I didn't see Petroc unless others were there too. That was as well. He was the one I feared. Surely he would know his own wife. But even so there was something I knew about Petroc. He wasn't the same. The gaiety had gone, the light-heartedness. He blamed himself. The servants were talking. They said it was *meant.* And it happened right under the picture of that other bride. It was no good going against what was meant. Barbarina was meant, to die, so that Lowella Pendorric could rest from the haunting. They wouldn't go near the gallery after dark. They believed Barbarina was haunting Pendorric. So she is. She haunted Petroc till the day he died. So the story was true. The Bride of Pendorric had died just as the story said she should and she couldn't rest in her grave.

'I couldn't go. I couldn't leave the children. They call me Aunt Deborah now. I *am* Deborah. I'm calm and serene. Carrie knows, though. Sometimes she calls me Miss Barbarina. I'm afraid of Carrie. But she'd never hurt me; she loves me too well. I was always her favourite. I was everybody's favourite. It's different now, though. People are different towards me. They call me Deborah and what is happening is that Deborah still lives and it is Barbarina who is dead.

'*January 1st*. I shall not write any more. There is nothing to write. Barbarina is dead. She had a fatal accident. Petroc hardly spoke to me again. I believe he thought that I was jealous of her, and that I did it hoping he'd marry me; he doesn't want to know too much about it in case it's true. I don't care about Petroc any more. I'm devoted to the children. It doesn't matter now that Petroc is never here. I'm not his wife any more; I'm his sister-in-law, taking care of his motherless children. I'm happier than I ever was since my marriage; though sometimes I think of my sister and it's as though she's with me. She comes to me at night when I'm alone and her eyes are mournful and accusing. She can't rest. She haunts me and she haunts Petroc. It's in the legend; and she'll continue to haunt Pendorric until another young bride takes her place; then she will rest for evermore.

'*March 20th*. I have been reading this book. I shall not read it any more. I shall not write in it any more. I shall hide it away. It worries me. Barbarina is dead and I am Deborah; I am calm and serene and I have devoted myself to Roc and Morwenna. Barbarina haunts me; that's because it's in the story that she should – until another bride takes her place. But reading this book upsets me. I shall not do it any more.'

There was one last entry. It stated simply:

'One day, there'll be a new bride at Pendorric and then Barbarina shall have her rest.'

So it was Barbarina who had brought me to this house, who had lured me to the vault, who had sought to kill me.

I did not know what to do. What could I do to-night? I was alone in this house with Barbarina and Carrie, for the Hansons would be in their cottage in the grounds.

I must lock my door. I attempted to get out of bed but my legs seemed unable to move, and even in my agitated state I could not fight the drowsiness which had taken possession of me. A thought came into my head that I was asleep and dreaming: and in that moment the book had slipped from my fingers and falling asleep was like entering a deep dark cave.

I awoke with a start. For a few seconds I was still in that deep, dark cave of oblivion; then objects started to take shape. Where was I? There was the hexagonal table. I remembered the diary, and then where I was.

I knew too that something had awakened me, and the knowledge quickly followed that I was not alone. Someone was in this room.

I had fallen asleep so suddenly that I was lying on my back. I had been aware of the hexagonal table by turning my eyes towards it without moving my head. The heavy sleepiness was still upon me and the deep darkness of the cave was threatening to close about me once more.

I was so tired . . . too tired to be afraid . . . too tired to care that I was not alone in the room.

I'm dreaming, I thought. Of course I'm dreaming. For from out of the shadows came a figure. It was a woman dressed in a blue house-coat. As the moonlight touched her face I knew who she was.

My heavy lids were pressing down over my eyes; vaguely I heard her voice.

'This time, little bride, there shall be no way out. They will no longer talk of Barbarina's ghost . . . but yours.'

I wanted to call out; but some waking instinct warned me not to, and I began to wonder whether after all I was in a dream.

Never before in my life had I been so frightened. Yet never had I been so sleepy, and terror was trying to ward off my sleepiness. What was happening to me? I longed to be in my bedroom at Pendorric with Roc beside me. That was safety. This was danger.

'This is a nightmare,' I told myself. 'In a moment you will wake up.'

She was standing at the foot of my bed looking at me while I watched her through half-closed eyes, waiting for what she would do next.

An impulse came to me to speak to her, but something warned me that I must first find out what she intended to do. This had never happened to me before. I was asleep; yet I was awake. I was terrified; and yet it was as though I stood outside this scene, a watcher in the shadows. I was looking on at the frightened woman in the bed and the other whose purpose was evil.

An idea hit me. I am drugged. The milk was drugged. The milk Deborah brought me. No . . . not *Deborah*. I didn't drink it all. If I had I should now be in a deep, drugged sleep.

She was smiling. Then I saw her hands move in a gesture as though she were sprinkling something over my bed. She went to the window and stooped for a few seconds; and then she stood upright and without giving another glance at my bed, ran from the room.

I was aware of thinking: It is a dream. Then suddenly it seemed I was wide awake. I was looking at a wall of flame. The curtains were on fire. For one second, two seconds, I stared at them, while it was as though I emerged from that black cave to reality.

I smelt petrol and in terrible understanding leaped out of bed and made for the door. I was not a second too soon, for as I did so my bed was aflame.

It is difficult to recall what happened next. I was aware of the blazing bed as I pulled at the door-handle and for one hideous second believed that I was locked in this room as I had been locked in the vault. But that was only due to my anxiety to get out quickly. The door was not locked.

I pulled it open and had the sense to shut it behind me. I saw her then. She was running along the corridor, and I went after her shouting: 'Fire!' as I did so. She turned to look at me.

I cried: 'Quick! My room's on fire. We must give the alarm.'

She looked at me in bewilderment. I knew then that she was mad, and for those few dramatic seconds I even forgot the danger we were in.

'You tried to kill me . . . *Barbarina!*' I said.

Horror dawned in her face. I heard her whisper as though to herself: 'The diary ... Oh, my God, she's read the diary.'

I caught her arm. 'You've set my room on fire,' I said urgently. 'It'll spread ... quickly. Where's Carrie? On this floor? Carrie! Carrie! Come quickly.'

Barbarina's lips were moving; she went on muttering to herself: 'It's there ... in the diary ... She's seen the diary. ...'

Carrie came into the corridor, wrapping an old dressing-gown about her, her hair in a plait tied with a red tape.

'Carrie,' I shouted. 'My room's on fire. Phone the fire brigade quickly.'

'Carrie! Carrie! She ... *knows* ...' moaned Barbarina

I gripped Carrie's arm. 'Show me where the phone is. There's no time to lose. We must all get out of the house. Don't you understand?'

Still gripping Carrie I pulled her downstairs. I did not look back, being certain that Barbarina, knowing how deadly was the fire she had started, would follow us.

I never saw Barbarina again. By the time we had phoned for the brigade, the top floor was a mass of flame. All I knew was that Barbarina did not follow us downstairs. I have always believed that, rudely shaken out of her dream-world, she had had no thought of anything but the incriminating diary. To her it represented the only way of remembering what had actually happened; and to have lost it would have been to have lost touch with the past. Unbalanced as she was, she had made a futile attempt to save it. I do not like to think what happened to Barbarina when she burst into that room which by then must have been a roaring furnace.

It was nearly an hour before the fire brigade reached the isolated manor house, and by that time it was too late to save it. It was not until we had telephoned for the brigade and the Hansons had arrived that we missed Barbarina. Hanson bravely went up to try to rescue her. We had to prevent Carrie from dashing into the flames to bring out her mistress, for we knew it was hopeless.

Looking back it is hard to remember the sequence of events. But I do remember sitting in the Hansons' cottage drinking tea which Mrs. Hanson brought to me, when suddenly I heard a familiar voice.

'Roc!' I cried, and ran to him; we just stood together clinging.

And this was a Roc I had never known before because I had never seen him clearly through the fog of suspicion which surrounded him – strong in his power to protect, weak in his anxiety over my safety, ready to do battle with the powers of darkness for my sake, yet terrified for fear some harm had come to me.

Chapter Seven

It is a year since that night and yet the memory of it is with me as vividly as when it happened. Perhaps, if one has come near to violent death, as I did, it is an experience which is never far from the surface of the mind.

I often say to Roc: 'If it hadn't been that I was so absorbed in the diary I should have drunk all the milk; I should have been unconscious when Barbarina came into my room and that would have been the end of me.' To that Roc answers: 'All life is chance. If your father had never come to our coast, you would not have been here at all.'

And it is so.

It is difficult to understand everything that went on in Barbarina's mind; I am sure that for much of the time she believed she was Deborah. She could never have played the part so well if she had not; and her character must have changed after Deborah died so that she really did take on the personality of her twin. The more she behaved like Deborah, the more like her she grew, just as Deborah, when Petroc became her lover, began to be like Barbarina. The curse laid on the Brides of Pendorric became an obsession with her. It may have been that she believed Deborah's spirit had actually entered her body, and that she had become Deborah; and because she constantly thought of the sister whom she had sent to her death, she believed she was haunted by her and it was for this reason that she was anxious for another bride to take over the role of ghost at Pendorric.

But how can one follow the tortuous meandering of a sick mind?

My conjectures must have an element of truth in them, though, because there was no doubt that I had been in danger from the moment I had come to Pendorric.

Poor simple-minded Carrie, who had always been dominated by her charges, was easily caught up in this morbid dream-life of her mistress; Barbarina and Deborah were one and the same; and Carrie believed it, while she alone knew that the twin who had fallen to her death in the hall at Pendorric was Deborah. At times she could not understand Barbarina's interpretation of this strange phenomenon; namely that Deborah's mind and soul were now with Barbarina. Carrie could only accept this by telling herself that the two of them were really alive.

It was from Carrie that we gleaned a little understanding of Barbarina's madness; but the years during which she had devoted herself to Barbarina and her crazy conception of life had undermined her own sanity and Roc was anxious that she should not be upset. He sent her away in the care of an old nanny of his who had a cottage on the Devon coast, and there she is now.

It was not so easy with Hyson, for Barbarina had tried to draw the child into her orbit. She saw in Lowella and Hyson a repetition of herself and Deborah; and because for most of the time she believed she *was* Deborah, she had great sympathy for the less attractive twin. Barbarina's affection for the child was deep and possessive and Hyson was fascinated by the strangeness of Barbarina, who revealed herself more to the child than to anyone else. Hyson did not understand but she was aware of the strangeness and, like Barbarina, learned to project herself into that make-believe world; Barbarina had hinted that she still lived and Hyson believed her; she believed that Barbarina would lure me to my death, so that she might rest in her grave according to the legend.

It was from Carrie we learned that Barbarina had sometimes gone to the music room and played the violin, and that she sang Ophelia's song; and that it was she who had waited for me to leave Polhorgan and had removed the sign on the cliffs in the hope that I, less sure-footed than those accustomed to the path, would have a fatal accident. She it was who had locked me in the vault, for the only other key to the vault had been in her possession; she had often paid secret visits to the vault as, according to Carrie, she told her she wanted to be with Barbarina. She would never have come to the vault had not Hyson been missing and she, guessing where she was, had decided to abandon that method of disposing of me, for the sake of the child. She had quietly unlocked the door before going to find Roc. Then she had tampered with the car and chance again had stepped in so that it was Morwenna who had had an accident.

Often I reflect how easily the legend of the Brides might have gone on and on; for few people can have come as near to death as I did, and escape. If Barbarina had been a cold-blooded murderess I should never have escaped; but she was not that; if she had been, she would have planned more carefully; but she was caught in her world of make-believe; she was living on two levels and she could not see where reality and the dream-world merged. I discovered that she had trunks of Deborah's clothes and often wore them when she was in Devon. The Hansons were not aware of this, never having known Deborah, and when Carrie called her Barbarina they merely thought that Carrie was a little weak in the head. And Barbarina could lightly step back into the character of Deborah to assure them that this was so.

I often wondered what damage she would have done to Hyson if I had not come to Pendorric when I did. The child was neurotic, her head full of strange notions. She was already beginning to believe that she stood in the same relationship to Lowella as Deborah had to Barbarina. Barbarina had won her devotion by preferring her to her gayer sister; and that was when the damage began to be done.

But there again events worked against her. Hyson had endured the terrifying experience of being locked in the vault with me. She had known, because of the hints Barbarina loved to give the child, that something was going to happen that day. She believed that the figure she saw in the graveyard when she had hidden herself there was the ghost of Barbarina. Barbarina had been unwise to involve the child, but, because she was already identifying Hyson with Deborah, could not stop doing so. And when

Barbarina opened the door of the vault and sang the song which was to lure me inside, Hyson slipped in. Thus we were locked in together, and from that moment Hyson began to understand the horror of death, that it did not come lightly, that there must be suffering before oblivion was reached.

Then she saw her mother in the hospital and she must have known that Morwenna was lying where I was intended to be.

Death was hateful; it was frightening; and it touched those she loved. Her own mother. And even for me she had some affection.

She was frightened; and when she saw me going off with Barbarina in the car, guessing for what purpose, she broke into hysteria which so alarmed her father that he sent for Dr. Clement, but it was some time before they could understand the meaning of her incoherent words. Dr. Clement's first action was to telephone Roc; and Roc immediately drove to the manor.

Yet although I lived so dangerously up to that night when Roc came to me in Devon, it was during the following months that I learned so much more of life than I ever had before; the months of safety and serenity.

For one thing, I learned the story of the boy who lived in Louisa Sellick's house on the moor. Morwenna must have grown up too, because she confessed to Charles that he was hers. She had been afraid to do so before because the boy was the result of a brief passionate love affair which had occurred when she was seventeen.

Rachel Bective, who as a child had so longed to be asked to Pendorric that she had locked Morwenna in the vault in order to blackmail her into giving her an invitation, had proved a good friend. She had looked after Morwenna during her troubles, and of course Roc had been at hand. It had been his idea to ask Louisa's help, and he and Rachel took the child to her; Louisa had been only too glad to do what she could for Petroc's children.

As Roc said to me: 'I couldn't tell you the truth when I'd sworn to keep Morwenna's secret. But I did intend to persuade her that you should be brought in. The trouble was she was so afraid of Charles's knowing.'

There had been fear and drama in Pendorric before I arrived.

During the last year we have gone a long way towards turning Polhorgan into a home for orphans. I am going to be very busy keeping an eye on this particular project as I shall be starting my own family. Rachel Bective is going to be a nursery governess to the orphans, and Dr. Clement will be at hand to advise when we need him. The Dawsons will stay on and although there may be a little friction now and then between them and Rachel, that is inevitable, I suppose. I don't like Rachel – I doubt whether I ever shall – but I have wronged her in my thoughts so much that I try very hard to change my opinion. She was merely enamoured of a way of life which was not hers. The romantic big house must have been very appealing to an orphan, brought up by an aunt who had children of her own and didn't really want her. She saw her main opportunity in life when she was sent to a good school paid for with the money her parents had left with instructions that all of it be spent on their daughter's education. She had attached herself to Morwenna and clung; but she had been a good friend in Morwenna's trouble and often visited Bedivere House – as Roc did – to bring Morwenna news of the son she dared not see until she had confessed to Charles.

The twins have now gone to school – separate schools. Hyson had a holiday, a holiday at Bournemouth alone with her mother after Morwenna's recovery. They both needed to recuperate; and we feel that in time Hyson will grow away from that sinister influence which Barbarina cast about her. We shall have to be very careful in our treatment of Hyson.

This, then, has been an illuminating year.

We all seem to have grown up, become wise; but then I suppose it is experiences such as these which make us learn our lessons quickly.

Morwenna has cast off the burden which, like Christian in *Pilgrim's Progress*, she has carried for fourteen years, and Charles, she discovered, was less self-righteous than she had believed him to be. Indeed he was a little sad and reproachful that she had not trusted him all those years.

As a result, Ennis and Louisa are often at Pendorric. Morwenna would not take the boy from Louisa, but she does want to share him, and I have an idea that in time he will be to Charles as the son he did not have.

It may well be that one day we shall have to give up Pendorric as we know it. We shall probably have to throw it open to the public and have strangers walking through our rooms. We shall have our own apartments of course, but it will not be the same.

Roc is reconciled. 'You can't fight the times,' he says. 'It would be like trying to fight the sea.'

All the money I have will be used on Polhorgan, and that is how Roc wishes it to be.

He often teases me, reminding me that I once thought he schemed to marry an heiress and then planned to murder her.

'And yet,' he said, 'you loved me . . . after your fashion.'

He is right. During those months of danger I was deep in physical love with Roc; I knew only what I saw, what I heard, what I sensed.

But there are many facets of love, and of these I am learning more every day; and so is he. And that is why when we walk down the cliff gardens to Pendorric Cove and look towards Polhorgan, high on the cliff, or to Cormorant Cottage where Althea Grey once lived, we remember those doubts which, while they did not diminish our passion, yet were a sign that we had just begun that voyage of discovery which our life together will be.

Victoria
Holt

Mistress
of Mellyn

Chapter One

'There are two courses open to a gentlewoman when she finds herself in penurious circumstances,' my Aunt Adelaide had said. 'One is to marry, and the other to find a post in keeping with her gentility.'

As the train carried me through wooded hills and past green meadows, I was taking this second course; partly, I suppose, because I had never had an opportunity of trying the former.

I pictured myself as I must appear to my fellow travellers if they bothered to glance my way, which was not very likely: A young woman of medium height, already past her first youth, being twenty-four years old, in a brown merino dress with cream lace collar and little tufts of lace at the cuffs. (Cream being so much more serviceable than white, as Aunt Adelaide told me.) My black cape was unbuttoned at the throat because it was hot in the carriage, and my brown velvet bonnet, tied with brown velvet ribbons under my chin, was of the sort which was so becoming to feminine people like my sister Phillida but, I always felt, sat a little incongruously on heads like mine. My hair was thick with a coppery tinge, parted in the centre, brought down at the sides of my too-long face, and made into a cumbersome knot to project behind the bonnet. My eyes were large, in some lights the colour of amber, and were my best feature; but they were too bold – so said Aunt Adelaide; which meant that they had learned none of the feminine graces which were so becoming to a woman. My nose was too short, my mouth too wide. In fact, I thought, nothing seemed to fit; and I must resign myself to journeys such as this when I travel to and from the various posts which I shall occupy for the rest of my life, since it is necessary for me to earn a living, and I shall never achieve the first of those alternatives: a husband.

We had passed through the green meadows of Somerset and were now deep in the moorland and wooded hills of Devon. I had been told to take good note of that masterpiece of bridge-building, Mr. Brunel's bridge, which spanned the Tamar at Saltash and, after crossing which, I should have left England behind me and have passed into the Duchy of Cornwall.

I was becoming rather ridiculously excited about crossing the bridge. I was not a fanciful woman at this time – perhaps I changed later, but then a stay in a house like Mount Mellyn was enough to make the most practical of people fanciful – so I could not understand why I should feel this extraordinary excitement.

It was absurd, I told myself. Mount Mellyn may be a magnificent mansion; Connan TreMellyn may be as romantic as his name sounds; but that will be no concern of yours. You will be confined to below stairs, or perhaps to the attics above stairs, concerned only with the care of little Alvean.

What strange names these people had! I thought, staring out of the window. There was sun on the moorland but the grey tors in the distance looked oddly menacing. They were like petrified people.

This family to which I was going was Cornish, and the Cornish had a language of their own. Perhaps my own name, Martha Leigh, would sound odd to them. Martha! It always gave me a shock when I heard it. Aunt Adelaide always used it, but at home when my father had been alive he and Phillida never thought of calling me Martha. I was always Marty. I could not help feeling that Marty was a more lovable person than Martha could ever be, and I was sad and a little frightened because I felt that the River Tamar would cut me off completely from Marty for a long time. In my new post I should be Miss Leigh, I supposed; perhaps Miss, or more undignified still – Leigh.

One of Aunt Adelaide's numerous friends had heard of 'Connan Tre-Mellyn's predicament.' He needed the right person to help him out of his difficulties. She must be patient enough to care for his daughter, sufficiently educated to teach her, and genteel enough for the child not to suffer through the proximity of someone who was not quite of her own class. Obviously what Connan TreMellyn needed was an impoverished gentlewoman. Aunt Adelaide decided that I fitted the bill.

When our father, who had been vicar of a country parsonage, had died, Aunt Adelaide had swooped on us and taken us to London. There should be a season, she told us, for twenty-year-old Martha and eighteen-year-old Phillida. Phillida had married at the end of that season; but after four years of living with Aunt Adelaide, I had not. So there came a day when she pointed out the two courses to me.

I glanced out of the window. We were drawing into Plymouth. My fellow passengers had alighted and I sat back in my seat watching the activities on the platform.

As the guard was blowing his whistle and we were about to move on, the door of the carriage opened and a man came in. He looked at me with an apologetic smile as though he were hinting that he hoped I did not mind sharing the compartment with him, but I averted my eyes.

When we had left Plymouth and were approaching the bridge, he said: 'You like our bridge, eh?'

I turned and looked at him.

I saw a man, a little under thirty, well dressed, but in the manner of the country gentleman. His tail coat was dark blue, his trousers grey; and his hat was what in London we called a 'pot hat' because of its resemblance to that vessel. This hat he laid on the seat beside him. I thought him somewhat dissipated, with brown eyes that twinkled ironically as though he were fully aware of the warnings I must have received about the inadvisability of entering into conversation with strange men.

I answered: 'Yes, indeed. I think it is a very fine piece of workmanship.'

He smiled. We had crossed the bridge and entered Cornwall.

His brown eyes surveyed me and I was immediately conscious of my somewhat drab appearance. I thought: He is only interested in me because there is no one else to claim his attention. I remembered then that Phillida had once said that I put people off by presuming, when they showed interest, that I believed it was because no one else was available. 'See yourself as a makeshift,' was Phillida's maxim, 'and you'll be one.'

'Travelling far?' he asked.

'I believe I have now only a short distance to go. I leave the train at Liskeard.'

'Ah, Liskeard.' He stretched his legs and turned his gaze from me to the tips of his boots. 'You have come from London?' he went on.

'Yes,' I answered.

'You'll miss the gaiety of the big city.'

'I once lived in the country so I know what to expect.'

'Are you staying in Liskeard?'

I was not sure that I liked this catechism, but I remembered Phillida again: 'You're far too gruff, Marty, with the opposite sex. You scare them off.'

I decided I could at least be civil, so I answered: 'No, not in Liskeard. I'm going to a little village on the coast called Mellyn.'

'I see.' He was silent for a few moments and once more turned his attention to the tips of his boots.

His next words startled me. 'I suppose a sensible young lady like you would not believe in second sight . . . and that sort of thing?'

'Why . . .' I stammered. 'What an extraordinary question!'

'May I look at your palm?'

I hesitated and regarded him suspiciously. Could I offer my hand to a stranger in this way? Aunt Adelaide would suspect that some nefarious advances were about to be made. I thought in this case she might be right. After all I was a woman, and the only available one.

He smiled. 'I assure you that my only desire is to look into the future.'

'But I don't believe in such things.'

'Let me look anyway.' He leaned forward and with a swift movement secured my hand.

He held it lightly, scarcely touching it, contemplating it with his head on one side.

'I see,' he said, 'that you have come to a turning point in your life . . . You are moving into a strange new world which is entirely different from anything you have known before. You will have to exercise caution . . . the utmost caution.'

I smiled cynically. 'You see me taking a journey. What would you say if I told you I was visiting relatives and could not possibly be moving into your strange new world?'

'I should say you were not a very truthful young lady.' His smile was puckish. I could not help feeling a little liking for him. I thought he was a somewhat irresponsible person, but he was very lighthearted and, being in his company, to some extent made me share that lightheartedness. 'No,' he went on, 'you are travelling to a new life, a new post. There's no mistake about that. Before, you lived a secluded life in the country, then you went to the town.'

'I believe I implied that.'

'You did not need to imply it. But it is not the past which concerns us on occasions like this, is it? It is the future.'

'Well, what of the future?'

'You are going to a strange house, a house full of shadows. You will have to walk warily in that house, Miss er—'

He waited, but I did not supply what he was asking for, and he went on: 'You have to earn your living. I see a child there and a man. . . . Perhaps it is the child's father. They are wrapped in shadows. There is someone else there . . . but perhaps she is already dead.'

It was the deep sepulchral note in his voice rather than the words he said which momentarily unnerved me.

I snatched my hand away. 'What nonsense!' I said.

He ignored me and half closed his eyes. Then he went on: 'You will need to watch little Alice, and your duties will extend beyond the care of her. You must most certainly beware of Alice.'

I felt a faint tingling which began at the base of my spine and seemed to creep up to my neck. This, I supposed, was what is known as making one's flesh creep.

Little Alice! But her name was not Alice. It was Alvean. It had unnerved me for the moment because it had sounded similar.

Then I felt irritated and a little angry. Did I look the part then? Was it possible that I already carried the mark of the penurious gentlewoman forced to take the only course open to her? A governess!

Was he laughing at me? He lay back against the upholstery of the carriage, his eyes still closed. I looked out of the window as though he and his ridiculous fortune-telling were of not the slightest interest to me.

He opened his eyes then and took out his watch. He studied it gravely, for all the world as though this extraordinary conversation had not taken place between us.

'In four minutes' time,' he said briskly, 'we shall pull into Liskeard. Allow me to assist you with your bags.'

He took them down from the rack. 'Miss Martha Leigh,' was clearly written on the labels, 'Mount Mellyn, Mellyn, Cornwall.'

He did not appear to glance at these labels and I felt that he had lost interest in me.

When we came into the station, he alighted and set my bags on the platform. Then he took off the hat which he had set upon his head when he picked up the bags, and with a deep bow he left me.

While I was murmuring my thanks I saw an elderly man coming towards me, calling: 'Miss Leigh! Miss Leigh! Be you Miss Leigh then?' And for the moment I forgot about my travelling companion.

I was facing a merry little man with a brown, wrinkled skin and eyes of reddish brown; he wore a corduroy jacket and a sugar-loaf hat which he had pushed to the back of his head and seemed to have forgotten. Ginger hair sprouted from under this, and his brows and moustaches were of the same gingery colour.

'Well, Miss,' he said, 'so I picked you out then. Be these your bags? Give them to me. You and me and old Cherry Pie 'ull soon be home.'

He took my bags and I walked behind him, but he soon fell into step beside me.

'Is the house far from here?' I asked.

'Old Cherry Pie'll carry us there all in good time,' he answered, as he loaded my bags into the trap and I climbed in beside him.

He seemed to be a garrulous man and I could not resist the temptation of trying to discover, before I arrived, something about the people among whom I was going to live.

I said: 'This house, Mount Mellyn, sounds as though it's on a hill.'

'Well, 'tis built on a cliff top, facing the sea, and the gardens run down to the sea. Mount Mellyn and Mount Widden are like twins. Two houses, standing defiant like, daring the sea to come and take 'em. But they'm built on firm rock.'

'So there are two houses,' I said. 'We have near neighbours.'

'In a manner of speaking. Nansellocks, they who are at Mount Widden, have been there these last two hundred years. They be separated from us by more than a mile, and there's Mellyn Cove in between. The families have always been good neighbours until—'

He stopped and I prompted: 'Until—?'

'You'll hear fast enough,' he answered.

I thought it was beneath my dignity to probe into such matters so I changed the subject. 'Do you keep many servants?' I asked.

'There be me and Mrs. Tapperty and my girls, Daisy and Kitty. We live in the rooms over the stables. In the house there's Mrs. Polgrey and Tom Polgrey and young Gilly. Not that you'd call her a servant. But they have her there and she passes for such.'

'Gilly!' I said. 'That's an unusual name.'

'Gillyflower. Reckon Jennifer Polgrey was a bit daft to give her a name like that. No wonder the child's what she is.'

'Jennifer? Is that Mrs. Polgrey?'

'Nay! Jennifer was Mrs. Polgrey's girl. Great dark eyes and the littlest waist you ever saw. Kept herself to herself until one day she goes lying in the hay – or maybe the gillyflowers – with someone. Then, before we know where we are, little Gilly's arrived; as for Jennifer – her just walked into the sea one morning. We reckoned there wasn't much doubt who Gilly's father was.'

I said nothing and, disappointed by my lack of interest, he went on: 'She wasn't the first. We knowed her wouldn't be the last. Geoffry Nansellock left a trail of bastards wherever he went.' He laughed and looked sideways at me. 'No need for you to look so prim, Miss. He can't hurt you. Ghosts can't hurt a young lady, and that's all Master Geoffry Nansellock is now . . . nothing more than a ghost.'

'So he's dead too. He didn't . . . walk into the sea after Jennifer?'

That made Tapperty chuckle. 'Not him. He was killed in a train accident.

You must have heard of that accident. It was just as the train was running out of Plymouth. It ran off the lines and over a bank. The slaughter was terrible. Mr. Geoff, he were on that train, and up to no good on it either. But that was the end of him.'

'Well, I shall not meet him, but I shall meet Gillyflower, I suppose. And is that all the servants?'

'There are odd boys and girls – some for the gardens, some for the stables, some in the house. But it ain't what it was. Things have changed since the mistress died.'

'Mr. TreMellyn is a very sad man, I suppose.'

Tapperty lifted his shoulders.

'How long is it since she died?' I asked.

'It would be little more than a year, I reckon.'

'And he has only just decided that he needs a governess for little Miss Alvean?'

'There have been three governesses so far. You be the fourth. They don't stay, none of them. Miss Bray and Miss Garrett, they said the place was too quiet for them. There was Miss Jansen – a real pretty creature. But she was sent away. She took what didn't belong to her. 'Twas a pity. We all liked her. She seemed to look on it as a privilege to live in Mount Mellyn. Old houses were her hobby, she used to tell us. Well, it seemed she had other hobbies besides, so out she went.'

I turned my attention to the countryside. It was late August and, as we passed through lanes with banks on either side, I caught occasional glimpses of fields of corn among which poppies and pimpernels grew; now and then we passed a cottage of grey Cornish stone which looked grim, I thought, and lonely.

I had my first glimpse of the sea through a fold in the hills, and I felt my spirits lifted. It seemed that the nature of the landscape changed. Flowers seemed to grow more plentifully on the banks; I could smell the scent of pine trees; and fuchsias grew by the roadside, their blossoms bigger than any we had ever been able to cultivate in our vicarage garden.

We turned off the road from a steep hill and went down and down nearer the sea. I saw that we were on a cliff road. Before us stretched a scene of breath-taking beauty. The cliff rose steep and straight from the sea on that indented coast; grasses and flowers grew there, and I saw sea pinks and red and white valerian mingling with the heather – rich, deep, purple heather.

At length we came to the house. It was like a castle, I thought, standing there on the cliff plateau – built of granite like many houses I had seen in these parts, but grand and noble – a house which had stood for several hundred years, and would stand for several hundred more.

'All this land belongs to the Master,' said Tapperty with pride. 'And if you look across the cove, you'll see Mount Widden.'

I did look and saw the house. Like Mount Mellyn it was built of grey stone. It was smaller in every way and of a later period. I did not give it much attention because now we were approaching Mount Mellyn, and that was obviously the house which was more interesting to me.

We had climbed to the plateau and a pair of intricately wrought-iron gates confronted us.

'Open up there!' shouted Tapperty.

There was a small lodge beside the gates and at the door sat a woman knitting.

'Now, Gilly girl,' she said, 'you go and open the gates and save me poor legs.'

Then I saw the child who had been sitting at the old woman's feet. She rose obediently and came to the gate. She was an extraordinary looking girl with long straight hair almost white in colour and wide blue eyes.

'Thanks, Gilly girl,' said Tapperty as Cherry Pie went happily through the gates. 'This be Miss, who's come to live here and take care of Miss Alvean.'

I looked into a pair of blank blue eyes which stared at me with an expression impossible to fathom. The old woman came up to the gate and Tapperty said: 'This be Mrs. Soady.'

'Good day to you,' said Mrs. Soady. 'I hope you'll be happy here along of us.'

'Thank you,' I answered, forcing my gaze away from the child to the woman. 'I hope so.'

'Well, I do hope so,' added Mrs. Soady. Then she shook her head as though she feared her hopes were somewhat futile.

I turned to look at the child but she had disappeared. I wondered where she had gone, and the only place I could imagine was behind the bushes of hydrangeas which were bigger than any hydrangeas I had ever seen, and of deep blue, almost the colour of the sea on this day.

'The child didn't speak,' I observed as we went on up the drive.

'No. Her don't talk much. Sing, her do. Wander about on her own. But talk . . . not much.'

The drive was about half a mile in length and on either side of it the hydrangeas bloomed. Fuchsias mingled with them, and I caught glimpses of the sea between the pine trees. Then I saw the house. Before it was a wide lawn and on this two peacocks strutted before a peahen, their almost incredibly lovely tails fanned out behind them. Another sat perched on a stone wall; and there were two palm trees, tall and straight, one on either side of the porch.

The house was larger than I had thought when I had seen it from the cliff path. It was of three stories, but long and built in an L shape. The sun caught the glass of the mullioned windows and I immediately had the impression that I was being watched.

Tapperty took the gravel approach to the front porch and, when we reached it, the door opened and I saw a woman standing there. She wore a white cap on her grey hair; she was tall, with a hooked nose and, as she had an obviously dominating manner, I did not need to be told that she was Mrs. Polgrey.

'I trust you've had a good journey, Miss Leigh,' she said.

'Very good, thank you,' I told her.

'And worn out and needing a rest, I'll be bound. Come along in. You shall have a nice cup of tea in my room. Leave your bags. I'll have them taken up.'

I felt relieved. This woman dispelled the eerie feeling which had begun, I realized, since my encounter with the man in the train. Joe Tapperty had done little to disperse it, with his tales of death and suicide. But Mrs. Polgrey was a woman who would stand no nonsense, I was sure of that. She seemed to emit common sense, and perhaps because I was fatigued by the long journey I was pleased about this.

I thanked her and said I would greatly enjoy the tea, and she led the way into the house.

We were in an enormous hall which in the past must have been used as a banqueting room. The floor was of flagged stone, and the timbered roof was so lofty that I felt it must extend to the top of the house. The beams were beautifully carved and the effect decorative. At one end of the hall was a dais and at the back of this a great open fireplace. On the dais stood a refectory table on which were vessels and plates of pewter.

'It's magnificent,' I said involuntarily; and Mrs. Polgrey was pleased.

'I superintend all the polishing of the furniture myself,' she told me. 'You have to watch girls nowadays. Those Tapperty wenches are a pair of flibbertigibbets, I can tell 'ee. You'd need eyes that could see from here to Land's End to see all they'm up to. Beeswax and turpentine, that's the mixture, and nothing like it. All made by myself.'

'It certainly does you credit,' I complimented her.

I followed her to the end of the hall where there was a door. She opened this and a short flight of some half a dozen steps confronted us. To the left was a door which she indicated and after a moment's hesitation, opened.

'The chapel,' she said, and I caught a glimpse of blue slate flagstones, an altar and a few pews. There was a smell of dampness about the place.

She shut the door quickly.

'We don't use it nowadays,' she said. 'We go to the Mellyn church. It's down in the village, the other side of the cove . . . just beyond Mount Widden.'

We went up the stairs and into a room which I saw was a dining room. It was vast and the walls were hung with tapestry. The table was highly polished and there were several cabinets in the room within which I saw beautiful glass and china. The floor was covered with blue carpet and through the enormous windows I saw a walled courtyard.

'This is not *your* part of the house,' Mrs. Polgrey told me, 'but I thought I would take you round the front of the house to my room. It's as well you know the lay of the land, as they say.'

I thanked her, understanding that this was a tactful way of telling me that as a governess I would not be expected to mingle with the family.

We passed through the dining room to yet another flight of stairs and mounting these we came to what seemed like a more intimate sitting room. The walls were covered with exquisite tapestry and the chair backs and seats were beautifully wrought in the same manner. I could see that the furniture was mostly antique and that it all gleamed with beeswax and turpentine and Mrs. Polgrey's loving care.

'This is the punch room,' she said. 'It has always been called so because it is here that the family retires to take punch. We follow the old custom still in this house.'

At the end of this room was another flight of stairs; there was no door leading to them, merely a heavy brocade curtain which Mrs. Polgrey drew aside, and when we had mounted these stairs we were in a gallery, the walls of which were lined with portraits. I gave each of them a quick glance, wondering if Connan TreMellyn were among them; but I could see no one depicted in modern dress, so I presumed his portrait had not yet taken its place among those of his ancestors.

There were several doors leading from the gallery, but we went quickly along it, to one of those at the far end. As we passed through it I saw that we were in a different wing of the house, the servants' quarters I imagined, because the spaciousness was missing.

'This,' said Mrs. Polgrey, 'will be *your* part of the house. You will find a staircase at the end of this corridor which leads to the nurseries. Your room is up there. But first come to my sitting room and we'll have that tea. I told Daisy to see to it as soon as I heard Joe Tapperty was here. So there shouldn't be long to wait.'

'I fear it will take some time to learn my way about the house,' I said.

'You'll know it in next to no time. But when you go out you won't go the way I brought you up. You'll use one of the other doors; when you've unpacked and rested awhile, I'll show you.'

'You're very kind.'

'Well, I do want to make you happy here with us. Miss Alvean needs discipline, I always say. And what can I do about giving in to her, with all I have to do! A nice mess this place would be in if I let Miss Alvean take up *my* time. No, what she wants is a sensible governess, and 'twould seem they'm not all that easy to come by. Why, Miss, if you show us that you can look after the child, you'll be more than welcome here.'

'I gather I have had several predecessors.' She looked a trifle blank and I went on quickly. 'There have been other governesses.'

'Oh yes. Not much good, any of them. Miss Jansen was the best, but it seemed she had habits. You could have knocked me down with a feather. She quite took *me* in!' Mrs. Polgrey looked as though she thought that anyone who could do that must be smart. 'Well, I suppose appearances are deceptive, as they say. Miss Celestine was real upset when it came out.'

'Miss Celestine?'

'The young lady at Widden. Miss Celestine Nansellock. She's often here. A quiet young lady and she loves the place. If I as much as move a piece of furniture she knows it. That's why she and Miss Jansen seemed to get on. Both interested in old houses, you see. It was such a pity and such a shock. You'll meet her sometime. As I say, scarcely a day passes when she's not here. There's some of us that think. . . . Oh, my dear life! 'twould seem as though I'm letting my tongue run away with me, and you longing for that cup of tea.'

She threw open the door of the room and it was like stepping into another world. Gone was the atmosphere of brooding antiquity. This was a room which could not have fitted into any other time than the present, and I realized that it confirmed my impression of Mrs. Polgrey. There were antimacassars on the chair; there was a 'what-not' in the corner of the room filled with china ornaments including a glass slipper, a gold pig and a cup with 'A present from Weston' inscribed on it. It seemed almost impossible to move in a room so crammed with furniture. Even on the mantelpiece Dresden shepherdesses seemed to jostle with marble angels for a place. There was an ormolu clock which ticked sedately; there were chairs and little tables everywhere, it seemed. It showed Mrs. Polgrey to me as a woman of strong conventions, a woman who would have a great respect for the right thing – which would, of course, be the thing she believed in.

Still, I felt something comfortingly normal about this room as I did about the woman.

She looked at the main table and tutted in exasperation; then she went to the bell rope and pulled it. It was only a few minutes later when a black-haired girl with saucy eyes appeared carrying a tray on which was a silver teapot, a spirit lamp, cups and saucers, milk and sugar.

'And about time too,' said Mrs. Polgrey. 'Put it here, Daisy.'

Daisy gave me a look which almost amounted to a wink. I did not wish to offend Mrs. Polgrey so I pretended not to notice.

Then Mrs. Polgrey said: 'This is Daisy, Miss. You can tell her if you find anything is not to your liking.'

'Thank you Mrs. Polgrey, and thank you, Daisy.'

They both looked somewhat startled and Daisy dropped a little curtsy, of which she seemed half ashamed, and went out.

'Nowadays . . .' murmured Mrs. Polgrey, and lighted the spirit lamp.

I watched her unlock the cabinet and take out the tea canister which she set on the tray.

'Dinner,' she went on, 'is served at eight. Yours will be brought to your room. But I thought you would be needing a little reviver. So when you've had this and seen your room, I'll introduce you to Miss Alvean.'

'What would she be doing at this time of day?'

Mrs Polgrey frowned. 'She'll be off somewhere by herself. She goes off by herself. Master don't like it. That's why 'e be anxious for her to have a governess, you see.'

I began to see. I was sure now that Alvean was going to be a difficult child.

Mrs. Polgrey measured the tea into the pot as though it were gold dust, and poured the hot water on it.

'So much depends on whether she takes a fancy to you or not,' went on Mrs. Polgrey. 'She's unaccountable. There's some she'll take to and some she won't. Her was very fond of Miss Jansen.' Mrs. Polgrey shook her head sadly. 'A pity she had habits.'

She stirred the tea in the pot, put on the tea cosy and asked me: 'Cream? Sugar?'

'Yes, please,' I said.

'I always do say,' she remarked, as though she thought I needed some consolation, 'there ain't nothing like a good cup of tea.'

We ate tea biscuits with the tea, and these Mrs. Polgrey took from a tin which she kept in her cabinet. I gathered, as we sat together, that Connan TreMellyn, the Master, was away.

'He has an estate farther west,' Mrs. Polgrey told me. 'Penzance way.' Her dialect was more noticeable when she was relaxed as she was now. 'He do go to it now and then to see to it like. Left him by his wife, it were. Now *she* was one of the Pendletons. They'm from Penzance way.'

'When does he return?' I asked.

She looked faintly shocked, and I knew that I had offended because she said in a somewhat haughty way: 'He will come back in his own time.'

I saw that if I was going to keep in her good books, I must be strictly conventional; and presumably it was not good form for a governess to ask questions about the master of the house. It was all very well for Mrs. Polgrey to speak of him; she was a privileged person. I could see that I must hastily adjust myself to my own position.

Very soon after that she took me up to my room. It was large with big windows equipped with window seats from which there was a good view of the front lawn, the palm trees and the approach. My bed was a four-poster and seemed in keeping with the rest of the furniture; and although it was a big bed it looked dwarfed in a room of this size. There were rugs on the floor, the boards of which were so highly polished that the rugs looked somewhat dangerous. I could see that I might have little cause to bless Mrs. Polgrey's love of polishing everything within sight. There was a tallboy and a chest of drawers; and I noticed that there was a door in addition to the one by which I had entered.

Mrs. Polgrey followed my gaze. 'The schoolroom,' she said. 'And beyond that is Miss Alvean's room.'

'I see. So the schoolroom separates us.'

Mrs. Polgrey nodded.

Looking round the room I saw that there was a screen in one corner and as I approached this I noticed that it shielded a hip bath.

'If you want hot water at any time,' she said, 'ring the bell and Daisy or Kitty will bring it to you.'

'Thank you.' I looked at the open fireplace and pictured a roaring fire there on winter days. 'I can see I'm going to be very comfortable here.'

'It's a pleasant room. You'll be the first governess to have it. The other governesses used to sleep in a room on the other side of Miss Alvean's room. It was Miss Celestine who thought this would be better. It's a more pleasant room, I must say.'

'Then I owe thanks to Miss Celestine.'

'A very pleasant lady. She thinks the world of Miss Alvean.' Mrs. Polgrey shook her head significantly and I wondered whether she was thinking that it was only a year since the master's wife had died, and that perhaps one day he would marry again. Who more suitable to be his wife than his neighbour who was so fond of Miss Alvean? Perhaps they were only waiting for a reasonable lapse of time.

'Would you like to wash your hands and unpack? Dinner will be in two hours' time. But perhaps first you would like to take a look at the schoolroom.'

'Thank you, Mrs. Polgrey,' I said, 'but I think I'll wash and unpack first.'

'Very well. And perhaps you'd like a little rest. Travelling is so fatiguing, I do know. I'll send Daisy up with hot water. Meals could be taken in the schoolroom. Perhaps you'd prefer that?'

'With Miss Alvean?'

'She takes her meals nowadays with her father, except her milk and biscuits last thing. All the children have taken meals with the family from the time they were eight years old. Miss Alvean's birthday was in May.'

'There are other children?'

'Oh, my dear life, no! I was talking of the children of the past. It's one of the family rules, you see.'

'I see.'

'Well, I'll be leaving you. If you cared for a stroll in the grounds before dinner, you could take it. Ring for Daisy or Kitty and whoever is free will show you the stairs you will use in future. It will take you down to the kitchen garden, but you can easily get from there to wherever you want to go. Don't 'ee forget though – dinner at eight.'

'In the schoolroom.'

'Or in your own room if you prefer it.'

'But,' I added, 'in the governess's quarters.'

She did not know what to make of this remark, and when Mrs. Polgrey did not understand, she ignored. In a few minutes I was alone.

As soon as she had gone the strangeness of the house seemed to envelop me. I was aware of silence – the eerie silence of an ancient house.

I went to the window and looked out. It seemed a long time ago that I had driven up to the house with Tapperty. I heard the august notes of a bird which might have been a linnet.

I looked at the watch pinned to my blouse and saw that it was just past six o'clock. Two hours to dinner. I wondered whether to ring for Daisy or Kitty and ask for hot water; but I found my eyes turning to the other door in my room, the one which led to the schoolroom.

The schoolroom was, after all, my domain, and I had a right to inspect it, so I opened the door. The room was larger than my bedroom but it had the same type of windows and they were all fitted with window seats on which were red plush fitted cushions. There was a table in the centre of the room. I went over to it and saw that there were scratches on it and splashes of ink, so I guessed that this was the table where generations of TreMellyns had learned their lessons. I tried to imagine Connan TreMellyn as a little boy, sitting at this table. I imagined him a studious boy, quite different from his erring daughter, the difficult child who was going to be my problem.

A few books lay on the table. I examined them. They were children's readers, containing the sort of stories and articles which looked as if they were of an uplifting nature. There was an exercise book on which was scrawled 'Alvean TreMellyn. Arithemetic.' I opened it and saw several sums, to most of which had been given the wrong answers. Idly turning the pages I came to a sketch of a girl, and immediately I recognized Gilly, the child whom I had seen at the lodge gates.

'Not bad,' I muttered. 'So our Alvean is an artist. That's something.'

I closed the book. I had the strange feeling, which I had had as soon as I entered the house, that I was being watched.

'Alvean!' I called on impulse. 'Are you there, Alvean? Alvean, where are you hiding?'

There was no answer and I flushed with embarrassment, feeling rather absurd in the silence.

Abruptly I turned and went back to my room. I rang the bell and when Daisy appeared I asked her for hot water.

By the time I had unpacked my bags and hung up my things it was nearly eight o'clock, and precisely as the stable clock was striking eight Kitty appeared with my tray. On it was a leg of roast chicken with vegetables and, under a pewter cover, an egg custard.

Daisy said: 'Are you having it in here, Miss, or in the schoolroom?'

I decided against sitting in that room where I felt I was overlooked.

'Here, please, Daisy,' I answered. Then, because Daisy looked the sort of person who wanted to talk, I added: 'Where is Miss Alvean? It seems strange that I have not seen her yet.'

'She's a bad 'un,' cried Daisy. 'Do 'ee know what would have happened to Kit and me if we'd got up to such tricks? A good tanning – that's what we'd have had – and in a place where 'tweren't comfortable to sit down on after. Her heard new Miss was coming, and so off her goes. Master be away and we don't know where her be until the house boy comes over from Mount Widden to tell we that she be over there – calling on Miss Celestine and Master Peter, if you do please.'

'I see. A sort of protest at having a new governess.'

Daisy came near and nudged me. 'Miss Celestine do spoil the child. Dotes on her so's you'd think she was her own daughter. Listen! That do sound like the carriage.' Daisy was at the window beckoning me. I felt I ought not to stand at the window with a servant spying on what was happening below, but the temptation to do so was too strong for me.

So I stood beside Daisy and saw them getting out of the carriage ... a young woman, whom I judged to be of my own age or perhaps a year or so older, and a child. I scarcely looked at the woman; my attention was all on the child. This was Alvean on whom my success depended, so naturally enough in those first seconds I had eyes for no one but her.

From what I could see she looked ordinary enough. She was somewhat tall for her eight years; her light brown hair had been plaited, and I presumed it was very long, for it was wound round her head; this gave her an appearance of maturity and I imagined her to be terrifyingly precocious. She was wearing a dress of brown gingham with white stockings and black shoes with ankle straps. She looked like a miniature woman and, for some vague reason, my spirits fell.

Oddly enough she seemed to be conscious that she was being watched, and glanced upwards. Involuntarily I stepped back, but I was sure she had seen the movement. I felt at a disadvantage before we had met.

'Up to tricks,' murmured Daisy at my side.

'Perhaps,' I said as I walked into the centre of the room, 'she is a little alarmed at the prospect of having a new governess.'

Daisy let out a burst of explosive laughter. 'What, her! Sorry, Miss, but that do make me laugh, that do.'

I went to the table and, sitting down, began to eat my dinner. Daisy was about to go when there was a knock on the door and Kitty entered.

She grimaced at her sister and grinned rather familiarly at me. 'Oh, Miss,' she said, 'Mrs. Polgrey says that when you'm finished will you go down to the punch room. Miss Nansellock be there and her would like to see you. Miss Alvean have come home. They'd like 'ee to come down as soon as you can. 'Tis time Miss Alvean were in her own room.'

'I will come when I have finished my dinner,' I said.

'Then would you pull the bell when you'm ready, Miss, and me or Daisy'll show you the way.'

'Thank you.' I sat down and, in a leisurely fashion, finished my meal.

I rose and went to the mirror which stood on my dressing table. I saw that I was unusually flushed and that this suited me; it made my eyes look decidedly the colour of amber. It was fifteen minutes since Daisy and Kitty had left me and I imagined that Mrs. Polgrey, Alvean and Miss Nansellock would be impatiently awaiting my coming. But I had no intention of becoming the poor little drudge that so many governesses were. If Alvean was what I believed her to be, she needed to be shown, right at the start, that I was in charge and must be treated with respect.

I rang the bell and Daisy appeared.

'They'm waiting for you in the punch room,' she said. 'It's well past Miss Alvean's supper time.'

'Then it is a pity that she did not return before,' I replied serenely.

When Daisy giggled, her plump breasts, which seemed to be bursting out of her cotton bodice, shook. Daisy enjoyed laughing, I could see. I judged her to be as lighthearted as her sister.

She led the way to the punch room through which I had passed with Mrs. Polgrey on my way to my own quarters. She drew aside the curtains and with a dramatic gesture cried: 'Here be Miss!'

Mrs. Polgrey was seated in one of the tapestry-backed chairs, and Celestine Nansellock was in another. Alvean was standing, her hands clasped behind her back. She looked, I thought, dangerously demure.

'Ah,' said Mrs. Polgrey, rising, 'here is Miss Leigh. Miss Nensellock have been waiting to see you.' There was a faint reproach in her voice. I knew what it meant. I, a mere governess, had kept a *lady* waiting while I finished my dinner.

'How do you do?' I asked.

They looked surprised. I suppose I should have curtsied or made some gesture to show that I was conscious of my menial position. I was aware of the blue eyes of the child fixed upon me; indeed I was aware of little but Alvean in those first few seconds. Her eyes were startlingly blue. I thought, she will be a beauty when she grows up. And I wondered whether she was like her father or mother.

Celestine Nansellock was standing by Alvean, and she laid a hand on her shoulder.

'Miss Alvean came over to see us,' she said. 'We're great friends. I'm Miss Nansellock of Mount Widden. You may have seen the house.'

'I did so on my journey from the station.'

'I trust you will not be cross with Alvean.'

I answered, looking straight into those defiant blue eyes: 'I could hardly scold for what happened before my arrival, could I?'

'She looks on me . . . on us . . . as part of her own family,' went on Celestine Nansellock. 'We've always lived so close to each other.'

'I am sure it is a great comfort to her,' I replied; and for the first time I gave my attention solely to Celestine Nansellock.

She was taller than I, but by no standards a beauty. Her hair was of a nondescript brown and her eyes were hazel. There was little colour in her face and an air of intense quietness about her. I decided she had little personality, but perhaps she was overshadowed by the defiance of Alvean and the conventional dignity of Mrs. Polgrey.

'I do hope,' she said, 'that if you need my advice about anything, Miss Leigh, you won't hesitate to call on me. You see, I am quite a near neighbour, and I think I am looked on here as one of the family.'

'You are very kind.'

Her mild eyes looked into mine. 'We want you to be happy here, Miss Leigh. We all want that.'

'Thank you. I suppose,' I went on, 'the first thing to do is to get Alvean to bed. It must be past her bedtime.'

Celestine smiled. 'You are right. Indeed it is. She usually has her milk and biscuits in the schoolroom at half past seven. It is now well past eight. But to-night I will look after her. I suggest that you return to your room, Miss Leigh. You must be weary after your journey.'

Before I could speak Alvean cried out: 'No, Celestine. I want *her* to. She's my governess. She should, shouldn't she?'

A hurt look immediately appeared in Celestine's face, and Alvean could not repress the triumph in hers. I felt I understood. The child wanted to feel her own power; she wanted to prevent Celestine from superintending her retirement simply because Celestine wished so much to do it.

'Oh, very well,' said Celestine. 'Then there's no further need for me to stay.'

She stood looking at Alvean as though she wanted her to beg her to stay, but Alvean's curious gaze was all for me.

'Good night,' she said flippantly. And to me: 'Come on. I'm hungry.'

'You've forgotten to thank Miss Nansellock for bringing you back,' I told her.

'I didn't forget,' she retorted. 'I never forget anything.'

'Then your memory is a great deal better than your manners,' I said.

They were astonished – all of them. Perhaps I was a little astonished myself. But I knew that if I were going to assume control of this child I should have to be firm.

Her face flushed and her eyes grew hard. She was about to retort, but, not knowing how to do so, she ran out of the room.

'There!' said Mrs. Polgrey. 'Why, Miss Nansellock, it was good of you—'

'Nonsense, Mrs. Polgrey,' said Celestine. 'Of course I brought her back.'

'She will thank you later,' I assured her.

'Miss Leigh,' said Celestine earnestly, 'it will be necessary for you to go carefully with that child. She has lost her mother . . . quite recently.' Celestine's lips trembled. She smiled at me. 'It is such a short time ago and the tragedy seems near. She was a dear friend of mine.'

'I understand,' I replied. 'I shall not be harsh with the child, but I can see she needs discipline.'

'Be careful, Miss Leigh.' Celestine had taken a step closer and laid a hand on my arm. 'Children are delicate creatures.'

'I shall do my best for Alvean,' I answered.

'I wish you good luck.' She smiled and then turned to Mrs. Polgrey. 'I'll be going back now. I want to get back before dark.'

Mrs. Polgrey rang the bell and Daisy appeared.

'Take Miss to her room, Daisy,' she commanded. 'And has Miss Alvean got her milk and biscuits?'

'Yes, M'am,' was the answer.

I said good night to Celestine Nansellock, who inclined her head. Then I left with Daisy.

I went into the schoolroom where Alvean sat at a table drinking milk and eating biscuits. She deliberately ignored me as I went to the table and sat beside her.

'Alvean,' I said, 'if we're going to get along together, we'd better come to an understanding. Don't you think that would be advisable?'

'Why should I care?' she replied curtly.

'But of course you'll care. We shall all be happier if we do.'

Alvean shrugged her shoulders. 'If we don't,' she told me brusquely, 'you'll have to go. I'll have another governess. It's of no account to me.'

She looked at me triumphantly and I knew that she was telling me I was merely a paid servant and that it was for her to call the tune. I felt myself shiver involuntarily. For the first time I understood the feelings of those who depended on the goodwill of others for their bread and butter.

Her eyes were malicious and I wanted to slap her.

'It should be of the greatest account,' I answered, 'because it is far more pleasant to live in harmony than in discord with those about us.'

'What does it matter, if they're *not* about us . . . if we can have them sent away?'

'Kindness matters more than anything in the world.'

She smiled into her milk and finished it.

'Now,' I said, 'to bed.'

I rose with her and she said: 'I go to bed by myself. I am not a baby, you know.'

'Perhaps I thought you were younger than you are because you have so much to learn.'

She considered that. Then she gave that shrug of her shoulders which I was to discover was characteristic.

'Good night,' she said, dismissing me.

'I'll come and say good night when you are in bed.'

'There's no need.'

'Nevertheless, I'll come.'

She opened the door which led to her room from the schoolroom. I turned and went into mine.

I felt very depressed because I was realizing the size of the problem before me. I had no experience of handling children, and in the past when I thought of them I had visualized docile and affectionate little creatures whom it would be a joy to care for. Here I was with a difficult child on my hands. And what would happen to me if it were decided that I was unfit to undertake her care? What did happen to penurious gentlewomen who failed to please their employers?

I could go to Phillida. I could be one of those old aunts who were at the beck and call of all and lived out their miserable lives dependent on others. I was not the sort of person to take dependence lightly. I should have to find other posts.

I accepted the fact that I was a little frightened. Not until I had come face to face with Alvean had I realized that I might not succeed with this job. I tried not to look down the years ahead when I might slip from one post to another, never giving satisfaction. What happened to women like myself, women who, without those attractions which were so important, were forced to battle against the world for a chance to live?

I felt that I could have thrown myself on my bed and wept, wept with anger against the cruelty of life, which had robbed me of two loving parents and sent me out ill-equipped into the world.

I imagined myself appearing at Alvean's bedside, my face stained with tears. What triumph for her! That was no way to begin the battle which I was sure must rage between us.

I walked up and down my room, trying to control my emotions. I went to the window and looked out across the lawns to the hilly country beyond. I could not see the sea because the house was so built that the back faced the coast and I was at the front. Instead I looked beyond the plateau on which the house stood, to the hills.

Such beauty! Such peace without, I thought. Such conflict within. When I leaned out of the window I could see Mount Widden across the cove. Two houses standing there over many years; generations of Nansellocks, generations of TreMellyns had lived here and their lives had intermingled so that it could well be that the story of one house was the story of the other.

I turned from the window and went through the schoolroom to Alvean's room.

'Alvean,' I whispered. There was no answer. But she lay there in the bed, her eyes tightly shut, too tightly.

I bent over her.

'Good night, Alvean. We're going to be friends, you know,' I murmured. There was no answer. She was pretending to be asleep.

Exhausted as I was, my rest was broken that night. I would fall into sleep and then awake startled. I repeated this several times until I was fully awake.

I lay in bed and looked about my room in which the furniture showed up in intermittent moonlight like dim figures. I had a feeling that I was not alone; that there were whispering voices about me. I had an impression that there had been tragedy in this house which still hung over it.

I wondered if it was due to the death of Alvean's mother. She had been dead only a year; I wondered in what circumstances she had died.

I thought of Alvean who showed a somewhat aggressive face to the world. There must be some reason for this. I was sure that no child would be eager to proclaim herself the enemy of strangers without some cause.

I determined to discover the reason for Alvean's demeanour. I determined to make her a happy, normal child.

It was light before sleep came; the coming of day comforted me because I was afraid of the darkness in this house. It was childish, but it was true.

I had breakfast in the schoolroom with Alvean, who told me, with pride, that when her father was at home she had breakfast with him.

Later we settled to work, and I discovered that she was an intelligent child; she had read more than most children of her age and her eyes would light up with interest in her lessons almost in spite of her determination to preserve a lack of harmony between us. My spirits began to rise and I felt that I would in time make a success of this job.

Luncheon consisted of boiled fish and rice pudding, and afterwards when Alvean volunteered to take me for a walk, I felt I was getting on better with her.

There were woods on the estate, and she said she wished to show them to me. I was delighted that she should do so and gladly I followed her through the trees.

'Look,' she cried, picking a crimson flower and holding it out to me. 'Do you know what this is?'

'It's betony, I believe.'

She nodded. 'You should pick some and keep it in your room, Miss. It keeps evil away.'

I laughed. 'That's an old superstition. Why should I want to keep evil away?'

'Everybody should. They grow this in graveyards. It's because people are buried there. It's grown there because people are afraid of the dead.'

'It's foolish to be afraid. Dead people can hurt no one.'

She was placing the flower in the buttonhole of my coat. I was rather touched. Her face looked gentle as she fixed it and I had a notion that she felt a sudden protective feeling towards me.

'Thank you, Alvean,' I said gently.

She looked at me and all the softness vanished from her face. It was defiant and full of mischief.

'You can't catch me,' she cried; and off she ran.

I did not attempt to do so. I called: 'Alvean, come here.' But she disappeared through the trees and I heard her mocking laughter in the distance.

I decided to return to the house, but the wood was thick, and I was not sure of my direction. I walked back a little way but it seemed to me that it was not the direction from which we had come. A panic seized me, but I told myself this was absurd. It was a sunny afternoon and I could not be half an hour's walk from the house. Moreover, I did not believe that the wood could be very extensive.

I was not going to give Alvean the satisfaction of having brought me to the wood to lose me. So I walked purposefully through the trees; but as I walked they grew thicker and I knew that we had not come this way. My anger against Alvean was rising when I heard the crackle of leaves as though I were being followed. I was sure the child was somewhere near, mocking me.

Then I heard singing; it was a strange voice, slightly off key, and the fact that the song was one of those which were being sung in drawing rooms all over the country did nothing to reassure me.

> *'Alice, where art thou?*
> *One year back this even*
> *And thou wert by my side,*
> *Vowing to love me,*
> *Alice, what e'er may betide—'*

'Who is there?' I called.

There was no answer, but in the distance I caught a glimpse of a child with lint-white hair, and I knew that it was only little Gilly who had stared at me from the hydrangea bushes by the lodge gates.

I walked swiftly on and after a while the trees grew less dense and through them I saw the road. I came out into this and realized that I was on the slope which led up to the plateau and the lodge gates.

Mrs. Soady was sitting at the door of the lodge as she had been when I arrived, her knitting in her hands.

'Why, Miss,' she called. 'So you've been out walking then?'

'I went for a walk with Miss Alvean. We lost each other in the woods.'

'Ah yes. So her run away, did her.' Mrs. Soady shook her head, as she came to the gate trailing her ball of wool behind her.

'I expect she'll find her way home,' I said.

'My dear life, yes. There ain't an inch of them woods Miss Alvean don't know. Oh, I see you've got yourself a piece of betony. Like as not 'tis as well.'

'Miss Alvean picked it and insisted on putting it in my buttonhole.'

'There now! You be friends already.'

'I heard the little girl, Gilly, singing in the woods,' I said.

'I don't doubt 'ee. Her's always singing in the woods.'

'I called to her but she didn't come.'

'Timid as a doe, she be.'

'Well, I think I'll be getting along. Goodbye, Mrs. Soady.'

'Good day to 'ee, Miss.'

I went up the drive, past the hydrangeas and the fuchsias. I realized I was straining my ears for the sound of singing, but there was no sound but that of an occasional small animal in the undergrowth.

I was hot and tired when I reached the house. I went straight up to my room and rang for water and, when I had washed and brushed my hair, went into the schoolroom where tea was waiting for me.

Alvean was at the table; she looked demure and made no reference to our afternoon's adventure; nor did I.

After tea I said to her: 'I don't know what rules your other governesses made, but I propose we do our lessons in the morning, have a break between luncheon and tea, and then start again from five o'clock until six, when we will read together.'

Alvean did not answer; she was studying me intently.

Then suddenly she said: 'Miss, do you like my name? Have you ever known anyone else called Alvean?'

I said I liked the name and had never heard it before.

'It's Cornish. Do you know what it means?'

'I have no idea.'

'Then I will tell you. My father can speak and write Cornish.' She looked wistful when she spoke of her father, and I thought: He at least is one person she admires and for whose approval she is eager. She went on: 'In Cornish, Alvean means Little Alice.'

'Oh!' I said, and my voice shook a little.

She came to me and placed her hands on my knees; she looked up into my face and said solemnly: 'You see, Miss, my mother was Alice. She isn't here any more. But I was called after her. That's why I am little Alice.'

I stood up because I could no longer bear the scrutiny of the child. I went to the window.

'Look,' I said, 'two of the peacocks are on the lawn.'

She was standing at my elbow. 'They've come to be fed. Greedy things! Daisy will soon be coming with their peas. They know it.'

I was not seeing the peacocks on the lawn. I was remembering the mocking eyes of the man on the train, the man who had warned me that I should have to beware of Alice.

Chapter Two

Three days after my arrival at Mount Mellyn, the Master of the house returned.

I had slipped into a routine as far as my duties were concerned. Alvean and I did lessons each morning after breakfast, and apart from an ever present desire to disconcert me by asking questions which, I knew, she hoped

I should not be able to answer, I found her a good pupil. It was not that she meant to please me; it was merely that her desire for knowledge was so acute that she could not deny it. I believe that there was some plot in her head that if she could learn all I knew she could then confront her father with a question: Since there is no more Miss can teach me, is there any point in her remaining here?

I often thought of tales I had heard of governesses whose declining years were made happy by those whom they had taught as children. No such happy fate would be mine – at least as far as Alvean was concerned.

I had been shocked when I first heard the name of Alice mentioned, and after the daylight had passed I would consequently feel that the house was full of eerie shadows. That was pure fancy of course. It had been a bad beginning, meeting that man in the train and his talk of second sight.

I did wonder, when I was alone in my room and the house was quiet, of what Alice had died. She must have been quite a young woman. It was, I told myself, because she was so recently dead – for after all a year was not a very long time – that her presence seemed to haunt the place.

I would wake in the night to hear what I thought were voices, and they seemed to be moaning: 'Alice. Alice. Where is Alice?'

I went to my window and listened, and the whispering voices seemed to be carried on the air.

Daisy who, like her sister, was by no means a fanciful person, explained away my fancies the very next morning when she brought my hot water.

'Did 'ee hear the sea last night, Miss, in old Mellyn Cove? Sis . . . sis . . . sis . . . woa . . . woa . . . woa . . . all night long. Just like two old biddies having a good gossip down there.'

'Why, yes, I heard it.'

"Tis like that on certain nights when the sea be high and the wind in a certain direction.'

I laughed at myself. There was an explanation to everything.

I had grown to know the people of the household. Mrs. Tapperty called me in one day for a glass of her parsnip wine. She hoped I was comfortable at the house; then she told me of the trial Tapperty was to her because he couldn't keep his eyes nor his hands from the maidens – and the younger the better. She feared Kitty and Daisy took after their father. It was a pity for their mother was, according to herself, a Godfearing body who would be seen in Mellyn Church every Sunday, night and morning. Now the girls were grown up she had not only to wonder whether Joe Tapperty was after Mrs. Tully from the cottages, but what Daisy was doing in the stables with Billy Trehay or Kitty with that house boy from Mount Widden. It was a hard life for a Godfearing woman who only wanted to do right and see right done.

I went to see Mrs. Soady at the lodge gates and heard about her three sons and their children. 'Never did I see such people for putting their toes through their stockings. It's one body's work to keep them in stockings.'

I was very eager to learn about the house in which I lived, and the intricacies of heel-turning did not greatly excite me; therefore I did not often call on Mrs. Soady.

I tried on occasions to catch Gilly and talk to her; but although I saw her now and then, I did not succeed. I called her, but that only made her run away more swiftly. I could never hear her soft crooning voice without being deeply disturbed.

I felt that something should be done for her. I was angry with these country folk who, because she was unlike they were, believed her to be mad. I wanted to talk to Gilly if that were possible. I wanted to find out what went on behind that blank blue stare.

I knew she was interested in me, and I believed that in some way she had sensed my interest in her. But she was afraid of me. Something must have happened to frighten her at some time, because she was so unnaturally timid. If I could only discover what, if I could teach her that in me at least she had nothing to fear, I believed I could help her to become a normal child.

During those days I believe I thought more of Gilly than I did of Alvean. The latter seemed to me to be merely a naughty spoilt child; there were thousands such. I felt that the gentle creature called Gillyflower was unique.

It was impossible to talk to Mrs. Polgrey about her granddaughter, for she was such a conventional woman. In her mind a person was either mad or sane, and the degree of sanity depended on the conformity with Mrs. Polgrey's own character. As Gilly was as different from her grandmother as anyone could be, Gilly was therefore irremediably crazy.

So although I did broach the subject with Mrs. Polgrey she was grimly uncommunicative and told me by her looks alone to remember that I was here to take charge of Miss Alvean, and that Gilly was no concern of mine.

This was the state of affairs when Connan TreMellyn returned to Mount Mellyn.

As soon as I set eyes on Connan TreMellyn he aroused deep feelings within me. I was aware of his presence, indeed, before I saw him.

It was afternoon when he arrived. Alvean had gone off by herself and I had sent for hot water to wash before I went for a stroll. Kitty brought it and I noticed the difference in her from the moment she entered the room. Her black eyes gleamed and her mouth seemed a little slack.

'Master be home,' she said.

I tried not to show that I was faintly disturbed; and at that moment Daisy put her head round the door. The sisters looked very much alike just then. There was about them both a certain expectancy which sickened me. I thought I understood the expression in the faces of these lusty girls. I suspected that neither of them was virgin. There was suggestion in their very gestures and I had seen them in scuffling intimacy with Billy Trehay in the stables and with the boys who came in from the village to work about the place. They changed subtly when they were in the presence of the opposite sex and I understood what that meant. Their excitement over the return of the Master, of whom I gathered everyone was in awe, led me to one conclusion, and I felt faintly disgusted, not only with them but with myself for entertaining such thoughts.

Is he *that* sort of man then? I was asking myself.

'He came in half an hour ago,' said Kitty.

They were studying me speculatively and once more I thought I read their thoughts. They were telling themselves that there would be little competition from me.

My disgust increased and I turned away.

I said coolly: 'Well, I'll wash my hands and you can take the water away. I am going for a walk.'

I put on my hat and, even as I went out quickly by way of the back stairs, I sensed the change. Mr. Polgrey was busy in the gardens, and the two boys who came in from the village were working as though their lives depended on it. Tapperty was cleaning out the stables; he was so intent on his work that he did not notice me.

There was no doubt that the whole household was in awe of the Master.

As I wandered through the woods I told myself that if he did not like me I could leave at any time. I supposed I could stay with Phillida while I looked round. At least I had some relations to whom I could go. I was not entirely alone in the world.

I called on Alvean, but my voice was lost in the thickness of the trees and there was no response. Then I called: 'Gilly! Are you there, Gillyflower? Do come and talk to me if you are. I won't hurt you.'

There was no answer.

At half past three I went back to the house and, as I was mounting the back stairs to my quarters, Daisy came running after me.

'Master have been asking for you, Miss. He do wish to see you. He be waiting in the punch room.'

I inclined my head and said: 'I will take off my things and then go to the punch room.'

'He have seen you come in, Miss, and have said for you to go right away.'

'I will take off my hat first,' I answered. My heart was beating fast and my colour was heightened. I did not know why I felt antagonistic. I believed that I should soon be packing my bags and going back to Phillida; and I decided that if it had to be done it should be done with the utmost dignity.

In my room I took off my hat and smoothed my hair. My eyes were certainly amber to-day. They were resentful, which seemed ridiculous before I had met the man. I told myself as I went down to the punch room that I had built up a picture of him because of certain looks I had seen in the faces of those two flighty girls. I had already assured myself that poor Alice had died of a broken heart because she had found herself married to a philanderer.

I knocked at the door.

'Come in.' His voice was strong – arrogant, I called it even before I set eyes on him.

He was standing with his back to the fireplace and I was immediately conscious of his great height; he was well over six feet tall, and the fact that he was so thin – one could almost say gaunt – accentuated this. His hair was black but his eyes were light. His hands were thrust into the pockets of his riding breeches and he wore a dark blue coat with a white cravat. There was an air of careless elegance about him as though he cared nothing for his clothes but could not help looking well in them.

He gave an impression of both strength and cruelty. There was sensuality in that face, I decided – that came through; but there was much else which was hidden. Even in that moment when I first saw him I knew that there were two men in that body – two distinct personalities – the Connan TreMellyn who faced the world, and the one who remained hidden.

'So, Miss Leigh, at last we meet.'

He did not advance to greet me, and his manner seemed insolent as though he were reminding me that I was only a governess.

'It does not seem a long time,' I answered, 'for I have only been in your house a few days.'

'Well, let us not dwell on the time it has taken us to get together. Now you are here, let that suffice.'

His light eyes surveyed me mockingly, so that I felt awkward and unattractive, and that I stood before a connoisseur of women when even to the uninitiated I was not a very desirable specimen.

'Miss Polgrey gives me good reports of you.'

'That is kind of her.'

'Why should it be kind of her to tell me the truth? I expect that from my employees.'

'I meant that she has been kind to me and that has helped to make this good report possible.'

'I see that you are a woman who does not use the ordinary clichés of conversation but means what she says.'

'I hope so.'

'Good. I have a feeling that we shall get on well together.'

His eyes were taking in each detail of my appearance, I knew. He probably was aware that I had been given a London season and what Aunt Adelaide would call 'every opportunity", and had failed to acquire a husband. As a connoisseur of women he would know why.

I thought, at least I shall be safe from the attentions which I feel sure he tries to bestow on all attractive women with whom he comes into contact.

'Tell me,' he said, 'how do you find my daughter? Backward for her age?'

'By no means. She is extremely intelligent, but I find her in need of discipline.'

'I am sure you will be able to supply that lack.'

'I intend to try.'

'Of course. That is why you are here.'

'Please tell me how far I may carry that discipline.'

'You are thinking of corporal punishment?'

'Nothing was farther from my thoughts. I mean, have I your permission to apply my own code? To restrict her liberty, shall we say, if I feel she needs such punishment.'

'Short of murder, Miss Leigh, you have my permission to do what you will. If your methods do not meet with my approval, you will hear.'

'Very well, I understand.'

'If you wish to make any alterations in the . . . curriculum, I think is the word . . . you must do so.'

'Thank you.'

'I believe in experiments. If your methods have not made an improvement in say . . . six months . . . well, then we could review the situation, could we not?'

His eyes were insolent. I thought: He intends to get rid of me soon. He was hoping I was a silly, pretty creature not averse to carrying on an intrigue with him while pretending to look after his daughter. Very well, the best thing I can do is to get out of this house.

'I suppose,' he went on, 'we should make excuses for Alvean's lack of good manners. She lost her mother a year ago.'

I looked into his face for a trace of sorrow. I could find none.

'I had heard that,' I answered.

'Of course you had heard. I'll swear there were many ready to tell you. It was doubtless a great shock to the child.'

'It must have been a great shock,' I agreed.

'It was sudden.' He was silent for a few seconds and then he continued: 'Poor child, she has no mother. And her father . . .?' He lifted his shoulders and did not complete his sentence.

'Even so,' I said, 'there are many more unfortunate than she is. All she needs is a firm hand.'

He leaned forward suddenly and surveyed me ironically.

'I am sure,' he said, 'that you possess that necessary firm hand.'

I was conscious in that brief moment of the magnetism of the man. The clear-cut features, the cool, light eyes, the mockery behind them – all these I felt were but a mask hiding something which he was determined to keep hidden.

At that moment there was a knock on the door and Celestine Nansellock came in.

'I heard you were here, Connan,' she said, and I thought she seemed nervous. So he had that effect even on those of his own station.

'How news travels!' he murmured. 'My dear Celestine, it was good of you to come over. I was just making the acquaintance of our new governess. She tells me that Alvean is intelligent and needs discipline.'

'Of course she is intelligent!' Celestine spoke indignantly. 'I hope Miss Leigh is not planning to be too harsh with her. Alvean is a *good* child.'

Connan TreMellyn threw an amused glance in my direction. 'I don't think Miss Leigh entirely agrees with that,' he said. 'You see our little goose as a beautiful swan, Celeste my dear.'

'Perhaps I am over fond—'

'Would you like me to leave now?' I suggested, for I had a great desire to get away from them.

'But I am interrupting,' cried Celestine.

'No,' I assured her. 'We had finished our talk, I believe.'

Connan TreMellyn looked in some amusement from her to me. It occurred to me that he probably found us equally unattractive. I was sure that neither of us was the least like the woman he would admire.

'Let us say it is to be continued,' he said lightly. 'I fancy, Miss Leigh, that you and I will have a great deal more to discuss, regarding my daughter.'

I bowed my head and left them together.

In the schoolroom tea was laid, ready for me. I felt too excited to eat, and when Alvean did not appear I guessed she was with her father.

At five o'clock she still had not put in an appearance, so I summoned Daisy and sent her to find the child and to remind her that from five to six we had work to do.

I waited. I was not surprised because I had expected Alvean to rebel. Her father had arrived and she preferred to be with him rather than come to me for an hour of our reading.

I wondered what would happen when the child refused to come to the schoolroom. Could I go down to the punch room or the drawing room or wherever they were and demand that she return with me? Celestine was with them and she would take her stand on Alvean's side against me.

I heard footsteps on the stairs. The door of Alvean's room which led into the schoolroom was opened, and there stood Connan TreMellyn holding Alvean by the arm.

Alvean's expression astonished me. She looked so unhappy that I found myself feeling sorry for her. Her father was smiling and I thought he looked like a satyr, as though the situation which caused pain to Alvean and embarrassment to me amused him – and perhaps for these reasons. In the background was Celestine.

'Here she is,' announced Connan TreMellyn. 'Duty is duty, my daughter,' he said to Alvean. 'And when your governess summons you to your lessons, you must obey.'

Alvean muttered and I could see that she was hard put to it to restrain her sobs: 'But it is your first day, Papa.'

'But Miss Leigh says there are lessons to be done, and she is in command.'

'Thank you, Mr. TreMellyn,' I said. 'Come and sit down, Alvean.'

Alvean's expression changed as she looked at me. All the wistfulness was replaced by anger and a fierce hatred.

'Connan,' Celestine said quietly, 'it *is* your first day back, you know, and Aleavn so looked forward to your coming.'

He smiled but I thought how grim his mouth was.

'Discipline,' he murmured. 'That, Celeste, is of the utmost importance. Come, we will leave Alvean with her governess.'

He inclined his head in my direction, while Alvean threw a pleading glance at him which he quite obviously ignored.

The door shut leaving me alone with my pupil.

That incident had taught me a great deal. Alvean adored her father and he was indifferent to her. My anger against him increased as my pity for the child grew. Small wonder that she was a difficult child. What could one expect when she was such an unhappy one? I saw her . . . ignored by the father whom she loved, spoiled by Celestine Nansellock. Between them they were doing their best to ruin the girl.

I would have liked Connan TreMellyn better, I told myself, if he had decided to forget discipline on his first day back, and devote a little time to his daughter's company.

Alvean was rebellious all that evening, but I insisted on her going to bed at her usual time. She told me she hated me, though there was no need for her to have mentioned a fact which was apparent.

I felt so disturbed when she was in her bed that I slipped out of the house and went into the woods, where I sat on a fallen tree trunk, brooding.

It had been a hot day and there was a deep stillness in the woods.

I wondered whether I was going to keep this job. It was not easy to say at this stage, and I was not sure whether I wanted to go or stay.

There were so many things to keep me. There was, for one thing, my interest in Gillyflower; there was my desire to wipe the rebellion from Alvean's heart. But I felt less eagerness for these tasks now that I had seen the Master.

I was a little afraid of the man although I could not say why. I was certain that he would leave *me* alone, but there was something magnetic about him, some quality which made it difficult for me to put him out of my mind. I thought more of dead Alice than I had before, because I could not stop myself wondering what sort of person she could have been.

I amused him in some way. Perhaps because I was so unattractive in his eyes; perhaps because he knews that I belonged to that army of women who are obliged to earn their living and are so dependent on the whim of people like himself. Was there a streak of sadism in his nature? I believed so. Perhaps poor Alice had found it intolerable. Perhaps she, like poor Gilly-flower's mother, had walked into the sea.

As I sat there I heard the sound of footsteps coming through the wood and I hesitated, wondering whether to wait there or go back to the house.

A man was coming towards me, and there was something familiar about him which made my heart beat faster.

He started when he saw me; then he began to smile and I recognized him as the man I had met on the train.

'So we meet,' he said. 'I knew our reunion would not be long delayed. Why, you look as though you have seen a ghost. Has your stay at Mount Mellyn made you look for ghosts? I've heard some say that there *is* a ghostly atmosphere about the place.'

'Who are you?' I asked.

'My name is Peter Nansellock. I have to confess to a little deception.'

'You're Miss Celestine's brother?'

He nodded. 'I knew who you were when we met in the train. I deliberately bearded you in your carriage. I saw you sitting there, looking the part, and I guessed. Your name on the labels of your baggage confirmed my guess for I knew that they were expecting Miss Martha Leigh at Mount Mellyn.'

'I am comforted to learn that my looks conform with the part I have been called upon to play in life.'

'You really are a most untruthful young lady. I remember I had reason to reprimand you for the same sort of thing at our first meeting. You are in fact quite discomfited to learn that you were taken for a governess.'

I felt myself grow pink with indignation. 'Because I am a governess that is no reason why I should be forced to accept insults from strangers.'

I rose from the tree trunk, but he laid a hand on my arm and said pleadingly: 'Please let us talk awhile. There is much I have to say to you. There are things you should know.'

My curiosity overcame my dignity and I saw down.

'That's better, Miss Leigh. You see I remember your name.'

'Most courteous of you! And how extraordinary- that you should first notice a mere governess's name and then keep it in your memory.'

'You are like a hedgehog,' he retorted. 'One only has to mention the word "governess" and up come your spines. You will have to learn resignation. Aren't we taught that we must be content in that station of life to which we have been called?'

'Since I resemble a hedgehog, at least I am not spineless.'

He laughed and then was immediately sober. 'I do not possess second sight, Miss Leigh,' he said quietly. 'I know nothing of palmistry. I deceived you, Miss Leigh.'

'Do you think I was deceived for a moment?'

'For many moments. Until this one, in fact, you have thought of me with wonder.'

'Indeed, I have not thought of you at all.'

'More untruths! I wonder if a young lady with such little regard for veracity is worthy to teach our little Alvean.'

'Since you are a friend of the family your best policy would be to warn them at once.'

'But if Connan dismissed his daughter's governess, how sad that would be! I should wander through these woods without hope of meeting her.'

'I see you are a frivolous person.'

'It's true.' He looked grave. 'My brother was frivolous. My sister is the only commendable member of the family.'

'I have already met her.'

'Naturally. She is a constant visitor to Mount Mellyn. She dotes on Alvean.'

'Well, she is a very near neighbour.'

'And we, Miss Leigh, shall in future be very near neighbours. How does that strike you?'

'Without any great force.'

'Miss Leigh, you are cruel as well as untruthful. I hoped you would be grateful for my interest. I was going to say, if ever things should become intolerable at Mount Mellyn you need only walk over to Mount Widden. There you would find me most willing to help. I feel sure that among my wide circle of acquaintances I could find someone who is in urgent need of a governess.'

'Why should I find life intolerable at Mount Mellyn?'

'It's a tomb of a place, Connan is overbearing, Alvean is a menace to anyone's peace, and the atmosphere since Alice's death is not congenial.'

I turned to him abruptly and said: 'You told me to beware of Alice. What did you mean by that?'

'So you remember?'

'It seemed a strange thing to say.'

'Alice is dead,' he said, 'but somehow she remains. That's what I always feel at Mount Mellyn. Nothing was the same after the day she . . . went.'

'How did she die?'

'You have not heard the story yet?'

'No.'

'I should have thought Mrs. Polgrey or one of those girls would have told you. But they haven't, eh? They're probably somewhat in awe of the governess.'

'I should like to hear the story.'

'It's a very simple one. The sort of thing which must happen in many a home. A wife finds life with her husband intolerable. She walks out . . . with another man. It's ordinary enough, you see. Only Alice's story had a different ending.'

He looked at the tips of his boots as he had when we were travelling in the train to Liskeard together. 'The man in the case was my brother,' he went on.

'Geoffry Nansellock!' I cried.

'So you have heard of him!'

I thought of Gillyflower, whose birth had so distressed her mother that she had walked into the sea.

'Yes,' I said, 'I've heard of Geoffry Nansellock. He was evidently a philanderer.'

'It sounds a harsh word to apply to poor old Geoff. He had charm . . . all the charm of the family, some say.' He smiled at me. 'Others may think he did not get it all. He was not a bad sort. I was fond of old Geoff. His great weakness was women. He loved women; he found them irresistible. And women love men who love them. How can they help it? I mean, it is such a compliment, is it not? One by one they fell victim to his charm.'

'He did not hesitate to include other men's wives among his victims.'

'Spoken like a true governess! Alas, my dear Miss Leigh, it appeared he did not . . . since Alice was among them. It is true that all was not well at Mount Mellyn. Do you think Connan would be an easy man to live with?'

'It is surely not becoming for a governess to discuss her employer in such a manner.'

'What a contrary young lady you are, Miss Leigh. You make the most of your situation. You use the governess when you wish to, and then expect others to ignore her when you do not wish her to be recognized. I believe that anyone who is obliged to live in a house should know something of its secrets.'

'What secrets?'

He bent a little closer to me. 'Alice was afraid of Connan. Before she married him she had known my brother. She and Geoffry were on the train . . . running away together.'

'I see.' I drew myself away from him because I felt it was undignified to be talking of past scandals in this way, particularly as these scandals had nothing whatever to do with me.

'They identified Geoffry although he was badly smashed up. There was a woman close to him. She was so badly burned that it was impossible to recognize her as Alice. But a locket she was wearing was recognized as one she was known to possess. That was how she was identified . . . and of course there was the fact that Alice had disappeared.'

'How dreadful to die in such a way!'

'The prim governess is shocked because poor Alice died in the act of forming a guilty partnership with my charming but erring brother.'

'Was she so unhappy at Mount Mellyn?'

'You have met Connan. Remember he knew that she had once been in love with Geoffry, and Geoffry was still in the offing. I can imagine life was hell for Alice.'

'Well, it was very tragic,' I said briskly. 'But it is over. Why did you say, "Beware of Alice," as though she were still there?'

'Are you fey, Miss Leigh? No, of course you are not. You are a governess with more than your fair share of commonsense. You would not be influenced by fantastic tales.'

'What fantastic tales?'

He grinned at me, coming even closer, and I realized that in a very short time it would be dark. I was anxious to get back to the house, and my expression became a little impatient.

'They recognized her locket, not her. There are some who think that it was not Alice who was killed on the train with Geoffry.'

'Then if it was not, where is she?'

'That is what some people ask themselves. That is why there are long shadows at Mount Mellyn.'

I stood up. 'I must get back. It will soon be dark.'

He was standing beside me – a little taller than I – and our eyes met.

'I thought you should know these things,' he said almost gently. 'It seems only fair that you should know.'

I began walking back in the direction from which I had come.

'My duties are with the child,' I answered somewhat brusquely. 'I am not here for any other purpose.'

'But how can even a governess, overburdened with common sense though she may be, know to what purposes fate will put her?'

'I think I know what is expected of me.' I was alarmed because he walked beside me; I wanted to escape from him that I might be alone with my thoughts. I felt this man impaired my precious dignity to which I was clinging with that determination only possible to those who are in constant fear of losing what little they possess. He had mocked me in the train. I felt he was waiting for an opportunity to do so again.

'I am sure you do.'

'There is no need for you to escort me back to the house.'

'I am forced to contradict you. There is every reason.'

'Do you think I am incapable of looking after myself?'

'I think none more capable of doing that than yourself. But as it happens I was on my way to call, and this is the most direct way to the house.'

I was silent until we came to Mount Mellyn.

Connan TreMellyn was coming from the stable.

'Hallo there, Con!' cried Peter Nansellock.

Connan TreMellyn looked at us in mild surprise, which I supposed was due to the fact that we were together.

I hurried round to the back of the house.

It was not easy to sleep that night. The events of the day crowded into my mind and I saw pictures of myself and Connan TreMellyn, pictures of Alvean, of Celestine, and of myself in the woods with Peter Nansellock.

The wind was in a certain direction that night, and I could hear the waves thundering into Mellyn Cove.

In my present mood it certainly seemed that there were whispering voices down there, and that the words they said to each other were: 'Alice! Alice! Where is Alice? Alice, where are you?'

Chapter Three

In the morning the fancies of the previous night seemed foolish. I asked myself why so many people – including myself – wanted to make a mystery of what had happened in this house. It was an ordinary enough story.

I know what it is, I told myself. When people consider an ancient house like this, they make themselves believe it could tell some fantastic stories if it could only speak. They think of the generations who have lived and suffered within these walls, and they grow fanciful. So that when the mistress of the house is tragically killed they imagine her ghost still walks and that, although she is dead, she is still here. Well, I am a sensible woman, I hope. Alice was killed on a train, and that was the end of Alice.

I laughed at my folly in allowing myself to be caught up in such notions. Had not Daisy or Kitty explained that the whispering voices, which I heard in the night, were merely the sound of waves thundering in the cove below?

From now on I was entertaining no more such fantastic thoughts.

My room was filled with sunshine and I felt differently from the way I had felt on any other morning. I was exhilarated. I knew why. It was due to that man, Connan TreMellyn. Not that I liked him – quite the reverse; but it was as though he had issued a challenge. I was going to make a success of this job. I was going to make of Alvean not only a model pupil but a charming, unaffected, uninhibited little girl.

I felt so pleased that I began to hum softly under my breath.

Come into the Garden, Maud . . . That was a song Father used to like to play while Phillida sang, for in addition to her other qualities Phillida possessed a charming voice. Then I passed to *Sweet and Low*, and I for a moment forgot the house I was in and saw Father at the piano, his glasses slipping down his nose, his slippered feet making the most of the pedals.

I was almost astonished to find that I had unconsciously slipped into the song I had heard Gilly singing in the woods: *Alice, where are thou—*

Oh no, not that, I said sharply to myself.

I heard the sound of horses' hoofs and I went to the window to look out. No one was visible. The lawns looked fresh and lovely with the early morning dew on them. What a beautiful sight, I thought; the palm trees gave the scene a tropical look and it was one of those mornings when there was every promise of a beautiful day.

'One of the last we can expect this summer, I daresay,' I said aloud; and I threw open my window and leaned out, my thick coppery plaits, the ends tied with pieces of blue ribbon for bedtime, swinging out with me.

I went back to *Sweet and Low* and was humming this when Connan TreMellyn emerged from the stables. He saw me before I was able to draw back, and I felt myself grow scarlet with embarrassment to be seen with my hair down and in my nightgown thus.

He called jauntily: 'Good morning, Miss Leigh.'

In that moment I said to myself: So it was his horse I heard. And has he been riding in the early morning, or out all night? I imagined his visiting one of the gay ladies of the neighbourhood if such existed. That was my opinion of him. I was angry that he should be the one to show no embarrassment whatsoever while I was blushing – certainly in every part that was visible.

'Good morning,' I said, and my voice sounded curt.

He was coming swiftly across the lawn, hoping, I was sure, to embarrass me further by a closer look at me in my night attire.

'A beautiful morning,' he cried.

'Extremely so,' I answered.

I withdrew into my room as I heard him shout: 'Hallo, Alvean! So you're up too.'

I was standing well back from the window now and I heard Alvean cry: 'Hallo, Papa!' and her voice was soft and gentle with that wistful note which I had detected when she spoke of him on the previous day. I knew that she was delighted to have seen him, that she had been awake in her room when she had heard his voice, and had dashed to her window, and that it would make her extremely happy if he stopped awhile and chatted with her.

He did no such thing. He went into the house. Standing before my mirror, I looked at myself. Most unbecoming, I thought. And quite undignified. Myself in a pink flannelette nightdress buttoned high at the throat, with my hair down and my face even now the colour of the flannelette!

I put on my dressing gown and on impulse crossed the schoolroom to Alvean's room. I opened the door and went in. She was sitting astride a chair and talking to herself.

'There's nothing to be afraid of really. All you have to do is hold tight and not be afraid . . . and you won't fall off.'

She was so intent on what she was doing that she had not heard the door open, and I stood for a few seconds watching her, for she had her back to the schoolroom door.

I learnt a great deal in that moment. He was a great horseman, this father of hers; he wanted his daughter to be a good horsewoman, but Alvean, who desperately wanted to win his approval, was afraid of horses.

I started forward, my first impulse to talk to her, to tell her that I would teach her to ride. It was the one thing I could do really well because we had always had horses in the country, and at five Phillida and I were competing in local shows.

But I hesitated because I was beginning to understand Alvean. She was an unhappy child. Tragedy had hit her in more ways than one. She had lost her mother, and that was the biggest tragedy which could befall any child; but when her father did not seem anything but indifferent to her, and she adored him, that was a double tragedy.

I quietly shut the door and went back to my room. I looked at the sunshine on the carpet and my elation returned. I *was* going to make a success of this job. I was going to fight Connan TreMellyn, if he wanted it that way. I was going to make him proud of his daughter; I was going to force him to give her that attention which was her right and which none but a brute would deny her.

Lessons were trying that morning. Alvean was late for them, having breakfasted with her father in accordance with the custom of the family. I pictured them at the big table in the room which I had discovered was used as a dining room when there were no guests. They called it the small dining room, but it was only small by Mount Mellyn standards.

He would be reading the paper, or looking through his letters, I imagined; Alvean would be at the other end of the table hoping for a word, which of course he would be too selfish to bestow.

I had to send for her to come to lessons; and that she deeply resented.

I tried to make lessons as interesting as I could, and I must have succeeded, for in spite of her resentment towards me she could not hide her interest in the history and geography lessons which I set for that morning.

She took luncheon with her father while I ate alone in the schoolroom, and after that I decided to approach Connan TreMellyn.

While I was wondering where I could find him I saw him leave the house and go across to the stables. I immediately followed him and, when I arrived at the stables, I heard him giving orders to Billy Trehay to saddle Royal Russet for him.

He looked surprised to see me; and then he smiled and I was sure that he was remembering the last time he had seen me – in dishabille.

'Why,' he said, 'it is Miss Leigh.'

'I had hoped to have a few words with you,' I said primly. 'Perhaps this is an inconvenient time.'

'That depends,' he said, 'on how many words you wish us to exchange.' He took out his watch and looked at it. 'I can give you five minutes, Miss Leigh.'

I was aware of Billy Trehay, and if Connan TreMellyn was going to snub me I was eager that no servant should overhear.

Connan TreMellyn said: 'Let us walk across the lawn. Ready in five minutes, Billy?'

'Very good, Master,' answered Billy.

With that Connan TreMellyn began to walk away from the stables, and I fell into step beside him.

'In my youth,' I said, 'I was constantly in the saddle. I believe Alvean wishes to learn to ride. I am asking your permission to teach her.'

'You have my permission to try, Miss Leigh,' he said.

'You sound as though you doubt my ability to succeed.'

'I fear I do.'

'I don't understand why you should doubt my ability to teach when you have not tested my skill.'

'Oh, Miss Leigh,' he said almost mockingly, 'you wrong me. It is not your ability to teach that I doubt; it is Alvean's to learn.'

'You mean others have failed to teach her?'

'I have failed.'

'But surely—'

He lifted a hand. 'It is strange,' he said, 'to find such fear in a child. Most children take to it like breathing.'

His tone was clipped, his expression hard; I wanted to shout at him: What sort of father are you! I pictured the lessons, the lack of understanding, the expectation of miracles. No wonder the child had been scared.

He went on: 'There are some people who can never learn to ride.'

Before I could stop myself I had burst out: 'There are some people who cannot teach.'

He stopped to stare at me in astonishment, and I knew that nobody in this house had ever dared to talk to him in such a way.

I thought: This is it. I shall now be told that my services are no longer required, and at the end of the month I may pack my bags and depart.

There was a violent temper there, and I could see that he was fighting to control it. He still looked at me and I could not read the expression in those light eyes. I believed it was contemptuous. Then he glanced back at the stables.

'You must excuse me, Miss Leigh,' he said; and he left me.

I went straight back to Alvean. I found her in the schoolroom. There was the sullen defiant look in her eyes, and I believed she had seen me talking to her father.

I came straight to the point. 'Your father has said I may give you riding lessons, Alvean. Would you like that?'

I saw the muscles of her face tighten, and my heat sank. Would it be possible to teach a child who was as scared as that?

I went on quickly, before she had time to answer: 'When we were your age my sister and I were keen riders. She was two years younger than I and we used to compete together in the local shows. The exciting days in our lives were those when there was a horse show in our village.'

'They have them here,' she said.

'It's great fun. And once you've really mastered the trick you feel quite at home in the saddle.'

She was silent for a moment, then she said: 'I can't do it. I don't like horses.'

'You don't like horses!' My voice was shocked. 'Why, they're the gentlest creatures in the world.'

'They're not. They don't like me. I rode Grey Mare and she ran fast and wouldn't stop, and if Tapperty hadn't caught her rein she would have killed me.'

'Grey Mare wasn't the mount for you. You should have a pony to start with.'

'Then I had Buttercup. She was as bad in a different way. She wouldn't go when I tried to make her. She took a mouthful of the bushes on the bank and I tugged and tugged and she wouldn't move for me. When Billy Trehay said "Come on, Buttercup," she just let go and started walking away as though it were all my fault.'

I laughed and she threw me a look of hatred. I hastened to assure her that was the way horses behaved until they understood you. When they did understand you they loved you as though you were their very dear friend.

I saw the wistful look in her eyes then and I exulted because I knew that the reason for aggressiveness was to be found in her intense loneliness and desire for affection.

I said: 'Look here, Alvean, come out with me now. Let's see what we can do together.'

She shook her head and looked at me suspiciously. I knew she felt that I might be trying to punish her for her ungraciousness towards me by making her look foolish. I wanted to put my arm about her, but I knew that was no way to approach Alvean.

'There's one thing to learn before you can begin to ride,' I said as though I had not noticed her gesture, 'and that is to love your horse. Then you won't be afraid. As soon as you're not afraid, your horse will begin to love you. He'll know you're his master, and he wants a master; but it must be a tender, loving master.'

She was giving me her attention now.

'When a horse runs away as Grey Mare did, that means that she is frightened. She's as frightened as you are, and her way of showing it is to run. Now when you're frightened you should never let her know it. You just whisper to her, "it's all right, Grey Mare ... I'm here." As for Buttercup – she's a mischievous old nag. She's lazy and she knows that you can't handle her, so she won't do as she's told. But once you let her know you're the master she'll obey. Look how she did with Billy Trehay!'

'I didn't know Grey Mare was frightened of me,' she said.

'Your father wants you to ride,' I told her.

It was the wrong thing to have said; it reminded her of past fears, past humiliations; I saw the stubborn fear return to her eyes, and felt a new burst of resentment towards that arrogant man who could be so careless of the feelings of a child.

'Wouldn't it be fun,' I said, 'to surprise him. I mean ... suppose you learned and you could jump and gallop, and he didn't know about it ... until he saw you do it.'

It hurt me to see the joy in her face and I wondered how any man could be so callous as to deny a child the affection she asked.

'Alvean,' I said. 'Let's try.'

'Yes,' she said, 'let's try. I'll go and change into my things.'

I gave a little cry of disappointment, remembering that I had no riding habit with me. During my years with Aunt Adelaide I had had little opportunity for wearing it. Aunt Adelaide was no horsewoman herself and consequently was never invited to the country to hunt. Thus I had no opportunity for riding. To ride in Rotten Row would have been far beyond my means. When I had last looked at my riding clothes I had seen that the moth had got at them. I had felt resigned. I believed that I should never need them again.

Alvean was looking at me and I told her: 'I have no riding clothes.'

Her face fell and then lit up. 'Come with me,' she said. She was almost conspiratorial and I enjoyed this new relationship between us which I felt to be a great advance towards friendship.

We went along the gallery until we were in that part of the house which Mrs. Polgrey had told me was not for me. Alvean paused before a door and I had the impression that she was steeling herself to go in. She at length threw open the door and stood aside for me to enter, and I could not help feeling that she wanted me to go in first.

It was a small room which I judged to be a dressing room. In it was a long mirror, a tallboy, a chest of drawers and an oak chest. Like most of the rooms in the house this room had two doors. These rooms in the gallery appeared to lead from one to another, and this other door was slightly opened and, as Alvean went to it and looked round the room beyond, I followed her.

It was a bedroom in there. A large room beautifully furnished, the floor carpeted in blue, the curtains of blue velvet; the bed was a four-poster and, although I knew it to be large, it was dwarfed by the size of the room.

Alvean seemed distressed to see my interest in the bedroom. She went to the communicating door and shut it.

'There are lots of clothes here,' she said. 'In the chests and the tallboy. There's bound to be riding clothes. There'll be something you can have.'

She had thrown up the lid of the chest and it was something new for me to see her so excited. I was delighted to have discovered a way to her affections that I allowed myself to be carried along.

In the chest were dresses, petticoats, hats and boots.

Alvean said quickly: 'There are a lot of clothes in the attics. Great trunks of them. They were grandmamma's and great grandmamma's. When there were parties they used to dress up in them and play charades—'

I held up a lady's black beaver hat – obviously meant to be worn for riding. I put it on my head and Alvean laughed with a little catch in her voice. That laughter moved me more than anything had done since I had entered this house. It was the laughter of a child who is unaccustomed to laughter and laughs in a manner which is almost guilty. I determined to have her laughing often and without the slightest feeling of guilt.

She suddenly controlled herself as though she remembered where she was. 'You look so funny in it, Miss,' she said.

I got up and stood before the long mirror. I certainly looked unlike myself. My eyes were brilliant, my hair looked quite copper against the black. I decided that I looked slightly less unattractive than usual, and that was what Alvean meant by 'funny'.

'Not in the least like a governess,' she explained. She was pulling out a dress, and I saw that it was a riding habit made of black woollen cloth and trimmed with braid and ball fringe. It had a blue collar and blue cuffs and it was elegantly cut.

I held it up against myself. 'I think,' I said, 'that this would fit.'

'Try it on,' said Alvean. Then . . . 'No, not here. You take it to your room and put it on.' She suddenly seemed obsessed by the desire to get out of this room. She picked up the hat and ran to the door. I thought that she was eager for us to get started on our lesson, and there was not a great deal of time if we were to be back for tea at four.

I picked up the dress, took the hat from her and went back to my room. She hurried through to hers, and I immediately put on the riding habit.

It was not a perfect fit, but I had never been used to expensive clothes and was prepared to forget it was a little tight at the waist, and that the sleeves were on the short side, for a new woman looked back at me from my mirror, and when I set the beaver hat on my head I was delighted with myself.

I ran along to Alvean's room; she was in her habit, and when she saw me her eyes lit up and she seemed to look at me with greater interest than ever before.

We went down to the stables and I told Billy Trehay to saddle Buttercup for Alvean and another horse for myself as we were going to have a riding lesson.

He looked at me with some astonishment, but I told him that we had little time and were impatient to begin.

When we were ready I put Buttercup on a leading rein and took her with Alvean on her back into the paddock.

For nearly an hour we were there and when we left it I knew that Alvean and I had entered into a new relationship. She had not accepted me completely – that would have been asking too much – but I did believe that from that afternoon she knew that I was not an enemy.

I concentrated on giving her confidence. I made her grow accustomed to sitting her horse, to talking to her horse. I made her lean back full length on Buttercup's back and look up at the sky; then I made her shut her eyes. I gave her lessons in mounting and dismounting. Buttercup did no more than walk round that field, but I do believe that at the end of the hour I had done a great deal towards making Alvean lose her fear; and that was what I had determined should be the first lesson.

I was astonished to find that it was half past three, and I think Alvean was too.

'We must return to the house at once,' I said, 'if we are to change in time for tea.'

As we came out of the field a figure rose from the grass and I saw to my surprise that it was Peter Nansellock.

He clapped his hands as we came along.

'Here endeth the first lesson,' he cried, 'and an excellent one. I did not know,' he went on, turning to me, 'that equestrian skill was included in your many accomplishments.'

'Were you watching us, Uncle Peter?' demanded Alvean.

'For the last half hour. My admiration for you both is beyond expression.'

Alvean smiled slowly. 'Did you really admire us?'

'Much as I could be tempted to compliment two beautiful ladies,' he said placing his hand on his heart and bowing elegantly, 'I could never tell a lie.'

'Until this moment,' I said tartly.

Alvean's face fell and I added: 'There is nothing very admirable in learning to ride. Thousands are doing it every day.'

'But the art was never so gracefully taught, never so patiently learned.'

'Your uncle is a joker, Alvean,' I put in.

'Yes,' said Alvean almost sadly, 'I know.'

'And,' I added, 'it is time that we returned for tea.'

'I wonder if I might be invited to schoolroom tea?'

'You are calling to see Mr. TreMellyn?' I asked.

'I am calling to take tea with you two ladies.'

Alvean laughed suddenly; I could see that she was not unaffected by what I supposed was the charm of this man.

'Mr. TreMellyn left Mount Mellyn early this afternoon,' I said. 'I have no idea whether or not he has returned.'

'And while the cat's away . . .' he murmured, and his eyes swept over my costume in a manner which I could only describe as insolent.

I said coolly: 'Come along, Alvean, we must go at once if we are to be in time for tea.'

I let the horse break into a trot, and holding Buttercup's leading rein, started towards the house.

Peter Nansellock walked behind us, and when we reached the stables I saw him making for the house.

Alvean and I dismounted, handed our horses to two of the stable boys, and hurried up to our rooms.

I got out of the riding habit and into my dress and, glancing at myself, I thought how drab I looked in my grey cotton. I made a gesture of impatience at my folly and picked up the riding habit to hang in my cupboard, deciding that I would take the first opportunity of asking Mrs. Polgrey if it was in order for me to use it. I was afraid I had acted on impulse by doing so this afternoon, but I had been stung into prompt action, I realized, by the attitude of Connan TreMellyn.

As I lifted the habit I saw the name on the waist band. It gave me a little start, as I suppose everything in that connection would do for some time. 'Alice TreMellyn' was embossed in neat and tiny letters on the black satin facings.

Then I understood. That room had been her dressing room; the bedroom I had glimpsed, her bedroom. I wondered that Alvean had taken me there and given me her mother's clothes.

My heart felt as though it were leaping into my throat. This, I said to myself, is absurd. Where else could we have found a modern riding habit? Not in those chests in the attics she had spoken of; the clothes in those were used for charades.

I was being ridiculous. Why should I not wear Alice's riding habit? She had no need for it now. And was I not accustomed to wearing cast-off clothes?

Boldly I picked up the riding dress and hung it in my cupboard.

I was impelled to go to my window and looked along the line of windows, trying to place that one which would have been that of her bedroom. I thought I placed it.

In spite of myself I shivered. Then I shook myself. She would be glad I used her habit, I told myself. Of course she would be glad. Am I not trying to help her daughter?

I realized that I was reassuring myself – which was ridiculous.

What had happened to my commonsense? Whatever I told myself I could not hide the fact that I wished the dress had belonged to anyone but Alice.

When I had changed there was a knock on my door and I was relieved to see Mrs. Polgrey standing there.

'Do come in,' I said. 'You are just the lady I wished to see.'

She came into my room, and I was very fond of her in that moment. There was an air of normality about her such as must inevitably put fancy to flight.

'I have been giving Miss Alvean a riding lesson,' I said quickly, for I was anxious to have this matter of the dress settled before she could tell me why she had come. 'And as I had no riding habit with me she found one for me. I believe it to have been her mother's.' I went to my wardrobe and produced it.

Mrs. Polgrey nodded.

'I wore it this once. Perhaps it was wrong of me.'

'Did you have the Master's permission to give her this riding lesson?'

'Oh yes, indeed. I made sure of that.'

'Then there is nothing to worry about. He would have no objection to your wearing the dress. I can see no reason why you should not keep it in your room, providing of course you only wear it when giving Miss Alvean her riding lesson.'

'Thank you,' I said. 'You have set my mind at rest.'

Mrs. Polgrey bowed her head in approval. I could see that she was rather pleased that I had brought my little problem to her.

'Mr. Peter Nansellock is downstairs,' she said.

'Yes, we saw him as we came in.'

'The Master is not at home. And Mr. Peter has asked that you entertain him for tea – you and Miss Alvean.'

'Oh, but should we . . . I mean should I?'

'Well, yes, Miss, I think it would be in order. I think that is what the Master would wish, particularly as Mr. Peter suggests it. Miss Jansen, during the time she was here, often helped to entertain. Why, there was an occasion I remember, when she was invited to the dinner table.'

'Oh!' I said, hoping I sounded duly impressed.

'You see, Miss, having no mistress in the house, makes it a little difficult at times; and when a gentleman expressly asks for your company – well, I really don't see what harm there could be in it. I have told Mr. Nansellock that tea will be served in the punch room and that I am sure you will be ready to join him and Miss Alvean. You have no objection?'

'No, no. I have no objection.'

Mrs. Polgrey smiled graciously. 'Then will you come down?'

'Yes, I will.'

She sailed out as majestically as she had arrived; and I found myself smiling not without a little complacence. It was turning out to be a most enjoyable day.

When I reached the punch room, Alvean was not there but Peter Nansellock was sprawling in one of the tapestry-covered chairs.

He leaped to his feet on my entrance.

'But this is delightful.'

'Mrs. Polgrey has told me that I am to do the honours in the absence of Mr. TreMellyn.'

'How like you, to remind me that you are merely the governess!'

'I felt,' I replied, 'that it was necessary to do so, since you may have forgotten.'

'You are such a charming hostess! And indeed I never saw you look less like a governess than when you were giving Alvean her lesson.'

'It was my riding habit. Borrowed plumes. A pheasant would look like a peacock, if it could acquire the tail.'

'My dear Miss Pheasant, I do not agree. "Manners makyth the man" – or woman – not fine feathers. But let me ask you this before our little Alvean appears. What do you think of this place? You are going to stay with us?'

'It is really more a question of how this place likes me, and whether the powers that be decide to keep me.'

'Ah – the powers that be in this case are a little unaccountable, are they not? What do you think of old Connan?'

'The adjective you use is inaccurate, and it is not my place to give an opinion.'

He laughed aloud showing white and perfect teeth. 'Dear Governess,' he said, 'you'll be the death of me.'

'I'm sorry to hear it.'

'Though,' he went on, 'I have often thought that to die of laughing must be a very pleasant way to do so.'

This banter was interrupted by the appearance of Alvean.

'Ah, the little lady herself!' cried Peter. 'Dear Alvean, how good it is of you and Miss Leigh to allow me to take tea with you.'

'I wonder why you want to,' replied Alvean. 'You never have before . . . except when Miss Jansen was here.'

'Hush, hush! You betray me,' he murmured.

Mrs. Polgrey came in with Kitty. The latter set the tray on a table, while Mrs. Polgrey lighted the spirit lamp. I saw that a canister of tea was on the tray. Kitty laid a cloth on a small table and brought in cakes and cucumber sandwiches.

'Miss, would you care to make the tea yourself?' asked Mrs. Polgrey. I said I would do so with pleasure, and Mrs. Polgrey signed to Kitty, who was staring at Peter Nansellock with an expression close to idolatry.

Kitty seemed reluctant to leave the room and I felt it was unkind to have dismissed her. I believed that Mrs. Polgrey was also to some extent under the spell of the man. It must be, I told myself, because he is such a contrast to the master. Peter managed to flatter with a look, and I had noticed that he was ready to lavish this flattery on all females; Kitty, Mrs. Polgrey and Alvean, no less than on myself.

So much for its worth! I told myself and I felt a little piqued, for the man had that comforting quality of making any woman in his company feel that she was an attractive one.

I made tea and Alvean handed him bread and butter.

'What luxury!' he cried. 'I feel like a sultan with two beautiful ladies to wait on me.'

'You're telling lies again,' cried Alvean. 'We're neither of us ladies, because I'm not grown up and Miss is a governess.'

'What sacrilege!' he murmured, and his warm eyes were on me, almost caressingly. I felt uncomfortably embarrassed under his scrutiny.

I changed the conversation briskly. 'I think Alvean will make a good horsewoman in time,' I said. 'What was your opinion?'

I saw how eagerly the girl waited on his words.

'She'll be the champion of Cornwall; you see!'

She could not hide her pleasure.

'And,' he lifted a finger and wagged it at her – 'don't forget whom you have to thank for it.'

The glance Alvean threw at me was almost shy, and I felt suddenly happy, and glad that I was here. My resentment against life had never been so far away; I had ceased to envy my charming sister. At that moment there was only one person I wanted to be: That person was Martha Leigh, sitting in the punch room taking tea with Peter Nansellock and Alvean TreMellyn.

Alvean said: 'It's to be a secret for a while.'

'Yes, we're going to surprise her father.'

'I'll be as silent as the grave.'

'Why do people say "silent as the grave"?' asked Alvean.

'Because,' put in Peter, 'dead men don't talk.'

'Sometimes they have ghosts perhaps,' said Alvean looking over her shoulder.

'What Mr. Nansellock meant,' I said quickly, 'was that he will keep our little secret. Alvean, I believe Mr. Nansellock would like some more cucumber sandwiches.'

She leapt up to offer them to him; it was very pleasant to have her so docile and friendly.

'You have not paid a visit to Mount Widden yet, Miss Leigh,' he said.

'It had not occurred to me to do so.'

'That is a little unneighbourly. Oh, I know what you're going to say. You did not come here to pay calls; you came to be a governess.'

'It is true,' I retorted.

'The house is not as ancient nor as large as this one. It has no history, but it's a pleasant place and I'm sure my sister would be delighted if you and Alvean paid us a visit one day. Why not come over and take tea with us?'

'I am not sure . . .' I began.

'That it lies within your duties? I'll tell you how we'll arrange it. You shall bring Miss Alvean to take tea at Mount Widden. Bringing her to us and taking her home again, I am sure, would come well within the duties of the most meticulous governess.'

'When shall we come?' asked Alvean.

'This is an open invitation.'

I smiled. I knew what that meant. He was again talking for the sake of talking; he had no intention of asking me to tea. I pictured him, coming over to the house, attempting a flirtation with Miss Jansen who, by all accounts, was an attractive young woman. I knew his sort, I told myself.

The door opened suddenly and, to my embarrassment – which I hoped I managed to hide – Connan TreMellyn came in.

I felt as though I had been caught playing the part of mistress of the house in his absence.

I rose to my feet, and he gave me a quick smile. 'Miss Leigh,' he said, 'is there a cup of tea for me?'

'Alvean,' I said, 'ring for another cup, please.'

She got up to do so immediately but she had changed. Now she was alert, eager to do the right thing and please her father. It made her somewhat clumsy, and as she rose from her chair she knocked over her cup of tea. She flushed scarlet with mortification.

I said: 'Never mind. Ring the bell. Kitty will clear it up when she comes.'

I knew that Connan TreMellyn was watching with some amusement. If I had known he would return I should have been very reluctant to entertain Peter Nansellock to tea in the punch room, which I was sure my employer felt was definitely not my part of the house.

Peter said: 'It was most kind of Miss Leigh to act as hostess. I begged her to do so, and she graciously consented.'

'It was certainly kind,' said Connan TreMellyn lightly.

Kitty came and I indicated the mess of tea and broken china on the carpet. 'And please bring another cup for Mr. TreMellyn,' I added.

Kitty was smirking a little as she went out. The situation evidently amused her. As for myself, I felt it ill became me. I was not the type to make charming play with the teacups and, now that the Master of the house had appeared, I felt awkward, even as I knew Alvean had. *I* must be careful to avoid disaster.

'Had a busy day, Connan?' asked Peter.

Connan TreMellyn then began to talk of complicated estate business, which I felt might have been to remind me that my duties consisted of dispensing tea and nothing else. I was not to imagine that I was in truth a hostess. I was there as an upper servant, nothing more.

I felt angry with him for coming in and spoiling my little triumph. I wondered how he would react when I presented him with the good little horsewoman I was determined Alvean was to become. He would probably make some slighting remark and show us such indifference that we should feel our trouble was wasted.

You poor child, I thought, you are trying to win the affections of a man who doesn't know the meaning of affection. Poor Alvean! Poor Alice!

Then it seemed to me that Alice had intruded into the punch room. In that moment I pictured her more clearly than I had ever done before. She was a woman of about my height, a little more slender at the waist – but then I had never gone in wholeheartedly for tight lacing – a trifle shorter. I could fit this figure into a black riding habit with blue collar and cuffs and black beaver hat. All that was vague and shadowy was the face.

The cup and saucer was brought to me and I poured out his tea. He was watching me, expecting me to rise and take it to him.

'Alvean,' I said, 'please pass this to your father.'

And she was very eager to do so.

He said a brief 'thanks,' and Peter took advantage of the pause to draw me into the conversation.

'Miss Leigh and I met on the train on the day she arrived.'

'Really?'

'Indeed, yes. Although of course she was not aware of my identity. How could she be? She had never heard then of the famous Nansellocks. She did not even know of the existence of Mount Widden. I knew her of course. By some strange irony of chance I shared her compartment.'

'That,' said Connan, 'is very interesting.' And he looked as though nothing could be less so.

'So,' went on Peter, 'it was a great surprise to her when she found that we were near neighbours.'

'I trust,' said Connan, 'that it was not an unpleasant one.'

'By no means,' I said.

'Thank you, Miss Leigh, for those kind words,' said Peter.

I looked at my watch, and said: 'I am going to ask you to excuse Alvean and me. It is nearly five o'clock and we have our studies between five and six.'

'And we must,' said Connan, 'on no account interfere with those.'

'But surely,' cried Peter, 'on such an occasion there could be a little relaxation of the rules.'

Alvean was looking eager. She was unhappy in her father's presence but she could not bear to leave it.

'I think it would be most unwise,' I said, rising. 'Come along, Alvean.'

She threw me a look of dislike and I believed that I had forfeited the advance I had made that afternoon.

'Please, Papa . . .' she began.

He looked at her sternly. 'My dear child, you heard what your governess said.'

Alvean blushed and looked uncomfortable, but I was already saying 'Good afternoon' to Peter Nansellock and making my way to the door.

In the schoolroom Alvean glared at me.

'Why do you have to spoil everything?' she demanded.

'Spoil?' I repeated. 'Everything?'

'We could have done our reading any time . . . any time—'

'But we do our reading between five and six, not any time,' I retorted, and my voice sounded the colder because I was afraid of the emotion which was rising in me. I wanted to explain to her: You love your father. You long for his approval. But, my dear child, you do not know the way to make it yours. Let me help you. But of course I said no such thing. I had never been demonstrative and could not begin to be so now.

'Come,' I went on, 'we have only an hour, so let us not waste a minute of that time.'

She sat at the table sullenly glaring at the book which we were reading. It was Mr. Dickens's *Pickwick Papers* which I had thought would bring light relief into my pupil's rather serious existence.

She had lost her habitual enthusiasm; she was not even attending, for she looked up suddenly and said: 'I believe you hate him. I believe you cannot bear to be in his company.'

I replied: 'I do not know to whom you refer, Alvean.'

'You do,' she accused. 'You know I mean my father.'

'What nonsense,' I murmured; but I was afraid my colour would deepen. 'Come,' I said, 'we are wasting time.'

And so I concentrated on the book and told myself that we could not read together the nightly adventure concerning the elderly lady in curlpapers. That would be most unsuitable for a child of Alvean's age.

That night when Alvean had retired to her room I went for a stroll in the woods. I was beginning to look upon these woods as a place of refuge, a place in which to be quiet and think about my life while I wondered what shape it would take.

The day had been eventful, a pleasant day until Connan TreMellyn had come into it and disturbed the peace. I wondered if his business ever took him away for long periods – really long periods, not merely a matter of a few days. If this were so, I thought, I might have a chance of making Alvean into a happier little girl.

Forget the man, I admonished myself. Avoid him when possible. You can do no more than that.

It was all very well but, even when he was not present, he intruded into my thoughts.

I stayed in the woods until it was almost dusk. Then I made for the house, and I had not been in my room more than a few minutes when Kitty knocked.

'I thought I 'eard 'ee come in, Miss,' she said. 'Master be asking for 'ee. He be in his library.'

'Then you had better take me there,' I said, 'for it is a room I have never visited.'

I should have liked to comb my hair and tidy myself a little, but I had a notion that Kitty was constantly looking for one aspect of the relationship between any man or woman and I was not going to have her thinking that I was preening myself before appearing before the master.

She led me to a wing of the house which I had as yet not visited, and the vastness of Mount Mellyn was brought home to me afresh. These, I gathered, were the apartments which were set aside for his especial use, for they seemed more luxurious than any other part of the house which I had so far seen.

Kitty opened a door, and with that vacuous smile on her face announced: 'Miss be here, Master.'

'Thank you, Kitty,' he said. And then, 'Oh, come along in, Miss Leigh.'

He was sitting at a table on which were leather-bound books and papers. The only light came from a rose quartz lamp on the table.

He said: 'Do sit down, Miss Leigh.'

I thought: He has discovered that I wore Alice's riding habit. He is shocked. He is going to tell me that my services are no longer required.

I held my head high, even haughtily, waiting.

'I was interested to learn this afternoon,' he began, 'that you had already made the acquaintance of Mr. Nansellock.'

'Really?' The surprise in my voice was not assumed.

'Of course,' he went on, 'it was inevitable that you would meet him sooner or later. He and his sister are constant visitors at the house, but—'

'But you feel that it is unnecessary that he should make the acquaintance of your daughter's governess,' I said quickly.

'That necessity, Miss Leigh,' he replied reprovingly, 'is surely for you or him to decide.'

I felt embarrassed and I stumbled on: 'I imagine that you feel that, as a governess, it is unbecoming of me to be ... on terms of apparently equal footing with a friend of your family.'

'I beg you, Miss Leigh, do not put words into my mouth which I had no intention of uttering. What friends you make, I do assure you, must be entirely your own concern. But your aunt, in a manner of speaking, put you under my care when she put you under my roof, and I have asked you to come here that I may offer you a word of advice on a subject which, I fear, you may think a little indelicate.'

I was flushing scarlet and my embarrassment was not helped by the fact that this, I was sure, secretly amused him.

'Mr. Nansellock has a reputation for being ... how shall I put it ... susceptible to young ladies.'

'Oh!' I cried, unable to suppress the exclamation, so great was my discomfort.

'Miss Leigh.' He smiled, and for a moment his face looked almost tender. 'This is in the nature of a warning.'

'Mr. TreMellyn,' I cried, recovering myself with an effort, 'I do not think I am in need of such a warning.'

'He is very handsome,' he went on, and the mocking note had come back to his voice. 'He has a reputation for being a charming fellow. There was a young lady here before you, a Miss Jansen. He often called to see her. Miss Leigh, I do beg of you not to misunderstand me. And there is another thing I would also ask: Please do not take all that Mr. Nansellock says too seriously.'

I heard myself say in a high-pitched voice unlike my habitual tone: 'It is extremely kind of you, Mr. TreMellyn, to concern yourself with my welfare.'

'But of course I concern myself with your welfare. You are here to look after my daughter. Therefore it is of the utmost importance to me.'

He rose and I did the same. I saw that this was dismissal.

He came swiftly to my side and placed his hand on my shoulder.

'Forgive me,' he said. 'I am a blunt man, lacking in those graces which are so evident in Mr. Nansellock. I merely wish to offer you a friendly warning.'

For a few seconds I looked into those cool light eyes and I thought I had a fleeting glimpse of the man behind the mask. I was sobered suddenly and, in a moment of bewildering emotions, I was deeply conscious of my loneliness, of the tragedy of those who are alone in the world with no one who really cares for them. Perhaps it was self-pity. I do not know. My feelings in that moment were so mixed that I cannot even at this day define them.

'Thank you,' I said; and I escaped from the library back to my room.

Each day Alvean and I went to the field and had an hour's riding. As I watched the little girl on Buttercup I knew that her father must have been extremely impatient with her, for the child, though not a born rider perhaps, would soon be giving a good account of herself.

I had discovered that every November a horse show was held in Mellyn village, and I had told Alvean that she should certainly enter for one of the events.

It was enjoyable planning this, because Connan TreMellyn would be one of the judges and we both imagined his astonishment when a certain rider, who came romping home with first prize, was his daughter who he had sworn would never learn to ride.

The triumph in that dream was something Alvean and I could both share. Hers was of course the more admirable emotion. She wanted to succeed for the sake of the love she bore her father; for myself I wanted to imply: See, you arrogant man, I have succeeded where you failed!

So every afternoon, I would put on Alice's riding habit (I had ceased to care to whom it had previously belonged, for it had become mine now) and we would go to the field and there I would put Alvean through her paces.

On the day we tried her first gallop we were elated.

Afterwards she returned to the stables with me and I watched her run on ahead after we had left the horses there. Every now and then she would jump into the air – a gesture, I thought, of complete joyousness. I knew she was seeing herself at the show anticipating that glorious moment when her father stared at her in astonishment and cried: 'You . . . Alvean! My dear child, I am proud of you.'

I was smiling to myself as I crossed the lawn in her wake. When I entered the house she was nowhere to be seen, and I pictured her taking the stairs several at a time.

This was more like the normal, happy child I intended her to become.

I mounted the first flight of stairs and came to a dark landing, when there was a step on the next flight, and I heard a quick gasp and voice which said: 'Alice!'

For a second my whole body seemed to freeze. Then I saw that Celestine Nansellock was standing on the stairs; she was gripping the banisters and was so white that I thought she was going to faint.

I understood. It was she who had spoken. She had seen me in Alice's riding habit and she believed in that second that I *was* Alice . . . or her ghost.

'Miss Nansellock,' I said quickly to reassure her, 'Alvean and I have been having a riding lesson.'

She swayed a little; her face had turned a greyish colour.

'I'm sorry I startled you,' I went on.

She murmured: 'For the moment I thought—'

'I think you should sit down, Miss Nansellock. You've had a shock.' I bounded up the stairs and took her arm. 'Would you care to come into my bedroom and sit down awhile?'

She nodded, and I noted that she was trembling.

'I am so sorry to have upset you,' I said as I threw open the door of my room. We went in, and I put her gently into a chair.

'Shall I ring for brandy?' I asked.

She shook her head. 'I'm all right now. You did startle me, Miss Leigh. I see now it is the clothes.'

'It is a little dark on that landing,' I said.

She repeated: 'For the moment, I thought. . . .' Then she looked at me again, fearfully, perhaps hopefully. I believed she was thinking that I was an apparition which had assumed the face of Martha Leigh, the governess, and would change at any moment.

I hastened to reassure her. 'It's only these clothes,' I said.

'Mrs. TreMellyn had a habit exactly like that. I remember the collar and cuffs so well. We went riding together . . . only a day or so before . . . You see, we were great friends, always together, and then. . . .' She turned away and wiped her eyes.

'You thought I was Mrs. TreMellyn returned from the dead.' I said. 'I understand.'

'It was so foolish of me. It seems so odd that you should have a riding habit . . . so exactly like hers.'

'This was hers,' I said.

She was startled. She put out a hand and touched the skirt. She held it between thumb and forefinger and her eyes had a hazy look as though she were staring into the past.

I went on quickly: 'I have to give Alvean riding lessons, and I lacked the suitable clothes. The child took me to what I now know to have been her mother's apartments, and found this for me. I asked Mrs. Polgrey if it were in order for me to wear it and she assured me that it was.'

'I see,' said Celestine. 'That explains everything. Please don't mention my folly, Miss Leigh. I'm glad no one else saw it.'

'But anyone might have been startled, particularly as—'

'As what?'

'As there seems to be this feeling about Alice . . . about Mrs. TreMellyn.'

'What feeling?'

'Perhaps there isn't a feeling. Perhaps it is my imagination only, but I did imagine that there was a belief in the house that she was not . . . at rest.'

'What an extraordinary thing to say! Why should she not be at rest? Who told you this?'

'I . . . I'm not sure,' I floundered. 'Perhaps it is merely my imagination. Perhaps no one suggested anything, and the idea just came to me. I'm sorry that I upset you.'

'You must not be sorry, Miss Leigh. You have been kind to me. I feel better now. She stood up. 'Don't tell anyone I was so silly. So you are giving Alvean riding lessons. I am glad. Tell me, are you getting along with her better now? I fancied, when you arrived, that there was a little antagonism . . . on·her part.'

'She is the kind of child who would automatically be antagonistic to authority. Yes, I think we are becoming friends. These riding lessons have helped considerably. By the way, they are secret from her father.'

Celestine Nansellock looked a little shocked, and I hurried on: 'Oh, it is only her good progress which is a secret. He knows about the lessons. Naturally I asked his permission first. But he does not realize how well she is coming along. It is to be a surprise.'

'I see,' said Celestine. 'Miss Leigh, I do hope she is not over-strained by these lessons.'

'Strained? But why? She is a normal healthy child.'

'She is highly strung. I wonder whether she has the temperament to make a rider.'

'She is so young that we have a chance of forming her character, which will have its effect on her temperament. She is enjoying her lessons and is very eager to surprise her father.'

'So she is becoming your friend, Miss Leigh. I am glad of that. Now I must go. Thank you again for your kindness. And do remember . . . not a word to anyone.'

'Certainly not, if it is your wish.'

She smiled and went out.

I went to the mirror and looked at myself – I'm afraid this was becoming a habit since I had come here – and murmured: 'That might be Alice . . . apart from the face.' Then I half closed my eyes and let the face become blurred while I imagined a different face there.

Oh yes, it must have been a shock for Celestine.

And I was not to say anything. I was very willing to agree to this. I wondered what Connan TreMellyn would say if he knew that I was going about in his wife's clothes and frightened practical people like Celestine Nansellock when they saw me in dim places.

I felt he would not wish me to continue to look so like Alice.

So, since I needed Alice's clothes for my riding lessons with Alvean, and since I was determined they should continue, that I might have the pleasure of saying, I told you so! to Alvean's father, I was as anxious as Celestine Nansellock that nothing should be said about our encounter on the landing.

A week passed and I felt I was slipping into a routine. Lessons in the schoolroom and the riding field progressed favourably. Peter Nansellock came over to the house on two occasions, but I managed to elude him. I was deeply conscious of Connan TreMellyn's warning and I knew it to be reasonable. I faced the fact that I was stimulated by Peter Nansellock and that I could very easily find myself in a state of mind when I was looking forward to his visits. I had no intention of placing myself in that position for I did not need Connan TreMellyn to tell me that Peter Nansellock was a philanderer.

I thought now and then of his brother Geoffry, and I concluded that Peter must be very like him; and when I thought of Geoffry I thought also of Mrs. Polgrey's daughter of whom she had never spoken; Jennifer with the 'littlest waist you ever saw,' and a way of keeping herself to herself until she had lain in the hay or the gillyflowers with the fascinating Geoffry – the outcome of which had been that one day she walked into the sea.

I shivered to contemplate the terrible pitfalls which lay in wait for unwary women. There were unattractive ones like myself who depended on the whims of others for a living; but there were those even more unfortunate creatures, those who attracted the roving eyes of philanderers and found one day that the only bearable prospect life had to offer was its end.

My interest in Alvean's riding lessons and her father's personality had made me forget little Gillyflower temporarily. The child was so quiet that she was easily forgotten. Occasionally I heard her thin reedy voice, in that peculiar off-key singing out of doors or in the house. The Polgreys' room was immediately below my own, and Gillyflower's was next to theirs, so that when she sang in her own room her voice would float up to me.

I used to say to myself when I heard it: If she can learn songs she can learn other things.

I must have been given to day-dreams, for side by side with that picture of Connan TreMellyn, handing his daughter the first prize for horse-jumping at the November horse show and giving me an apologetic and immensely admiring and appreciative glance at the same time, there was another picture. This was of Gilly sitting at the schoolroom table side by side with Alvean, while I listened to whispering in the background: 'This could never have happened but for Miss Martha Leigh. You see she is a wonder with the children. Look what she had done for Alvean . . . and now for Gilly.'

But at this time Alvean was still a stubborn child and Gillyflower elusive and, as the Tapperty girls said: 'With a tile loose in the upper story.'

Then into those more or less peaceful days came two events to disturb me.

The first was of small moment, but it haunted me and I could not get it out of my mind.

I was going through one of Alvean's exercise books, marking her sums, while she was sitting at the table writing an essay; and as I turned the pages of the exercise book a piece of paper fell out.

It was covered with drawings. I had already discovered that Alvean had a distinct talent for drawing, and one day, when the opportunity offered itself, I intended to approach Connan TreMellyn about this, for I felt she should be encouraged. I myself could teach her only the rudiments of the art, but I believed she was worthy of a qualified drawing teacher.

The drawings were of faces. I recognized one of myself. It was not bad. Did I really look as prim as that? Not always, I hoped. But perhaps that was how she saw me. There was her father . . . several of him. He was quite recognizable too. I turned the page and this was covered with girls' faces: I was not sure who they were meant to be. Herself? No . . . that was Gilly, surely. And yet it had a look of herself.

I stared at the page. I was so intent that I did not realize she had leaned across the table until she snatched it away.

'That's mine,' she said.

'And that,' I retaliated, 'is extremely bad manners.'

'You have no right to pry.'

'My dear child, that paper was in your arithmetic book.'

'Then it had no right to be there.'

'You must take your revenge on the paper,' I said lightly. And then more seriously: 'I do beg of you not to snatch things in that ill-mannered way.'

'I'm sorry,' she murmured still defiantly.

I turned back to the sums, to most of which she had given inaccurate answers. Arithmetic was not one of her best subjects. Perhaps that was why she spent so much of her time drawing faces instead of getting on with her work. Why had she been so annoyed? Why had she drawn those faces which were part Gilly's, part her own?'

I said: 'Alvean, you will have to work harder at your sums.'

She grunted sullenly.

'You don't seem to have mastered the rules of practice nor even simple multiplication. Now if your arithmetic were half as good as your drawing I should be very pleased.'

Still she did not answer.

'Why did you not wish me to see the faces you had drawn? I thought some of them quite good.'

Still no answer.

'Particularly,' I went on, 'that one of your father.'

Even at such a time the mention of his name could bring that tender, wistful curve to her lips.

'And those girl's faces. Do tell me who they were supposed to be – you or Gilly?'

The smile froze on her lips. Then she said almost breathlessly: 'Who did you take them for, Miss?'

'Whom,' I corrected gently.

'*Whom* did you take them for then?'

'Well, let me look at them again.'

She hesitated, then she brought out the paper, and handed it to me; her eyes were eager.

I studied the faces. I said: 'This one could be either you or Gilly.'

'You think we're alike then?'

'N . . . no. I hadn't thought so until this moment.

'And now you do,' she said.

'You are of an age, and there often seems to be a resemblance between young people.'

'I'm not like her!' she cried passionately. 'I'm not like that . . . idiot.'

'Alvean, you must not use such a word. Don't you realize that it is extremely unkind?'

'It's true. But I'm not like her. I won't have you say it. If you say it again I'll ask my father to send you away. He will . . . if I ask him. I only have to ask and you'll go.'

She was shouting, trying to convince herself of two things, I realized. One that there was not the slightest resemblance between herself and Gilly, and the other that she only had to ask her father for something, and her wishes would be granted.

Why? I asked myself. What was the reason for this vehemence?

There was a shut-in expression on her face.

I said, calmly looking at the watch pinned to my grey cotton bodice: 'You have exactly ten minutes in which to finish your essay.'

I drew the arithmetic book towards me and pretended to give it my attention.

The second incident was even more upsetting.

It had been a moderately peaceful day, which meant that lessons had gone well. I had taken my late evening stroll in the woods and when I returned I saw two carriages drawn up in front of the house. One I recognized as from Mount Widden so I guessed that either Peter or Celestine was visiting. The other carriage I did not know, but I noticed a crest on it, and it was a very fine carriage. I wondered to whom it belonged before I told myself that it was no concern of mine.

I went swiftly up the back stairs to my apartment.

It was a warm night and as I sat at my window I heard music coming from another of the open windows. I realized that Connan TreMellyn was entertaining guests.

I pictured them in one of the rooms which I had not even seen. Why should you, I asked myself. You are only a governess. Connan TreMellyn, his gaunt body clothed elegantly, would be presiding at the card table or perhaps sitting with his guests listening to music.

I recognized the music as from Mendelssohn's *Midsummer Night's Dream* and I felt a sudden longing to be down there among them; but I was astonished that this desire should be greater than any I had ever had to be present at Aunt Adelaide's *soirées* or the dinner parties Phillida gave. I was overcome with curiosity and could not resist the temptation to ring the bell and summon Kitty or Daisy who always knew what was going on and were only too happy to impart that knowledge to anyone who was interested to hear it.

It was Daisy who came. She looked excited.

I said: 'I want some hot water, Daisy. Could you please bring it for me?'

'Why yes, Miss,' she said.

'There are guests here to-night, I understand.'

'Oh yes, Miss. Though it's nothing to the parties we used to have. I reckon now the year's up, the Master will be entertaining more. That's what Mrs. Polgrey says.'

'It must have been very quiet during the last year.'

'But only right and proper . . . after a death in the family.'

'Of course. Who are the guests to-night?'

'Oh, there's Miss Celestine and Mr. Peter of course.'

'I saw their carriage.' My voice sounded eager and I was ashamed. I was no better than any gossiping servant.

'Yes, and I'll tell you who else is here.'

'Who?'

'Sir Thomas and Lady Treslyn.'

She looked conspiratorial as though there was something very important about these two.

'Oh?' I said encouragingly.

'Though,' went on Daisy, 'Mrs. Polgrey says that Sir Thomas bain't fit to go gallivanting at parties, and should be abed.'

'Why, is he ill?'

'Well, he'll never see seventy again and he's got one of those bad hearts. Mrs. Polgrey says you can go off sudden with a heart like that, and don't need no pushing either. Not that—'

She stopped and twinkled at me. I longed to ask her to continue, but I felt it was beneath my dignity to do so. Disappointingly she seemed to pull herself up sharply.

'*She's* another kettle of fish.'

'Who?'

'Why, Lady Treslyn of course. You ought to see her. She's got a gown cut right down to here and the loveliest flowers on her shoulder. She's a real beauty, and you can see she's only waiting—'

'I gather she is not the same age as her husband.'

Daisy giggled. 'They say there's nearly forty years' difference in their ages, and she'd like to pretend it was fifty.'

'You don't seem to like her.'

'Me? Well, if I don't, some do!' That sent Daisy into hysterical laughter again, and as I looked at her ungainly form in her tight clothes and listened to her wheezy laughter, I was ashamed of myself for sharing the gossip of a servant, so I said: 'I *would* like that hot water, Daisy.'

Daisy subsided and went off to get it, leaving me with a clearer picture of what was happening in that drawing room.

I was still thinking of them when I had washed my hands and unpinned my hair preparatory to retiring for the night.

The musicians had been playing a Chopin waltz and it had seemed to spirit me away from my governess's bedroom and tantalize me with pleasures outside my reach – a dainty beauty, a place of salons such as that somewhere in this house, wit, charm, the power to make the chosen man love me.

I was startled by such thoughts. What had they to do with a governess such as myself.

I went to the window. The weather had been fine and warm for so long that I did not believe it could continue. The autumn mists would soon be with us and I heard that they and the gales which blew from the south-west were, as Tapperty would say, 'something special in these parts.'

I could smell the sea and hear the gentle rhythm of the waves. The 'voices' were starting up in Mellyn Cove.

And then suddenly I saw a light in a dark part of the house and I felt the goose-pimples rise on my flesh. I knew that window belonged to the room to which Alvean had taken me to choose my riding habit. It was Alice's dressing room.

The blind had been down. I had not noticed that before. Indeed I was sure it had not been like that earlier in the evening because, since I had known that that was Alice's room, I had made a habit – which I regretted and of which I had tried to cure myself – of glancing at the window whenever I looked out of my own.

The blind was of thin material, for behind it I distinctly saw the light. It was a faint light but there was no mistaking it. It moved before my astonished eyes.

I stood at my window staring out and, as I did so, I saw a shadow on the blind. It was that of a woman.

I heard a voice close to me saying: 'It is Alice!' and I realized that I had spoken aloud.

I'm dreaming, I told myself. I'm imagining this.

Then again I saw the figure silhouetted against the blind.

My hands which gripped the window sill were trembling as I watched that flickering light. I had an impulse to summon Daisy or Kitty, or go to Mrs. Polgrey.

I restrained myself, imagining how foolish it should look. So I remained staring at the window.

And after a while all was darkness.

I stood at my window for a long time watching, but I saw nothing more.

They were playing another Chopin waltz in the drawing room, and I stood until I was cold even on that warm September night.

Then I went to bed but I could not sleep for a long time.

And at last, when I did sleep, I dreamed that a woman came into my room; she was wearing a riding habit with blue collar and cuffs, trimmed with braid and ball fringe. She said to me: 'I was not on that train, Miss Leigh. You wonder where I was. It is for you to find me.'

Through my dreams I heard the whispering of the waves in the caves below; and the first thing I did on rising next morning – which I did as soon as dawn appeared in the sky – was to go to my window and look across at the room which – little more than a year ago – had belonged to Alice.

The blinds were drawn up. I could clearly see the rich blue velvet curtains.

Chapter Four

It was about a week later when I first saw Linda Treslyn.

It was a few minutes past six o'clock. Alvean and I had put away our books and had gone down to the stables to look at Buttercup who we thought had strained a tendon that afternoon.

The farrier had seen her and given her a poultice. Alvean was really upset, and this pleased me because I was always delighted to discover her softer feelings.

'Don't 'ee fret, Miss Alvean,' Joe Tapperty told her. 'Buttercup 'll be right as two dogs on a bright and frosty morning afore the week's out; you see! Jim Bond, he be the best horse-doctor between here and Land's End, I do tell 'ee.'

She was cheered and I told her that she should take Black Prince in Buttercup's place to-morrow.

She was excited about this for she knew Black Prince would test her mettle, and I was glad to see that her pleasure was only faintly tinged with apprehension.

As we came out of the stables I looked at my watch.

'Would you care for half an hour's stroll through the gardens?' I asked. 'We have half an hour to spare.'

To my surprise she said she would, and we set off.

The plateau on which Mount Mellyn stood was a piece of land a mile or so wide. The slope to the sea was steep but there were several zigzag paths which made the going easier. The gardeners spent a great deal of time on this garden which was indeed beautiful with the flowering shrubs which grew so profusely in this part. At various points arbours had been set up, constructed of trellis work around which roses climbed. They were beautiful even as late as this and their perfume hung on the air.

One could sit in these arbours and gaze out to sea; and from these gardens the south side of the house was a vision of grandeur, rising nobly, a pile of grey granite there on the top of the cliff like a mighty fortress. It was inevitable that the house should have a defiant air, as though it represented a challenge, not only to the sea but to the world.

We made our way down those sweet-smelling paths and were level with the arbour before we noticed that two people were there.

Alvean gave a little gasp and, following her gaze, I saw them. They were sitting side by side and close. She was very dark and one of the most beautiful women I had ever seen; her features were strongly marked and she wore a gauzy scarf over her hair, and in this gauze sequins glistened. I thought that she looked like someone out of *A Midsummer Night's Dream* – Titania perhaps, although I had always imagined her fair. She had that quality of beauty which attracts the eyes as a needle is attracted by a magnet. You have to look whether you want to or not; you have to admire. Her dress was pale mauve of some clinging material such as chiffon and it was caught at the throat with a big diamond brooch.

Connan spoke first. 'Why,' he said, 'it is my daughter with her governess. So, Miss Leigh, you and Alvean are taking the air.'

'It is such a pleasant evening,' I said, and I made to take Alvean's hand, but she eluded me in her most ungracious manner.

'May I sit with you and Lady Treslyn, Papa?' she asked.

'You are taking a walk with Miss Leigh,' he said. 'Do you not think that you should continue to do so?'

'Yes,' I answered for her. 'Come along, Alvean.'

Connan had turned to his companion. 'We are very fortunate to have found Miss Leigh. She is . . . admirable!'

'The perfect governess this time, I hope for your sake, Connan,' said Lady Treslyn.

I felt awkward, as though I were in the position of a horse standing there while they discussed my points. I was sure he was aware of my discomfiture and rather amused by it. There were times when I believed he was a very unpleasant person.

I said, and my voice sounded very chilly: 'I think it is time we turned back. We were merely taking an airing before Alvean retires for the night. Come, Alvean,' I added. And I seized her arm so firmly that I drew her away.

'But,' protested Alvean, 'I want to stay. I want to talk to you, Papa.'

'But you can see I am engaged. Some other time, my child.'

'No,' she said. 'It is important . . . now.'

'It cannot be all that important. Let us discuss it tomorrow.'

'No . . . no . . . Now!' Alvean's voice had a hysterical note in it; I had never before known her defy him so utterly.

Lady Treslyn murmured: 'I see Alvean is a very determined person.'

Connan TreMellyn said coolly: 'Miss Leigh will deal with this matter.'

'Of course. The perfect governess. . . .' There was a note of mockery in Lady Treslyn's voice, and it goaded me to such an extent that I seized Alvean's arm roughly and almost dragged her back the way we had come.

She was half sobbing, but she did not speak until we were in the house. Then she said: 'I hate her. You know, don't you, Miss Leigh, that she wants to be my new mamma.'

I said nothing then. I thought it dangerous to do so because I always felt that it was so easy to be overheard. It was only when we reached her room and I had followed her in and shut the door that I said: 'That was an extraordinary remark to make. How could she wish to be your mamma when she has a husband of her own?'

'He will soon die.'

'How can you know that?'

'Everybody says they are only waiting.'

I was shocked that she should have heard such gossip and I thought: I will speak to Mrs. Polgrey about this. They must be careful what they say in front of Alvean. Is it those girls, Daisy and Kitty ... or perhaps Joe Tapperty or his wife?

'She's always here,' went on Alvean. 'I won't let her take my mother's place. I won't let anybody.'

'You are becoming quite hysterical about improbabilities, and I must insist that you never allow me to hear you say such things again. It is degrading to your papa.'

That made her thoughtful. How she loves him! I thought. Poor little Alvean, poor lonely child!

A little while before, I had been sorry for myself as I stood in that beautiful garden and was forced to be quizzed by the beautiful woman in the arbour. I had said to myself: 'It is not fair. Why should one person have so much, and others nothing? Should I be beautiful in chiffon and diamonds? Perhaps not as Lady Treslyn was, but I am sure they would be more becoming than cotton and merino and a turquoise brooch which had belonged to my grandmother.'

Now I forgot to be sorry for myself, and my pity was all for Alvean.

I had seen Alvean to bed and had returned to my room, conscious of a certain depression. I kept thinking of Connan TreMellyn out there in the arbour with Lady Treslyn, asking myself if he were still there and what they talked about. Each other! I supposed. Of course Alvean and I had interrupted a flirtation. I felt shocked that he should indulge in such an undignified intrigue, for it seemed wholly undignified to me, since the lady had a husband to whom she owed her allegiance.

I went to the window and I was glad that it did not give me a view of the south gardens and the sea. I leaned my elbows on the sill and looked out at the scented evening. It was not quite dark yet but the sun had disappeared and the twilight was on us. My eyes turned to the window where I had seen the shadow on the blind.

The blinds were drawn up and I could see the blue curtains clearly. I stared at them, fixedly. I don't know what I expected. Was it to see a face appear at the window, a beckoning hand? There were times when I could laugh at myself for my fancies, but the twilight hour was not one of them.

Then I saw the curtains move, and I knew that someone was in that room.

I was in an extraordinary mood that evening. It had something to do with meeting Connan TreMellyn and Lady Treslyn together in the arbour, but I had not sufficiently analysed my feelings at this date to understand it. I felt our recent encounter to have been humiliating but I was ready to risk another which might be more so. Alice's room was not in my part of the house but I was completely at liberty to walk in the gardens if I wished to. If I were caught I should look rather foolish. But I was reckless. I did not care. Thoughts of Alice obsessed me. There were times when I felt such a burning desire to discover what mystery lay behind her death that I was prepared to go to any lengths.

So I slipped out of my room. I left my wing of the house and went along the gallery to Alice's dressing room. I knocked lightly on the door and, with my heart beating like a sledge hammer, I swiftly opened it.

For a second I saw no one. Then I detected a movement by the curtains. Someone was hiding behind them.

'Who is it?' I asked, and my voice successfully hid the trepidation I was feeling.

There was no answer, but whoever was behind those curtains was very eager not to be discovered.

I strode across the room, drew aside the curtains and saw Gilly cowering there.

The lids of her blank blue eyes fluttered in a terrified way. I put out a hand to seize her and she shrank from me towards the window.

'It's all right, Gilly,' I said gently. 'I won't hurt you.'

She continued to stare at me, and I went on: 'Tell me, what are you doing here?'

Still she said nothing. She had begun to stare about the room as though she were asking someone for help and for a moment I had the uncanny feeling that she *saw* something – or someone – I could not see.

'Gilly,' I said, 'you know you should not be in this room, do you not?' She drew away from me, and I repeated what I had said.

Then she nodded and immediately afterwards shook her head.

'I am going to take you back to my room, Gilly. Then we'll have a little talk.'

I put my arm about her; she was trembling. I drew her to the door but she came very reluctantly, and at the threshold of the room she looked back over her shoulder; then she cried out suddenly: 'Madam . . . come back, Madam. Come . . . *now!*'

I led her firmly from the room and shut the door behind us, then almost had to drag her along to my bedroom.

Once there I firmly shut my door and stood with my back against it. Her lips were trembling.

'Gilly,' I said, 'I do want you to understand that I won't hurt you. I want to be your friend.' The blank look persisted and taking a shot in the dark I went on: 'I want to be your friend as Mrs. TreMellyn was.'

That startled her and the blank look disappeared for a moment. I had stumbled on another discovery. Alice had been kind to this poor child.

'You went there to look for Mrs. TreMellyn, did you not?'

She nodded.

She looked so pathetic that I was moved to a demonstration of feeling unusual with me. I knelt down and put my arms about her; now our faces were level.

'You can't find her, Gilly. She is dead. It is no use looking for her in this house.'

Gilly nodded and I was not sure what she implied – whether she agreed with me that it was no use, or whether she believed that she could find Mrs. TreMellyn in the house.

'So,' I went on, 'we must try to forget her, mustn't we Gilly?'

The pale lids fell over the eyes to hide them from me.

'We'll be friends,' I said. 'I want us to be. If we were friends, you wouldn't be lonely, would you?'

She shook her head, and I fancied that the eyes which surveyed me had lost something of their blankness; she was not trembling now, and I was sure that she was no longer afraid of me.

Then suddenly she slipped out of my grasp and ran to the door. I did not pursue her and, as she opened the door and turned to look back at me, there was a faint smile on her lips. Then she was gone.

I believed that I had established a little friendliness between us. I believed that she had lost her fear of me.

Then I thought of Alice, who had been kind to this child. I was beginning to build up the picture of Alice more clearly in my mind.

I went to the window and looked across the L-shaped building to the window of the room, and I thought of that night when I had seen the shadow on the blind.

My discovery of Gilly did not explain that. It was no child I had seen silhouetted there. It had been a woman.

Gilly might hide herself in Alice's room, but the shadow I had seen on the blind that night did not belong to her.

It was the next day when I went to Mrs. Polgrey's room for a cup of tea. She was delighted to invite me. 'Mrs. Polgrey,' I had said, 'I have a matter which I feel to be of some importance, and I should very much like to discuss this with you.

She was bridled with pride. I could see that the governess who sought her advice must be, in her eyes, the ideal governess.

'I shall be delighted to give you an hour of my company and a cup of my best Earl Grey,' she told me.

Over the teacups she surveyed me with an expression bordering on the affectionate.

'Now, Miss Leigh, pray tell me what it is you would ask of me.'

'I am a little disturbed,' I told her, stirring my tea thoughtfully. 'It is due to a remark of Alvean's. I am sure that she listens to gossip, and I think it most undesirable in a child of her age.'

'Or in any of us as I am sure a young lady of your good sense would feel,' replied Mrs. Polgrey with what I could not help feeling was a certain amount of hypocrisy.

I told her how we had walked in the cliff gardens and met the master with Lady Treslyn. 'And then,' I went on, 'Alvean made this offensive remark. She said that Lady Treslyn hoped to become her mamma.'

Mrs. Polgrey shook her head. She said: 'What about a spoonful of whisky in your tea, Miss? There's nothing like it for keeping up the spirits.'

I had no desire for the whisky but I could see that Mrs. Polgrey had, and she would have been disappointed if I had refused to join her in her tea tippling, so I said: 'A small teaspoonful, please, Mrs. Polgrey.'

She unlocked the cupboard, took out the bottle and measured out the whisky even more meticulously than she measured her tea. I found myself wondering what other stores she kept in that cupboard of hers.

Now we were like a pair of conspirators and Mrs. Polgrey was clearly enjoying herself.

'I fear you will find it somewhat shocking, Miss,' she began.

'I am prepared,' I assured her.

'Well, Sir Thomas Treslyn is a very old man and only a few years ago he married this young lady, a play-actress, some say, from London. Sir Thomas went there on a visit and returned with her. He set the neighbourhood agog, I can tell you, Miss.'

'I can well believe that.'

'There's some that say she's one of the handsomest women in the country.'

'I can believe that too.'

'Handsome is as handsome does.'

'But it remains handsome outwardly,' I added.

'And men can be foolish. The Master has his weakness,' admitted Mrs. Polgrey.

'If there is gossip I am most anxious that it shall not reach Alvean's ears.'

'Of course you are, Miss. But gossip there is, and that child's got ears like a hare's.'

'Do you think Daisy and Kitty chatter?'

Mrs. Polgrey came closer and I smelt the whisky on her breath. I was startled, wondering whether she could smell it on mine. 'Everybody chatters, Miss.'

'I see.'

'There's some as say that they'm not the sort to wait for blessing of clergy.'

'Well, perhaps they are not.'

I felt wretched. I hate this, I told myself. It's so sordid. So horrible for a sensitive girl like Alvean.

'The Master is impulsive by nature and in his way he is fond of the women.'

'So you think—'

She nodded gravely. 'When Sir Thomas dies there'll be a new mistress in this house. All they have to wait for now is for him to go. Mrs. TreMellyn, her . . . her's already gone.'

I did not want to ask the question which came to my lips but it seemed as though there were some force within me which would not let me avoid it. 'And was it so . . . when Mrs. TreMellyn was alive?'

Mrs. Polgrey nodded slowly. 'He visited her often. It started almost as soon as she came. Sometimes he rides out at night and we don't see him till morning. Well, he'm Master and 'tis for him to make his own rules. 'Tis for us to cook and dust and housekeep, or teach the child . . . whatsoever we'm here for. And there's an end of it.'

'So you think that Alvean is only repeating what everyone knows? When Sir Thomas dies Lady Treslyn *will* be her new mamma.'

'There's some on us that thinks it's more than likely, and some that wouldn't be sorry to see it. Her ladyship's not the kind to interfere much with our side of the house; and 'tis better to have these things regularized, so I do say.' She went on piously: 'I'd sooner see the Master of the house I serve living in wedlock than in sin, I do assure you. And so would we all.'

'Could we warn the girls not to chatter, before Alvean, of these matters?'

'As well try to keep a cuckoo from singing in the spring. I could wallop them two till I dropped with exhaustion and still they'd gossip. They can't help it. It be in their blood. And there's nothing much to choose between one girl and the other. Nowadays—'

I nodded sympathetically. I was thinking of Alice, who had watched the relationship between her husband and Lady Treslyn. No wonder she had been prepared to run away with Geoffry Nansellock.

Poor Alice! I thought. What you must have suffered, married to such a man.

Mrs. Polgrey was in such an expansive mood that I felt I might extend the conversation to other matters in which I happened to be interested.

I said: 'Have you ever thought of teaching Gilly her letters?'

'Gilly! Why that would be a senseless thing to do. You must know, Miss, that Gilly is not quite as she should be.' Mrs. Polgrey tapped her forehead.

'She sings a great deal. She must have learned the songs. If she could learn songs, could she not learn other things?'

'She's a queer little thing. Reckon it was the way she come. I don't often talk about such things, but I'll swear you've been hearing about my Jennifer.' Mrs. Polgrey's voice changed a little, became touched with sentiment. I wondered if it had anything to do with the whisky and how many spoonfuls she had taken that day. 'Sometimes I think that Gillyflower is a cursed child. Us didn't want her; why, she was only a little thing in a cradle . . . two months old . . . when Jennifer went. The tide brought her body in two days after. 'Twas found there in Mellyn Cove.'

'I'm sorry,' I said gently.

Mrs. Polgrey shook herself free of sentiment. 'Her'd gone, but there was still Gilly. And right from the first her didn't seem quite like other children.'

'Perhaps she sensed the tragedy,' I ventured.

Mrs. Polgrey looked at me with hauteur. 'We did all we could for her – me and Mr. Polgrey. He thought the world of her.'

'When did you notice that she was not like other children?'

'Come to think of it it would be when she was about four years old.'

'That would be how many years ago?'

'About four.'

'She must be the same age as Alvean. She looks so much younger.'

'Born a few months after Miss Alvean. They'd play together now and then . . . being in the house, you do see, and being of an age. There was an accident when she was, let me see . . . she'd be approaching her fourth birthday.'

'What sort of accident?'

'She was playing in the drive there, not far from the lodge gates. The Mistress were riding along the drive to the house. She was a great horsewoman, the Mistress. Gilly, her darted out from the bushes and caught a blow from the horse. She fell on her head. It was a mercy she weren't killed.'

'Poor Gilly,' I said.

'The Mistress were distressed. Blamed herself although 'twas no blame to her. Gilly should have known better. She'd been told to watch the roads often enough. Darted out after a butterfly, like as not. Gilly has always been taken with birds and flowers and insects and such like. The Mistress made much of her after that. Gilly used to follow her about and fret when she was away.'

'I see,' I said.

Mrs. Polgrey poured herself another cup of tea and asked me if I would have another. I declined. I saw her tilt the teaspoonful of whisky into the cup. 'Gilly,' she went on, 'were born in sin. Her had no right to come into the world. It looks like God be taking vengeance on her, for it do say that the sins of the fathers be visited on the children.'

I felt a sudden wave of anger sweep over me. I was in revolt against such distortions. I felt I wanted to slap the face of the woman who could sit there calmly drinking her whisky and accepting the plight of her little grand-daughter as God's will.

I marvelled too at the ignorance of these people, who did not connect Gilly's strangeness with the accident she had had but believed it was due punishment for her parents' sins meted out to her by a vengeful God.

But I said nothing, because I believed that I was battling against strange forces in this house and, if I were going to succeed, I needed all the allies I could command.

I wanted to understand Gilly. I wanted to soothe Alvean. I was discovering a fondness for children in myself which I had not known I possessed before I came into this house. Indeed since I had come here I had begun to discover quite a lot about myself.

There was one other reason why I wanted to concentrate on the affairs of these two children; doing so prevented my thinking of Connan TreMellyn and Lady Treslyn. Thoughts of them made me feel quite angry; at this time I called my anger 'disgust.'

So I sat in Mrs. Polgrey's room, listening to her talk, and I did not tell her what was in my mind.

There was excitement throughout the house because there was to be a ball – the first since Alice's death – and for a week there was little talk of anything else. I found it difficult to keep Alvean's attention on her lessons; Kitty and Daisy were almost hysterical with delight, and I was constantly coming upon them clasped in each other's arms in attempts to waltz.

The gardeners were busy. They were going to bring in flowers from the greenhouses to decorate the ballroom and were eager that the blooms should do them credit; and invitations were being sent out all over the countryside.

'I fail to see,' I said to Alvean, 'why you should feel this excitement. Neither you nor I will take part in the ball.'

Alvean said dreamily: 'When my mother was alive there were lots of balls. She loved them. She danced beautifully. She used to come in and show me

how she looked. She was beautiful. Then she would take me into the
solarium and I would sit in a recess behind the curtains and look down on
the hall through the peep.'

'The peep?' I asked.

'Ah, you don't know.' She regarded me triumphantly. I suppose it was
rather pleasing to her to discover that her governess, who was constantly
shocked by her ignorance, should herself be discovered in that state.

'There is a great deal about this house that I do not know,' I said sharply.
'I have not seen a third of it.'

'You haven't seen the solarium,' she agreed. 'There are several peeps in
this house. Oh, Miss, you don't know what peeps are, but a lot of big houses
have them. There's even one in Mount Widden. My mother told me that
it is where the ladies used to sit when the men were feasting and it was
considered no place for them among the men. They could look down and
watch, but they must not *be* there. There's one in the chapel . . . a sort of
one. We call it the lepers' squint there. They couldn't come in because they
were lepers, so they could only look through the squint. But I shall go to the
solarium and look down on the hall through the peep up there. Why Miss,
you ought to come with me. Please do.'

'We'll see,' I said.

On the day of the ball Alvean and I took our riding lesson as usual, only
instead of riding Buttercup Alvean was mounted on Black Prince.

When I had first seen the child on that horse I had felt a faint twinge of
uneasiness, but I stifled this, for I told myself that if she were going to
become a rider she must get beyond the Buttercup stage. Once she had
ridden Prince she would gain more confidence, and very likely never wish
to go back to Buttercup.

We had done rather well for the first few lessons. Prince behaved admirably
and Alvean's confidence was growing. We had no doubt, either of us, that
she would be able to enter for at least one of the events at the November
horse show.

But this day we were not so fortunate. I suspect that Alvean's thoughts
were on the ball rather than on her riding. She was still diffident with me,
except perhaps during our riding lessons, when oddly enough we were the
best of friends; but as soon as we had divested ourselves of our riding kit we
seemed automatically to slip back to the old relationship. I had tried to
change this without success.

We were about half-way through the lesson when Prince broke into a
gallop. I had not allowed her to gallop unless she was on the leading rein;
and in any case there was little room for that sort of thing in the field; and
I wanted to be absolutely sure of Alvean's confidence before I allowed her
more licence.

All would have been well if Alvean had kept her head and remembered
what I had taught her, but as Prince started to gallop she gave a little cry
of fear and her terror seemed immediately to communicate itself to the
frightened animal.

Prince was off; the thud of his hoofs on the turf struck terror into me. I saw Alvean, forgetting what I had taught her, swaying to one side.

It was all over in a flash because as soon as it happened I was on the spot. I was after her immediately. I had to grasp Prince's bridle before he reached the hedge for I believed that he might attempt to jump and that would mean a nasty fall for my pupil. Fear gave me new strength and I had his rein in my hands and had pulled him up just as he was coming up to the hedge. I brought him to a standstill while a white-faced trembling Alvean slid unharmed to the ground.

'It's all right,' I said. 'Your mind was wandering. You haven't reached the stage when you can afford to forget for a moment what you're doing.'

I knew that was the only way to deal with her. Shaken as she was, I made her remount Prince; I knew that she had become terrified of horses through some such incident as this. I had overcome that fear and I was not going to allow it to return.

She obeyed me, although reluctantly. But by the time our lesson was finished she was well over her fright, and I knew that she would want to ride next day. So I was more satisfied that day that I would eventually make a rider of Alvean than I had been before.

It was when we were leaving the field that she suddenly burst out laughing.

'What is it?' I asked, turning my head, for I was riding ahead of her.

'Oh, Miss,' she cried. 'You've split!'

'What *do* you mean?'

'Your dress has split under the armhole. Oh . . . it's getting worse and worse.'

I put my hand behind my back and realized what had happened. The riding habit had always been a little too tight for me and during my efforts to save Alvean from a nasty fall the sleeve seam had been unable to stand the extra strain.

I must have shown my dismay, for Alvean said: 'Never mind, Miss. I'll find you another. There *are* more, I know.'

Alvean was secretly amused as we went back to the house. Odd that I had never seen her in such good spirits. It was however somewhat disconcerting to discover that the sight of my discomfiture could give her so much pleasure that she could forget the danger through which she had so recently passed.

The guests had begun to arrive. I had been unable to resist taking peeps at them from my window. The approach was filled with carriages, and the dresses I had glimpsed made me gasp with envy.

The ball was being held in the great hall which I had seen earlier that day. Before that I had not been in it since my arrival, for I always used the back staircase. It was Kitty who had urged me to take a peep. 'It looks so lovely, Miss. Mr. Polgrey's going round like a dog with two tails. He'll murder one of us if anything happens to his plants.'

I thought I had rarely seen a setting so beautiful. The beams had been decorated with leaves. 'An old Cornish custom,' Kitty told me, 'specially at Maytime. But what's it matter, Miss, if this be September. Reckon there'll be other balls now the period of mourning be up. Well, so it should be.

Can't go on mourning for ever, can 'ee. You might say this is a sort of Maytime, don't 'ee see? 'Tis the end of one old year and the beginning of another like.'

I said, as I looked at the pots of hothouse blooms which had been brought in from the greenhouses and the great wax candles in their sconces, that the hall did Mr. Polgrey and his gardeners great credit. I pictured how it would look when those candles were lighted and the guests danced in their colourful gowns, their pearls and their diamonds.

I wanted to be one of the guests. How I wanted it! Kitty had begun to dance in the hall, smiling and bowing to an imaginary partner. I smiled. She looked so abandoned, so full of joy.

Then I thought that I ought not to be here like this. It was quite unbecoming. I was as bad as Kitty.

I turned away and there was a foolish lump in my throat.

Alvean and I had supper together that evening. She obviously could not dine with her father in the small dining room, as he would be busy with his guests.

'Miss,' she said, 'I've put a new riding habit for you in your cupboard.'

'Thank you,' I said; 'that was thoughtful of you.'

'Well, you couldn't go riding in that!' cried Alvean, pointing derisively at my lavender gown.

So it was only that I might not miss a riding lesson for want of the clothes, that she had taken such trouble on my behalf! I should have known that.

I asked myself in that moment whether I was not being rather foolish. Did I expect more than people were prepared to give? I was nothing to Alvean except when I could help her to attain what she wanted. It was as well to remember that.

I looked down distastefully at my lavender cotton gown. It was the favourite of the two which had been specially made for me by Aunt Adelaide's dressmaker when I had obtained this post. One was of grey – a most unbecoming colour to me – but I fancied I looked a little less prim, a little less of a governess in the lavender. But how becoming it seemed, with its bodice buttoned high at the neck and the cream lace collar and the cream lace cuffs to match. I realized I was comparing it with the dresses of Connan TreMellyn's guests.

Alvean said: 'Hurry and finish, Miss. Don't forget we're going to the solarium.'

'I suppose you have your father's permission . . .' I began.

'Miss, I always peep from the solarium. Everybody knows I do. My mother used to look up and wave to me.' Her face puckered a little. 'To-night,' she went on, as though she were speaking to herself, 'I'm going to imagine that she's down there after all . . . dancing there. Miss, do you think people come back after they're dead?'

'What an extraordinary question! Of course not.'

'You don't believe in ghosts then. Some people do. They say they've seen them. Do you think they lie when they say they see ghosts, Miss?'

'I think that people who say such things are the victims of their own imaginations.'

'Still,' she went on dreamily, 'I shall imagine she is there ... dancing there. Perhaps if I imagine hard enough I shall see her. Perhaps I shall be the victim of my imagination.'

I said nothing because I felt uneasy.

'If she *were* coming back,' she mused, 'she would come to the ball, because dancing was one of the things she liked doing best.' She seemed to remember me suddenly. 'Miss,' she went on, 'if you'd rather not come to the solarium with me, I don't mind going alone.'

'I'll come,' I said.

'Let's go now.'

'We will first finish our meal,' I told her.

The vastness of the house continued to astonish me, as I followed Alvean along the gallery, up stone staircases through several bedrooms, to what she told me was the solarium. The roof was of glass and I understood why it had received its name. I thought it must be unbearably warm in the heat of the summer.

The walls were covered with exquisite tapestries depicting the story of the Great Rebellion and the Restoration. There was the execution of the first Charles, and the second shown in the oak tree, his dark face peering down at the Roundhead soldiers; there were pictures of his arrival in England, of his coronation and a visit to his shipyards.

'Never mind those now,' said Alvean. 'My mother used to love being here. She said you could see what was going on. There are two peeps up here. Oh, Miss, don't you want to see them?'

I was looking at the escritoire, at the sofa and the gilt-backed chairs; and I saw her sitting here, talking to her daughter here – dead Alice who seemed to become more and more alive as the days passed.

There were windows at each end of this long room, high windows curtained with heavy brocade. The same brocade curtains hung before what I presumed to be doors of which there appeared to be four in this room – the one by which we had entered, another at the extreme end of the room and one other on either side. But I was wrong about the last two.

Alvean had disappeared behind one of these curtains and called to me in a muffled voice, and when I went to her I found we were in an alcove. In the wall was a star-shaped opening, quite large but decorated so that one would not have noticed it unless one had been looking for it.

I gazed through it and saw that I was looking down into the chapel. I could see clearly all but one side of the chapel – the small altar with the triptych and the pews.

'They used to sit up here and watch the service if they were too ill to go down, my mother told me. They had a priest in the house in the old days. My mother didn't tell me that. She didn't know about the history of the house. Miss Jansen told me. She knew a lot about the house. She loved to come up here and look through the peep. She used to like the chapel too.'

'You were sorry when she went, Alvean, I believe.'

'Yes, I was. The other peep's on the other side. Through that you can see into the hall.'

She went to the other side of the room and drew back the hangings there. In the wall was a similar star-shaped opening.

I looked down on the hall and caught my breath for it was a magnificent sight. Musicians were on the dais and the guests, who had not yet begun to dance, stood about talking.

There were a great many people down there and the sound of the chatter rose clearly up to us. Alvean was breathless beside me, her eyes searching . . . in a manner which made me shiver slightly. Did she really believe that Alice would come from the tomb because she loved to dance?

I felt an impulse to put my arm about her and draw her to me. Poor motherless child, I thought. Poor bewildered little creature!

But of course I overcame that impulse. Alvean had no desire for my sympathy, I well knew.

I saw Connan TreMellyn in conversation with Celestine Nansellock, and Peter was there too. If Peter was one of the most handsome men I had ever seen, Connan, I told myself, was the most elegant. There were few in that brilliant assembly whose faces were known to me, but I did see Lady Treslyn there. Even among the magnificently brilliant gathering she stood out. She was wearing a gown which seemed to be composed of yards and yards of chiffon, which was the colour of flame, and I guessed that she was one of the few who would have dared to wear such a colour. Yet had she wanted to attract attention to herself she could not have chosen anything more calculated to bring this result. Her dark hair looked almost black against the flame; her magnificent bust and shoulders were the whitest I had ever seen. She wore a band of diamonds in her hair, which was like a tiara, and diamonds sparkled about her person.

Alvean's attention was caught by her even as mine was and her brows were drawn together in a frown.

'*She* is there then,' she murmured.

I said: 'Is her husband present?'

'Yes, the little old man over there talking to Colonel Penlands.'

'And which is Colonel Penlands?' She pointed the colonel out to me, and I saw with him a bent old man, white-haired and wrinkled. It seemed incredible that he should be the husband of that flamboyant creature.

'Look!' whispered Alvean. 'My father is going to open the ball. He used to do it with Aunt Celestine, and at the same time my mother used to do it with Uncle Geoffry. I wonder who he will do it with this time.'

'With whom he will do it,' I murmured absentmindedly, but my attention, like Alvean's was entirely on the scene below.

'The musicians are going to start now,' she said. 'They always start with the same tune. Do you know what it is? It's the *Furry* Dance. Some of our ancestors came from Helston way and it was played then and it always has been since. You watch! Papa and Mamma used to dance the first bar or so with their partners, and all the others fell in behind.'

The musicians had begun, and I saw Connan take Celestine by the hand and lead her into the centre of the hall; Peter Nansellock followed, and he had chosen Lady Treslyn to be his partner.

I watched the four of them dance the first steps of the traditional dance, and I thought, Poor Celestine! Even gowned as she was in blue satin she looked ill at ease in that quartette. She lacked the elegance and nonchalance of Connan, the beauty of Lady Treslyn and the dash of her brother.

I thought it was a pity that he had to choose Celestine to open the ball, but that was tradition. The house was filled with tradition. Such and such was done because it always had been done, and often for no other reason. Well, that was the way in great houses.

Neither Alvean nor I seemed to tire of watching the dancers. An hour passed and we were still there. I fancied that Connan glanced up once or twice. Did he know of his daughter's habit of watching? I thought that it must be Alvean's bedtime, but that perhaps on such an occasion a little leniency would be permissible.

I was fascinated by the way she watched the dancers tirelessly, fervently, as though she were certain that if she looked long enough she would see that face there which she longed to see.

It was now dark, but the moon had risen. I turned my eyes from the dance floor to look through the glass roof at that great gibbous moon which seemed to be smiling down on us. No candles for you, it seemed to say; you are banished from the gaiety and the glitter, but I will give you my soft and tender light instead.

The room, touched by moonlight, had a supernatural character all its own. I felt in such a room anything might happen.

I turned my attention back to the dancers. They were waltzing down there and I felt myself swaying to the rhythm. No one had been more astonished than myself when I had proved to be a good dancer. It had brought me partners at the dances to which Aunt Adelaide had taken me in those days when she had thought it possible to find a husband for me; alas for Aunt Adelaide, those invitations to the dances had not been extended to other pursuits.

And as I listened entranced I felt a hand touch mine and I was so startled that I gave an audible gasp.

I looked down. Standing beside me was a small figure, and I was relieved to see that it was only Gillyflower.

'You have come to see the dancers?' I said.

She nodded.

She was not quite so tall as Alvean and could not reach the star-shaped peep, so I lifted her in my arms and held her up. I could not see very clearly in the moonlight but I was sure the blankness had left her eyes.

I said to Alvean: 'Bring a stool and Gillyflower can stand on it; then she will be able to see quite easily.'

Alvean said: 'Let her get it herself.'

Gilly nodded and I put her on the floor; she ran to the stool and brought it with her. I thought, since she understands, why can she not talk with the rest of us?

Alvean did not seem to want to look now that Gilly had come. She moved away from the peep and as the musicians below began the opening bars of that waltz which always enchanted me – I refer to Mr. Strauss's *Blue Danube Waltz* – Alvean began to dance across the floor of the solarium.

The music seemed to have affected my feet. I don't know what came over me that night. It was as though some spirit of daring had entered into my body, but I could not resist the strains of the *Blue Danube Waltz*. I danced towards Alvean. I waltzed as I used to in those ballrooms to which I went accompanied by Aunt Adelaide, but I was sure that I never danced as I did that night in the solarium.

Alvean cried out with pleasure; I heard Gilly laugh too.

Alvean cried: 'Go on, Miss. Don't stop, Miss. You do it well.'

So I went on dancing with an imaginary partner, dancing down the moonlit solarium with the lopsided moon smiling in at me. And when I reached the end of the room a figure moved towards me and I was no longer dancing alone.

'You're exquisite,' said a voice, and there was Peter Nansellock in his elegant evening dress, and he was holding me as it was the custom to hold a partner in the waltz.

My feet faltered. He said: 'No . . . no. Listen, the children are protesting. You must dance with me, Miss Leigh, as you were meant to dance with me.'

We went on dancing. It was as though my feet, having begun would not stop.

But I said: 'This is most unorthodox.'

'It is most delightful,' he answered.

'You should be with the guests.'

'It is more fun to be with you.'

'You forget—'

'That you are a governess? I could, if you would allow me to.'

'There is no earthly reason why you should forget.'

'Only that I think you would be happier if we could all forget it. How exquisitely you dance!'

'It is my only drawing room accomplishment.'

'I am sure it is one of many that you are forced to squander on this empty room.'

'Mr. Nansellock, do you not think this little jest has been played out?'

'It is no jest.'

'I shall now rejoin the children.' We had come close to them and I saw little Gilly's face enrapt, and I saw the admiration in Alvean's. If I stopped dancing I should revert to my old position; while I went on dancing I was an exalted being.

I thought how ridiculous were the thoughts I was entertaining; but tonight I wanted to be ridiculous, I wanted to be frivolous.

'So here he is.'

To my horror I saw that several people had come into the solarium, and my apprehension did not lessen when I saw the flame-coloured gown of Lady Treslyn among them, for I was sure that wherever that flame-coloured dress was there Connan TreMellyn would be.

Somebody started to clap; others took it up. Then *The Blue Danube* ended.

I put my hand to my hair in my acute embarrassment. I knew that dancing had loosened the pins.

I thought: I shall be dismissed to-morrow for my irresponsibility, and perhaps I deserve it.

'What an excellent idea,' said someone. 'Dancing in moonlight. What could be more agreeable? And one can hear the music up here almost as well as down there.'

Someone else said: 'This is a beautiful ballroom, Connan.'

'Then let us use it for that purpose,' he answered.

He went to the peep and shouted through it: 'Once more – *The Beautiful Blue Danube.*'

Then the music started.

I turned to Alvean and I gripped Gilly by the hand. People were already beginning to dance. They were talking together and they did not bother to lower their voices. Why should they? I was only the governess.

I heard a voice: 'The governess. Alvean's, you know.'

'Forward creature! I suppose another of Peter's light ladies.'

'I'm sorry for the poor things. Life must be dull for them.'

'But in broad moonlight! What could be more depraved?'

'The last one had to be dismissed, I believe.'

'This one's turn will come.'

I was blushing hotly. I wanted to face them all, to tell them that my conduct was very likely less depraved than that of some of them.

I was furiously angry and a little frightened. I was aware of Connan's face in the moonlight for he was standing near to me, looking at me, I feared, in a manner signifying the utmost disapproval, which I was sure he was feeling.

'Alvean,' he said, 'go to your room and take Gillyflower with you.'

She dared not disobey when he spoke in those tones.

I said as coolly as I could: 'Yes, let us go.'

But as I was about to follow the children I found my arm gripped and Connan had come a little closer to me.

He said: 'You dance extremely well, Miss Leigh. I could never resist a good dancer. Perhaps it is because I scarcely excel in the art myself.'

'Thank you,' I said. But he still held my arm.

'I am sure,' he went on, 'that *The Blue Danube* is a favourite of yours. You looked . . . enraptured.' And with that he swung me into his arms and I found that I was dancing with him among his guests . . . I in my lavender cotton and my turquoise brooch, they in their chiffons and velvets, their emeralds and diamonds.

I was glad of the moonlight. I was so overcome with shame, for I believed that he was angry and that his intention was to shame me further.

My feet caught the rhythm and I thought to myself: Always in future *The Blue Danube* will mean to me a fantastic dance in the solarium with Connan TreMellyn as my partner.

'I apologize, Miss Leigh,' he said, 'for my guests' bad manners.'

'It is what I must expect and no doubt what I deserve.'

'What nonsense,' he said, and I told myself that I was dreaming, for his voice which was close to my ear sounded tender.

We had come to the end of the room and, to my complete astonishment, he had whirled me through the curtains and out of the door. We were on a small landing between two flights of stone stairs in a part of the house which I had not seen before.

We stopped dancing, but he still kept his arms about me. On the wall a paraffin lamp of green jade burned; its light was only enough to show me his face. It looked a little brutal I thought.

'Miss Leigh,' he said, 'you are very charming when you abandon your severity.'

I caught my breath with dismay for he was forcing me against the wall and kissing me.

I was horrified as much by my own emotions as by what was happening. I knew what that kiss meant: You are not averse to a mild flirtation with Peter Nansellock; therefore why not with me?

My anger was so great that it was beyond my control. With all my might I pushed him from me and he was so taken by surprise that he reeled backwards. I lifted my skirts and began to run as fast as I could down the stairs.

I did not know where I was but I went on running blindly and eventually found the gallery and so made my way back to my own room.

There I threw myself on to my bed and lay there until I recovered my breath.

There is only one thing I can do, I told myself, and that is get away from this house with all speed. He has now made his intentions clear to me. I have no doubt at all that Miss Jansen was dismissed because she refused to accept his invitations. The man is a monster. He appeared to think that anyone whom he employed belonged to him completely. Did he imagine he was an eastern pasha? How dared he treat me in such a way!

There was a constricted feeling in my throat which made me feel as though I were going to choke. I was more desperately unhappy than I had ever been in my life. It was due to him. I would not face the truth, but I really cared more deeply than I had about anything else that he should regard me with such contempt.

These were the danger signals.

I had need now of my common sense.

I rose from my bed and locked my door. I must make sure that my door was locked during the last night I would spend in this house. The only other way to my room would be through Alvean's room and the schoolroom, and I knew he would not attempt to come that way.

Nevertheless I felt unsafe.

Nonsense, I said to myself, you can protect yourself. If he should dare enter your room you could pull the bell rope immediately.

The first thing I would do would be to write to Phillida. I sat down and tried to do this but my hands were trembling and my handwriting was so shaky that the note looked ridiculous.

I could start packing.

I did this.

I went to the cupboard and pulled open the door. For a moment I thought someone was standing there, and I cried out in alarm; which showed the nervous state to which I had been reduced. I saw what it was almost immediately: The riding habit which Alvean had procured for me. She must have hung it in my wardrobe herself. I had forgotten all about this afternoon's little adventure for what had happened in the solarium and after had temporarily obliterated everything else.

I packed my trunk in a very short time, for my possessions were not many. Then, as I was more composed, I sat down and wrote the letter to Phillida.

When I had finished writing I heard the sound of voices below and I went to my window. Some of the guests had come out on to the lawn, and I saw them dancing down there. More came out.

I heard someone say: 'It's such a heavenly night. That moon is too good to miss.'

I stood back in the shadows watching, and eventually I saw what I had been waiting for. There was Connan. He was dancing with Lady Treslyn; his head was close to hers. I imagined the sort of things he was saying to her.

Then I turned angrily from the window and tried to tell myself that the pain I felt within me was disgust.

I undressed and went to bed. I lay sleepless for a long time and when I did sleep I had jumbled dreams that were of Connan, myself and Lady Treslyn. And always in the background of these dreams was that shadowy figure who had haunted my thoughts since the day I had come here.

I awoke with a start. The moon was still visible and in the room in my half awakened state I seemed to see the dark shape of a woman.

I knew it was Alice. She did not speak yet she was telling me something. 'You must not go from here. You must stay. I cannot rest. You can help me. You must help us all.'

I was trembling all over. I sat up in bed. Now I saw what had startled me. When I had packed I had left the door of the cupboard open, and what appeared to be the ghost of Alice was only her riding habit.

I was late up next morning because when I had slept I had done so deeply, and it was Kitty banging on the door with my hot water who awakened me. She could not get in and clearly she wondered what was wrong.

I leaped out of bed and unlocked the door.

'Anything wrong, Miss?' she said.

'No,' I answered sharply, and she waited a few seconds for my explanation of the locked door.

I was certainly not going to give it to her, and she was so full of last night's ball that she was not as interested as she would have been had there been nothing else to absorb her.

'Wasn't it lovely, Miss? I watched from my room. They danced on the lawn in the moonlight. My dear life, I never saw such a sight. It was like it used to be when the mistress was here. You look tired, Miss. Did they keep you awake?'

'Yes,' I said, 'they did.'

'Oh, well, it's all over now. Mr. Polgrey's already having the plants taken back. Fussing over them like a hen with her chicks, he be. The hall do look a sorry mess this morning, I can tell 'ee. It's going to take Daisy and me all day to get it cleared up, you see.'

I yawned and she put my hot water by the hip bath and went out. In five minutes' time she was back again.

I was half clothed, and wrapped a towel about me to shield myself from her too inquisitive eyes.

'It's Master,' she said. 'He's asking for you. Wants to see you right away. In the punch room. He said, "Tell Miss Leigh it is most urgent."'

'Oh,' I said.

'Most urgent, Miss,' Kitty repeated, and I nodded.

I finished washing and dressed quickly. I guessed what this meant. Very likely there would be some complaint. I would be given my notice because I was inefficient in some way. I began to think of Miss Jansen, and I wondered whether something of this nature had happened in her case. 'Here one day and gone the next.' Some trumped-up case against her. What if he should trump up a case against me?

That man is quite unscrupulous! I thought.

Well, I would be first. I would tell of my decision to leave, before he had a chance to dismiss me.

I went down to the punch room prepared for battle.

He was wearing a blue riding jacket and he did not look as though he had been up half the night.

'Good morning, Miss Leigh,' he said, and to my astonishment he smiled.

I did not return the smile. 'Good morning,' I said. 'I have already packed my bags and would like to leave as soon as possible.'

'Miss Leigh!' His voice was reproachful, and I felt an absurd joy rising within me. I was saying to myself: He doesn't want you to go. He's not asking you to go. He's actually going to apologize.

I heard myself say in a high, prim voice, which I should have hated in anyone else as selfrighteous and priggish: 'I consider it the only course open to me after—'

He cut in: 'After my outrageous conduct of last night. Miss Leigh, I am going to ask you to forget that. I fear the excitement of the moment overcame me. I forgot with whom I was dancing. I have asked you to overlook my depravity on this occasion, and to say generously – I am sure you are generous, Miss Leigh – we will draw a veil over that unpleasant little incident and go on as we were before.'

I had a notion that he was mocking me but I was suddenly so happy that I did not care.

I was not going. The letter to Phillida need not be posted. I was not to leave in disgrace.

I inclined my head and I said: 'I accept your apology, Mr. TreMellyn. We will forget this unpleasant and unfortunate incident.'

Then I turned and went out of the room.

I found that I was taking the stairs three at a time; my feet were almost dancing as they had been unable to resist dancing last night in the solarium.

The incident was over. I was going to stay. The whole house seemed to warm to me. I knew in that moment that if I had to leave this place I should be quite desolate.

I had always been given to self-analysis and I said to myself, Why this elation? Why would you be so wretched if you had to leave Mount Mellyn?

I had the answer ready: Because there is some secret here. Because I want to solve it. Because I want to help those two bewildered children; for Alvean is as bewildered as poor little Gillyflower.

But perhaps that was not the only reason. Perhaps I was a little more than interested in the Master of the house.

Perhaps had I been wise I should have recognized the danger signals. But I was not wise. Women in my position rarely are.

That day Alvean and I took our riding lesson as usual. It went off well and the only remarkable thing about it was that I wore the new riding habit. It was different from the other, for it consisted of the tightly fitting dress of light-weight material and with it was a jacket, tailored almost like a man's.

I was delighted that Alvean showed no sign of fear after her small mishap of the day before, and I said that in a few days' time we might attempt a little jumping.

We arrived back at the house and I went to my room to change before tea.

I took off the jacket, thinking of the shock these things had given me in the night, and I laughed at my fears, for I was in very high spirits that day. I slipped out of the dress with some difficulty (Alice had been just that little bit more slender than I), put on my grey cotton – Aunt Adelaide had warned me that it was advisable not to wear the same dress two days running – and was about to hang up the riding habit in the cupboard when I felt something in the pocket of the coat.

I thrust in my hand in surprise, for I was sure I had had my hands in the pockets before this and nothing had been there.

There was nothing actually in the pocket now but there was something beneath the silk lining. I laid the jacket on the bed and examining it soon discovered the concealed pocket. I merely had to unhook it and there it was; in it was a book, a small diary.

My heart beat very fast as I took it out because I knew that this belonged to Alice.

I hesitated for a moment but I could not resist the impulse to look inside. Indeed I felt in that moment that it was my duty to look inside.

On the fly leaf was written in a rather childish hand 'Alice TreMellyn.' I looked at the date. It was the previous year so I knew that she had written in that diary during the last year of her life.

I turned the leaves. If I had expected a revelation of character I was soon disappointed. Alice had merely used this as a record for her appointments. There was nothing in this book to make me understand her more.

I looked at the entries. 'Mount Widden to tea.' 'The Trelanders to dine.' 'C to Penzance.' 'C due back.'

Still it was written in Alice's handwriting and that made it exciting to me.

I turned to the last entry in the book. It was under the twentieth of August. I looked back to July. Under the fourteenth was written: 'Treslyns and Trelanders to dine at M.M.' 'See dressmaker about blue satin.' 'Do not forget to see Polgrey about flowers.' 'Send Gilly to dressmaker.' 'Take Alvean for fitting.' 'If jeweller has not sent brooch by sixteenth go to see him.' And on the sixteenth: 'Brooch not returned must go along to-morrow morning. Must have it for dinner party at Trelanders on eighteenth.'

It all sounded very trivial. What I had believed might be a great discovery was nothing very much. I put the book back into the pocket and went along to have tea in the schoolroom.

While Alvean and I were reading together a sudden thought struck me. I didn't know the exact date of Alice's death but it must have been soon after she was writing those trivial things in her diary. How odd that she should have thought it worth while to make those entries when she was planning to leave her husband and daughter for another man.

It suddenly became imperative to know the exact date of her death.

Alvean had had tea with her father because several people had come to pay duty calls and compliment Connan on last night's ball.

Thus I was free to go out alone. So I made my way down to Mellyn village and to the churchyard where I presumed Alice's remains would have been buried.

I had not seen much of the village before as I had had little opportunity of going so far except when we went to church on Sunday, so it was an interesting tour of exploration.

I ran almost all the way downhill and was very soon in the village. I reminded myself that it would be a different matter toiling uphill on my way back.

The village in the valley nestled about the old church, the grey tower of which was half covered in ivy. There was a pleasant little village green and a few grey stone houses clustered round it among which was a row of very ancient cottages which I guessed were of the same age as the church. I promised myself that I would make a closer examination of the village later. In the meantime I was most eager to find Alice's grave.

I went through the lych gate and into the churchyard. It was very quiet there at this time of the day. I felt I was surrounded by the stillness of death and I almost wished that I had brought Alvean with me. She could have pointed out her mother's grave.

How could I find it among these rows of grey crosses and headstones, I wondered as I looked about me helplessly. Then I thought, the TreMellyns would no doubt have some grand memorial to their dead; I must look for the most splendid vault, and I am sure I shall quickly find it that way.

I saw a huge vault of black marble and gilt not far off. I made for this and quickly discovered it to be that of the Nansellock family.

A sudden thought occurred to me. Geoffry Nansellock would lie here, and he died on the same night as Alice. Were they not found dead together?

I discovered the inscription engraved on the marble. This tomb contained the bones of defunct Nansellocks as far back as the middle seventeen hundreds. I remembered that the family had not been in Mount Widden as early as there had been TreMellyns at Mount Mellyn.

It was not difficult to find Geoffry's name for his was naturally the last entry on the list of the dead.

He died last year, I saw, on the 17th of July.

I was all eagerness to go back and look at the diary and check up that date.

I turned from the tomb and as I did so I saw Celestine Nansellock coming towards me.

'Miss Leigh,' she cried. 'I thought it was you.'

I felt myself flush because I remembered seeing her last night among the guests in the solarium, and I wondered what she was thinking of me now.

'I took a stroll down to the village,' I answered, 'and found myself here.'

'I see you're looking at my family tomb.'

'Yes. It's a beautiful thing.'

'If such a thing can be beautiful. I come here often,' she volunteered. 'I like to bring a few flowers for Alice.'

'Oh, yes,' I stammered.

'You saw the TreMellyn vault, I suppose?'

'No.'

'It's over here. Come and look.'

I stumbled across the long grass to the vault which rivalled that of the Nansellocks in its magnificence.

On the black slab was a vase of Michaelmas daisies – large perfect blooms that looked like mauve stars.

'I've just put them there,' she said. 'They were her favourite flowers.'

Her lips trembled, and I thought she was going to burst into tears.

I looked at the date and I saw it was that on which Geoffry Nansellock had died.

I said: 'I shall have to go back now.'

She nodded. She seemed too moved to be able to speak. I thought then: She loved Alice. She seems to have loved her more than anyone else.

It was on the tip of my tongue to tell her about the diary I had discovered, but I hesitated. The memory of last night's shame was too near to me. I might be reminded that I was, after all, only the governess. And what right had I, in any case, to meddle in their affairs.

I left her there and as I went away I saw her sink to her knees. I turned again later and saw that her face was buried in her hands and her shoulders were heaving.

I hurried back to the house and took out the diary. So on the 16th of July last year, on the day before Alice was supposed to have eloped with Geoffry Nansellock, she had written in her diary that if her brooch was not returned on the next day she must go along to the jeweller as she needed it for a dinner party to be held on the 18th.

That entry had not been made by a woman who was planning to elope.

I felt that I had almost certain proof in my hands that the body which had been found with Geoffry Nansellock's on the wrecked train was not Alice's.

I was back at the old question. What had happened to Alice? If she was not lying inside the black marble vault, where was she?

Chapter Five

I felt I had discovered a vital clue but it took me no further. Each day I woke up expectant, but of the days which passed one was very like another. Sometimes I pondered on several courses of action. I wondered whether I would go to Connan TreMellyn and tell him that I had seen his wife's diary and that it clearly showed she had not been planning to leave.

Then I told myself I did not quite trust Connan TreMellyn, and there was one thought concerning him which I did not want to explore too thoroughly. I had already begun to ask myself the question: Suppose Alice was not on the train, and something else happened to her, who would be most likely to know what that was? Could it be Connan TreMellyn?

There was Peter Nansellock. I might discuss this matter with him, but he was too frivolous; he turned every line of conversation towards the flirtatious.

There was his sister. She was the most likely person. I knew that she had been fond of Alice; they must have been the greatest friends. Celestine was clearly the one in whom I could best confide. And yet I hesitated. Celestine belonged to that other world into which I had been clearly shown on more than one occasion, I had no right to intrude. It was not for me, a mere governess, to set myself up as investigator.

The person in whom I might confide was Mrs. Polgrey, but again I shrank from doing this. I could not forget her spoonfuls of whisky and her attitude towards Gilly.

So I decided that for the time being I would keep my suspicions to myself. October was upon us. I found the changing seasons delightful in this part of the world. The blustering south-west wind was warm and damp, and it seemed to carry with it the scent of spices from Spain. I had never seen so many spiders' webs as I did that October. They draped themselves over the hedges like gossamer cloth sewn with brilliants. When the sun came out it was almost as warm as June. 'Summer do go on a long time in Cornwall,' Tapperty told me.

The sea mist would come drifting in, wrapping itself about the grey stone of the house so that from the arbour in the south gardens it would sometimes be completely hidden. The gulls seemed to screech on a melancholy note on such days as though they were warning us that life was a sorrowful affair. And in the humid climate the hydrangeas continued to flower - blue, pink and yellow - in enormous masses of bloom such as I should not have expected to find outside a hot-house. The roses went on flowering, and with them the fuchsias.

When I went down to the village one day I saw a notice outside the church to the effect that the date of the horse show was fixed for the 1st of November.

I went back and told Alvean. I was delighted that she had lost none of her enthusiasm for the event. I had been afraid that, as the time grew near, her fear might have returned.

I said to her: 'There's only three weeks. We really ought to get in a little more practice.'

She was quite agreeable.

We could, I suggested, rearrange our schedule. Perhaps we could ride for an hour both in the mornings and the afternoons.

She was eager. 'I'll see what can be done,' I promised.

Connan TreMellyn had gone down to Penzance. I discovered this quite by accident. Kitty told me, when she brought in my water, one evening.

'Master have gone off this afternoon,' she said ''Tis thought he'll be away for a week or more.'

'I hope he's back in time for the show,' I said.

'Oh, he'll be back for that. He be one of the judges. He'm always here for that.'

I was annoyed with the man. Not that I expected him to tell me he was going; but I did feel he might have had the grace to say good-bye to his daughter.

I thought a good deal about him and I found myself wondering whether he had really gone to Penzance. I wondered whether Lady Treslyn was at home, or whether she had found it necessary to pay a visit to some relative.

Really! I admonished myself. 'Whatever has come over you? How can you entertain such thoughts? It's not as though you have any proof!

I promised myself that while Connan TreMellyn was away there was no need to think of him, and that would be a relief.

I was not entirely lying about that. I did feel relaxed by the thought that he was out of the house. I no longer felt it necessary to lock my door; but I continued to do so, purely on account of the Tapperty girls. I did not want them to know that I locked it for fear of the Master – and although they were quite without education, they were sharp enough where such matters were concerned.

'Now,' I said to Alvean, 'we will concentrate on practising for the show.'

I procured a list of the events. There were two jumping contests for Alvean's age group, and I decided that she should take the elementary one, for I felt that she had a good chance of winning a prize in that; and of course the whole point of this was that she *should* win a prize and astonish her father.

'Look, Miss,' said Alvean, 'there's this one. Why don't *you* go in for this?'

'Of course I shall do no such thing.'

'But why not?'

'My dear child, I am here to teach you, not to enter for competitions.'

A mischievous look came into her eyes. 'Miss,' she said, 'I'm going to enter you for that. You'd win. There's nobody here can ride as well as you do. Oh, Miss, you must!'

She was looking at me with what I construed as shy pride, and I felt a thrill of pleasure. I enjoyed her pride in me. She wanted me to win.

Well, why not? There was no rule about social standing in these contests, was there?

I fell back on my stock phrase for ending an embarrassing discussion: 'We'll see,' I said.

One afternoon we were riding close to Mount Widden and met Peter Nansellock.

He was mounted on a beautiful bay mare, the sight of which made my eyes glisten with envy.

He came galloping towards us and pulled up, dramatically removing his hat and bowing from the waist.

Alvean laughed delightedly.

'Well met, dear ladies,' he cried. 'Were you coming to call on us?'

'We were not,' I answered.

'How unkind! But now you are here you must come in for a little refreshment.'

I was about to protest when Alvean cried: 'Oh, do let's, Miss. Yes, please, Uncle Peter, we'll come in.'

'I had hoped you would call before this,' he said reproachfully.

'We had received no definite invitation,' I reminded him.

'For you there is always welcome at Mount Widden. Did I not make that clear?'

He had turned his mare and we all three walked our horses side by side. He followed my gaze, which was fixed on the mare.

'You like her?' he said.

'Indeed I do. She's a beauty.'

'She's a real beauty, are you not, Jacinth my pet?'

'Jacinth. So that's her name.'

'Pretty, you're thinking. Pretty name for a pretty creature. She'll go like the wind. She's worth four of that lumbering old cart horse you're riding, Miss Leigh.'

'Lumbering old cart horse? How absurd! Dion is a very fine horse.'

'Was, Miss Leigh. *Was!* Do you not think that the creature has seen better days? Really, I should have thought Connan could have given you something better from his stables than poor old Dion.'

'It was not a matter of his giving her any horse to ride,' said Alvean in hot defence of her father. 'He does not know what horses we ride, does he, Miss. These are the horses which Tapperty said we could have.'

'Poor Miss Leigh! She should have a mount worthy of her. Miss Leigh, before you go, I would like you to take a turn on Jacinth. She'll quickly show you what it feels like to be on a good mount again.'

'Oh,' I said lightly, 'we're satisfied with what we have. They serve my purpose – which is to teach Alvean to ride.'

'We're practising for the show,' Alvean told him. 'I'm going in for one of the events, but don't tell Papa; it's to be a surprise.'

Peter put his finger to his lips. 'Trust me. I'll keep your secret.'

'And Miss is entering for one of the events too. I've made her!'

'She'll be victorious,' he cried. 'I'll make a bet on it.'

I said curtly: 'I'm not at all sure about this. It is only an idea of Alvean's.'

'But you must, Miss!' cried Alvean. 'I insist.'

'We'll both insist,' added Peter.

We had reached the gates of Mount Widden which were wide open. There was no lodge here as at Mount Mellyn. We went up the drive – where the same types of flowers grew in profusion – the hydrangeas, fuchsias and fir trees which were indigenous to this part of the country.

I saw the house, grey stone as Mount Mellyn was, but much smaller and with fewer outbuildings. I noticed immediately that it was not so well cared for as what in that moment I presumptuously called 'our' house and I felt an absurd thrill of pleasure because Mount Mellyn compared so favourably with Mount Widden.

There was a groom in the stables and Peter told him to take charge of our horses. He did so and we went into the house.

Peter clapped his hands and shouted: 'Dick! Where are you, Dick?'

The houseboy, whom I had seen when he had been sent over to Mount Mellyn with messages, appeared; and Peter said to him: 'Tea, Dick. At once, in the library. We have guests.'

'Yes, Master,' said Dick and hurried away.

We were in a hall which seemed quite modern when compared with our own hall. The floor was tessellated and there was a wide staircase at one end of it which led to a gallery containing oil paintings, presumably of the Nansellock family.

I laughed at myself for scorning the place, which was very much larger and much grander than the vicarage in which I had spent my childhood. But it had a neglected air – one might almost say one of decay.

Peter took us into the library, a huge room, the walls of which were lined with books on three sides. I noticed that the furniture was dusty and that dirt was visible in the heavy curtains. What they need, I thought, is a Mrs. Polgrey with her beeswax and turpentine.

'I pray you sit down, dear ladies,' said Peter. 'It is to be hoped that tea will not long be delayed, although I must warn you that meals are not served with the precision which prevails in our rival across the cove.'

'Rival?' I said in surprise.

'Well, how could there fail to be a little rivalry? Here we stand, side by side. But the advantages are all with them. They have the grander house, and the servants to deal with it. Your father, dear Alvean, is a man of property. We Nansellocks are his poor relations.'

'You are not our relations,' Alvean reminded him.

'Now is that not strange? One would have thought that, living side by side for generations, the two families would have mingled and become one. There must have been charming TreMellyn girls and charming Nansellock men. How odd that they did not join up and become relations! I suppose the mighty TreMellyns always looked down their arrogant noses at the poor Nansellocks and went farther afield to make their marriages. But now there is the fair Alvean. How maddening that we have no boy of your age to marry you, Alvean. *I* shall have to wait for you. There is nothing for it but that.'

Alvean laughed delightedly. I could see that she was quite fascinated by him; and I thought, Perhaps he is more serious than he pretends. Perhaps he has already begun courting Alvean in a subtle way.

Alvean began to talk about the show and he listened attentively. I occasionally joined in, and so the time passed until tea was brought to us.

'Miss Leigh, will you honour us by pouring out?' Peter asked me.

I said I should be happy to do so, and I placed myself at the head of the tea table.

Peter watched me with attention which I found faintly embarrassing because, not only was it admiring, but contented.

'How glad I am that we met,' he murmured as Alvean handed him his cup of tea 'To think that, if I had been five minutes earlier or five minutes later, our paths might not have crossed. What a great part chance plays in our lives.'

'Possibly we should have met at some other time.'

'There may not be much more time left to us.'

'You sound morbid. Do you think that something is going to happen to one of us?'

He looked at me very seriously. 'Miss Leigh,' he said 'I am going away.'

'Where, Uncle Peter?' demanded Alvean.

'Far away, my child, to the other side of the world.'

'Soon?' I asked.

'Possibly with the New Year.'

'But where are you going?' cried Alvean in dismay.

'My dearest child, I believe you are a little hurt at the thought of my departure.'

'Uncle, where?' she demanded imperiously.

'To seek my fortune.'

'You're teasing. You're always teasing.'

'Not this time. I have heard from a friend who was at Cambridge with me. He is in Australia, and there he has made a fortune. Gold! Think of it, Alvean. You too, Miss Leigh. Lovely gold . . . gold which can make a man . . . or woman . . . rich. And all one has to do is pluck it out of the ground.'

'Many go in the hope of making fortunes,' I said, 'but are they all successful?'

'There speaks the practical woman. No, Miss Leigh, they are not all successful; but there is something named hope which, I believe, springs eternal in the human breast. All may not have gold but they can all have hope.'

'Of what use is hope if it is proved to be false?'

'Until she is proved false she can give so much pleasure, Miss Leigh.'

'Then I wish that your hopes may not prove false.'

'Thank you.'

'But I don't want you to go, Uncle Peter.'

'Thank *you*, my dear. But I shall come back a rich man. Imagine it. Then I shall build a new wing on Mount Widden. I will make the house as grand as – no, grander than – Mount Mellyn. And in the years to come people will say it was Peter Nansellock who saved the family fortunes. For, my dear young ladies, someone has to save them . . . soon.'

He then began to talk of his friend who had gone to Australia a penniless young man and who, he was sure, was now a millionaire, or almost.

He began planning how he would rebuild the house, and we both joined in. It was a pleasant game – building a house in the mind, to one's own desires.

I felt exhilarated by his company. He at least, I thought, has never made me feel my position. The very fact of his poverty – or what to him seemed poverty – endeared him to me.

It was an enjoyable tea time.

Afterwards he took us out to the stables and both he and Alvean insisted on my mounting Jacinth, and showing them what I could do with her. My saddle was put on her, and I galloped her and jumped with her, and she responded to my lightest touch. She was a delicious creature and I envied him his possession of her.

'Why,' he said, 'she has taken to you, Miss Leigh. Not a single protest at finding a new rider on her back.'

I patted her fondly and said: 'She's a beauty.'

And the sensitive creature seemed to understand.

We then mounted our horses, and Peter came to the gates of Mount Mellyn with us, riding Jacinth.

As we went up to our rooms I decided that it had indeed been a very enjoyable afternoon.

Alvean came to my room and stood for a while, her head on one side. She said: 'He likes you, I think, Miss.'

'He is merely polite towards me,' I replied.

'No, I think he likes you rather specially . . . in the way he liked Miss Jansen.'

'Did Miss Jansen go to tea at Mount Widden?'

'Oh yes. I didn't have riding lessons with her, but we used to walk over there. And one day we had tea just as we did this afternoon. He'd just bought Jacinth then and he showed her to us. He said he was going to change her name to make her entirely his. Then he said her name was to be Jacinth. That was Miss Jansen's name.'

I felt foolishly deflated. Then I said: 'He must have been very sorry when she left so suddenly.'

Alvean was thoughtful. 'Yes, I think he was. But he soon forgot all about her. After all—'

I finished the sentence for her: 'She was only the governess, of course.'

It was later that day when Kitty came up to my room to tell me that there was a message for me from Mount Widden.

'And something more too, Miss,' she said; it was clearly something which excited her, but I refrained from questioning her since I should soon discover what this was.

'Well,' I said, 'where is the message?'

'In the stables, Miss.' She giggled. 'Come and see.'

I went to the stables, and Kitty followed at a distance.

When I arrived there I saw Dick, the Mount Widden houseboy; and, to my astonishment, he had the mare, Jacinth, with him.

He handed me a note.

I saw that Daisy, her father, and Billy Trehay were all watching me with amused and knowing eyes.

I opened the note and read it. It said:

> Dear Miss Leigh,
>   You could not hide from me your admiration for Jacinth. I believe she reciprocates your feelings. That is why I am making you a present of her. I could not bear to see such a fine and graceful rider as yourself on poor old Dion. So pray accept this gift.
>
> > Your admiring neighbour,
> > *Peter Nansellock*

In spite of efforts to control myself I felt the hot colour rising from my neck to my forehead. I knew that Tapperty found it hard to repress a snigger.

How could Peter be so foolish! Was he laughing at me? How could I possibly accept such a gift, even if I wanted to? Horses have to be fed and stabled. It was almost as though he had forgotten this was not my home.

'Is there an answer, Miss?' asked Dick.

'Indeed there is,' I said. 'I will go to my room at once, and you may take it back with you.'

I went with as much dignity as I could muster in front of such an array of spectators back to the house, and in my room I wrote briefly:–

> Dear Mr. Nansellock,
>   Thank you for your magnificent gift which I am, of course, quite unable to accept. I have no means of keeping a horse here. It may have escaped you that I am employed in this house as a governess. I could not possibly afford the upkeep of Jacinth. Thank you for the kind thought.
>
> > Yours truly,
> > *Martha Leigh*

I went straight back to the stables. I could hear them all laughing and talking excitedly as I approached.

'Here you are, Dick,' I said. 'Please take this note to your master with Jacinth.'

'But . . .' stammered Dick. 'I was to leave her here.'

I looked straight into Tapperty's lewd old face. 'Mr. Nansellock,' I said, 'is fond of playing jokes.'

Then I went back to the house.

The next day was Saturday and Alvean said that, as it was a half holiday, could we not take the morning off and go to the moors. Her Great-Aunt Clara had a house there, and she would be pleased to see us.

I considered this. I thought it would be rather pleasant to get away from the house for a few hours. I knew that they must all be talking about me and Peter Nansellock.

I guessed that he had behaved with Miss Jansen as he was behaving with me, and it amused them all to see the story of one governess turning out so much like another.

I wondered about Miss Jansen. Had she perhaps been a little frivolous? I pictured her stealing, whatever she was supposed to have stolen, that she might buy herself fine clothes to appear beautiful in the sight of her admirer.

And he had not cared when she was dismissed. A fine friend he would be!

We set out after breakfast. It was a beautiful day for riding for the October sun was not fierce and there was a soft south-west wind. Alvean was in high spirits, and I thought this would be a good exercise in staying power. If she could manage the long ride to her great aunt's house and back without fatigue I should be delighted.

I felt it was pleasant to get away from the watchful eyes of the servants, and it was delightful to be in the moorland country.

I found the great tracts of moor fitted my mood. I was enchanted by the low stone walls, the grey boulders and the gay little streams which trickled over them.

I warned Alvean to be watchful of boulders, but she was sure-seated and alert now, so I did not feel greatly concerned.

We studied the map which would guide us to Great-Aunt Clara's house – a few miles south of Bodmin. Alvean had travelled there   a carriage once or twice and she thought she would know the road; but the moor was the easiest place in the world in which to lose oneself, and I thought that we could profit by the occasion to learn a little map-reading.

But I had left a great deal of my severity behind and I found myself laughing with Alvean when we took the wrong road and had to retrace our steps.

But at length we reached The House on the Moors which was the picturesque name of Great-Aunt Clara's home.

And a charming house it was, set there on the outskirts of a moorland village. There was the church, the little inn, the few houses and The House on the Moors which was like a small manor house.

Great-Aunt Clara lived here with three servants to minister to her wants, and when we arrived there was great excitement as we were quite unexpected.

'Why, bless my soul if it b'aint Miss Alvean!' cried an elderly housekeeper. 'And who be this you have brought with 'ee, my dear?'

'It is Miss Leigh, my governess,' said Alvean.

'Well now! And be there just the two on you? And b'aint your papa here?'

'No. Papa has gone to Penzance.'

I wondered then whether I had been wrong in acceding to Alvean's wishes, and had forgotten my position by imposing myself on Great-Aunt Clara without first asking permission.

I wondered if I should be banished to the kitchen to eat with the servants. Such a procedure did not greatly disturb me and I would rather have done that than sit down with a haughty, disapproving old woman.

But I was soon reassured. We were taken into a drawing room and there was Great-Aunt Clara, a charming old lady seated in an armchair, white-haired, pink-cheeked with bright friendly eyes. There was an ebony stick beside her, so I guessed she had difficulty in walking.

Alvean ran to her and she was warmly embraced.

Then the lively blue eyes were on me.

'So you are Alvean's governess, my dear,', she said. 'Well, that is nice. And how thoughtful of you to bring her to see me. It is particularly fortunate, for I have my grandson staying with me and I fear he grows a little weary of having no playmates of his own age. When he hears Alvean has arrived he'll be quite excited.'

I did not believe that the grandson could be any more excited than Great-Aunt Clara herself. She was certainly charming to me, so much so that I forgot my diffidence and I really did feel like a friend calling on a friend, rather than a governess bringing her charge to see a relative.

Dandelion wine was brought out and we were pressed to take a glass. There were wine cakes with it and I must say I found the wine delicious. I allowed Alvean to take a very small glass of it but when I had taken mine I wondered whether I had been wise, for it was certainly potent.

Great-Aunt Clara wished to hear all the news of Mount Mellyn; she was indeed a garrulous lady, and I guessed it was due to the fact that she lived a somewhat lonely life in her house on the moors.

The grandson appeared – a handsome boy a little younger than Alvean – and the pair of them went off to play, although I warned Alvean not to go too far away as we must be home before dark.

As soon as Alvean had left us I saw that Great-Aunt Clara was eager for a real gossip; and whether it was due to the fact that I had taken her potent dandelion wine or whether I believed her to be a link with Alice, I am not sure; but I found her conversation fascinating.

She spoke of Alice as I had not until now heard her spoken of – with complete candour; and I quickly realized that from this gossipy lady I was going to discover a great deal more than I could from anyone else.

As soon as we were alone she said: 'And now tell me how things really are at Mount Mellyn.'

I raised my eyebrows as though I did not fully comprehend her meaning.

She went on: 'It was such a shock when poor Alice died. It was so sudden. Such a tragic thing to happen to such a young girl – for she was little more than a girl.'

'Is that so?'

'Don't tell me you haven't heard what happened.'

'I know very little about it.'

'Alice and Geoffry Nansellock, you know. They went off together . . . eloped. And then this terrible accident.'

'I have heard that there was an accident.'

'I think of them – those two young people – quite often, in the dead of the night. And then I blame myself.'

I was astonished. I did not understand how this gentle talkative old lady could blame herself for Alice's infidelity to her husband.

'One should never interfere in other people's lives. Or should one? What do you think, my dear? If one can be helpful—'

'Yes,' I said firmly, 'if one can be helpful I think one should be forgiven for interference.'

'But how is one to know whether one is being helpful or the reverse?'

'One can only do what one thinks is right.'

'But one might be doing right and yet be quite unhelpful?'

'Yes, I suppose so.'

'I think of her so much . . . my poor little niece. She was a sweet creature. But, shall I say, not equipped to face the cruelties of fate.'

'Oh, was she like that?'

'I can see that you, Miss Leigh, are so good for that poor child. Alice would be so happy if she could see what you've done for her. The last time I saw her she was with her . . . with Connan. She was not nearly so happy . . . so relaxed as she is to-day.'

'I'm so glad of that. I am encouraging her to ride. I think that has done her a world of good.' I was loath to interrupt that flow of talk from which I might extract some fresh evidence about Alice. I was afraid that at any moment Alvean and the grandson would return, and I knew that in their presence there would be no confidences. 'You are telling me about Alvean's mother. I am sure you have nothing with which to reproach yourself.'

'I wish I could believe that. It worries me sometimes. Perhaps I shouldn't weary you. But you seem so sympathetic, and you are there, living in the house. You are looking after little Alvean like . . . like a mother. It makes me feel very grateful to you, my dear.'

'I am paid for doing it, you know.' I could not resist that remark, and I thought of the smile it would have brought to Peter Nansellock's lips.

'There are some things in this world which cannot be bought. Love . . . devotion . . . they are some of them. Alice stayed with me before her marriage. Here . . . in this house. It was so convenient, you see. It was only a few hours' ride from Mount Mellyn. It gave the young people a chance to know each other.'

'The young people?'

'The engaged pair.'

'Did they not know each other then?'

'The marriage had been arranged when they were in their cradles. She brought him a lot of property. They were well matched. Both rich, both of good families. Connan's father was alive then and, you know, Connan was a wild boy with a will of his own. The feeling was that they should be married as soon as possible.'

'So he allowed this marriage to be arranged for him?'

'They both took it as a matter of course. Well, she stayed with me several months before the wedding. I loved her dearly.'

I thought of little Gilly and I said: 'I think a great many people loved her dearly.'

Great-Aunt Clara nodded; and at that moment Alvean and the grandson came in.

'I want to show Alvean my drawings,' he announced.

'Well, go and get them,' said his grandmother. 'Bring them down and show her here.'

I believed that she realized she had talked a little too much and was afraid of her own garrulity. It was clear to me that she was the sort of woman who could never keep a secret; how could she when she was ready to confide secret family history to me, a stranger?

The grandson returned with his portfolio, and the children sat at the table. I went over to them and I was so proud of Alvean's attempts at drawing that I determined to speak to her father about that at the first opportunity.

Yet as I watched, I felt frustrated. I was sure that Great-Aunt Clara had been on the point of confiding something to me which was of the utmost importance.

Aunt Clara gave us luncheon and we left immediately after.

We found our way back with the utmost care, but I was determined to ride out again, and that before long, to the house on the moors.

When I was strolling through the village one day I passed the little jeweller's shop there. But perhaps that was scarcely the term to use when describing it. There were no valuable gems in the window; but a few silver brooches and plain gold rings, some engraved with the word Mizpah, or studded with semi-precious stones such as turquoises, topaz, and garnets. I guessed that the villagers bought their engagement and wedding rings here and that the jeweller made a living by doing repairs.

I saw in the window a brooch in the form of a whip. It was of silver, and quite tasteful, I decided, although it was by no means expensive.

I wanted to buy that whip for Alvean and give it to her the night before the horse show, telling her that it was to bring her luck.

I opened the door and went down the three steps into the shop.

Seated behind the counter was an old man wearing steel-rimmed spectacles. He let his glasses fall to the tip of his nose as he peered at me.

'I want to see the brooch in the window,' I said. 'The silver one in the form of a whip.'

'Oh yes, Miss,' he said, 'I'll show it to you with pleasure.'

He brought it from the window and handed it to me.

'Here,' he said, 'pin it on and have a look at it.' He indicated the little mirror on the counter. I obeyed him and decided that the brooch was neat, not gaudy, and in the best of taste.

As I was looking at it I noticed a tray of ornaments with little tickets attached to them. They were clearly jewellery which he had received for repair. Then I wondered whether this was the jeweller to whom Alice had brought her brooch last July.

The jeweller said to me: 'You're from Mount Mellyn, Miss?'

'Yes,' I said; and I smiled encouragingly. I was becoming very ready to talk to anyone who I thought might have any information to offer me on this subject which appeared to obsess me. 'As a matter of fact I want to give the brooch to my pupil.'

Like most people in small villages he was very interested in those living around him.

'Ah,' he said, 'poor motherless little girl. It's heartening to think she has a kind lady like yourself to look after her now.'

'I'll take the brooch,' I told him.

'I'll find a little box for it. A nice little box makes all the difference when it be a matter of a present, don't you agree, Miss?'

'Most certainly.'

He bent down and from under the counter brought a small cardboard-box which he began to stuff with cotton-wool.

'Make a little nest for it, Miss,' he said with a smile.

I fancied that he was loth to let me go.

'Don't see much of them from the Mount these days. Mrs. TreMellyn, her was often in.'

'Yes, I suppose so.'

'See a little trinket in the window and she'd buy it ... sometimes for herself, sometimes for others. Why, she was in here the day she died.'

His voice had sunk to a whisper and I felt excitement grip me. I thought of Alice's diary which was still in the concealed pocket of her habit.

'Really?' I said encouragingly.

He laid the brooch in the cotton-wool and looked at me. 'I thought 'twas a little odd at the time. I remember it very clearly. She came in here and said to me: "Have you got the brooch done, Mr. Pastern? It's very important that I should have it. I'm anxious to wear it to-morrow. I'm going to a dinner party at Mr. and Mrs. Trelanders', and Mrs. Trelander gave me that brooch as a Christmas present so you see it's most important I should wear it to show her I appreciate it." ' His eyes were puzzled as they looked into mine. 'She were a lady who talked like that. She'd tell you where she was going, why she wanted a thing. I couldn't believe my ears when I heard she'd left home that very evening. Didn't seem possible that she could have been telling me about the dinner party she was going to the next day, you see.'

'No,' I said, 'it was certainly very strange.'

'You see, Miss, there was no need for her to say anything to me like. If she'd said it to some it might seem as though she was trying to pull the wool over their eyes. But why should she say such a thing to me, Miss? That's what I've been wondering. Sometimes I think of it ... and still wonder.'

'I expect there's an answer,' I said. 'Perhaps you misunderstood her.'

He shook his head. He did not believe that he had misunderstood. Nor did I. I had seen the entry in her diary and what I had read there confirmed what the jeweller had said.

Celestine Nansellock rode over next day to see Alvean. We were about to go for our riding lesson, and she insisted on coming with us.

'Now, Alvean,' I said, 'is the time to have a little rehearsal. See if you can surprise Miss Nansellock as you hope to surprise your father.'

We were going to practise jumping, and we rode down through the Mellyn village and beyond.

Celestine was clearly astonished by Alvean's progress.

'But you've done wonders with her, Miss Leigh.'

We watched Alvean canter round the field. 'I hope her father is going to be pleased. She has entered for one of the events in the show.'

'He'll be delighted, I'm sure.'

'Please don't say anything to him beforehand. We do want it to be a surprise.'

Celestine smiled at me. 'He'll be very grateful to you, Miss Leigh. I'm sure of that.'

'I'm counting on his being rather pleased.'

I was conscious of her eyes upon me as she smiled at me benignly. She said suddenly: 'Oh, Miss Leigh, about my brother Peter. I did want to speak to you confidentially about that matter of Jacinth.'

I flushed faintly, and I was annoyed with myself for doing so.

'I know he gave you the horse and you returned it as too valuable a gift.'

'Too valuable a gift to accept,' I answered, 'and too expensive for me to be able to maintain.'

'Of course. I'm afraid he is very thoughtless. But he is the most generous man alive. He's rather afraid he has offended you.'

'Please tell him I'm not offended, and if he thinks awhile he will understand why I can't accept such a gift.'

'I explained to him. He admires you very much, Miss Leigh, but there was an ulterior motive behind the gift. He wanted a good home for Jacinth. You know that he plans to leave England.'

'He did mention it.'

'I expect he will sell some of the horses. I shall keep a couple for myself, but there is no point in keeping an expensive stable with only myself at the house.'

'No, I suppose not.'

'He saw you on Jacinth and thinks you'd be a worthy mistress for her. That was why he wanted you to have her. He's very fond of that mare.'

'I see.'

'Miss Leigh, you would like to possess a horse like that?'

'Who wouldn't?'

'Suppose I asked Connan if it could be taken into his stables and kept there for you to ride. How would that be?'

I replied emphatically: 'It is most kind of you, Miss Nansellock, and I do appreciate your desire – and that of your brother – to please me. But I do not wish for any special favours here. Mr. TreMellyn has a full and adequate stable for the needs of us all. I should be very much against asking for special favours for myself.'

'I see,' she said, 'that you are very determined and very proud.'

She leaned forward and touched my hand in a very friendly manner. There was a faint mist of tears in her eyes. She was touched by my position, and understood how desperately I clung to my pride because it was my only possession.

I thought her kind and considerate, and I could understand why Alice had made a friend of her. I felt that I too could easily become her friend, for she had never made me in the least conscious of my social position in the house.

One day, I thought, I'll tell her what I've discovered about Alice.

But not yet. I was, as her brother had said, as spiky as a hedgehog. I did not think for a moment that I should be rebuffed by Celestine Nansellock, but just at this time I was not going to run any risk.

Alvean joined us, and Celestine complimented her on her riding. Then we went back to the house, and tea, over which I presided, was served in the punch room.

I thought what a happy afternoon that was.

Connan TreMellyn came back the day before the show. I was glad he had not returned before, because I was afraid that Alvean might betray her excitement.

I was entered for one of the early events in which points were scored, particularly for jumping. It was what they called a mixed event which meant that men and women competed together.

Tapperty, who knew I was going to enter, wouldn't hear of my riding on Dion.

'Why, Miss,' he said, the day before the show, 'if you'd have took Jacinth when she was offered you, you would have got first prize. That mare be a winner and so would you be, Miss, on her back. Old Dion, he's a good fellow, but he ain't no prize winner. How'd you say to taking Royal Rover?'

'What if Mr. TreMellyn objected?'

Tapperty winked. 'Nay, he'd not object. He'll be riding out to the show on May Morning, so old Royal 'ull be free. I'll tell 'ee what, just suppose master was to say to me "Saddle up Royal Rover for me, Tapperty." Right, then I'd saddle the Rover for him and it would be May Morning for you, Miss. Nothing 'ud please master more than for to see his horse win a prize.'

I was anxious to show off before Connan TreMellyn and I agreed to Tapperty's suggestion. After all, I was teaching his daughter to ride and that meant that I could, with the approval of his head stable man, make my selection from the stables.

The night before the show I presented Alvean with the brooch.

She was extremely delighted.

'It's a whip!' she cried.

'It will pin your cravat,' I said, 'and I hope bring you luck.'

'It will, Miss. I know it will.'

'Well, don't rely on it too much. Remember luck only comes to those who deserve it.' I quoted the beginning of an old rhyme which Father used to say to us.

'Your head and your heart keep boldly up,

Your chin and your heels keep down.' I went on: 'And when you take your jump together . . . go with Prince.'

'I'll remember.'

'Excited?'

'It seems so long in coming.'

'It'll come fast enough.'

That night when I went in to say good night to her I sat on her bed and we talked about the show.

I was a little anxious about her, because she was too excited, and I tried to calm her down. I told her she must go to sleep for if she did not she would not be fresh for the morning.

'But how does one sleep, Miss,' she asked, 'when sleep won't come?'

I realized then the magnitude of what I had done. A few months before, when I had come to this house, this girl had been afraid to mount a horse; now she was looking forward to competing at the horse show.

That was all well and good. I would have preferred her interest not to have been centred so wholeheartedly on her father. It was his approval which meant so much to her.

She was not only eager; she was apprehensive, so desperately did she long for his admiration.

I went to my room and came back with a book of Mr. Longfellow's poems.

I sat down by her bed and began to read to her, for I knew of nothing to turn the mind to peace than his narrative poem, 'Hiawatha.'

I often quoted it when I was trying to sleep and then I would feel myself torn from the events of this world in which I lived and in my imagination I would wander along through the primeval forests with the 'rushings of great rivers' . . . and their wild reverberations.'

The words flowed from my lips. I knew I was conjuring up visions for Alvean. She had forgotten the show . . . her fears and her hopes. She was with the little Hiawatha sitting at the feet of the good Nokomis and – she slept.

I woke up on the day of the horse show to find the mist had penetrated my room. I got out of bed and went to the window. Little wisps of it encircled the palm trees and the feathery leaves of the evergreen pines were decorated with little drops of moisture.

'I hope the mist lifts before the afternoon,' I said to myself.

But all through the morning it persisted, and there were anxious looks and whispers throughout the house where everyone was thinking of the show. Most of the servants were going. They always did, Kitty told me, because the master had special interest in it as one of the judges, and Billy Trehay and some of the stable boys were entrants.

'It do put master in a good mood to see his horses win,' said Kitty: 'but they say he's always harder on his own than on others.'

Immediately after luncheon Alvean and I set out; she was riding Black Prince and I was on Royal Rover. It was exhilarating to be on a good horse, and I felt as excited as Alvean; I fear I was just as eager to shine in the eyes of Connan TreMellyn as she was.

The show was being held in a big field close to the village church, and when we arrived the crowds were already gathering.

Alvean and I parted company when we reached the field and I discovered that the event in which I was competing was one of the first.

The show was intended to start at two-fifteen, but there was the usual delay, and at twenty past we were still waiting to begin.

The mist had lifted slightly, but it was a leaden day; the sky was like a grey blanket and everything seemed to have accumulated a layer of moisture.

The sea smell was strong but the waves were silent to-day and the cry of the gulls was more melancholy than ever.

Connan arrived with the other judges; there were three of them, all local worthies. Connan, I saw, had come on May Morning, as I expected, since I had been given Royal Rover.

The village band struck up a traditional air and everyone stood still and sang.

It was very impressive, I thought, to hear those words sung with such fervour in that misty field:

> *'And shall they scorn Tre Pol and Pen,*
> *And shall Trelawney die?*
> *Then twenty thousand Cornish men*
> *Will know the reason why.'*

A proud song, I thought, for an insular people; and they stood at attention as they sang. I noticed little Gillyflower standing there, singing with the rest, and I was surprised to see her; she was with Daisy and I hoped the girl would look after her.

She saw me and I waved to her, but she lowered her eyes at once, yet I could see that she was smiling to herself and I was quite pleased.

A rider came close to me and a voice said: 'Well, if it is not Miss Leigh, herself!'

I turned and saw Peter Nansellock; he was mounted on Jacinth.

'Good afternoon,' I said, and my eyes lingered on the perfection of Jacinth.

I was wearing a placard with a number on my back which had been put there by one of the organizers.

'Don't tell me,' said Peter Nansellock, 'that you and I are competitors in this first event.'

'Are you in it then?'

He turned, and I saw the placard on his back.

'I haven't a hope,' I said.

'Against me?'

'Against Jacinth,' I answered.

'Miss Leigh, you could have been riding her.'

'You must have been mad to do what you did. You set the stables talking.'

'Who cares for stable boys?'

'I do.'

'Then you are not being your usual sensible self.'

'A governess has to care for the opinions of all and sundry.'

'You are not an ordinary governess.'

'Do you know, Mr. Nansellock,' I said lightly, 'I believe all the governesses in your life were no ordinary governesses. If they had been, perhaps they would have had no place in your life.'

I gave Royal Rover a gentle touch on the flank and he responded immediately.

I did not see Peter again until he was competing. He went before I did. I watched him ride round the field. He and Jacinth seemed like one animal.

Like a centaur, I thought. Were they the creatures with the head and shoulders of a man and the body of a horse?

'Oh, perfect,' I exclaimed aloud as I watched him take the jumps and canter gracefully round the field. And who couldn't, I said to myself maliciously, on a mare like that!

A round of applause followed him as he finished his turn.

Mine did not come until some time later.

I saw Connan TreMellyn in the judges' stand. And I whispered: 'Royal Rover, help me. I want you to beat Jacinth. I want you to win this prize. I want to show Connan TreMellyn that there is one thing I can do. Help me, Royal Rover.'

The sensitive ears seemed to prick up as Royal Rover moved daintily forward and I knew that he heard me, and would respond to the appeal in my voice.

'Come on, Rover,' I whispered. 'We can do it.'

And we went round as faultlessly, I hoped, as Jacinth had. I heard the applause burst out as I finished, and walked my horse away.

We waited until the rest of the competitors were finished and the results were called. I was glad that they were announced at the end of each event. People were more interested immediately after they had seen a performance. The practice of announcing all winners at the end of the meeting I had always thought to be a sort of anti-climax.

'This one is a tie,' Connan was saying. 'Two competitors scored full marks in this one. It's most unusual, but I am happy to say that the winners are a lady and a gentleman: Miss Martha Leigh on Royal Rover, and Mr. Peter Nansellock on Jacinth.'

We trotted up to take our prizes.

Connan said: 'The prize is a silver rose bowl. How can we split it? Obviously we cannot do that so the lady gets the bowl.'

'Of course,' said Peter.

'But you get a silver spoon,' Connan told him. 'Consolation for having tied with a lady.'

We accepted our prizes, and as Connan gave me mine he was smiling, very well pleased.

'Good show, Miss Leigh. I did not know anyone could get so much out of Royal Rover.'

I patted Royal Rover and said, more for his hearing than anyone else's: 'I couldn't have had a better partner.'

Then Peter and I trotted off; I with my rose bowl, he with his spoon.

Peter said: 'If you had been on Jacinth you would have been the undisputed winner.'

'I should still have had to compete against you on something else.'

'Jacinth would win any race . . . just look at her. Isn't she perfection? Never mind, you got the rose bowl.'

'I shall always feel that it is not entirely mine.'

'When you arrange your roses you will always think, Part of this belonged to that man . . . what was his name? He was always charming to me, but I was a little acid with him. I'm sorry now.'

'I rarely forget people's names, and I feel I have nothing to regret in my conduct towards you.'

'There is a way out of this rose bowl situation. Suppose we set up house together. It could have a place of honour there. "Ours," we could say, and both feel happy about it.'

I was angry at this flippancy, and I said: 'We should, I am sure, feel far from happy about everything else:'

And I rode away.

I wanted to be near the judges' stand when Alvean appeared. I wanted to watch Connan's face as his daughter performed. I wanted to be close when she took her prize – which I was sure she would, for she was eager to win and she had worked hard. The jumps should offer no difficulty to her.

The elementary jumping contest for eight-year-olds began and I was feverishly impatient, waiting for Alvean's turn as I watched those little girls and boys go through their performances. But there was no Alvean. The contest was over and the results announced.

I felt sick with disappointment. So she had panicked at the last moment. My work had been in vain. When the great moment came her fears had returned.

When the prizes were being given I went in search of Alvean, but I could not find her, and as the more advanced jumping contest for the eight-year-old group was about to begin, it occurred to me that she must have gone back to the house. I pictured her abject misery because after all our talk, all our practice, her courage had failed her at the critical moment.

I wanted to get away, for now my own petty triumph meant nothing to me, and I wanted to find Alvean quickly, to comfort her if need be, and I felt sure she would need my comfort.

I rode back to Mount Mellyn, hung up my saddle and bridle, gave Royal Rover a quick rub-down and a drink, and left him munching an armful of hay in his stall while I went into the house.

The back door was unlatched and I went in. The house seemed very quiet. I guessed that all but Mrs. Polgrey were at the horse show. Mrs. Polgrey would probably be in her room having her afternoon doze.

I went up to my room and called Alvean as I went.

There was no answer so I hurried through the schoolroom to her room which was deserted. Perhaps she had not come back to the house. I then remembered that I had not seen Prince in the stables. But then I had forgotten to look in his stall.

I came back to my room and stood uncertainly at the window. I thought, I'll go back to the show. She's probably still there.

And as I stood at the window I knew that someone was in Alice's apartments. I was not sure how I knew. It may only have been a shadow across the window-pane. But I was certain that someone was there.

Without thinking very much of what I would do when I discovered who was there I ran from my room, through the gallery to Alice's rooms. My riding-boots must have made a clatter along the gallery. I threw open the door of the room and shouted: 'Who is here? Who is it?'

No one was in the room, but I saw in that fleeting second, the communicating door between the two rooms close.

I had a feeling that it might be Alvean who was there, and I was sure that Alvean needed me at this moment. I had to find her, and any fear I might have had, disappeared. I ran across the dressing room and opened the door of the bedroom. I looked round the room. I ran to the curtains and felt them. There was no one there. Then I ran to the other door and opened it. I was in another dressing room and the communicating door – similar to that in Alice's – was open. I went through and immediately I knew that I was in Connan's bedroom for I saw a cravat, which he had been wearing that morning, flung on the dressing table. I saw his dressing gown and slippers.

The sight of these made me blush and realize that I was trespassing in a part of the house where I had no right to be.

But someone other than Connan had been there before me. Who was it?

I went swiftly across the bedroom, opened the door and found myself in the gallery.

There was no sign of anyone there so I went slowly back to my room.

Who had been in Alice's room? Who was it who haunted the place?

'Alice,' I said aloud. 'Is it you, Alice?'

Then I went down to the stables. I wanted to get back to the show and find Alvean.

I had saddled Royal Rover and was riding out of the stable yard when I saw Billy Trehay hurrying towards the house.

He said: 'Oh Miss, there's been an accident. A terrible accident.'

'What?' I stammered.

'It's Miss Alvean. She took a toss in the jumping.'

'But she wasn't in the jumping!' I cried.

'Yes she were. In the eight-year-olds. Advanced class. It was the high jump. Prince stumbled and fell. They went rolling over and over . . .'

For a moment I lost control of myself; I covered my face with my hands and cried out in protest.

'They were looking for you, Miss,' he said.

'Where is she then?'

'She were down there in the field. They'm afraid to move her. They wrapped her up and now they'm waiting for Dr. Pengelly to come. They think she may have broken some bones. Her father's with her. He kept saying, "Where's Miss Leigh?" And I saw you leave so I came after you. I think perhaps you'd better be getting down there, Miss . . . since he was asking for you like.'

I turned away and rode as fast as I dared down the hill into the village, and as I rode I prayed, and scolded:

'Oh God, let her be all right. Oh Alvean, you little fool! It would have been enough to take the simple jumps. That would have pleased him enough. You could have done the high jumps next year. Alvean, my poor, poor child.'

And then: 'It's his fault. It's all his fault. If he had been a human parent this wouldn't have happened.'

And so I came to the field. I shall never forget what I saw there: Alvean lying unconscious on the grass, and the group round her and others standing about. There would be no more competitions that day.

For a moment I was terrified that she had been killed.

Connan's face was stern as he looked at me.

'Miss Leigh,' he said, 'I'm glad you've come. There's been an accident. Alvean . . .'

I ignored him and knelt down beside her.

'Alvean . . . my dear . . .' I murmured.

She opened her eyes then. She did not look like my arrogant little pupil. She was just a lost and bewildered child.

But she smiled.

'Don't go away . . .' she said.

'No, I'll stay here.'

'You did go . . . before . . .' she murmured, and I had to bend low to catch her words.

And then I knew. She was not speaking to Martha Leigh, the governess. She was speaking to Alice.

Chapter Six

Dr. Pengelly had arrived on the field and had diagnosed a broken tibia; but he could not say if any further damage had been done. He set the fractured bone and drove Alvean back to Mount Mellyn in his carriage while Connan and I rode back together in silence.

Alvean was taken to her room and given a sedative by the doctor.

'Now,' he said, 'there is nothing we can do but wait. I'll come back again in a few hours' time. It may be that the child is suffering acute shock. In the meantime we will keep her warm and let her sleep. She should sleep for several hours, and at the end of that time we shall know how deeply she has suffered from this shock.'

When the doctor had left, Connan said to me: 'Miss Leigh, I want to have a talk with you. Come to the punch room . . . now, will you please.'

I followed him there and he went on:

'There is nothing we can do but wait, Miss Leigh. We must try to be calm.'

I realized that he could never have seen me agitated as I was now, and he had probably considered me incapable of such deep feeling.

Impulsively I said: 'I find it hard to be as calm about my charge as you are about your daughter, Mr. TreMellyn.'

I was so frightened and worried that I wanted to blame someone for what had happened so I blamed him.

'Whatever made the child attempt such a thing?' he demanded.

'You made her,' I retorted. 'You!'

'I! But I had no idea that she was so advanced in her riding.'

I realized later that I was on the verge of hysteria. I believed that Alvean might have done herself some terrible injury and I felt almost certain that a child of her temperament would never want to ride again. I believed I had been wrong in my methods. I should not have tried to overcome her fear of horses; I had tried to win my way into her affections by showing her the way to win those of her father.

I could not rid myself of a terrible sense of guilt, and I was desperately trying to. I was saying to myself, This is a house of tragedy. Who are you to meddle in the lives of these people? What are you trying to do? To change Alvean? To change her father? To discover the truth about Alice? What do you think you are? God?

But I wouldn't blame myself entirely. I was looking for a scapegoat. I was saying to myself, He is to blame. If he had been different, none of this would have happened. I'm sure of that.

I had lost control of my feelings and on the rare occasions when people like myself do that, they usually do it more completely than those who are prone to hysterical outbursts.

'No,' I cried out, 'of course you had no idea that she was so advanced. How could you when you had never shown the slightest interest in the child? She was breaking her heart through your neglect. It was for that reason that she attempted this thing of which she was not capable.'

'My dear Miss Leigh,' he murmured. 'My dear Miss Leigh.' And he was looking at me in complete bewilderment.

I thought to myself, What do I care! I shall be dismissed, but in any case I have failed. I had hoped to do the impossible – to bring this man out of his own selfishness to care a little for his lonely daughter. And what have I done – made a complete mess of it and perhaps maimed the child for life. A fine one I was to complain of the conduct of others.

But I continued to blame him, and I no longer cared what I said.

'When I came here,' I went on, 'it did not take me long to understand the state of affairs. That poor motherless child was starved . . . Oh, I know she had her broth and her bread and butter at regular intervals. But there is another starvation besides that of the body. She was starved of the affection which she might expect from a parent and, as you see, she was ready to risk her life to win it.'

'Miss Leigh, please, I beg of you, do be calm, do be reasonable. Are you telling me that Alvean did that . . .'

But I would not let him speak. 'She did that for you. She thought it would please you. She has been practising for weeks.'

'I see,' he said. Then he took his handkerchief from his pocket and wiped my eyes. 'You do not realize it, Miss Leigh,' he went on almost tenderly, 'but there are tears on your cheeks.'

I took the handkerchief from him and angrily wiped my tears away.

'They are tears of anger,' I said.

'And of sorrow. Dear Miss Leigh, I think you care very much for Alvean.'

'She is a child,' I said, 'and it was my job to care for her. God knows, there are few others to do it.'

'I see,' he answered, 'that I have been behaving in a very reprehensible manner.'

'How could you . . . if you had any feeling? Your own daughter! She lost her mother. Don't you see that because of that she needed special care?'

Then he said a surprising thing: 'Miss Leigh, you came here to teach Alvean, but I think you have taught me a great deal too.'

I looked at him in amazement; I was holding his handkerchief a few inches from my tear-stained face; and at that moment Celestine Nansellock came in.

She looked at me in some astonishment, but only for a second. Then she burst out: 'What is this terrible thing I've heard?'

'There's been an accident, Celeste,' said Connan. 'Alvean was thrown.'

'Oh . . . no!' Celestine uttered a piteous cry. 'And what . . . and where . . .?'

'She's in her room now,' Connan explained. 'Pengelly's set the leg. Poor child. At the moment she is asleep. He gave her something to make her sleep. He's coming again in a few hours' time.'

'But how badly . . .?'

'He's not sure. But I've seen accidents like this before. I think she'll be all right.'

I was not sure whether he meant that or whether he was trying to soothe Celestine who was so upset. I felt drawn towards her; she was the only person, I believed, who really cared about Alvean.

'Poor Miss Leigh is very distressed,' said Connan. 'I think she fancies it is her fault. I do want to assure her that I don't think that at all.'

My fault! But how could I be blamed for teaching the child to ride? And having taught her, what harm was there in her entering for a competition? No, it was his fault, I wanted to shout. She would have been content to do what she was capable of, but for him.

I said with defiance in my voice: 'Alvean was so anxious to impress her father that she undertook more than she could do. I am sure that had she believed her father would be content to see her victorious in the elementary event she would not have attempted the advanced.

Celestine had sat down and covered her face with her hands. I thought fleetingly of the occasion when I had seen her in the churchyard, kneeling by Alice's grave. I thought, Poor Celestine, she loves Alvean as her own child, because she has none of her own and perhaps believes she never will have.

'We can only wait and see,' said Connan.

I rose and said: 'There is no point in my remaining here. I will go to my room.'

But Connan put out a hand and said almost authoritatively: 'No, stay here, Miss Leigh. Stay with us. You care for her deeply, I know.'

I looked down at my riding habit – Alice's riding habit – and I said: 'I think I should change.'

It seemed that in that moment he looked at me in a new light – and perhaps so did Celestine. If they did not look at my face I must have appeared to be remarkably like Alice.

I knew it was important that I change my clothes, for in my grey cotton dress with its severe bodice I should be the governess once more and that would help me to control my feelings.

Connan nodded. He said: 'But come back when you've changed, Miss Leigh. We have to comfort each other, and I want you to be here when the doctor returns.'

So I went to my room and I took off Alice's riding habit and put on my own grey cotton.

I was right. The cotton did help to restore my equilibrium. I began to wonder, as I buttoned the bodice, what I had said, in my outburst, to Connan TreMellyn.

The mirror showed me a face that was ravaged by grief and anxiety, eyes which burned with anger and resentment, and a mouth that was tremulous with fear.

I sent for hot water. Daisy wanted to talk, but she saw that I was too upset to do so and she went quickly away.

I bathed my face and when I had done so I went down to the punch-room and rejoined Connan and Celestine, there to await the coming of Dr. Pengelly.

It seemed a long time before the doctor returned. Mrs. Polgrey made a pot of strong tea and Connan, Celestine and I sat together drinking it. I did not feel astonished then, but I did later, because the accident seemed to have made them both forget that I was merely the governess. But perhaps I mean it made Connan forget; Celestine had always treated me without that condescension which I thought I had discerned in others.

Connan seemed to have forgotten my outburst and treated me with a courtly consideration and a new gentleness. I believed he was anxious that I should not blame myself in any way, and he knew that the reason I had turned on him so vehemently was because I wondered whether I had been at fault.

'She'll get over this,' he said. 'And she'll want to ride again. Why, when I was a little older than herself I had an accident which I'm sure was worse than this one. I got it in the collar-bone and was unable to ride for weeks. I could scarcely wait to get back on a horse.'

Celestine shivered. 'I shall never have a moment's peace if she rides again after this.'

'Oh Celeste, you would wrap her in cotton wool. And then what would happen? She would go out and catch her death of cold. You must not coddle children too much. After all, they've got to face the world. They must be prepared for it in some way. What does the expert have to say to that?'

He was looking at me anxiously. I knew he was trying to keep up our spirits. He knew how deeply Celestine and I felt about this, and he was trying to be kind.

I said: 'I believe one shouldn't coddle. But if children are really set against something I don't think they should be forced to do it.'

'But she was not forced to ride.'

'She did it most willingly,' I answered. 'But I cannot be sure whether she did it from a love of riding or from an intense desire to please you.'

'Well,' he said almost lightly, 'is it not an excellent thing that a child should seek to please a parent?'

'But it should not be necessary to risk a life for the sake of a smile.'

My anger was rising again and my fingers gripped the cotton of my skirt as though to remind me that I was not in Alice's riding habit now. I was the governess in my cotton gown, and it was not for me to press forward my opinions.

Both Celestine and Connan were surprised at my remark, and I went on quickly: 'For instance, Alvean's talents may lie in another direction. I think she has artistic ability. She has done some good drawings. Mr. TreMellyn, I have been going to ask you for some time whether you would consider letting her have drawing lessons.'

There was a tense silence in the room and I wondered why they both looked so startled.

I blundered on: 'I am sure there is great talent there, and I do not feel that it should be ignored.'

Connan said slowly: 'But Miss Leigh, you are here to teach my daughter. Why should it be necessary to engage other teachers?'

'Because,' I replied boldly, 'I believe she has a special talent. I believe it would be an added interest in her life if she were to be given drawing lessons. These should be given by a specialist in the art. She is good enough for that. I'm merely a governess, Mr. TreMellyn, I am not an artist as well.'

He said rather gruffly: 'Well, we shall have to go into this at some time.' He changed the subject, and shortly afterwards the doctor arrived.

I waited outside in the corridor while Connan and Celestine were with Alvean and the doctor.

A hundred images of disaster crowded into my mind. I imagined that she died of her injuries. I saw myself leaving the place, never to return. If I did that I should feel that my life had been incomplete in some way. I realized that if I had to go away I should be a very unhappy woman. Then I thought of her, maimed for life, more difficult than she had been previously, a wretched and unhappy little girl; and myself devoting my life to her. It was a gloomy picture.

Celestine joined me.

'This suspense is terrible,' she said. 'I wonder whether we ought to get another doctor. Dr. Pengelly is sixty. I am afraid . . .'

'He seemed efficient,' I said.

'I want the best for her. If anything happens to her . . .'

She was biting her lips in anguish, and I thought how strange it was that she, who always seemed so calm about everything else, should be so emotional over Alice and her daughter.

I wanted to put my arm about her and comfort her, but of course, remembering my position, I did no such thing.

Doctor Pengelly came out with Connan, and the doctor was smiling.

'Injuries,' he said, 'a fractured tibia. Beyond that . . . there's very little wrong.'

'Oh, thank God!' cried Celestine, and I echoed her words.

'A day or so and she'll be feeling better. It'll just be a matter of mending that fracture. Children's bones mend easily. There's nothing for you two ladies to worry about.'

'Can we see her?' asked Celestine eagerly.

'Yes, of course you can. She's awake now, and she asked for Miss Leigh. I'm going to give her another dose in half an hour, and that will ensure a good night's sleep. You'll see a difference in her in the morning.'

We went into the room. Alvean was lying on her back looking very ill, poor child; but she gave us a wan smile when she saw us.

'Hallo, Miss,' she said. 'Hallo, Aunt Celestine.'

Celestine knelt by the bed, took her hand and covered it with kisses. I stood on the other side of the bed and the child's eyes were on me.

'I didn't do it,' she said.

'Well, it was a good try.'

Connan was standing at the foot of the bed.

I went on: 'Your father was proud of you.'

'He'll think I was silly,' she said.

'No he doesn't,' I cried vehemently. 'He is here to tell you so.'

Connan came round to the side of the bed and stood beside me.

'He's proud of you,' I said. 'He told me so. He said it didn't matter that you fell. He said all that mattered was that you tried; and you'd do it next time.'

'Did he? Did he?'

'Yes, he did,' I cried; and there was an angry note in my voice because he still said nothing and the child was waiting for him to confirm my words.

Then he spoke. 'You did splendidly, Alvean. I *was* proud of you.'

A faint smile touched those pale lips. Then she murmured: 'Miss . . . oh Miss . . .' And then: 'Don't go away, will you. Don't *you* go away.'

I sank down on my knees then. I took her hand and kissed it. The tears were on my cheeks again.

I cried: 'I'll stay, Alvean. I'll stay with you always . . .'

I looked up and saw Celestine watching me from the other side of the bed. I was aware of Connan, standing beside me. Then I amended those words, and the governess in me spoke. 'I'll stay as long as I'm wanted,' I said firmly.

Alvean was satisfied.

When she was sleeping we left her and, as I was about to go to my room, Connan said: 'Come into my library a moment with us, Miss Leigh. The doctor wants to discuss the case with you.'

So I went into his library with him, Celestine and the doctor, and we talked of the nursing of Alvean.

Celestine said: 'I shall come over every day. In fact I wonder, Connan, whether I won't come over and stay while she's ill. It might make things easier.'

'You ladies must settle that,' answered Dr. Pengelly. 'Keep the child amused. We don't want her getting depressed while those bones are knitting together.'

'We'll keep her amused,' I said. 'Any special diet, Doctor?'

'For a day or so, light invalid foods. Steamed fish, milk puddings, custards and so on. But after a few days let her have what she wants.'

I was almost gay, and this swift reversal of feelings made me slightly light-headed.

I listened to the doctor's instructions and Connan's assurance that there was no need for Celestine to stay at the house; he was sure Miss Leigh would manage and it would be wonderfully comforting for Miss Leigh to know that in any emergency she could always ask for Celestine's help.

'Well Connan,' said Celestine, 'perhaps it's as well. People talk. And if I stayed here . . . Oh, people are so ridiculous. But they are always ready to gossip.'

I saw the point. If Celestine lived at Mount Mellyn, people would begin to couple her name with Connan's; whereas the fact that I, an employee of the same age, lived in the house aroused no comment. I was not of the same social standing.

Connan laughed and said: 'How did you come over, Celeste?'

'I rode over on Speller.'

'Right. I'll ride back with you.'

'Oh, thank you, Connan. It's nice of you. But I can go alone if you'd rather . . .'

'Nonsense! I'm coming.' He turned to me. 'As for you, Miss Leigh, you look exhausted. I should advise you to go to bed and have a good night's sleep.'

I was sure I could not rest, and my expression must have implied this for the doctor said: 'I'll give you a draught, Miss Leigh. Take it five minutes before retiring for the night. I think I can promise you a good night's sleep.'

'Thank you,' I said appreciatively, for I suddenly realized how exhausted I was.

I believed that to-morrow I should wake up my usual calm self, able to cope with whatever new situation should be the result of all that had happened to-day.

I went to my room, where I found a supper tray waiting for me. It contained a wing of cold chicken, appetising enough on most occasions, but to-night I had no appetite.

I toyed with it for a while and ate a few mouthfuls, but I was too upset to eat.

I thought it would be an excellent idea to take Dr. Pengelly's sleeping draught and retire for the night.

I was about to do so when there was a knock on my door.

'Come in,' I called; and Mrs. Polgrey came. She looked distraught. No wonder, I thought. Who in this household isn't?

'It's terrible,' she began.

But I cut in quickly: 'She'll be all right, Mrs. Polgrey. The doctor said so.'

'Oh yes, I heard the news. It's Gilly, Miss. I'm worried about her.'

'Gilly!'

'She didn't come back from the show, Miss. I haven't seen her since this afternoon.'

'Oh, she's wandering about somewhere, I expect. I wonder if she saw . . .'

'I can't understand it, Miss. I can't understand her being at the show. She'm afeared of going near the horses. You could have knocked me down with a feather when I heard she was there. And now . . . she's not come in.'

'But she does wander off alone, doesn't she?'

'Yes, but she'll always be in for her tea. I don't know what can have become of her.'

'Has the house been searched?'

'Yes, Miss. I've looked everywhere. Kitty and Daisy have helped me. So's Polgrey. The child's not in the house.'

I said: 'I'll come and help look for her.'

So instead of going to bed I joined in the search for Gillyflower.

I was very worried because on this day of tragedy I was prepared for anything to happen. What could have happened to little Gilly? I visualized a thousand things. I thought she might have wandered on to the beach and been caught by the tide, and I pictured her little body thrown up by the waves in Mellyn Cove as her mother's had been eight years ago.

That was morbid. No, Gilly had gone wandering and had fallen asleep somewhere. I remembered that I had seen her often in the woods. But she would not be lost if she were in the woods. She knew every inch of them.

I nevertheless made my way to the woods, calling 'Gilly! Gilly!' as I went; and the mist, which was rising again with the coming of evening, seemed to catch my voice and muffle it as though it were cotton wool.

I searched those woods thoroughly because my intuition told me that she was there, and that she was not lost but hiding.

I was right. I came across her lying in a clearing surrounded by small conifers.

I had seen her in this spot once or twice and I guessed it was a haven to her.

'Gilly!' I called. 'Gilly!' And as soon as she heard my voice she sprang to her feet. She was poised to run but she hesitated when I called to her: 'Gilly, it's all right. I'm here all alone and I won't hurt you.'

She looked like a wild fairy child, her extraordinary white hair hanging damply about her shoulders.

'Why, Gilly,' I said, 'You'll catch cold, lying on that damp grass. Why are you hiding, Gilly?'

Her big eyes watched my face, and I knew that it was fear of something which had driven her to this refuge in the woods.

If only she would talk to me! I thought. If only she would explain.

'Gilly,' I said, 'we're friends, aren't we? You know that. I'm your friend – as Madam was.'

She nodded and the fear slipped from her face. I thought, she has seen me in Alice's well-cut riding clothes and, I believe, in her confused little mind she had bracketed us together in some way.

I put my arm about her; her dress was damp and I could see the mist on her pale brows and lashes.

'Why, Gilly, you are cold.'

She allowed me to cuddle her. I said: 'Come on, Gilly, we're going back. Your grandmamma is very anxious. She is wondering what has become of you.'

She allowed me to lead her from the clearing, but I was aware of the reluctant drag of her feet.

I kept my arm firmly about her, and I said: 'You were at the horse show this afternoon.'

She turned to me and as she buried her face against me, her little hands gripped the cloth of my dress. I was conscious of her trembling.

Then in a flash of understanding I began to see what had happened. This child, like Alvean, was terrified of horses. Of course she was. Had she not been almost trampled to death by one?

I believed that, as Alvean had been suffering from temporary shock, so was this child; but the shock which had come to her was of longer duration, and she had never known anyone who had been able to help her fight the darkness which had descended upon her.

In that misty wood I felt like a woman who has a mission. I was not going to turn my face from a poor child who needed help.

She was suffering from a return of that earlier shock. This afternoon she had seen Alvean beneath a horse's hoofs as she herself had been – after all it happened only four years ago.

At that moment I heard the sound of horse's hoofs in the wood, and I shouted: 'Hallo, I've found her.'

'Hallo! Coming, Miss Leigh.' And I was exhilarated – almost unbearably so – because that was Connan's voice.

I guessed that he had returned from Mount Widden to discover that Gilly was lost, and that he had joined the search party. Perhaps he knew that I had come to the woods and decided to join me.

He came into sight and Gilly shrank closer to me, keeping her face hidden.

'She's here,' I called. He came close to us and I went on: 'She is exhausted, poor child. Take her up with you.'

He leaned forward to take her, but she cried out: 'No! No!'

He was astonished to hear her speak, but I was not. I had already discovered that in moments of stress she did so.

I said: 'Gilly. Go up there with the master. I'll walk beside you and hold your hand.'

She shook her head.

I went on: 'Look! This is May Morning. She wants to carry you, because she knows you're tired.'

Gilly's eyes turned to look at May Morning, and, in the fear I saw there, was the clue.

'Take her,' I said to Connan, and he stooped and swung her up in his arms and set her in front of him.

She tried to fight, but I kept on talking to her soothingly. 'You're safe up there. And we'll get back more quickly. You'll find a nice bowl of bread and milk waiting for you, and then there'll be your warm cosy bed. I'll hold your hand all the time and walk beside you.'

She no longer struggled but kept her hand in mine.

And so ended that strange day, with myself and Connan bringing in the lost child.

When she was lifted from the horse and handed to her grandmother, Connan gave me a smile which I thought was infinitely charming. That was because it held none of the mockery which I had seen hitherto.

I went up to my room, exultation wrapped about me as the mist wrapped itself about the house. It was tinged with melancholy but the joy was so strong that the mingling of my feelings was difficult to understand.

I knew of course what had happened to me. To-day had made it very clear. I had done a foolish thing – perhaps the most foolish thing I had ever done in my life.

I had fallen in love for the first time, and with someone who was quite out of my world. I was in love with the master of Mount Mellyn, and I had an uneasy feeling that he might be aware of it.

On the table by my bed was the draught which Dr. Pengelly had given me.

I locked the door, undressed, drank the draught and went to bed.

But before I got into bed I looked at myself in my pink flannelette nightdress, primly buttoned up to the throat. Then I laughed at the incongruity of my thoughts and said aloud in my best governess's tones: 'In the morning, after the good night's rest Dr. Pengelly's potion will give you, you'll come to your senses.'

The next few weeks were the happiest I had so far spent in Mount Mellyn. It soon became clear that Alvean had suffered no great harm. I was delighted to find that she had lost none of her keenness for riding and asked eager questions about Black Prince's slight injuries, taking it for granted that she would soon ride him again.

We resumed school after the first week; she was pleased to do so. I also taught her to play chess, and she picked up the game with astonishing speed; and if I handicapped myself by playing without my queen she was even able to checkmate me.

But it was not only Alvean's progress which made me so happy. It was the fact that Connan was in the house; and what astonished me was that, although he made no reference to my outburst on the day of the accident, he had clearly noted it and would appear in Alvean's room with books and puzzles which he thought would be of interest to her.

In the first days I said to him: 'There is one thing that pleases her more than all the presents you bring; that is your own company.'

He had answered: 'What an odd child she must be to prefer me to a book or a game.'

I smiled at him and he returned my smile; and again I was aware of that change in his expression.

Sometimes he would sit down and watch our game of chess. Then he would range himself on Alvean's side against me. I would protest and demand I be allowed to have my queen back.

Alvean would sit smiling, and he would say: 'Look, Alvean. We'll put our bishop there, and that'll make our dear Miss Leigh look to her defences.'

Alvean would giggle and throw me a triumphant glance, and I would be so happy to be with the two of them that I grew almost careless and nearly lost the game. But not quite. I never forgot that between Connan and me there was a certain battle in progress and I always wanted to prove my mettle. Though it was only a game of chess I wanted to show him I was his match.

He said one day: 'When Alvean's movable we'll drive over to Fowey and have a picnic.'

'Why go to Fowey,' I asked, 'when you have a perfect picnic beach here?'

'My dear Miss Leigh' – he had acquired a habit of calling me his dear Miss Leigh – 'do you not know that other people's beaches are more exciting than one's own?'

'Oh yes, Papa,' cried Alvean. 'Do let's have a picnic.'

She was so eager to get well for the picnic that she ate all the food which was brought to her and talked of the expedition continually. Dr. Pengelly was delighted with her; so were we all.

I said to Connan one day: 'But you are the real cure. You have made her so happy, because at last you let her see that you are aware of her existence.'

Then he did a surprising thing. He took my hand and lightly kissed my cheek. It was very different from that kiss which he had given me on the night of the ball. This was swift, friendly, passionless yet affectionate.

'No,' he said, 'it is you who are the real cure, my dear Miss Leigh.'

I thought he was going to say something more. But he did not do so. Instead he left me abruptly.

I did not forget Gilly. I determined to fight for her as I had for Alvean, and I thought the best way of doing so was to speak to Connan about it. He was in that mood, I believed, to grant me what I asked. I should not have been surprised if, when Alvean was about again, he changed to his old self – forgetful of her, full of mockery for me. So I decided to strike my blow for Gilly while I had a chance of success.

I boldly went down to the punch room, when I knew he was there one morning, and asked if I might speak to him.

'But of course, Miss Leigh,' he replied. 'It is always a pleasure to speak to you.'

I came straight to the point. 'I want to do something for Gilly.'

'Yes?'

'I do not believe she is half-witted. I think that no one has made any attempt to help her. I have heard about her accident. Before that, I understand, she was quite a normal little girl. Don't you see that it might be possible to make her normal once again?'

I saw a return of that mockery to his eyes as he said lightly: 'I believe that as with God, so with Miss Leigh, all things are possible.'

I ignored the flippancy. 'I am asking your permission to give her lessons.'

'My dear Miss Leigh, does not the pupil you came here to teach take up all your time?'

'I have a little spare time, Mr. TreMellyn. Even governesses have that. I would be ready to teach Gilly in my own time, providing of course you do not expressly forbid it.'

'If I forbade you I am sure you would find some way of doing it, so I think it would be simpler if I say: "Go ahead with your plans for Gilly. I wish you all success." '

'Thank you,' I said; and turned to go.

'Miss Leigh,' he called. I stood waiting.

'Let us go on that picnic soon. I could carry Alvean if necessary to and from the carriage.'

'That would be excellent, Mr. TreMellyn. I'll tell her at once. I know it will delight her.'

'And you, Miss Leigh, does it delight you?'

For a moment I thought he was coming towards me and I started back. I was suddenly afraid that he would place his hands on my shoulders and that at his touch I might betray myself.

I said coolly: 'Anything which is going to be so good for Alvean delights me, Mr. TreMellyn.'

And I hurried back to Alvean to tell her the good news.

So the weeks passed – pleasurable, wonderful weeks which I sometimes felt could never be repeated.

I had taken Gilly to the schoolroom and I had even managed to teach her a few letters. She delighted in pictures and quickly became absorbed in them. I really believed she enjoyed our lessons for she would present herself at the schoolroom each day at the appointed time.

She had been heard to speak a few words now and then and I knew that the whole household was watching the experiment with amusement and interest.

When Alvean was well enough to take lessons in the schoolroom I should have to be prepared for opposition. Alvean's aversion to Gilly was apparent. I had brought the child into the sick-room on one occasion and Alvean had immediately become sulky. I thought, when she is quite well I shall have to reconcile her to Gilly. But that was one of the problems of the future. I knew very well that when life returned to normal I could not expect these days of pleasure to continue.

There were plenty of visitors for Alvean. Celestine was there every day. She brought fruit and other presents for her. Peter came and she was always pleased to see him.

Once he said to her: 'Do you not think I am a devoted uncle to call and see you so often, Alvean?'

She had retorted: 'Oh, but you don't come to see me only, do you, Uncle Peter. You come mainly for Miss.'

He had replied in characteristic style: 'I come to see you both. How fortunate I am to have two such charming ladies on whom to call.'

Lady Treslyn called with expensive books and flowers for Alvean, but Alvean received her sullenly and would scarcely speak to her.

'She is an invalid still, Lady Treslyn,' I explained; and the smile which was flashed upon me almost took my breath away, so beautiful was it.

'Of course I understand,' Lady Treslyn told me. 'Poor child! Mr. TreMellyn tells me that she has been brave and you have been wonderful. I tell him how lucky he is to have found such a treasure. "They are not easy to come by," I said. I reminded him of how my last cook walked out in the middle of a dinner party. She was another such treasure.'

I bowed my head and hated her – not because she had linked me in her mind with her cook, but because she was so beautiful, and I knew that rumours persisted about her and Connan and I feared that there was truth in them.

Connan seemed different when this woman was in the house. I felt he scarcely saw me. I heard the sounds of their laughter and I wondered sadly what they said to each other. I saw them in the gardens and I told myself there was an unmistakable intimacy in the very way they walked together.

Then I realized what a fool I had been, for I had been harbouring thoughts which I would not dare express, even to myself. I tried to pretend they did not exist. But they did – and in spite of my better sense they kept intruding.

I dared not look into the future.

Celestine one day suggested that she should take Alvean over to Mount Widden for the day and look after her there.

'It would be a change,' she said.

'Connan,' she added, 'you shall come to dinner, and you can bring her back afterwards.'

He agreed to do so. I was disappointed not to be included in the invitation; which showed what a false picture I had allowed myself to make of the situation during these incredible weeks. Imagine myself – the governess – invited to dine at Mount Widden!

I laughed at my own foolishness, but there was a note of bitterness and sadness. It was like waking up to a chilly morning after weeks of sunshine so brilliant that you thought it was going to last for ever; it was like the gathering of storm clouds in a summer sky.

Connan drove Alvean over in the carriage and I was left alone, for the first time since I arrived here without any definite duties.

I gave Gilly her lesson but I did not believe in taxing the child too much and when I had returned her to her grandmother I wondered what I was going to do.

Then an idea struck me. Why should I not go for a ride, a long ride? Perhaps on the moors.

I immediately remembered that day when Alvean and I had ridden to her Great-Aunt Clara. I began to feel rather excited. I was remembering the mystery of Alice again, which I had forgotten during those halcyon weeks of Alvean's convalescence. I began to wonder whether I had been so interested in Alice's story because I needed some interest to prevent me from brooding on my own.

I thought to myself, Great-Aunt Clara will want to hear how Alvean is getting on. In any case she had made it clear that I should be welcomed any time I called. Of course it would be different, calling without Alvean; but then I believed that she had been more interested to talk to me than to the child.

So I made up my mind.

I went to Mrs. Polgrey and said: 'Alvean will be away all day. I propose to take a day's holiday.'

Mrs. Polgrey had become very fond of me since I had taken such an interest in Gilly. She really did love the child, I believed. It was merely because she had assumed that Gilly's strangeness had been the price which had to be paid for her parents' sins that she had accepted her as *non compos mentis.*

'And none deserves a holiday more, Miss,' she said to me. 'Where are you going?'

'I think I'll go on to the moors. I'll take luncheon at an inn.'

'Do you think you should, Miss, by yourself?'

I smiled at her. 'I am very well able to take care of myself, Mrs. Polgrey.'

'Well, there be bogs on the moor and mists and the Little People, some say.'

'Little People indeed!'

'Ah, don't 'ee laugh at 'em, Miss. They don't like people to laugh at 'em. There's some as say they've seen 'em. Little gnome-like men in sugarloaf hats. If they don't like 'ee they'll lead 'ee astray with their fairy lanterns, and afore you knows where you be you'm in the middle of a bog that sucks 'ee down and won't let 'ee go however much you do struggle.'

I gave a shiver. 'I'll be careful, and I wouldn't dream of offending the Little People. If I meet any I'll be very polite.'

'You'm mocking, Miss, I do believe.'

'I'll be all right, Mrs. Polgrey. Don't have any fears about me.'

I went to the stables and asked Tapperty which horse I could have to-day.

'There's May Morning if you'd like her. She be free.'

I told him I was going to the moors. 'A good chance to see the country,' I added.

'Trust you, Miss. Bain't much you miss.' And he laughed to himself as though enjoying some private joke.

'You be going with a companion, Miss?' he asked slyly.

I said that I was going alone, but I could see that he did not believe me.

I felt rather angry with him because I guessed that his thoughts were on Peter Nansellock. I believed that my name had been coupled with his since he had been so foolish as to send Jacinth over for me.

I wondered too if my growing friendship with Connan had been noted. I was horrified at the possibility. Oddly enough I could bear to contemplate their sly remarks which I was sure were exchanged out of my hearing, about

Peter and me; it would be a different matter if they talked in that way of me and Connan.

How ridiculous! I told myself as I walked May Morning out of the stables and down to the village.

There is nothing to talk about between you and Connan. But there is, I answered myself; and I fell to thinking of those two occasions when he had kissed me.

I looked across the cove at Mount Widden. Wistfully I hoped that I should meet Connan coming back. But I didn't of course; he would stay there with Alvean and his friends. Why should I imagine that he would want to come back to be with me? I was letting this foolish habit of day dreaming get the better of my common sense.

But I continued to hope until I had left the village well behind me and I came to the first grey wall and boulders of the moor.

It was a sparkling December morning and there were great golden patches of gorse dotted over the moor.

I could smell the peaty soil, and the wind which had veered a little to the north was fresh and exhilarating.

I wanted to gallop across the moor with that wind in my face. I gave way to my desire and while I did so I imagined that Connan was riding beside me and that he called me to stop that he might tell me what a difference I had made to his life as well as Alvean's, and that, incongruous as it seemed, he was in love with me.

In this moorland country it was possible to believe in fantastic dreams; as some told themselves that these tracts of land were inhabited by the Little People, so I told myself that it was not impossible that Connan TreMellyn would fall in love with me.

At midday I arrived at The House on the Moor. It was very like that other occasion; the elderly housekeeper came out to welcome me and I was taken into Great-Aunt Clara's sitting room.

'Good day to you, Miss Leigh! And all alone to-day?'

So no one had told her of Alvean's accident. I was astonished. I should have thought Connan would have sent someone over to explain, since the old lady was obviously interested in her great-niece.

I told her about the accident and she looked very concerned. I hastily added that Alvean was getting on well and would soon be about again.

'But you must be in need of some refreshment, Miss Leigh,' she said. 'Let us have a glass of my elderberry wine; and will you stay to luncheon?'

I said it was most kind of her to invite me and if it were not causing too much inconvenience I should be delighted to do so.

We sipped our elderberry wine, and once more I was conscious of that heady feeling which I had experienced after her dandelion wine on the previous occasion. Luncheon consisted of mutton with caper sauce exceedingly well cooked and served; and afterwards we retired to the drawing room for what she called a little chat.

This was what I had been hoping for, and I was not to be disappointed. 'Tell me,' she said, 'how is dear little Alvean? Is she happier now?'

'Why . . . yes, I think she is very much happier. In fact I think she has been more so since her accident. Her father has been so attentive, and she is so fond of him.'

'Ah,' said Great-Aunt Clara, 'her father.' She looked at me, and her bright blue eyes showed her excitement. I knew she was one of those women who cannot resist talking; and since she spent so much of her time with only her own household, the coming of a visitor such as myself was an irresistible temptation.

I was determined to make the temptation even more irresistible. I said tentatively: 'There is not the usual relationship between them, I fancy.'

There was a slight pause, and then she said quickly: 'No. I suppose it is inevitable.'

I did not speak. I waited breathlessly, afraid that she might change her mind. She was hovering on the edge of confidences and I felt that she could give me some vital clue to the situation at Mount Mellyn, to the story of the TreMellyns which I was beginning reluctantly to admit might very well become my story.

'I sometimes blame myself,' she said, as though she were talking to herself; and indeed her blue eyes looked beyond me as though she were looking back over the years and was quite unconscious of my presence.

'The question is,' she went on, 'how much should one interfere in the lives of others.'

It was a question which had often interested me. I had certainly tried to interfere in the lives of people I had met since I entered Mount Mellyn.

'Alice was with me after the engagement,' she went on. 'Everything could have changed then. But I persuaded her. You see, I thought *he* was the better man.'

She was being a little incoherent, and I was afraid to ask her to elucidate lest I broke the spell. She might remember that she was betraying confidences to a young woman who was more curious than she should be.

'I wonder what would have happened if she had acted differently then. Do you ever play that game with yourself, Miss Leigh? Do you ever say, now if at a certain point I . . . or someone else . . . had done such and such . . . the whole tenor of life for that person would have changed?'

'Yes,' I said. 'Everybody does. You think that things would have been different for your niece and for Alvean.'

'Oh yes . . . for her – Alice – more than most. She had come to a real turning-point. A cross-roads, one might say. Go this way and you have such and such a life. Go that way and everything will be quite different. It frightens me sometimes because if she had turned to the right instead of the left . . . as it were . . . she might be here to-day. After all, if she had married Geoffry there would not have been any need to run away with him, would there?'

'I see you were in her confidence.'

'Indeed yes. I'm afraid I had quite a big part in shaping what happened. That's what alarmed me. Did I do right?'

'I am sure you did what you thought was right, and that is all any of us can do. You loved your niece very much, did you not?'

'Very much. My children were boys, you see, and I'd always wanted a girl. Alice used to come and play with my family . . . three boys and no girl. I used to hope that she might marry one of them. Cousins though. Perhaps that would not have been so good. I didn't live in this house then. We were in Penzance. Alice's parents had a big estate some few miles inland. That's her husband's now of course. She had a good fortune to bring to a husband. All the same, perhaps it would not have been good for cousins to marry. In any case they were set on the marriage with the TreMellyns.'

'So that was arranged.'

'Yes. Alice's father was dead, and her mother – she was my sister – had always been very fond of Connan TreMellyn . . . the elder I mean. There have been Connans in that family for centuries. The eldest son was always given the name. I think my sister would have liked to marry the present Connan's father, but other marriages were arranged for them, and so they wanted their children to marry. They were betrothed when Connan was twenty and Alice eighteen. The marriage was to take place a year later.'

'So it was indeed a marriage of convenience.'

'How odd it is! Marriages of convenience often turn out to be marriages of inconvenience, do they not? They thought it would be a good idea if she came to stay with me. You see, I was within a few hours' riding distance from Mount Mellyn, and the young people could meet often like that . . . without her staying at the house. Of course you might say, why did not her mother take her to stay at Mount Mellyn? My sister was very ill at that time and not able to travel. In any case it was arranged that she should stay with me.'

'And I suppose Mr. TreMellyn rode over to see her often.'

'Yes. But not as often as I should have expected. I began to suspect that they were not as well matched as their fortunes were.'

'Tell me about Alice,' I said earnestly. 'What sort of girl was she?'

'How can I explain her to you. The word light comes to my mind. She was light-hearted, light-minded. I do not mean she was light in her morals – which is a sense in which some people use the word. Although of course, after what happened . . . But who shall judge? You see, he came over here to paint. He did some beautiful pictures of the moors.'

'Who? Connan TreMellyn?'

'Oh, dear me, no! Geoffry. Geoffry Nansellock. He was an artist of some reputation. Did you not know that?'

'No,' I said. 'I know nothing of him except that he was killed with Alice last July twelvemonth.'

'He came over here often while she was with me. In fact he came more often than Connan did. I began to wonder how matters stood. There was something between them. They would go off together and he'd have his painting things with him. She used to say she was going to watch him at work. She would be a painter herself one day. But of course it was not painting they did together.'

'They were . . . in love?' I asked.

'I was rather frightened when she told me. You see, there was going to be a child.'

I caught my breath in surprise. Alvean, I thought. No wonder he could not bring himself to love her. No wonder my statement that she possessed artistic talent upset him and Celestine.

'She told me two weeks before the day fixed for her wedding. She was almost certain, she said. She did not think she could be mistaken. She said, "What shall I do, Aunt Clara? Shall I marry Geoffry?"

'I said: "Does Geoffry want to marry you, my dear?" And she answered: "He would have to, would he not, if I told him."

'I know now that she should have told him. It was only right that she should. But her marriage was already arranged, Alice was an heiress and I wondered whether Geoffry had hoped for this. You see the Nansellocks had very little and Alice's fortune would have been a blessing to them. I wondered . . . as one does wonder. He had a certain reputation too. There had been others who found themselves in Alice's condition, and it was due to him. I did not think she would be very happy with him for long.'

There was silence, and I felt as though vital parts of a puzzle were being fitted together to give my picture meaning.

'I remember her . . . that day,' the old lady continued. 'It was in this very room. I often go over it. She talked to me about it . . . unburdening herself as I'm unburdening myself to you. It's been on my conscience for the last year . . . ever since she died. You see, she said to me: "What shall I do, Aunt Clara? Help me. . . . Tell me what I should do."

'And I answered her. I said: "There's only one thing you can do, my dear; and that is go on with your marriage to Connan TreMellyn. You're betrothed to him. You must forget what happened with Geoffry Nansellock." And she said to me: "Aunt Clara, how can I forget? There'll be a living reminder, won't there?" Then I did this terrible thing. I said to her: "You must marry. Your child will be born prematurely." Then she threw back her head and laughed and laughed. It was hysterical laughter. Poor Alice, she was near breaking-point.'

Great-Aunt Clara sat back in her chair; she looked as though she had just come out of a trance. I really believe she had been seeing, not me sitting opposite her, but Alice.

She was now a little frightened because she was wondering whether she had told me too much.

I said nothing. I was picturing it all; the wedding which would have been a ceremonial occasion; the death of Alice's mother almost immediately afterwards; and Connan's father had died the following year. The marriage had been to please them and they had not lived long to enjoy it. And Alice was left with Connan – my Connan – and Alvean, the child of another man, whom she had tried to pass off as his. She had not succeeded – that much I knew.

He had kept up the pretence that Alvean was his daughter, but he had never accepted her as such in his mind. Alvean knew it; she admired him so much; but she suspected something was wrong and she was uncertain; she longed to be accepted as his daughter. Perhaps he had never really discovered whether she was or not.

The situation was fraught with drama. And yet, I thought, what good can come of brooding on it? Alice is dead; Alvean and Connan are alive. Let them forget what happened in the past. If they were wise they would try to make happiness for each other in the future.

'Oh, my dear,' sighed Great-Aunt Clara, 'how I talk! It is like living it all again. I have wearied you.' A little fear crept into her voice. 'I have talked too much and you, Miss Leigh, have played no part in all this. I trust you will keep what I have said, to yourself.'

'You may trust me to do so,' I assured her.

'I knew it. I would not have told you otherwise. But in any case, it is all so long ago. It has been a comfort to talk to you. I think about it all sometimes during the night. You see, it might have been right for her to marry Geoffry. Perhaps she thought so, and that was why she tried to run away with him. To think of them on that train! It seems like the judgment of God, doesn't it?'

'No,' I said sharply. 'There were many other people on that train who were killed. They weren't all on the point of leaving their husbands with other men.'

She laughed on a high note. 'How right you are! I knew you had lots of common sense. And you don't think I did wrong? You see, I sometimes tell myself that, if I had persuaded her not to marry Connan, she wouldn't. That is what frightens me. I pointed the way to her destiny.'

'You must not blame yourself,' I said. 'Whatever you did you did because you thought it was best for her. And we after all make our own destinies. I am sure of that.'

'You do comfort me, Miss Leigh. You will stay and have tea with me, won't you?'

'It is kind of you, but I think I should be back before dark.'

'Oh yes, you must be back before dark.'

'It grows dark so early at this time of year.'

'Then I must not be selfish and keep you. Miss Leigh, when Alvean is well enough, you will bring her over to see me?'

'I promise I shall.'

'And if you yourself feel like coming over before that. . . .'

'Depend upon it, I shall come. You have given me a very pleasant and interesting time.'

The fear came back into her eyes. 'You will remember it was in confidence?'

I reassured her. I knew that this charming old lady's greatest pleasure in life must have been sharing confidences, telling a little more than was discreet. Well, I thought, we all have our little vices.

She came to the door to wave me on when I left.

'It's been so pleasant,' she reiterated. 'And don't forget.' She put her finger to her lips and her eyes sparkled.

I imitated the gesture and, waving, rode off.

I was very thoughtful on the way home. This day I had learned so much.

I was nearly at Mellyn village when the thought struck me that Gilly was Alvean's half-sister. I remembered then the drawings I had seen of Alvean and Gilly combined.

So Alvean knew. Or did she merely fear? Was she trying to convince herself that her father was not Geoffry Nansellock – which would make her Gilly's half-sister? Or did her great desire for Connan's approval really mean that she was longing for him to accept her as his daughter?

I felt a great desire to help them all out of this morass of tragedy into which Alice's indiscretion had plunged them.

I can do it, I told myself. I will do it.

Then I thought of Connan with Lady Treslyn, and I was filled with disquiet. What absurd and impossible dreams I was indulging in. What chance had I – a governess – of showing Connan the way to happiness?

Christmas was rapidly approaching, and it brought with it all that excitement which I remembered so well from the old days in my father's vicarage.

Kitty and Daisy were constantly whispering together, and Mrs. Polgrey said that they nearly drove her crazy, and that their work was more skimped than usual, though that had to be seen to be believed. She went about the house sighing 'Nowadays. . . .' and shaking her head in sorrow. But even she was excited.

The weather was warm, more like the approach of spring than of winter. On my walks in the woods I noticed that the primroses had begun to bloom.

'My dear life,' said Tapperty, 'primroses in December be nothing new to we. Spring do come early to Cornwall.'

I began to think about Christmas presents and I made a little list. There must be something for Phillida and her family, and Aunt Adelaide; but I was mainly concerned with the people at Mount Mellyn. I had a little money to spend, as I used very little and had saved most of what I had earned since I had taken my post at Mount Mellyn.

One day I went into Plymouth and did my Christmas shopping. I bought books for Phillida and her family and had them sent direct to her; I bought a scarf for Aunt Adelaide and that was sent direct too. I spent a long time choosing what I would give the Mellyn household. Finally, I decided on scarves for Kitty and Daisy, red and green which would suit them; and a blue one for Gilly to match her eyes. For Mrs. Polgrey I bought a bottle of whisky which I was sure would delight her more than anything else, and for Alvean some handkerchiefs in many colours, with A embroidered on them.

I was pleased with my purchases. I was beginning to grow as excited about Christmas as Daisy and Kitty were.

The weather continued very mild, and on Christmas Eve I helped Mrs. Polgrey and the girls to decorate the great hall and some of the other rooms.

The men had been out the previous day and brought in ivy, holly, box and bay. I was shown how the pillars in the great hall were entwined with these leaves and Daisy and Kitty taught me how to make Christmas bushes; they were delightedly shocked by an ignorance like mine. I had never before heard of a Christmas bush! We took two wooden hoops – one inserted into the other – and this ball-like framework we decorated with evergreen leaves and furze; then we hung oranges and apples on it; and I must say this made a pretty show. These we hung in some of the windows.

The biggest logs were carried in for the fireplaces, and the house was filled with laughter, while the servants' hall was decorated in exactly the same manner as the great hall.

'We do have our ball here while the family be having theirs,' Daisy told me; and I wondered to which ball I should go. Perhaps to neither. A governess's position was somewhere in between, I supposed.

'My life!' cried Daisy, 'I can scarcely wait for the day. Last Christmas was a quiet one . . . had to be on account of the house being in mourning. But we in the servants' hall managed pretty well. There was dash-an-darras and metheglin to drink, and Mrs. Polgrey's sloe gin had to be tasted to be believed. There was mutton and beef, I remember, and hog's pudding. No feast in these parts ain't complete without hog's pudding. You ask Father!'

All through Christmas Eve the smell of baking filled the kitchen and its neighbourhood. Tapperty, with Billy Trehay and some of the boys from the stables, came to the door just to smell it. Mrs. Tapperty was up at the house all day working in the kitchen. I scarcely recognized the usually calm and dignified Mrs. Polgrey. She was bustling about, her face flushed, purring, stirring and talking ecstatically of pies which bore the odd names of squab and lammy, giblet, muggety and herby.

I was called in to help. 'Do 'ee keep your eye on that saucepan, Miss, and should it come to the boil tell I quickly.' Mrs. Polgrey's dialect became more and more broad as the excitement grew, and I could scarcely understand the language which was being bandied about in the kitchen that Christmas.

I was smiling fatuously at a whole batch of pasties which had just come out of the oven, golden-brown pastry with the smell of savoury meats and onions, when Kitty came in shouting: 'Ma'am, the curl singers be here.'

'Well, bring 'em, bring 'em in, ye daftie,' cried Mrs. Polgrey, forgetting dignity in the excitement and wiping her hand across her sweating brow. 'What be 'ee waiting for? Don't 'ee know, me dear, that it be bad luck to keep curl singers waiting?'

I followed her into the hall, where a company of village youths and girls had gathered. They were already singing when we arrived, and I understood that the curl singers were what were known in other parts of the country as carol singers.

They rendered 'The Seven Joys of Mary,' 'The Holly and the Ivy,' 'The Twelve Days of Christmas' and 'The First Noël.' We all joined in.

Then the leader of the group began to sing:

> 'Come let me taste your Christmas beer
> That is so very strong,
> And I do wish that Christmas time,
> With all its mirth and song,
> Was twenty times as long.'

Then Mrs. Polgrey signed to Daisy and Kitty, who were already on their way, I guessed, to bring refreshment to the party after this gentle reminder.

Metheglin was served to the singers with blackberry and elderberry wine, and into their hands were thrust great pasties, some containing meat, some fish. The satisfaction was evident.

And when they had finished eating and drinking, a bowl – which was tied with red ribbons and decorated with furze – was handed to Mrs. Polgrey who very majestically placed some coins in it.

When they had gone Daisy said: 'Well, now that lot have come a-gooding, what's to be next?'

She delighted in my ignorance of course when I had to ask what a-gooding meant.

'My dear life, you don't know all, Miss, do 'ee now. To go a-gooding means to go collecting for Christmas wine or a Christmas cake. What else?'

I realized that I had a great deal to learn concerning the habits of the Cornish, but I did feel that I was enjoying their way of celebrating Christmas.

'Oh, Miss, I forgot to tell 'ee,' cried Daisy. 'There be a parcel in your room. I took it up just afore them come a-gooding, and forgot to tell 'ee till now.' She was surprised because I lingered. 'A parcel, Miss! Don't 'ee want to see what it is? 'Twas so size, and 'twas a box like as not.'

I realized that I had been in a dream. I felt that I wanted to stay here for ever, and learn all the customs of this part of the world. I wanted to make it my part of the world.

I shook myself out of that dream. What you really want, I told myself, is some fairy-tale ending to your story. You want to be the mistress of Mount Mellyn. Why not admit it?

I went up to my room, and there I found Phillida's parcel.

I took out a shawl of black silk on which was embroidered a pattern in green and amber. There was also am amber comb of the Spanish type. I stuck the comb in my hair and wrapped the shawl about me. I was startled by my reflection. I looked exotic, more like a Spanish dancer than an English governess.

There was something else in the parcel. I undid it quickly and saw that it was a dress – one of Phillida's which I had greatly admired. It was of green silk, the same shade of green as in the shawl. A letter fell out.

'*Dear Marty,*

How is the governessing? Your last letter sounded as though you found it intriguing. I believe your Alvean is a little horror. Spoilt child, I'll swear. Are they treating you well? It sounded as if that side of it was not too bad. What is the matter with you, by the way? You used to write such amusing letters. Since you've been in that place you've become uncommunicative. I suspect you either love it or hate it. Do tell.

The shawl and comb are my Christmas gift. I hope you like them because I spent a lot of time choosing. Are they too frivolous? Would you rather have had a set of woollen underwear or some improving book? But I heard from Aunt Adelaide that she was sending you the former. There is a distinctly governessy flavour in your letters. All sound and fury, Marty, my dear, signifying nothing. I am wondering whether you'll be sitting down to dine with the family this Christmas or presiding in the servants' hall. I'm sure it will be the former. They couldn't help but ask you. After all it is Christmas. You'll dine with the family even if there's one of those dinner parties where a guest doesn't turn up and they say, "Send for the governess. We cannot be thirteen." So our Marty goes to dine in my old green and her new scarf and comb, and there she attracts a millionaire and lives happily ever after.

Seriously, Marty, I did think you might need something for the festivities. So the green gown is a gift. Don't think of it as a cast-off. I love the thing and I'm giving it to you, not because I'm tired of it, but because it always suited you better than me.

I shall want to hear all about the Christmas festivities. And, dear sister, when you're the fourteenth at the dinner table don't freeze likely suitors with a look or give them one of your clever retorts. Be a nice gentle girl and, kind lady, I see romance and fortune in the cards for you.

Happy Christmas, dear Marty, and do write soon sending the real news. The children and William send their love. Mine to you also.

Phillida.'

I felt rather emotional. It was a link with home. Dear Phillida, she did think of me often then. Her shawl and comb were beautiful, even if a little incongruous for someone in my humble position; and it was good of her to send the dress.

I was startled by a sudden cry. I spun round and saw Alvean at the door which led to the schoolroom.

'Miss!' she cried. 'So it's you!'

'Of course. Who did you think it was?'

She did not answer, but I knew.

'I've never seen you look like that, Miss.'

'You've never seen me in a shawl and comb.'

'You look . . . pretty.'

'Thank you, Alvean.'

She was a little shaken. I knew who she had thought it was standing in my room.

I was the same height as Alice, and if I were less slender that would not be obvious with the silk shawl round me.

Christmas Day was a day to remember all my life.

I awoke in the morning to the sounds of excitement. The servants were laughing and talking together below my window.

I opened my eyes and thought: Christmas Day. And then: My first Christmas at Mount Mellyn.

Perhaps, I said to myself trying to throw a cold douche over my exuberance which somehow made me apprehensive because it was so great, it will be not only your first but your last.

A whole year lay between this Christmas and the next. Who could say what would happen in that time?

I was out of bed when my water was brought up. Daisy scarcely stopped a moment, she was so full of excitement.

'I be late, Miss, but there be so much to do. You'd better hurry now or you'll not be in time to see the wassail. They'll be coming early, you can depend on that. They know the family 'ull be off to church, so they mustn't be late.'

There was no time to ask questions so I washed and dressed and took out my parcels. Alvean's had already been put by her bed the previous night.

I went to the window. The air was balmy and it had that strong tang of spices in it. I drew deep breaths and listened to the gentle rhythm of the waves. They said nothing this morning; they merely swished contentedly. This was Christmas morning when for a day all troubles, all differences might be shelved.

Alvean came to my room. She was carrying her embroidered handkerchiefs rather shyly. She said: 'Thank you, Miss. A happy Christmas!'

I put my arms about her and kissed her, and although she seemed a little embarrassed by this demonstration she returned my kiss.

She had brought a brooch so like the silver whip I had given her that I thought for a moment that she was returning my gift.

'I got it from Mr. Pastern,' she said. 'I wanted one as near mine as possible, but not too near, so that we shouldn't get them mixed up. Yours has got a little engraving on the handle. Now we'll each have one when we go riding.'

I was delighted. She had not ridden since her accident, and she could not have shown me more clearly that she was ready to start again.

I said: 'You could not have given me anything I should have liked better, Alvean.'

She was very pleased, although she murmured in an offhand way: 'I'm glad you like it, Miss.' Then she left me abruptly.

This, I told myself, is going to be a wonderful day. It's Christmas.

My presents proved to be a great success. Mrs. Polgrey's eyes glistened at the sight of the whisky; as for Gilly, she was delighted with her scarf. I suppose the poor child had never had anything so pretty before; she kept stroking it and staring at it in wonder. Daisy and Kitty were pleased with their scarves too; and I felt I had been clever in my choice.

Mrs. Polgrey gave me a set of doilies with a coy whisper: 'For your bottom drawer, me dear.' I replied that I would start one immediately, and we were very gay. She said that she would make a cup of tea and we'd sample my whisky, but there wasn't the time.

'My dear life, when I think of all there has to be done to-day!'

The wassail singers arrived in the morning and I heard their voices at the door of the great hall.

> *'The Master and Mistress our wassail begin*
> *Pray open your door and let us come in*
> *With our wassail, wassail, wassail.*
> *And joy come to our jolly wassail.'*

They came into the hall, and they also carried a bowl into which coins were dropped; and all the servants crowded in and, as Connan entered, the singing grew louder and the verse was repeated.

'The Master and the Mistress . . .'

I thought, Two years ago, Alice would have stood there with him. Does he remember? He showed no sign. He sang with them and ordered that the stirrup cup, the dash-an-darras, be brought out with the saffron cake and pasties and gingerbread, which had been made for the occasion.

He moved nearer to me.

'Well, Miss Leigh,' he said under cover of singing, 'what do you think of a Cornish Christmas?'

'Very interesting.'

'You haven't seen half yet.'

'I should hope not. The day has scarcely begun.'

'You should rest this afternoon.'

'But why?'

'For the feasting this evening.'

'But I . . .'

'Of course you will join us. Where else would you spend your Christmas Day? With the Polgreys? With the Tappertys?'

'I did not know. I wondered whether I was expected to hover between the great hall and the servants' hall.'

'You look disapproving.'

'I am not sure.'

'Oh, come, this is Christmas. Do not wonder whether you should be sure or not. Just come. By the way, I have not wished you a merry Christmas yet. I have something here . . . a little gift. A token of my gratitude, if you like. You have been so good to Alvean since her accident. Oh, and *before* of course, I have no doubt. But it has been brought to my notice so forcibly since . . .'

'But I have only done my duty as a governess. . . .'

'And that is something you would always do. I know it. Well, let's say this is merely to wish you a merry Christmas.'

He had pressed a small object into my hand, and I was so overcome with pleasure that I felt it must show in my eyes and betray my feelings to him.

'You are very good to me,' I said. 'I had not thought . . .'

He smiled and moved away to the singers. I had noticed Tapperty's eyes on us. I wondered whether he had seen the gift handed to me.

I wanted to be alone, for I felt so emotionally disturbed. The small case he had pressed into my hand was demanding to be opened. I could not do so here.

I slipped out of the hall and ran up to my room.

It was a small, blue plush case, the sort which usually contained jewellery.

I opened it. Inside, on oyster-coloured satin, lay a brooch. It was in the form of a horseshoe, and it was studded with what could only be diamonds.

I stared at it in dismay. I could not accept such a valuable object. I must return it of course.

I held it up to the light and saw the flash of red and green in the stones. It must be worth a great deal of money. I possessed no diamonds, but I could see that these were fine ones.

Why did he do it? If it had been some small token I should have been so happy. I wanted to throw myself on to my bed and weep.

I could hear Alvean calling me. 'Miss, it's time for church. Come on, Miss. The carriage is waiting to take us to church.'

I hastily put the brooch into its box and put on my cape and bonnet as Alvean came into the room.

I saw him after church. He was going across to the stables and I called after him.

He hesitated, looked over his shoulder and smiled at me.

'Mr. TreMellyn. It is very kind of you,' I said as I ran up to him, 'but this gift is far too valuable for me to accept.'

He put his head on one side and regarded me in the old mocking manner.

'My dear Miss Leigh,' he said lightly. 'I am a very ignorant man, I fear. I have no notion how valuable a gift must be before it is acceptable.'

I flushed hotly and stammered: 'This is a very valuable ornament.'

'I thought it so suitable. A horseshoe means luck, you know. And you have a way with horses, have you not?'

'I . . . I have no occasion to wear such a valuable piece of jewellery.'

'I thought you might wear it to the ball to-night.'

For a moment I had a picture of myself dancing with him. I should be wearing Phillida's green silk dress, which would compare favourably with those of his guests because Phillida had a way with clothes. I would wear my shawl, and my diamond brooch would be proudly flaunted on the green silk, because I treasured it so much, and I treasured it because he had given it to me.

'I feel I have no right.'

'Oh,' he murmured, 'I begin to understand. You feel that I give the brooch in the same spirit as Mr. Nansellock offered Jacinth.'

'So . . .' I stammered, 'you knew of that?'

'Oh, I know most things that go on here, Miss Leigh. You returned the horse. Very proper and what I would expect of you. Now the brooch is given in a very different spirit. I give it to you for a reason. You have been good to Alvean. Not only as a governess but as a woman. Do you know what I mean? There is more to the care of a child, is there not, than arithmetic and grammar. You gave her that little extra. The brooch belonged to Alvean's mother. Look upon it like this, Miss Leigh: It is a gift of appreciation from us both. Does that make it all right?'

I was silent for a few moments. Then I said: 'Yes . . . that is different, of course. I accept the brooch. Thank you very much, Mr. TreMellyn.'

He smiled at me – it was a smile I did not fully understand, because it seemed to hold in it many meanings.

I was afraid to try to understand.

'Thank you,' I murmured again; and I hurried back to the house.

I went up to my room and took out the brooch. I pinned it on my dress, and immediately my lavender cotton took on a new look.

I would wear the diamonds to-night. I would go in Phillida's dress and my comb and shawl, and on my breast I would wear Alice's diamonds.

So on this strange Christmas Day I had a gift from Alice.

I had dined in the middle of the day in the small dining room with Connan and Alvean, the first meal I had taken with them in this intimacy. We had eaten turkey and plum pudding and had been waited on by Kitty and Daisy. I could feel that certain significant looks were being directed towards us.

'On Christmas Day,' Connan had said, 'you could not be expected to dine alone. Do you know, Miss Leigh, I fear we have treated you rather badly. I should have suggested that you should go home to your family for Christmas. You should have reminded me.'

'I felt I had been here too short a time to ask for a holiday,' I answered. 'Besides . . .'

'In view of Alvean's accident, you felt you should stay,' he murmured. 'It is good of you to be so thoughtful.'

Conversation in the small dining room was animated. The three of us discussed the Christmas customs, and Connan told us stories of what had happened in previous years, how on one occasion the wassailers had arrived late so that the family had gone to church and they had to wait outside and serenade them all the way home.

I imagined Alice with him now. I imagined her sitting in the chair I now occupied. I wondered what the conversation was like then. I wondered if now, seeing me there, he was thinking of Alice.

I kept reminding myself that it was merely because it was Christmas that I was sitting here. That after the festivities were over I should revert to my old place.

But I was not going to think of that now. To-night I was going to the ball. Miraculously I had a dress worthy of the occasion. I had a comb of amber and a brooch of diamonds. I felt, To-night I shall mingle with these people on my own terms. It will be quite unlike that occasion when I danced in the solarium.

I took Connan's advice that afternoon and tried to rest so that I might stay fresh until the early morning. Much to my surprise I did manage to sleep. I must have slept lightly for I dreamed, and as so often in this house, my dreams were of Alice. I thought that she came to the ball, a shadowy wraith of a figure whom no one but I could see, and she whispered to me as I danced with Connan: 'This is what I want, Marty. I like to see this. I like to see you sitting in my chair at luncheon. I like to see your hand in that of Connan. You . . . Marty . . . you . . . not another. . . .'

I awoke with reluctance. That was a pleasant dream. I tried to sleep again, tried to get back to that half-world where ghosts came back from the tomb and told you that they longed for you to have all that you most wanted in life.

Daisy brought me a cup of tea at five o'clock. On Mrs. Polgrey's instructions, she told me.

'I've brought 'ee a piece of Mrs. Polgrey's fuggan to take with it,' she said, indicating a slice of raisin cake. 'If there's more you do want, 'tis only for you to say.'

I said: 'This will be ample.'

'Then you'll be wanting to get ready for the ball, will 'ee not, Miss?'

'There's plenty of time,' I told her.

'I'll bring 'ee hot water at six, Miss. That'll give 'ee plenty of time to dress. The Master 'ull be receiving the guests at eight. That's how it always was. And don't forget – 'tis but buffet supper at nine, so there's a long time to go afore you get more to eat. Are you sure you wouldn't like something more than that there piece of fuggan?'

I was sure I was going to find it difficult to eat what she had brought so I said: 'This is quite enough, Daisy.'

'Well, 'tis for you to say, Miss.'

She stood at the door a moment, her head on one side, watching me. Speculatively? Was she regarding me with a new interest?

I pictured them in the servants' hall, Tapperty leading the conversation.

Were they always wondering what new relationship had begun – or was about to begin – between the Master of the house and the governess?

I was at the ball in Phillida's green dress with the tight, low-cut bodice and the billowing skirt. I had dressed my hair differently, piling it high on my head; it was necessary to do so in order to do justice to the comb. On my dress sparkled the diamond brooch.

I was happy. I could mingle with the guests as one of them. No one would know, unless told, that I was only the governess.

I had waited until the ballroom was full before I went down. Then I could best mingle with the guests. I had only been there a few minutes when Peter was at my elbow.

'You look dazzling,' he said.

'Thank you. I am glad to surprise you.'

'I'm not in the least surprised. I always knew how you could look, given the chance.'

'You always know how to pay the compliment.'

'To you I always say what I mean. One thing I have not yet said to you, and that is "A happy Christmas." '

'Thank you. I wish you the same.'

'Let us make it so for each other. I have brought no gift for you.'

'But why should you?'

'Because it is Christmas, and a pleasant custom for friends to exchange gifts.'

'But not for . . .'

'Please . . . please . . . no reminders of governessing to-night. One day I am going to give you Jacinth, you know. She is meant for you. I see Connan is about to open the ball. Will you partner me?'

'Thank you, yes.'

'It's the traditional dance, you know.'

'I don't know it.'

'It's easy. You only have to follow me.' He began humming the tune to me. 'Haven't you seen it done before?'

'Yes, through the peep in the solarium at the last ball.'

'Ah, that last ball! We danced together. But Connan cut in, didn't he?'

'It was somewhat unconventional.'

'Very, for our governess. I'm really surprised at her.'

The music had begun, and Connan was walking into the centre of the hall holding Celestine by the hand. To my horror I realized that Peter and I would have to join them and dance those first few bars with them.

I tried to hold back, but Peter had me firmly by the hand.

Celestine was surprised to see me there; but if Connan was he gave no sign. I imagined that Celestine reasoned: It is all very well to ask the governess as it is Christmas. But should she immediately thrust herself into such a prominent position?

However, I believed her to be of too sweet a nature to show her astonishment after that first start of surprise. She gave me a warm smile.

I said: 'I shouldn't be here. I don't really know the dance. I didn't realize . . .'

'Follow us,' said Connan.

'We'll look after you,' echoed Peter.

And in a few seconds the others were falling in behind us.

Round the hall we went to the tune of *The Furry Dance.*

'You're doing excellently,' said Connan with a smile as our hands touched.

'You will soon be a Cornishwoman,' added Celestine.

'And why not?' demanded Peter. 'Are we not the salt of the earth?'

'I am not sure that Miss Leigh thinks so,' replied Connan.

'I am becoming very interested in all the customs of the country,' I added.

'And in the inhabitants, I hope,' whispered Peter.

We danced on. It was simple enough to learn, and when it was over I knew all the movements.

As the last bars were played I heard someone to say: 'Who is the striking-looking young woman who danced with Peter Nansellock?'

I wanted for the answer to be: 'Oh, that's the governess.'

But it was different: 'I've no idea. She certainly is . . . unusual.'

I was exultant. I doubt that I had ever been so happy in my life.

I knew that in the time to come I should treasure every minute of that wonderful evening, for I was not only at the ball, I was a success at the ball.

I did not lack partners; and even when I was forced to admit that I was the governess, I continued to receive the homage due to an attractive woman. What had happened to change me, I wondered. Why couldn't I have been like this at Aunt Adelaide's parties? But if I had, I should never have come to Mount Mellyn.

Then I knew why I had not been like this. It was not only the green dress, the amber comb and the diamond brooch; I was in love, and love was the greatest beautifier of all.

Never mind if I was ridiculously, hopelessly in love. I was like Cinderella at the ball, determined to enjoy myself until the stroke of twelve.

A strange thing happened while I was dancing. I was with Sir Thomas Treslyn, who turned out to be a courteous old gentleman, a little wheezy during the dance so I suggested that he might prefer to sit out the rest of it. He was very grateful to me and I felt quite fond of him. I was ready to be fond of anyone on that night.

He said: 'I'm getting a little too old for the dance, Miss er . . .'

'Leigh,' I said. 'Miss Leigh. I'm the governess here, Sir Thomas.'

'Oh indeed,' he said. 'I was going to say, Miss Leigh, it is extremely kind of you to think of my comfort when you must be longing to dance.'

'I'm quite happy to sit for a while.'

'I see that you are kind as well as very attractive.'

I remembered Phillida's instructions and accepted the compliments nonchalantly as though I had been accustomed to them all my life.

He was relaxed and confidential. 'It's my wife who likes to come to these affairs. She has so much vitality.'

'Ah yes,' I said, 'she is very beautiful.'

I had noticed her, of course, the very moment I entered the ballroom; she was in pale mauve chiffon over an underskirt of green; she evidently had a passion for chiffon and such clinging materials, and it was understandable considering her figure; she wore quantities of diamonds. The mauve toning down the green was exquisite and I wondered whether my own vivid emerald was not a little blatant compared with hers. She looked outstandingly beautiful, as she would in any assembly.

He nodded, a little sadly I thought.

And as I sat talking, my eyes, wandering round the hall, went suddenly to the peep high in the wall, that star-shaped opening which merged so perfectly into the murals that none would have guessed it was there.

Someone was watching the ball through the peep, but it was impossible to see who it was.

I thought: Of course it is Alvean. Did she not always watch the ball through the peep? Then I was suddenly startled for, as I was sitting there, watching the dancers, I saw Alvean. I had forgotten that this was a special occasion – Christmas Day – and just as, on such a day, the governess might come to the ball, so might Alvean.

She was dressed in a white muslin dress with a wide blue sash and I saw that she wore the silver whip pinned to the bodice of her dress. All these things I noticed with half my attention. I looked swiftly up to the peep. The face, unrecognizable, indefinable, was still there.

Supper was served in the dining room and the punch room. There was a buffet in both these rooms and guests helped themselves, for according to custom the servants on this day of days were having their own ball in their own hall.

I saw that these people who so rarely waited on themselves now found it quite good fun to do so. Piled on dishes were the results of all that kitchen activity; small pies of various kinds, called here pasties – not the enormous ones which were eaten frequently in the kitchen, but dainty ones. There were slices of beef, and chicken and fish of various descriptions. There was a great bowl of hot punch; another of mulled wine; there was mead, whisky and sloe gin.

Peter Nansellock, with whom I had had the supper dance, led me into the punch room. Sir Thomas Treslyn was already there with Celestine, and Peter led me to the table at which they were sitting.

'Leave it to me,' he said. 'I'll feed you all.'

I said: 'Allow me to help you.'

'Nonsense,' he replied. 'You remain with Celeste.' He whispered banteringly: 'You're not the governess to-night, Miss Leigh; you're a lady like the rest of them. Don't forget it; then no one else will.'

But I was determined that I would not be waited on and I insisted on going to the buffet with him.

'Pride,' he murmured, slipping his hand through my arm. 'Wasn't that the sin by which fell the angels?'

'It may have been ambition; I am not sure.'

'Well, I'll warrant you're not without a dash of that either. Never mind. What will you eat? Perhaps it is as well you came. Our Cornish food often seems odd to you foreigners from the other side of the Tamar.'

He began loading one of the trays which had been put there in readiness.

'Which sort of pie will you have? Giblet, squab, nattling or muggety? Ha, here's taddage too. I can recommend the squab: layers of apple and bacon, onions and mutton and young pigeon. The most delicious Cornish fare.'

'I'm ready to try it,' I said.

'Miss Leigh,' he went on, 'Martha . . . has anyone ever told you that your eyes are like amber?'

'Yes,' I answered.

'Has anyone ever told you you're beautiful?'

'No.'

'Then that oversight should be and is rectified immediately.'

I laughed and at that moment Connan came into the room with Lady Treslyn.

She sat down with Celestine, and Connan came over to the buffet.

'I am enlightening Miss Leigh about our Cornish food. She doesn't know what a "fair maid" is. Is that not odd, Con, seeing that she is one herself?'

Connan looked excited; his eyes smiling into mine were warm. He said: 'Fair maids, Miss Leigh, is another name for pilchards served like this with oil and lemon.' He took a fork and put some on two plates. 'It is a contraction of the old Spanish fumado, and we always say here that it is food fit for a Spanish don.'

'A relic, Miss Leigh,' interrupted Peter, 'of those days when the Spaniards raided our shores and took too great an interest in another kind of fair maid.'

Alvean had come in and was standing beside me. I thought she looked tired.

'You should be in bed,' I said.

'I'm hungry,' she told me.

'After supper we'll go up.'

She nodded and with sleepy pleasure she piled food on a plate.

We sat round the table, Alvean, Peter, Celestine, Sir Thomas, Connan and Lady Treslyn.

It seemed like a dream that I should be there with them. Alice's brooch glittered on my dress, and I thought: Thus, two years ago, she would have sat . . . as I am sitting now. Alvean would not have been here then; she would have been too young to have been allowed to come, but apart from that and the fact that I was in Alice's place, it must have been very like other occasions. I wondered if any of the others thought this.

I remembered the face I had seen at the peep, and what Alvean had said on the night of that other ball. I could not remember the exact words but I knew that it had been something about her mother's love of dancing and how, if she came back, she would come to a ball. Then Alvean had half-hoped to see her among the dancers . . . What if she watched from another place? I thought of that ghostly solarium in moonlight and I said to myself: 'Whose face did I see at the peep?'

Then I thought: Gilly! What if it were Gilly? It must have been Gilly. Who else could it have been?

My attention was brought back to the group at the table when Connan said: 'I'll get you some more whisky, Tom.' He rose and went to the buffet. Lady Treslyn got up quickly and went to him. I found it difficult to take my eyes from them. I thought how distinguished they looked – she in green shaded mauve draperies, the most beautiful woman at the ball and he, surely the most distinguished of the men.

'I'll help you, Connan', she said, and I heard them laughing together.

'Look out,' said Connan, 'we're spilling it.'

They had their backs to us, and as I watched them I thought that with the slightest provocation I could have burst into tears because now I clearly saw the ridiculousness of my hopes.

She had slipped her arm through his as they came back to the table. The intimate gesture wounded me deeply. I suppose I had drunk too much of the mead, or metheglin as they called it. Mead. It was such a soft and gentle name. But the mead which was made at Mount Mellyn was very potent.

I said to myself coldly: It is time you retired.

As he gave the glass to Sir Thomas – who emptied it with a speed which surprised me – I noticed that there were smudges of shadow under Alvean's eyes, and I said: 'Alvean, you look tired. You should be in bed.'

'Poor child!' cried Celestine at once. 'And she only just recovering. . . .'

I rose. 'I will take Alvean to bed now,' I said. 'Come along, Alvean.'

She was half-asleep already and made no protest but rose meekly to her feet.

'I will say good night to you all,' I said.

Peter rose to his feet. 'We'll see you later,' he said.

I did not answer. I was desperately trying not to look at Connan, for I felt he was not aware of me; that he would never be aware of anyone when Lady Treslyn was near.

'*Au revoir*,' said Peter, and as the others echoed the words absentmindedly I went out of the punch room, holding Alvean by the hand.

I felt as Cinderella must have felt with the striking of the midnight hour. My brief glory was over. Lady Treslyn had made me realize how foolish I had been to dream.

Alvean was asleep before I left her room. I tried not to think of Connan and Lady Treslyn while I went to my room and lighted the candles on my dressing table. I looked attractive; there was no doubt of it. Then I said to myself, Anyone looks attractive by candlelight.

The diamonds winked back at me, and I was immediately reminded of the face I had seen at the peep.

I thought afterwards that I must have drunk too freely of the metheglin, because on impulse I went down to the landing below my own. I could hear the shouts coming from the servants' hall. So they were still merry-making down there. The door to Gilly's room was ajar, and I went in. There was enough moonlight for me to see that the child was in her bed, but sitting up, awake.

'Gilly,' I said.

'Madam!' she cried and her voice was joyful. 'I knew you'd come to-night.'

'Gilly, you know who this is.' What had made me say such a foolish thing?

She nodded.

'I'm going to light your candle,' I said, and I did so.

Her eyes regarded my face with that blank blue stare, and came to rest on the brooch. I sat on the edge of the bed. I knew that when I had first come in she had thought I was someone else.

She was contented though, which showed the confidence she was beginning to feel in me.

I touched the brooch and said: 'Once it was Mrs. TreMellyn's.'

She smiled and nodded.

I said: 'You spoke when I came in. Why do you not speak to me now?'

She merely smiled.

'Gilly,' I said, 'were you at the peep in the solarium tonight? Were you watching the dancers?'

She nodded.

'Gilly, say "Yes." '

'Yes,' said Gilly.

'You were up there all alone? You weren't afraid?'

She shook her head and smiled.

'You mean no, don't you, Gilly? Say "no." '

'No.'

'Why weren't you afraid?'

She opened her mouth and smiled. Then she said: 'Not afraid because . . .'

'Because?' I said eagerly.

'Because,' she repeated.

'Gilly,' I said. 'Were you alone up there?'

She smiled and I could get her to say no more.

After a while I kissed her and she returned my kiss. She was fond of me, I knew. I believed that in her mind she confused me with someone else, and I knew who that person was.

Back in my room I did not want to take off my dress. I felt that as long as I wore it, I could still hope for what I knew to be impossible.

So I sat by my window for an hour or so. It was a warm night and I was comfortable with my silk shawl about me.

I heard some of the guests coming out to their carriages. I heard the exchange of good-byes.

And while I was there I heard Lady Treslyn's voice. Her voice was low and vibrant, but she spoke with such intensity that I caught every syllable and I knew to whom she was speaking.

She said: 'Connan, it can't be long now. It won't be long.'

Next morning when Kitty brought my water, she did not come alone. Daisy was with her. I heard their raucous voices mingling and, in my half-waking state, thought they sounded like the gulls.

'Morning, Miss.'

They wanted me to wake up quickly; they had exciting news. I saw that in their faces.

'Miss . . .' they were both speaking together, both determined to be the one to impart the startling information, 'last night . . . or rather this morning . . .'

Then Kitty rushed on ahead of her sister: 'Sir Thomas Treslyn was taken bad on the way home. He was dead when they got to Treslyn Hall.'

I sat up in bed, looking from one excited face to the other.

One of the guests . . . dead! I was shocked. But this was no ordinary death, no ordinary death.

I realized, no less than Kitty and Daisy, what such news could mean to Mount Mellyn.

Chapter Seven

Sir Thomas Treslyn was buried on New Year's Day.

During the preceding week gloom had settled on the house, and it was all the more noticeable because it followed on the heels of the Christmas festivities. All the decorations had been left about the house, and there was divided opinion as to which was the more unlucky – to remove them before Twelfth Night or to leave them up and thereby show lack of respect.

They all appeared to consider that the death touched us closely. He had died between our house and his own; our table was the last at which he had sat. I realized that the Cornish were a very superstitious people, constantly on the alert for omens, eager to placate supernatural and malignant powers.

Connan was absentminded. I saw little of him, but when I did he seemed scarcely aware of my presence. I imagined he was considering all that this meant to him. If he and Lady Treslyn had been lovers there was no obstacle now to their regularizing their union. I knew that this thought was in the minds of many, but no one spoke of it. I guessed that Mrs. Polgrey would consider it unlucky to do so until Sir Thomas had been buried for some weeks.

Mrs. Polgrey called me to her room and we had a cup of Earl Grey laced with a spoonful of the whisky I had given her.

'This is a shocking thing,' she said. 'Sir Thomas to die on Christmas Day as he did. Although 'tweren't Christmas Day but Boxing Day morning,' she added in a slightly relieved tone, as though this made the situation a little less shocking. 'And to think,' she went on, reverting to her original gloom, 'that ours was the last house he rested in, my food was the last that passed his lips! The funeral is a bit soon, do you not think, Miss?'

I began to count the days on my fingers. 'Seven days,' I said.

'They could have kept him longer, seeing it's winter.'

'I suppose they feel that the sooner it's over the sooner they'll recover from the shock.'

She herself looked shocked indeed. I think she thought it was disrespectful or unlucky to suggest that anyone would want to recover quickly from their grief.

'I don't know,' she said, 'you hear tales of people being buried alive. I remember years ago, when I was a child, there was a smallpox epidemic. People panicked and buried quick. It was said that some was buried alive.'

'There is surely no doubt that Sir Thomas is *dead*.'

'Some seem dead and are not dead, after all. Still seven days should be long enough to tell. You'll come to the funeral with me, Miss?'

'I?'

'But why not? I think we should show proper respect to the dead.'

'I have no mourning clothes.'

'My dear life, I'll find a bonnet for 'ee. I'll give 'ee a black band to sew on your cloak. Reckon that 'ud be all right if we were just at the grave. 'Twouldn't do for 'ee to go into the church like, but then 'twouldn't be right either . . . you being the governess here, and them having so many friends as will attend to fill Mellyn Church to the full.'

So it was agreed that I should accompany Mrs. Polgrey to the churchyard.

I was present when Sir Thomas's body was lowered into the tomb.

It was an impressive ceremony, for the funeral had been a magnificent one in accordance with the Treslyn's rank in the duchy. Crowds attended, but Mrs. Polgrey and I hovered only in the distance. I was glad of this; she deplored it.

It was enough for me to see the widow in flowing black draperies yet looking as beautiful as she ever had. Her lovely face was just visible among the flowing black, which seemed to become her even as green and mauve had on the night of the Christmas ball. She moved with grace and she looked even more slender in her black than in the brilliant colours I had seen her wear, intensely feminine and appealing.

Connan was there, and I thought how elegant and distinguished he looked; I tried to fathom the expression on his face that I might discover his feelings. But he was determined to hide those feelings from the world; and I thought, in the circumstances, that was just as well.

I watched the hearse with the large waving black plumes and I saw the coffin, carried by six bearers and covered with velvet palls of deep purple and black, taken into the church. I saw the banks of flowers and the mourners in their deathly black, the only colour being the white handkerchiefs which the women held to their eyes – and they had wide black borders.

A cold wind had swept the mists away and the winter sun shone brightly on the gilt of the coffin as it was lowered into the grave.

There was a deep silence in the churchyard, broken only by the sudden cry of gulls.

It was over and the mourners, Connan, Celestine and Peter among them, went back to their carriages which wound their way to Treslyn Hall.

Mrs. Polgrey and I returned to Mount Mellyn, where she insisted on the usual cup of tea and its accompaniment.

We sat drinking, and her eyes glittered. I knew she was finding it difficult to restrain her tongue. But she said nothing of the effect this death might have on us all at Mount Mellyn. So great was her respect for the dead.

Sir Thomas was not forgotten. I heard his name mentioned often during the next few weeks. Mrs. Polgrey shook her head significantly when the Treslyns were mentioned, but her eyes were sharp and full of warning.

Daisy and Kitty were less discreet. When they brought my water in the mornings they would linger. I was a little cunning, I think. I longed to know what people were saying but I did not want to ask, yet I managed to draw them out without, I hoped, seeming to do so.

It was true they did not need a lot of encouragement.

'I saw Lady Treslyn yesterday,' Daisy told me, one morning. 'Her didn't look like a widow, in spite of the weeds.'

'Oh? In what way?'

'Don't 'ee ask me, Miss. She was quite pale and not smiling, but I could see something in her face . . . if you do get my meaning.'

'I'm afraid I don't.'

'Kit were with me. She said the same. Like as though she were waiting and content because she wouldn't have to wait long. A year though. Seems a long time to *me*.'

'A year? What for?' I asked, although I knew very well what for.

Daisy looked at me and giggled.

''Twon't do for them to be seeing too much of each other for a bit, will it, Miss. After all, him dying here . . . almost on our doorstep. 'Twould seem as though they'd almost willed him to it.'

'Oh, Daisy, that's absurd. How could anybody?'

'Well, that's what you can't say till you know, 'twould seem.'

The conversation was getting dangerous. I dismissed her with 'I must hurry. I see I'm rather late.'

When she had gone, I thought: So there is talk about them. They are saying he was willed to die.

As long as that's all they say, that won't do much harm.

I wondered how careful they were being. I remembered hearing Phillida say that people in love behaved like ostriches. They buried their heads in the sand and thought, because they saw no one, no one saw them.

But they were not two inexperienced lovers.

No, I thought bitterly, it is clear that both are very experienced. They knew the people among whom they lived. They would be careful.

It was later that day, when I was in the woods, that I heard the sounds of horses' hoofs walking nearby and then I heard Lady Treslyn say: 'Connan. Oh, Connan!'

They had met then . . . and to meet as near the house as this was surely foolish.

In the woods their voices carried. The trees hid me, but snatches of their conversation came to me.

'Linda! You shouldn't have come.'

'I know . . . I know. . . .' Her voice fell and I could not hear the rest.

'To send that message . . .' That was Connan. I could hear him more clearly than her, perhaps because I knew his voice so well. 'Your messenger will have been seen by some of the servants. You know how they gossip.'

'I know, but . . .'

'When did this come . . .?'

'This morning. I had to show it to you right away.'

'It's the first?'

'No, there was one two days ago. That's why I had to see you, Connan. No matter what . . . I'm frightened. . . .'

'It's mischief,' he said. 'Ignore it. Forget it.'

'Read it,' she cried. 'Read it.'

There was a short silence. Then Connan spoke. 'I see. There's only one thing to be done. . . .'

The horses had begun to move. In a few seconds they might come past the spot where I was. I hurried away through the trees.

I was very uneasy.

That day Connan left Mount Mellyn.

'Called away to Penzance,' Mrs. Polgrey told me. 'He said he was unsure how long he would be away.'

I wondered if his sudden departure had anything to do with the disquieting news which Lady Treslyn had brought to him that morning in the woods.

Several days passed. Alvean and I resumed our lessons and Gilly too came to the schoolroom.

I would give Gilly some small task while I worked with Alvean, such as trying to make letters in a tray of sand, or on a slate, or counting beads on an abacus. She was contented to do this and I believed that she was happy in my company, that from me she drew a certain comfort which had its roots in security. She had trusted Alice and she was transferring that trust to me.

Alvean had rebelled at first but I had pointed out the need to be kind to those less fortunate than ourselves, and at length I had worked on her sympathy so that she accepted Gilly's presence, although a little sullenly. But I had noticed that now and then she would throw a glance at the child, and I was sure that at least she was very interested in her.

Connan had been away a week and it was a cold February morning when Mrs. Polgrey came into the schoolroom. I was very surprised to see her, for she rarely interrupted lessons; she was holding two letters in her hand and I could see that she was excited.

She made no excuses for her intrusion and said: 'I have heard from the Master. He wants you to take Miss Alvean down to Penzance at once. Here is a letter for you. No doubt he explains more fully in that.'

She handed me the letter and I was afraid that she would see that my hand shook a little as I opened it.

> *My dear Miss Leigh,* I read,
> I will be here for a few weeks, I think, and I am sure you will agree that it would be very desirable for Alvean to join me here. I do not think she should miss her lessons, so I am asking you to bring her and be prepared to stay for a week or so.
> Perhaps you could be ready to leave to-morrow. Get Billy Trehay to drive you to the station for the 2.30 train.
>
> *Connan TreMellyn*

I knew that the colour had rushed to my face. I hoped I had not betrayed the extreme joy which took possession of me.

I said: 'Alvean, we are to join your father to-morrow.'

Alvean leapt up and threw herself into my arms, a most unusual display, but it moved me deeply to realize how much she cared for him.

This helped me to regain my own composure. I said: 'That is for to-morrow. To-day we will continue with our lessons.'

'But, Miss, there's our packing to do.'

'We have this afternoon for that,' I said primly. 'Now, let us return to our work.'

'I turned to Mrs. Polgrey. 'Yes,' I said, 'Mr. TreMellyn wishes me to take Alvean to him.'

She nodded. I could see that she thought it very strange, and this was because he had never before shown such interest in the child.

'And you're leaving to-morrow.'

'Yes. Billy Trehay is to be given instructions to drive us to the station in time for the 2.30 train.'

She nodded.

When she had gone I sat down in a daze. I could not concentrate more than Alvean could. It was some time before I remembered Gilly. She was looking at me with that blank expression in her eyes which I had dreamed of banishing.

Gilly understood more than one realised.

She knew that we were going away and that she would be left behind.

I could scarcely wait to begin my packing. Alvean and I had luncheon together in the schoolroom but neither of us was interested in food, and immediately after the meal we went to our rooms to do the packing.

I had very little to pack. My grey and mauve dresses were clean, for which

I was thankful, and I would wear my grey merino. It was not very becoming but it would be too difficult to pack.

I took out the green silk dress which I had worn at the Christmas ball. Should I take it? Why not? I had rarely possessed anything so becoming, and who knew, there might be an occasion when I could wear it.

I took out my comb and shawl, stuck the comb in my hair and let the shawl fall negligently about my shoulders.

I thought of the Christmas ball – that moment when Peter had taken my hand and had drawn me into the *Furry Dance*. I heard the tune in my head and began to dance, for the moment really feeling I was in the ballroom and that it was Christmas night again.

I had not heard Gilly come in, and I was startled to see her standing watching me. Really, the child did move too silently about the house.

'I stopped dancing, flushing with embarrassment to have been caught in such silly behaviour. Gilly was regarding me solemnly.

She looked at the bag on my bed and the folded clothes beside it, and imediately my pleasure left me for I understood that Gilly was going to be very unhappy if we went away.

I stooped down and put my arms about her. 'It'll only be for a little while, Gilly.'

She screwed her eyes up tightly and would not look at me.

'Gilly,' I said, 'listen. We'll soon be back, you know.'

She shook her head and I saw tears squeeze themselves out of her eyes.

'Then,' I went on, 'we'll have our lessons. You shall draw me more letters in the sand, and soon you will be writing your name.'

But I could see that she refused to be comforted.

She tore herself from me and ran to the bed and began pulling the things out of my trunk.

'No, Gilly, no,' I said. I lifted her up in my arms and went to a chair. I sat for a while rocking her. I went on: 'I'm coming back, you know, Gilly. In less than no time I'll be here. It will seem as though I've never been away.'

She spoke then: 'You won't come back. She . . . She . . .'

'Yes, Gilly, yes?'

'She . . . went.'

For the moment I forgot even the fact that I was going to Connan, because I was certain now that Gilly knew something, and what she knew might throw some light on the mystery of Alice.

'Gilly,' I said, 'did she say good-bye to you before she went?'

Gilly shook her head vehemently, and I thought she was going to burst into tears.

'Gilly,' I pleaded, 'try to talk to me, try to tell me. . . . Did you see her go?'

Gilly threw herself at me and buried her face against my bodice. I held her tenderly for a moment, then withdraw myself and looked into her face; but her eyes were tightly shut.

She ran back to the bed and again started to pull the things out of my trunk.

'No. . . .' she cried. 'No . . . no. . . .'

Swiftly I went to her. 'Look, Gilly,' I said, 'I'm coming back. I'll only be away a short time.'

'She stayed away!'

We were back at that point where we started. I did not believe I could discover anything more from her at this stage.

She lifted her little face to mine and all the blankness had gone from the eyes; they were tragic.

I saw in that moment how much my care of her had meant to her, and that it was impossible to make her understand that if I went away it was not for ever. Alice had been kind to her and Alice had gone. Her experiences had taught her that that was the way of life.

A few days . . . a week in the life of Gilly . . . would be like a year to most of us. I knew then that I could not leave Gilly behind.

Then I asked myself what Connan would say if I arrived with both children.

I believed that I could adequately explain my reasons. However, I was not going to leave Gilly behind. I could let Mrs. Polgrey know that the master expected the two children; she would be pleased; she trusted Gilly with me, and she had been the first to admit that the child had improved since I had tried to help her.

'Gilly,' I said. 'I'm going away for a few days. Alvean and you are coming with me.' I kissed her upturned face. And I repeated because she looked so bewildered: 'You are coming with me. You'll like that, won't you.'

It was still some seconds before she understood, and then she shut her eyes tightly and lowered her head; I saw she smiled. That moved me more than any words could have done.

I felt I was ready to brave Connan's displeasure to bring such happiness to this poor child.

The next morning we set out early, and the whole household turned out to see us go. I sat in the carriage with a child on either side of me, and Billy Trehay in TreMellyn's livery sat jauntily in the driver's seat talking to the horses.

Mrs. Polgrey stood, her arms folded across her bosom, and her eyes were on Gilly. It was clear that she was delighted to see her little granddaughter riding with myself and Alvean.

Tapperty stood with his daughters on either side of him; and their twinkling eyes, all so much alike, were full of speculation.

I did not care. I felt so light-headed as we drove off that it was all I could do to prevent myself breaking into song.

It was a bright sunny morning and there was a slight frost in the air which sparkled on the grass, and the thin layer of ice on the ponds and streams.

We rattled along at a good speed over the rough roads. The children were in high spirits; Alvean chattered a good deal, and Gilly sat contentedly beside me. I noticed that she clutched my skirt with one hand, and the gesture filled me with tenderness for her. I was deeply aware of my responsibility towards this child.

Billy was talkative, and when we passed a grave at a crossroads, he uttered a prayer for the poor lost soul who was buried there.

'Not that the soul will rest, me dears. A person who meets death that way never rests. 'Tis the same if they meet death any way violent like. They can't stay buried underground. They *walks*.'

'What nonsense!' I said sharply.

'Them that knows no better call wisdom nonsense,' retorted Billy, piqued.

'It seems to me that many people have too lively imaginations.'

The children's eyes I noticed were fixed on my face.

'Why,' I said quickly as we passed a cob cottage with beehives in the garden, 'look at those hives! What's that over them?'

'Tis black crêpe,' said Billy. 'It means death in the family. Bees would take it terrible hard if they weren't told of the death and helped to share in the mourning.'

I was glad when we arrived in the station.

We were met at Penzance by a carriage and then began the journey to Penlandstow. It was growing dark when we turned into a drive and I saw a house loom up before us. There was a man in the porch with a lantern who called out: 'They be here. Run and tell master. He did say to let him know the minute they did come.'

We were a little stiff and both children were half-asleep. I helped them down and as I turned, I saw Connan standing beside me. I could not see him very clearly in the dim light but I did know that he was pleased to see me. He took my hand and pressed it warmly.

Then he said an astonishing thing. 'I've been anxious. I visualized all sorts of mishaps. I wished I'd come and brought you here myself.'

I thought: He means Alvean, of course. He is not really talking to me.

But he was facing me, and smiling; and I felt I had never been quite so happy in the whole of my life.

I began: 'The children . . .'

He smiled down at Alvean.

'Hallo, Papa,' she said. 'It's lovely to be here with you.'

He laid a hand on her shoulder, and she looked up at him almost pleadingly, as though she were asking him to kiss her. That, it seemed, was asking too much.

He merely said: 'I'm glad you've come, Alvean. You'll have some fun here.'

Then I brought Gilly forward.

'What . . .' he began.

'We couldn't leave Gilly behind,' I said. 'You know you gave me your permission to teach her.'

He hesitated for a moment. Then he looked at me and laughed. I knew in that moment that he was so pleased to see me – me, not the others – that he would not have cared whom I brought with me as long as I came myself.

It was no wonder that as I walked into Alice's old home I felt as though I were entering an enchanted place.

During the next two weeks it seemed that I had left behind me the cold hard world of reality and stepped into one of my own making, and that everything I desired was to be mine.

From the moment I arrived at Penlandstow Manor I was treated, not as a governess, but as a guest. In a few days I had lost my sensitivity on this point and, when I had cast that off, I was like the high-spirited girl who had enjoyed life in the country vicarage with her father and Phillida.

I was given a pleasant room next to Alvean's and when I asked that Gilly should be put near me this was done.

Penlandstow was a house of great charm which had been built in the Elizabethan era. It was almost as large as Mount Mellyn and as easy to lose oneself in.

My room was large and there were padded window seats upholstered in red velvet, and dark red curtains. My bed was a fourposter hung with silk embroidered curtains. The carpet was of the same deep red, and this would have given warmth to the room even if there had not been a log fire burning in the open grate.

My bag was brought up to this room and one of the maids proceeded to unpack while I stood by the fire watching the blue flames dart among the logs.

The maid curtsied when she had laid my things on the bed, and asked if she might put them away. This was not the manner in which to treat a governess, I thought. Kind and friendly as Daisy and Kitty had been, they had not been ready to wait on me like this.

I said I would put my things away myself but would like hot water to wash.

'There be a little bathroom at the end of the landing, Miss,' I was told. 'Shall I show it to 'ee and bring 'ee hot water up there?'

I was taken along to the room in which there was a big bath; there was also a hip bath.

'Miss Alice had the room afore her married and went away,' I was told; and with a little shock I remembered that I was in Alice's old home.

When I had washed and changed my dress – I put on the lavender cotton – I went along to see Alvean. She had fallen asleep on her bed so I left her. Gilly was also asleep in her room. And when I returned to my own the maid who had shown me the bathroom came in and said that Mr. TreMellyn had asked that, when I was ready, I would join him in the library.

I said I was ready then and she took me to him.

'It is indeed pleasant to see you here, Miss Leigh,' he said.

'It will be very agreeable for you to have your own daughter here . . .' I began.

And he interrupted me with a smile. 'I said it was pleasant to see you here, Miss Leigh. I meant exactly that.'

I flushed. 'That is kind of you. I have brought certain of the children's lesson books along. . . .'

'Let us give them a little holiday, shall we? Lessons I suppose there must be, if you say so, but need they sit at their desks all the time?'

'I think their lessons might be curtailed on an occasion like this.'

He came and stood close to me. 'Miss Leigh,' he said, 'you are delightful.'

I drew back startled, and he went on: 'I'm glad you came so promptly.'

'Those were your orders.'

'I did not mean to order, Miss Leigh. Merely to request.'

'But . . .' I began; and I was apprehensive because he seemed different from the man I had known. He was almost like a stranger – a stranger who fascinated me no less than that other Connan TreMellyn, a stranger who frightened me a little, for I was unsure of myself, unsure of my own emotions.

'I was so glad to escape,' he said. 'I thought you would be too.'

'Escape . . . from what?'

'From the gloom of death. I hate death. It depresses me.'

'You mean Sir Thomas. But . . .'

'Oh, I know. A neighbour merely. But still it did depress me. I wanted to get right away. I am so glad you have joined me . . . with Alvean and the other child.'

I said on impulse: 'I hope you did not think it was presumptuous of me to bring Gillyflower. She would have been heartbroken if I had not brought her.'

Then he said a thing which set my senses swimming: 'I can understand her being heartbroken if she had to part from you.'

I said quickly: 'I suppose the children should have a meal of some sort. They are exhausted and sleeping now. But I do feel they need some refreshment before they go to bed. It has been a tiring day for them.'

He waved a hand. 'Order what you wish for them, Miss Leigh. And when you have seen to them, you and I will dine together.'

I said: 'Alvean dines with you . . . does she not?'

'She will be too tired to-night. We will have it alone.'

So I ordered what I wanted for the children, and I dined with Connan in the winter parlour. It was a strange and exhilarating experience to dine with that man in candlelight. I kept telling myself that it could not be real. If ever anything was the stuff that dreams were made of, this was.

He talked a great deal; there was no sign of the taciturn Connan that evening.

He told me about the house, how it had been built in the shape of an E as a compliment to the queen who had been reigning when it was built. He drew the shape to show me. 'Two three-sided courtyards,' he said, 'and a projecting centre block, if you see what I mean. We are in the central block now. The main feature of it is the hall, the staircase and the gallery, and these smaller rooms such as the winter parlour which, I think you will agree, is ideally suited for a small company.'

I said I thought it was a delightful house, and how fortunate he was to possess two such magnificent places.

'Stone walls do not bring satisfaction, Miss Leigh. It is the life one lives within these walls which is of the greatest importance.'

'Yet,' I retaliated, 'it is some comfort to have charming surroundings in which to live one's life.'

'I agree. And I cannot tell you how glad I am that you find my homes so charming.'

When we had eaten he took me to the library and asked me if I would play a game of chess with him. I said I would be delighted.

And we sat there in that beautiful room with its carved ceiling and thick piled carpet, lighted by lamps the bowls of which were made of artistically painted china of oriental origin. I was happier than I had ever dreamed I could be.

He had set out the ivory pieces on the board, and we played in silence.

It was a deep, contented silence, or so it seemed to me. I knew I should never forget the flickering firelight, the ticking of the gilded clock which looked as though it might have belonged to Louis XIV, as I watched Connan's strong lean fingers on the ivory pieces.

Once, as I frowned in concentration, I was conscious of his eyes fixed on me and, lifting them suddenly, I met his gaze. It was of amusement, and yet of speculation. In that moment I thought: He has asked me here for a purpose. What is it?

I felt a shiver of alarm, but I was too happy to entertain such feelings.

I moved my piece and he said: 'Ah!' And then: 'Miss Leigh, oh my dear Miss Leigh, you have, I think, walked straight into the trap I have set for you.'

'Oh . . . no!' I cried.

He moved a knight which immediately menaced my king. I had forgotten that knight.

'I believe it is . . .' he said. 'Oh no, not entirely. Check, Miss Leigh. But not checkmate.'

I saw that I had allowed my attention to wander from the game. I sought hurriedly to save myself, but I could not. With every move the inevitable end was more obvious.

I heard his voice, gentle, full of laughter. 'Checkmate, Miss Leigh.'

I sat for a few seconds staring at the board. He said: 'I took an unfair advantage. You were tired after the journey.'

'Oh no,' I said quickly. 'I suspect you are a better player than I am.'

'I suspect,' he replied, 'that we are very well matched.'

I retired to my room soon after that game.

I went to bed and tried to sleep, but couldn't. I was too happy. I kept going over in my mind his reception of me, our meal together, his words: 'We are very well matched.'

I even forgot that the house in which I now lay had been Alice's home – a fact which at one time would have seemed of utmost interest to me – I forgot everything but that Connan had sent for me and, now that I was here, seemed so delighted to have me.

The next day was as pleasant and unpredictable as the first. I did a few lessons with the children in the morning and in the afternoon Connan took us for a drive. How different it was, riding in his carriage than jogging along behind Tapperty or Billy Trehay.

He drove us to the coast and we saw St. Michael's Mount rising out of the water.

'One day,' he said, 'when the spring comes, I'll take you out there and you can see St. Michael's chair.'

'Can we sit in it, Papa?' asked Alvean.

'You can if you are prepared to risk a fall. You'll find your feet dangling over a drop of seventy feet or so. Nevertheless, many of your sex think it worth while.'

'But why, Papa, why?' demanded Alvean, who was always delighted when she had his undivided attention.

'Because,' he went on, 'there is an old saying that if a woman can sit in St. Michael's chair before her husband, she will be the master of the house.'

Alvean laughed with pleasure and Gilly, who I had insisted on bringing with us, stood there smiling.

Connan looked at me. 'And you, Miss Leigh,' he said, 'would you think it worth while to try?'

I hesitated for a second, and then met his gaze boldly. 'No, Mr. TreMellyn, I don't think I should.'

'Then you would not desire to be the master in the house?'

'I do not think that either a husband or his wife should be master in that sense. I think they should work together and, if one has an opinion which he or she feels to be the only right one, he or she should adhere to it.'

I flushed a little; I imagined how Phillida would smile if she heard that.

'Miss Leigh,' said Connan, 'your wisdom puts our foolish folklore to shame.'

We drove back in winter sunshine and I was happy.

I did not dine with him that evening because I had asked that I might have my meals in the schoolroom with Gilly. Alvean dined with her father. And afterwards I sat in the room reading. He did not ask me to join him that evening.

I went to bed early and lay for a long time thinking of the strange turn life had taken, and I knew that when I awoke next morning I should do so with a feeling of expectation, because I believed that something wonderful was about to happen to me.

I awoke with a start. Someone was in my room. There was a movement by my bed. I started up. It was early morning. I knew this because I could see that the sky was streaked with pale pink light.

'Who is there?' I cried.

Then I saw Gilly.

She was wearing one of Alvean's old dressing gowns which I had altered to fit her, and her feet were in a pair of slippers which I had brought for her.

I said: 'What are you doing here, Gilly?'

She opened her mouth as though to speak. I waited, but she smiled at me and nodded.

'I said: 'What has happened, Gilly? It is something, I know. You must tell me.'

She pointed to the door and stared at it.

I felt a shiver run down my spine because Gilly often made me think that she could see things which I could not.

'There's nothing there,' I said.

She nodded again and then she spoke: 'She's here. She's here.'

I felt my heart beat fast. I thought: She means that Alice is here. This was Alice's home. She has found Alice here.

'Mrs. TreMellyn . . .' I whispered.

She smiled rapturously and continued to nod.

'You . . . you've seen her?'

Gilly nodded again.

'In this house?'

Again the nod.

'I'll take you to her.' The words tumbled out. 'She wants me to.'

I got out of bed and with trembling fingers wrapped my dressing gown about me and put my feet into my slippers.

Gilly took my hand.

We went through a gallery and down a short staircase. Gilly rapped with her fingers on the door and appeared to listen.

She looked up at me and nodded as though she had heard someone tell her to enter. I had heard nothing. It was very uncanny.

Then she opened the door. We were in a room which was shadowy, for the day was young yet.

Gilly pointed, and for a few seconds I thought I saw a woman standing there. She was dressed in a ball dress and her fair hair fell about her shoulders in long silken curls.

I stared, and then I saw that I was looking at a life-size oil painting.

I knew I was face to face with Alice.

I went close to the painting and looked up at it. The blue eyes looked straight out of the picture at me and it seemed as though words were forming themselves on those red lips.

I forced myself to say: 'What a good artist must have painted that picture!'

But perhaps because it was not yet quite light, because this grey house was sleeping, because Gilly had brought me here in her own strange way, I felt that this was more than a picture.

'Alice,' I whispered. And I stared at that painted face, and, practical woman that I was, I half expected her to step out of the frame and talk to me.

I wondered when that had been painted . . . before or after the disastrous marriage, before she 'had known she was to have Geoffry's child or after.

'Alice,' I said to myself, 'where are you now, Alice? You are haunting me, Alice. Since I have known you I have known what haunting means.'

Gilly was holding my hand.

I said: 'It's only a picture, Gilly.'

She reached out a small finger and touched the white ball-dress.

Gilly had loved her. I looked into that soft young face and thought I understood why.

Poor Alice, who had been caught up in too many emotions, what had become of her?

I suddenly realized that it was a winter's morning and I was lightly clad.

'We'll catch our deaths,' I said practically; and taking Gilly's hand in mine I firmly shut the door on Alice.

I had been at Penlandstow a week, and I was wondering how much longer this idyllic interlude could last, when Connan spoke to me of what was in his mind.

The children were in bed and Connan asked me if I would join him in a game of chess in the library.

There I found him, the pieces set out on the board, sitting looking at them.

The curtains had been drawn and the fire burned cheerfully in the great fireplace. He rose as I entered and I quickly slipped into my place opposite him.

He smiled at me and I thought his eyes took in every detail of my appearance, in a manner which I might have found offensive in anyone else.

I was about to move king's pawn when he said: 'Miss Leigh, I did not ask you down here to play. There is something I have to say to you.'

'Yes, Mr. TreMellyn?'

'I feel I have known you a very long time. You have made such a difference to us both – Alvean and myself. If you went away, we should miss you very much. I am certain that we should both want to ensure that you do not leave us.'

I tried to look at him and failed because I was afraid he would read the hopes and fears in my eyes.

'Miss Leigh,' he went on, 'Will you stay with us . . . always?'

'I . . . I don't understand. I . . . can't believe . . .'

'I am asking you to marry me.'

'But . . . but that is impossible.'

'Why so, Miss Leigh?'

'Because . . . because it is so incongruous.'

'Do you find me incongruous . . . repulsive? Do please be frank.'

'I . . . No indeed not! But I am the governess here. . . .'

'Precisely. That is what alarms me. Governesses sometimes leave their employment. It would be intolerable for me if you went away.'

I felt I was choking with my emotions. I could not believe this was really happening to me. I remained silent. I dared not try to speak.

'I see that you hesitate, Miss Leigh.'

'I am so surprised.'

'Should I have prepared you for the shock?' His lips twitched slightly at the corner. 'I am sorry, Miss Leigh. I thought I had managed to convey to you something of my feelings in this matter.'

I tried to picture it all in those few seconds – myself going back to Mount Mellyn as the wife of the Master, slipping from the role of governess to that of Mistress of the house. Of course I would do it and in a few months they would forget that I had once been the governess. Whatever else I lacked I had my dignity – perhaps a little too much of it, according to Phillida. But I should have thought that a proposal would have been made in a different way. He did not take my hand; he did not touch me; he merely sat at the table watching me in an almost cool and calculating manner.

He went on: 'Think of how much good this could bring to us all, my dear Miss Leigh. I have been so impressed by the manner in which you have helped Alvean. The child needs a mother. You would supply that need . . . admirably.'

'Should two people marry for the sake of a child, do you think?'

'I am a most selfish man. I never would.' He leaned forward across the table and his eyes were alight with something I did not understand. 'I would marry for my own satisfaction.'

'Then . . .' I began.

'I confess I was not considering Alvean alone. We are three people, my dear Miss Leigh, who could profit from this marriage. Alvean needs you. And I. . . . I need you. Do you need us? Perhaps you are more self-sufficient than we are, but what will you do if you do not marry? You will go from post to post, and that is not a very pleasant life. When one is young, handsome and full of spirit it is tolerable . . . but sprightly governesses become ageing governesses.'

I said icily: 'Do you suggest that I should enter into this marriage as an insurance against old age?'

'I suggest only that you do what your desires dictate, my dear Miss Leigh.'

There was a short silence during which I felt an absurd desire to burst into tears. This was something I had longed for, but a proposal of marriage should have been an impassioned declaration, and I could not rid myself of the suspicion that there was something other than Connan's love for me which had inspired it. It seemed to me as though he were offering me a list of reasons why we should marry, for fear I should discover the real one.

'You put it on such a practical basis,' I stammered. 'I had not thought of marriage in that way.'

His eyebrows lifted and he laughed, looking suddenly very gay. 'How glad I am. I thought of you always as such a practical person, so I was trying to put it to you in the manner in which I felt it would appeal to you most.'

'Are you seriously asking me to marry you?'

'I doubt if I have ever been so serious in my life as I am at this moment. What is your answer? Please do not keep me in suspense any longer.'

I said I must have time to consider this.

'That is fair enough. You will tell me to-morrow?'

'Yes,' I said. 'I will tell you to-morrow.'

I rose and went to the door. He was there before me. He laid his fingers on the door handle and I waited for him to open it, but he did no such thing. He stood with his back to the door and caught me up in his arms.

He kissed me as I had never been kissed, never dreamed of being kissed; so that I knew that there was a life of the emotions of which I was totally ignorant. He kissed my eyelids, my nose, my cheeks, my mouth and my throat until he was breathless, and I was too.

Then he laughed.

'Wait until the morning!' he mocked. 'Do I look the sort of man who would wait until the morning? Do you think I am the sort of man who would marry for the sake of his daughter? No, Miss Leigh ...' he mocked again, 'my dear, *dear* Miss Leigh ... I want to marry you because I want to keep you a prisoner in my house. I don't want you to run away from me, because, since you came, I have thought of little else but you, and I know I am going on thinking of you all my life.'

'Is this true?' I whispered. 'Can this be true?'

'Martha!' he said. 'What a stern name for such an adorable creature! And yet, how it fits!'

I said: 'My sister calls me Marty. My father did too.'

'Marty,' he said. 'That sounds helpless, clinging ... feminine. ... You can be a Marty sometimes. For me you will be all three. Marty, Martha and Miss Leigh, my very dear Miss Leigh. You see you *are* all three, and my dearest Marty would always betray Miss Leigh. I knew from her that you were interested in me. Far more interested than Miss Leigh would think proper. How enchanting! I shall marry not one woman but three!'

'Have I been so blatant?'

'Tremendously so ... adorably so.'

I knew that it was foolish to pretend. I gave myself up to his embrace, and it was wonderful beyond my imaginings.

At length I said: 'I have a terrible feeling that I shall wake up in bed at Mount Mellyn and find I have dreamed all this.'

'Do you know,' he said seriously, 'I feel exactly the same.'

'But it is so different for you. You can do as you will ... go where you will ... dependent on no one.'

'I am dependent no longer. I depend on Marty, Martha, my dear Miss Leigh.'

He spoke so seriously that I could have wept with tenderness. The changing emotions were almost too much for me to bear.

This is love! I thought. The emotion which carries one to the very heights of human experience and, because it can carry one so high, one is in continual danger of falling; and one must never forget, the higher the delight, the more tragic the fall.

But this was not the moment to think of tragedy. I loved, and miraculously I was loved. I had no doubt in that library of Penlandstow that I was loved.

For love such as this, one would be prepared to risk everything.

He put his hands on my shoulders and looked long into my face.

He said: 'We'll be happy, my darling. We'll be happier than either you or I ever dreamed possible.'

I knew that we should be. All that had gone before would give us a finer appreciation of this joy we could bring each other.

'We should be practical,' he said. 'We should make our plans. When shall we marry? I do not like delay. I am the most impatient man alive, where my own pleasures are concerned. We will go home to-morrow, and there we

will announce our engagement. No, not to-morrow ... the day after. I have
one or two little commitments here to-morrow. And as soon as we are home
we will give a ball to announce our engagement. I think that in a month
after that we should be setting out on our honeymoon. I suggest Italy, unless
you have any other ideas?'

I sat with my hands clasped. I must have looked like an ecstatic schoolgirl.

'I wonder what they will think at Mount Mellyn.'

'Who, the servants? You may be sure they have a pretty shrewd idea of
the way things are; servants have, you know. Servants are like detectives in
the house. They pick up every little clue. You shiver. Are you cold?'

'No, only excited. I still believe I'm going to wake up in a moment.'

'And you like the idea of Italy?'

'I would like the idea of the North Pole in some company.'

'By which, my darling, I hope you mean mine.'

'That was my intention.'

'My dear Miss Leigh,' he said, 'how I love your astringent moods. They
are going to make conversation throughout our lives so invigorating.' I had
an idea then that he was making comparisons between Alice and myself,
and I shivered again as I had when he had made that remark about the
detectives.

'You are a little worried about the reception of the news,' he went on.
'The servants ... the countryside ... Who cares? Do you? Of course you
do not. Miss Leigh has too much good sense for that. I am longing to tell
Peter Nansellock that you are to be my wife. To tell the truth I have been
somewhat jealous of that young man.'

'There was no need to be.'

'Still I was anxious. I had visions of his persuading you to go to Australia
with him. That was something I should have gone to great lengths to
prevent.'

'Even so far as asking me to marry *you*?'

'Farther than that if the need had arisen. I should have abducted you and
locked you up in a dungeon until he was far away.'

'There was no need for the slightest apprehension.'

'Are you quite sure? He is very handsome, I believe.'

'Perhaps he is. I did not notice.'

'I could have killed him when he had the effrontery to offer you Jacinth.'

'I think he merely enjoys being outrageous. He probably knew I should
not accept it.'

'And I need not fear him?'

'You need never fear anyone,' I told him.

Then once more I was in that embrace, and I was oblivious of all but the
fact that I had discovered love, and believed, as doubtless hosts of lovers have
before, that there was never love such as that between us two.

At length he said: 'We'll go back the day after to-morrow. We'll start
making arrangements immediately. In a month from now we'll be married.
We'll put up the banns as soon as we return. We will have a ball to announce
our engagement and invite all our neighbours to the wedding.'

'I suppose it must be done in this way?'

'Tradition, my darling. It is one of the things we have to bow down to. You'll be magnificent, I know. You're not nervous?'

'Of your country neighbours, no.'

'You and I will open the ball this time together, dearest Miss Leigh.'

'Yes,' I said; and I pictured myself in the green dress wearing the amber comb in my hair with the diamond horseshoe glittering on the green background.

I had no qualms about taking my place in his circle.

Then he began to talk of Alice. 'I have never told you,' he said, 'of my first marriage.'

'No,' I answered.

'It was not a happy one.'

'I'm sorry.'

'A marriage which was arranged. This time I shall marry my own choice. Only one who has suffered the first can realize the joy of the second. Dearest, I have not lived the life of a monk, I fear.'

'I guessed it.'

'I am a most sinful man, as you will discover.'

'I am prepared for the worst.'

'Alice . . . my wife . . . and I were most unsuited, I suppose.'

'Tell me about her.'

'There is little to tell. She was a gentle creature, quiet, anxious to please. She seemed to have little spirit. I understood why. She was in love with someone else when she married me.'

'The man she ran away with?' I asked.

He nodded. 'Poor Alice! She was unfortunate. She chose not only the wrong husband but the wrong lover. There is little to choose between us . . . myself and Geoffry Nansellock. We were of a kind. In the old days there was a tradition of the *droit de seigneurs* in these parts. Geoffry and I did our best to maintain that.'

'You are telling me that you have enjoyed many love affairs.'

'I am a dissolute, degenerate philanderer. I am going to say *was*. Because from this moment I am going to be faithful to one woman for the rest of my life. You do not look scornful or sceptical. Bless you for that. I mean it, dearest Marty. I swear I mean it. It is because of those experiences of the past that I know the difference between them and this. This is love.'

'Yes,' I said slowly, 'you and I will be faithful together because that is the only way we can prove to each other the depth and breadth of our love.'

He took my hands and kissed them, and I had never known him so serious. 'I love you,' he said. 'Remember that . . . always remember it.'

'I intend to.'

'You may hear gossip.'

'One does hear gossip,' I admitted.

'You have heard of Alice and that Alvean is not my daughter? Oh, darling, someone told you and you do not want to betray the teller. Never mind. You know. It is true. I could never love the child. In fact I avoided the sight of her. She was an unpleasant reminder of much that I wished to forget. But when you came I felt differently. You made me see her as a lonely child, suffering from the sins of grown-up people. You see, you changed me, Marty dear. Your coming changed the whole household. That is what confirms me in my belief that with us it is going to be different from anything that has ever happened to me before.'

'Connan, I want to make that child happy. I want to make her forget that there is a doubt as to her parentage. Let her be able to accept you as her father. It is what she needs.'

'You will be a mother to her. Then I must be her father.'

'We are going to be so happy, Connan.'

'Can you see into the future?'

'I can see into ours, for our future is what we make it, and I intend that it shall be one of complete happiness.'

'And what Miss Leigh decides shall be, will be. And you will promise me not to be hurt if you hear gossip about me?'

'You are thinking of Lady Treslyn, I know. She has been your mistress.'
He nodded.

Then I said: 'She will never be again. That is all over.'

He kissed my hand. 'Have you not sworn eternal fidelity?'

'But, Connan,' I said, 'she is so beautiful and she will still be there.'

'But I am in love,' he answered, 'for the first time in my life.'

'And you were not in love with her?'

'Lust, passion,' he answered, 'they sometimes wear the guise of love; but when one meets true love one recognizes them for what they are. Dearest, let us bury all that is past. Let us start afresh from this day forth . . . you and I . . . for better for worse. . . .'

I was in his arms again. 'Connan,' I said, 'I am not dreaming, am I? Please say I am not dreaming.'

It was late when I left him. I went to my room in a haze of happiness. I was afraid to sleep for fear I should wake up and find it had all been a dream.

In the morning I went to Alvean's room and told her the news.

For a few seconds a satisfied smile appeared at the corners of her mouth; then she assumed indifference, but it was too late. I knew that she was pleased.

'You'll stay with us all the time now, Miss,' she said.

'Yes,' I assured her.

'I wonder if I shall ever ride as well as you.'

'Probably better. You'll be able to have more practice than I ever could.'
Again that smile touched her lips. Then she was serious.

'Miss,' she said, 'what shall I call you? You'll be my stepmother, won't you?'

'Yes, but you can call me what you like.'

'Not Miss!'

'Well, hardly. I shan't expect Miss any more.'

'I expect I shall have to call you Mamma.' Her mouth hardened a little.

'If you do not like that you could call me Martha in private. Or Marty. That's what my father and sister always called me.'

'Marty,' she repeated. 'I like that. It sounds like a horse.'

'What could be better praise,' I cried, and she regarded my amusement with continued seriousness.

I went to Gilly's room.

'Gilly,' I said, 'I'm going to be Mrs. TreMellyn.'

The blankness left the blue eyes and her smile was dazzling. Then she ran to me and buried her head in my bodice. I could feel her body shaking with laughter.

I could never be quite sure what was going on among all the shadowy vagueness of Gilly's mind, but I knew she was contented. She had bracketed me with Alice in her mind and I felt that she was less surprised than I or Alvean, or anyone else, would be.

To Gilly it was the most natural thing in the world that I should take Alice's place.

I believe that, from that moment, for Gilly I became Alice.

It was a merry journey home. We sang Cornish songs all the way to the station. I had never seen Connan so happy. I thought, this is how it will be all the rest of our lives.

Alvean joined in the singing, so did Gilly; and it was astonishing to hear that child, who scarcely ever spoke, singing quietly as though to herself.

We sang the 'Twelve Days of Christmas.' Connan had a rich baritone voice which was very pleasant to hear and I felt I had reached the very peak of happiness as he sang the first lines.

> *'The first day of Christmas my true love sent to me*
> *A partridge in a pear tree.'*

We went through the song and I had difficulty in remembering all the gifts after the five golden rings; and we laughed together hilariously while we argued as to how many maids there were a-milking, and how many geese a-laying were sent.

'But they were not very sensible things,' said Alvean, 'except of course the five gold rings. I think he was pretending he loved her more than he really did.'

'But he was her true love,' I protested.

'How could she be sure?' asked Alvean.

'Because he told her so,' answered Connan.

'Then he ought to have given her something better than a partridge in a pear tree. I expect the partridge flew away and the pears were those hard ones which are used for stewing.'

'You must not be hard on lovers,' Connan cried. 'All the world loves them, and you have to keep in step.'

And so we laughed and bantered until we boarded the train.

Billy Trehay met us with the carriage and I was astonished when we reached the house, for I then realized that Connan must have sent a message to arrive before we did. He wanted me to be received with honours. Even so I was unprepared for the reception which was waiting for us in the hall.

The servants were all there – the Polgrey and Tapperty families and others from the gardens and stables, and even the village boys and girls who came to help and whom I scarcely knew.

They were lined up ceremoniously, and Connan took my arm as we entered the hall.

'As you know,' he said, 'Miss Leigh has promised to marry me. In a few weeks' time she will be your Mistress.'

The men bowed and the women curtsied, but I was conscious, as I smiled at them and walked along the line with Connan, that there was a certain wariness in their eyes.

As I had guessed, they were not ready to accept me as mistress of the house . . . yet.

There was a big fire in my room and everything looked cosy and welcoming. Daisy brought my hot water. She was a little remote, I thought. She did not stop and chat with me as she had hitherto.

I thought: I will regain their confidence, but of course I had to remember that, as the future Mistress of the house, I must not gossip as I once had.

I dined with Connan and Alvean and afterwards I went up with Alvean; and when I had said good night to her I joined Connan in the library.

There were so many plans to make, and I gave myself up to the complete joy of contemplating the future.

He asked me if I had written to my family, and I told him that I had not yet done so. I still could not quite believe this was really happening to me.

'Perhaps this token will help you to remember,' he said. Then he took a jewel case from a drawer in the bureau and showed me a beautiful square-cut emerald set in diamonds.

'It's . . . quite beautiful, far too beautiful for me.'

'Nothing is too beautiful for Martha TreMellyn,' he said, and he took my left hand and put the ring on the third finger.

I held it out and stared at it.

'I never thought to possess anything so lovely.'

'It's the beginning of all the beautiful things I shall bring to you. It's the partridge in the pear tree, my darling.'

Then he kissed my hand and I told myself that, whenever I doubted the truth of all that was happening to me I could look at my emerald and know I was not dreaming.

Next morning when I went down Connan had gone out on business, and after I had given Alvean and Gilly their lessons – for I was eager that everything should go on as before – I went to my room, and I had not been there for more than a few minutes when there was a discreet knock.

'Come in,' I said; and Mrs. Polgrey entered.

She looked a little furtive, and I knew that something significant had happened.

'Miss Leigh,' she said, 'there will be things which we have to discuss. I was wondering if you would come to my room. I have the kettle on. Could you drink a cup of tea?'

I said I would like that. I was very anxious that there should be no difference in our relationship which, from my point of view, had always been a very pleasant and dignified one.

In her room we drank tea. There was no suggestion of whisky this time, and this secretly amused me although I made no reference to it. I should be the mistress of the house, and it was very different for *her* to know of the tea-tippling than the mere governess.

She again congratulated me on my engagement and told me how delighted she was. 'In fact,' she said, 'the whole household is delighted.' She asked me then if I intended to make changes, and I answered that, while the household was so efficiently run by herself, I should make none at all.

This was a relief to her, I could see, and she settled down to come to the point.

'While you've been away, Miss Leigh, there's been a bit of excitement in these parts.'

'Oh?' I said, feeling that we were now coming to the reason for my visit.

'It's all along of the sudden death of Sir Thomas Treslyn.'

My heart had begun to leap in a disconcerting manner.

'But,' I said, 'he is buried now. We went to his funeral.'

'Yes, yes. But that need not be the end, Miss Leigh.'

'I don't understand, Mrs. Polgrey.'

'Well, there's been rumours . . . nasty rumours, and letters have been sent.'

'To . . . to whom?'

'To her, Miss Leigh . . . to the widow. And, it seems, to others . . . and as a result they're going to dig him up. There's going to be an examination.'

'You mean . . . they suspect someone poisoned him?'

'Well, there's been these letters, you see. And him dying so sudden. What I don't like is that he was here last . . . It's not the sort of thing one likes to have connected with the house. . . .'

She was looking at me oddly. I thought I saw speculation in her eyes.

I wanted to shut from my mind all the unpleasant thoughts which kept coming to me.

I saw again Connan and Lady Treslyn in the punch room together, their backs towards me . . . laughing together. Had Connan loved me then? One would not have thought so. I thought of the words they had spoken in my hearing when the party was over. 'It will not be long . . . now.' She had said that . . . and to him. And then there was the conversation I had partly overheard in the woods.

What did this mean?

There was a question that hammered in my brain. But I would not let my mind dwell on it.

I dared not. I could not bear to see all my hopes of happiness shattered. I had to go on believing, so I would not ask myself questions.

I looked expressionlessly into Mrs. Polgrey's face.

'I thought you'd want to know,' she said.

Chapter Eight

I was afraid, more afraid than I had ever been since I came to this house.

The body of Sir Thomas Treslyn, who had died after supping at Mount Mellyn, was to be exhumed. People were suspicious of the manner in which he died and, as a result, there had been anonymous letters. Why should they be suspicious? Because his wife wanted him out of the way; and it was known that Connan and Linda Treslyn had been lovers. There had been two obstacles to their union – Alice and Sir Thomas. Both had died suddenly.

But Connan had no wish to marry Lady Treslyn. He was in love with me.

A terrible thought had struck me. Did Connan know that there was to be this exhumation? Had I been living in a fool's paradise? Was my wonderful dream-come-true nothing but a living nightmare?

Was I being used by a cynic? Why did I not use the harsher word? Was I being used by a *murderer*?

I would not believe it. I loved Connan. I had sworn to be faithful to him all my life. How could I make such a vow when I believed the worst of him at the first crisis?

I tried to reason with myself. You're crazy, Martha Leigh. Do you really think that a man such as Connan TreMellyn could suddenly fall in love with *you*!

Yes, I do. I do, I retorted hotly.

But I was a frightened woman.

I could see that the household was divided between two topics of conversation: the exhumation of Sir Thomas and the proposed marriage of the master and the governess.

I was afraid to meet the stern eyes of Mrs. Polgrey, the lewd ones of Tapperty and the excited ones of his daughters.

Did they, as I had begun to do, connect these two events?

I asked Connan what he thought of the Treslyn affair.

'Mischief-makers,' he said. 'They'll have an autopsy and find he died a natural death. Why, his doctor had been attending him for years and has always told him that he must expect to go off like that.'

'It must be very worrying for Lady Treslyn.'

'She will not worry unduly. Indeed, since she has been pestered by letter-writers she may well be relieved to have the matter brought to a head.'

I pictured the medical experts. They would no doubt be men who knew the Treslyns and Connan. As Connan was going to marry me – and he was very eager to spread the news – was it possible that they would approach the matter in a different spirit from that in which they would if they believed Lady Treslyn was eager to marry again? Who could say?

I must drive away these terrible thoughts. I would believe in Connan, I had to; if I did not I must face the fact that I had fallen in love with a murderer.

The invitations for the ball had gone out hastily – too hastily, I thought. Lady Treslyn, being in mourning and with the autopsy pending, was of course not invited. It was to take place only four days after our return from Penlandstow.

Celestine and Peter Nansellock rode over the day before the ball.

Celestine put her arms about me and kissed me.

'My dear,' she said, 'how happy I am. I have watched you with Alvean and I know what this is going to mean to her.' There were tears in her eyes. 'Alice would be so happy.'

I thanked her and said: 'You have always been such a good friend to me.'

'I was so grateful that at last the child had found a governess who really understood her.'

I said: 'I thought Miss Jansen did that.'

'Miss Jansen, yes. We all thought so. It was a pity she was not honest. Perhaps though it was the temptation of a moment. I did all I could to help her.'

'I'm so glad somebody did.'

Peter had come up. He took my hand and kissed it lightly. Connan's look of displeasure made my heart beat fast with happiness, and I was ashamed of my suspicions.

'Fortunate Connan,' cried Peter exuberantly. 'No need to tell you how much I envy you, is there! I think I've made it clear. I've brought over Jacinth. I told you I'd make you a present of her, didn't I? Well, she's my wedding present. You can't object to that, can you?'

I looked at Connan. 'A present for us both,' I said.

'Oh no,' said Peter. 'She's for you. I'll think of something else for Con.'

'Thank you, Peter,' I said. 'It's most generous of you.'

He shook his head. 'Couldn't bear the thought of her going to anyone else. I feel sentimental about that mare. I want a good home for her. You know I'm going at the end of next week.'

'So soon?'

'Everything has been speeded up. There's no point in delaying further.' He looked at me significantly; 'Now,' he added.

I saw that Kitty, who was serving us with wine, was listening with all attention.

Celestine was talking earnestly to Connan, and Peter went on: 'So it's you and Con after all. Well, you'll keep him in order, Miss Leigh. I'm sure of that.'

'I'm not going to be his governess, you know.'

'I'm not sure. Once a governess, always a governess. I thought Alvean seemed not displeased by the new arrangement.'

'I think she's going to accept me.'

'I think you're an even greater favourite than Miss Jansen was.'

'Poor Miss Jansen! I wonder what became of her.'

'Celeste did something for her. She was rather worried about the poor girl, I think.'

'Oh, I'm so glad.'

'Helped her to find another place ... with some friends of ours actually. The Merrivales who have a place on the edge of Dartmoor. I wonder how our gay Miss Jansen likes Hoodfield Manor. Finds it a bit dull, I should imagine, with Tavistock, the nearest town, quite six miles away.'

'It was very kind of Celestine to help her.'

'Well, that's Celestine all over.' He lifted his glass. 'To your happiness, Miss Leigh. And whenever you ride Jacinth, think of me.'

'I shall ... and of Jacinth's namesake, Miss Jansen.'

He laughed. 'And if,' he went on, 'you should change your mind ...'

I raised my eyebrows.

'About marrying Connan, I mean. There'll be a little homestead for you on the other side of the world. You'll find me ever faithful, Miss Leigh.'

I laughed and sipped my wine.

The next day Alvean and I went riding together, and I was mounted on Jacinth. She was a wonderful creature and I enjoyed every moment of the ride. I felt that this was another of the glorious things which were happening to me. I even had my own mount now.

The ball was a great success and I was surprised how ready the neighbourhood was to accept me. The fact that I had been Alvean's governess was forgotten. I felt that Connan's neighbours were reminding each other that I was an educated young woman and that my family background was passibly good. Perhaps those who were fond of him were relieved because he was engaged to be married, for they would not wish him to be involved in the Treslyn scandal.

The day after the ball Connan had to go away again on business.

'I neglected a great deal during our stay in Penlandstow,' he said. 'There were things I simply forgot to do. It is understandable. My mind was on other matters. I shall be away a week, I think, and when I come back it'll be but a fortnight before our wedding. You'll be getting on with your preparations, and darling, if there's anything you want to do in the house ... if there's anything you want to change, do say so. It mightn't be a bad idea to ask Celestine's advice; she's an expert on old houses.'

I said I would, because it would please her, and I wanted to please her.

'She was kind to me right from the first,' I said. 'I shall always have a soft feeling for her.'

He said good-bye and drove off while I stood at my window, waving. I did not care to do so from the porch because I was still a little shy of the servants.

When I went out of my room I found Gilly standing outside the door. Since I had told her that I was to be Mrs. TreMellyn she had taken to following me around. I was beginning to understand the way her mind worked. She was fond of me in exactly the same way that she had been fond of Alice and, with the passing of each day, the two of us became in her mind merged into one. Alice had disappeared from her life; she was going to make sure that I did not.

'Hallo, Gilly,' I said.

She dropped her head in that characteristic way of hers and laughed to herself.

Then she put her hand in mind and I led her back to my room.

'Well, Gilly,' I said, 'in three weeks' time I am going to be married, and I am the happiest woman in the world.'

I was really trying to reassure myself, for sometimes talking to Gilly was like talking to oneself.

I thought of what Connan had said about altering anything I wished to in the house, and I remembered that there were some parts of it which I had not even seen yet.

I suddenly thought of Miss Jansen and what I had been told about her having a different room from the one I occupied. I had never seen Miss Jansen's room and I decided that I would now go along and inspect it. I need have no qualms now about going to any part of the house I wished, for in a very short time I should be mistress of it.

'Come along, Gilly,' I said. 'We'll go and see Miss Jansen's room.'

She trotted along contentedly by my side, and I thought how much more intelligent she was than people realized, for it was she who led me to Miss Jansen's room.

There was nothing very unusual about it. It was smaller than mine. But there was a rather striking mural. I was looking at this when Gilly tugged my arm and drew me close to it. She pulled up a chair and stood on it. Then I understood. There, in this wall, was a peep like that in the solarium. I looked through it and saw the chapel. It was of course a different view from that to be seen in the solarium, as it was from the opposite side.

Gilly looked at me, delighted to have shown me the peep. We went back to my room, and clearly she did not want to leave me.

I could see that she was apprehensive. I understood of course. Her somewhat confused mind had so clearly associated me with Alice that she expected me to disappear as Alice had done.

She was determined to keep an eye on me so that this should not happen.

All through the night a south-west gale was blowing in from the sea. The rain which came with it was driven horizontally against our windows, and even the solid foundations of Mount Mellyn seemed to shake. It was one of the wettest nights I had known since my arrival in Cornwall.

The next day the rain continued; everything in my room – mirrors, the furniture – was misty and damp. It was what happened often enough, Mrs. Polgrey told me, when the south-west wind came bringing rain with it, which it invariably did.

Alvean and I could not go out riding that day.

By the following morning the skies had cleared a little, and the heavy rain gave way to a light drizzle. Lady Treslyn called, but I did not see her. She did not ask for me; it was Mrs. Polgrey who told me she had called and that she had wished to see Connan.

'She seemed very distressed,' said Mrs. Polgrey. 'She'll not rest until this terrible business is over.'

I felt sure that Lady Treslyn had come over to talk to Connan about his engagement to me and that she was probably distressed because he was not at home.

Celestine Nansellock also called. We had a chat about the house. She said she was so pleased because I was becoming very interested in Mount Mellyn.

'Not only as a home,' she said, 'but as a house.' She went on: 'I have some old documents about Mount Mellyn and Mount Widden. I'll show them to you one day.'

'You must help me,' I told her. 'It'll be fun discussing things together.'

'You'll make some changes?' she asked.

'If I do,' I assured her, 'I shall ask your advice.'

She left before luncheon, and in the afternoon Alvean and I went down to the stables for the horses.

We stood by while Billy Trehay saddled them for us.

'Jacinth be frisky, to-day, Miss,' he told me.

'It's because she had no exercise yesterday.' I stroked her muzzle and she rubbed against my hand to show she shared my affection.

We took our usual ride down the slope, past the cove and Mount Widden; then we went along the cliff path. The view here was particularly beautiful with the jagged coast stretched out before us and Rame Head lying in the water, hiding Plymouth and its Sound from view.

Some of the paths were narrow, cut into the cliffs at spots where it had been convenient to do so. Up and down we went; sometimes we were almost down to the sea; at others we climbed high.

It was not very easy going, for the rain had whipped up the mud and I began to feel a little anxious about Alvean. She sat firmly in her saddle – no novice now – but I was conscious of Jacinth's mood and I expected Black Prince's was not much different, although, of course, he hadn't Jacinth's fiery temperament. At times I had to rein her in firmly; a gallop would have been more to her taste than this necessarily slow careful walk along paths which were a good deal more dangerous than when we had come this way on our last ride.

There was one spot on this cliff path which was particularly narrow; above the path loomed the cliff face, dotted with bushes of gorse and brambles; below it, the cliff fell almost sheer to the sea. The path was safe enough ordinarily; but I felt a little nervous about Alvean's using it on a day like this.

I noticed that some of the cliff had fallen in places. This was continually happening. Tapperty had often said that the sea was gradually claiming the land, and that in his grandfather's day there had been a road which had now completely disappeared.

I thought of turning back, but if we did I would have to explain my fears to Alvean; I did not want to do this while she was mounted.

No, I thought, we'll continue on this path until we can climb to the top road. Then we'll go home a roundabout way, but on firm land.

We had come to that danger spot and I noticed that the ground was even more slippery here, and that there had been a bigger fall of cliff than I had seen on other portions of the path.

I held Jacinth in and walked her slowly in front of Alvean and Black Prince, for we naturally had to go in single file.

I pulled up and looked over my shoulder, saying: 'We're going very slowly here. You just follow.'

Then I heard it. I turned quickly as the boulder came tumbling down bringing in its wake shale, turf and vegetation. It passed within a few inches of Jacinth. I stared, in fascinated horror, as it went hurtling down to the sea.

Jacinth reared. She was terrified and ready to plunge anywhere . . . over the cliff . . . down to the sea . . . to escape what had startled her.

It was fortunate for me that I was an experienced rider, and that Jacinth and I knew each other so well. Thus it was all over in a matter of seconds. I had her under control. She grew calm as I began to talk to her in a voice which was meant to be soothing but which shook a little.

'Miss! What happened?' It was Alvean.

'It's all over,' I answered, trying to speak lightly. 'You managed perfectly.'

'Why, Miss, I thought Black Prince was going to start a gallop.'

He would, I thought, if Jacinth had.

I was terribly shaken and afraid to show it, either to Alvean or Jacinth.

I suddenly felt the need to get off that dangerous path immediately. I glanced nervously up and said: 'It's not safe to be on these paths . . . after the weather we've been having.'

I don't know what I expected to see up there, but I was staring at the thickest of the bushes. Did I see a movement there, or did I imagine it? It would be easy for someone to hide up there. What if a boulder had become dislodged by the recent rains. What an excellent opportunity if someone wanted to be rid of me. It merely had to be rolled down at that moment when I was on the path – a perfect target. Alvean and I had made a habit of coming along this path at a certain time.

I shivered and said: 'Let's go on. We'll get on to the top road and won't go back along the cliff path.'

Alvean was silent; and when in a few minutes we were on the road she looked at me oddly. I saw that she was not unaware of the danger through which we had passed.

It was not until we were back in the house that I realized how alarmed I was. I was telling myself that a terrifying pattern was being formed. Alice had died; Sir Thomas Treslyn had died; and now I, who was to be Connan's wife, might easily have met my death on the cliff path this day.

I longed to tell Connan of my fears.

But I was a sensible, practical woman. Was I going to refuse to look facts in the face because I was afraid of what I might see there if I did so?

Suppose Connan had not really gone away. Suppose he had wanted an accident to happen to me while he was believed to be away from home. I thought of Lady Treslyn at the Christmas ball. I thought of her beauty, her sensuous, voluptuous beauty. Connan had admitted that she had been his mistress. Had been? Was it possible that anyone, knowing her, could want me?

The proposal had been so sudden. It had come at a time when his mistress's husband was about to be exhumed.

It was small wonder that the practical governess had become a frightened woman.

To whom could I go for help?

There was Peter or Celestine . . . only those two, I thought. No, I could not betray these terrible suspicions of Connan to them. It was bad enough that I entertained them myself.

'Don't panic,' I cautioned myself. 'Be calm. Think of something you can do.'

I thought of the house, vast and full of secrets, a house in which it was possible to peep from certain rooms into others. There might be peeps as yet undiscovered. Who could say? Perhaps someone was watching me now.

I thought of the peep in Miss Jansen's room and that set me thinking of her sudden dismissal. Then I was saying to myself: 'Hoodfield Manor near Tavistock.'

I wondered if Miss Jansen was still there. There was a good chance that she might be for she must have gone there about the same time as I came to Mount Mellyn.

Why should I not try to meet her? She might have some light to throw on the secrets of this house.

I was desperately afraid, and at such times it is always conforting to take action.

I felt better when I had written the letter.

Dear Miss Jansen.

I am the governess at Mount Mellyn and I have heard of you. I should like to meet you. I wonder if that would be possible. If so, I should like our meeting to be as soon as you can manage it.

Yours sincerely,
Martha Leigh.

I went out quickly to post the letter before I could change my mind. Then I tried to forget it.

I longed for a message from Connan. There was none. Each day I looked for his return. I thought: When he comes home I am going to tell him of my fears, because I must do so. I am going to tell him of what happened on the cliff path. I am going to ask him to tell me the truth. I am going to say to him: Connan, why did you ask me to marry you? Was it because you love me and want me to be your wife, or was it because you wished to divert suspicion from yourself and Lady Treslyn?

The devilish scheme which I had invented seemed to gain credibility with every passing moment.

I said to myself: Perhaps Alice died by accident, and that gave them the idea of ridding themselves of Sir Thomas, who was the only obstacle to their marriage. Did they slip something into his whisky? Why not? It could not have been merely by chance that the boulder came hurtling down at the precise moment. Now there was to be an exhumation of Sir Thomas and the countryside knew of the relationship between Connan and Lady Treslyn. So Connan became engaged to the governess in order to divert suspicion. The governess is now an obstacle even as Alice was, even as Sir Thomas was. So the governess could have an accident on her newly acquired mare to which it might be said that she had not yet grown accustomed.

The road is clear for the guilty lovers and all they need do is wait until scandal has blown over.

How could I imagine such things of the man I loved? Could one love a man and think such thoughts of him?

I do love him, I told myself passionately. So much that I would rather meet death at his hands than leave him and be forced to endure an empty life without him.

Three days later there was a letter from Miss Jansen, who said she was eager to meet me. She would be in Plymouth the following day and if I would meet her at the White Hart, which was not far from the Hoe, we might have luncheon together.

I told Mrs. Polgrey that I was going into Plymouth to shop. That seemed plausible enough since my wedding was due to take place in three weeks' time.

I made straight for the White Hart.

Miss Jansen was already there – an extremely pretty fair-haired girl. She greeted me with pleasure and told me that Mrs. Plint, the innkeeper's wife, had said that we might have luncheon together in a small room of our own.

We were conducted to this private room and there took stock of each other.

The innkeeper's wife talked with enthusiasm of duck and green peas and roast beef, but we were, neither of us, very interested in food.

We ordered roast beef, I think it was, and as soon as we were alone, Miss Jansen said to me: 'What do you think of Mount Mellyn?'

'It's a wonderful old place.'

'One of the most interesting houses I ever saw,' she replied.

'I did hear, from Mrs. Polgrey I think, that old houses specially interested you.'

'They do. I was brought up in one. However, the family fortunes declined. That's what happens to so many of us who become governesses. I was sorry to leave Mount Mellyn. You have heard why I went?'

'Y . . . yes,' I said hesitantly.

'It was a very distressing affair. I was furiously angry to be unjustly accused.'

She was so frank and sincere that I believed her, and I made that clear.

She looked pleased; and then the food was brought in.

As we sat eating it in a somewhat desultory way she told me of the affair.

'The Treslyns and the Nansellocks had been having tea at the house. You know the Treslyn's and the Nansellocks of course?'

'Oh yes.'

'I mean, I expect you know quite a lot about them. They are such friends of the family, are they not?'

'Indeed yes.'

'I had been treated rather specially.' She flushed slightly, and I thought, Yes, you are so pretty. Connan would have thought so. I was aware of a flash not so much of jealousy as uneasiness as I wondered whether in the years to come I was going to be continually jealous of Connan's appreciation of the attractive members of my sex.

She went on: 'They had called me in to tea, because Miss Nansellock wanted to ask some questions about Alvean. She did dote on that child. Does she still?'

'Indeed yes.'

'She is such a kind person. I don't know what I should have done without her.'

'I am so glad somebody was kind to you.'

'I think that she looks upon Alvean as her child. There was a rumour that Miss Nansellock's brother was the father of Alvean, which would make her Miss Nansellock's niece. Perhaps that is why . . .'

'She certainly does feel strongly about Alvean.'

'So I was called down to talk to her, and I was given tea and chatted with them – as though I were a guest as they were. I think that Treslyn woman resented it . . . she resented my presence there altogether. Perhaps they were a little too attentive to me – I mean Mr. Peter Nansellock and Mr. TreMellyn. Lady Treslyn has a hot temper, I am sure. In any case I believe she arranged the whole thing.'

'She couldn't be so vile!'

'Oh, but I am sure she could, and she was. You see, she was wearing a diamond bracelet and the safety chain had broken. It had caught in the upholstery of the chair, I think. She said, "I won't wear it. I'll take it down to old Pastern to get it repaired as soon as we leave." She took it off and put it on the table. I left them at tea and went to the schoolroom to do some work with Alvean. It was while we were there that the door was thrown open and they all stood there looking at me accusingly.

'Lady Treslyn said something about having a search made because her diamond bracelet was missing. She was truculent. One would have thought she was already the mistress of the house. Mr. TreMellyn said very kindly that Lady Treslyn was asking that my room be searched, and he hoped I would not object. I was very angry and I said: "Come on, search my room. Nothing will satisfy me, but that you should."

'So we all went into my room, and there in a drawer, hidden under some of my things was the diamond bracelet.

'Lady Treslyn said I was caught red-handed, and she was going to have me sent to prison. The others all pleaded with her not to make a scandal. Finally they agreed that if I went at once the matter would be forgotten. I was furious. I wanted an inquiry. But what could I do? They had found the thing there, and whatever I had to say after that they wouldn't believe me.'

'It must have been terrible for you,' I began to shiver.

She leaned across the table and smiled in a kindly way at me. 'You are afraid that they may do something similar to you. Lady Treslyn is determined to marry Connan TreMellyn.'

'Do you think so?'

'I do. I am sure there was something between them. He was, after all, a widower and not the sort of man, I think, to live without women. One knows his sort.'

I said: 'I suppose he made advances to you?'

She shrugged her shoulders. 'At least Lady Treslyn imagined that I might be a menace, and I am sure she chose that way to get rid of me.'

'What a foul creature she is! But Miss Nansellock was kind.'

'Very kind. She was with them, of course, when they found the bracelet; and when I was packing she came to my room. She said: "I'm very distressed, Miss Jansen, that this should have happened. I know they found the bracelet in your drawer, but you didn't put it there, did you?" I said: "Miss Nansellock, I swear I didn't." I can tell you, I was hysterical. It had all happened so suddenly. I didn't know what was to become of me. I had very little money and I would have to go to some hostel to look for work, and I knew I could not expect a testimonial. I shall never forget her kindness to me. She asked me where I was going and I gave her this address in Plymouth. She said: "I know the Merrivales are going to want a governess for a month or so. I am going to see that you get that job." She lent me some money, which I have now paid back, although she did not want me to do so; and that's how I lived until I went to the Merrivales. I have written, thanking Miss Nansellock, but how can one thank people adequately who do so much for one when one is in such dire need?'

'Thank goodness there was someone to help.'

'Heaven knows what would have become of me if she had not been there. Ours is a precarious profession, Miss Leigh. We are at the mercy of our employers. No wonder so many of us become meek and down-trodden.' She brightened. 'I try to forget all that. I'm going to be married. He is a doctor who looks after the family. In six months' time my governessing days will be over.'

'Congratulations! As a matter of fact I, too, am engaged to be married.'

'How wonderful!'

'To Connan TreMellyn,' I added.

She stared at me in astonishment. 'Why . . .' she stammered, 'I wish you the best of luck.'

I could see that she was a little embarrassed and trying to remember what she had said about Connan. I felt too that she thought I should need that good luck.

I could not explain to her that I would rather have one stormy year with Connan than a lifetime of peace with anyone else.

'I wonder,' she said after a pause, 'why you wanted to see me.'

'It is because I had heard of you. They talk of you often. Alvean was fond of you and there are things I want to know.'

'But you, who are soon to be a member of the family, will know so much more than I can tell you.'

'What do you think of Gilly – Gillyflower?'

'Oh, poor little Gilly. A strange, mad Ophelia-like creature. I always felt that one day we should find her floating on the stream with rosemary in her hands.'

'The child had a shock.'

'Yes, the first Mrs. TreMellyn's horse nearly trampled her to death.'

'You must have gone there soon after the death of Mrs. TreMellyn.'

'There were two others before me. I heard they left because the house was too spooky. A house couldn't be too spooky for me.'

'Oh yes, you're an expert on old houses?'

'Expert! Indeed I'm not. I just love them. I've seen a great many and I've read a great deal about them.'

'There was a peep in your room. Gilly showed it to me the other day.'

'Do you know, I lived in that room three weeks without knowing it was there.'

'I'm not surprised. The peeps are so cleverly concealed in the murals.'

'That's an excellent way of doing it. Do you know those in the solarium?'

'Oh yes.'

'One overlooking the hall, the other, the chapel. I think there's a reason for that. You see, the hall and the chapel would be the most important parts of the house at the time that was built.'

'You know a great deal about period and so on. At what period was Mount Mellyn built?'

'Late Elizabethan. At the time when people had to keep the presence of priests in their houses secret. I think that's why they had all these peeps and things.'

'How interesting.'

'Miss Nansellock is an expert on houses. That was something we had in common. Does she know we're meeting?'

'No one knows.'

'You mean, you came here without telling even your future husband?'

Confidences trembled on my lips. I wondered if I dared share them with this stranger. I wished it were Phillida sitting opposite me. Then I could have poured out my heart to her; I could have listened to her advice, which I was sure would be good.

But, although I had heard Miss Jansen's name mentioned so much since I had come to Mount Mellyn, she was still a stranger to me. How could I say to a stranger: I suspect the man I am engaged to marry of being involved in a plot to murder me.

No! It was impossible.

But, I reasoned, she had suffered accusation and dismissal. There was a kind of bond between us.

How far, I asked myself, are hot-blooded people prepared to go for the satisfaction of their lust?

I could not tell her.

'He is away on business,' I said. 'We are to be married in three weeks' time.'

'I wish you the best of luck. It must have happened very suddenly.'

'It was August when I went to the house.'

'And you had never met before?'

'Living in the same house one quickly gets to know people.'

'Yes, I suppose that is so.'

'And you yourself must have become engaged in almost as short a time.'

'Oh yes, but . . .'

I knew what she was thinking. Her pleasant country doctor was a very different person from the Master of Mount Mellyn.

I went on quickly: 'I wanted to meet you because I believed you had been falsely accused. I am sure that many people at the house think that.'

'I'm glad.'

'When Mr. TreMellyn returns I shall tell him that I have seen you, and I shall ask if something can be done.'

'It is of little consequence now. Dr. Luscombe knows what happened. He is very indignant. But I have made him see that no good purpose could be served by bringing up the matter again. If Lady Treslyn ever tried to make more mischief, then something could be done. But she won't; her only desire was to get rid of me, and that she did . . . quite effectively.'

'What a wicked woman she is! She did not consider the effect on you. But for the kindness of Miss Nansellock. . . .

'I know. But don't let's talk of it. You will tell Miss Nansellock that you have seen me?"

'Yes, I will.'

'Then tell her that I am engaged now to Dr. Luscombe. She will be so pleased. And there's something else I would like her to know. Perhaps you'll be interested too. It's about the house. The house will soon be your home, won't it? I envy you the house. It's one of the most interesting places I've ever seen.'

'What were you going to tell me to pass on to Miss Nansellock?'

'I've been doing a little research on architecture, and so on, of the Elizabethan period, and my fiancé arranged for me to see Cotehele, the Mount Edgcumbes' place. They were delighted to let me see it because they are understandably proud of it. It's more like Mount Mellyn than any house I've ever seen. The chapel is almost identical, even to the lepers' squint. But the squint at Mount Mellyn is much bigger, and the construction of the walls is slightly different. As a matter of fact I've never seen a squint quite like that at Mount Mellyn before. Do tell Miss Nansellock. She would be most interested, I'm sure.'

'I'll tell her. I expect she'll be more interested to hear that you are so happy and that you are going to marry.'

'Don't forget to tell her too that I remember I owe it all to her. Give her my kindest regards and my best thanks.'

'I will,' I said.

We parted, and on my journey home I felt I had obtained from Miss Jansen some fresh light on my problem.

There was no doubt that Lady Treslyn arranged for Miss Jansen's dismissal. Miss Jansen was very pretty indeed. Connan admired her and Alvean was fond of her. Connan would consider marriage because he would want sons; and Lady Treslyn, possessive as a tigress, was not going to allow him to marry anyone but herself.

I believed now that Lady Treslyn was planning to remove me as she had removed Miss Jansen; but because I was already engaged to Connan she would have to use more drastic methods in my case.

But Connan did not know of this attempt on my life.

I refused to believe that of him and, refusing, I felt a great deal happier.

Moreover, I had made up my mind. When Connan came back I was going to tell him everything – all I had discovered, all I had feared.

The decision brought me great comfort.

Two days passed, and still Connan had not returned.

Peter Nansellock came over to say good-bye. He was leaving late that night for London on his way to join the ship which would carry him to Australia.

Celestine was with him when he came to say good-bye. They thought Connan would have returned by now. As a matter of fact while they were there a letter arrived from Connan. He was coming back if possible late that night; if not, as early as possible next day.

I felt tremendously happy.

I gave them tea and, as we talked, I mentioned Miss Jansen.

I saw no reason why I should not do so in front of Peter, because it was he who had told me that Celestine had found her a job with the Merrivales.

'I met Miss Jansen the other day,' I began.

They were both startled.

'But how?' asked Peter.

'I wrote and asked her to meet me.'

'What made you do that?' asked Celestine.

'Well, she had lived here, and there was a mystery about her, and I thought it would be rather interesting, so, as I was going to Plymouth.·....'

'A charming creature,' mused Peter.

'Yes. You'll be pleased to hear that she's engaged to be married.'

'How interesting,' cried Celestine, her face growing pink. 'I'm delighted.'

'To the local doctor,' I added.

'She'll make an excellent doctor's wife,' said Celestine.

'Her husband's male patients will all be in love with her,' put in Peter.

'That could be disconcerting,' I replied.

'But good for business,' murmured Peter. 'Did she send us greetings?'

'Particularly to your sister,' I smiled at Celestine. 'She is so grateful to you; you were wonderful to her. She says she'll never forget.'

'It was nothing. I could not let that woman do what she did and stand by doing nothing.'

'You think Lady Treslyn deliberately planted that theft on her? I know Miss Jansen does.'

'There is no doubt of it,' said Celestine firmly.

'What an unscrupulous woman she must be!'

'I believe that to be so.'

'Well, Miss Jansen is happy now, so good came out of evil. By the way, I have a special message for you. It's about the house.'

'What house?' asked Celestine with great interest.

'This one. Miss Jansen has been to Cotehele and has been comparing their squint, in the chapel, with ours. She says ours is quite unique.'

'Oh really! That's very interesting.'

'It's bigger, she says – I mean ours is. And there's something about the construction of the walls.'

'Celestine is aching to go down and have a look at it,' said Peter.

She smiled at me: 'We'll look at it together sometime. You're going to be the Mistress of the house, so you ought to take an interest in it.'

'I'm becoming more and more interested. I'm going to ask you to teach me lots about it.'

She smiled at me warmly. 'I'll be glad.'

I asked Peter what train he was catching, and he answered that it would be the ten o'clock from St. Germans.

'I'll ride to the station,' he said, 'and stable the horse there. The baggage has gone on ahead of me. I shall go alone. I don't want any fond farewells at the station. After all, I shall no doubt be home this time next year ... with a fortune. *Au revoir*, Miss Leigh,' he went on. 'I'll come back one day. And if you do feel like coming with me ... it's not too late even now.'

He spoke flippantly, and his eyes were full of mischief. I wondered what he would say if I suddenly agreed to his proposal, if I suddenly told him that I was filled with terrible doubts about the man I had promised to marry.

I went down to the porch to say my last farewells. The servants were there for he was a great favourite. I guessed that he had bestowed many a sly kiss on Daisy and Kitty, and they were sad to see him go.

He looked very handsome in the saddle and beside him Celestine seemed insignificant.

We stood waving to them.

His last words were: 'Don't forget, Miss Leigh ... if you should change your mind!'

Everybody laughed and I joined in with them. I think we all felt a little sad that he was going.

As we were going back into the house, Mrs. Polgrey said to me: 'Miss Leigh, could I have a word with you?'

'But certainly. Shall I come to your room?'

She led the way there.

'I've just had word,' she said. 'The result of the autopsy. Death through natural causes.'

I felt floods of relief sweeping over me.

'Oh, I'm so pleased about that.'

'So are we all. I can tell you, I didn't like the things that were being said ... and him dying after he'd had supper here.'

'It seems as though it was all a storm in a teacup,' I said.

'Something like that, Miss Leigh. But there you are – people talk and something has to be done.'

'Well, it must be a great relief to Lady Treslyn.'

She looked a little embarrassed and I guessed she was wondering what she had said to me in the past about Connan and Lady Treslyn. It must have been disconcerting to discover that I was going to be Connan's wife. I decided to sweep aside her embarrassment for ever, and said: 'I hoped you were going to offer me a cup of your special Earl Grey.'

She was pleased and rang for Kitty.

We talked of household affairs while the kettle boiled, and when tea was made she tentatively brought out the whisky and when I nodded a tea-spoonful was put into each cup. I felt then that we had indeed resumed the old friendly relationship.

I was glad, because I could see this made her happy, and I wanted everyone about me to be as happy as I was.

I kept on telling myself: If Lady Treslyn really did attempt to kill me by sending that boulder crashing down in front of me when I was mounted on Jacinth, Connan knew nothing about it. Sir Thomas died a natural death, so there was nothing to hide; he had no reason to ask me to marry him except the one which he gave me; he loves me.

It was nine o'clock and the children were in bed. It had been a warm and sunny day and there were signs of spring everywhere.

Connan was coming home either to-night or to-morrow and I was happy.

I wondered what time he would arrive. Perhaps at midnight. I went to the porch to look for him because I had imagined I heard horses' hoofs in the distance.

I waited. The night was still. The house always seemed very quiet at times like this for all the servants would be in their own quarters.

I guessed that Peter would be on his way to the station by now. It was strange to think that I might never see him again. I thought of our first meeting in the train; he had begun by playing his mischievous tricks on me even then.

Then I saw someone coming towards me. It was Celestine, and she had come by way of the woods, not along the drive as usual.

She was rather breathless.

'Why, hallo,' she said. 'I came to see you. I felt so lonely. Peter's gone. It's rather sad to think that I shan't see him for a long time.'

'It does make one sad.'

'He played the fool a great deal, of course, but I am very fond of him. Now I've lost both my brothers.'

'Come in,' I said.

'Connan's not back, I suppose?'

'No. I don't think he can possibly be here before midnight. He wrote that he had business to attend to this morning. I expect he'll arrive to-morrow. Won't you come in?'

'Do you know, I rather hoped you'd be alone.'

'Did you?'

'I wanted to have a look at the chapel . . . that squint, you know. Ever since you gave me Miss Jansen's message I've been eager to see it. I didn't say so in front of Peter. He's apt to laugh at my enthusiasm.'

'Do you want to have a look at it now?'

'Yes, please. I've a theory about it. There may be a door in the panelling which leads to another part of the house. Wouldn't it be fun if we could discover it and tell Connan about it when he arrives?'

'Yes,' I agreed, 'it would.'

'Let's go now then.'

We went through the hall and, as we did so, I glanced up at the peep, because I had an uncanny feeling that we were being watched. I thought I saw a movement up there, but I was not sure, and said nothing.

We went along to the end of the hall, through the door, down the stone steps, and were in the chapel.

The place smelt damp. I said: 'It smells as though it hasn't been used for years.' And my voice echoed weirdly through the place.

Celestine did not answer. She had lighted one of the candles which stood on the altar. I watched the long shadow which the flickering light threw against the wall.

'Let's get into the squint,' she said. 'Through this door. There is another door in the squint itself which opens on to the walled garden. That was the way the lepers used to come in.'

She carried the candle high and I found that we were in a small chamber.

'This is the place,' I said, 'which is bigger than most of its kind.'

She did not answer. She was pressing different parts of the wall.

I watched her long fingers at work.

Suddenly she turned and smiled at me. 'I've always had a theory that somewhere in this house there is a priest's hole . . . you know, the hidy hole of the resident priest into which he scuttled when the queen's men arrived. As a matter of fact I know that one TreMellyn did toy with the idea of becoming a Catholic. I'll swear there is a priest's hole somewhere. Connan would be delighted if we found it. He loves this place as much as I do . . . as much as you're going to. If I found it . . . it would be the best wedding present I could give him, wouldn't it? After all, what can you give people who have all they want?'

She hesitated, and her voice was high with excitement. 'Just a minute. There's something here.' I came close to her, and caught my breath with amazement, for the panel had moved inward and shown itself as a long narrow door.

She turned to look at me and she looked unlike herself. Her eyes were brilliant with excitement. She put her head inside the aperture and was about to go forward when she said: 'No, you first. It's going to be your house. You should be the first to enter it.'

I had caught her excitement. I knew how pleased Connan would be.

I stepped ahead of her and was aware of an unrecognizable pungent odour.

She said: 'Have a quick look. It's probably a bit foul in there. Careful. There are probably steps.' She held the candle high, and I saw there were two of them. I went down those steps and, as I did so, the door shut behind me.

'Celestine!' I cried in terror. But there was no answer. 'Open that door,' I screamed. But my voice was caught and imprisoned in the darkness, and I knew that I was a prisoner too – Celestine's prisoner.

The darkness shut me in. It was cold and eerie – foul, evil. Panic seized me. How can I explain such terror? There are no words to describe it. Only those who have suffered it could understand.

Thoughts – hideous thoughts – seemed to be battering on my brain. I had been a fool. I had been trapped. I had accepted what seemed obvious, I had walked the way she who wished to be rid of me had directed; and like a fool I had asked no questions.

My fear numbed my brain as it did my body.

I was terrified.

I mounted the two steps. I beat my fists against what now seemed to be a wall. 'Let me out. Let me out . . .' I cried.

But I knew that my voice would not be heard beyond the lepers' squint. And how often did people go to the chapel?

She would slip away . . . no one would know she had even been in the house.

I was so frightened I did not know what to do. I heard my own voice sobbing out my terror, and it frightened me afresh because, for the moment, I did not recognize it as my own.

I felt exhausted and limp. I knew that one could not live for long in this dark, damp place. I pulled at the wall until I tore my nails and I felt the blood on my hands.

I began to look about me because my eyes were becoming familiar to the gloom. Then I saw that I was not alone.

Someone had come here before me. What was left of Alice lay there. At last I had found her.

'Alice,' I screamed. 'Alice. It is you then? So you were here in the house all the time?'

There was no answer from Alice. Her lips had been silent for more than a year.

I covered my face with my hands. I could not bear to look. There was the smell of death and decay everywhere.

I wondered: How long did Alice live after the door had closed on *her*? I wanted to know because so long I might expect to live.

I think I must have fainted for a long time and I was delirious when I came to. I heard a voice babbling; it must have been my own because it could not have belonged to Alice.

I was mercifully only half-conscious. But it was as though a part of me understood so much.

During that time I spent in the dark and gruesome place I was not sure who I was. Was I Martha? Was I Alice?

Our stories were so much alike. I believed the pattern was similar. They had said she ran away with Geoffry. They would say I had run away with Peter. Our departure had been cleverly timed. 'But why . . .' I said, 'but why. . . .'

I knew whose shadow I had seen on the blind. It was hers . . . that diabolical woman. She had known of the existence of that little diary which I had discovered in Alice's coat pocket and she was searching for it because she knew it could provide one of those small clues which might lead to discovery.

I knew that she did not love Alvean, that she had tricked us all with her gentle demeanour. I knew that she was incapable of loving anyone. She had used Alvean as she had used others, as she was going to use Connan.

It was the house that she loved.

I pictured her during those delirious moments looking from her window at Mount Widden across the cove – coveting a house as fiercely as man ever coveted woman or woman man.

'Alice,' I said. 'Alice, we were her victims . . . you and I.'

And I fancied Alice talked to me . . . and told me of the day Geoffry had caught the London train and how Celestine had come to the house and told her of the great discovery in the chapel.

I saw Alice . . . pale, pretty, fragile Alice crying out in pleasure at the discovery, taking those fatal steps forward to death.

But it was not Alice's voice I heard. It was my own.

Yet I thought she was with me. I thought that at last I had found her, and that we had comfort to offer each other as I waited to go with her into the shadowy world which had been hers since she was led by Celestine Nansellock into the lepers' squint.

There was a blinding light in my eyes. I was being carried.

I said: 'Am I dead then, Alice?'

And a voice answered: 'My darling . . . my darling . . . you are safe.'

It was Connan's voice, and it was his arms which held me.

'Are there dreams in death then, Alice?' I asked.

I was conscious of a voice which whispered: 'My dearest . . . oh, my dearest. . . .' And I was laid upon a bed, and many people stood about me.

Then I saw the light glinting on hair which looked almost white.

'Alice, there is an angel.'

Then the angel answered and said: 'It's Gilly. Gilly brought them to you. Gilly watched and Gilly saw. . . .'

And oddly enough it was Gilly who brought me back to the world of reality. I knew that I was not dead, that some miracle had happened; that it was in truth Connan's arms which I had felt about me, Connan's voice I heard.

I was in my own bedroom from the window of which I could see the lawns and the palm trees and the room which had once been Alice's, on the blind of which I had seen the shadow of Alice's murderer who had sought to kill me too.

I called out in terror. But Connan was beside me.

I heard his voice, tender, soothing, loving. 'It's all right, my love . . . my only love. I'm here . . . I'm with you for evermore.'

Afterwards

This is the story I tell my great-grandchildren. They have heard it many times, but there is always a first time for some.

They ask for it again and again. They play in the park and in the woods; they bring me flowers from the south gardens, a tribute to the old lady who can always charm them with the story of how she married their great-grandfather.

To me it is as clear as though it happened yesterday. Vividly I remember my arrival at the house and all that preceded those terrifying hours I spent in the dark with dead Alice.

The years which followed with Connan have often been stormy ones. Connan and I were both too strong-willed, I suppose, to live in perpetual peace; but they were years in which I felt I had lived life richly, and what more could one ask than that?

Now he is old, as I am, and three more Connans have been born since that day we married – our son, grandson and great-grandson. I was glad I was able to give Connan children. We have five sons and five daughters, and they in their turn were fruitful.

When the children hear the story they like to check up all the details. They want every incident explained.

Why was it believed that the woman who died in the train was Alice? Because of the locket she wore. But it was Celestine who identified the locket as one which, she said, she had given Alice, but which, of course, she had never seen before in her life.

She had been eager that I should accept Jacinth when Peter had first offered the mare to me – I suppose because she feared it was just possible that Connan might be interested in me and therefore she was ready to encourage the friendship between myself and Peter; and it was she who later, discovering the loosened boulder on the cliff, had lain in wait for me and attempted to kill or maim me.

She was the sender of the anonymous letters to Lady Treslyn and the public prosecutor, commenting on the suspicious circumstances of Sir Thomas's death. She had believed that if there was a big enough scandal, marriage between Connan and Lady Treslyn would have been impossible for years. She had reckoned without Connan's feelings for me; thus when she knew that I was engaged to marry him, she immediately planned to remove me. She failed to do this on the cliff path; therefore I was to join Alice; the fact that Peter was leaving for Australia on that day must have made her decide on this method. The whole household knew that Peter's attitude to me had been a flirtatious one, and it would appear that I had run away with him.

It was Celestine who had put the diamond bracelet in Miss Jansen's room because the governess was learning too much about the house and the knowledge would inevitably lead her to the lepers' squint and Alice. She had worked on Lady Treslyn's jealousy of the pretty young governess for she had known Lady Treslyn to be a vindictive woman who, given the opportunity, would bring all her malice to bear on Miss Jansen.

She was in love – passionately in love with Mount Mellyn and she wanted to marry Connan only because thus she would be Mistress of the house. So in the first place, discovering the secret of the squint she had kept it to herself, and had chosen her opportunity to murder Alice. She knew of the love affair between Alice and her brother Geoffry; she knew that Alvean was his child. It worked out so easily because she had waited for her opportunity. If it had not been possible to make Alice's death appear to have occurred in the train accident she would have found some other way of disposing of her as she had intended to dispose of me through Jacinth.

But she had reckoned without Gilly. Who would have thought that a poor simple child should play such a big part in this diabolical plan? But Gilly had loved Alice as later she was to love me. Gilly had known Alice was in the house for Alice had made a habit of coming to say good night to her when she did the same to Alvean; she had always done it before she went out to a dinner party. Because she had never forgotten, Gilly did not believe she had forgotten this time. Gilly therefore continued to believe that Alice had never left the house, and had gone on looking for her. It was Gilly's face which I had seen at the peep. Gilly knew all the peeps in the house and used them frequently, because she was always watching for Alice.

Thus she had seen Celestine and myself enter the hall from the solarium. I imagined her crossing the room and looking through the peep on the other side of the room so that she saw us enter the chapel. We crossed to the squint, but that side of the chapel could not easily be seen from the solarium peep, and so Gilly sped along to Miss Jansen's room, where from that peep she could have a good view of the squint. She was just in time to see us disappearing through the door, and waited for us to come out. She waited and waited, for Celestine naturally left by the door to the courtyard and slipped away so that, since she believed that no one had seen her come into the house except myself, she could let it appear that she had not been there at all.

Thus, while I lived through that period of horror in Alice's death-chamber, Gilly was standing on her stool in Miss Jansen's room, watching the door to the lepers' squint.

Connan returned at eleven and expected the household to give him a welcome.

Mrs. Polgrey received him. 'Go and tell Miss Leigh that I am here,' he said. He must have been a little piqued because he was – and still is – the sort of man who demands the utmost affection and attention, and the fact that I could be sleeping when he came home was inconceivable to him.

I pictured the scene: Mrs. Polgrey reporting that I was not in my room, the search for me, that terrible moment when Connan believed what Celestine had intended he should believe.

'Mr. Nansellock came over this afternoon to say good-bye. He caught the ten o'clock from St. Germans. . . .'

I have wondered often how long it would have been before they discovered that I had not run away with Peter. I could imagine what might have happened. Connan's losing that belief in life which I believed I was beginning to bring back to him, perhaps continuing his *affaire* with Linda Treslyn. But it would not have led to marriage, Celestine would have seen to that. And in time she would have found some way of making herself mistress of Mount Mellyn; insidiously she would have made herself necessary to Alvean and to him.

How strange, I thought, that all this might have come to pass and the only two who could have told the truth would have been two skeletons behind the walls of the lepers' squint. Who would have believed that even at this day the story of Alice and Martha would never have been known, had not a simple child, born in sorrow, living in shadow, led the way to the truth.

Connan told me often of the uproar in the house when I was missing. He told me of the child, who came and stood patiently beside him, waiting to be heard; how she tugged at his coat and sought for the words to explain.

'God forgive us,' he says, 'it was some time before we would listen to her, and so we delayed bringing you out of that hellish place.'

But she had led them there . . . through the door into the lepers' squint. She had seen us, she said.

And for a moment Connan had thought that Peter and I had left the house together, slipping out that way so that we should not be noticed.

It was dusty in the squint – for no one had entered it since Alice had gone there with her murderer; but in the dust on the wall was the mark of a hand, and when Connan saw it he began to take Gilly seriously.

It was not easy to find the secret spring in the door even if it had been known that it was there. There was an agonizing search of ten minutes while Connan was ready to tear the walls down.

But they found it and they found me. They found Alice too.

They took Celestine to Bodmin where she was eventually to be tried for the murder of Alice. But before the trial could take place she was a raving lunatic. At first I believed that this was yet another scheme of hers. It may have started that way, but she did not die until twenty years after, and all that time she spent locked away from the world.

Alice's remains were buried in the vault where those of an unknown woman lay. Connan and I were married three months after he had brought me out of the darkness. That experience had affected me even more than I realized at the time, and I suffered from nightmares for a year or more. It was a great shock to have been buried alive even though one's tomb was opened before life was extinguished.

Phillida came to my wedding with William and the children. She was delighted. So was Aunt Adelaide, who insisted that the wedding take place from her town house. Thus Connan and I had a smart London wedding. Not that we cared, but it pleased Aunt Adelaide who, for some reason, seemed to have the idea in her head that it was all her doing.

And so we honeymooned, as we had originally intended, in Italy and then we came home to Mount Mellyn.

I dream over the past when I have told the story to the children. I think of Alvean happily married to a Devonshire squire. As for Gilly, she never left me. She is with me now. At any moment she will appear on the lawn with the eleven o'clock coffee which on warm days we take in that arbour in the south gardens where I first saw Lady Treslyn and Connan together.

I must confess that Lady Treslyn continued to plague me during the first years of my married life. I discovered that I could be a jealous woman – and a passionate one. Sometimes I think Connan liked to tease me, in repayment, he said, for the jealousy he had felt of Peter Nansellock.

But she went to London after a few years, and we heard she married there.

Peter came back some fifteen years after he left. He had acquired a wife and two children but no fortune; he was, however, as gay and full of vitality as ever. In the meantime Mount Widden had been sold; and later one of my daughters married the owner, so the place has become almost as much home to me as Mount Mellyn.

Connan said he was glad when Peter came back, and I laughed at the thought of his ever feeling he needed to be jealous. When I told him this, he replied: 'You're even more foolish about Linda Treslyn.'

That was one of those moments when we both knew that there was no one for us but each other.

And so the years passed and now, as I sit here thinking of it all, Connan is coming down the path from the gardens. In a moment I shall hear his voice.

Because we are alone he will say: 'Ah, my dear Miss Leigh ...' as he often does in his most tender moments. That is to remind me that he does not forget those early days; and there will be a smile on his lips which tells me that he is seeing me, not as I am now, but as I was then, the governess somewhat resentful of her fate, desperately clinging to her pride and her dignity – falling in love in spite of herself – his dear Miss Leigh.

Then we shall sit in the warm sunshine, thankful for all the good things which life has brought us.

Here he comes and Gilly is behind him ... still a little different from other people, still speaking rarely, singing as she works, in the off-key voice that makes us think she is a little out of this world.

As I watch her I can see so clearly the child she once was, and I think of the story of Jennifer, the mother who one day walked into the sea, and how that story was part of my story, and how delicately and intricately our lives were woven together.

Nothing remains, I thought, but the earth and the sea which are here just as they were on the day Gilly was conceived, on the day Alice walked unheeding into her tomb, on the day I felt Connan's arms about me and I knew he had brought me back to life.

We are born, we suffer, we live, we die, but the waves continue to beat upon the rocks; the seed time and the harvest come and go, but the earth remains.